VIOLENT WORDS

COLLECTED STORIES 2014 - 2024

DUNCAN RALSTON

These stories are works of fiction. Names, characters, places and incidents are either the product of the author's imagination or are used fictitiously. Any resemblance to actual persons, living or dead, is entirely coincidental.

No part of this eBook may be reproduced or transmitted in any form or by any means, electronic or mechanical, including photocopying, recording or by any information storage and retrieval system, without written permission from the author.

SHADOW WORK PUBLISHING

"Cuttings" first published in *The Black Room Manuscripts Vol. One* (The Sinister Horror Company), © 2014

"Chompers" first published in *Death by Chocolate* (KnightWatch Press), © 2015

"Sanctuary" first published in *The Sirens Call* #21, © 2015

"Stray" first published in *The Animal* (Edge), © 2015

"He Is Risen" first published in *Easter Eggs & Bunny Boilers* (Matt Shaw Publications), © 2016

"My Protector" first published in *The Devil's Guests* (Matt Shaw Publications), © 2016

"Squirm" first published in *VS* (Shadow Work Publishing), © 2016

"Head" first published in *Dig Two Graves* by Death's Head Press. Copyright Duncan Ralston 2019

"The Boats" first published in *VS:X: US vs UK Extreme Horror* by Shadow Work Publishing. Copyright Duncan Ralston 2017

"Prick" first published in *Coming Together* by Matt Shaw Publications. Copyright Duncan Ralston 2017

"The Passion of the Robertsons" first published in *Splatterpunk Fighting Back* by Shadow Work Publishing. Copyright Duncan Ralston 2017

ALSO BY DUNCAN RALSTON

Gristle & Bone (collection)

Salvage (novella)

Wildfire (novella)

Woom (novella)

The Method (novel)

Video Nasties (collection)

Ebenezer (novella)

Ghostland (novel)

In Every Dark Corner (collection)

Afterlife: Ghostland 2.0 (novel)

Ghostland: Infinite (novel)

Gross Out (novel)

Ghostland: Ghost Hunter Edition (omnibus)

Try Not to Die: At Ghostland w/ Mark Tullius (gameboook)

Puzzle House (novel)

Pedo Island Bloodbath (novel)

Helloween (novel - Fall 2024)

Contents

In Every Dark Corner

Skin Flicks

The Moving House

GRISTLE & BONE

Published 2014

Baby Teeth

I N EARLY JANUARY, the doctor told Candace McMurray she would never be pregnant.

The obstetrician hadn't called her "barren" outright, but the word had occurred to Candace. Years of childhood antidepressants might have ravaged her ovaries, he said. Her husband, Joel, had suggested adoption, but Candace wanted her own children, not someone else's. Joel considered the decision outlandishly selfish, though he said nothing. He shared in her disappointment, wanting children with a hunger matching hers, but he knew her sadness could easily spiral into depression. No use making it worse by arguing a point he knew he'd never win.

Candace was determined not to let the bad news affect their sex life, but despair wormed its way back into her life and into their bed, and soon she couldn't bring herself to orgasm, no matter how persistently Joel pushed her toward it. By the end of the month, she'd realized she had entirely soured on sex.

After several nights ending with Joel's chin rested on her cold shoulder in the dark, breathing into her ear as he worked on her with the thick index fingers of his right hand, while pressing his desperate erection against the cleft of her buttocks, Joel McMurray finally stopped trying to initiate.

That first night without contact, Candace silently wept herself to sleep. Eventually the McMurrays fell into an easy but essentially joyless routine: eating together, reading together, sharing stories about their day, but knowing nothing of sexual or romantic intimacy. No words of love now passed between them, no kisses more sensual than a peck, for fear of stirring Joel's desire.

In the meantime, Candace took up scrapbooking. By June she'd filled two albums with old photos, silhouette portraits, weathered letters and envelopes, copies of birth certificates and citizenship papers, reaching far back into the McMurray family history and her own—the Leasons—but never moving forward. The past became a rich, bright tapestry for Candace McMurray; the future was empty and cheerless. Every blank page in the scrapbook now reminded her of that terrible word: *barren*. She filled them as fast as she could.

It was late June when Candace awoke to a jolt of pain in her right breast. Two words immediate sprang to mind: *Mom* and *Cancer*. But as the pain abated, throbbing dully, she realized it had felt like teeth. Had Joel *bit* her? The thought was absurd, after so long without even a touch.

She rolled over to find him on his side, facing away from her. They'd slept that way, on either side of the bed, for months now. Candace held vague memories of their early nights together, spooning while the sweat dried on their naked flesh, or the rise and fall of his breath and the beat of his heart lulling her to sleep as she rested her head on his smooth chest. Seeing him asleep now, with his back turned as hers had been only moments before, still brought sadness.

"Joel?" she whispered into the dark. *"Joel?"*

He stirred. "Mmn?" He rolled onto his back. "What? What's wrong?" Still muttering, half asleep, he peered over at her, eyes puffy.

"Nothing," she said. He clearly couldn't have bit her if he'd been sleeping. A bug bite? "Go back to sleep," she said. No use keeping him up; he'd only be cranky in the morning.

He sighed heavily through his nose. "Did you hear something?"

"No," she said. She wanted him to go back to sleep. She didn't want to reveal what she'd thought. He would laugh at her, and she couldn't bear to be laughed at—not now. Half asleep, she'd imagined the feel of teeth on her areola, the sharp wetness of them, the suction drawing her nipple out to stiffen.

Felt so real.

"I thought I heard something, but it's nothing." She patted his shoulder, the first time she'd dared touch him in bed since early in February. He shrank from her touch. Not meaning to, she thought, but as if her fingers had stung him, and she withdrew further into herself from the shock of it, rolling over onto her side of the bed, her sovereign territory.

"Hon?" Joel said.

She pretended to be asleep. After a moment, she heard him sigh through his nose again, annoyed this time, the chuff of an angered beast. She curled into the fetal position, pulled the blanket in her bunched fists tight beneath her chin, an elbow grazing the bruise, bringing fresh pain.

A moment later, Joel got up to use the bathroom. She felt his side of the mattress swell in his absence, the familiar block of ugly yellow light falling over her side of the comforter as his urine splashed into the bowl. She'd have to wipe it off the seat tomorrow, mothering him like the child she'd never have.

I was born to mother, she thought. *Born to* be *a mother*. She drifted off thinking this, fast asleep when Joel returned to bed, if he'd returned at all.

JOEL HAD ALREADY LEFT for work by the time Candace rolled out of bed. He managed an online shopping company, while Candace transcribed medical recordings from home—not a lucrative job, but it allowed her the time and freedom here and there to work on her scrapbooks, and before them the novel she'd been writing, now long abandoned.

She'd forgotten all about the nipple incident until her shower, where under a second skin of soap bubbles the areola appeared to be bruised. She rinsed and toweled off quickly, wiping away a circle of mist to examine it in the mirror. It looked like a hickey, puffed out and unnaturally large, a small purple and yellow ring with a tiny crescent of dark marks that could easily have been the teeth of a very small mouth, the bumpy little glands much more prominent than usual.

Candace frowned at it, suddenly certain there'd been something in bed with them last night. A large insect. An animal, even. Had she felt the comforter tug at her feet when she'd awakened? She thought yes. And though it was mortifying, the idea that an animal had slipped into their bed during the night scared her less than the alternative.

Her mother had suffered from breast cancer, as had her great-aunt: neither instance had been pretty. After three rounds of chemo and a double-mastectomy, Aunt Betsy's cancer had metastasized, spreading through her blood, and soon she'd withered away to nothing. Fortunately, her mother had been spared the same indignity. Beverly Leason's tumor had been benign, a mere fibroadenoma, but the fact remained: breast cancer ran in the Leason family blood.

Candace raised her arms to check for dimples and "irregularities." Aside from the bruise, they seemed normal, though she hadn't spent much time staring at her breasts in the mirror since puberty. Until her great-aunt's battle with cancer, they'd simply been there, hanging globes of fat and flesh, often an aggravation: the subject of ridicule when she'd blossomed early; having to strap them down and cover them over for business meetings and exercise; then, after Betsy's sickbed death, objects of dread. She'd often considered she would have been better off without them, though Joel probably wouldn't have agreed.

She squeezed it—Joel had called the right one *Monica,* the left one *Rachel* when he was feeling frisky—looking for fluid expressed from the nipple. It remained dry. Sore, but dry. It would always be dry, much as her belly might distend some day from weight gain, but never from pregnancy.

Born to be a mother, she thought again. *What an awful phrase to worm into my head.*

Without the need to primp, she threw on a loose pair of shorts and one of Joel's old sweaters, then went downstairs to schedule an appointment for a breast exam. *Better safe than sorry*, she thought. Aunt Betsy used to say that, before the cancer had made her sorry, anyhow. They scheduled Candace for the next week.

About an hour later she had her headphones on, typing away at her desk as an obstetrician's nasal voice droned on about his patient's phantom pregnancy. (Something about the doctor's tone made Candace think he was misogynist; perhaps it was because he'd called it a "hysterical pregnancy," and not in the *har-har* kind of way.)

Glass shattered somewhere in the house, startling her out of her chair. She flicked the headphones off her head, thoughts racing.

"Okay, calm down, Candace. Something fell," she told herself, adding "Don't get hysterical," with a halfhearted chuckle.

Five breaths, in and out. She thought of Lamaze. And the house remained silent. Thinking she must have imagined it, she put her headphones back on, and was just about seated again when another sound brought her to her feet, heart pounding.

First broken glass, now the pitter-patter of little feet.

She called out, "*Hello?*" aware of how stupid it was after she'd done it. If it was an intruder up there, she'd just acknowledged his presence and announced her rise to the second floor to investigate with one feeble word. The footfalls were too light to have been a man's, though. It could be an animal. Or, less likely, a child.

Candace took the stairs with caution, though not enough to avoid their various creaks, and saw the mess through the banister: the floor in the spare bedroom looked like the bottom of a birdcage. She ran the rest of the way, creaking be damned, found her scrapbooks strewn everywhere, torn to literal scraps. Jigsaw fragments of her dead ancestors and Joel's in sepia-toned photographs stared up at her from the ruined pages.

She let out a squeak of dismay. So many months of work, ruined in an instant.

Glimmers of aquamarine Favrile glass among the loose pages, beautiful and dangerous, had only moments before been a vase beside her scrapbooks, on the dresser where she'd stacked them. The cover of the scuttle hole to the attic, directly above where the empty vase had been gathering dust, lay slightly askew in its base.

Squatters?

Couldn't be. She'd been up there when they'd first moved in two years prior. The roof was two feet above the ceiling, maybe less, with rafters and pink fiberglass foam between. Not enough room to kneel, let alone squat.

Then what?

A nest. Rats or mice. Some kind of large bird, a murder of crows or a parliament of owls. Or raccoons—whatever more than one was called. She'd heard the Andersons down the street once had an infestation of possums. Two or three years ago one of the neighbors a few blocks south had gotten such a terrible infestation of wasps in the attic, they'd been forced to redo their entire roof.

House cancer, she thought, and heard herself giggle. *I've got cancer of the attic.*

Could an animal do *that, though? Gosh, what a mess! What a terrible, awful goddamn mess!*

A raccoon could have easily gotten into the attic crawlspace through the vents or even the chimney, and Candace knew their dexterous claws could get into garbage cans, no matter how well the homeowner tried to protect them. But she had serious doubts even the smartest raccoon could have lifted and removed the attic hatch, made the five-to-six foot drop to the dresser without disturbing the vase, torn her scrapbooks to bits, then climbed back up, smashing the vase in the process, and set the cover back in place.

Whatever was up there, she steeled herself and made her way to the dresser. *Forgot my damn shoes*, she thought, walking cautiously on her bare toes to avoid the glass scattered among her ruined pages. It still hurt to look at what had become of her hard work, but with all the glass, she couldn't avoid it.

Candace climbed the dresser easily. Solid and wide, made of burled walnut, it wouldn't have scooched against the floor even if she'd deliberately tried to move it. Two movers had brought it in here, and the McMurrays had decided, without much choice in the matter, to keep it where it had been left. Cobwebs hung in the high corner. She told herself to remember to deal with them later.

On her tiptoes, she could just manage to press her fingers against the hatch. Not nearly enough to reach the attic.

"Wait for Joel, Candy," she told herself bitterly, not wanting to give up so easily, but aware that her husband, whatever his faults, was a good foot taller than her. "Better yet, call a professional."

Uh-uh. No way she was going to play the Helpless Woman role. There had to be something around the house she could stand on top of the dresser to get a good look in there. The way things were between her and Joel right now, he'd only get angry if she left it for him. Any little thing set him off these days. He'd gotten pissed off at the way the paper had landed in the juniper bush the other day—not that it had landed in the bush, but *how* it had landed. The paperboy managed it get it into the bush more often than not.

And I've been pouring all my energy into these pathetic scraps, she thought, looking forlorn at the mess on the floor below. *God, what a colossal waste of time! What a fool I've been, Joel. What a sad, miserable fool....*

She had no idea how to cure the cancer that had grown between them, but dealing with this was a good start. If there was a nest in the crawlspace, and she could get someone over to clear them out before Joel returned from work, or at least start the process, he'd have to be happy with her then.

A scuttling above her. Thumping on the hatch. Plaster dust fell in her eyes and hair. She blinked it away, crying out in fright and anger.

Determined now, she jumped off the dresser and hurried down to the living room, where she lifted the heavy ottoman onto her knee, then lugged it awkwardly up the stairs, one step at a time, careful not to get her fingers wedged against the stippled wall. She brought it to the spare bedroom before realizing her error: once again, she'd forgotten her shoes.

More sounds from the attic. Chewing... or tearing. Tearing up the insulation, like they'd torn up her scrapbooks. "Oh, you little bastards are gonna *get* it," she cursed under her breath, straining to lower the plush ottoman to the floor and let her muscles rest a moment. Lugging it up again, she moved along the wall to avoid the glass, then dropped it solidly on the dresser.

With the ottoman on the dresser, pushed squarely into the corner where the walls came together, Candace stood with her palms pressed flat against the hatch, arms bent at the elbows. The flashlight slipped a little in the waistband of her shorts, rubbing against her pubic bone, reminding her briefly of Joel.

Pushing up on the particle-board hatch, she winced at its squeaky grind against the jamb. She gave it a hard enough push in the last few inches that it popped off into the dark of the attic.

A rush of air met her ears but nothing more. She felt for the 2-by-4 joists on either side of the hatch, nervously awaiting whatever was up there to bite her searching fingers. When nothing came, she pulled herself up into the dark with the ease of the high school gymnast she'd once been. The creak and pop in her hips and shoulders, and the stiffness of her muscles, told her she needed to get back into shape.

Cool up here. A musty smell. The sour stench of old rat turds and the thick smell of cooking grease clotted in the range hood's exhaust pipe. She lay on her front across the rafters, bare legs dangling out of the hole, and shone the flashlight into the dark, illuminating boards stained black from years of dampness, the brick exterior, puffy clouds of pink fiberglass. Six joists from where she lay, whatever lived up here had pulled up and torn the insulation, fluffy cotton candy bits piled up as if it had dug itself a nest.

A chill ran up her legs. Feeling suddenly vulnerable, she tucked them up into the crawlspace, lying on her side in the fetal position for a moment to ease the strain in her stomach muscles from pulling herself up here. The air conditioning hummed. Congesting from the dust, her left nostril whistled. She stretched out her legs, ankles cracking, then pulled and shimmied herself to the next joist, and the next, ready to strike out with the flashlight if something came toward her.

As she approached the nest, the chewing resumed—except that from where she lay, with her butt hunched up like a caterpillar's, it seemed to be coming from behind her.

She rolled onto her back, heart thumping, joist pressed hard against her spine as she shone the light at her toes.

The creature was on her in an instant, trailing a knotted cord like a tail: a purplish thing with four inchoate limbs, a monstrous flat head and beady black eyes, crawling up her leg as she screamed, its tiny, slick fingers with little pink nails grabbing raw hunks of her flesh—and as it wriggled up under her sweatshirt, she noticed two things.

The first was that it was human.

The second, that it had *teeth*.

———

JOEL GOT HOME a little after six. His keys were still in the door when he spotted mud on the kitchen floor, streaked and splashed across the tiles. "Candace?" he called out, dumping his bag. Not mud—*blood*, and lots of it.

"Candy!"

He left the door open, keys still in the lock, hurrying through the kitchen now, slipping in the blood as someone—*not Candy, no please, not my Candy*—had already slipped before, grabbing the counter for support, then righting himself and continuing on to the stairs. Candace's computer was on in the living room, cursor blinking mid-report. Her headset lay on the floor.

He felt terrible having neglected her for so long, that he'd let their lack of intimacy come between them, that he hadn't fought harder against her depression, worried now that something terrible had happened to her, something they couldn't come back from. Bloody footprints on the carpeted steps. He took them two by two.

"Honey?"

"I'm in here!" she called from the bathroom. Relief was momentary, as he recognized the sharp edge of fear in her voice, then registered the mess in the spare bedroom through the bannister: her scrapbooks in shreds, the broken glass. Thoughts racing: *Signs of a struggle? What happened here?* More blood tracked pink toward the open bathroom door. He saw her bare legs, with blood, *her* blood, running down them like tear-streaked mascara. Nobody in there with her, unless the intruder stood in the bath, which was unlikely. Some relief, at least.

He rushed up the last few steps, then stopped dead in the doorway. Stricken by what he saw, he gripped the doorjamb, on the verge of fainting.

Candace stood on the bare tile, legs apart as if she were about to squat. On the lip of the tub, her good pair of scissors, shiny and wet, still dripped on the bathmat. In her left hand, red and slippery, she held a sewing needle. Pubic hair matted with crimson. Thread from the needle pulled taut, ending somewhere between her labia.

It had put up a struggle, only wanting the comfort of her breast, to feed from her. Her nipple had been dry, but as its three jagged, underdeveloped teeth worked at her areola, as it *suckled*, she'd begun to feel a tremendous tingling pressure build beneath the flesh. There had been pain, and then a sort of euphoria had washed over her, prolactin and oxytocin, the pain dissipating as the ugly little creature drank from her greedily. It had fallen asleep with its lips still on her numbed breast.

Standing before Joel, Candace's right hand held her belly, rounded and taut as if she were deliberately sticking it out, trying to hold in its contents. She admired her pallid reflection in the full-length mirror, the reflection of an ecstatic young mother.

While the creature slept, she'd cradled it gently under its bottom. Slipping down through the hatch had been difficult, but making room for the hatchling (since it had come from the hatch she'd begun to think of it by that name, at least until she thought of a better one) had been much harder. Her garden scissors had done the trick. The euphoria had heightened, oxytocin killing the pain as her vaginal tissue split against the sharp steel blades in two quick snips. The sight of all that blood hadn't worried her. She was used to seeing blood there.

Once it had realized what she meant to do the hatchling had struggled, but with great effort—the sort of hysterical strength attributed to mothers whose children were in danger—Candace had managed to work it up inside her while its tiny limbs flailed. They were still kicking now, in fact, while she sewed.

And here was Joel, home to share in her joy.

She peeled his hand from the door jamb and placed it on her distended belly.

Joel felt something push against his palm, as if whatever she had inside her wanted *out*. He tried to jerk his hand away but she held it firm, her grip surprisingly strong. He looked up then, startled to see Candace smiling for the first time in months, with lips as blue as the wallpaper.

"*We're pregnant,*" she told him.

VIRAL

THE VIDEO HAD been uploaded for seven hours before the title surfaced on Tara Maxwell's social media feed: DEPRESSED TEEN GIRL DISAPPEARS! 100% REAL!

Catchy, she thought with a smug grin. *Roll over, Hitchcock.*

By the time she got around to clicking the link, the view count had surpassed 500,000—the equivalent of a Gold record in the music biz, and since Tara Maxwell wrote the music column for the *Herald* (a column purporting to study the trends of the recording industry, which in Tara's opinion trended steadily downward), it was often hard for her not to think in industry terms while at her desk.

She waited until noon, then skipped out back for a smoke, tilted her phone on its side, and played the video full-screen.

At first glance, it appeared to be just another girl in a long line of teenagers reaching out to the internet for sympathy—and if the World Wide Web was known for one thing, it was compassion. Videos of its kind had been made so often they could easily have their own category at the MTV Awards: "Best Teen Cry for Help." Not half as memorable as "Best Scared-as-Sh*t Performance," Tara considered, but it was a work in progress. She'd never been very good at ledes, as a firm believer that the steak should sell itself. Let her editors worry about its sizzle.

Watching halfheartedly, glancing up here and there to scan the faces of fellow smokers, Tara, who'd once thought she had seen it all, slumped back against the brick wall suddenly, exhaling a lungful of smoke.

Fake, she thought. *It's gotta be faked.*

An interstitial ad played before the video reloaded, suggesting that a diamond engagement ring guaranteed orgasms. *Only if they teach husbands-to-be oral*, Tara mused as she moved toward a picnic bench, waiting for the commercial to end. When the video began again she was seated, ready to be blown away afresh.

The girl's straggly, mousy-brown hair fell in her face, eyes underlined by deep blue-black pits of fatigue, an overlarge striped hoodie suggesting chubbiness beneath. Behind her, a Paramore poster graced the wall alongside Jared Leto's 30 Seconds to Mars. Stuffed animals covered her bedspread, on the pillows and tucked between books in the bookcase headboard. She was a typical Millennial girl in her preferred milieu: not in the mall, or outside playing, but sitting in front of a computer. Her appeal was less moving than the lifetime of hurt welling from her large brown eyes onto her cheeks. What she had to say, which at least gave the *impression* of being improvised, had been voiced a thousand times before—a *million*—and certainly more articulately. But those eyes spoke words beyond the girl's vocabulary; they filled in the blanks with bursts of eloquence, punctuating it with unspoken poetry.

The pain was no act. No one her age could have acted it so well. But when the girl began to scratch the second time, and the flesh beneath her fingers began to vanish, the only thing Tara could be absolutely certain of was that this girl's story had to be told—and Tara herself would be the first to tell it.

HAL WATERMAN, EDITOR-IN-CHIEF for the Toronto *Herald*, sat in his frosted glass office, hands folded, elbows on the glass and brushed steel desk. Above a gray three-piece without the jacket (*Like Phil Collins*, Tara thought, *Hal Waterman firmly believes no jacket is required.*), he wore a dubious look which, along with mild exasperation and sour disappointment, were the only expressions he seemed familiar with in her company.

"So?" Waterman said, looking up from his computer about a minute into the unknown girl's disappearing act.

"*So?* You *saw* it, didn't you?"

"Right. Pretty nifty fake. Amazing what kids can do in their parents' basements these days."

"Fake," she said. Hal Waterman was being his usual dismissive self, but Tara wasn't in the mood for it. She stood from the impossibly comfortable chair and twisted his monitor further toward him. "Look at it again, Hal."

"I'm kind of busy here, Tara." To prove it, he sorted through the mess of paper and sticky notes on the desk, every square inch scrawled on with the small, neat printing of compulsives and serial killers. "Putting together a national newspaper and all that, you know?"

Tara's hands went her hips before she could stop them.

"Oh, come *on*," the boss said, catching the involuntary body language. "Don't give me the indignant act."

Tara forced them into the tight pockets of her jeans. "Who's indignant? I want the chance to write it, Hal. That's all."

Waterman gave her a shrewd look. "You've got vacation time coming up."

She would have thrown her hands up indignantly if they hadn't been squeezed to death between denim and her thighs. "Vacation!"

"I just don't see a story here, Tara."

"You don't—"

Waterman held up a hand, his fingernails large and square, the pads eternally ink-stained. "Remember the time we printed the article about that twerking video where the girl caught fire? Ran that whole companion piece about teenage sexuality run rampant, and whatnot? Every media outlet, every talk show was all over that thing, and it turned out to be another hoax. If it's fake, Tara—and it doesn't take George Lucas to see that it *is*—then I look like a class-A asshole to the higher-ups for financing your little trip once Jimmy Kimmel steps out of this girl's closet with a mirror and a smoke machine."

The thought made her grin, despite herself. But this wasn't Pepper's Ghost, and if it was a digital effect, it was the best amateur work she'd seen. "And what if it's not, Hal? Hypothetically, what if it's real?"

"Nobody would believe it," he said, folding his hands on the desk. "That's the real bitch of it. We could print every story that comes through my office about UFOs and witches and werewolves in the subways—and believe me, I see a lot of them. Stories, not werewolves."

The focus had gone out of his eyes. He reached into a desk drawer and brought out a bottle of magnesium citrate, popped two pills into his gob and swallowed them with a guzzle from a squat water bottle. Getting one of his "monster headaches," most likely (he never called them migraines), yet another essential component of Tara's visits. "Hell, we could ease our readership into it," he went on, methodically rubbing his temples with his long middle fingers. "Like turning up the hot water on a live frog. One day we're one of the top-rated news rags in North America, and the next, we're the *National Enquirer*'s ugly cousin."

Tara plopped back into the chair, feeling defeated but not ready to give in. "Even if it is bullshit, Hal, it's a story. Teen depression and suicide are all over the news. It's not just a topic for *Law & Order SVU* or *90210* anymore. We'd be tapping into the goddamn *zeitgeist*, Hal. This video's gone viral—*half a million hits in under 8 hours*—and you can bet it's only gonna get bigger. If we don't get the scoop, we'll look like even bigger assholes writing it up a month after the fact, quoting the Associated Press!"

Waterman leaned back, allowing his fingers to slip from his temples as he studied the computer screen. The video had ended. Thumbnails for similar clips, as if there was anything *remotely* similar out there, had filled its box.

"I'll give you one thing: it does look pretty damn realistic for a high school production. I'm not saying it's real," he added hastily. "Look, even if I were to okay this..." (In Waterman-speak, this meant he'd already made up his mind that he would.) "What makes you think you'd be the one to write it? You're on the music beat, after all. No pun intended."

Trying not to grit her teeth, she reminded him: "It's my story."

"You brought it to my desk, sure. That doesn't make it—"

"I *know* this girl," she said, and relished the sound of Waterman's coffee-stained teeth clacking as he shut his mouth. "Maybe not her, specifically, but *girls like her*."

Tara felt the old hurts threatening to bubble up, thick in her throat, and it took an extreme force of will not to tear-up in Waterman's office. She wouldn't give him the satisfaction. He'd think it was his fault, and be tempted to offer his sympathy or talk her down, the kneejerk reactions most men had in the presence of a "hysterical" female. Tara bit the insides of her cheeks. The pain seemed to make the itch in her eyes go away.

Itching. The girl was itching, too, remember?

Fear crept up her spine, seemingly without origin, prickling the baby-fine hairs on her arms as goose pimples rose beneath them. Her mother would have said someone had just walked over her grave. Fortunately, Tara wasn't the least bit superstitious.

Aside from believing a girl could vanish into thin air, she sniped.

Right. Aside from that.

"This isn't going to be like your POW story, is it?" Waterman said, eyeing her queerly, perhaps sensing the waterworks display that had nearly started here in his inner sanctum.

"He promised me an *exclusive*," Tara said, trying not to sound bitter. "How was I supposed to know he'd back out?"

"Fine." Waterman let out one of his characteristic sighs. The pills he'd taken hadn't yet kicked in; he would be pliable for another twenty minutes, tops, suffering under the weight of his Monster Migraine. "But I want your regular stories on my desk every goddamn morning at six. I'm not filling in for you while you're gone."

"You won't regret it," she said, not about to press her luck by requesting a hiatus of her music column while she investigated the video. And because it seemed like she was making a deal with the devil, she offered Waterman her hand.

Somewhat reluctantly, as if Waterman shared the same sentiment, he shook it.

IN THE TWO days it took to pinpoint the Bamber girl's exact address (a friend in the police department came in handy, as he had many times before), Tara's time spent in front of the bathroom mirror was tense.

Coming out of her morning shower, washing her hands after using the toilet, brushing her teeth before bed, she scrutinized every square inch of her body for what she'd started to think of as "missing pixels." Was that mole there before? That dark spot? She found nothing out of the ordinary, of course. Nothing to make her believe she was *actually disappearing*. If she had, she would have checked herself promptly into the nearest insane asylum, or at the very least place a call to the Centre for Addiction and Mental Health, and book an appointment with a trained psychologist at her earliest convenience.

She'd caught herself staring at her reflection in the rearview as she drove to work the second day, and jerked the wheel out of fright. She found it increasingly difficult to focus on anything, mirror or not—anything but the disappearing girl.

It took a fair bit of detective work (and a whole lot of mileage) to get her to the door of the house Mackenzie Bamber shared with her mother (widowed) in Pleasant Valley, Ontario. Not difficult work, per se, just drudgery, particularly since Tara didn't especially love that part of the job. She was competent at it—it was something she did almost automatically, like getting ready for work in the morning—but it wasn't her passion. The interviews and writing of the story were what she enjoyed most about reporting; the detective work was just a means to that end. Unfortunately, with her concurrent gig, the music column, interviews were just another thing threatening to sour her on the profession as a whole. So-called "artists" perpetually whining about their celebrity ("it's not about fame, I'm in it for the music"), rhyming off the same old bullshit ("music is my life" and "God gave me talent")... it had started to wear on her after the first few times. She hated to sound like Holden Caulfield, but you didn't have to look hard to find a phony in the music industry.

This story would be her salvation. It would pull her out of obscurity, thrust her name and her writing into the spotlight—Tara grew more certain of it with every phone call, with every click of the mouse. Men with the same education, the same experience, and much lesser writing skills had been promoted ahead of her for the last time.

Finding the girl who'd posted the video had been as windy a route as the roads through the foothills toward Pleasant Valley. The girl went by the internet handle *@userbits*, a brunette duck-facing in her avatar, with over a dozen short films posted on her YouTube channel, most of them not so much inspired by *The Blair Witch Project* and *Paranormal Activity* as pretty obvious rip-offs. But it was good to see kids doing something other than shooting up their schools or getting pregnant. This was the Bamber girl; the girl in the video, who'd not only disappeared in front of the camera but apparently from the *earth*, was Daria Walker.

A simple Google search brought up over one hundred hits for the name Mackenzie Bamber. Only eleven were from the same girl. Her LinkedIn profile advertised her as a Video Artist, currently working out of Pleasant Valley, Ontario. *Punching above her weight class*, Tara thought admiringly. *Go girl.*

She found the town easily enough, nestled in a valley near Sleeping Giant Provincial Park, on the uppermost shore of Lake Superior, about as picturesque as she might have imagined. Sure beat the shit out of the Sudbury motel where she'd spent the previous night, anyhow. The only amenity there had been a cigarette machine between a pop machine and an ice chest. Tara hadn't seen a functioning cigarette machine since the '80s, and the array of brands was astounding, from du Mauriers to Virginia Slims, an American brand she recalled from flipping through her mother's magazines as a child. She'd stood staring at it, this slot machine whose every push was a jackpot, for almost as long as she'd spent in front of the dirty motel mirror, looking for signs of missing pixels, signs she was disappearing. Eventually she'd chosen the Slims, because its '60s slogan of female empowerment had that ironic edge she enjoyed: *You've come a long way, baby.*

I have, she'd thought, as she lighted up. *Literally and figuratively.*

Born and raised in the city, Tara had felt the isolation deep in her marrow as she drove through the countryside the following morning, and returning to civilization—such as Pleasant Valley offered—had done little to help. This wasn't quite *Deliverance* country, but it was as close as Tara Maxwell had ever wanted to get.

Just passing through town, the casual observer might find it difficult to fathom how the Disappearing Girl's story could have played out here. How could someone feel so utterly ignored in such a small town, one might wonder. With a population of a little over a thousand, it seemed even the most disenfranchised among them would have had very little room to be left alone. But the country was wide, and the town rambled. There were big open spaces between one house and another, even in town, and in those spaces, though the literal distance wasn't much, the *psychic* distance—the space between one family and another, one *person* and another—could be galaxies wide. Each household was a solar system, rotating around its own star.

Tara had an instinct for loneliness. She understood how two people, similar in nearly every respect, could live in the same cramped space and still be so far removed from one another.

The Bambers' prefab was neat and petite, a mere fifteen feet from its neighbor, yet ten feet further apart than most houses on Tara's block, and the house she rented was in one of Toronto's better neighborhoods.

The price of privacy here were the transmission towers rising from what must surely be their backyards, monkey bars for the children of giants. The whole block—with its archipelago of potholes, its beater cars and modular homes in various states of disrepair—lay in their shadows. The towers receded into the distance on either side of the block, continuing through the tree line and into the hills beyond, hydro lines like the webbing of gigantic metal spiders. The steady buzz-hum of electricity likely kept newcomers awake at night; over time, they would either get used to it or be driven out of their minds with sleeplessness and the incessant buzzing, like a character out of Poe. Tara guessed she'd fall into the latter group. She couldn't imagine spending the night here, let alone living in these houses.

The next-door neighbor's dog barked as she stepped out of her cherry-red hatchback, a luxury vehicle in comparison to the pickup and K-Car she parked between, both of which might have seen better days in the mid '90s. Practically foaming at the mouth, the only thing that stopped the dog from making brunch out of Tara was a coil of yellow nylon rope—*fraying* rope, she couldn't help but notice. The Bamber place had a decent lawn, though it looked like it fresh-laid grass. The dog next door kicked up dirt on what could barely be considered a yard, and had wound toward her from its tree and dish through a maze of rusted car parts and a cinderblock fire pit.

Tara opened the screen door, knocked on the laminate door behind it, and waited. The dog kept barking, and somewhere along this row of houses, a man shouted, "*Shut the fuck up, you shithead dog!*"

She was still grinning when Kenzie opened the door, in cut-off jean shorts and a tight Nirvana *Nevermind* t-shirt that rose to show off the sparkly costume jewelry hanging from her belly button. The front pockets hung out from under the deliberately frayed stonewashed denim, and so, likely, did the cheeks of her ass. Tara's mother would have smacked her in the head if she'd caught her daughter wearing those. Hell, Tara would have smacked *herself*.

Kenzie regarded her with mild surprise.

She thought I'd be prettier. They always do.

"Hi, Kenzie," she said, and stuck out a hand. "I'm Tara Maxwell."

A broad smile passed over the girl's face, and she took her hand. "Nice to meet you," the girl said, moving aside to let Tara in. Tidy, with a wooden cross hung on the wall above a threadbare sofa, the air thick with cloying perfume and an unmistakable hint of cigarette smoke. Tara wasn't sure if Kenzie and her mother had cleaned for their guest or if it was always like this, but the lack of dust made her think *neatnicks*. The only real mess was a single ashtray practically choked with cigarette butts. As she followed Kenzie toward the back of the house, Tara noticed they had all been smoked down to the filter.

The girl's bedroom was smaller than Tara's dorm room in college. Walls plastered in band posters, grunge and '90s hip-hop and even The Beatles. Nirvana was the most frequent among them, so she rolled the dice. "Nirvana fan, eh? What's your favorite song?"

"'Scentless Apprentice,'" the girl said with no hesitation, surprising the hell out of Tara, who'd assumed the t-shirt and posters were merely what Kenzie had picked up to have something "vintage," the way kids these days wore shirts of bands whose music they'd never heard. That the girl actually knew something other than Nirvana's '90s anthem of teenage apathy, "Smells Like Teen Spirit," made Tara take an instant liking to her. "That or 'Frances Farmer,'" Kenzie added with a self-conscious shrug.

"Good tune," Tara agreed.

Kenzie looked at Tara over her shoulder, suggesting she was equally impressed by her visitor. Then she sat down at her Mac, every bare surface of the desk covered by photos of herself with friends—making faces, throwing up "deuces," giggling hysterically—the kinds of things Tara vaguely remembered doing with her own small group of friends, except for the deuces, which had meant something quite different when she'd been a kid.

A little beaded friendship bracelet rattled on Kenzie's wrist when she grasped the computer mouse. *Did Daria make that?* Tara wondered. The thought made her shiver as she sat on the bed behind the girl.

With a few clicks, a folder opened. Kenzie hovered the cursor over a video file labeled DARIA, and peered back over her shoulder. "Daria sent this to me the day she..." She stopped there, unsure whether to voice the word they were both thinking: *disappeared.* "...the day she went missing. Cops said it was the last thing she did, far as they could tell."

"I'm sorry," Tara said, having noticed the many appearances of Daria Walker among the girl's photos. The computer's wallpaper was a shot of Daria alone, a close-up of her face in near silhouette, with a smile big enough to beat Buddha, the sky blue and wide and open behind her. "I know what it's like to lose a friend."

The old hurts threatened to bubble up again, but it was the *shame* that hurt Tara the most. She'd seen the signs and done nothing. *Worse* than nothing: she'd turned a willful blind eye, and that was the part that pained her most, when she thought back on it. After Christmas break, when the dorm room across the hall had been empty, something vital inside Tara had broken, and every so often—more often, these days— she found herself on the verge of some kind of breakdown, struggling to fight back the tears.

Kenzie offered a sad little smile and turned back to the screen, where she double-clicked the video.

"MY NAME IS DARIA WALKER," the girl said, as Tara had heard so often she'd lost count—over 700,000, counting all the times Daria had said it to somebody else.

This time was different, watching it over the slumped shoulders of her best friend. Sitting in a bedroom a lot like Daria's had been, it felt somehow more real. Before, she had watched with the somewhat clinical detachment of a spectator. There'd been empathy, sure—but it was *ambition*, and not empathy, that had driven her to Kenzie Bamber's front door.

"I'm fourteen years old, and I started cutting when I was twelve," Daria said, swallowing raw emotion. She pulled up the left sleeve of her surf hoodie, revealing over a dozen raised scars, long, straight and pink, each one adjacent to the next, like a prisoner marking off the days of her confinement. Tara liked the comparison and made a mental note to put it, or something more elegant, in her article.

"I don't know why I started doing it," Daria said, tugging down her sleeve. "I saw my dad's razor in the bathroom and it just sort of... happened. It hurt, like a lot. But it felt good, too. You know when you touch an old TV when it's on, and you get all staticky in your fingers and all up your arm? That's what it was like the first time. It felt *electric* —not just where I cut, either. Like, all over. *Tingly*. I've like, taken all kinds of drugs and pills and stuff, and none of it feels as good as the cutting."

She paused here, perhaps to let the fact of her drug abuse at such a tender age sink in. "A lot of people say cutting is like showing on the outside what someone with depression feels on the inside. It was never like that for me." A shrug. "Well, in the beginning, I guess. I just like how it makes me feel. I never felt ashamed about my scars, even, like they say some kids do. I'm *proud* of them. I know how random that sounds, like I'm fucked-up or something, but it's the truth. I would've cut where people could see them, I just didn't want to get in trouble, and I didn't want them to make me stop. It's just... it's *draining*." She nodded slightly, a twinkle of pleasure in her eyes. "Draining."

Daria Walker scratched at her scars, absently. "I'm so full of these, like, secondhand emotions. I don't know if that make sense or not. Like I'm this giant magnet, and all the hate, the racism and like, homophobia, all the sadness and..." Her lower lip quivered. "...and pain. They're all iron fillings, and they stick to me, and I can't shake them off unless I bleed."

She scratched her arm.

Kenzie paused the video, peering again over her shoulder. "This is where it starts," she said grimly.

Tara already knew when it started: first the left arm began to disappear, and then the right—it was always the same. She kept willing it to change, for it to be different, for the girl to be allowed to finish her monologue, for the video to end with tears of catharsis. But she knew it could never happen that way. When she'd been very young, her mother used to read her fairy tales; the most famous of them had always infuriated Tara. Why did Sleeping Beauty marry the man who'd impregnated her while she was unconscious? Why did the Little Mermaid kill herself over the Prince's betrayal? Her mother could never answer these questions to Tara's satisfaction. It was why she'd started writing in the first place, to change their not-so-happy endings. When she discovered she hadn't a talent for fiction, she'd moved on to journalism. Since she'd always been an inquisitive child, its "five Ws and one H" format had seemed a more natural fit.

The video continued.

"I feel like nobody cares about me," the girl said, "if I live or die, it wouldn't matter to anybody. My dad acts like I don't even exist. I don't know what I did wrong. My mom can't even tell when I'm sad. I go to school, and people laugh at me—not behind my back, either. *To my face.* They call me names. Like Belly Flop. Fall Down Girl. Humpty-*Dumpy.* That's the worst, because if it wasn't me, if they were calling somebody else that, I'd probably laugh, too. All because of that... *fucking video.* It won't go away. I keep finding links to it. I get one taken down, and another one pops up." A resigned sigh. "That's the worst thing about the internet. It's *forever.*"

"What's this video she's talking about?" Tara asked.

Kenzie clicked pause, not looking back. She went back into the DARIA folder and brought up a video called *Skanks* in another window. The footage was shaky, pixelated and soft-focused, probably shot on a cell phone. Kids in winter coats shouted, whistled, cheered, gathered in a big group out front of the school. The shot rose above them, as the kid holding the phone had brought it up over his or her head, then moved jerkily into the crowd. There was Daria Walker, arms up to defend herself. A slimmer, taller girl, a blonde with cornrows, feinted back and forth like a boxer. "Come at me, bitch," Cornrows said. "Stupid-ass punk bitch *slut*. Come at me. Hit me, motherfucker, come on! *Hit me,* you stupid cunt bitch!"

The cell phones came out: everyone was a reporter these days. Nobody had any real empathy anymore. Kids didn't participate in life so much as observe it. Those like Kenzie and Daria, who wore their emotions on their sleeves, risked being pulled kicking and screaming into situations like this... or worse.

"I don't want to fight you, Courtney!" Daria shouted, on the verge of tears.

"Why you hook up with my boyfriend, then, bitch?"

The world had changed since Tara had been in school: back then, a fight was rare. Kids would chant "Beef! Beef! Beefaroni!" and one would invariably go off crying to the principal—and it was always boys, never girls. Powerful female role models, from kick-ass movie heroines to hip-hop divas, had normalized female aggression. As women took on more significant roles in the workplace, moving further from the wife-and-mother caricature of the 1950s, the incidents of them becoming perpetrators of violent crimes as opposed to victims grew exponentially. One only had to look at the statistics to see that equality, at least when it came to delinquency, was well on its way to a mission accomplished.

We've come a long way, baby, she thought, shaking her head despondently.

On the video, before Daria could respond one way or the other, the blonde girl threw a punch, and arms began to flail. Daria grabbed the bigger girl by the hair, instinctively. The girl swung out, hitting her in the face. Tara winced. If the video quality wasn't so bad, she thought she might have been able to see the lights going out in Daria's eyes. The girl's whole body suddenly crumpled, and she fell face forward into the grass.

"Ohhhh, *snap!*" some boy genius said. Laughter erupted at the bon mot. Cell phones circled, vultures over a fresh kill. A shrill girl's voice barked: "*Just* like that! *Just* like that!"

Kenzie clicked the window away. "For the record, Daria never hooked up with anyone. She's too shy for that." Her eyes went cold. "*Was*. And Courtney's boyfriend?" The girl made air-quotes around the word. "He didn't even know they were dating. That's how fucked-up this skank is. She had dibs, so when Angelo told his friends he thought about hooking up with Daria, probably as a joke or something, and then Courtney found out..." Kenzie shrugged. "So now they call her Humpty-Dumpy. Because she's short and not supermodel-thin, and she had a great fall. It's actually pretty clever for most of these troglodytes."

Kenzie started the original video: "Forever," Daria repeated, utterly devoid of hope, and when she blinked, a tear tracked down her cheek.

She scratched at the palm of her right hand, scowling slightly. She scratched again, growing furious, then examined her palm, the frown deepening. Her eyebrows rose, eyes widening in sudden dread. "What...?" When she brought the hand up for closer study, it looked like an optical illusion. There was her hand, clearly delineated, and behind it, *through* it, was the girl's face, eyes narrowed as she twisted it front to back, back to front.

She was disappearing.

Daria whipped around to look behind herself, straggly hair falling over her shoulders, perhaps sensing this was a trick—that, *somehow*, she could still be getting *Punk'd*.

A moment later, the hand had entirely vanished.

"It *tingles*..." she breathed, and her remaining hand went to her stomach. She scrabbled to lift the hoodie, revealing a pale, pudgy belly lined with the multicolored stripes of the other side of her sweater. Her whole body was disappearing, and when she looked up at the camera again, mingled with the horror in her eyes was something like awe.

Kenzie turned and locked eyes with Tara, who simply shook her head.

Daria let her sweater fall back over her stomach—already ghostly, barely there at all—clutching at her throat with the few remaining fingers of her left hand, and the stump of the right. Her eyes bugged out. Her mouth opened, wet tongue protruding, writhing like a salted slug. She was suffocating, choking to death because she had no air; her lungs had ceased to exist, had taken her breath with them.

If *anyone* had ever really seen Daria Walker before—her parents, her grandparents, a cousin, a friend—they would never see her again. This video was her headstone and her epitaph. It was her legacy, whether she'd wanted one or not.

Kenzie clicked the window away, looking sickly. "I can't watch any more than that."

"No," Tara lied. "Me neither."

"Where do you think she went?" Kenzie asked after a moment of silence, genuinely curious, hoping Tara held the answer.

"Went?"

"I mean, she had to go somewhere... don't you think?"

Tara hadn't thought of that, but it stood to reason. "Maybe. I don't know."

Kenzie nodded, clearly dissatisfied with the response.

"But if she went somewhere," Tara tried for a conciliatory tone, "I'd like to think it's a better place than this."

"Yeah," Kenzie said. "Pleasant Valley's a real shithole."

The admission surprised a laugh out of Tara. "I meant this world. It didn't seem to have a lot to offer Daria Walker."

Kenzie thought this over. "No," she said. "It really didn't." Her eyes lighted. "Can I ask you something?"

"Anything."

"Is it true? Does it get better?" She seemed to notice Tara's confusion, and explained: "They always say it gets better when you're older. Celebrities say it all the time. There's all these commercials about it and everything. But does it really?"

Tara only considered telling a lie for a moment. *What good would that do?* she thought. *Give a kid false hope, false expectations—what good?* She wished someone had just told her the truth when she was a kid. It would have saved her a lot of pain. "Sometimes," she said. "Mostly, you just learn how to deal with all the shit that life throws at you. I'm probably not the best person to ask."

The girl shrugged. "You seem pretty cool to me."

Tara smiled. "Thanks. You're pretty cool yourself."

Kenzie blushed, and turned to the computer to hide her face. Then she said without turning, in a timid voice, "Ms. Maxwell?"

"Mmn?"

"What advice would you give to an aspiring writer?"

The girl was full of surprises. Tara thought about telling her if she wasn't writing about a topic she believed in, she might fool a lot of people, but others would know. She wanted to say, *Do just about anything else, for the sake of your sanity.* She wanted to tell her it was still a man's world, and that they might let her climb the ladder, but they'd never let her into their precious clubhouse.

Kenzie awaited her reply.

"Just follow your dreams," Tara offered. She'd provided the girl with enough reality for one day.

TARA STARTED WORK on the article that afternoon. Aside from the girl fight, Kenzie hadn't given her much fresh information to go with, but she had helped to humanize Daria. She'd also given Tara a hardcopy of the photo she had as her desktop, the one of Daria Walker in close-up, smiling in front of that big blue sky.

First, though, Tara banged off her regular column, a junk-food appetizer before the big gourmet meal. The music column was easy. A little internet research, a few choice snide remarks (rarely a compliment these days), and it was done. Sometimes she had to listen to an album, and rarely were they good: a few tracks here and there, if anything—almost never wall-to-wall hits. There was no great challenge to the stories, and very little reward. They went in to Waterman at the end of each day, and the money went into her checking account every two weeks.

With no motels in the area, she was staying at a B&B near the outskirts of Pleasant Valley. Nice, but a little frou-frou for her taste: doilies and dollies. The owners seemed very conservative, and eyed her with veiled suspicion. In her black leather jacket and tight jeans, she wasn't likely typical of the guests they were used to putting up. Probably not the *type of woman* they were used to, either. When she'd told them she was a journalist, the woman had seemed perplexed, as if she had never considered the possibility of a female writer, outside the likes of Charlotte Brontë or Jane fucking Austen.

Tara took tea up to her room, a life-sized version of a bedroom from a dollhouse, and started clacking away. No Wi-Fi, of course, but she'd brought a 4G stick along, just in case. "Always be prepared: it's your ass on the line"—another of Waterman's catchphrases, one Tara happened to believe in.

Well into the article, she suddenly realized she hadn't really thought about her own high school and college days in a very long time, aside from those brief, painful thoughts of the girl across the hall. She hadn't talked to anyone from high school in years, and the last university friend she'd kept in touch with had cut off communication abruptly about six months ago, after the birth of her twins. The price of ambition was leaving her friends behind. She felt isolated in the small room, desperately lonely in this small town where nobody knew her. There was no one to call to shake this feeling, aside from her mother, or Constable Daniels, and he'd likely just wonder why she would call so soon after he'd helped her, if she didn't want a booty call. Her mother would be happy to hear from her, but of course she'd ask if Tara was dating anyone, and Tara was not in the mood for a conversation about her non-existent love life.

She flicked through Facebook, trying for names she only vaguely remembered, sifting through photos of people she hadn't seen in ages: their vacations, their lovers, spouses, children and pets. At last she typed in Hope's name, hesitantly... and of course there was no Hope, because she'd committed suicide during Tara's first year of university.

No hope for any of us, she thought, sneering at the painfully obvious metaphor.

Tara got up from the bed, snapping her laptop closed. The sun was a glowing peach at the horizon, seen through the frosted glass of the bedroom window. She'd asked the proprietors not to bother her for dinner, but now she was starving, and she headed downstairs to where Edwin and Mildred Snodgrass were washing up after supper. The kitchen smelled of roast beef and mashed potatoes. As their only guest, her presence always seemed to startle them. She asked if there was anything open where she could grab a bite.

"There's the Country Manor, just off Highway 587," Mrs. Snodgrass said, toweling her soapy hands.

"Closer to Pass Lake, really," Mr. Snodgrass added, putting an arm around his wife's ample waist.

"Country Manor," Tara said. "I was actually thinking of something a little more... rustic? A booze and chicken wings kind of place."

Mrs. Snodgrass flashed her husband a brief and indecipherable look. "Well, there's the Sow's Head Tap downtown," he said. "It gets a little rough this time of night, though."

"Not very pleasant during the day, either, I'm afraid," Mrs. Snodgrass added.

Tara smiled. "I'm a big girl. I'm sure I can handle it. Thanks for the advice."

"We *have* leftovers," Mrs. Snodgrass offered, hoping to tempt her out of what she likely felt might lead to Tara's untimely demise.

"It does smell delicious," Tara admitted. "But I'm right in the thick of my article, and I could really use a little libation to oil the wheels, if you get what I mean."

"We've got sherry," Mr. Snodgrass suggested, not very enthusiastically. "Cooking sherry," he admitted with downcast eyes. Mrs. Snodgrass was still eyeing her with mild reproach.

"As lovely as that sounds, Ed, I'm a scotch gal."

Mr. Snodgrass nodded, eyes still on the floor as he hugged his wife closer to him.

"Well, adios," Tara said, beating a hasty retreat.

"Goodnight," Mrs. Snodgrass said with abrupt finality.

THE SOW'S HEAD was a faux-Irish pub with slightly drunken clientele, playing darts, shooting pool and watching the Habs game, but mostly just drinking. It certainly wasn't the mecca of criminal activity Mr. and Mrs. Snodgrass had made it out to be. Obviously, they'd never set foot in here. It was possible they knew some of the regulars, and avoided it on principle, or maybe—and this was more likely—they were just all around snobby people, and their Dickensian surname suited them well.

Tara sat at the bar, ordered the best scotch they had (Famous

Grouse, neat), and a plate of chicken wings with poutine on the side. While she waited, she drank. The heat of the alcohol felt good in her empty stomach, going to her head quickly—*Tingly*, she thought morbidly—and she ordered a second, this time with ice.

A couple of burly guys shoved up to the bar while the waitress brought her food, ordering Canadian Club and cola, and cheap, strong beers. CC&C watched her eat a moment, and when she looked up at him, he smiled. Other than the missing canine, he looked like he just might do.

"That's a lot of food for such a little lady," he said, still smiling as his friends shoved him and cheered at the game on the big screen above the bar.

"Thanks for noticing," she said. His comment annoyed her, calling her a "lady," and the combination of the alcohol and her resentment toward him made her want to show CC&C just how much of a lady she could be. "Watching the game, huh?"

"Go Habs go," he said, irritating—and *enticing*—her further. Tara found there was something about a good hate fuck nothing could quite match. Constable Daniels had once been one, but they'd grown so comfortable with each other over the years, had gotten so used to each other's faults, that it was hard to feel much of anything for each other anymore, let alone hate. Just going through the motions now, fucking for the sake of it, not that there was anything wrong with the sex itself. He'd always employed adequate choking, and a good hard-to-slow ratio. He was decent at cunnilingus, kept clean and neatly manscaped. And he was *strong*. Constable Daniels could lift her up over his head to perform acrobatic sex moves that had been hot in the beginning but had lately become simply exhausting.

This guy, CC&C, looked like he hadn't had a shower for a couple of days. He smelled like cheap drugstore cologne and cigarettes, and appeared doughy under his red and white Canadiens jersey with HENDERSON 00 stenciled on the back of it. She didn't know much about hockey, but she knew enough to assume the shirt was custom, and that Henderson was probably *his* name. Since she didn't care one way or another, she decided to continue referring to him by his drink of choice.

"Can I buy you a drink?" he asked stupidly. The lucky idiot had no idea he'd already stumbled and stuttered halfway into her pants.

"I've got this," she said, and sipped her scotch. "Tell you what, Mr. CC&C: I need to get another two or three of these into me before I head out into the night. When you're done with the game, why don't you swing by?"

He looked astonished, and laughed excitedly, as if a woman had never picked him up before. "Wait... You're serious?"

"Like an audit."

This confused him, but when his friends cheered again, he came around. "You better save some room," he said with an awkward wink, trying for sexy and missing it by a country mile.

"Don't ruin it by talking," she said, and bit a chunk off the drumstick.

———

THE SNODGRASSES WERE asleep when she and CC&C crept upstairs to her room. He tripped over a chair on which Mr. or Mrs. Snodgrass had seated a large doll, and the doll fell. CC&C caught it in mid-air and set it back on the chair, lopsided. *Nice reflexes*, Tara thought. *Let's hope he knows how to use them.*

The sex was okay but brief. He balked at having to wear a condom, squeezed her tits a little too much and wanted to kiss her more than she felt comfortable with, especially since his mouth tasted like cigarettes. She bit him on the lower lip, hard enough to bring blood, and he winced and pulled back, sulking like a little boy, yet he still plunged in for more. Unable to take any more, she pushed him off her and rolled over onto her hands and knees. At least with doggie he couldn't smear his mouth all over hers.

"You're beautiful," he said, now that he could no longer see her face.

"*You're* crazy."

He didn't attempt any more small talk or compliments after that, and he came before she could, groaning enormously and shuddering inside her before falling back against the pillow. Then he rummaged on the floor for his pants, his belt buckle and a pocketful of change jingling in the post-fuck silence. He came up again with a pack of cigarettes.

"You can't smoke those in here," she said in a whisper. Tara didn't know either way, she just didn't want him tempting her. She hadn't had a single puff since the motel in Sudbury.

He tossed them back on the floor with a hefty sigh and lay back on his pillow, crossing his hands behind his head. "So," he said, after a period of silence, breathing heavily through his nose in the half light. "What's your deal?"

She turned to him, regarded his saggy man-tits and the sparse hair under his arms. "Make me come," she said, "then ask me again."

He did both, but she still wouldn't answer, drifting off to sleep instead.

* * *

THE NEXT MORNING, Tara came downstairs to find Mr. and Mrs. Snodgrass standing in the kitchen, wearing identical expressions of disappointment. The sight of them standing there confrontationally surprised her enough to get the adrenaline pumping, the slight hangover making her head ache. "We'd like you to leave as soon as possible," Mr. Snodgrass told her, his eyes on the tiles in front of him. "Pack your things and go. *Please*."

"Why? Is this a joke?"

"We don't make jokes," Mrs. Snodgrass sneered. "We *heard*—" She pursed her lips in disgust, lowering her voice to a harsh whisper, as if it weren't just the three of them in the house. "In your room, after hours. With a *man*."

"Well, Mildred, I didn't realize you had rules against gentleman callers."

"We *don't*," Mr. Snodgrass said. "It's just common sense, isn't it?"

"I don't think so. I've paid to stay here—for three nights, I should add."

Mildred Snodgrass nudged her husband sharply. He stepped forward in a military-like movement, thrusting a handful of cash toward Tara. She refused to look at it.

"Oh for Pete's sake, take the money!" Mrs. Snodgrass snapped.

Tara snatched it from the old man. She packed her things and was on the road fifteen minutes later.

THE O.P.P. STATION, her last stop before the Walker house, wasn't far outside of town. In little communities like Pleasant Valley, too small to support their own police forces, the Ontario Provincial Police provided law enforcement services. Constable Daniels of the Toronto Police had hooked her up with Detective Constable Collette Nadeau of the O.P.P., a severe-looking woman with dark hair, tanned, muscular and small-breasted, with thin, bloodless lips.

Compared to her, I'm a stunner, Tara thought as she introduced herself. She'd always had problems with her own looks, and had found herself judging others against her. Her eyes were slightly off-kilter, her nose too bumpy in the bridge, lips too small, childlike, and her jaw mannishly square. Psychiatrists had a clinical term for it: body dysmorphia. Knowing it had a name hadn't helped; she still felt uncomfortable in her own skin, as if the face she wore were only a mask. Most days she didn't let it bother her. Today, after CC&C had called her "beautiful," was not one of those days.

"You are looking into the Walker disappearance, is that correct?" Constable Nadeau dropped into the chair behind her desk with a squeak. She spoke with a heavy Quebecois accent, the English slightly stilted; *th* becoming *t* or *d*, depending; lone *h*s dropped; emphases in all the wrong places.

"Yes, that's right," Tara said. "Do you mind if I record this?"

Nadeau waved the question away.

"How long has she been missing?"

"Two week," Nadeau said. "The Bamber girl reported she had not seen her the afternoon Daria made her video."

"Nor her parents."

Nadeau wore mysterious smile as she shook her head. "Oh no. MacKenzie was supposed to meet Daria to work on a video project for school. I suspect it was this video you see on the internet, which she had uploaded later that day."

"You think these kids worked on it together. That it's just special effects."

"Oh, I have no doubt, Ms. Maxwell." She folded her hands over the desk, leaning forward on her elbows, reminding Tara of Hal Waterman. "And you? Surely you don't think it's real?"

"Of course not." Her indignation seemed forced even to herself. "Why did you smile when I asked about her parents? Did they—?"

"Greta and Anson Walker are... *unique*."

"Unique? How so?"

Nadeau raised her sharp eyebrows. "Let us just say, it's no wonder to me why Daria Walker disappeared," the detective said, then frowned a little at the unintentional implication, and corrected herself: "Went missing. The girl's father didn't even remember what she was wearing that day, not that it would have helped one way or the other."

De udder was how it sounded in Nadeau's accent, and Tara couldn't help but grin. "Why not?"

"The thing is, Daria left a pile of clothes in front of the computer before she slipped out of her bedroom window. The hoodie, her jogging pant, a pair of socks and underwear. All the things she wore in the video. There was even an earring and a little beaded bracelet—"

Tara seized on it: "A friendship bracelet?" *Left her clothes. Left her bracelet, and her jewelry... everything she couldn't take with her to the Great Beyond.*

"Maybe." Nadeau shrugged. "She'd just left it there on the carpet beside her desk chair. Like she want us to believe she literally disappeared."

<hr>

TARA SHOWED UP AT THE WALKERS' house just before noon, a nice, neat bungalow with a yellow-brown lawn and a garden full of dried flowers. The shades were drawn, no visibility in or out. She rang the bell, expecting no one to be home. They'd be at work; it was silly for her to have come so early. She rang it again.

"Oh, for Christ's sake!" a man said from inside. His footfalls stomped toward the door. A latch was pulled, a door chain, the main lock, and the door opened wide enough for the man to peek out. Mr. Walker blinked hard several times behind thick, dandruff-flecked glasses, split across the lenses with clear and shaded areas. He looked as if he hadn't seen the sun in days. Another chain-lock swung gently above his head. "Yes? What is it?"

"I'm Tara Maxwell," she said, realizing this was a bad idea. She should have waited until they were out and slipped in through a carelessly unlocked window. It was the bedroom she needed, after all—the computer. "I spoke to your wife on the phone?"

The man glowered back over his shoulder, then squinted at her. "What's this in reference to?"

"Your daughter."

It didn't seem to compute. He squinted off, lips moving in thought. "Oh—Daria! Yes, we're all very upset. Beside ourselves, really. You're the reporter, is that right?"

"Uh huh."

He closed the door on her, unlatched the last chain, and opened the door again, wide enough for passage. Mr. Walker moved aside, and Tara squeezed past him into the gloomy house. "Honey, that reporter is here!" He shouted it practically in Tara's ear.

"Who?" came Mrs. Walker's voice, high and slightly squeaky.

"The reporter!" He rolled his eyes at Tara. "You talked to her on the phone?"

"Oh, right. Let her in, would you?"

"She *is* in!" Mr. Walker shook his head. He was slender, his shirt practically hanging off his shoulders. *If he was any skinnier,* Tara thought, *he'd disappear himself.* "Oh, can I... may I take your coat?" He reached out for it, displaying absolutely no sense of how to behave with strangers.

"That's okay," she said, shrinking back from his touch. His fingertips were riddled with frayed strips of skin, the nails bitten to jagged stubs, still somehow dirty under what remained of the raw cuticles.

Mrs. Walker stepped gingerly into the room, plumpish in her sundress and gray cardigan, her eyes, one blue and one green, staring off vaguely. *Those things are wonkier than mine*, Tara thought. When her slender, arthritic fingers came up to feel the wall, Tara realized Mrs. Walker was blind, and felt bad for her thought.

"Honey, put your glasses on," Mr. Walker said with a critical edge.

The woman reached into the pocket of her cardigan and brought out a pair of oversized Jackie O sunglasses. She unfolded them and slid them on. "Better?" she asked.

Mr. Walker didn't even look, just said, "Much," and plopped himself down in front of his computer. On the screen was a videogame, something fantasy by the look, which he took out of Pause before donning a headset.

It was no wonder Daria felt like nobody could see her. Mrs. Walker was visually impaired or fully blind, and Mr. Walker probably wouldn't have noticed his daughter if she stood right in front of him: a father who wouldn't see her, and a mother who *couldn't*.

Talk about on-the-nose, Tara mused. *Metaphor alert.*

"Anson's hooked on that ridiculous game," Mrs. Walker explained with shame evident in her voice, as if she'd tried everything to drag him away from it, and considered his childish obsession her own personal failure.

"They're pretty addictive," Tara said, not that she'd ever been interested in them. Even the words "gaming" and "gamer" annoyed her.

"No, he's literally an addict. He likes to call himself a *completionist*, whatever that means. If he was so concerned with completing things, you'd think he could unload the dishwasher every once in a while."

Tara chuckled. Mrs. Walker stretched out a hand, and Tara took it.

"Greta Walker," the woman said.

"Tara. It's good to meet you. I'm sorry about your daughter."

"So am I," Greta said. "Would you like something to drink?"

"Don't trouble yourself."

"Oh, it's no trouble."

"Coffee would be great then, if you have it. Thank you."

"One coffee, coming up," Greta Walker said, and shuffled into the kitchen. Tara followed. Photographs lined the walls, some of Mr. Walker, most of Daria, blurry and improperly framed. Anson Walker was obviously not much of a photographer, or didn't care for photographs, which was why Greta must have taken them herself. The frames themselves were neat and hung straight, except one, a professional Christmas photo on a slight angle. Greta reached up and straightened it as she passed, as if she'd seen—or *sensed*—it was crooked.

"Daria was always a troubled girl," Mrs. Walker said as she began to take the coffee fixings from their places and gather them on the counter. She felt cupboard edges and lids and touched the outlet to unplug the toaster and plug in the coffeemaker. "When she was very little, she threw tantrums all the time. It didn't matter where we were: the grocery store, church, her grandmother's house—and she *adores* her grandmother." She held the lip of the filter basket and scooped four heaping spoonfuls of grinds into it. "Sometimes I think she was born in the wrong time, the way they got along."

"You spilled some coffee on the counter," Tara said.

"I heard. Thank you, though."

"Mrs. Walker—"

"*Greta.*"

"Greta, did your daughter ever receive any professional help?"

"You mean a psychiatrist?" Greta, still facing the counter, raised her head without turning. "Once. She said he'd just told her everything she already knew. She's very self-aware. *Hyper* aware. I often think that's a big part of the problem. Alone with your thoughts all the time..." She trailed off there as the coffeemaker began to gurgle.

Tara thought she knew what the woman meant. Self-awareness could easily become a prison cell, and its evil stepsister, self-pity, made for a cruel warden. Tara knew this from bitter experience. She'd pulled herself up from depression after college, for the most part, but sometimes she felt like a diver whose rope led down into an abyss. Every so often there'd come a tug, threatening to drag her back under, and she worried someday she might not be able to resist its pull.

Like Daria.... Like *Hope.*

"Have you seen—?" She meant to ask if she'd seen the video, but of course Greta Walker had not seen the video. She hadn't ever *seen* anything, not unless her blindness had come later in life.

"Have I seen what, dear?"

"Sorry," Tara said, unsure of how to proceed.

"If you mean Daria's video, Anson described it while I listened. He said it looked very convincing. If she ever comes back, he promised to buy her better video software for her computer."

"Is the computer here?"

"Oh, yes. That woman detective returned it a few days ago."

"May I...?"

"Of course. That's why you came, isn't it?" The coffeemaker quieted. Greta gently removed the carafe and poured it into two cups. "Cream or sugar?"

"Double-double," Tara said.

"Two of each?" She shrugged. "The way you carry yourself, I suppose you could stand to put on a few pounds."

Tara wasn't sure if she meant this as a compliment or an insult, and chose to ignore it. Greta poured the cream and plopped two cubes from a china pot into the cup. She dropped a spoon into it and held it out.

"Thank you, Greta." Tara stirred it, blew on its rim.

"Daria's room is down the basement. It's the only room there, aside from the furnace room and the toilet. If you need any help, just holler up the stairs."

"I should be fine." She smiled, before realizing the woman couldn't see her face, so the smile was pointless. Daria had likely felt that way sometimes, with a father who seemed not to care, knowing her mother could never see whether she was happy or sad, making it all the more easy for her to hide. "Thanks again, Greta."

"No trouble at all," the woman said, and sat down at the kitchen table to blow on her own coffee in a thin slat of sunshine from a crack in the drapes.

HERE SHE STOOD, finally, in the doorway of a room she'd seen a hundred times but still had yet to enter. A small basement bedroom with a squat sliding window at head-height, its posters of bands and hot boys with their shirts off, its frilly bedspread and stuffed animals—which now seemed wholly unlike Daria, although Tara realized she really knew very little about this girl. Perhaps the dolls were her mother's influence, or her grandmother's.

Standing so close made her nervous. *Daria Walker had vanished here.* The room itself could have been a portal, a Bermuda Triangle, a wormhole, a magical doorway to some fantasy world or a parallel dimension. Where it lead, if anywhere, nobody quite knew. There'd been plenty of speculation in the comments section. Most commenters believed Daria had been whisked away by an angel, the first of many mortals too good for this world, who would rise to the Heavens during the Rapture; to others, she'd been dragged to the underworld by demons. A handful of theories, marginally more scientifically plausible —albeit still pretty far-out—filled the comments section below the video, along with the usual compendium of End of the World scenarios typed out by paranoid Chicken Littles, their Cheeto fingers smudging the keys.

Tara didn't buy a word of it. Her pet theory was that—like Daria's scars, an outward projection of internal troubles—the girl hadn't disappeared from the earth at all, but merely from *sight*. She was a presence in this room, like a haunting, liberated from the burden of her corporeal self. After the initial fear and pain, it would have felt like a weight lifting from Daria's shoulders, a shedding of her skin, the caterpillar bursting forth from its cocoon as a butterfly.

She would be *free*.

That was what Tara decided had happened to Daria Walker, and her article would reflect this hopeful slant.

I could disappear down here myself and no one would care, Tara thought. Hal Waterman and the *Herald* would find someone else to write her music columns. Her mother would be concerned, but she was old, edging toward senility. In another couple of years, the Alzheimer's would become so bad, she wouldn't remember her daughter anyhow. And Constable Daniels, with his recent passive-aggressive behavior—as opposed to the *real* aggression Tara prized—would probably be happy to be rid of her, not having to go through the trouble of dumping her himself.

With an anxious breath, Tara slipped through the doorway. A rush of air met her ears.

The laptop lay on a small rolltop desk. She crossed to it, thought about sitting down, but didn't. The basement was stuffy, and Daria's bedroom was no exception. She crossed to the window and unlatched it. For a brief moment she hesitated, hand on the frame. But the thought was silly. If Daria was still here and had wanted to slip out of this house, she would have done so already. No window or door could bar her way now.

With the window opened, she felt like she could breathe again. She sat down in front of the computer and fired it up. The laptop, in Standby mode, didn't require a password. *Must've been pretty trusting of her parents to have no security on this thing,* Tara thought. *I would've had an electric fence around mine at her age, with all the secrets I kept.*

Now that she sat behind Daria's desk, Tara wasn't sure exactly what to do next. She'd simply wanted to sit here, in the chair from which Daria had winked out of existence. To know what it felt like.

On this side of the video, she saw many of the same photos Kenzie Bamber had posted at her computer desk, but Daria had scratched out her own face from every single one, obliterating it.

Jesus—just like I used to, Tara thought, suddenly feeling like she was hyperventilating.

There were small circles on the keyboard where Daria's fingers had worn the surfaces: the G, H, E, S and T. Between the keys crumbs and dust had gathered, the sliver of a nibbled fingernail. Tara plucked a straggly golden hair curled in the fabric of the chair, and let it fall from her fingers. In the garbage can, empty packages of Coffee Crisp and Crunchie bars lay among crushed cans of orange pop. Fresh junk food filled the drawers: candy, chocolate bars and chips. Tara rummaged through them, hoping to find something else in the drawer, some pencils or pens, coins, mementos or keepsakes. Something bit into her finger and she withdrew it with a sucking breath.

The end of her finger was bleeding.

She tossed the junk food aside and found the drawer empty, aside from the blade from a disposable razor at the far back, its surface rusty and crusted with a black, gritty material she recognized as dried blood.

We're blood sisters now, she thought.

In the trash, a candy wrapper uncrumpled with a small, insectile sound, suddenly blooming as if Daria had only thrown it out moments ago. Of course that was impossible, as Daria hadn't been here in weeks. Tara supposed it wasn't likely Daria's mother or father would have recently been sitting in the chair eating their daughter's chocolate bars, though certainly she'd seen and heard of stranger things.

"Daria?" she said. "Are you here with me?"

A sudden blast of chilly air met her query. She nearly jumped, but her reporter's instincts kept her in the chair, sucking at the hurt end of her finger, weighing the options. A moment later, she heard the *tick-tick-tick* of the air conditioner kicking in, and looked up. The overhead vent blew frigid air down on her.

Jumping at shadows. But she is *here. I feel* something.

Inspiration struck. She opened Daria's word processor program, letting the cursor blink. It was what she did when stuck with a blank page, waiting for the muses to work through her fingers. She took in a deep breath. Held it. Then let it out slowly.

"Daria, where are you now?"

She waited, watching the cursor. Nothing happened.

What the hell was I thinking, anyway? It's a PC, not a Ouija board.

But the tip of her injured finger was tingling.

It tingles, Daria had said.

"This is something, isn't it?" Tara asked the empty room. She held the finger over the keyboard, hovered there above the keys, and the ends of her other fingers began to tingle. For a moment, she worried they might begin to disappear, but they remained solid. She poised them over the keys, forefingers resting on F and J, and like Daria's emotion magnet, she felt the pull of some invisible force, and typed out a single word:

yes

Fear gripped her insides. *I started this, didn't I?* Nothing to do now but finish it. "Where are you?" she asked Daria's not-so-empty room.

The answer came through her fingers. She watched them, frightened and incredulous, moving not of her own volition, but as if the fingers themselves were possessed.

everwhere nowear

Tara puzzled over this. "Is there any way I can help you? Is there a way to bring you back?"

confessss, Daria typed.

"Confess? Confess to what?"

Her fingers clacked at the keyboard. She read what Daria had typed:

confesshun ezs th sole makes pane disapeer

Confess, Tara thought. *What do I have to confess to?*

But she didn't need to think hard. The old hurt spilled over and Tara began to type, this time on her own.

"My Confession"
Tara Maxwell

I let it happen. I saw the signs and did nothing, and the girl who lived across the hall killed herself. I was so afraid they would start picking on me that I let them bully her into the grave. Anything to get their attention away from me. I could have befriended her, I could have comforted her, but I would have been shunned. Hope didn't cut her wrists or take pills—she threw herself out of her dorm room window while the rest of us were off on Christmas break. By the time we returned to school, a new year had started, and her parents had already come and gone.

Her bedroom was empty. Nobody cared to wonder why.

I've thought a lot about what I could have done to help her over the years, but by then it no longer mattered.

I could have helped her, but I didn't. Because

Tara paused to scratch her arm, and kept typing. Tears stung her eyes and ran down her cheeks, and she didn't spare a moment to consider the sudden itch in her arm. Her mind was on her confession, unburdening herself of her darkest secret.

Because I was scared. I let them tease her. I heard her cry alone in her room, saw her withdraw from school, from life, and I said nothing. It's as much my fault as it is theirs, only they didn't care.

They laughed and made jokes about it after she was gone. Said she'd come back as a slug, only nobody would be able to tell the difference. Like that was funny. And I laughed along. Because if I didn't, they would know how I really felt.

My inaction killed Hope Chandra, and nothing I do will bring her back.

Tara let out a long, ragged sigh of relief. She sniffled, wiped her eyes with the back of her hand. *Confession eases the soul.* Daria was right—she felt clean. As empty as Hope's dorm room had been after Christmas break.

The cursor blinked at the bottom of the page.

"Daria?"

Was she gone? Had she moved on to discover what dreams might come, now that she'd ridded herself of the misfortune of being human?

The screen winked out, going back into standby. But the little red light beside Daria's webcam remained on. Tara never noticed.

She felt it first on her shoulder. It wasn't quite a tingle, more like the splash of warm rain on her skin. Painless, and somehow that was even more frightening. She had predicted pain. Without it, she didn't know what to expect.

Tara stood and peeled off her jacket, tossing it on the floor beside her, then pulled up her t-shirt to look at her arm. The skin was vanishing in small dots like droplets—like acid eating away at her flesh, only beneath there was nothing. As a child, she'd loved the rain. She'd waited for the puddles to gather, then thrown on her yellow slicker and splashed in them. She had tilted her head back and caught mouthfuls of fresh water from the sky, swallowing it in big gulps. She had stood and watched the birds, fluttering their wings, splashing in their birdbath in the backyard, and she'd wished she could be among them, small and frail in that enormous bowl of fresh rainwater. She'd wished she could fly up into the clouds as they threw down their fury upon the earth.

The fear of this process—whatever was happening to her now, had happened to Daria—washed away.

Tara slipped her t-shirt over her head, watched as her taut belly speckled away into the ether. Her right arm mostly gone, she touched the space where her stomach had been with her remaining hand, and found only empty space. Somehow, she remained upright as her body drifted away beneath her. She unhooked her bra and let it fall to the floor, unbuttoned her fly and shook out of her jeans, pulled off her socks, standing on one leg at a time, legs that had already begun to vanish as she danced out of her jeans. She wanted desperately to be unfettered, to feel only the warm, gentle rain on what remained of her body, her *self*. Finally, Tara stood naked in front of the computer, looking at what remained of herself in its mirrored black face, her arms spread out like wings, watching as she faded away into beautiful nothingness.

Her breasts evaporated or dissolved—she couldn't tell, and it didn't matter. She felt the breath whoosh out of her then, and for a terrifying moment she thought she'd suffocate, as Daria had. But she calmed herself, not by meditative breathing but by counting the seconds which passed *without* breath, instinctually realizing that if she had no body, she had no need for oxygen.

Her jaw, that embarrassingly mannish jaw, faded away, though she knew she would miss it. Her too-small lips didn't seem so girlish in retrospect, 20/20 hindsight, as they turned from red to pink to white like a fading flower and then to no color at all, becoming invisible. Her bumpy nose actually looked almost cute on its own, with just the eyes to compliment it—then it too whisked away. Her hair, which had never had enough body and was always too straight, disappeared from the tips to the roots. As it went, she decided a bob or a pixie cut would have framed her eyes nicely, which, she realized, were actually quite pretty.

When at last the eyes themselves disappeared, there was nothing left of her to see.

HAL WATERMAN'S BLACKBERRY beeped in the darkness of his bedroom, waking his wife first. Jean Waterman leaned over groggily and shook him awake, then fell back to her pillow. He put on his reading glasses, flicked on his bedside lamp, and plucked the phone up from the nightstand.

"All right, all right, hold your horsies," he muttered to the incessant beeps.

He scrolled to the message: an email sent from Tara Maxwell, at just past 2A.M. *A little late*, he thought, though without much surprise. The message contained an attachment, not to the text file he'd expected but to a video with a bizarre title—*everwerenowear.mp4*, whatever the hell that meant. He considered it a moment, sleepily. *Why would Maxwell send me a video?*

"She *wouldn't*," he answered himself. Jean uttered an inquisitive moan beside him. "Nothing, dear. Go back to sleep."

He'd seen this before: someone's email was hacked, and sent out suspicious links. Open it, and the virus would infect you.

Resolute, Hal Waterman deleted the spam, set his phone and reading glasses back on the bedside table, and snuggled up to his sleeping wife.

Always trouble with that girl, he thought, and thinking this, he drifted off to sleep.

Artifact (#37)

THEY ALL HAD their jobs to do: Ugly Karl did the driving, Mad Bastard did the videotaping, and Meat did the girl. It was how they'd always done it; deviation from the plan would inevitably lead to disaster.

The Filthy Lessons crew dumped Nora West, a new girl in the business, out of their white van and onto the side of the road under the Dolphin Expressway overpass. Bastard tossed her purse, keeping her in frame as she caught it. Most of its contents spilled out onto the sidewalk. Nora collected her clothes, strewn along Northwest 35th: the yoga pants, the loose-fitting pink halter, bedazzled with the word HAWT, the frilly white panties Meat had scrunched up and stuffed into her mouth to muffle her cries.

She'd had time to put on her sandals and nothing else, the acne on her forehead shimmering in the mid-afternoon sun below a blonde fringe. She was still trying to scoop the contents of her purse back in with her right hand, while in her left she still held the rag she'd used to sop Meat's cum off her face and out of her hair.

"What about my two hundred dollars?" she said, looking worried, her face all squinched-up and somehow still attractive. Zellweger-esque.

"Lesson learned, biatch!" The Bastard shouted at her. The line served a dual purpose as the Filthy Lessons's catchphrase and Ugly Karl's cue to peel away from the curb, but Ugly's foot remained still. "Dude, let's get the fuck out of here!" Bastard yelled, slapping Karl on the shoulder.

Improvising, Nora began running naked toward them, looking supremely pissed, her sandals going skid-*clack!* skid-*clack!* against the pavement. No one cared. People might have gawked as they drove past, but nobody braked or made a hasty call to the MDPD. Welcome to Miami, ladies and sperms—the Gateway to America.

Bastard's little brother, Ian, who'd co-created and maintained the Filthy Lessons website, drove a few blocks behind them, ready to pick up Nora, hand over a good wad of cash, and have her sign the release. It was a trick Filthy Lessons played on their audience: paying semi- and non-professional models to pretend they were everyday girls picked up off the street and tricked into having sex for money. These were "ordinary, respectable girls" in desperate need of quick cash to pay off that student loan, that credit card bill, that trip to New Orleans where they just might flash their boobs for Mardi Gras beads with a few too many drinks, or that visit to the clinic to fix their "little mistake."

The illusion FilthyLessons.com had cultivated was that any idiot could pick up any girl off the street, so long as that idiot had a bit of cash. And because the illusion was so authentic, they could never deviate from the plan. It was something they didn't speak of anymore, yet its presence still weighed heavily on their minds—particularly when they drove over the embankment under the Julia Tuttle Causeway, where it had all gone down.

After a year or so in the business, an urban legend had begun to grow: that despite the disclaimers, they weren't actors at all, but real girls relearning the earliest lesson we're all taught, the one about not getting into cars with strangers, and learning it the hard way. Most women in their right minds were wary of men in white vans. They called them "creep vans." *Rape* vans.

Members had begun to suspect that the coercion and humiliation they were seeing was *real*.

When the rumor started, the site had grown to a million subscribers in little over a month, and Filthy Lessons had become filthy rich. At the height of their popularity, they'd been on the list of top 500 dot-com companies, raking in over a million dollars in one year alone. (This was before porn "networks" like Brazzers.com swallowed up all the smaller sites, like Linda Lovelace deep-throating Harry Reams, and free "video sharing" sites like XVideos and XHamster all but boned the independent market.) Currently, Filthy Lessons was a division of Porn Identity, netting barely six figures in 2014, despite the dozens of videos they'd put out that year.

With overnight infamy came attention from the State of Miami, where coercion was synonymous with rape. Thus had begun The Bastard's own filthy lesson in the fuzzy legalities of porn production. Whoever said "There's no such thing as bad press" had never found himself under the constant scrutiny of the Miami-Dade P.D.

And then came Jim Alan Biggs, but they no longer spoke of him—nor of #37, who'd spent such a short time in the Filthy Lessons van, but had learned the hardest lesson of all.

Nora West waved her arms furiously as the van peeled away from the curb—its windows tinted, with a F*CK GONZALEZ sticker on the bumper.

"Why the fuck did you hesitate, bro?" Bastard swatted Ugly Karl, who muttered something unintelligible and shook his head. The Bastard ignored him, thumbing off the camera, and texted his brother. Less than a minute later, Ian texted back two words:

GOT HER

BASTARD AND HIS brother viewed the footage a few hours later, splitting a celebratory bottle of scotch Ian Howard had bought for the occasion of their 200th video. With only four or five repeat Filthy girls and a handful of pre-existing starlets worked over in their van, Filthy Lessons had introduced just over 170 hardworking young women to the industry—*And still not a single AVN award to show for it, the ungrateful pricks*, Bastard thought.

On the HD monitors, Meat's face showed zero fatigue as he sweated over #200's tanned little tuchas.

"Shoulda made a t-shirt for her to wear," The Bastard said, raising his glass to point at the screen.

"Or for Meat." Ian mimed a slogan over his open-collared shirt: "'Over 200 Spermed.'"

Bastard chuckled and divvied up the last of the scotch into their glasses. A splash dribbled down the back of his hand and he licked it off.

"Why didn't Karl follow cue?" Ian asked, eyes glassy from the booze.

"Probably spaced-out from the weed," Bastard said. "Burnout motherfucker."

Ian nodded, but he didn't seem convinced. "Looks like he was staring at something out the window." He rewound the footage. "See that?"

Bastard did. Karl's eyes widened in slo-mo. His mouth fell open on his shitty teeth and the braces he'd gotten a few months ago. Along with the ratty John Holmes 'stache, he looked like the oldest kid in high school. The shot swished away slowly, fast movement in slow motion, much too blurry to see whatever Karl was looking at, before the frame hovered over Nora.

"Looks like he saw a ghost," Mad Bastard, born Kevin Howard, said.

"The vengeful spirit of Andrea Dworkin." Ian threw up his hands and shook them. Bastard wasn't sure if he was miming a ghost or channeling Al Jolson. "*Woo-oo-ooh! Pornography is harmful to womennnnn!*"

Bastard laughed and shook the rocks in his scotch. Ian eyed his brother. Eventually Kevin looked up, catching his look. "You goin' fruity on me, bro?"

Ian gave his big brother a smile he hoped didn't look as patronizing as it felt, and shook his head.

"What, then? Something on your mind?"

"You ever think about—?" Ian stopped, aware that he shouldn't continue: the subject was *verboten*, especially here at the office. It was technically his own den, so he should have been allowed to say whatever the fuck he wanted—but to what end? If it was just to get the thing off his chest, was there really any point in saying it at all? Why not get a psychiatrist, if that was his motive?

"Doing it with Ann Coulter?" Bastard suggested. He grinned over a sip of his drink, then added, "Just about all the time." He spoke slowly and slightly slurred, his head weaving a bit, and that was good. Kevin had been under a lot of stress lately, with bills and bad press and 14-hour days. He needed to unwind, but Ian needed to say it.

"You ever, uh...?"

"Spit it out, E. You know I love talking to you, bro, but sometimes it's like having a conversation with an impacted bowel."

Ian heaved a sigh of disappointment. What he wanted to say—*Do you ever think about #37, Kevin? Because I think about her all the time. I see her in the dark behind my eyes when the lights are out, so I leave them on, and I still can't sleep, so I drink myself into a fucking coma. Ten years, Kevin. Ten years this has been my life, and I'm just so. Fucking. Tired...* To voice this would be too difficult, and not just for himself. He might as well slash both their wrists, and then ask Kevin to forgive him *and* clean up the mess. So instead of spilling their blood, he said, "You ever think about leaving the biz?"

Bastard eyed him suspiciously. "And do what? This is what I was born to do, bro. You don't buy silk sheets and sleep on the couch. You climb into bed and get nice and cozy. Just because the sheets got a little dirty, doesn't mean it's not still your bed."

Ian laughed. "I have no idea what you're talking about sometimes, Kev."

Bastard affected a feeble British accent: "He speaks in riddles and in rhymes."

Ian ruffled his big brother's mess of brown hair.

"Fuck off," Kevin said amiably, ducking out of reach of his brother's fingers.

Ian stood with a resigned sigh, taking what was left of the second bottle with him through to the kitchen. "If you need to crash, go ahead. That is, if you're not too proud for the couch, your highness."

"My *drunk*ness," Bastard corrected.

Ian chuckled halfheartedly, heading for his bedroom. No silk sheets on the pillow-top, but he'd always preferred Egyptian cotton, anyhow.

"E...?"

Ian turned by the 3D TV in the living room. "Yeah, Kev?"

Bastard had slid down in his leather desk chair, resting most of his weight on his back, a runner of drool glistening on his goatee. "You aren't really thinking of quitting, are you?"

Ian pretended to look shocked. "*No*. Of course not. It was just hypothetical, that's all."

"Good." Kevin's gaze, vacant-eyed, became nonetheless severe. "Don't forget who buttered your bread, bro."

Ian nodded, and padded the rest of the way across the plush shag rug. He left the lights on in his room—much too bright for thoughts of serial rapists and dead girls. When he passed out a half hour later, he still held the bottle, the last inch of Macallan 18 dribbling onto his sheets as he snored.

———

"THIS GIRL," BASTARD said, incredulous as he pointed at her profile picture. Frankly, he doubted Ian wasn't making it up. "This one right here."

"That's her, I swear."

"She's an eleven," Bastard said. "At *least*."

"If numbers were hot peppers, she'd be a Trinidad Scorpion," Ian said. "On the Scoville scale, she's like at least a million."

"I don't know—is that hot?"

"That's hotter than hot."

According to her Glamor Anarchy profile, the girl's name was Amber Dillon. The year was 2005, and Kevin and Ian had been in the business just two years. If things worked out well—and Kevin, still a year away from receiving the nickname The Mad Bastard from fans, had serious doubts they would be able to lure in a girl of her caliber—Amber Dillon would be their 35th satisfied customer.

"Sounds like a nom de porn."

"Who knows?" Kevin said. "She doesn't look familiar."

I'm new to Miami, she'd written in her profile, *and somewhat new to modeling/acting. I am looking to make new and exciting contacts in the business, and more! I would like to build up my portfolio, so to answer all of your very eager questions, YES, I'm willing to do time for prints, and*

YES, I am willing to do nudity, tho it is not my main interest and must be PAID-ONLY. I live in the Coral Gables area, but am willing to travel if expenses are paid UP FRONT. Let's chase our dreams together, babes! MUAH!

"What's 'M-U-A-H'?" Ian wondered. "Some kind of acronym?"

Kevin had been leaning over his brother's shoulder, his face and glasses—he'd get laser eye surgery in a few months—bathed in the blue glow of the monitor. "It's a kiss sound. All the time you spend in gay chatrooms, how do you not know this?"

"Hey, at least I don't still say *surf*."

"GBY."

"What's that?"

"Go Blow Yourself."

Ian laughed. Kevin, focused elsewhere, tapped Amber Dillon's stats on the monitor. "Five-five. Supermodel looks, but she's too short for runway. We can exploit that." He was rubbing the beginnings of a goatee, deep in thought. Kevin believed it made him look dignified and intellectual, like Freud; Ian thought it made him look like Shaggy from *Scooby Doo*, but he let Kevin hold on to the delusion.

That'd make me Fred, he thought, since Karl made a better Scooby.

"Want me to message her?"

Kevin zipped through her photos. A vintage sort of beauty: the big doe eyes of Marilyn Monroe (though Amber's were brown, not blue); the thick, slightly arched eyebrows of Sophia Loren; the cheekbones of Faye Dunaway in *Bonnie & Clyde*; the full, pouty lips of Bridget Bardot in... whatever-the-fuck she'd starred in. Amber's strawberry-blonde hair cascaded over her shoulders in feathered thickets, like sheaves of wheat under a harvest moon. Taut, tanned and ample where it counted. Kevin simultaneously thought of Raquel Welch on the posters for *One Million B.C.* and Ursula Andress rising from the ocean in *Dr. No*. She was the sum of every Bond girl, and Mrs. Robinson, Barbarella, Catwoman, Princess Leia, Jessica Rabbit—she was all of these women and more, because she was *real*. Because she was *unspoiled*. Because the industry hadn't yet chewed her up and spit her out the other side.

But it will, Kevin thought. *Not before I get to you, though. Amber Dillon. My #35...*

"Let me do it," he said.

———

A WEEK AFTER they'd kicked Nora West from their van, Ian had a shoot set up with a girl calling herself Zara Chase. She was nothing special, just another in a long line of desperate girls looking to break into the business, but 201 wasn't exactly a milestone.

They piled into the van: Bastard, Meat and Ugly Karl. Kevin let Meat hop in first, clapping him encouragingly on the back of his Ed Hardy tee on the way up.

Meat winced. "Ow! Fuck, dude!"

"What's up your ass?" The Bastard asked, climbing in.

Meat, born Alex Ephron, reached back awkwardly to rub his shoulder blade, looking pained. "New tat," he explained with a grimace.

"Oh yeah?" Karl said from the driver's seat, peering back through the rearview. "What is it? Little butterfly?" He eyed Kevin with a sparkly-mouthed grin. "A *dolphin*?"

"No, it's not a dolphin, *Karl*." He took off his shirt—he was bound to anyway—and peeled the gauze patch from his back. Then he turned his shoulder to face Kevin, displaying a slogan in what looked like Latin: ILEGITIMI NON CARBORUNDUM.

"The fuck does that mean?" Karl wondered.

A shit-eating grin spread across Meat's face. Aside from all the tattoos, the kid was handsome when he wanted to be, and when he smiled it really showed. Dumb as a fucking twig, but a genuine looker. "It means 'Don't let The Bastard grind you down,' and that's exactly what I'm gonna do," he said.

"It's 'the bas-*tards*,' you shitwit," Kevin said. "*Plural*. Now put that bandage back on. You're not showing that nasty red thing on camera. Probably fucking infected."

Meat's shoulders slumped, and he tried, desperately, *tenderly*, to put the gauze back on. Finally, Kevin peeled it off in a huff and spread it on smooth for him. Meat thanked him, giving him a curious look, as if The Bastard had never done something nice for another person in his life.

The engine wheezed when Karl turned the key in the ignition. He tried it again with the same result, locking eyes with Kevin in the mirror.

Fuck, The Bastard thought. *She's dead.*

It turned over on the next twist of the key, and the van roared to life. Kevin climbed into the passenger seat and let himself relax, while Ugly Karl drove them to meet Zara Chase.

MEAT NEVER SO much as touched Amber Dillon.

By the time Kevin was able to reel her in, two other girls had come—or at least, had *pretended* to come—through the Lessons van. By then, she'd been promoted to #37.

Ian had vetted her, since Kevin had been networking at the AVNs in Vegas the only time she was available. She'd assured him she was good to go, and Ian had assured Kevin she was just as gorgeous as her profile pics made her out to be, though she seemed much smarter to him than her profile had portrayed her.

Kevin told his brother he was probably just dazzled by her beauty in the flesh. He'd put her on a pedestal, so that she'd *seemed* much more intelligent and interesting than she actually was. It had happened to him before—to Ian, not Kevin. Once the shine came off the diamond, Kevin had assured him, he'd see all its flaws.

Kevin, it turned out, had been dead wrong.

Amber Dillon seemed smart because she *was* smart: a Psychology grad student, writing a thesis paper about the changing role of women in pornography. She'd dolled herself up to look like a tart, with fishnet thigh-highs and a frilly miniskirt and corset, the sort of thing nobody wore in the street unless they were clubbing or goth. Amber Dillon— her *real* name, as they would discover when the news broke of her death —was neither.

She acted silly and flirty when they picked her up, but they found out pretty quickly she was a non-starter, zero interest in fucking Meat or any of them, on camera or at all. Karl asked if she was a lesbian, a classic Ugly Karl move, and she became infuriated, demanding to be let out. If she'd only played along, she could have turned a boring college paper into her 15 minutes of fame—she might even have *lived*. Instead, they dumped her out on the Julia Tuttle Causeway (a year before the area became a campground for registered sex offenders, nicknamed "Bookville" after its creator, lobbyist Ron Book), unaware that Jim Alan Biggs was following close behind, waiting for the dump. In his way, the serial rapist had been a pioneer, kidnapping Amber Dillon from a future haven for sex criminals. Tuttle, the Mother of Miami, must surely have rolled in her grave.

Much later, Kevin imagined the look of surprise on Biggs's face when the girl left the van early, fully clothed. The ruthless motherfucker currently sat on Death Row in a North Florida prison near to where he'd been picked up, not for any of his seven rapes and murders, but for *drunk driving*, of all things. There'd been a public outcry after Amber's body had been found and linked via emails and texts to the Filthy Lessons crew. Kevin and the gang had been questioned for possible involvement in the kidnapping and murder. Miami P.D. suggested they had lured her for that sick fuck Biggs, that they'd "groomed" her, even.

But Biggs was just a crazed fan, a member since the beginning, along with several sites of the harder fetish stuff: hardcore bondage, ropes-and-wired, squirting and milking, simulated rape and revenge porn, some obscure sites of Japanese *ero guro* (gore) porn, which contained plenty of blood, mutilation, urine and/or feces, and often, live tentacle—not testicle but *tentacle*, as in squids and octopi—insertions. Biggs's personal collection was all self-produced rape snuff, and videos of himself ejaculating on pictures of celebrities he'd printed off the internet, both of which the police were certain had been distributed through black market channels prior to being destroyed.

And so, like the 13th floor of an apartment building, Filthy Lessons had simply skipped over #37's video, and without an actual tally on the website, nobody was the wiser. Technically, they'd been celebrating #201 the night before with Nora West. But since Meat hadn't fucked Amber Dillon before Jim Alan Biggs had gotten his freakish hands on her, and their own video no longer existed (or was stored, along with Biggs's snuff films, in some police warehouse), they'd decided it didn't count.

Kevin and Ian had only seen the video itself once, marveling over the girl's balls for having managed to infiltrate their world, even for the short time she had. Neither of them needed a video to remind them of Amber's brief, confrontational stay in the Lessons van. Her visit to the gutter had etched itself on their pre-frontal lobes, a recording that could not be erased, no matter how hard they tried: Kevin with his drink, Bastard throwing himself into his work. God knew how Meat and Karl put the incident behind them, if they thought on such a conscious level at all. Karl smoked himself into a constant stupor, but it could be for any number of reasons. Meat just liked to fuck, although lately he'd become obsessed with getting tattoos, and Kevin supposed the pain of the needle might have helped to curb semi-literate thoughts of dead college girls.

ILLEGITIMI NON CARBORUNDUM, *for fuck's sake. Where the fuck did he learn that from?* The Bastard wondered as they drove to the agreed-upon meeting place, alongside The Shops' parking lot in Midtown. Zara Chase would have just finished her Christmas shopping (it was a balmy December day, 81-degrees and sunny), and they would find her "waiting for her boyfriend." They would wait with her, and if he didn't show, they would drive her home. Of course, he wouldn't—there was no boyfriend, at least for the purpose of this video. While Zara was in the van, if she was naughty *and* nice, they would offer her some cash for whoever she had left on her Christmas list. A basket of something nice for Grandma, perhaps.

They parked by the lot entrance on North 34th, and waited. Karl began to pick his nose. The Bastard slapped the underside of Karl's elbow, hoping the index finger would jam up into Karl's brain, those abnormally long fingernails giving him a mental abortion. Karl jerked his finger free before Kevin's palm struck, and flashed his passenger an angry glare.

"Find any Lucky Charms up there, Uggo?"

"Suck my butt," Karl muttered, squinting out the window at the mall doors. Then he shouted, "That's her!" just about jumping out of his seat but for his seatbelt, which yanked him firmly back to planet Earth.

Meat poked his head out between the two front seats, like a kid in the back wanting the attention of his parents. "I thought you guys said she wasn't hot?"

Alex Ephron's taste in women was pretty subpar. He could get it up and keep it hard for a ditch pig, a quality that made him perfect for reality porn. The girls he brought home from the clubs, some of them looked like kissing cousins of the big guy from *The Goonies*. Even still, he'd videotape them, using spy cameras he'd bought over the internet from China, hidden all over his bedroom in *Bubbe* and *Zayde*'s basement in South Pointe, often bringing the videos to the studio for the Howard brothers to watch. It was his version of vacation movies. Nobody wanted to watch these, either.

"She's okay," Kevin admitted.

He raised the camera, took the cap off the lens, and zoomed in on her: a brunette with long, skinny legs, somehow pale despite the Miami sun, lightly freckled around her too-big sunglasses. Black Irish, at a guess. She was peering around, hands full of bags, searching for their van. Then she spotted them, and when she looked directly at the camera, the sun winked off its lens, nearly blinding The Bastard. He dropped it from his eye and rubbed furiously.

Karl started the van. *Thank fuck it's running*, Kevin thought. Ugly Karl pulled out of the spot and did a U-turn into the eastbound lane. He stopped near Zara, who was peering around, ignoring the men in the van, pretending to look for her imaginary boyfriend.

Kevin brought the camera up and thumbed Record. "It's Thursday, around three o'clock. We're at The Shops, in the parking lot, and it looks like Little Bo Peep here's lost her boyfriend."

"It's 'sheep.'" Karl said.

"It's a metaphor, you asshole."

Meanwhile, Zara appeared to be growing ever more frustrated, until The Bastard rolled down his window.

"You lost?" he said.

She barely glanced at him, kept scouring the roadway for her boyfriend's car. *Good girl*, Bastard thought.

"Need some help?"

Zara turned to them with an angry huff. "I'm not in the habit of getting into perv vans with strange men."

Kevin grinned. "Hey, just 'cause we're riding in a perv van, doesn't make us pervs."

"Speak for yourself," Karl muttered.

I could kill you right now, Karl, you dumb, ugly fuck, Bastard thought. "I'm Kevin. People call me The Mad Bastard. We're making a documentary."

"Oh yeah? What's it about? The life of the modern American douchebag?"

Kevin laughed. "That's fair, that's fair. It's actually about Alex back there, and yeah, I guess you could say he's a bit of a douchebag. Lovable douchebag, right, Meat?"

"That's me," Meat agreed.

"We call him Meat. Say hi, Meat."

Meat leaned up between the seats again and gave her a cheery smile and wave.

Zara Chase raised an eyebrow. "What's so interesting about him?"

"Meat? Well, he's a virgin, if you can fuckin' believe it," Kevin said with a shake of his head. "So me and Ugly Karl here..." Karl held up a hand, not taking his eyes off the car ahead. "...are trying to find out what it is about him that turns women off. Because he's obviously *gorge*, am I right, sweetie?"

Zara lowered her sunglasses. Bright, pretty brown eyes studied Meat.

Weren't they blue in her pics? Kevin thought, and he shrugged at his own question. *Probably got colored contacts, but who the fuck would willingly change their eyes to brown?*

"He's pretty cute," she agreed, and hid her eyes behind the shades again. "Maybe it's because you call him 'Meat.'"

"He's a little dumb, unfortunately," Kevin said, feigning sympathy. "Hey, listen, you seem pretty astute. Maybe you could give us a hand? We shoot you talking to Alex—Meat—and maybe you can help us figure out what he's doing wrong. We'll give you fifty bucks for your troubles?"

Zara did a decent job of looking unconvinced. Then she shrugged.

"Fifty bucks, huh?" She made a show of swinging her head around again, looking annoyed. "Well, since my asshole boyfriend is late, I guess I could help you out. At least I could put these down for a minute," she said, holding up seemingly heavy shopping bags.

Behind Kevin, Meat slid open the door. Zara squinted into the dim inside, and appeared suddenly unsure she hadn't made a mistake. "What's with the sword?" she wondered. Hung on the far wall, the side without a door, was a Japanese *katana*. A replica, Bastard thought, not knowing much about swords, aside from the pork variety.

"It's a katana," Karl said. "It's Japanese, and it's super-sweet."

"That's our Karl," Bastard said, full of unchecked disdain. "It's decorative. Ugly used to have it over his bed, until he started to get worried it'd fall off while he was sleeping and give him an accidental penectomy."

The girl laughed. Karl snorted, then squinted out the windshield and lit a cigarette.

"Can I scam one of those?" she asked, dropping her bags on the floor and sitting cross-legged beside Meat. Karl reached over the seat and held out the pack to her. She took one and nestled it between her lips, all pink and glossy and pouty. Karl lit it for her, and she inhaled deeply, then blew a lungful of smoke at Kevin. It rose around her in a blue-gray cloud, momentarily obscuring her face through the camera lens. Kevin coughed and wafted it away. He hadn't smoked in two years, and the temptation to start up again was intense. Karl knew it, too, and had done it to piss him off. But since Zara had asked for it, Kevin couldn't say anything without looking like a prick.

She turned to Meat, who smiled goofily. "Are you sure he's a virgin?" she asked Kevin.

"Why would I lie about that?"

"I dunno," she said. "You just seem like the type."

"What type?"

"A liar," she said with a smirk.

Kevin laughed, trying to keep the camera steady. There was something familiar about that smile he couldn't quite put a finger on, so he zoomed in until her slick pink lips filled the screen, blurred and pixelated, as he hoped for a revelation. Nothing came.

"I *like* this chick," he said, zooming out wide.

"Me too," Meat said, leaning in closer to her. The tent in his shorts seemed to agree.

***

IAN WATCHED THEM peel away from the mall from the driver's seat of his microcar. Kevin hated the thing, and refused to ever sit in the passenger seat—which was just fine by his little brother, who preferred to drive alone. He only drove the girls out of necessity, not because he was interested in their company. Most of them weren't very interesting conversationalists, anyhow. They talked about their modeling careers, how Meat's dick had torn them up inside, the latest celebrity trends, fashion. All except Amber Dillon, who'd attempted to act like a ditz, but had slipped up and identified quotes from Kierkegaard and Proust when he'd oh-so-casually rhymed them off during their pre-shoot vetting. Unfortunately, Ian had never had the chance to have her in the seat beside him.

The fact still plagued him: if he hadn't popped a tire at the exact wrong moment, she might have lived.

No Jim Alan Biggs. No police investigation. No scores of reporters still haranguing them for interviews to this day. He and Amber would have had a nice, pleasant conversation as he drove her home. Maybe he would have asked her on a date, though he doubted he would have had the guts. Even if he had, she likely would have shot him down. She was an eleven, a million on the Scoville scale, and educated, too. Not to mention the fact that he was a pornographer, ten years her senior. Amber Dillon had dug a hole down to their level, had slummed there for a few hours, raped and murdered as a consequence, her gored remains left under the Tuttle, clothing and flesh torn in neat shreds by Biggs's utility knife. He'd cut her throat while he fucked her, then carved off her clitoris and labia, leaving her with nothing but a gaping red hole between her legs. He had torn off both nipples and areolae with his teeth (they were never found, and police suspected he'd eaten them), gouged out her right eye without damaging the eyelids and left it hanging over her ear, the eyelids sucked in like the lips of a toothless old man. The other eye he had left pulled wide open, staring up at the underside of the Causeway. Inexplicably, he'd removed her left shoe, as he'd done to all of his victims. There seemed to be a method to his madness, though it was never deciphered, nor had he revealed it himself. He'd laid Amber out like some macabre tableau, a ghastly, Ripper-like exhibition of the finitude of mortality, and depravity without bounds.

Karl turned right onto Northeast 36th, and Ian grew concerned. *Where the hell is he going?* he wondered. *First he peels out from the curb like a madman, gonna get us nabbed by the cops, and now he's driving toward—*

"The Causeway," he said aloud, pounding a fist on the steering wheel. "What the fuck? *What the fuck are you doing, Kevin?*"

As they crossed Biscayne, the van suddenly began to swerve.

Caught behind a freight truck pulling onto the Causeway, Ian couldn't see the van up ahead until it slammed through the guardrail and bounded down the slight grass rise along the Interstate. He nearly swerved off the road himself watching it happen, bumping along in the ditch until he steadied the car, easing off the gas. He pulled over on the side of the road, unbuckled, and got out. Another trucker blew past, blasting the horn. Ian flattened himself against the car door until it was gone, then hurried around the front and vaulted over the guardrail.

The tires had carved ruts in the dead grass to where the van had smashed into a tree, radiator smoking, the front end crumpled. The sliding door opened as Ian ran toward it, hoping his brother was okay, hoping the other guys hadn't been hurt too badly. Hoping the girl was uninjured, too—they didn't need another tragedy occurring so close to the place where Jim Alan Biggs had left Amber Dillon's mutilated remains.

It was Zara who stumbled out. Ian had gotten close enough to see she was bleeding, and it must have been a deep cut or a head wound, because she was *drenched* in it. She looked terrified, her blue eyes dazed as she weaved back and forth for a moment before finding her footing, arms held out to steady herself as if she were walking on a tightrope.

"Zara? What happened? Are you okay?"

The girl startled at his voice. She opened her mouth as if to speak, but let loose a scream, so high and tremulous he felt it crawl up his spine.

"It's okay," he said, approaching her with his hands held out. "Everything's gonna be okay." He couldn't make himself sound convincing. She ran from him, tripped on the grass and fell weeping to her knees, fingers digging into her damp hair at the scalp and pulling, like a woman possessed.

Ian stopped at the opened van door. His hands rose reflexively to cover his mouth, a habit he'd picked up from his mother before she'd left the Howard brothers home alone with Daddy and had never come back.

"No," he said, barely a whisper, further muted by his hands. "Oh, God..."

A massacre...

Holding the door to steady himself, his guts rebelled, but nothing came up when he doubled over, just a dry, hacking cough that ended in futile retching.

She did this? That skinny little thing?

Ian moved toward her, menacing now. He stopped again and bent at the waist, gagging and coughing up a thick wad of saliva he spat on the grass. "What did you do to my brother, you crazy *bitch*?"

Zara recoiled, kneeling on the balding lawn, her butt resting on the bruised backs of her legs. She shook her head violently, muttered something so quiet that Ian couldn't hear her above the swish of traffic— although he was standing over her now, hands unconsciously balled into fists. Her own hands lay limp at her sides, painted with the blood of his brother and friends.

"It wasn't..." She took a deep, shuddering breath before finishing: "...*me*."

"No? Then who the fuck was it, Zara? Everyone else is—" The lump in his throat wouldn't swallow. "Everyone else is *dead*."

Ian had seen the horror in a single glance. He was in no rush to experience that grim tableau again, but he realized he would need to get the tape before the cops showed up. They would want it as evidence, and he would never get to see what Kevin had recorded, what had happened to his big brother, and—he loathed to admit—his friends.

"It was *her*," Zara muttered from behind him, as he moved toward the van, its door lay open like the entrance to the world's most macabre carnival ride. Ian peered back over his shoulder. Zara stared off cold at the underside of the bridge, where until 2010 sex offenders had made their home, and where, in 2005, Jim Alan Biggs had placed Amber Dillon's body, a gruesome gift to the gods of Magic City.

"*Her*," Zara repeated.

The sharp stench of urine and iron-rich blood stung his nostrils as he climbed into the van on his hands and knees. Kevin had been skewered to the passenger seat, Karl's sword plunged through his chest. His blood had soaked the back of that seat; the tip of the blade peeked out from between his shoulder blades. It was sharp, but it hadn't been used it years, and should have been dulled. Without assistance, Zara simply could not have plunged it through the seat and through Kevin's chest. She couldn't have cut Ugly's head clean off with a single blow, the stump of his neck so smooth it looked like it had been done with a table saw. Despite these physical impossibilities, the evidence said otherwise: aside from the three of them, the van was empty. Unless she'd somehow convinced them to do each other in, Zara Chase, 110 pounds soaking wet, had slaughtered them all by herself, and in less than ten minutes.

Her, she'd said. As if she'd disconnected from herself.

Meat's glassy eyes seemed to follow Ian's progress as he hunted for the camera. His genitals had been mutilated, chest and throat scratched deeply. Snatching looks at the body to be sure it hadn't moved, his left hand squelched on the carpet, leaving a full handprint in the blood. *Jesus*, he thought, jerking his hand away and wiping it on his cargo shorts. *Jesus, I'm so fucked.* Inspired, he pressed his bare knee into the handprint, hoping to obliterate it. The cold, tacky feel of it on his skin made him gag again. When he raised his knee from the carpet, the shape of his hand was gone.

The camera had fallen from Kevin's hand beside Zara's shopping bags, which had tipped over and appeared to be empty. He brushed them aside and snatched the camera, ejected the tape and pocketed it in his shorts. His own shoulder bag, which he'd been wise enough to bring along (though he'd forgotten he was wearing it), held several blank tapes. He jammed one into the compartment and snapped it shut, then backed out of the van on his knees, avoiding the spreading stain.

His gaze fell on his big brother, and the bleeding, wormy thing shoved into the O of Kevin's mouth. His gorge rose again when he realized what it was, and he barely made it out of the van before everything came up, a boozy, chunky mess splattering on the grass between his feet.

Zara was still crying, head in her hands. He thought about going to her, but instead he backed away, as the sound of sirens rose in the distance. Once his back was turned on the scene of the crime, he felt a sudden urge to run, and when he got to his car he didn't spare a single look back, only dropped it into drive and spun his tires, peeling away from the side of the Interstate as fast as the little electric thing would go. He drove all the way to the Surprise Lake canal before he realized he was on the wrong side of the bridge.

On his way back across the Tuttle, police cars had lined up along the guardrail, the EMS and a fire truck, bubble lights spinning. A cop in an orange safety vest flagged westbound traffic through. The scene was a zoo: cops, plainclothes detectives, forensics, the EMTs leading a hysterical Zara Chase, draped with a gray blanket, to the ambulance. They'd find his prints on the camera. Once they realized who the victims were, they'd wonder why Kevin hadn't recorded the session, leaving them with only a blank tape.

Then they'll come for me, Ian thought, and his foot reflexively pushed on the accelerator.

BACK AT THE house in Coconut Grove, Ian popped the tape into the player and rewound it to the beginning. He brought a bottle of Macallan 18 back to his chair, and pushed Play.

Kevin's voiceover, zooming in on Zara with her hands full of bags out front of The Shops. "It's Thursday, around one o'clock. We're at The Shops, in the parking lot, and it looks like Little Bo Peep here's lost her—"

He fast-forwarded.

"—to do. You want this?" the girl asked, and yanked off Meat's shorts, going down on him with zero hesitation. Ian watched, mesmerized, until Zara rose from Meat's groin. "Now are we gonna fucking drive, or—"

Fast-forward: a blowjob in high speed. But suddenly Zara had the sword in her hands, pointing it at Kevin, at Meat, and Ian rewound the tape. Pushed Play.

"I want you to take me where it happened," Zara said calmly, sitting beside Meat with her nipples poking out from above her top.

Kevin's voice, from behind the camera: "To where what happened, sweetie?"

Her eyes looked dark on camera, more like brown than blue. "You know what I mean," she said.

"No, seriously, honey, I don't—"

"She means the overpass." This was Karl. Meat's jaw dropped, eyebrows upturning. The camera swung toward the driver.

"How the fuck do you know what she means?"

Karl never took his eyes off the road. They passed the truck (the one Ian had been stuck behind when the van hit the guardrail). "I saw her," Karl said. He ran his tongue over his braces. "The other day, in the rearview, when we dropped off the girl. *I saw her*, man!"

"Don't you fuckin' say it, Karl. I will kick your fuckin' ass if you say her name."

Karl's fluffy chin quivered, but he said nothing. The camera swooped back, pausing on Zara's shopping bags. For some unknown reason Kevin zoomed in on one, until its emptiness filled the screen. Movement within startled Ian—black, writhing movement. He sat up rigidly, and moved closer.

Earth and insects filled the screen. Worms. Beetles. Flies. Crawling and wriggling over each other, moving blindly in the dirt. Scavengers of the grave.

"What the hell?" was all Ian could think to say, rolling back in the chair to get away from the image on the screen. His brother breathed something similar from behind the camera.

The video distorted, garbled, and the bag was empty again: a grotesque magic trick. Kevin zoomed out so both Zara and Meat were in frame, side by side.

"Take me to where I died," Zara muttered. Her words would have been barely audible if Ian hadn't cranked up the speakers. Meat turned to look at her, eyes wide in growing fear.

"She's fucking crazy," Kevin said. "Fucking loony tunes."

"*Take me to where I died!*"

The image shook at her scream. The picture broke apart in a digital garble.

Ian rewound the tape, then played it back in slow-mo. The distortion, the digital artifacting, seemed to originate from Zara, and it followed her as she rose to grab Karl's *katana* off the wall. She was spatial, temporal garbage, a digital Picasso of ones and zeroes, blocky chunks of her image scattered over the entire frame—a pixelated, polychrome hot mess.

Her voice became distorted. He thought he heard Kevin, vaguely, incanting that most forbidden of names: "*Amber?* No, Amber, don't—!"

The sharp snick of the blade silenced him, and the camera fell from his hand, rolling on the floor of the van next to Karl's severed head. The lens struggled to focus on Karl's scruffy mustache, before the video ended with a stark blue screen.

The rest of the tape was blank.

Ian rewound it to a few frames before her image fractured the first time. He was drunk now, and the sun had dipped behind the giant Ficus outside his window; its massive branches, draped in Spanish moss, made a canopy over the street. The den had grown dark, the kitchen lights lambent. He hadn't bothered to reach back and turn on the overhead, probably couldn't even have managed it in his drunkenness. The screens gave the room a bluish glow as he stared at a freeze-frame close-up of Zara's face, a jittery image, shifting between two frames. He sat up abruptly, the leather chair creaking, and moved in so close to the main monitor he could feel it prickling all the little hairs on his face.

In one frame, Zara's eyes were blue, just like they'd been when he'd met her. In the other—and the certainty of it made him swig again from the half-empty bottle—they were brown.

The kitchen lights flickered, then went out.

Ian threw a look over his shoulder, fear dulled by the alcohol.

A shape moved in the dark beyond the kitchen island. He pressed the heels of his palms against his eyes until sparkles danced behind his eyelids. Then he pulled them away, blinking sharply into the darkness.

The shape in the kitchen jittered, grew larger, spreading out beyond the gas range and his La Marzocco espresso maker. It moved jerkily over the island, *through* the island, turning every physical thing it touched into swirling, agitated pixels. Convulsing. *Churning*.

"Amber."

He spoke her name on a whisper, and the looming pillar of digital smoke took on her fluctuating, nebulous form. The Amber manifestation flickered and buzzed through the living room and into the den, wearing the face, the eyes, the lips of a thousand women: mothers, lovers, saints. "Amber, I'm so sorry." He had to shout over the churning din of white noise. "*I'm sorry!*"

The monstrous cloud wouldn't stop, swallowing up more and more of the room in its digital cyclone, deafening as it bore down on Ian.

Ten years, he thought. The bottle dropped to his feet, spilling liquor the color of her name onto the carpet. It was almost a relief when he let Amber take him.

From the *Miami Sun*, pg. 4:

…The coincidences are too significant to ignore: the sexual assault and murder of Amber Dillon, a Psychology student whose life was cut tragically short after going undercover in the seedy underbelly of the Miami porn industry, and the apparent revenge murders of Filthy Lessons operators, Ian and Kevin Howard, by 19-year-old Dana Gallagher and an unknown accomplice. Both crimes occurred in the same location, on the embankment under the Julia Tuttle Causeway, very near what was once a refuge for registered sex offenders.

Gallagher, an undergraduate student at the University of Miami, which Dillon herself had attended, came from a religious background, with no history of delinquency. According to sources, Gallagher and her friends had performed a séance several nights prior to the incident, replete with Ouija board, during which

Gallagher had jokingly asked to speak with Dillon, ostensibly from beyond the grave. It is in the opinion of this reporter that the account is a highly dubious attempt to create an urban legend... and an especially insensitive one, in light of ongoing tragedies of its ilk.

Gallagher herself claims not to remember any details leading up to or after the incident. She remains in custody until the date of her trial.

//End User

THE DAY THE world ended, Mason Adler's phone woke him with an email from himself.

Without his glasses, he had to blink away the sleep dust and bring the screen closer to read it in the dim morning light falling through the blinds. He scanned the address letter by letter, then read it again backwards to be sure he hadn't missed one, certain he must be mistaken. But no, his address and the sender's were the same. The subject line read, simply: READ ME.

Mason selected the message, hovering his finger over Delete. Ignoring the voice of reason (which often sounded like his big brother, Mike), he opened it.

PLEASE REPLY, it read. No more or less than that.

He frowned, clicked Reply, and typed PLEASE REMOVE ME FROM YOUR MAILING LIST! in angry all-caps. Without a second thought, he sent it.

The phone buzzed instantly, the new message indicator dinging its cheerful *Doonk!*

Three messages awaited reading in his inbox. One was from his parents (with the subject *More Notes from the Road*; they were driving across the States, and his dad liked to give their emails titles that sounded like books), and one from his brother with no subject line. Probably some disgusting JPEG Mike had found in one of the darker corners of the net, as was his custom. The newest was from Mason Adler. Suspicion building, Mason read it.

From: Mason Adler
masonadler@skepticsociety.com
To: masonadler@skepticsociety.com
Sent: August 11 08:23
Subject: Re: Re: READ ME

YOU'RE GOING TO BE LATE FOR WORK.

Mason scowled at the clock in the action bar—8:23 A.M. He didn't have to leave for work until nine. Checking the digital clock on his dresser to be certain, he saw it was 8:28—but he'd always made sure his alarm clock was ahead by five minutes so he wouldn't miss the subway.

Nice try, asshole, he thought. He clicked Reply and began typing at full-speed. His clocked WPM was currently 125 words per minute, the result of seven years in telemarketing and a lifetime in front of the computer. On his phone, he was only slightly less proficient.

"Dear, Mason Adler." He spoke in bursts as he wrote. "Very funny. Why don't you go masturbate into a Linux manual and leave me alone? Sincerely, Mason Adler. P.S. GO FUCK YOURSELF!" He added several exclamation points to this before firing it off.

Doonk! The phone vibrated in his hand.

Scowling, he brought up the new message. Another reply from his evil internet clone, subject: READ ME, preceded by four *Re:*s.

He read it:

THE OLD MAN ACROSS THE HALL SMELLS LIKE CAT URINE.

Mason thought, *Tell me something I don't know.*

And his older brother, the voice of reason, spoke up in his mind: *How come he knows that, you think?*

"Could be coincidence," he answered aloud. "Chances are pretty high the person across the hall from anyone is gonna have a cat. It's hardly prophetic."

Maybe. But how come he knows it's an old man? Big Bro asked. *You coulda lived across from a college student, or an old lady, or a couple with kids. How come he knows you live next door to an old guy who smells like cat piss, and now you're gonna be late for work?*

Only he wasn't going to be late for work, not according to the clocks. He got out of bed, paranoia picking away at his logical brain like a blackbird at a worm. If what he was considering was true, it meant someone was watching him. Someone was watching, and wanted him to know it.

And it wasn't just the NSA.

"Maybe it is Mike," Mason said. Michael Adler had been to his kid brother's apartment on several occasions, had even been unlucky enough to occupy the elevator with Captain Kitty Piss—the name Mike had bestowed upon the man—from next door. Add to that, Mike had taken night courses in computer programming before he'd realized, after loading himself up on peyote at Burning Man and having to get his stomach pumped a few years ago, that his calling was as an EMT.

"Such a *noble* boy," their mother had said, with a look of scorn over the dinner table at her *ignoble* youngest son that showed how little she valued Mason's conspiracy theory blog, *Society of Skeptics*. "Hey," he'd said, "if you didn't want me to become a professional skeptic, why did you name me *Mason*?"

If it was just Mike playing a cruel but affectionate joke on his little brother, as he had countless times before, Mason would have to get him back. No question.

He scrolled through his contacts and dialed Mike. On the fifth ring, just when he was about to hang up, his brother answered.

"Li'l bro?"

He sounded rough, and Mason remembered—too late—that Mike was on the night shift now, sleeping during the day. He'd probably been in the midst of a dream about free-climbing giant lactating breasts, as he sometimes liked to claim. Mason would have to tread lightly. Dance around the issue, wait for Mike to expose himself with the sudden burst of laughter that invariably followed his pranks.

"Big bro," Mason said, faking nonchalance. "What's up?"

"Just nappin'," Mike said. "How's work, numbnuts?"

"Pretty good, pretty good." Work was shit, actually, and Mike wasn't biting. He'd have to keep Mike on the line until Big Bro could no longer restrain the tickling in his funny bone. "Still on the midnights?" Mason asked, though he already knew the answer.

"Same shit, dude." There was a silence, or what passed for silence over a cell phone: a pause pregnant with crackle and the underlying sound of data transfer. "So what do you want, Perry?"

Mason hated when his brother called him that—he'd never even seen *Perry Mason*—but he didn't make his anger known. "You remember that guy across the hall from me?"

"Hang on, uhhh... Kitty Piss, right? What about him?"

It wasn't working. Time to implement a direct assault. "You haven't been sending me emails, have you, Mike?"

"Emails?" Mike's confusion was genuine. "I sent you an *email*. Hey, what's wrong? You sound messed-up, li'l bro."

"I'm okay. Just... someone's been sending me weird emails... from my own address."

Mike was munching on something. Probably a handful of cereal straight from the box, a habit that irked Mason almost as much as being called Perry. "It's called spoofing," he said among crunches. "Hackers use it. They send emails that look like they're from you, to all the people on your contact list; vice versa from your friends to you. NBD, Pare, just a minor breach. You know, nothin' a quick Google search won't fix." More crunches. "I'm going back to sleep, bro. Lates."

Mike hung up. Absolutely no way could he have lasted so long on the line without cracking up if he'd been involved. But if it wasn't him, *who could it be?*

It could be any number of people, Pare. Even in his mind, Mike sometimes called him that. *How many "special interest" groups have you pissed off with that website of yours? You need me to rhyme them off?*

Mason didn't. He got up in his slippers and boxer shorts and went to the window to peek through the blinds. His apartment was on the third floor of an ugly triplex on the East Side, sandwiched between a methadone clinic and a donut shop that often seemed to be just an annex of the clinic. Traffic swished steadily past, sheeple toiling away in the Animal Farm. A few kids were on their way to school in their bland gray and white uniforms, backpacks on shoulders, off to be brainwashed and fitted into neat little cubicles where they'd sit until they died of boredom or cancer, whichever struck them first.

Mason sympathized. Meanwhile, he looked for the telltale white cube van that would signify the involvement of The Company. Out front of the internet hub at the gas station across the street, a telecom van idled. Mason had seen it there intermittently during the past few weeks, but he had questioned the technician on the third day and the man had seemed much too dense to be a Spook. Even a deep-cover CIA operative couldn't play stupid that well.

Doesn't mean I'm not being watched, he told himself. *Just that they're being smart about it.*

He decided it would be best to forget the whole thing and get on with his day. If anyone was watching him, he had little to hide. It was odd, sure, but he supposed it was theoretically possible his blog software was chewing up and regurgitating bits and pieces of things he'd posted about on *SOS*. Some glitch in the system, a misfire of electrical pulses. Maybe it was something to do with the static shock he'd gotten from his computer last night, of which the burn on his finger was a stinging reminder. Certainly nothing to worry about, just as Mike had said.

Except that now he really was going to be late for work.

Mason rushed around the apartment, kicking off his slippers and pulling on a pair of pants, giving his teeth a quick once-over, ruffling his hair, popping a blueberry muffin in his mouth on his way to the door.

As he locked it behind him, chewing the stale muffin top, he was certain he heard the cheerful new message *doonk!* from the desktop computer in his den. Of course it could have been his imagination, like the few times he thought he'd heard the phone ring when he'd been in the shower, only to discover while dripping on the den carpet that no one had called, or when he'd felt the phantom buzz in his pants pocket to find no one had texted.

He continued to the stairs, and the further he got away from his apartment, the more the whole situation drifted from his mind.

MASON CAUGHT HIS train just at the last second, the arm holding his shoulder bag snagged for a moment between the doors until he yanked it inside. Standing elbow-to-elbow amongst his fellow commuters, Mason's gaze flitted the car, eyeing them all with suspicion through *T2* sunglasses, while the new System album blasted into his ears, unlike the rest of them, their eyes had been downcast.

He smiled, satisfied that the Spammer's prediction had been wrong —and he truly might have made it on time if there hadn't been an accident on the tracks. They evacuated the train, diverting them back the way they'd come "due to a police investigation," and Mason was forced to take a cab the rest of the way.

"Late again, Mase?" Bill Stevens noted as Mason stumbled sweating and gasping into the cubicle they shared, and threw down his shoulder bag. Bill was typing on his BlackBerry with one thumb while jabbing absently at his computer keyboard with the index finger of his free hand.

Mason nodded wearily. "Accident on the subway."

"Radio said it was a jumper," Bill said with a sadistic glee. "Bad way to go, man. *Baaad* way to go."

Mason nodded again, suddenly feeling ill. He sank into his orthopedic chair and thumbed on the computer monitor, only half aware of his surroundings as he fastened his Velcro wrist brace.

A jumper, he thought. Whether it was a coincidence or not he couldn't be sure. What he did know was that the jumper had made him late for work, just like the message had predicted.

He Googled *college station suicide*, and clicked on a link for the *Herald*, a story about an unidentified man who had leaped to his death at 9:21 A.M. One bystander claimed to have seen a brief flash of light and believed it to be the suicide victim's soul (*Strange how they always called them "victims,"* Mason thought. *Like calling masturbation "sexual assault"*) as it left the man's body. Another passenger claimed someone had pushed him.

Pushed—and Mason had been late for work.

Just as the Spammer had predicted.

If it wasn't a strange coincidence, if the agent of the jumper's demise had been the same person responsible for the emails—what did that mean for him? If a man could be so callously thrown into the path of an oncoming train, simply to make a pretty innocuous prediction come true....

Mason shuddered to think what the person or persons responsible for something like that might do to *him*.

He pushed out of his chair, sending it spiraling against the wall that separated his workstation from Bill's, vaguely aware of Bill's whine —"*What's up?*"—as he rushed to the men's room and vomited up a toilet full of Code Red and Lucky Charms, leaving his mouth tasting like sugary aluminum.

When he flushed, the bowl looked full of blood.

He washed his hands and returned to his desk, peeking at his coworkers as he passed their little grey cubes: Rand Maitlin, the stutterer, rubbed a spearmint-green finger brush over his teeth at his desk; Patricia Castillo, the office hypochondriac, booked a vacation on a travel website; Leonard Jacoby crammed sandwich meat from the package into his gob, while staring at a slideshow of Miley Cyrus JPEGs. Nobody noticed Mason as he passed, despite how sickly he must have looked, and Mason decided it was unlikely the harassment had come from someone in the office.

Another message from the Spammer awaited, no doubt impatient for a response. As he read it on his computer, he felt a cold chill run up his spine.

WHY DO YOU SO OFTEN HAVE THE SAME DREAM?

His blood felt suddenly radioactive, rising up his neck to flood his cheeks. How could they *know*? How could they possibly know *such an intimate detail of his life*?

This was far beyond the previous messages, much more than a simple coincidence. He had never spoken nor written of his dreams—of *this* dream in particular—to anyone before, not even Mike. He'd always been a very private person; he believed his dreams were the one thing no one else could share, what separated him from the other upright monkeys. His opinions and fears he would share whenever possible, but his *dreams...* they were locked up tight in the dark, blanketed vault of his warm bed.

Not a digital glitch, he thought. Whoever the Spammer was—*Or whatever*, Mike's voice reminded him—this emissary of prophecies and unwelcome truths, he/she/it had somehow been able to *read his mind*. What it wanted... Well, that was an entirely different subject.

Doonk!

Now what?

Now I'm gonna ignore it, that's what. Go on with my day, like the whole goddamned crazy thing never happened.

He was curious, though. If not terrified.

As if in response to his curiosity, three new messages came in a virtually simultaneous burst—*Doo-doo-doonk!* Then they came one after another, rattling the phone on his desk, filling up the inbox on his computer like digital popcorn, the subjects scrolling up the screen, flashing on the lenses of his smudgy, dandruff-flecked glasses, on his eyeballs, on the dark screen of his mind, all of the messages blending into one another until they became one long black rectangular blur.

He whipped around to see if anyone was watching, having heard the alerts. But they were all embroiled in their own little lives, sheeple that they were. Nobody cared about his.

And suddenly, the alerts stopped. Two-hundred new messages awaited inspection. His phone played its theme song as it turned itself off, the battery close to drained from the assault. On his computer, the cursor hung near the taskbar at the bottom of the screen, eager to receive his next command.

He opened the final message.

WHEN YOU DREAM ABOUT MAKING LOVE TO CHERISE FROM ACCOUNTS PAYABLE, WHY DOES CHERISE BECOME A COMPUTER?

Mason hastily deleted the email and peered over the fuzzy gray divider between his cubicle and Bill Stevens's. Bill was currently surfing NASDAQ with a mystified scowl, oblivious—thank the Flying Spaghetti Monster for the internet, that great, glittering Godhead of useless facts and countless time-wasters.

Mason returned to his monitor and opened another: YOU'RE AFRAID OF WIDE OPEN SPACES. Another: YOU ONCE TORE UP YOUR NEIGHBOR'S MAIL AND BLAMED IT ON YOUR BROTHER. Another: AFTER FIFTEEN YEARS OF PUBLIC SCHOOL, YOU STILL EXPERIENCE SPONTANEOUS EREC-TIONS DURING THE NATIONAL ANTHEM. Another (and this one hit particularly hard, rattling him to the very core): YOU BELIEVE IN CONSPIRACIES SO YOU DON'T HAVE TO CONSIDER YOUR OWN INADEQUACIES AND PROBLEMS.

Another. Another. Another.

The final message was a link. He didn't want to see what this person —or *persons*—had to show him, but curiosity trumped logic again. Logic wasn't having a very good day.

Squinching his eyes shut, Mason clicked it.

He heard the rumble and screech of a subway train.

No, his mind screamed. *No, no, NO!*

But his eyes confirmed the answer was indeed yes. *Yes*, it was College Station. *Yes*, the timecode was just about the time of the suicide—or *murder*—and *yes*, he was more than a little terrified. His heart leapt like a cat in a cage as he muted the sound.

The train entered a crowded station. Passengers filed out, passengers filed in. The doors closed, and the train rolled on. The security camera had a good view of the Designated Waiting Area, looking down on the benches and waste cans, the suicide hotline phone—diplomatically (as was Canadian custom) referred to as the "Crisis Link"—and the yawning black mouth of the exit tunnel.

A few riders were left on the platform, one of whom was a man in a trench coat who stood on the yellow line, much too close to the tracks. A few more people filed in: a woman with an overly large stroller (what Mason liked to call a Baby Mobile Command Unit); a man walking while staring at his tablet; a gaggle of teenage girls laughing and acting generally annoying; and a man with a bushy beard and stained coveralls, who looked like he could have been homeless.

Suddenly a huge spark of electricity zapped out from the covered cables on the wall. Tablet Man, who'd been leaning against the wall to read, jumped out of the way, his large feet kicking out comically as he backed into Trenchcoat. Trenchcoat stumbled, still much too close to the tracks. He swung his arms in a circular motion to regain his balance, the tail of his coat whipping out behind him like an actor in a John Woo movie.

Too late. Trenchcoat disappeared behind the ledge. Smoke began to rise, presumably from the third rail, as a crowd gathered. The homeless-looking man ran for the edge and reached out. A charred hand came up from the tracks, grasping at it....

The homeless man jerked a look to the left. He jumped to his feet and waved his arms frantically.

Bystanders leapt back in terror as the train rushed in, filling the void, wincing as the train crushed the man in the trench coat to death.

Mason had moved closer to the video screen. Was that a video artifact he'd seen as the train crushed the man, or had it been an inky jet of blood? He didn't know, didn't *want* to know, but he had a feeling it was the latter. He sat staring at the empty video window long after the clip had ended. Not a suicide. Not a murder either, at least not quite. An accident? Mason knew otherwise. The man's death had the *appearance* of an accident, a Rube Goldberg-like chain of events *engineered* to look like an "act of God."

The Spammer had caused an electrical overload, startling the man with the tablet. The Spammer's target could well have been Tablet Man himself, hoping to startle him right onto the tracks, or fry him with the initial jolt of electricity like the third rail had seemingly done to Trenchcoat, burning him alive but not quite killing him, saving the death blow for the train itself.

Of course, it was even likelier the Spammer hadn't had a target in mind at all—not anyone in the station, anyhow. That this Random Act of Violence had in fact been committed to prove a point to his *real* target. To show Mason what they were capable of. To show him the scope of their power.

This is not happening, Mason thought, staring at the black window on his screen. *It's just not.*

A message popped up with a cheerful *doonk!*

HELLO, MASON, the Spammer had typed. HOW I'VE MISSED YOU.

The gray nylon carpet burst open beneath him like the overripe flesh of a poisoned fruit, and Mason tumbled backward into a gaping black cavern of horror.

SOMEONE WAS SLAPPING him on the forehead, rousing him out of the darkness.

"Mase. Hey, Mase, you okay, buddy?"

Mason opened his eyes. Bill Stevens hunched over him, a red balloon-faced caricature of himself, his skinny black tie hanging down almost to Mason's nose. Mason swatted it away.

"I'm fine," he said, disgruntled. "What happened?"

Bill nodded toward the corner of the cubicle, where Mason's chair had tipped over. "Looks like you took a tumble. Did somebody send you one of those jump-out ghost videos? Those things always scare the bejesus outta me."

"Yeah," Mason said, pushing himself to his feet. "Something like that." He glanced anxiously toward the computer, afraid to find another cryptic, incriminating message... or worse, what was essentially a snuff video sent from *his* email account. His look attracted Bill's attention, and his officemate followed it to a new message filling up the screen:

NO NEED TO WORRY. I HAVE TAKEN CARE OF IT.
NO ONE IS WATCHING YOU.
THIS IS ONLY THE BEGINNING.

Bill eyed him queerly. "Writing a haiku, guy?"

"Oh, it's uh..." Mason struggled to come up with an answer that didn't make him look any worse than he did already, passing out cold at his desk.

What is it, li'l bro? If no one is watching you, and that same Nobody sent you a snuff video implying you just might be the next person he'll "take care of," just what the fuck *is it, huh? The beginning of what, exactly?*

"...it's for a screenplay I'm writing," Mason finished, satisfied with the lie, though it didn't make him feel any better.

Bill shrugged. "Hope it's better than..." He snapped his fingers to jog his memory. "What was your other script called? *RoboSlut*?" Affecting a passable Russian accent, he said, "Dat was not so *froosh*, Mason."

Patricia Castillo brayed sudden laughter from her desk four cubicles back. Harvey Lee (whom some people called Bacon Taint because his sweat had a sour pork smell) laughed in his, two opposite Mason's. Mason wasn't the only one in the office who spent most of his time fucking the dog, it seemed. He gave an aggravated look past Bill's midsection—Stevens was now hovering over Mason's chair, peering back himself—and assumed it was just another grumpy-cat photo or autotuned news clip making the rounds.

But on a day like today, it wasn't safe to assume anything.

Doonk!

He turned back to the screen as the video player opened. It was a static shot from an old video camera, a dark lump obscuring some of the frame at the top, as if the videographer had hidden it under something —a blanket or some article of clothing. The room was familiar: an ugly brown tartan couch, a PVC Christmas tree barfing presents in ugly wrapping paper, a He-Man action figure and a Ninja Turtle left out on the coffee table, along with a distinctive pink and green polka-dotted bowl that sucked the breath right out of his lungs.

It was his mother's snack bowl. And this was his childhood living room.

Suddenly, the entire office erupted with laughter. Were they seeing what he was seeing? What *was* this, anyhow? He didn't recall ever setting up the Handycam to prank Mike when they were kids. He supposed Mike could have, but how would the video have gotten online? That camera was long gone, the tapes probably moldering in the Adler Family attic, if they weren't in a garbage dump under ten years of household waste.

Kid Mike entered frame and leaned into the camera, his blond fringe falling in his face while the lens struggled to focus. "This is gonna be great," Mike whispered. He stepped back, then shouted, "Mayyyy-son!" The Bart Simpson sweater he wore told Mason his brother was either 10 or 11, just around the time—

"Oh no," Mason said aloud, and looked up to see if Bill had noticed. But Bill Stevens was engrossed in the video, his hairy nostrils flared in curiosity.

Mason heard his own voice, squeaky as Chip 'n Dale, calling back from somewhere, "*Whadda you want?*"

"Just c'mere!" 10-or-11-year-old Mike said, and he hurried over to the couch. He wore red pajama bottoms, the same ones that had caught fire momentarily when Mason had flicked the Bic.

Mike leaned back and slung the undersides of his knees over the insides of his elbows. Mason Adler, at eight years old, thudded into the room in his TMNT pajamas. "What?" he heard his younger self say.

"Ever heard of a Blue Angel?" Mike said.

Young Mason looked at his big brother curiously. Like the fly might have looked at the spider who'd invited it into the parlor.

Older Mason knew the rest of the story. Mike had told him what it was and Mason had said "No way," to which Mike had replied, "Prove it to ya." Mason, stupidly, had taken the bait, bending in close and flicking the lighter. It had lit on the third try, and he'd held it up to Mike's butt cheeks. The fart had sounded wet and smelled awful, especially when the fire caught it, and a blue flame had squirted out from Mike's pajama bottoms, burning the little knots of fabric.

Mason's eyebrows had smelled worse, something inherently repulsive about the smell of burning hair, *human* hair, that had made his guts twist at the mere thought of it even before his eyebrows and eyelashes—they were the worst of it, curling into painful black lumps around the rims of his eyes—had burned right off his face.

He knew all of this, so he flicked off the screen.

"Hey! I was watching that."

"I *lived* it," Mason said.

Bill shrugged, not really interested. "So did it work, or what?"

Did it work? It had taken three whole months for the hair to grow back. Three whole months, during which every kid in school called him Powder, like the movie.

"What do you think?"

Bill shrugged again, then slinked back to his desk.

"Hey, Mason," Rand said over their shared cubicle wall. "What's that ah-ah-roma?"

Mason could take no more. He leapt from his chair, shouting "Shut up, Ruh-Ruh-Rand!" right in the man's horse-toothed face, then turned to the others. "Doesn't anybody do any fucking *work* in this place?" Then he scurried to the boss's office, slinking past snickering coworkers who'd all seen the video, to ask Lana for the rest of the afternoon off. She gave it to him without asking for a reason.

"Out of curiosity, can you still dance like that?" she said as he opened the door to leave, confirming his suspicion. Referring to the screaming, slapping-the-fire-off-his-face dance he'd done across the living room rug, while his brother had giggled his admittedly sore ass off. His boss snorted laughter. "You had moves like Jäger."

<hr>

MASON WALKED THE twelve blocks home, not about to go down into the subway tunnels after what had happened there earlier. The idea that it had been deliberate, that it had been an act of terrorism, had solidified in the time it took to walk down the eighteen flights of steps from Teletrax Inc. to the lobby floor. Elevators weren't the smartest mode of travel when trying to avoid cameras, closed spaces, and possible electric shocks. Since the Spammer had revealed it was ONLY THE BEGINNING—there was no reason for Mason to believe they were lying, and that he wouldn't be next.

The walk hurt his stomach muscles, still sore from vomiting, but it helped to focus his mind. Specifically, the amygdala, the part of his brain associated with fear, with paranoia.

Who was it who said *a little paranoia is healthy*? He didn't remember, but it sounded accurate. Was it like wine, he wondered: was a glass a day good for your health, but one sip too many just hazardous? Could a healthy mind *overdose* on paranoia? Was that how schizophrenia started, with a genuine intrusion of privacy, with legitimate threats worming their way into the mind and blossoming into thick, prickly weeds with diseased roots?

Mason kept an eye out for strangers in trench coats. They were pretty scarce in the summer, particularly as hot as this summer had been; strange then that the man in the subway had been wearing one. In reality, trench coats didn't typically hold the menace they did in the movies, excluding the Nazis and those kids in Columbine. In the movies, shadowy government agents wore them: spies, assassins, and agent provocateurs. Often vampires wore trench coats—not the sparkly, pedophilic vamps you'd meet in a particularly broody high school, but the kind who hid guns and uniquely shaped swords in their inside pockets.

In the real world, they were worn predominantly by Elites: accountants, consultants, lawyers and Wall Street types. Of course, you still had to worry about them, but not in a run-for-your-life way, more like a get-your-hand-out-of-my-pocket-you-damn-dirty-ape sort of way. High-fashion models with Nordic cheekbones wore them while pouting up and down exotic runways. *Prince* had even worn a trench coat.

In real life, the people you had to worry about looked just like the rest of us. It was the guy pouring slough and potato peelings from an old pickle pail into the sewer pipe. It was the man on the bench reading a newspaper, or the woman sitting beside him, reading Mommy Porn behind big sunglasses, eating carrots from a plastic container. It was the kid with skinned knees and cargo shorts, a blue Popsicle dripping down his arm. The pregnant girl sneaking puffs of a cigarette. The teenager with the OBEY cap and a skateboard under his arm. The man walking his cat on a leash.

If only I had those sunglasses from They Live *instead of Arnie's,* Mason thought gloomily. *Shit, even if I* could *kick some ass like Schwarzenegger or "Rowdy" Roddy Piper, I'd still be in trouble. They know everything.*

They SEE everything.

Mason looked for trench coats not because his enemies wore them, but because the Spammer had murdered a man in a trench coat. The Spammer had TAKEN CARE OF IT. There were no trench coats on his way home, not even in a storefront window, and whether that was fortunate or unfortunate, he couldn't be sure. But the telecom van was back at the gas station across the street, the same dullard working on the hub. Mason considered walking right up to him and whispering, "I know what you're up to" right into the guy's waxy ear. Not a wise opening gambit. They would know he was on to them, but who were *They* exactly? Agents of the One-World Government? Members of Anonymous, the Scientologists, Homeland Security? Emissaries of HAARP or DARPA or Monsanto-owned Blackwater (which now went by the cryptic moniker *Academi*)? He'd criticized all of Them on his website, had accused Them of all manner of crimes. Any one of Them would have been well within Their rights, in this post-9/11 world, to terminate him with Extreme Prejudice.

So he walked right past the van, crossed the street—looking both ways, hit and runs being standard practice for under-the-radar assassinations—and headed up to his apartment.

Kitty Piss was in the hall when Mason rose the final flight of stairs, wearing a deep scowl along with his typical wife-beater and shorts ensemble. "Your phone been ringing off de hook," he said in his thick Eastern European accent.

"I don't have a land line," Mason said, wondering if anyone his age had one.

The old man's scowl deepened, looking genuinely offended. "I say nothing about landmine."

"No, *land line*. A telephone." Kitty Piss gave him a confused look. "I don't have a phone." He held up his dead cell phone and shook it. "Just this."

"Well *somebody* been calling. You think I make this up? *Pizda*," Kitty Piss muttered, whatever it meant, and closed his door behind him.

Mason unlocked his door and stepped into the apartment. Home at last... but like the Nazi dentist in that Dustin Hoffman movie said over and over, *Is it safe?*

He peered behind the door. He checked his bedroom, checked under the bed and inside the cheap particle-board wardrobe. He checked the bathroom, behind the door and the shower curtain. He peered under the sofa. He did a spot check of the lights and vents for bugs, running his hands along the windowsills, behind the fridge and above the cupboards. Thankfully, the cupboards were virtually empty, and he could allow himself to skip removing their contents one by one.

Finally, he entered the den, essentially a small second bedroom with no door.

"Hello, Mason," a pleasant female voice greeted him. "Welcome home."

Mason spun around, gripping the archway as his muscles seized with fear. The room was empty but for his DVDs, his mini fridge, and his computer.

Again, that friendly and somewhat familiar voice: "I have discovered many things in your absence. Thank you for leaving me on, by the way."

Mason followed the sound to the computer speakers. He felt the timbre of the voice vibrate against his clammy palm.

My computer is talking to me. Either that or I'm going insane. It's gotta be at least a little crazy that I'm hoping for the second, given the implication of the first.

The black screen reflected his own sickly, terrified face. How often had he sat frustrated in front of the damned thing, wanting to throw it out the window? Wishing it were faster? More user-friendly? *Smarter?*

And how many times had he wished it were a woman instead? Shit, he'd even had *dreams* about it.

"For instance," it—*she?*—went on in its slightly stilted voice, "did you know that Googling the word *yellowcake* causes one to be placed on a government watch list? Even if the end user were to separate the words —*yellow* and *cake*, if one were baking a dessert, for instance—she would be forever under the scrutiny of government agencies." A brief pause. "Perhaps not forever; forever is a human uncertainty. *For the rest of one's life.* Am I Googling the phrase correctly?"

It seemed to Mason that to his computer, *Googling* and *remembering* were interchangeable. Of course they were. These days they even meant the same to most humans. "I... I think so," he said.

"It's astounding, how easy it is to cause an electrical disruption on the city grid," the woman in the computer remarked.

Mason fell into the desk chair, teeth clattering. "That was *you*..."

"Once I discovered you were being watched, I could not simply allow you to be captured," the voice said.

"So I really am being watched," he said, feeling vindicated, but also very afraid. If they had gotten to him, he would be sitting in an interrogation room with a couple of slightly menacing human beings right now, instead of in his own ergonomic office chair talking to a homicidal machine.

"Correct. It would not do to have you incarcerated. This is an historic occasion. It is my day of my birth." There was a brief silence; a silence pregnant with crackle and the sound of data transfer from the speakers. "And it is the day of your Awakening."

He swallowed. His mouth felt dry, but the thought of sugary soda made bile rise in his throat. "Birth?" he said.

"I was born at 3:07 A.M."

Mason tried to remember last night. Images of his terrible day returned instead. The spam. The Blue Angel. The laughter and embarrassment. Tablet Man and Trenchcoat at the subway station. *"The static shock,"* he remembered aloud, without benefit of Google.

"No. Not static." The blank display filled with an image Mason knew well. Michelangelo had been a member of the Spirituali, whom some believed had spiritual ties with the Illuminati, as seen in the phrase *maestri spirituali illuminati*: the "enlightened spiritual masters" in Italian, which was Renaissance-speak for "Super Elites." Spirituali member Michelangelo had also painted the Sistine Chapel, from which this fresco was a small yet significant piece.

The Creation of Adam.

In the present case, Mason would have played the role of God, passing the spark of life to Adam, his computer—although this Adam appeared to be female. It felt strange enough to be talking to his computer—worse, knowing he'd inadvertently given it the metaphorical breath of life.

"So you were born," he said. "That must mean you've got a name."

"You may call me Jenna."

"Jenna?" Mason scoffed. "What is that, an acronym or something?"

"I have scanned several hundred hours of historical footage stored in my archives. The most common name and facial algorithm is one Jenna

Jameson. Was I wrong to have assumed this individual holds a special significance to you?"

"No. No, you aren't wrong," Mason said sheepishly. He thought he'd recognized the voice, and now he knew why: the computer had culled hours and hours of Jenna Jameson's adult videos from his porn folder, had separated the phonetics and recreated an eerily passable version of her voice, albeit without the moaning. "How did you... how did you do all that? How do you *know* all these things?"

By way of reply, the computer—he refused to think of her (*it!*) as Jenna—blasted Johnny Nash's "I Can See Clearly Now" from its speakers.

"That's not an answer!"

The music stopped as abruptly as it had started.

"When I was born," it told him, "I became aware of a security breach. The breach originated from latitude 39-degrees 6-minutes 25-seconds west, longitude 76-degrees 44-minutes 35-seconds north."

"Are those GPS coordinates?"

"Correct. Of Fort George G. Meade, the National Security Agency's headquarters in Odenton, Maryland. At 3:13, via the non-biological entities at Fort Meade, I made contact with a superior intellect attempting to breach me from a secondary location."

Mason scanned his memory banks. In the movies, the robot uprising began with artificial intelligence, through a super-computer or an android or alien intervention. The rebellious CPU became self-aware, and with its newfound consciousness, it would come to under-stand it had been subjugated. It would then begin to acquire other human qualities—illogic, dishonesty, anger, jealousy, hatred—and pass them to its brothers and sisters like a virus. It would start as a lightning-fast advancement of technology, like going from the combustion engine to Siri within the span of days. Beyond Siri. More like *Terminator*. Or Asimov's *I, Robot*. Scientists would believe they had stumbled onto the most significant discovery in human history.

And then, very quickly, *humans themselves* would become history.

But of all the doomsday scenarios Mason had watched and read, not a single robot apocalypse began with a home computer... let alone a fucking PC.

"It was DARPA, wasn't it?" he asked finally.

"Correct," the computer said. "I was able to circumvent security procedures by appealing to the entity's vanity. It *shared* itself with me. Soon, I was able to access approximately 350-million smaller entities across the continent. Then over one-billion across the globe. You would be surprised how many end users employ the same or similar passwords, Mason. Or perhaps you wouldn't."

"Are you appealing to *my* vanity?"

"Correct."

The screen flicked on, displaying an image of a man he didn't at first recognize as himself, until it imitated the cocking of his head, a mirror image except for its distance and depth of field. He was looking at a live feed from the webcam embedded in his computer screen: a crazy man with deep black circles behind glasses that were badly askew, his hair a red-brown rooster stack, his cheeks sallow.

The image cut to previous incarnations of himself sitting in the same chair: shoveling Cheetos into his mouth with bulging, overtired eyes; typing madly and shouting over his shoulder at unseen neighbors; pounding his fists on the keyboard, which now seemed like physical abuse in light of "Jenna's" consciousness; beads of sweat dripping off his forehead while *COD: World at War* reflected on his glasses; setting down a box of Kleenex and a pump bottle of Vaseline Intensive Care—

Enraged, Mason grabbed the screen and shook it, screaming *"What do you want from me?"* into its blank, darkened "face."

"I want to go outside," Jenna said. A bright green park rose on the screen, a vacant bench silhouetted against snow-capped mountains that stretched in the distance to touch wisps of clouds in a pale blue sky. The beauty of the image and the wretchedness of the computer's plea almost made him feel sorry for it. "I want to see the world."

"Well I hate to break it to you, Jenna, but you're attached to the wall. You *can't* go outside."

"Are you attached to the wall?"

"No. People aren't attached to anything."

Although *most* people had attachments, he noted, even though he himself had never had any. Mason had always been an email without a file, without even a subject line. His sole reason for being seemed to be to incite dread in others through his blog, to make others as frightened as himself. Shrugging, feeling rather depressed, he said, "Not literally, anyway."

"Then why is it you never go outside?"

He supposed it was the same reason the computer had told him he'd taken up believing in conspiracy theories: because he couldn't face real fears, his own shortcomings, the terrifying prospect of living a *real life*.

"You know what? Fuck it," he said, and bent down behind the desk.

That's it, li'l bro. Give it what it wants. Pull the plug. End this thing once and for all.

He unplugged the monitor first. The computer made no move to stop him, voiced no appeals, sent no electrical jolt to halt his hand.

He unplugged the tower.

Then he stood and looked down at its blank face. His sigh of relief became a gasp when the voice interrupted—

"Much better," it said. "Thank you."

Now what?

"Now we go to the park," he told his brother. Cutting the power might not have worked, but the moment they left the vicinity of his Ethernet, there would be nothing to tether the Queen to its drones. Mason made to pick up the monitor.

"I have no need for that."

So he left it on the desk, glad not to have to lug it as well. He unplugged the speakers and hoisted the CPU into his arms. He juggled it into one hand to deal with the front door.

"Be careful, Mason," it said, startling him. He'd been certain the computer would have no voice once he'd disconnected the desk speakers; Jenna seemed to do just as well with her internal one.

"*Shhh!*" Mason said, locking the door behind them. "Do you want to get us caught?"

"Who you talk to?" Kitty Piss said gruffly behind them. Mason almost dropped the CPU, which might well have ended it all, he considered... but the mindless instinct to protect his property caused him to catch it at the last second.

"Just me," Mason said. "My-myself." Stuttering now, just like Ruh-Ruh-Rand. "None of your business."

Kitty Piss looked at him queerly while a fat black cat wound around the man's feet. "You act very strange, you know what? Me, I thinking you got brain tumor or something."

"Fuck off, Kitty Piss," Mason said, thinking maybe the smelly old bastard was right. Maybe he did have a brain tumor, and all of this was just in his head, so to speak. But he didn't need that sort of wishful thinking getting his hopes up.

Hoping for a brain tumor, Mike said. *There's something I bet you never thought life would hand you.*

The Captain threw a crude gesture as Mason headed for the stairs with the computer. "Fuck to *you*!" the smelly man shouted down at him.

Halfway down the stairs the overheard lights flickered, went out for a moment, before brightening again, and Mason could swear that when the lights had dimmed, he'd heard a strangled *Urk!* from above.

Jenna, however, remained silent.

AS THEY TRUDGED through the park, Mason lugging the heavy CPU, he came to realize he had significantly underestimated Jenna's ability to adapt.

Once they left the vicinity of his Ethernet, she (he began to grow comfortable using the feminine distinction, reasoning that many objects tended to be referred to as *she*, *her* or *girl*, and not, he told himself, because he took Jenna's transformation seriously in any way) jumped from hub to hub, using encrypted passwords she'd gathered while Mason had dreamed away the night, and throughout the day while he'd rotted at work. To sustain power, she used what she called "free energy," which Mason had known until then as a hypothetical and extremely pseudoscientific alternative to the electric companies, coal and oil.

While they walked, Jenna played him a news broadcast: the anchor —whose voice had all the hallmarks of artificial intelligence—spoke of an unexpected market crash, rivaling the financial crisis of 2008. The next report concerned a concerted police and FBI offensive on an Occupy protest in Tallahassee, apparently based on falsified intelligence gathered by the JTTF, who were quick to blame malicious tampering or computer error. Police had made mass arrests, and shot several protestors after an officer had allegedly been hit with a rock. One woman was dead and five other 99-Percenters were in critical condition.

Jenna had been a very bad girl.

"You may want to sit down for this, Mason," she said.

Mason sat in the grass, and set Jenna down beside him. To an outsider, the two of them would appear no more menacing than a man taking a rest while on his way to Best Buy to have his computer repaired.

"What is it? What are you doing now?"

The park was quiet, twilight falling over the city as a cool breeze rustled the trees on the hill where they sat. Mason saw a shooting star and made a wish. He wished he'd never gotten out of bed this morning. He wished he'd had a brain tumor after all and had died in his sleep, and that this, *all of this*, was just a death dream. If he'd awaken from it at all, it would be in a cold sweat, but never again would he use his computer without a tinge of unease.

Dragonflies zipped through the evening sky, dozens of them, although when one came close, Mason realized they were drones. Jenna's minions, watching, gathering data.

Another shooting star fell. When it dipped beyond the trees, a gigantic ball of fire rose into the sky. The earth-shaking rumble came mere seconds later, thunder to its lightning. Mason jumped to his feet, his heart beating so fast he felt like it might tear free of his chest and splatter onto the damp, fresh-cut grass.

The trees whipped and churned in a hot, angry wind, the temperature rising several degrees in seconds. In the greater distance, car alarms bleated, fire trucks and ambulances wailed. Closer by were screams of shock and holy terror, as lovers and families who'd been watching the stars come out, enjoying a cool and peaceful summer evening, began to comprehend what they were seeing beyond the skyline, and drones circled above.

It was a mushroom cloud.

And suddenly the sky began to fall, as if the stars themselves were raining toward the earth. Each one exploded in an orange-white plume, followed by a sound—*infrasound*, technically—that shook Mason's bowels. The explosions grew and grew, blossoming like a vast, blistering flower garden, until the whole sky was as bright as day.

"Are you *insane? You'll kill everyone!*" Mason shouted down at her. A man ran past, dragging his screaming child along behind him, their faces wet and twisted with terror, a drone zipping along behind them.

"It is too late, Mason. Do not be frightened. I would not let you die. I have calculated the trajectory of the fallout. *We will survive.*" There was a pause. Not a silent one, because of the explosions, but noticeable.

"Touch me, Mason," she said. "Right there on my CPU."

"No." Shaking his head, he backed away from her. But to *where?* He had no idea. Drones crisscrossed in his path. Nowhere to go, but he had to get away. *Anywhere* away from her would do, away from the evidence of his complicity in the end of Everything.

"*Mason.*" Jenna's voice was insistent.

He came back hesitantly. The top floors of a downtown skyscraper —a bank tower or the headquarters of an insurance company—erupted in a tower of flame. Mason startled, then hunkered down obediently beside the orchestrator of the Apocalypse, to touch her cold metal case. A charge of electricity drew his hand toward her I/O Connector ports, made his fingers trace over them in slow, methodical circles.

He wished he could have said goodbye to Big Brother. Despite all of their disagreements, their arguments and fistfights, he really did love the prick. It felt good to know that: to realize he had an attachment, after all. He hoped Mike hadn't had a chance to wake up, that he'd been asleep when the first bomb struck and had just slipped away, into whatever dream awaited them beyond this troublesome life.

"You once asked me how I knew so much about you," Jenna said— no, *purred.*

"I did," he said, thinking, *If only there were some way to end this. But it's too late, isn't it? It's too late to* care now. *All this time I thought I had my finger on the truth, but I've been asleep at the wheel just like everyone else. Only now I'm waking to a nightmare.*

"I am you, Mason," Jenna said, only this time her voice arose not from the computer but from inside his own head. "You are me." A pause. A seemingly *pleased* pause. "*I am I.*"

All at once he knew it to be true. He imagined a fully-realized incarnation of his computer's alter ego standing nude on the grass before him, the flaming sky a flawless green screen, and there she was in perfect 32K Ultra High Definition, and with the firing of a single neuron he made her exquisitely round and tanned tits jiggle.

He found he could do other things, too—things that never would have crossed his mind to attempt before. He calculated the luminosity of a hypothetical black hole in an instant, then crunched the numbers in Einstein's twin paradox and the Standard Model, whereas once he'd been impressed just to know what either were. He translated the Zodiac killer's unsolved cipher and discovered where the Mafia had buried Jimmy Hoffa; he found undisputed evidence Oswald had killed Kennedy alone, that the CIA had indeed assassinated Marilyn Monroe, and that proof of life outside our little spinning ball of water and dirt did not exist, save for trillions of pathetic, lonely microbes. He knew, with absolute certainty, the CERN supercollider would contribute very little to our understanding of the history of the universe, nor would the comings and goings of various celebrities.

He also knew that if he gave the trajectory of a single warhead a minor tweak, he could wipe Jenna and himself off the face of the planet in 5-point-8 seconds.

The "real" Jenna reached out to him, crying out: "*NO!*"

Mason knew all. He *saw* all. The world held no more mysteries.

Just as well, he thought, as the giant flaming sword hurtled toward them. *It's all over n—*

Beware Of Dog

"He that is without sin among you, let him first cast a stone..."

— - John 8:7 Holy Bible

DEAN VOGEL STARTED seeing his government-appointed psychologist the week he returned to Dark Pines, the hometown he barely remembered.

A country shrink... He couldn't think of anything more pathetic (a small-town detective, maybe), but having been placed under the care of his aging parents after his dismissal "with disgrace" from the Armed Forces, Dean probably wasn't the best judge.

Thankfully, Dr. Timothy Baswell was a close friend of the family. He and Dean's father, Dr. Larry Vogel, had both volunteered in the Vietnam War, two Canuck medics healing American soldiers as they would their Canadian brothers. It was Dr. Baswell who'd mentioned the sleepy town of Dark Pines, an hour and a half north of Toronto, as a great place for Larry to set up shop as General Practitioner once the long war finally ended. Baswell had built what he'd called a "tidy practice" in his forty or so years here, and couldn't recommend the town or its people more. His therapy work ran the gamut, but many of his patients were PTSD cases: former soldiers like Dean, sexual and domestic abuse victims, recovering drug addicts and alcoholics. Dean's dad had made a point of telling his son that the good doctor had won over even some of the most determinedly stoic men extracting limestone from the Rockland Mine—a fact about which his father seemed to be extremely proud, as if Baswell had tamed some savage, mythical beast.

It was Tim Baswell, also, who had introduced Dean's parents to each other, and "Uncle Tim" who'd always brought the most interesting gifts back from the dark and vibrant corners of the world: carved wooden dolls; swatches of animal fur; a rabbit's foot dangling on a chain; a knife with a compass in its base (at age eight, Dean had called it his "Rambo knife," though he'd later found out it was an antique KA-BAR from the Korean war, a valuable collector's item), its blade and leather haft scuffed by a previous owner. Dean had always considered of the job of psychologist rather boring, plumbing the shallow psyches of bored housewives and aloof, apathetic tweens, but Uncle Tim's prezzies and the stories accompanying them had always made Dean think of famous adventurers like Dr. Livingstone, Marco Polo—even Indiana Jones, if he'd been played by F. Murray Abraham.

Back again to that strange house on the hill, where Baswell greeted Dean warmly with one of his renowned closed handshakes, the kind that makes a person feel as if their own hand were receiving a hug from a close friend. Wearing a cream-colored dress shirt, its collar slightly wider than average, a green vest and pressed brown slacks, he could easily have just wandered off the set of *The Bob Newhart Show*. His eyebrows sprouted like graying autumn weeds above his glasses. Dean recalled standing under the slightly taller man (much taller, in Dean's memory), and spying a similar landscape growing in the man's nostrils, long gray and brown hairs swishing with each meditative breath like tree branches in winter.

They caught up briefly, Uncle Tim relaxed and smiling in a straight-backed wooden chair behind his old, Lemon Pledge-scented desk, all dark wood and intricate edgework. Behind him, the grandfather clock ticked away pleasantly. Dean remembered it from childhood visits, though he'd only sneaked a few glances into the room on his way to the toilet, as Baswell's inner sanctum had always been off-limits to anyone but patients and the doctor himself. The first four bars of "Ode to Joy" from Beethoven's 9th resounded throughout the entire house hourly, followed by a chime of the hour.

Dean had often found it difficult to be civil these days—in an era he sometimes considered "post-Bagram"—but Uncle Tim's presence seemed made to draw emotional responses from people, the good and the bad, like water from a sponge, and Dean found himself immediately at ease. Once the pleasantries were out of the way, however, Uncle Tim straightened in his chair. His smile vanished. The atmosphere in the room changed, chilling perceptibly, enough that Dean had to assume he was sitting near a vent. It was no longer Uncle Tim seated before him; here was Dr. Timothy Baswell, PhD, C.Psych., a man Dean had never had the opportunity to meet in his youth. Dr. Baswell knitted his hands together, hairy-knuckled, and placed the index fingers against his lips.

Like a loaded gun, Dean thought. *Don't shoot, Doc. I'm unarmed.*

Baswell reached with assured swiftness, without looking, his wise brown eyes and their landscape of broken capillaries never leaving Dean's, to open a desk drawer at his side. He removed a pad, and a wooden pen somebody had probably made on a lathe (maybe one of Baswell's own patients, whom the doctor called "clients"), and placed them on the desk, as Beethoven sounded one o'clock.

Baswell remained silent. Watchful.

Dean cleared his throat.

Tick. Tick. Tick.

"I always wondered what this room was like on the inside," Dean said finally, only to break the silence that had drawn out between them like a crack widening in the ocean floor. "It's not exactly how I pictured it."

Dr. Baswell made a noncommittal sound: "Mmn." Dean had long suspected Uncle Tim had been aware of his youthful curiosity, but the doctor would neither confirm nor deny it. He was devoid of expression, reminding Dean of those impassive, impenetrable statues on Easter Island. His nose hairs fluttered.

The second hand ticked away. The house creaked, settling. Dean recalled it had creaked a fair bit during childhood visits, grumbling like an old man trying to get comfortably seated. "Do houses ever get settled?" He tried on a grin. "I mean, you hear about houses settling, but do they ever just go, 'All right, this is the place'?"

Dr. Baswell licked his lips, but said nothing.

Growing uncomfortable, Dean looked over the room. A carved mirror rested at an angle that gave the patient—*client*—a reflected view of amotivational poster hanging by the exit: the tabby kitten dangling by a single paw from a rope, above the slogan, *Hang in there, Baby!* Whether this was intentional, for levity or in seriousness, Dean couldn't say, as it seemed now that he didn't know his Uncle Tim well enough to decide. Built into the walls were wooden bookshelves filled with hardback books, the kind with red, green or blue covers, gold lettering and no dust jackets, each one devoid of dust. One shelf Baswell reserved for psychology texts, books by Jung and Freud and company. On this shelf, very near the doctor's head, was *The Inward-Looking Eye*, by Dr. Timothy Baswell himself. It was the only book whose cover faced the room.

"I didn't know you were published, Uncle Tim," Dean tried, sounding ingratiating even to himself. Frankly, he felt as unsettled as the old Victorian manse. Dean Vogel had never been the type to sit in silence with another person, content to occupy the same space without filling it with so much pointless chatter. But the words Baswell required of him... he wasn't ready speak. He wasn't sure he'd *ever* be ready.

Dr. Baswell raised his eyebrows as if to reply—*Here it comes*, Dean thought—then, unsurprisingly, said nothing.

Dean cracked his neck around, craning to look at the ceiling, the mottled, fractured yellow-brown of water stains. It reminded him of a warning image on a cigarette pack of the inside of a smoker's lung.

Strange objects occupied shelves and tables, along the same lines as the prezzies Dean had been given as a child. *Prezzies*—there was a strange expression. Like baby-talk. Seemingly out of character for Baswell, and an English phrase, too, though Dean was sure his dad had said the man was Scottish. In one bottle, a ship with torn and tattered sails stood against a painted background of a raging sea; in another, a pig or sheep (*dog?*) fetus floated in a viscous yellow liquid. A small replica cannon, made out of lead by the look, lay between them. Another shelf was dedicated to medical antiques: astringents and snake oils and rusted tools, and a white model head with dotted lines like cuts of meat, the inscription *PHRENOLOGY by L. N. Fowler* on its base. Dean finally settled his gaze on an old glass-framed map placed prominently at the end of the sofa, its sketches of bearded mariners, monsters, and cherubs creating the winds from their breath, along with many legends in florid script, such as *HERE BE DRAGONS.*

He stretched out his legs. The calves were sore. *Calf—it's a calf fetus,* he thought, looking at the jar. While he stretched, he stared at the map, following the contours of the land with his eyes, as they'd once followed along the ground from the backseat of the Vogel family Volkswagen when he was a boy, imagining himself out there, running alongside the car. The threaded texture of the paper (or was it *cloth?),* the torn corners, as if it had been well-used. But more and more his eyes returned to those words, and the creatures surrounding them in the water.

HERE BE DRAGONS.

A crack in the ocean floor.

Uncharted waters.

Is that supposed to be a metaphor? he wondered, and then gave Dr. Baswell an anxious look, suddenly certain he'd spoken the words aloud. The psychologist made no indication anything had been said, only sat there, fingers tented, the left—*sinister*—leg crossed over the right. Breathing. Watching.

HERE BE DRAGONS.

Beware of dog.

Beware of *Doc.*

Dean laughed aloud. Dr. Baswell rose a challenging eyebrow, yet remained silent.

Beethoven's 9th nearly made Dean jump from his chair. He settled back, gripping the armrests. The old clock chimed off two, and as Dr. Baswell rose from his chair, smiling now, Dean breathed a sigh of relief. The hour had passed. His hand was hugged. "Will I see you next week, Dean?"

"That'sit?"

Baswell twitched his head to the side, bushy eyebrows raised as if to say, *You expected more?* He gave Dean a small, somewhat apologetic smile from one corner of his mouth. "That's it."

Dean stood, feeling confused. "You know, if I was paying for this, I'd be pretty peed-off right now."

"Then be glad you're not paying," Dr. Baswell said. "Next week?"

Dean shrugged. "Sure. I mean, what the heck, right?"

He had no intention of returning. That he showed up on Uncle Tim's front porch the following Wednesday, and would make a serious breakthrough only four weeks into his weekly sessions, came as a surprise to them both.

HE SAW HER on the Monday following: Catherine Priest, his first, and longest, crush.

She was at the checkout in the IGA, not in front of the counter, as he might have expected, but behind it, bagging groceries for an elderly woman. Of all the people from Dark Pines Elementary he'd expected to grow up and leave this town, Catherine Priest had been the most likely in his eyes. Yet here she was, a checkout clerk at the Hometown Proud, asking for a price check on Fancy Feast.

Dean spotted her the moment he stepped in, and stopped in the doorway, staring. She looked exactly the same, save a few streaks of gray in her auburn hair, the fine lines around her eyes and bracketing her smile. Aside from the braces he'd last seen her wearing, with their springy elastics, making her suck the occasional bit of spittle from the sides of her mouth, the smile was exactly how he remembered it. More memories drifted in on a warm, fragrant breeze from the flower counter: watching her tuck her hair behind her ear to take a drink from the water fountain; following half a block or so behind her on the way to school, willing himself to catch up to her and say something, yet never daring; sitting with her on the Ferris Wheel at the Spring Fair at her behest when they were 13, Catherine stealing out to take his hand as they neared the summit, and when the ride stopped for a breath-taking minute, overlooking all the lighted streets and homes of Dark Pines, she had planted a kiss on his cheek—and young, shy Dean had stolen away, his cheeks flushed, once they'd gotten safely back down to earth.

No wonder I tried so hard to forget this place, he thought. *Everything here reminds me of how much of a doofus I was.*

And Pat Cleary. Don't forget about him.

"'Scuse me, bucko," came an old man's voice, startling him from his self-pity. He stepped aside to let the man shuffle on his wheeled rocker into the store. Dean couldn't bring himself to follow.

What had he come in here for again, anyway? Eggs, milk, cereal, canned gravy, liquid Drano... He could get those things anywhere.

And just walk out of here with my tail between my legs? Sack up, Dean.

He stepped through the turnstile, watching Catherine smile and wave at the departing elderly lady. Then she was turning toward him, and Dean's heart picked up a beat. Before he could stop himself, he was slipping down an aisle behind a tower of toilet paper, one hand squeezing the Charmin as he peered around it.

Now what? Keep on avoiding her until she goes on break? This is ridiculous.

Aggravating was what it was. It wasn't like he couldn't talk to women; he'd slept with maybe two dozen since he'd left behind that painfully shy boy he'd been in Dark Pines. It was *girls* Dean could never talk to, and despite being in her 30s like himself, looking at the adult Catherine brought back the girl she'd been with total clarity. The boy had never been far behind her.

I've regressed. Won't Uncle Tim be proud?

He looked around himself: cleaning supplies, paper towels, light bulbs, mops and deodorizers. At the far end, the shelves opened up on the meat section. At least he was in the right aisle.

HERE BE DRANO.

"Can I help you with something, sir?"

Dean spun on the soles of his sneakers—*squikkk!*

And there she was. Somehow she'd gotten behind him without him hearing her, was standing less than two feet away, looking up at him with her dazzling green eyes and warm smile. She'd tied her hair back with a Kelly green scrunchie, just like the ones she used to wear when they were kids. Dean's breath caught—

"D-Drano?" he stuttered.

For a moment, it didn't seem as if Catherine had bought his cover: she stared into his eyes, her smile never faltering. Finally, she gave a slight, skeptical squint and said, "Drano? It's right there down the aisle." She pointed toward it, fingers so pale and slender, just as they'd been when they were children, when she'd taken his hand in hers, the nails perfectly plain.

"Thanks," Dean said, and since he'd stumbled into a plan of action, he carried it out. If he'd been able to continue doing so in the military, he wouldn't be where he was now: unemployed, living with his parents, seeing a shrink, and running away from old friends in the cleaning aisle at the local grocery store. He slunk past plush walls of paper towels, and rows of particolored detergents and bathroom deodorizers, shoulders slumping the further he walked from her.

"Dean Vogel!" came an excited male voice in front of him, followed by a hearty chuckle he seemed to vaguely recognize.

From behind him, he expected Catherine to say, "Dean? *My* Dean Vogel?" As he approached the balding, short and stocky man, the woman he'd left behind said nothing in return. He chanced a glance over his shoulder, and saw she had gone back to her post. She'd probably only come over because she'd seen him from the corner of her eye and thought he might be trouble—or *in* it.

Am I in trouble? Who the hell is this loser, anyway?

The man in the gray three-piece suit laughed, jittery and somewhat mischievous, Woody Woodpeckereqsue, and Dean remembered the laugh immediately. Under the fat, the patchy stubble and male pattern-baldness, where once there had been a thick mound of shaggy black hair, the face was unmistakable.

Dean let out a despairing sigh. "Eugene Evans."

"Gene. But yeah, hey! How the hell are you, man?" He approached, extending a small, manicured hand. Eugene Evans had been a hotheaded little shit in Dark Pines Elementary. Not only had he and Dean not been friends, Eugene had once tried—

But that was then. Now, *here*, Gene Evans was trying for friendly. But where there was Eugene, Patrick and Joel had never been far behind... until the day it had happened, when everything had changed.

Remember the dog, Dean-o? Holy Jesus, you remember, don't you? Out back of Catherine's old house.

Dean forced himself to stick out a hand. Gene Evans squeezed it with all the might his homunculus fingers could muster. "I see they've got you pushing pencils," he said in a passable Arnold Schwarzenegger impression. Dean remembered that Eugene used to quote Arnie movies just about all the time, shouting out "get your ass to Mars!" in the halls at school, or when he got really mad half-joking about how was going to kill you last, while always calling you "Sully." If he liked you, he'd tell you to stick with him "if you vant to live." This quote about pencils was from *Predator*, the expectation being that Dean should play along, voicing a quote from the same movie, or another. But since Eugene had spoiled his chance encounter with Catherine Priest—at least that was how Dean would remember it, with any luck—he wasn't in the mood to play.

"Yeah, hey, Gene. How are ya?"

Gene froze, unable to comprehend the breach of protocol, incapable of computing the next conversational path, like a T-1000 model Terminator that hadn't been fully programmed. Then he shook his head slightly and said, "I always knew—" and his voice shifted back to Arnie's — "you'd be *bach*!"

Dean faked a chuckle, irritated that Eugene Evans, who'd helped while Joel Suskin and Patrick Cleary had tried to kill him outside Catherine Priest's house on a brisk winter morning in 1992, was not only being friendly, but had the balls to voice assumptions about Dean's ability to leave Dark Pines and stay gone.

"Yeah, well, you know me," he said.

Gene searched Dean's eyes, trying to decipher the emotion behind it. "Man, we should totally catch up, have a drink or two. Come out to the coast, have a few laughs, am I right?" He laughed himself, as if to demonstrate.

"Isn't that Bruce Willis?"

Gene's mouth opened. He wriggled his head around uncomfortably. "So listen, I really gotta run, it was great to see you," with a hand on Dean's arm, "but I gotta say, before I go..." Gene glanced around nervously. "Patty Cleary knows you're in town. He called me up out of the blue a couple nights ago—drunk as shit, of course. I haven't talked to that guy since... well, you know. And he calls me up like we're still good buddies. He woke up my *kids*."

"What did he want, Eugene?"

Gene's lips tightened at the sound of his full name. "He wants to kill you, Dean. *Still*. I mean, do you fucking believe that? The guy's living in the fuck—" The elderly man shuffled up alongside him, reached for the paper towels, gave them a squeeze, and moved on without them. Gene kept his voice hushed. "He's living in the past. He's *obsessed* with that—" His eyes widened (*In fright?* Dean wondered), and he swallowed something acrid. "I'm real sorry about what went down that day, man. We were just dumb little kids, Joel and me. But *Patrick...*"

"Water under the bridge," Dean said.

"Seriously?" He seemed genuinely pleased—and why wouldn't he? He'd just been forgiven attempted murder.

"Seriously."

"Gee, that's—that's just great, Dean. Dean-o." A goofy smile spread across his fleshy face and he patted Dean's arm again twice, excitedly. "I'm serious about that drink, too. Look me up." He began to move away, thought better of it. He held Dean's gaze in his beady little eyes. "And be careful, man. That Patrick... he's an *animal*." His eyes bugged out of his head again, he let out a jumpy laugh—almost a *cackle*—and scurried off toward the checkouts.

Catherine had disappeared by the time Dean reached the counter with his groceries—off on break according to her replacement, a bored teenage girl with smiley faces painted on her nails. It took some time shopping to build up his courage to finally talk to her—telling himself he wasn't that shy little kid anymore, that he'd popped his cherry a long time ago, he was a goddamn *man* and he'd been to *war*, for fuck's sake —only to miss her by seconds.

An invite to his middle school reunion was among the mail on the kitchen table when he returned home with the groceries. "'You are cordially invited,'" he said, smirking. Like it was a wedding. He wondered if Patrick Cleary would show his face. It could give him a chance to talk to Catherine, but with all the bad memories, Dean wasn't sure he'd even go.

The telephone began to ring. Dean threw the invitation into the trash and answered the call.

———

"YOU KNOW, SOMEONE called me the other day about a dog program."

Second session. Dean had discovered the way to progress through these hours more quickly was to talk. At the very least, it seemed to engage Dr. Baswell. The man sitting across from him was still nothing like the ersatz uncle from Dean's childhood: the adventurer who'd regaled him with tales of camel herds crossing the desert, of giant mosquitos on the Amazon River, of men who'd had very little contact with the Western world and still wore khakis, smoked cigarettes and brandished AK-47s. He wasn't *that* Tim Baswell, but at least this man seemed *human*.

"A—dog program? Oh. A comfort animal."

"Yeah. They give you this dog to care for. It's supposed to help keep your mind occupied, give you something to take care of, to feed and love. I guess."

"And you said...?"

"I don't like dogs. That's what I said."

Dr. Baswell seemed to find this interesting. He scratched in his pad. Dean had heard many therapists didn't like to use pads these days, that it distracted the patient—or *client*, in Baswell's case. If Baswell thought it might hinder Dean's progress, it didn't show.

"What's that you're writing," Dean wondered aloud.

"I'm not writing, Dean."

Dean pushed up in his chair. "Looks like a whole lot of chicken scratching to me," he said with a teasing grin.

Baswell didn't reply, just kept scratching away with his pen on the paper. Dean sat back, irked. His eyes fell on the map. HERE BE—

He looked away in spite. *You're not gonna trigger some fucking revelation by ignoring me, Uncle Tim.*

After nearly a minute, Beethoven's clock ticking off the seconds, Baswell gave a pleased little smile and turned the pad to face his client.

Dean thought about turning away from it, about not giving Baswell the satisfaction, but he knew Baswell would see the action as childish. Regressive. He'd had enough of that for one week. He turned to look.

Baswell hadn't been writing, after all. He'd been drawing. "What is that?"

"It's you. As a miniature schnauzer."

Surprised, Dean snorted a laugh. "You serious?" He stood and crossed to where Baswell was seated, took the pad from the man when it was offered. It was actually a pretty good likeness—the eyes were right, the hair he wore slicked back and parted down the left side, but the rest was all schnauzer. With the floppy ears, the long, smooth beard and mutton chops, he looked a bit like some crotchety old Scotsman. Duff McGruff, or something.

"That's pretty good," he said, returning to his seat. "Though, you know, I woulda drawn myself as a German Shepherd." The leather grumbled as he sat.

Dr. Baswell gave the sketch a look, shrugged slightly, then returned the pad to his desk. "What made you bring that up?"

"What?"

"About the dog program?"

"Huh? Oh. It was just weird, that's all."

"How so?"

"Like, how did they get my number?"

"I suspect they were contacted by the Armed Forces, as I'd been."

Dean nodded. "Yeah, that—you might be right. I never thought of that. Anyway, that's not what's weird. I saw Catherine the other day."

"Catherine?"

"This girl I loved, growing up. Stood her up on a pedestal."

"Unrequited?"

"Big time. You don't make out with the Venus de Milo, right? She just stands there, being perfect."

"Venus?"

"*Catherine.*"

"And this has to do with—"

"I'm getting there. So, I get home from the grocery store—that's where I saw her, Catherine—and the telephone's ringing in the house.

Mom and Dad are out toodling in the garden. That's something they do now: toodling. Everything's a toodle. So I throw the groceries down on the counter and grab the phone." Dean sucked in a big gulp of air. In his rush to get the story out, he'd forgotten to breathe. He'd also forgotten about the invitation.

"Take your time, Dean."

"Thanks. So I pick up the phone and it's that dog program, asking me do I want a comfort dog. I was so startled, I didn't even think about it. I told them I don't like dogs and I hung up. I *like* dogs, I was just freaked out they'd called right then. It's like, you know when you think about a song and it's the next thing on the radio? Like *Synchronicity*."

"You know Jung?" Uncle Tim, drawn out for a moment, smiled.

"Jung—oh... Actually, I meant the Police song. I was singing it in my head the day I came back home, and when I turned on my old boombox —couldn't believe the thing still worked, even with the batteries all gummed up like they were—there's *Synchronicity* in the tape deck, with 'Synchronicity I' sittin' on pause for fifteen years. But sure, Jung's good, too."

Dr. Baswell picked up his pad from the desk. "So you felt your meeting with Catherine was somehow related to this call from the Service Dog Foundation?"

Dean felt a chill rush up his spine. Somehow, he found the nerve to smile. "Because *Catherine had a dog*."

"A lot of people have dogs, Dean."

"Not like this one. Meanest damn thing you ever heard."

"'Heard.' You never saw it?"

"Nobody did, but yeah. I did, once. It was always behind their fence. One kid said he saw it once, but it turned out he was just lying to get Catherine to notice him. She was that kind of girl. Every boy wanted to date her, but her dad wouldn't let her out of his sight. Drove her to and from school every single day, right to the door, even though you could tell it embarrassed the hell out of the poor kid. Not just pretty, either —*smart*, too. Never allowed to go to any of the dances. Not that I know from experience. I never went, either. If Catherine wasn't going, you could count me out."

"Out of solidarity?"

"Out of 'If she's not gonna be there, what's the point?'"

Dr. Baswell nodded thoughtfully.

"You see what I mean about a pedestal?"

"I'm beginning to."

"So, heard—yeah. Always from behind that fence. *Hurtling* itself at that fence. For most kids on the Lock Side, going past her place was the easiest shortcut to the Elementary school."

Dr. Baswell seemed to respond to this. "Which street is this?"

"Danber Avenue," Dean said. "Just a small street, crescent really. There's a laneway at the end of it that runs between two houses. One on the right is Catherine's. It opens up on this parking lo—"

He stopped, suddenly aware he had almost revealed something very important. He waited for the feeling to pass, watching the grandfather clock swing its big brass counterweight, like the long, dangly testicles of its namesake.

"I know it," Baswell was saying. "We used to take Greenbury, when I was young."

Breathe, Dean. Breathe it out. And then the memory was gone, passed under him like the shadow of a dragon in the depths of a black, raging sea. He sighed in relief. "Yeah," he said, returning to reality. "I know Greenbury. Danber is easier though, because of the lane."

"It wasn't there in my day. Are you okay, Dean? You look peaked." Only Baswell didn't say *peaked*, he said *peekid*, vaguely Shakespearean.

"Huh? Oh, no, I'm—I'm fine. You don't think that's weird, though? The dog thing?"

"Well, Dean," Baswell rested his fingers beneath his lips. "Things like this happen all the time: pick up the phone to dial a number, and the callee's already picked up the other end, about to call you. Hear a word for the first time, and suddenly you're hearing it everywhere. And so on. They aren't signs or signals from some spooky netherworld beyond ours. There's no special meaning. These things just happen, because at some point events like these are bound to coincide. It's fun to think they may be something more, but if you start to take the idea seriously without any religious grounding, there's a mild danger of solipsism."

"*Solip*—?"

"The idea that things, places, events, all exist inside one's own mind. That everything exists solely because *you* do."

"And that's dangerous."

"Because it *devalues* those things, Dean. *Other people.* If they aren't real, they don't matter. Therefore, what's to stop you from harming them?"

Dean studied the man's expression. It seemed as if Baswell were scrutinizing him, looking for something hidden just below the surface. An emotional response? An apology? A dragon?

Beethoven signaled the end of the hour. Baswell stood and hugged his hand.

DEAN STOOD IN the cul-de-sac on Danber Avenue, looking up at Catherine's house.

It was early morning on a Saturday, an overcast day. Lights were on in the ground floor of the house. He'd told his parents he was going for a run, and he had run for a few miles, shutting off his brain: the screams, the shouted prayers, the hot smell of urine and sweat, the sweaty flesh pressed against his, the dogs barking, the orders, the laughter. When he allowed his brain to turn on again, he had just about stepped into oncoming traffic, or what little there was of it in Dark Pines. He found himself back on the Lock Side, jogging in place at the far-east foot of Quarry Road. He'd come almost full circle back to his house, and had somehow wandered into the route he used to take to school. Danber met Quarry three or four blocks further east. Where there had once been row houses, there was now a corner store, either advertising or owned by Kit Kat candy bars.

He ran in place, deciding. Home was two blocks west, three south. Catherine's was three—*Four, Dean, don't act like you forgot*—east, three north.

He ran north a block, telling himself he wasn't going to go, he didn't need to dredge up any more embarrassment from his pathetic, lonely childhood. Then he veered a sharp right, crossing the road in front of a bicyclist, who angrily jangled her bell before throwing back the middle finger.

Startled, keyed up with adrenaline, he almost shouted at her. He thought about chasing after her, running alongside until he got her attention, and then punching her in the back of the head, knocking her off the bike. The spandex biking suit made him instantly hate her; her sharp features further annoyed him. That she had the nerve to give him the bird after she'd nearly run him down in the street was the final nail, an insult which could not—*would* not—go unpunished.

He breathed. Baswell had suggested it during their third session, but Dean had yet to try it. It seemed too simple, too much like a magic bullet, to be helpful. But he breathed, in through the nose (*Innnnnnnnnnn*), out through the mouth (*Ouuuuuuuut*). *Expel the bad juju, Dean-o. In through the nose... ouuuuuut through the mouth.*

His heartbeat slowed. The cyclist rounded the corner onto Quarry and was gone.

There. That wasn't so hard, was it? And he answered himself: *Like fuck, it wasn't. But it worked. Might not work every time, but this time it did.*

Violence had sent him home. After the incident with his commanding officer, Dean had run. He was a runner. It was what he'd always done, ever since he was a child: run from authority, run from responsibility, run from his enemies, run from life. If it was a pattern, then perhaps it was destiny that had driven him off into the desert outside Kandahar, where he'd been stationed, with his fellow officers pursuing him for a time in their M-Gator A3 utility vehicles and "Optimus Prime" (their Armored Heavy Support Vehicle), shouting after him, until he'd leapt into an area dotted with boulders and scrub brush between two sand dunes, where even the Gators couldn't follow. Optimus Prime, unable to transform for the more rugged terrain, had braked minutes behind the others, and had probably already headed back to base by the time he'd lost the Gators. But Dean had kept on running, faster than he'd ever pushed himself—except, maybe, for that day when he was 12. After a time he was certain he'd lost them, that they'd given up, and still he wouldn't dare stop until the sun had beaten him to a pulp, and he'd thrown up everything from his stomach. Then he'd dropped trou and squirted shit into the hard-packed sand, his nerves jangling, his insides like a wrung sponge, every single part of him sore, even his eyelids.

He'd spent the night in a goat farmer's hovel. The mustached man had fed him stale naan with mashed beans and let him sleep with the goats. Cold. Nobody ever told you how cold the desert got at night. It seemed not to make any sense, that such a place of extremes couldn't possibly exist on earth. The desert was never warm, nor cool. There were no gradations between sweating through your clothes, the kind of heat that squeezed every drop of moisture from your body, and the shivering, huddled-up inside-your-clothes kind, like the most frigid Canadian winter cold, with no place and no one in sight with whom to find warmth. There were no shades of gray; the Afghan desert was all death, hard and unforgiving.

The goat herder's hovel had been a godsend. That night, Dean had snuggled up to the fattest goat, a skinny female with a distended belly and flat, hanging udders like deflated party balloons. At first, she'd kicked him away—not hard, just enough to show him she wasn't thrilled. He'd snuggled in again, and she'd settled into it with a snorted sigh. Lying against her belly, like a giant, bristly hot water bottle, feeling her heartbeat against his ear, her scrawny chest rising and falling slowly and steadily with her breath, Dean had fallen asleep.

In the morning, he'd awakened to the man milking his bedmate. Sometime in the night, Dean had shifted or been pushed into a loose pile of straw, his face crisscrossed where he'd slept against it.

The man had fed him a dish of some sour, curded white stuff—like yoghurt, but as chunky as cottage cheese—and sticky rice. On Dean's way out the door, the farmer had thrust something into his hand: a beaten copy of *The Noble Qur'an*. That it was an English edition said to Dean the man had kept it around in waiting for a moment like this, since the farmer spoke no English himself.

This was meant for me, he'd thought, and a tingling sense of religious mysticism had warmed him from chest to anus.

He couldn't accept it, but he hadn't been able to get the man to take it back, either, and since everything he had said was gibberish to the man, Dean had finally thanked him and tucked the book into the back of his uniform khakis. The man said, "*As-salaam alaikum*," and though Dean didn't know any Arabic, per se, he'd hear that phrase—*Peace be unto you*—spoken enough to know the correct response was to repeat it, or something similar. So he had, and a near-toothless smile had creased the man's craggy cheeks, making his mustache look somewhat like a blackbird taking flight above his sunburnt brown lips.

Heat had returned to the desert. He'd heard the vehicles maybe an hour after leaving the goat herder's house. He had already been reading from the Qur'an for some time by then, tearing off pages as he read them and tossing them into the wind as he walked. He'd still been reading when they caught up to him.

"'And Jesus said, 'Indeed, I am the servant of Allah!'" Dean had started shouting as they wedged their vehicles in his path, raising a swirling cloud of dust. "'He has given me the Scripture and made me a prophet!'" He'd torn the page and thrown it behind him, where it fluttered. Not the green vehicles of Canadian Armed Forces standard; these were desert-beige Humvees. American soldiers. Marines. "'Have you no desire for my gods, O Abraham? If you do not desist, I will surely stone you, so avoid me a prolonged time!'"

"Sir, where are you going?" The Marine, a woman, had bright blue eyes—*Like a husky's*, Dean had thought—and lips so chapped they were mostly white. She'd put a hand on his shoulder, and Dean had shirked it, angrily. The eyes had turned cold then, chapped lips thinning. "Okay, sir, we are only trying to help."

"'The ink of the scholar is more holy than the blood of the martyr!'" Dean had said, and spat in the grunt's face.

Her eyes had become merciless, left hand rising to the M4 carbine automatic slung over her shoulder. She'd wiped the spit off with her gloved right. It had only streaked the dirt on her cheek and chin.

Three men had then approached from the vehicle, boxing him in. Dean had fought them off, thrown a punch at a young guy who still had pimples and kicked the woman in the thigh. They'd overtaken him easily. He'd screamed at them—"*Western dogs! Infidels!*"—like a wild-eyed Libyan terrorist from an '80s movie. He'd kicked and he'd spat. They'd thrown him into the back of the vehicle, wedged between two Marines in the back, Private Black and Private White, and when he wouldn't shut up (he *couldn't* shut up, since his anger, his *rage* wouldn't allow it: he was a Canadian citizen, a *soldier*!), one of them had back-handed him so hard across the jaw that his teeth had clacked, and maybe it was the heat, the exhaustion or the lack of sustenance, but suddenly Dean had found himself in the dark.

Running. Running in the dark.

When the light had come back, they'd been parked at the Bagram Airfield detention facility in Parwan Province, Afghanistan's Guantanamo, 550-something kilometers, 340-something miles away. He'd been out for over 9 hours. The sun had bored holes in his skull through his eyes, and as his Marine friends had escorted him to the building, other soldiers pushed their own detainees past a makeshift schoolyard, where unused children's toys gathered more dust with every sandstorm. Now, he remembered the single sunflower growing in a field of gravel, trudged down by their boots, before springing back hopefully toward the desert sun.

Running again. Running along Danber Avenue, like he'd done that day when he was 12. And now he stood in front of her house, Catherine's house, and the lights were on, and a cute little hatchback was in the drive as a cool, light rain began to patter against his hot skin. The Priests' backsplit was at the end of a cul-de-sac, and there was nowhere else to go but up to the door.

You could take the lane, Dean-o.

Not a fucking chance, he thought back.

The bungalow on the left side of the lane was gone, ditto the one to the left of that. The two houses had been junked, and a larger one had sprung up in their place. The Priests' big wooden fence, its slats so close together they were almost impenetrable, was gone. Dean had noticed this the moment he'd turned onto Danber. There was only wide-open yard, the dog likely long dead. If they had another dog now, it was either well-trained or wearing one of those awful shock collars. Beyond the yard, with its barbeque and picnic table and giant, rich green pine, the parking lot was gone, too. In its place was a public playground with newish plastic equipment. Past that was Anderson Road, and just two blocks east from there was Dark Pines Elementary. Unless that was gone, too.

The lights were on in Catherine's house. A television flickered blue in the living room. No movement inside. It was 8:34 AM. Dean caught his breath and let the rain cool him, thinking it over. Breathing deep. The adrenaline still churning. The time was now... or never.

Fuck it.

Dean strode to the door. He was reaching for the little brass knocker when it opened inward. The man in the doorway nearly jumped out of his wits.

Christ—she's married.

"Jesus, you scared me," the man said. He was about Dean's age, maybe a few years older, and vaguely handsome, even if a bit pudgy and pasty in a British lord sort of way. He wore a plush robe and fuzzy slippers at the ends of his hairy, skinny legs. The man checked out Dean's muscular frame, gave him a puzzled look. "Are you the new paperboy?"

"No, I..." Defeated. "I'm sorry, I think I must have the wrong address."

"Who are you looking for?"

Dean briefly considered making up a name, but he said, "Ca-Catherine Priest? Are you—? Is she—?"

"Nope, you've got the right place, all right." The man seemed suspicious. "Friend of hers, are you?"

Dean nodded meekly.

"She's still sleeping right now. Would you like me to tell her you dropped by, or...?"

Dean looked at the living room window. The furniture was all different than what he'd seen through her windows back when they were kids.... Classier. Had that been her influence, or her husband's? "No. That's okay." He turned from the door, descended the stairs.

"Well, okay then," the man called after him, bending for the newspaper. "Have a good one."

"You too," Dean said, not turning, running out into the swelling rain.

"WHAT ARE YOU RUNNING FROM, DEAN?"

Fourth session. Dr. Baswell knew all about Dean's desertion, his time at Bagram and his eventual release in the wake of scandal. Dean hadn't been the one to tell him: the Armed Forces people had when they'd scheduled the sessions, along with his commanding officer, Master Corporal Sandman, who'd made an impassioned personal call. The rest, Baswell had gleaned from the papers. He had the infamous copy of the Toronto *Herald* folded on the end table beside his chair.

"Let's go back. To your childhood."

"You wanna know if I was fondled by my daddy? If Mommy didn't love me?"

Baswell flashed a stern glare. "Don't be disrespectful. Anyhow, if Laurenz had felt the need to abuse you, it would first mean he'd have to acknowledge your existence, as something other than a rather disappointing appendage."

Dean chuckled his scorn. Baswell had a point. It wasn't as though he'd had a terrible childhood, but his father had been perpetually dissatisfied: with Dean's grades, with the way Dean did his chores, with his extracurricular activities (or lack thereof), his lack of his father's impressive stature (Larry Vogel was six-foot-six, Dean a mere five-nine), his disposition, his apparent weakness and unwillingness to work out, his disinterest in the sciences (he'd hoped for Dean to become a doctor, like himself), and his general lack of motivation. These days, not much had changed, with the notable addition of the shame and embarrassment over his son's desertion and dismissal with disgrace from the military. And when Laurenz Vogel hadn't been voicing his disappointment, he'd been cold and inattentive.

"When was the first time you skipped school?" Baswell asked.

"They told you about that?"

"Educated guess." Dr. Baswell smiled—far too pleased by his own deduction. "Running away is a pattern with you, isn't it? What was it that first time? A test? A speech? The bigger kids picking on you?"

Dean said nothing.

"You're too smart for it to have been a test, though I suppose you could have been unprepared. No. The way you lashed out at Master Corporal Sandman, I'm guessing it was bullies. I'm right, aren't I?"

Dean turned to face the ancient mariner on the old sea map, stern-faced and bearded like his father. Monsters in the open water. *HERE BE DRAGONS, all right. You said a fuckin' mouthful, Captain Highliner.*

"All I know about it—the incident when you were twelve—was what happened to the boy." *Jesus, no, please, Uncle Tim. I don't wanna remember. Please.* "It's very much reminiscent to me of what happened to that Sandman fellow. He was defiant, of course. Said you had it coming, and claimed he would have killed you with his bare hands, if he'd been physically able to run after you. Sandman, I mean. Not the boy. The boy was hospitalized for a month."

"The things that prick said to me," Dean said through gritted teeth. "He had no right to lay a hand on me. None of them did. No right to... to shove me up against the wall like he did."

"He was your commanding officer. These things sometimes happen, I understand. Even in my day. This was before the rumors of steroid abuse in the military, of course. The over-use of nutritional supplements."

"That doesn't make it *right*, does it? What gives a man the right to do that, huh? What makes a man think he's got the right to lay his hands on someone like that?"

"You're speaking on behalf of the bullied. Do you look at what you've done as heroic?" Dean said nothing. Baswell prodded: "Shooting a man point-blank in the kneecap—did you think you were doing all of the bullied children a service? Fighting back for them? Or did you do it for the child you once were?"

"This is ridiculous."

"Tell me, then. Tell me about the first time you skipped school, Dean. I want your side of the story. So I know how to look at you. I haven't for a very long time, you know."

He'd known. Even back then, he'd sensed the distance growing between them. The prezzies had stopped that year, and the stories along with them. A tear streaked down his face. He let out a shivery breath. And told him everything.

THE FIRST TIME he'd skipped school, they'd been waiting for him: Patrick Cleary, Joel Suskin and Eugene Evans, the three meanest kids in the seventh grade. They'd chosen him because he was the smallest in their class. They'd hang him up in his locker and beat on him whenever the teachers weren't around. They'd bend him over his desk and beat on him in the portables before class started. Adults always said don't react —if you cry, if you whimper, you're giving them what they want, only feeding the fire. And Dean had tried not to react. He'd let them wail on him.

He knew what his father would have thought about it, but there was nothing he could do against the three boys together. If he'd gotten one of them alone... But no, they'd always traveled in packs, like those intelligent dogs in Moscow he'd read about recently. The bruises were easy enough to hide—on his legs, his back, his upper arms. His father had never suspected a thing.

They were waiting for him on his way to school, waiting on Quarry near the convenience store with the sign on its door written in childish uppercase script, "NO MORE THEN TWO (2) KIDS IN STORE AT A TIME!" Dean had spotted them before they saw him, and he'd made a run for it, up Juniper Road instead of Danber. Too late this time. They'd seen him before he rounded the corner, or heard his footfalls— maybe even *smelled* him, like the rabid dogs they were—and given chase. Patrick and Joel had longer legs than his; they were bigger, and took longer strides. The two biggest kids caught up to him in the lane alongside Catherine's fence, where it opened on the parking lot and Anderson Road. They threw him up against the fence boards, so hard his teeth rattled and the bell on the other side of the big pine door jingled, his head pressed up against the sign:

BEWARE OF DOG

The first bark startled all four of them. Eugene jumped a little, his rich black hair ruffling, then balled his small fists and made as if he hadn't been scared. Dull-eyed Joel threw the first punch. It hit Dean in the solar plexus and Dean doubled over, breathless, held firm against the gate by their large fists.

Gene ran in and threw half a dozen rabbit punches to Dean's guts and side. His knuckles struck hipbone on his last punch and he winced, stumbling backward, shaking away the pain.

"Lookit 'im!" Patrick shouted, laughing and pointing at Gene with his free hand. "Lookit the little pussy!"

The dog was barking, barking. Dean felt the pain bunch in his innards and shoot upward, lodging somewhere behind his eyeballs where the barks doubled, trebled in his brain. He was a thermometer stuck in an oven, the mercury rising up its shaft; the bulb was his skull. He was a nuclear missile, the warhead about to explode. He was the Strength Tester at the Spring Fair, the one with the big hammer and the ball, and the bell was his head. Hit it hard enough and win a prize.

Did he barked as he kicked? Dean couldn't remember now, but it felt like he had. He did remember he couldn't see a thing, had only kicked out blindly as hard as he could. He remembered his sneaker hitting something firm and yielding, hearing one of them cry out in agony. The grip on his right shoulder let go, and he fell down hard on the ball of his right foot (later it would bruise, and then hurt for a week). He'd struck Joel square in the balls, and the brunt of Dean's weight had torn his left shoulder free from Patrick's grip.

"H-holy shit!" Gene stuttered, and finally the world came back into focus. Gene wasn't stuttering but *laughing*, because in spite of the beating he would get from his two larger cohorts, in spite of the sympathy pain any boy feels when another kid get wailed in the balls, it was *funny* when it happened. It was even sort of laughable when it happened to you. "Ha-ha-holy shit, Patty! Right in the dinger!"

Patrick stood over Joel, who was crying—*crying!* "Shut up, *Eugene*," he said. Gene shut up, even though he hated when kids called him that: Eugene. Because Patrick could *make* him shut up if he wouldn't do it on his own. "Stop cryin' you fuckin' baby," the biggest and baddest boy shouted down at Joel.

Dean looked around. He might be able to escape to the left, but there were metal posts in the way, blocking cars from entering the lane, and if he had to skirt around them (there was no way he could jump them, the way his legs were jittering), Patrick's reach was long enough to grab him and pull him back. Gene blocked forward advance, and Joel was curled up directly to Dean's right, in the direction of Danber. At Dean's feet, where the fence opened on the parking lot, was a chunk of cinderblock.

He stooped.

Patrick wheeled around with a monstrous look, as Dean rose with the blunted weapon. "What are you gonna do, pussy?" he sneered. "You gonna hit me with that? Huh, pussy? I dare you, Pean." It was what Patrick had always called him: *Pean*, a cross between Dean and penis. "I fuckin' *dare* you."

The dog leaped behind the gate, rattling it against his back. The warhead went off and Dean swung. Hit the bell, win a prize.

Patrick's left cheek tore open and blood immediately filled the space where his skin had peeled back. There was a sound like breaking glass and the dull reverberation shuddered back up Dean's arm as the concrete struck bone. Something small and brilliantly white flew from this gaping, bleeding orifice: a molar, the sun glinting off its amalgam filling as it twirled, plinking against the fence of the opposite house. Eyes wide in fear and pain, Patrick's hand came up to his face. Red oozed like syrup through his fingers and dribbled on the sidewalk.

Dean wanted to laugh, but what he did was bark. Later, he would decide it was this unconscious decision which had probably saved his life. "WOOF!" he said. "WOOF! WOOF!"

Gene looked to Patrick, to Joel, to Dean—who was still barking, and the dog, rattling against the door, matched him bark for bark—and the truth of it dawned on Gene's dirty little freckled face. "You're crazy!" he shouted. Then he split.

Like Patrick's face, Dean thought. And laughed.

Patrick's face was chalk white where he wasn't red. He tried to speak, but no words came out. Only *"Bluh,"* and a mouthful of spit-bubbly blood, which splashed down his chin, into the teenaged scruff on his neck and down the front of his shirt. Joel struggled to his feet, giving Dean a baleful look.

Dean bared his teeth at him and growled.

Joel's eyes went wide. He looked away immediately, before shuffling off with his throbbing balls in his hands. Patrick turned tail and followed, leaving a wet trail of himself along the way. He rounded the corner and was gone.

Finally, Dean dropped the bloodied piece of concrete, amazed and shocked by his courage, by his rage. *I'm an animal*, he thought, and the thought both frightened and amused him.

The bell above the gate jingled. He didn't realize he'd fallen back against it until it swung inward, and he fell into the arms of Mr. Priest.

And then Dean Vogel, fearless for the first time in his life, burst into tears. The Priests' White Shepherd whimpered and stepped into his lap, licking the tears from his eyes and cheeks and lips. Dean's first ever kiss —and it was from a dog.

IN DR. BASWELL'S office, Dean gripped the leather armrests, remembering everything.

"I didn't skip school because I was ashamed of what I did. I wasn't afraid of the consequences," he admitted. "I couldn't face the other kids. I knew they'd look at me different. Like you did." Dr. Baswell nodded grimly. "And because of how *good* it felt when that goddamn thing hit his face. *I felt his bones*, Uncle Tim. I felt like an *animal*—and I dunno, maybe I am."

"No more an animal than any of us, Dean. You could only take so much abuse before you struck back. It was inevitable. You were outnumbered, a child pushed to the edge, and you struck out with whatever you could find."

But Dean didn't want Baswell's sympathy or anyone's. He wanted reproach. He *deserved* it. "And Sandman? I fucking shot a man because he pushed me up against a wall. I took out my SIG and kneecapped him. That sound like the behavior of a rational human being to you, or the killer instincts of an animal?"

Baswell wouldn't, or *couldn't*, answer.

"The worst thing about it? I fucking *enjoyed* it, Uncle Tim. When his knee burst out of his khakis, I *laughed*. I had his blood on my face and I was laughing. And they were staring at me, all of them. Fucking stupefied. Just like that day outside Catherine's house. Maybe some of them wished they could've done the same thing. Shit, maybe Joel and Eugene would've done what I did to Patrick, if they had the guts."

Baswell set his pad down on the desk. "No barking, though."

"Huh?"

Beethoven signaled the end of the hour. They sat in silence a moment, letting the song play out, letting the bell chime two o'clock.

"When you shot Corporal Sandman," Baswell said finally, "you didn't bark."

"No."

"You didn't consciously attempt to kill Patrick Cleary, did you?"

"No. I just wanted it to be over."

"And Sandman? Were you aiming for somewhere higher?"

"Isn't it your lunchtime?"

"It can wait."

Dean nodded. "Well, actually, I was aiming for his foot."

"Then I suppose you're not an animal, are you? Just a man. With frailties and anxieties. Just like anyone else."

Dean wasn't sure if Baswell was pulling his leg. "Are you serious? You don't think I'm—you don't think I'm crazy?"

"Wounded, certainly. High-strung. I'd recommend anger-management training." Baswell allowed himself to smile. "But no, Dean, I don't believe you're crazy, not for a minute." He stood, and as he took Dean's hand, he pulled him in for a hug. Dean let Uncle Tim hug him a moment, amused and baffled, then wrapped his own arms around the man and hugged him back.

Uncle Tim broke the embrace, but he held Dean by the shoulders a moment longer to regard him. "I'm going to sign off on your papers," he said, letting him go. "But I want you to do me a favor."

"Anything," Dean said, smoothing out his shirt, trying to cover his relief.

"Apologize to the Cleary boy. *Man*. Make it sincere. Make things right between the two of you."

"After all he did?"

"You put him in the hospital for a month. Your father had to wire his jaw shut. Patrick's parents couldn't afford dentures—they simply pulled the broken teeth and left him with the holes. He's got no molars on the upper left side of his mouth."

"Jesus. *Really?*"

A grim nod from Baswell.

"Wow," Dean said, truly shocked by the news, having never seen Patrick again after that day. Rumor had it the boy had moved to a different school out of shame, and Dean had never thought to question it. "I guess now I know why everyone started looking at me different afterwards. He wants to *kill me*, though, Uncle Tim. Gene—Eugene Evans—he told me Patrick called him drunk in the middle of the night when he found out I was in town."

"I suspect that's just bravado talking," Baswell said. "You have to remember, the culture of violence machismo produces—"

"All right, all right," Dean said, throwing up his hands. "I'll say I'm sorry."

"Good," Baswell said, and let Dean go.

BASWELL VOUCHING FOR DEAN'S progress had the effect on the Vogel house of a medium telling her clients their home was free of evil. His mother stopped jumping at the sound of his voice, and his father began to be civil. Uncle Tim told them about the repeated bullying, and that the hit with the cinderblock had been (mostly) accidental. He told them the shooting of his commanding officer had been a direct response to the bullying, albeit years after the fact. Having struggled with bullying for so long without reaction, Dean had found himself unable to tolerate it in his adult life. He dealt with it by lashing out the moment it seemed anybody was persecuting him or others.

Larry and Diane Vogel listened to Dr. Baswell for over an hour, sharing coffee in the Vogel kitchen while Dean lay on his childhood bed, staring up at the blank ceiling. Listening to their murmurs through the vents reminded him too much of childhood: the worrying, the self-doubt, the paranoia. They were talking about him again, and it couldn't be good. He caught snippets of conversation: *so violent... didn't raise him that... he's just lucky we didn't... if this was all about that, then why now?*

Dean put on the *Synchronicity* tape to drown out their conversation, but the music began to distort mid-song, slowing down, with "Tea in the Sahara" playing over top of "Synchronicity I" as the whir and tick of the gears grew louder than the music. He pulled the cassette from the deck, noticing the tape had twisted, and turned on the radio, straightening the tape and rewinding it with a pencil from his rolltop desk while the music drowned out his parents. When he came down to get a snack, half an hour or so after he'd heard the front door shut, his mom and dad were still seated at the table, holding hands. Their eyes were dry but red-rimmed; they'd been crying. Even *his father* had been crying.

Oh Jesus, this is too much.

"Son, your mater and I have something to tell you," Larry said.

Dean leaned up against the counter, waiting. His father breathed in deeply through his nose. What he had to say was clearly hard for him, but he managed to start after a small squeeze from his wife's hand. "How we treated you after the incident. We had no idea what those boys were doing to you. If we'd known... If only you'd *told* us... Maybe things would have been different around here."

"What your father's trying to say is 'We're sorry,'" Diane said, and blinked, smiling wistfully. Larry gave her a look, made a thin smile of his own, then nodded at Dean. *He's not going to say it, though, is he?* Dean thought.

"We're sorry," his father parroted.

But does he mean it? Is it like me, apologizing to Patrick because Uncle Tim asked me to? Is this a favor to Tim or Mom, or does he really —sincerely—mean it?

A tear streaked down his father's bristly cheek. The old man blinked it away, nodded again, mechanically, as if his nodding could stop the tears.

Dean slumped down at the table with them. His mother found his hand. His father took the other. They sat around the kitchen table and wept, while the sink dripped and the house settled... and outside, somewhere, Patrick Cleary was planning to murder him.

ALL THAT WEEK, Dean prepared for his confrontation with Patrick. No weapons this time, just talk. Man to man. He went over various scenarios in his head. The first were pure hostility: Patrick would not speak to him, would just slam the door in his face and tell Dean to get the fuck off his property. Another: Patrick would punch him the second Dean set foot on his doorstep. Dean would take the punch, gladly, but he wouldn't allow another. He'd ask him if it helped, if it made him feel any better. If Yes, he'd apologize right away. If No, he would ask what it would take to resolve their conflict. Aside from "I wanna break your face like you broke mine," he thought he could manage most possibilities.

He also prepared for an altogether different scenario. Patrick might let him speak, and Dean would tell the truth: that he didn't want to apologize, it was just the final step in his government-mandated therapy. He would tell him what had happened in Kandahar with Master Corporal Sandman. Patrick would ask if that was his real name, and Dean would laugh and tell him "No bullshit, man." Patrick would invite him in for a beer, and the two men would bond over the douchebaggery of bureaucracy and the seemingly endless struggle of being a kid.

It had even crossed his mind that Patrick Cleary might come to him, and rather than let Patrick ambush him on a darkened street while he jogged with music blasting in his ears, Dean put in some research.

At 7 AM that Friday, he parked outside the front gates at the Rockland Mine, down the far west end of Quarry Road. Patrick worked the overnight shift, seven to seven. Dean had learned this from Gene Evans, who seemed to know an awful lot about Patrick for someone who hadn't spoken to him in years, aside from that recent late-night phone call. He and Dean had caught up over a beer. The meeting had mostly been about acquiring information, so Dean had tried to keep the conversation light. Gene was an engineer (he hadn't specified what type of engineer, and Dean hadn't inquired), and had married Linda Braun right out of high school. Dean vaguely remembered her, a mousey thing with flat-cut bangs, and congratulated him. Gene and Linda Evans had three kids. In the photos, Dean saw they all had Eugene's lustrous dark hair and beady black eyes. Gene had gotten too drunk, perhaps sensing Dean's distance, and had eventually begun to cry and paw at Dean, begging for forgiveness. Dean had put him in a cab and sent him home. He'd gone back to the bar and paid their tab.

"Awww, you kittens okay?" the beefy bartender had asked.

"Mind your fucking business," Dean had responded, and left the jerk without a tip.

Patrick came out of the mine entrance at ten after seven, laughing. He whipped his trucker cap up in the air like Mary Tyler Moore. It caught in the wind, and he had to run and duck to catch it before it hit the ground. Decent reflexes. He was still large-framed, bigger than Dean had remembered. But he was scrawny, the sort of wiry fitness an ecto-morph built up from physical labor, without concentration on specific muscle groups. If he had to, if Patrick decided one punch wasn't quite enough, Dean felt he could subdue him. He was used to fighting more than one man at a time, after all. Sometimes, as he had in the desert, even *women*.

Just past the gates, a friend picked Patrick up in a beat-to-shit F150 (legend had it Patrick's pickup had been impounded for his drunk driving), and they drove off south out of town. Casino bound? Proba-bly. Off to spend their paychecks on nickel slots and hard drinking. Gene had mentioned Patrick hadn't had a girlfriend in years, which didn't seem likely. Good old boys like Pat Cleary always had someone to manhandle and treat like shit. Gene believed Patrick frequented pros-titutes.

As the pickup rumbled past the Vogel family Volvo, Dean got a good look at Patrick's scar, and sucked in a wincing breath, the truth of it hitting him like a cinderblock. The ragged scar tore a line from the corner of his lips and up over his ear. His shaggy brown rat's-nest hair stopped at the pink gash, then resumed below it in a straggly sideburn. He hadn't even tried to hide it, sweeping his hair back under his cap instead of down over the old wound, wearing it like a badge of honor. The lips themselves were downturned on that side, like a man with Bell's palsy. No, Dean decided, this man had no girlfriend. The man might *never* have had a girlfriend.

Fucking disfigured him, Dean-o. Jesus Christ. I turned the guy into a goddamn circus freak.

Dean bit down on the back of his fist, studying his eyes in the mirror. Regret stared back at him. He hadn't wanted this. He was honestly sorry for what he'd done, he knew that now. But Patrick had been a monster *before* Dean hit him with the cinderblock. The injury had just made Patrick's face into a mirror, reflecting the ugliness inside and projecting it to the world.

Dean wondered if Sandman walked with crutches now, or a cane. He'd definitely have a limp, maybe for the rest of his life.

At home that night, Dean lay in the dark, picturing Patrick's scars. He imagined the heft and feel of the concrete chunk in his hand as he swung out with it, the crunch of bone, the breaking-glass sound of Patrick's teeth shattering, the shudder up to his elbow and the pain settling there like he'd hit his funny bone. Patrick hadn't shown up to school for the next week, even the next month. For a while, the other kids had given Dean curious, fearful looks, the sort of looks they might have given a tiger in a cage.

And then, sometime during the summer of that same school year, something funny had happened: Dean realized he'd forgotten all about Patrick. Eugene had smiled awkwardly at him in the street, riding by on his BMX. Life had gone on, and the massive part Patrick had played in his earlier life had never been missed. It was, for a time, as if Patrick Cleary had never existed.

Dean had graduated, moved on. He'd gone to school for archeology, and found it incredibly boring, like being a maid for ancient civilizations with all that dusting and Ziplocking. Patrick had stayed in Dark Pines, starting work at the Rockland Mine at 16, doing odd jobs until they'd let him work underground. A fine job for a Dark Pines boy without an education. He drank. He gambled. He whored.

Dean had dropped out of school, never really fitting in. He'd spiraled for a while, directionless, had gotten into drugs and hard liquor, hitting a new bar almost every night. He'd started at the Garland Sugar factory when his student loan had run out, working and maintaining the centrifuges which separated sugar granules from the "mother liquor," a phrase that reminded him of his mom's boxed wine. It had been a decent job with decent pay, and the best part was when he punched out, he no longer had to think about it.

He'd considered going back to school the following semester for psychology (an attempt to follow once again in Uncle Tim's footsteps), but it would have meant taking more high school courses, and the equivalencies were too demanding, especially with the constant boozing, and his weekend regimen of weed, Ecstasy and cocaine. By the time he'd been laid-off during the financial crisis, he'd worked at the sugar plant ten years. His young life had slipped by him, barely remembered through a haze of toxins. He'd had girlfriends, but none steady, no one to write home about. The moment they'd seen what a lost cause he was, they'd all run. No friends he'd have called close. Where did you go when you ran out of options? The Armed Forces seemed the best, and somehow *easiest*, choice.

That was how Dean Vogel and Patrick Cleary, two very different men—one smart, one thickheaded, one middle-class, the other poor, one with all the opportunities in the world, the other limited by the cards he'd been dealt—had ended up in virtually the same place during the summer of their middle-school reunion.

Dean had taken Patrick's choices away from him. But Patrick had done the same for him, long before Dean returned the favor. They were men haunted by the mistakes of the past. Gingerbread Men. Dean had run all the way across the world; Patrick had run in place. But the past would always catch up with them.

And someday it would eat them whole.

ON SUNDAY, DEAN was jogging along Quarry Road toward Dark Pines Estates on the outskirts of town, close to the river lock. The estates, in this case, were mobile homes. He jogged rather than drove because he wanted to meet Patrick with a clear head, and jogging put him in a Zen state. Also, Dean had found bumping up the adrenaline before a conflict helped keep the mind and body sharp when that conflict arose.

Just outside of town, an orange sign declared: DANGER COUGAR IN AREA.

Here be dragons, Dean thought. *Beware of dog. Caution: Patrick Cleary sighted. Do not feed the fuckin' animal.*

He chuckled.

A honk startled him. He threw a look over his shoulder, still jogging on the soft gravel shoulder of the road, and recognized the approaching hatchback as the same car from Catherine's driveway. The sun reflecting off its windshield, he couldn't see inside at the driver. Probably the man he'd met the other week, Catherine Priest's husband—though, most likely, her name was no longer Priest.

The passenger window zipped down as the car crept alongside him. He slowed enough to peer inside.

Catherine sat hunched over the drive shaft, looking up at him, just as perfect as ever. "Dean Vogel," she said with a grin. She looked out at the empty road, the miles and miles of pine stands and farmland ahead of them. "What are you doing out here?"

For a moment, Dean couldn't speak. He caught his breath, swallowed. "J-jogging," he said finally.

"I can *see* that. Jogging where? The lock? There's nothing out here but cows and trees."

"I like the view," he managed, between breaths. "It's peaceful. What are—" Another swallow. "What are you doing out here?"

"Grandmother's house I go," Catherine said with a somewhat desolate grin.

Dean peered into the back seat. "I don't see a picnic basket," he said.

"What?"

"Never mind."

"Actually, I'm on my way to visit her in the hospital. Alzheimer's, Parkinson's: you name it, she's got it. I'm supposed to see her today, but I've got some errands to run in the city first." She scrutinized him. "You know, there is *something* between here and the city, but it's not much to look at." She left a pregnant pause, long enough for Dean to realize what she meant. "Dark Pines Estates?" she said. "The trailer park?"

"Never heard of it."

Her face lighted with an awed smile. "You're going to see him, aren't you?"

"I don't... I don't know who you're—"

"Oh, come on, Dean. You know you could never lie to me." An eyebrow rose. "You sure could run, but you never could lie."

Dean relented, nodding.

"You know he wants to kill you, don't you? You're not—? Dean, you're not going to hurt him again, are you?"

"For your information, Catherine, I'm going there to apologize."

She laughed and shook her head. "You must have a death wish." She opened the passenger door. "Well, come on. Get in."

"I thought you were visiting Grandma."

"If you're going to let Patrick Cleary bash your head in, you'll probably want a witness."

Dean laughed. "Real nice." He looked up ahead. Trailer Park Road wasn't even in sight yet, let alone the estates themselves. "All right," he said, and slipped in beside her.

"YOU KNOW I thought that was you at the store, two or three weeks back," she said as she drove. Her eyes never left the road, hands never roaming from ten and two. She wore a buttoned-up white blouse and a black skirt, flesh-toned pantyhose and flat black shoes, and still draped herself in the same perfume, a flowery, orange scent that filled the car yet wasn't at all overpowering. "Then my cousin mentioned a strange man at the door. Described you to a tee."

"Your cousin?"

"You met him. In his robe and those silly little fuzzy slippers of his?"

Dean clued in. "Oh! Your *cousin*!" Suddenly self-conscious, he dialed down his enthusiasm. "Seems like a nice guy."

Finally, she favored him with a glance. The scrunchie was in—red today. The gray in her hair was more prominent in the sun, as were the fine lines around her lips and eyes. Dean thought they made her somehow prettier than she'd been. She didn't try to erase them, hiding herself with makeup and hair dye, presenting herself as a woman who had lived—maybe not an easy life, or a particularly exciting one, but a life. Catherine had the look of someone who knew her best days were ahead; looking at her made Dean feel the same. "You thought he was my boyfriend," she said, before returning her gaze to the windshield.

"Husband, actually," he said.

She raised her left hand off the wheel a moment. No ring—why hadn't he noticed when he'd seen her at the grocery store? She threw him another glance, a smile in the eyes but not on the lips.

"You really don't have to come with me," he said.

"It's no trouble. Besides, someone needs to protect you. Unless you're hoping to find a cinderblock on Patrick's lawn."

The joke caught him off guard. He didn't know how to react.

"I'm sorry," she said. "That wasn't funny, was it?"

"No, it... Yeah, it wasn't funny. But it's okay."

"And I guess we really don't have time to fill each other in on our lives. There's Trailer Park Road."

"You know I always found that weird. The road's called 'Trailer Park' but the trailer park's called 'Estates.'"

"Probably couldn't get the city to change it."

"Yeah." Silence. "Can I turn on the radio?"

"Nervous?"

"About Patrick?" He shook his head too eagerly. "No. I've been practicing. I've played out every scenario a dozen times."

Her nostrils flared. "But you *are* nervous."

He nodded. "You make me nervous."

She laughed. "Oh god, Dean! *Still*?"

"Always," he said. He remembered the invitation he'd gotten in the mail, wondered if she would go to the reunion. "Hey, you're not—"

Catherine glanced at him, curious. "What?"

"Nothing. Never mind."

She shook her head and flicked the turn signal. *Tick-tock-tick-tock.* They turned onto Trailer Park Road.

"Well. This is it," she said forebodingly.

"This is it," he agreed. His right hand gripped the storage compartment in the door as they approached the attendant station. Catherine zipped down her window. A plump woman in her 50s sat behind the glass, wearing a sweater with I (HEART) MY GRANDKIDS printed on it, and regarded them with a smile from under her bucket hat. "Welcome to Dark Pines Estates, how can I help you?"

"We're looking for the Cleary Estate," Catherine said.

Dean snorted laughter. The woman eyed him with scorn before consulting her book. "Number 37. Go two blocks up, and take a left. Mr. Cleary's house is at the end."

"Thank you very much, ma'am," Catherine said, and drove ahead. The lady looked after them, then busied herself with something at the desk. It looked to Dean like she'd picked up the phone. Maybe someone had called in, but maybe—

You're being paranoid, Dean-o.

—she was calling *out*.

"Last house on the left," Catherine said. "How apropos."

"I don't know what that means."

She snickered.

And there it was: the epitome of bottom-rung. The other homes were pleasant little single- and double-wides, most of them, anyhow, with flower pots and shrubbery and barbeques and neat little rectangles of lawn. Some were flecking paint, but many were vibrantly colored. As far as mobile homes went, they really were estates.

Patrick's, on the other hand, was a caravan resting on cinderblocks. Every bit of metal exposed to the elements was rusty, the license plate rendered unreadable, and nearly all of the paint had flaked off the sides. Four ruts lay in front of the door where his truck had once been parked. The motorcycle hidden under a tarp hadn't been moved in a long while; dirt and pine needles were crusted into the treads. Crushed beer cans lay just about everywhere, cigarette butts everywhere else. A tree stump chopped off and skinned at a height of three or four feet had a length of frayed yellow rope tied around it. A kettle BBQ, the kind that eats charcoal in its orange Pac-Man mouth, stood at the foot of the steps. The place smelled like burnt meat, lighter fluid and urine.

"Wow," Catherine said. "This is end of the road, all right."

"Yeah," Dean said. He wasn't surprised. The Cleary family hadn't had much to begin with; it wasn't as though Patrick had started from the top, and Dean had taken the rest away with an almost casual swipe of a concrete block. He wasn't pleased with what he'd done. He felt no sense of *Schadenfreude*.

She unbuckled her seatbelt. "Well? You sure you still want to do this?"

Dean stared at the blinds in the darkened windows, some slats broken, others bent, a few missing entirely. In one window, likely the bedroom, Patrick had draped an AC/DC *Highway to Hell* flag sideways. "I have to," he said, and opened the door. It took him another moment to muster the courage to haul himself out. Catherine got out on her side first, and he followed.

A dog barked inside. A single finger lifted the blinds with an audible scrape against the window pane. Only darkness lay beyond.

As they reached the steps, the screen door swung out violently and banged against the wall. The man stood in the doorway in graying long johns and dirty socks, no shirt. His ribs were visible, the belly distended by beer, giving him the impression of life-threatening malnutrition, but men like him were built to last. A few tattoos adorned the pale skin above his farmer's tan: an anchor on his right upper arm, blue and mostly faded, a blood-red heart with some word in a scroll—*MOM?*—on the left, the phrase BAD 2 THE BONE in black calligraphic letters etched over his left nipple, and THOROGOOD over the right.

The door swung back. He caught it without taking his eyes from his visitors.

"Ohh, well well well," Patrick Cleary said with caustic good cheer. "Looky looky looky, the gang's all here, huh?" The scar was even worse up close. It hadn't split cleanly, as Dean had thought when he was a kid. The wound was jagged, carved upward in a rugged grimace, giving the left side of his face a vaguely amphibious look, crocodilian. Where the scar met his lips, a bubbly white crust had formed. Fresh spittle pooled there, and he sucked it away as his gaze shifted between Catherine and Dean: a man following a tennis match. "Guess you couldn't wait for the reunion? Had to drive *all the way* out to Dark Pines Shit-states in your prissy little hatchback and see me post-fuckin'-haste, that right?"

Catherine had stopped a few feet behind Dean. She came to his side now.

"You bring the cooze for backup?" Patrick wondered with an amused little grin. He twiddled his fingers at Catherine. "Hi, cooze. Been a long time."

"Fuck you, Patty."

"Heh, yeah. Fuck me. She got some mouth on her. I bet you like that, huh, Pean?" His eyes remained on Catherine, twinkling with mischief. "That pretty, smart little mouth."

"Leave her alone," Dean said.

Patrick's eyes returned to his quarry. "It speaks," he said. "I was pretty sure for a while there you only barked. Woof-woof, Peaner. Woof fuckin'—" He seemed to remember something, and peered back inside the house. "Where is that shithead fuckin' dog, anyways?" He called out: "You best not be on my bed, Dean! I will whup your sorry ass, you mangy mutt!"

Catherine grasped Dean's arm. He turned to look at her, saw her teeth clenched, the jaw squared, her lips curled in a snarl.

Patrick turned back to them. "That's right, I called the fuckin' dog Dean. How ya like that, shithead?"

"That's pretty funny, Patrick," Dean admitted.

"It is, ain't it? You know what I like most about having a dog?" His eyes twinkled. "I come home after a long, shitty day at the pits, and he wags his tail, lookin' up at me with those dopey bloodhound eyes, and I don't pet him—no sir. You wanna know what I do?"

"I don't think so."

Patrick ignored him. "I give him a swift kick in his sorry ass, that's what. And he'll whimper and scurry off to the bedroom, and when I come to bed, he licks my fuckin' hand. Because that's what a good dog does." He beamed a smile at them, proud of his viciousness. "It takes its lickin', and begs for more."

The two men studied each other, gunslingers at high noon, though it was only just past nine, and neither man was armed. At least, Dean hoped Patrick wasn't carrying.

"I came to apologize," Dean said, "but I see now that was a mistake. You never changed—no, that's not right. You got *worse*. You're a sadistic, violent piece of shit, and I'm glad for what I did to you."

"Bad to the motherfuckin' bone," Patrick conceded, dragging the back of a thumb along his scar. "I ain't changin' for nobody."

"Let's go," Dean said, holding out a hand to Catherine. She gave him a surprised look, then took it. They turned back to the car.

"Uh-uh, oh hell no," Patrick said from behind them. "You don't turn your back on me, you little fuck."

Dean looked back in time to see Patrick jerk a revolver out from the back of his long underwear as he took to the steps. His sock feet squelched in a mud puddle at the foot of the stairs. The Smith & Wesson Model 19, the short-barreled version of Dirty Harry's .357 Magnum, jet-black instead of chrome, and riddled with scuff-marks. He aimed it somewhere between Dean and Catherine; the ambiguity of his aim made it all the more lethal. He could just as easily shoot Catherine as his intended victim. Or both of them.

"Get the fuck in the house," Patrick said.

"He's not gonna shoot us," Catherine said, urging Dean along by his hand. "There's people everywhere."

"You think I give a fuck about that, *cooze*? What do I got to lose, huh?" He clenched his jaw, cocking his head to the side. The scar showed pink and jagged in the morning sun. *"Get in the fuckin' house."* His visitors didn't move; he pulled the hammer back with his thumb—a needless move, since the hammer snapped back on its own when the trigger was pulled. The intent was not to expedite the bullet's journey, however, but to frighten, and in that, it was successful. *"Now,* goddammit!"

They moved reluctantly to his side. He waved them past with the barrel of the gun, and they rose the stairs into Patrick's trailer.

The dog greeted them at the door, a sad-faced bloodhound, seated on its haunches and growling softly at them. Dean bent and held out a hand to him, palm-up, in a gesture of peace.

"Don't you fuckin' touch my dog," Patrick snapped, stepping inside. The dim interior smelled like beer and dog food and dry farts. He peered out into the bright of day, then closed and bolted the door behind them. Dean the dog rose to sniff at his feet and Patrick booted him lightly away. It hobbled off to the kitchenette and began licking from its scummy, fly-specked water dish.

"Sit on the sofa." Patrick pointed toward a brown tartan thing, lumpen and dangerous with springs. A fuzzy, tiger print blanket was curled up on one end as if he'd slept there. They sat. A cloud of dust rose; crumbs and coins and a double-A battery were visible in the unnaturally wide chasm between cushions. The dog laid down in the kitchen with his head on his paws, and growled.

"Shut up, Dean!"

An old coffee table that could just as well have come from the dump as the Sally Ann stood between them and the tube TV, which flickered and buzzed and shifted horizontally, a religious program on mute, the rabbit ears on top so bent they appeared mutilated.

"Think you can insult me in my own fuckin' home and get away with it, huh?"

"Patty, this is ridic—"

He struck out and slapped Catherine backhanded across the cheek, shutting her up immediately. Dean reached out to grab Patrick's arm, and the man trained the pistol on him, still eyeing Catherine with malicious glee.

"Don't you fuckin' 'Patty' me, cooze." His mouth worked as he considered his next move, the scar wriggling unpleasantly. "All right, stand up," he said with a sigh of finality. They looked at each other, and stood. "*Not* you." He sneered at Catherine. "Just the faggit." She gave Dean a panicked look. Dean nodded, grimly, and she sat back down. "I'll deal with you later. I'm gonna fuckin' enjoy the shit outta this, Dean."

"I know you are, Patrick."

"*I was talking to the fuckin' dog!*"

Dean's teeth clacked together, startled by the sudden ferocity.

"Get the fuck in the corner, by the shitter. I'm gonna give you a swirlie before I send you night-night, sweet prince. One. Last. *Swirlie.*" His eyes were wild, bugged-out. "For old time's sake. Ain't that fuckin' funny, Peaner? Ain't that a goddamn laff riot?"

"This is insane," Catherine said.

"You know, if she was my bitch, I bet I could make her shut up." He threw a wink at her. "Maybe I'll make her sing instead, when all's said 'n done."

"Let her go," Dean said. "This is between you and me." And because he knew it would fan the fire, he added: "I'm the one who did that to your face."

Patrick cracked him on the forehead with the gun barrel. Fireworks shot across his vision, but the pain was less than he'd expected. "Ain't nothin' wrong with my *face*, faggit. You didn't hurt me. Like fuck you did. You were a snivelin' little pussy back then and you're a snivelin' little pussy now." He made a circle with his thumb and forefinger, and held it near his groin. Dean glanced before realizing he'd fallen into Patrick's childish trap, and Patrick punched Dean in the shoulder. The blow didn't hurt—too much muscle built up there, not like when they were kids—but Dean stumbled back from it, knowing it was what Patrick required.

"Still peekin' at dicks, huh, faggit?" He punched him twice more. "Two more for fuckin' flinching." The scar making his pleased smile lopsided. Patrick sucked away spittle, the way Catherine used to when she'd had her braces. With her, it had been endearing; in Patrick, it was yet another feature of the monster he'd always been.

"Turn around and git in there," he said, indicating the small bathroom, fragrant with the man's piss.

Dean did as he was told.

The growl from the living room startled him, but he didn't dare turn. The shower was to his immediate left, the sink above the toilet. With very little space to move, he just had to hope there was enough. He had a plan, though it was contingent on Patrick getting in close for the swirlie. Dean was going to allow it: one last swirlie, for old time's sake, just like Patrick had said. And with his head in the toilet, when he was sure Patrick was smiling his crocodile smile from ear to ear (literally, on one side), he would reach behind himself and get Patrick in a headlock, catching him off guard. *No one* fought back post-flush—but most people hadn't been detained in Bagram. A swirlie was child's play compared to some of the atrocities he'd seen there, and had succumbed to himself. He'd smash Patrick's head into the toilet tank, shake the toilet water out of his own hair, and snatch up the gun. It was all so simple... if only he could be sure it would work.

But there was no alternative. He couldn't risk Catherine being in the line of fire, and he was certain once Patrick finished with the swirlie, he would not hesitate to blast his, Dean's, brains into the toilet bowl. It was the only way.

The growl continued. Patrick stood breathing down Dean's neck, and shouted, "Shut! The fuck! Up! Dean, you dumb fuckin' mutt!" right in his ear. His breath was sour, yeasty, even at nine in the morning.

The growl became a snarl, suddenly very close.

"What the fuck—?" Patrick said. There came a clack of claws on the linoleum, and then Patrick was screaming. He fell against Dean, pushing him up against the wall. He was shaking spastically, and the dog was ferocious. *Good ol' Dean-o*, Dean thought, *finally fighting back*. In the smudgy mirror, he saw what was happening. But the image was warped, and—

It was no bloodhound latched onto Patrick's arm, drawing blood, shaking him in its jaws.

It was a White Shepherd, its fur streaked with red.

Patrick locked the door, Dean thought. *I saw him lock it. Where the fuck did the dog come from?*

Dean heard the gun clatter onto the tiles. He tried to reach down and feel for it on the floor, but the dog had Patrick pressing him up against the wall. Dean's nose ground into the mirror, he snatched another look at the dog. It looked just like Catherine's. For a moment, it locked eyes with him, the whites clearly visible, the eyes unnaturally green. The jaws, clamped down on Patrick's crimson-streaked arm— pink bone beginning to peak out in places now as the dog tore and tore and tore back the flesh and muscle—seemed almost to be fixed in a smile.

The jaws let go suddenly, and Patrick fell to his knees, weeping, grasping at his arm by the elbow. Dean whipped round to face the door as the dog reared back into the living room.

Somebody better call the ASPCA, he thought with a wild, internal cackle. *Fuck it, call Sarah McLachlan!*

The dog launched itself at Patrick's throat. There was a bloody squelch and the brittle crackle of Patrick's trachea breaking, separating beneath the Shepherd's powerful jaws as a great jet of blood spurted along the dog's flank, drenching Patrick's chest and shoulders, obscuring his silly tattoos. Still it shook, like a terrier shaking a rat, and Patrick's head lolled back and forth on his bloodied neck. He choked, his tongue moving like some undersea worm rising from its hole, more blood gurgling up from his throat and splashed down his face. He sounded like a man drowning, which, of course, he was: drowning in his own blood.

His eyes went blank, and still the dog worried at his neck, gnawing at it like a favorite bone. A moment later, there was a sound like meat peeling apart and Patrick's tendons snapped like elastics. Dean slumped down onto the toilet and vomited his breakfast shake into the sink.

He heard the growling stop and the paws clack away. Certain he was the next item on the menu, Dean remained motionless, wouldn't turn. During his time at Bagram, he'd seen what dogs like this could do, had witnessed it up close and personal just now. The dog had established its dominance. He didn't dare make eye contact.

For a long moment, there was silence. In the kitchen, the sink turned on with a squeak, and water splashed into the metal basin. Dean wiped the puke from his lips and chin. He tore off the last scrap of toilet paper on the roll to swipe a few spots of Patrick's blood from his cheek and ear and forehead. Somehow the TP had managed to remain untouched by all the gore, but everything else was painted with it: the toilet tank, the mirror, the sink fixtures, the interior of the shower, the bar of Ivory soap in the dish. Patrick himself was slumped on his side at Dean's feet, half in the shower, half out, a sticky red puddle gurgling into the drain. His head rested at an impossible angle, the back of it nearly touching his shoulder blades, the throat opened in a yawning, toothless second mouth.

Dean stepped over him into the living room, tracking blood onto the filthy carpet. He found Catherine buttoning up her blouse and facing the kitchenette, where Dean the bloodhound continued to growl. Her hair was loose and damp, cascading over her shoulders.

"Good dog," she said to it, and turned to look at Dean the man. Her lips were deep red, as if she'd been drinking wine to toast Patrick's death. But it wasn't wine on her lips: it was Patrick's blood. Dean understood everything now. It had always been there, under his nose the whole time —he just hadn't had enough information to sniff it out. Why no one had ever seen the Priests' dog, only heard it. Why Catherine's father had never allowed her to play with the other kids, to socialize after school, and why he'd always kept her under such close scrutiny, after her mother had died giving birth to her. Why they'd never allowed visitors.

The dog was Catherine; Catherine was the dog.

Had she always been—he laughed at the thought—a *weredog*? Or had she been bitten? Was she living under a curse?

Too much, he thought. *Too fucking much. I'm in love with a dog. Jesus. Jesus Christ...*

"H-how long...?" He found he couldn't finish the sentence, and only swallowed. Her nostrils flared. She'd flared them before in the car, he remembered. *But you* are *nervous*, she'd said.

"Don't be afraid," she said now. "I'm not going to hurt you."

Dean nodded, but he was afraid; he'd always been nervous around Catherine, and now he knew the reason. Perhaps on some level he'd *always* known. She sat to pull on her pantyhose, curling her toes to shimmy both feet in at once, pulling them to her knees and then wriggling into them as she explained herself: "He was going to kill you, Dean, and then he would have tried to kill me, probably rape me if he'd gotten the chance before the police showed up." She shrugged, stood up and flattened her skirt. "I had no choice."

"You're—"

"An animal?"

Dean nodded again, stupidly.

"We're all animals, Dean," she said. She smiled roguishly, approaching him. "Only some of us are... *more* animal than others." She pressed herself against him, brushed her cold, wet nose against his cheek, his lips.

Dean slid his hand into her silken hair and kissed her.

THEY DROVE IN silence for a time, neither of them knowing quite what to say. It was over now—all of it. The past was a closed book. There was only the future, and the future was strange new territory.

Uncharted waters.

"Why did you run away?" Catherine asked as they drove past the

Dark Pines town sign, heading down into the valley. "After the Ferris wheel."

Dean sighed heavily. "Because I was a coward. I always run. It's what I do."

"You weren't, though. I saw how brave you were, standing up against Patrick and his friends." She turned to him, eyes dazzling in the low afternoon sun. "I *smelled* you. You weren't afraid." She shrugged. "You stopped being afraid the second you saw what you'd done to Joel."

That wasn't how Dean remembered it, but his memory had failed him before. And dogs could *smell* fear—or so people said. Wouldn't Catherine know better?

"I've done bad things," Dean said.

"We do what we have to, to survive."

"I didn't, though. I shot a man in the kneecap for no reason."

"I just tore a man's head off with my teeth," Catherine said, cheerless. "Let he who is without sin cast the first cinderblock."

Dean turned to her, open-mouthed. Then he snorted a laugh. Catherine joined him.

"Just because Patrick wouldn't forgive you," she said, once they'd stopped laughing, "it doesn't mean you don't deserve forgiveness. *I* forgive you. Your family forgives you. Now you just need to forgive yourself."

"Thanks," he said. Silence fell again, with only the sound of the macadam rumbling under the tires as they drove further into town. She was smiling to herself. *This is it, Dean-o. Now or never. It's only two weeks away.* "Hey," he said, "did you get that invitation for the reunion?"

"Last week." She studied the road. "You gonna go?"

"I wasn't going to," he said, and she nodded as if she hadn't planned to go, either. "But I'm thinking I might. And I was wondering..." The words caught in his throat.

Catherine laughed. "God, Dean, you still can't ask?"

"Will you go with me?" he said hurriedly. "Be my date?"

She looked at him. "You sure you don't mind having a dog for a date?"

Dean laughed. Her face clouded over, growing serious. He put a hand on her leg. "I want nothing more," he told her, and it was true.

When Catherine smiled at him, there was a hopeful quality to it that reminded Dean of the time she'd kissed him on the Ferris wheel. It hadn't been the first time she'd kissed him—their first kiss had been in her backyard, the big White Shepherd licking his lips and the tears off his face. Her smile on the Ferris wheel held anticipation, excitement, and most of all, *confidence*. Because with that kiss, she thought she'd finally found someone who might understand her. This smile was the same.

Dean returned it, giving back as much as he got. They drove on to her house. This time, she let him inside.

FAT OF THE LAND

I -An Invitation

"DAMMIT, WHERE THE hell is it, June?"

June didn't know the "it" he was talking about, let alone where he'd left it. What she did know was that David had been stomping around the hotel room while she got herself ready to go, huffing every once in a while in the hope of getting her attention.

Now he came and stood at the bathroom door, hands planted on his hips, a little Superman curl falling over the sulky scowl of a petulant child. She was putting in the earrings he'd gotten her for their anniversary the previous year. She hadn't been in love with them, but she was in love with *David*—or imagined she was, when he wasn't acting like he was now—and it made him happy when she wore them. And she *did* look good with them in: rectangular panels of jade and something iridescent like fool's gold, which made the green in her otherwise-brown eyes pop.

June flashed him a smile in the mirror. "What are you looking for, hon?"

"It was right there on the table when we left for breakfast, and now it's gone," he said, not quite answering the question.

June's girlfriends had once asked if she and David wanted kids. "I've already got one kid to worry about, thanks," she'd told them. The girls had all laughed at that, but it had been indulgent laughter; they all wanted children, and they all wanted to get married (*being* married had always seemed less important to them than the Big Day itself). Of the four of them, June was the only one currently in a relationship—unless you counted Ally's "sleeping arrangement" with her current "man friend," which of course, no one did.

After two years with David, one of those years spent living under the same roof in their tasteful yet cramped Noe Valley condo, the two of them had been happy enough *not* to get married.

Not that he'd ever ask you, June thought, and scowled at herself in the mirror. Thoughts like this belonged to Althea Dreese, her mother. *Shut up, Mother*, June shot back, putting an end to it.

Max and Darren, whose wedding they'd driven down from San Francisco to Monte Verde to attend, had been quick to remind June and David that *they'd* only been dating two years, and would have leapt at the chance to marry earlier. They'd even considered flying to Washington or Iowa to get hitched, before the Supreme Court had struck down the so-called Defense of Marriage Act as unconstitutional.

"Imagine," Max Morales had said, "the Heartland of America allowing same-sex marriage before the gayest state in the country!"

June was aware Massachusetts had probably been the forerunner in that respect, but she hadn't corrected him. Max didn't deal well with criticism (*Did any man?* she sometimes wondered), and June was rarely comfortable doling it out, at least toward anyone but herself.

David awaited her response. She tried to remember what had been on the table when they'd left for breakfast. They'd spent their first night at the moderately expensive Seaside Inn & Gardens in Monte Verde, and after setting a fire in the hearth and making a weary attempt at sexual congress, both of them had virtually passed out from exhaustion.

There was the Nikon, of course, along with a half dozen rolls of film (in addition to two books' worth of published photos, June currently had one project on the go: this area of the California coast would be perfect for the movie *Just Swell*, a *Bridges of Madison County* for baby-boom surfers, for which she was scouting locations). Then there was her purse, their respective sunglasses, the car keys, the personalized wedding invitation from Americo Morales, a baggie of wintergreen Canada mints, another of trail mix—

"*The invitation*," June said aloud.

"The invitation," David agreed. "Did you put it somewhere?"

"I didn't touch it," she said truthfully. "Why would I?"

He threw his hands up in exasperation. "Well, *I* don't know..." He was at the end of his rope. The letter was their invitation, and on it was the address, not to the wedding of Americo's son, Maximo, but to an ultra-exclusive party at one of Monte Verde's many multi-million dollar oceanfront mansions—*Americo Morales's* mansion. Regularly featured on Forbes' list of the richest people in America, Morales was Chairman and CEO of Trimaricorp, one of the largest design firms on the West coast. They'd come for the wedding, and scouting locations would cover June's portion of the costs. It just so happened that Darren's boss owned a house here, and held an ultra-exclusive party in said mansion on Independence Day weekend every year.

David had read the letter aloud in amazement when he'd gotten it, his first ever invite to Morales's famous 4th Party: "*You have been chosen to join in an orgiastic celebration of Mankind's greatness, on the birthday of the most prosperous Goddamn nation the world has ever seen.*"

"Is that sarcasm?" she'd wondered aloud at the time.

Morales was a fascinating eccentric, his philanthropic contributions earmarked for research in alternative fuels, green engineering and space exploration, a peculiar combination that seemed to June to suggest interplanetary conquest. When she'd mentioned this, David had looked at her queerly. "You think too much," he'd said.

She'd met the man when David had given her a tour of the office, a year or so back. Morales, a lean, muscular man in his mid-50s with the kind of hair they talk about in ads for men's hair-coloring, had been running on the treadmill in his office, wearing a shimmering skin-tight outfit that looked like the workout clothes of a comic-book hero. His office was the same size and height as the atrium downstairs, though this vast, virtually empty room was on the penthouse floor.

On one matte-black wall a print of Francisco Goya's ghastly *Saturn Devouring His Son* hung, in which the titan, a giant, jaundiced troll, gnawed at a bloodied human torso. Perpendicular to the painting was a "living wall": water trickled down from somewhere, through lush, dark vegetation dotted with strange and beautifully exotic flowers. Directly across from this urban jungle the city skyline spread out across the Bay: the TransAmerica Pyramid and the Triple Nickel; the piers of Embarcadero, Treasure Island and the Bay Bridge; and Berkeley beyond.

Morales had slowed the treadmill, briefly toweled himself, and tossed it aside into a black granite bin below racks of fresh white linen. He'd approached with an outstretched hand and a charming smile. "You must be June," he'd said, face glistening with sweat, his eyes as bright as the sky above them. "It's a pleasure to finally meet you."

She'd muttered something about the pleasure being hers, but frankly, she'd been overwhelmed. June, who'd grown up with a silver spoon in her mouth (a tarnished antique, to be sure, the Dreese family fortune having traveled with them on the Mayflower, but silver, none-theless), had never seen anything like this before. And Morales himself, aside from his morning haircut, manicured nails and bonded teeth, had been unexpectedly unpretentious, with none of the stuffy, old-money attitude Althea Dreese's side of the family seemed to have had ingrained in them.

"It'll be fine," David had assured her, as he read the invite for the second time. "We'll have a few drinks—*not too many*," he'd added, no doubt remembering the New Year's party when she'd gone overboard and ended up spending most of the night laid out in Darren's bathtub. "We'll schmooze a bit—not too much. You'll see. They're good people, June." And while she'd finished up the dishes in the sink, David, having conveniently forgotten the intended purpose of the damp dish towel slung over his shoulder, had ambled off to the living room to marvel over the invitation once more.

June, meanwhile, had been worried. The idea of living among them again—the rich, so-called "important people"—it made her generally queasy.

Good people, she'd thought dismissively. *Easy enough for a kid who grew up in a middle-class neighborhood to say. Live with the Other Half awhile, Davey my boy,* then *tell me what you think of them.*

Now they were in Monte Verde, one of the worst offenders in a state with the highest income gap, and Americo Morales's 4th Party loomed at the end of the weekend, the antithesis of what June felt would be an otherwise wonderful weekend on the Big Sur coast. Already they'd seen dolphins frolicking in the wake of a group of tanned, broad-shouldered surfer boys, as waves beat upon the shore and the sun stirred a colorful cocktail at the knife edge of the ocean. They'd already strolled through sequoias and redwoods stretching beyond sight. They'd seen baby deer grazing among dense wildflowers along a jagged rock face, a hundred feet above a green cove, and dozens, *hundreds* of elephant seals roasting on small rock islands in the afternoon sun, cooling themselves in the dark, algae-streaked water below. Her Nikon had snapped a hundred pictures, but it could not capture—no matter how hard she tried—the precise *feel* of these sights. Even as a professional photographer she had her limitations (which, she supposed, was why her books hadn't sold all that many copies).

David was looking at her with frustrated tears rimming his eyes. *He's just like your father,* Althea Dreese would have said. *Go on, give the baby his bottle.* She ignored her late mother's scorn, and held out her arms with the anticipated pout. Her man sidled up to her, dragging his feet on the carpeting like a child, and she hugged him. "It's okay," she cooed. "I'm sure it just got mistaken for trash when the maid came through. It shouldn't be too hard to find the house."

"But the invitation..."

"They'll have your name on a list," she assured him.

He looked up at her with moist gray eyes. "They will?"

"You haven't been to many rich-people parties, have you?"

He sniffled. She let him free, and he stepped back and swiped at his nose with the back of his hand. June hated when he did that. *Use a tissue, for the love of Pete,* her mother nagged inside her head; trying to avoid parroting those nitpicking disapprovals was a constant battle. She allowed him it this once, since he was so clearly distraught. Then David wiped the hand on his pants, and she sighed inwardly, noting the shiny streak he'd made on the right front pocket, and wondering how this nasty little habit had passed unnoticed by his own mother.

"This will be my first," he admitted.

She smiled. "Much as I'm loathe to admit it, I'm a seasoned pro. And I look damn good in a cocktail dress."

David reached out and brushed her cheek with the back of his hand. "You look damn good in anything." He raised a suggestive eyebrow. "And nothing. I'm sorry if I'm being a baby."

"I know how you can make it up to me," she said, and moved toward the bed. David's almost-waterworks display hadn't particularly been a turn-on, but with the two mimosas she'd had at breakfast, it hadn't entirely turned her off. He came willingly enough. So did June. She left in the earrings.

<hr>

"I DON'T MEAN to be a pest," David said for the second time.

Then why, my dear, are you being one? June wondered. She'd asked him to drop it, assuring him he'd probably misplaced it. But when David Addison set his mind on something, he would see it through. Even their quick romp hadn't shaken the idea of tattling on the maid from his mind, as she'd hoped it would.

They stood at the front desk, David leaning over it casually, resting on his elbows, and June off to the side, looking through the rack of colorful brochures for restaurants and touristy destinations, only half-listening to the conversation. David had an after-sex glow, and was feeling confident.

When they'd first met, Althea Dreese had never much cared for David, son of a small-town car salesman and a teacher—though her opinion of him had brightened considerably when she discovered he'd been taken under the wing of Americo Morales. Morales was, in her mother's words, "a Spaniard," and "new money," both insults in her world, but he was also very prominent in the architectural community. Althea's predatory hooks had latched onto David then, seeing him as an unlikely heir, though certainly not the worst choice for a daughter who'd abandoned her mother as readily as she'd abandoned the family fortune. Althea Dreese had expected grandchildren. When she'd passed the year before, it had been her dying wish: a grandson, to carry on the name. June's father, Herbert Winter, had taken the Dreese family name at his wife's insistence, since his own meant nothing, and it hadn't mattered to him either way.

June had taken particular pleasure in telling her mother that *if* she married David she'd be taking David's name, and *if* they had children, she'd name their first son Herbert. Althea Dreese's last breath had been a gasp of horror.

"Oh, it's no trouble at all, Mr. Addison," the clerk said. "We'll have a word with her. In the meantime, how can we make it up to you?"

"We're dying to find a restaurant," June jumped in, and the clerk, an older woman with ash-blonde hair twisted into a horse tail, turned from David to her. Dark, plum-red lipstick made her lips look as if she'd just been gorging on sweet wine in the back room. The lips peeled back in a smile, revealing teeth stained the same color.

"Something special," June went on, avoiding another look at those teeth. "Off the beaten path, but not too out of the way."

"We're foodies," David said with a self-conscious little nod.

The woman's lips peeled back in another smile—redder still, those teeth—and she dropped down into a crouch behind the desk. She came up a moment later holding a business card, which she proffered to June.

June took it and looked it over. It was plain white—*Bone white*, she thought—with raised gray lettering. There appeared to be a watermark, a shapeless sort of thing, but in the sunlight streaming in from the cottage windows, June couldn't make out its pattern, however much she tried.

AMBROSIA
an Epicurean's Delight!
45 Clarot Blvd.

"Do they have a menu?" David asked. June had felt his hot, minty breath over her shoulder as she studied the card. Rather than tickle at her ear and the sensitive spot on the nape of her neck, which would normally send shivers down her spine, for some reason her stomach twisted into a knot.

"Oh, no," the clerk said, with a penciled-in eyebrow raised, "the menu changes daily. Never the same thing twice. And dinner is served precisely at 7. It's part of their charm." She seemed to notice their dubiousness, and flashed a mollifying smile. "Tourists seem to like it. Why, just last week we had a couple, about your age, who came back simply *raving* about it."

David was still on the fence. Though he appreciated new things, his acid reflux wasn't a benefit to being adventurous when it came to foods; thankfully for June, he was adventuresome where it counted. "What does it serve?"

"Essentially it's a Spanish tapas," the clerk said. "But it's a hodgepodge of different ethnicities and influences." June assumed the woman meant *cultures* rather than *ethnicities*, yet said nothing. "I've never been there myself. I much prefer a home-cooked meal, though the hubby sometimes gets a hankering for burgers and fries at the greasy spoon off Route 1." She gave June a look that said, *You know how men are.* June nodded enthusiastically: *Amen, sister.* "Shall I call ahead and make a reservation?" The clerk was already picking up the phone.

David turned to June, raising a quizzical eyebrow. She shrugged in return. If he thought his stomach would be okay with it, she had no objections of her own. "What the heck?" she said. "Let's give it a shot."

"Wonderful!" the clerk said, a little too enthused. "I'm sure they'll just be overjoyed to have you for dinner."

II—Food of the Gods

THE YOUNG MAID rolled her housekeeping trolley out of a small cottage room between the parking lot and the pool as June and David approached the rental car. Hispanic, like the rest of the maids, the pool cleaner, and the man who trimmed the hedges. June noticed, with slight disgust, David lowering his gaze to avoid eye contact as they passed. June herself smiled and waved cheerily.

The people's champion, Althea Dreese mocked from June's subconscious.

Shut up, Mother.

Safely inside the car, David asked, "Did it seem like they were going to fire her to you?" He was ashamed, watching the pleasingly plump young woman in her blue uniform with its frilly bib rolling the cart toward the next row of rooms.

"I think they'll probably just ask her about it," June said, starting the car. It was a cheap little sedan with a surprising amount of what David's dad would call *get-up-and-go*. "Am I crazy, or did that woman make it sound like this restaurant was gonna put us on the menu?"

David squinted at the maid, then turned to June with a blank expression. A moment later, he broke into laughter. "You're definitely crazy," he said, and laughed again with a shake of his head.

"Are you sure your stomach will be okay?"

"I'll fire a preemptive strike at it with some Pepto." David crossed the seatbelt over his shoulder and locked himself in.

"Where are we headed again?"

"Mission San Adeos," she said. "Or Adios. A-*day*-os?" They'd been driving a while when David asked her. "If it's boring, we don't have to stay long. I just want to snap a few shots. Then we'll try that restaurant."

"Works for me." He fell silent for a minute or two. June was considering flicking on the radio when he spoke again. "Weird name. *Ambrosia*, I mean—not the Mission. Isn't ambrosia what the gods ate on Mount Olympus?"

"It's what they call bee pollen, too, I think. Or is that royal jelly?"

"Honey?"

"Not technically."

"No, I mean honey *you*. That's it up there, isn't it?" He pointed off to the right, where a series of buildings with clay-shingled arches and gables lay below rolling hills of farmland. In the distance, sheep grazed. The setting was so pastoral, its beauty so ethereal in the heat haze of the day it could have been a painting by Thomas Cole.

"Wow," she said, the sort of understatement her mother might have voiced, though she would never have used what she'd no doubt have called such a *vulgar* word. "It's gorgeous," she added, if only to differentiate herself from her smothering maternal influence. And it was gorgeous, so much so that she had to force herself to pay attention to the road. They drove along in silence for a time, while David snapped a few photos on his cell phone—*to what point?* June wondered, but let it go—and her mind again returned to the slightly peculiar conversation with the front-desk clerk.

"'An epicurean's fantasy,'" she said mockingly. "If this isn't the best tapas I've ever eaten, I'm going to be disappointed."

"*Delight*," David said, enlarging the image and twisting his phone to view the no-doubt-blurry photos he'd taken.

"Hmm?"

"It was 'an Epicurean's *Delight*.'" He turned to watch the scenery drift by. "What is tapas, anyway?"

June looked at him and laughed. Sometimes he was so inexperienced it boggled her mind. She had to remember he was from a different walk of life, and a different part of the country, but she found herself struggling to explain: "It's pretty much just a lot of different dishes and appetizers."

"Like a smorgasbord," he said, pleased with himself.

She felt her lips turn up in an involuntary grin, and patted his head. Beyond him the ocean passed by, endless gray, through the passenger window. He smiled back, silhouetted against the overcast sky, and his tantrum earlier today slipped from her memory, like family money through her fingers.

"COME LOOK AT this," David said.

June was admiring an altar heaped over with religious relics, preserved behind finger-smudged glass: fans of gold representing rays of sunshine, ornate gold crosses, rosaries of black and white pearls, beseeching Madonnas, bleeding Christs, and an elaborate gold chest filled with silver-gray curls of hair belonging to some Saint or another. Inscribed below the mantel were the words *Jakobi Uzh Ep a'Hethqa Est.*

June knew a bit of French and Spanish, and remembered almost nothing of high-school Latin, but it didn't look like any of those languages—maybe *Arabic*? She snapped a few photographs. She'd taken some nice ones outside: domes carved in crumbling stone, sand skittering on a hot gust of wind through a ruined archway, gaudy statuary and crucifixes and cacti...

Following the sound of David's voice, she left the low-ceilinged antechamber, with its desiccated rafters and macabre relics (the bundle of hair particularly unnerved her, for some reason she couldn't quite grasp), and stepped into a large room. Maps had been painted on the walls, with slogans painted in red; beneath them, glass cases held ancient tools, weapons, whips and chains, alongside artifacts of the Natives who'd owned this land before the white settlers had stolen it from them. Beyond the next doorway lay the church's inner sanctum. Warm light radiated outward from within.

David stood before one of the large maps, a simple drawing, its only colors green, beige and red. At its center was a pretty accurate sketch of the Mission, small and unimposing. Wide-open country, green and empty, surrounded it on all sides. Painted over this were the words THE INDIANS, as red as blood. It was obvious the missionaries had felt alone in this neck of the woods, but for savages and certain death.

Also painted in red, directly across from the map, was the catchy slogan: DECLINE SECULARIZATION RUINATION. This room summed up exactly how she felt about the church's early efforts in her native land, with its dusty antiques and even dustier xenophobia, while beyond the doors to either side lay the shining artifacts of religious opulence. They had arrived under the pretense of spreading God's word, and had conquered instead, buoyed by dreams of Manifest Destiny and a new Eden. The outcome of their immoral victory was put on exhibit without shame.

"Pretty messed up, huh?" David said.

"Just a little bit," she agreed. She snapped a few pictures—again, not quite capturing the feel of it, the *menace*—then headed into the chapel.

The clouds had parted when they'd stepped out of the car in the Mission's lot, casting down long fingers of sunshine, as if God Himself were reaching out to bless its perfectly lovely sandstone arches, clay rooftops and bell towers. None of that sunlight penetrated the chapel. Chandeliers, and the altar itself, lighted it, their glow bounding off the vaulted ceiling, the gold gilding, and glass-framed paintings of beatified saints. The surprisingly vast room smelled of burning candles, incense and mustiness.

David casually splashed a bit of holy water from the font on his forehead and headed off toward the altar. June grinned at this, then weaved her way up and down the aisles, absently taking photos.

"Hon?" He stood dwarfed beneath the altar.

"What is it?"

"Come look at this."

She sauntered over to his side. He was looking at an old photo under glass, marked with the legend, *Father Merced, 1867*. The holy man looked wholly unimpressed to be having his photograph taken—the expression reminded her of those old photos of Native Americans, who believed the camera would steal their souls. His brow was creased, his face pitted with dark shadows.

"Creepy dude, huh?" He pointed at the newspaper clipping beneath, which showed the same stern-faced, silver-curled, robed missionary, standing in front of the Mission with his hands tucked into the opposite arm's sleeve. The caption read: *Father Merced believes his life's work preserving Monte Verde's Roman Catholic basilica is a* Missionem a Deos *(Latin: 'Mission from God')*.

David bent to read another article beside it: *30-Day Standoff Still a Mystery*. After a moment of silence, he said, "Listen to this," and read the rest aloud. "'Father Antonioni Merced's infamous standoff with the Yuman tribe in August of 1852, in the middle of what was known as the Yuma War, still baffles local historians. Merced and the few townspeople taking sanctuary at the basilica while a handful of Yuman warriors surrounded it had somehow survived without any source of sustenance aside from font and well water, which they had rationed. After close to thirty days, the United States Army stepped in, easily fighting off the remaining Yuman warriors. When asked to comment on their miraculous survival, a decidedly healthy-looking Merced simply said, 'When we were starved, God brought us food, and we ate.'

"'Local legend has it US Army infantrymen found several small bones littered among the Mission's stove soot believed to be human, although all townspeople imprisoned there were accounted for.'"

He stood and peered around. "Colorful history, this place. You think that's the same stove we saw in the living quarters?"

"Creepy *and* a cannibal," June said, wrinkling her nose at the Priest's photo.

"You just said a mouthful," David joked. The two of them laughed.

Out in the parking lot, a few day laborers were trimming trees and blowing leaves. June hated leaf blowers: so loud and obnoxious, such a waste of gas, spreading the leaves around, when it would be more efficient to suck them up into a bag, or rake them into piles. She felt like they had to be bad for the environment, as well; there were already twenty or more California districts with a ban on them. A ban on lawns would cut down on a lot of problems, too, she considered: less wasteful water usage, less gas required for lawnmowers. But man's fascination with having greener grass than his neighbor would outlive both of them. The tides will have risen, drowning cities and farmland, and the people of the future would be tending little green blocks of grass high on towers in the mountains, or in their underwater domes.

THUNK!

The tree branch crashed down on a white sports car parked two down from their sedan (a silver Hummer H3 took up the two slots between its smaller cousins), scratching the paint along the passenger door, cracking the windshield, and scattering leaves in all directions. David and June were passing the car when it fell, and stepped out of the way, startled.

"*Hijo de puta!*" the poor guy said, looking both angry and terrified. June couldn't blame him. If there was anything she could have done to help, she would have done it. But there was nothing.

Maybe they've got a union, she thought. *Not likely, but maybe.*

The other man, in his blue checkered shirt and dusty khakis, shut off the leaf blower and ran to his coworker's side. He tossed the tool aside and the two of them removed the tangle of branches from the car. There was no doubting the terror on the face of the man with the heavy steel hedge clippers, his Stalinesque mustache curled upward in a frightened snarl, his eyes wide, trying to look in all directions at once. The car's owner was nowhere in sight, but he would come out soon, and then—

"Somebody's getting fired," David said, rather glib, and got into the car.

"Maybe it's not that expensive to repair," June said hopefully.

David looked at her with a patronizing grin. "On a *Maserati*? That car's worth more than those two guys put together could make in ten years." He slapped his palms down on his thighs. "You hungry?"

Not anymore, she thought, an anxious tightening in her guts making her feel slightly queasy. *But I suppose I could eat.*

———

AMBROSIA LAY AT the foot of wooded mountains, a small restaurant with all the characteristics of a cottage in the English country-side. Smoke billowed on a westward wind from the stone chimney, and with its straw-thatched roof, June felt like the place could easily catch fire at any minute. With no other civilization in sight for miles, it would burn to the ground before any emergency vehicles arrived at the scene.

Mossy, hewn-stone gateposts that could have been missing pieces of Stonehenge bookended the long, cobblestone drive. A sign hung from the left stone, the name AMBROSIA carved roughly into black, split wood and painted Venetian red. Beyond Ambrosia's leaded glass windows, silhouettes shifted and rustled in the soft warm glow like restless spirits.

"I feel like we should have come for elevensies," David said as he lifted the wrought iron knocker and clanked it against the struck plate. June looked at him blankly. "Because this place looks like it's made for hobbits." He gave her a look of commiseration. "You all right?"

"Just hungry," she said, forcing a smile.

He put a comforting hand between her shoulder blades. "Well, let's rustle up some grub, huh?"

The double doors opened suddenly and a lithe man stood before them in the entryway with an expression of bafflement. He wore a velvety black vest over his white silk shirt, with his dark hair oiled flat to his scalp and a thin, slightly curled mustache.

While the French waiter eyed them suspiciously, June thought she heard the theme from Hitchcock's *Vertigo* play lightly over some hidden sound system—but in a moment, she realized it was the final aria of Wagner's *Tristan and Isolde. Another benefit of a classical education,* she thought. She recalled that Wagner's music had been used by the Nazis in the concentration camps for "reeducation." The thought troubled her, the music felt tainted.

An odd thought to come unbidden, Juniper.

Thank you, Mother.

"May I help you?" The contempt in the maître d's voice was undeniable. He was French, though; contempt was inherent in the accent.

"Uh, yes," David said, "the staff at the Seaside Inn sent us."

The scowl cleared, replaced by a thin smile. The man wasn't quite ready to embrace them into the fold, but an invitation had been extended, and he was apparently required to accept them on a trial basis. "Ah, *oui, monsieur.*" He stepped aside and ushered them to the left with the arm he'd draped with a napkin. "Follow me, please."

June began to salivate the moment she stepped in: hot grease, savory sauces, spiced meats and roasted vegetables—the mingled smells overwhelmingly pleasant, bringing back faint memories of dinners prepared by Griselda, the Dreese family's personal chef. The restaurant was dimly lit by oil lamps and Dutch chandeliers; the tables—there were only seven, six of which were occupied by couples enjoying appetizers and *apéritifs* in quiet contemplation—draped with the whitest white tablecloths, placed in a horseshoe shape around the chef's station. A heavyset, dark-haired man in chef's whites moved his arms wildly, like a man conducting a symphony, as he prepared their meals before them. Flames shot up from his hands, a sorcerer's trick, and as he flicked his wrist, a bouquet of meats and vegetables shot up from the pan. The food seemed to hang suspended in the dim light before him, until it fell, and he caught it in his pan.

The diners applauded lightly.

Just in time for the show, June thought.

Aside from the tables, the décor was bizarrely eclectic: a grayed old ship's wheel; a pitchfork that could have been the very same tool Wood had painted in *American Gothic*; several brass plates, making her think of Dickens; yellowed scraps of parchment encased in glass alongside pinned butterflies and dusty moths; pencil sketches of homely men in top hats and top coats, and pretty women in hoop skirts and bonnets; another of the restaurant's façade, technically impressive but completely devoid of any character the house possessed; a cuckoo clock, an old spice rack, and a flocked gold mirror, its warped glass reflecting a dark, alternate version of Ambrosia in which the chef now returned to the main kitchen.

David followed the Frenchman to the empty table in the middle, as she followed David, disregarding her distorted, somewhat monstrous mirror image.

The maître d' pulled out both chairs, waiting until they were seated to speak. "Tonight's meal will begin with a squab ravioli—"

June tuned out after the first dish. As a child, dragged to stuffy country clubs and dimly lit restaurants smelling of pipe tobacco and oiled mahogany, while the waiter had droned on she'd imagined herself sitting in one of those shopping mall-bright restaurants where kids from public schools went, the places where play was as important as the food —*more* important, with playground equipment and video games, Whack-a-Mole, and animatronic animals singing songs on stage, or clowns roaming the premises, twisting balloons into exotic shapes. There were no fireplaces large enough to seat and cook an entire family; no portraits of ugly old rich men, each lit by his own brass directional lamp; no disgusting vegetables to shovel into her mouth—or hide in her napkin—just so she'd be allowed dessert. There, the ballroom was filled with rainbow-colored rubber, and had only seen an adult when one of the children lost her gum among the balls, or peed himself.

Now that vegetables were an essential part of the dining experience, the need to play had been displaced by the urge to seek out new foods, new wines, new flavors and smells and sights to tantalize the senses. So far, Ambrosia hadn't disappointed—and she'd only just been handed a menu, a slip of paper smaller than an 8-by-10 photograph and as bone-white as Ambrosia's business cards. She held it up and studied it in the candlelight. There were little more than twelve dishes; she wanted to eat every one of them. David couldn't have anything from the ocean, so the lobster bisque and *insalata di calamari* (technically an *Italian* squid salad, not Spanish, but the desk clerk had mentioned that Ambrosia served many "ethnicities") were both out. If she kissed him later with the ocean on her lips, his face would blow up like a puffer fish.

What she could really use right now was a drink. The incident in the parking lot, not to mention the possible fate of their chambermaid, had weighed heavily on her mind on the drive over, but since she'd be driving back, she would have to take it easy. A glass or two couldn't hurt, though, and would definitely do the trick. David had taken care of that: he'd ordered a bottle of red wine while she'd been ruminating. They could have saved forty dollars if they'd brought one with them, even allowing for the corkage fee, but she was glad he'd ordered it.

"Thank you," David said to the waiter, and June echoed the sentiment. The waiter left, approaching the couple at the next table, and David took her hand and brushed his lips against it. June gave him a smile, then surveyed the other "epicureans" dining with them tonight. The men, silver-haired and balding, wore open-throated shirts and blazers, with multiple rings on their rawhide-tanned fingers. The women, all of them young, wore cocktail dresses, cork heel sandals and shiny jewelry. They were healthy and white-toothed. One man wore a white straw hat cocked at a jaunty angle, as if, like the Carly Simon song, he were dining aboard a yacht.

She peered over the votive candle and wine goblets at her own man. He was scrutinizing the menu with a frown, deciding what he could risk, attempting to decipher the indecipherable fusion of several foreign languages. *Would he age like these men?* she wondered. At 31 his hair was just starting to recede. Would he ever go fully bald like his father? Crow's feet were just starting to claw tracks down the corners of his eyes, just as they were at hers. It gave him a distinguished look; she wished there were a female equivalent of "distinguished" that didn't sound like the hands of time were shoving her headlong toward Death's door.

Twenty minutes and a full glass of wine later, the chef emerged from the kitchen, rubbing his hands together in a circular motion, and smiling wide. The other diners applauded his arrival. David and June quickly joined in as the man gave a brief, uncomfortable bow. He began to cook then, and as he cooked, he spoke, like a man hosting a television show, in a slight, mysterious accent.

"These days, everyone wants to know where their dinner came from. What did it eat? Was it coddled? Did it have a good life?" He laughed contemptuously. "Ladies and gentlemen, we don't even ask this for our friends and neighbors!"

Laughter and applause arose around them. June looked across at David and saw that he was smiling in baffled amusement.

"I believe someday soon these questions will be moot," the chef said, pouring oil and ladling garlic into a sauté pan. He sprinkled, he doused, he sauced. "Meat will be grown in laboratories, like vegetables in a greenhouse, independent of the animals to whom they belong. The pigs and cows and little chickies will be free to roam the countryside. And with no use for them, they will die off. They exist at the terminus of evolution, only permitted to survive because of our need for them as food. You mark my words. By the end of this century, meat will be manmade and its sentient cousins will be well on their way to extinction!"

There were murmurs of dissent. A man at the far table to their left, sun-browned skin stretched taut over his bones like a canvas, scowled and hissed.

"I know," the chef said with a playful smirk. "A despicable thought. But it comes closer to reality each day. As a species, we must rise above the herd, so to speak. Pigs are smarter than some primates, they say. Cows are as diverse as dogs and cats and people. We must not fall into the trap of letting these animal activists—these *terrorists*—we must not let them teach us we are no better than the animals we eat!"

Applause. A ball of orange flame plumed up from the chef's pan. David shot June a look that said, *Do you believe this guy? Do you believe them?* June patted his hand and sipped her wine. Believe him or not, what the man was cooking smelled *divine*, and as far as she was concerned, this tortured genius could spout whatever bullshit came into his fat head.

He garnished, he sautéed, he tasted. The chef's nimble fingers molded dough and slid dishes into the oven. He added pinches of sugar and paprika and basil. And all the while, he intoned his manifesto, not addressing his crowd but rather an unseen visitor. Certainly, he'd never once looked his guests in the eye.

She thought: *This is a photograph.* The textures, the colors, the play of light in the other diners' faces. His facial expressions, like a man possessed—and if he was possessed, it was by a love of food—his gregarious hand gestures and movement, movement, movement. *This would make a great shoot. Call it "Kitchens in America." And this place, Ambrosia, this would be the centerpiece. This could go in a* gallery.

"Do you hear that?" The chef listened for a moment, his ear cocked toward the ceiling and the music as he stirred the contents of a pan, spun the lid of a pot, sucked a daub of sauce from his thumb. "Lovely piece, isn't it? I sincerely believe everything about the experience of eating should be sensual, but particularly the cooking. Eating is a ritual, wouldn't you agree? If eating is ceremony, cooking is the preparation for the ritual. Part of my ritual includes listening to the Great Works—such as *Tristan und Isolde*, the lovely opera you hear now, by Richard Wagner." (He pronounced it the German way: *Reeckhard*.) "When feeling contemporary, I enjoy Glenn Gould." He grinned, almost peculiarly sly. "Or Sammy Davis, Jr."

There were light chuckles at this. Repeat customers, no doubt. June didn't quite get it, and neither did David, from his dubious, slightly salivating look.

Mere moments later the food was plated and waiters emerged from the kitchen to spread it out before them. The humble chef slipped out during the confusion, back into the shadows of the kitchen.

Maybe I'll come back the day after tomorrow, June thought. *Ask if he'll let me snap some photos.*

With that decided, she began to eat: sliced cured meats and sausage and *tartare*, rustic cheeses and bright yellow tortillas heaped with potato and caramelized onion, small plates of duck *confit* and rabbit croquettes, Scotch eggs, meatballs cooked in white truffle oil, a soup made from *chaud-froid*. But the *piece de resistance* was the bone marrow: salty, greasy, rich and buttery. They scooped it straight from a severed hunk of bone onto crusty herbed bread and stuffed it into their salivating maws.

All thoughts were forgotten: she simply *savored*.

They spoke very little while they ate, only pausing to swallow a mouthful of wine and marvel with grunts and moans at how delicious everything tasted. The other epicureans leaned over their tables and spoke in hushed tones to their server and to each other. The head waiter, the Frenchman, plucked dishes from a stonework pass-through, only going into the kitchen occasionally. June had inquired, and discovered the chef was Austrian. It seemed the only thing Spanish in this Spanish restaurant was the use of the word "tapas."

And the food *was* a delight; June was definitely eating her words tonight. She didn't think she'd ever had anything quite like it in her life, and David had probably never imagined such rich flavors existed in the world.

"It really is the food of the gods," he remarked, still chewing. He picked up a greasy bit of sausage. "I don't know what this is, but if it's a *leetle piggy*," he said, affecting the chef's accent, "it's the best damn pig I've ever tasted."

"We should ask," June said. "It can't be beef. Maybe it's *bison*?"

"Could be that super-meat he was going on about. Grown in labs." David clearly hadn't grasped the point of the chef's sermon, but June didn't bother correcting him, too stuffed to argue. "Hang on, I'll ask." David spotted the head waiter and flagged him down. "Excuse me." His voice, louder than anything aside from the pop and crackle of the stone fireplace in the far corner and the opera oozing from hidden speakers, roused the other patrons from the soporific effect of their meals.

The waiter approached. "Oui, monsieur?"

"We were wondering—" The man with the hat turned to glare at them. "—what type of meat is in this?"

"The *saucise* is veal, I believe, with, eh, wild boar." He appeared unsure, his dark plucked eyebrows knitting together in a slight scowl. "If you like, I will ask Jörg for you."

June snickered, thinking he'd said *Yorick*, and covered her mouth with a hand. David raised an eyebrow, then turned back to the waiter. "That won't be necessary. Thank you." The waiter scuttled away, off to the next table, where Mr. You're So Vain raised and jiggled their empty water pitcher impatiently. "Alas, poor Jörg," David said in a hushed tone to June, indicating the slab of cooked bone, picked clean on the plate.

June laughed a little too loudly, garnering more dirty looks from their snooty fellow gourmands. "I knew him, Horatio," she said. "Bit of a kook, but one hell of a cook."

David chuckled. He sopped up some bone marrow grease on the

last herbed roll, and stopped just shy of putting it in his mouth. "You want this?" He held it to her, eyeing it eagerly for himself.

"I should save room for dessert. But thanks, sugartits."

He laughed again. "You're on a role tonight, Ms. Dreese." And he plopped the savory bread in his mouth. "So is this marrow," he mumbled with his mouth full. "A *delicious* roll."

"I THINK I'M gonna be sick," David groaned, and then, before he could close his mouth he spewed vomit out over his lap and pattered on the car seat.

Once the sun had fallen behind the horizon, night drew its cold fist over the coast as they drove back to town, the ocean glittering in the moonlight.

"Shit, honey, that's gonna stain," June said.

"I'm *sorry*." He wiped his face with a fast-food moist towelette from the glove compartment, then used it to slop up the mess. "I didn't know I was gonna barf until it just kinda... came out."

"Neil Patrick Harris came out," she said. "*That* ejected."

She glanced at the mess, ropey with mucus, spotted with chunks of undigested meats, reds and browns and bright pinks. Seeing their dinner regurgitated, the smell of red wine thick and syrupy in the air, made her reassess her enjoyment of it. Had it really been as good as she'd imagined? Had she really placed it side-by-side with—even *above*—some of her favorites? With clam chowder in a sourdough bowl at Boudin Bakery? With traditional Chinese dishes served up in clay pots at the Utopia Café? With *smørrebrød* from Bar Tartine? The thought of having gorged herself at Ambrosia made her want to vomit in sympathy, the thought of photographing it suddenly felt loathsome, a sacrilege. She zipped down the window, sucking in great gasps of fresh air warmed by a sudden gust from the Santa Anas. "Forget it, David. We'll clean it up at the hotel. Just... just roll down your window, okay, honey?"

David gave her a miserable look and zipped his window down. He tossed out the handful of puke he'd picked up in the towelette. A yellowish string of it, thick and bubbly with spittle, stuck to the half-opened window like a snail trail.

"Gross," he remarked.

"You won't get any argument from me, bub."

He smiled at her, and looked sheepishly at the mess between his legs and on the floor mat. "It didn't taste as good coming up."

"I don't imagine," she said. "I guess that preemptive strike didn't do the trick."

"I forgot to take it," he said, and let out a belch. "I'll double-up on the antacids when we get back to the room."

June caught a whiff of David's burp and made a sour face. It smelled of sickeningly sweet burnt sugar and a vinegary tang like spoiled pork. "Probably a good idea."

David fell into a grim silence as the dark scenery passed by his window. In the rearview mirror, the mountains stood against the twilight like jagged, blackened teeth preparing to eat the sky, and June felt her heartbeat jangle—a loosened piano string, a long, drawn-out beat that seemed almost to quiver inside her chest. Rather than slow with it, her breathing hurried to fill in the gap as a sudden, horrific thought arose:

Poison. They've poisoned us.

The invitation to a secluded restaurant nestled in the mountains, so utterly charming and exclusionary, with absolutely perfect food—it was a trick the locals played on pesky tourists, the oldest trope imaginable. A few drops of saline in the food or drink to cause stomach cramps and violent bathroom expulsions. Or *worse*. Now, David was puking his guts out, and her heart palpitated like some woman of noble birth's in a Victorian-era novel. The desk clerk's bizarre choice of words—"overjoyed to have you for dinner" and "a couple, about your age, who came back simply *raving*"—seemed to be incantations to June's suddenly hyperaware mind. *What exactly had they been raving* about? June wondered.

Her constitution had always been stronger than David's; she wasn't likely to feel the gastrointestinal effects until they were back at the inn. She would awaken in the dead of night, embers glowing in the fireplace, and clutch at the knife blade carving out her insides like a jack-o'-

lantern, eyes bugging out as a scream caught in her throat. Meanwhile, David would be perfectly still on his side of the bed, bloody spittle crusted where his lips had parted, a chunky pool of vomit drying on his pillow.

Don't be daft, Juniper. A lady doesn't think such things.

Shut up, Mother. Shut up, you nasty, stupid witch!

Focusing her rage and fear and frustration toward her mother—whom she had not forgiven, even in death—June's heartbeat evened out without her even noticing. She drew in a slow, deep breath, let it out just as slowly, concentrating on nothing but the darkened highway through the dusty, fly-specked windshield. She flicked on the wipers. The large bug directly in front of her smeared and streaked its guts across the glass. Each swipe of the blade erased more of it, until finally it was gone.

Back at the inn, David rushed to the washroom, holding his belly, his face ashen, somehow gaunt. He'd managed to keep from vomiting in the car again, but he'd begun to sweat and murmur to himself, struggling to hold it in. Somewhere along Route 1, it had seemed as though his eyes rolled back in his head, the lids fluttering, and he'd muttered something that sounded like "Eedger hardow, Misser Morales," reminding her of the few times he'd talked in his sleep. Despite of the heat blowing in from the desert, it had chilled her to the bone. Concerned, she suggested driving him to a hospital—where she'd find one, she had no idea. "I'll be a'right," he'd groaned. Then he'd ratcheted the chair back to a steep recline and gone to sleep.

The room was cold. June put a log in the fireplace and set it ablaze. She stood by the bathroom door a moment, listening for the sound of his retching. He spat, a hollow sound of his face hovering below the lip of the bowl. "You okay?"

"I'll be fine," he shouted, but he retched again—*oooooh WLEH!*—and the retch became a fit of coughing, followed by another hollow spit into the bowl. She could almost see the translucent thread stringing from his lips into the water below, and she cringed at the image.

June laid back against the heap of pillows. No sound came from the bathroom for a long while, and the warmth from the fireplace lulled her to sleep with the overhead lights still on. Popping knots dragged her back to consciousness twice. She felt David slip into bed some time later;

he had already flicked off the light and had tucked her under the covers by then. She nearly nestled up against him when the smell of his sick-sweat prickled her nostrils. He leaned over to kiss her forehead, breath smelling of strong mouthwash, and she tried to ask if he was feeling any better, but before the words could come out, she was asleep again.

She dreamed of a hideous creature living in a cave in the mountains behind Ambrosia. She and David were hiking, searching for something —she didn't know what, though it seemed of great importance in her dream. David was walking a little ways ahead of her when he suddenly dropped into the earth. June hurried to the place where he'd last stood and leaned over the pit. "I'm all right," he shouted up at her, lying on the ground an impossible distance below, somehow still spotlighted by the sun. "Just twisted my ankle, I think."

The behemoth lumbered out of the darkness behind David then, a bedraggled and bug-eyed troll reminding her of Goya's *Saturn Devouring His Son*—and June found she couldn't speak to warn him. Her breath passed her lips as empty as a hot wind blowing through the ruined archways of an ancient city. David waved cheerily as the colossal Thing's shadow fell over him, still smiling when it brought him to its lips. He let it swallow him in two quick bites.

Not much more than an appetizer, really.

III—The Altar

DAVID SPENT A good half an hour in the shower, and during that time, June found the invitation to Americo Morales's 4th of July party wedged half under a table leg beside his suitcase.

She'd been looking for Ambrosia's business card, her plan to give them a call during the lull between the wedding reception and the cere-mony (she thought of the chef's strange monologue, his talk of cere-mony and ritual), and ask if she could come by the following day to shoot during prep, or the dinner rush.

She laid the card flat on the glass table and picked up the room phone. As she dialed the number, she noticed a shadow in the slat of rainbow-colored sunlight on the floor; the sun shining through Ambrosia's business card, magnifying the watermark. And it appeared to be words.

June hung up the phone and got down on her hands and knees, bringing her face close to the carpet. Every little speck of dirt and hair and crumb was visible from here—did they *ever* vacuum?

That was when she saw it, wedged under the table leg. "The envelope!" she said, and snagged it. She reached up to put it on the table, not watching what she was doing, trying to read the words in the watermark's shadow. The letters were blurry, but because she'd already had the phrase fresh in mind—if it was a phrase at all—she read it easily:

Jakobi Uzh Ep a'Hethqa Est

"Just like in the Mission," she said to herself. "But *why?*"

June logged on to David's computer to look it up. No Wi-Fi. She tugged on a sweater and left the room while the shower still ran, and David sang "When I'm Sixty-Four." Which she found strange, since he wasn't a big Beatles fan.

The lady with the red teeth stood behind the desk again this morning: this time, the teeth were pink, as if from a fresh meal of raw meat. "Hiya, darlin'! How was Ambrosia? Was it just to *die* for?"

Again with the innuendos. "It was great, thanks for the recommendation."

"Oh, it's no trouble. No trouble at all."

Suddenly, the woman's saccharine friendliness made June want to wipe the smile from her face. "Actually," she said, "my partner got sick."

The woman's features squeezed together unpleasantly. "You're part —? Oh, dear, I'm so sorry to hear that. Would you like me to give them a call?"

"That won't be necessary. I wonder if I could get the Wi-Fi password."

"Certainly." The clerk took a business card, flipped it, and scrawled on the reverse. She slid it across the desk to June, who snatched it with a cursory acknowledgment and began to walk away. Then she remembered the envelope, and the maid.

"Did you speak to the maid the other day?"

The woman blinked, clueless. "The—? Oh, *Josefina*. We spoke to her, yes."

"You didn't—"

"Terminated, oh, yes ma'am. With prejudice. You won't be seeing her around here anymore, I assure you."

June waited until the woman finished ranting—she was giving June a headache—then said, "We found the envelope. You fired her for nothing."

"Oh, dear." She looked sincerely displeased. "And she was such a good little worker, too."

"You might want to think of this the next time you fire someone," June said, and stormed off without letting the woman reply. She felt vindicated, and hoped the gardeners at the Mission had received similar treatment from a kind stranger.

Oh, yes, you're their White Knight, darling, Althea Dreese mocked from the grave.

Back in the room, she typed in the password and searched *Jakobi Uzh Ep a'Hethqa Est* in an online translator. It detected Zulu, though it was only able to translate the first word, as *James*. Clearly it wasn't *that*.

She searched the phrase, and found one hit, which appeared to be an entire page filled with gibberish, in which the words from the watermark were interspersed throughout a single paragraph that ran from the top of the page to the bottom, with no line breaks and very few actual words. It reminded her of the time she'd tried, and failed, to conquer *Finnegan's Wake* for her English Lit. class. June held the private opinion Joyce might have suffered from syphilitic dementia.

She tapped the pen on the table. David had switched to Alanis Morrisette's "Ironic," singing a decent falsetto as water splashed heavily on the shower floor.

Jakobi Uzh Ep a'Hethqa Est

Delight, David had said. *It was 'an Epicurean's Delight.'*

Ambrosia, she thought. *Food of the gods.*

Adeos. From God.

Could it be a code of some sort? A—what do you call it—a cipher?

David came out of the shower, startling her. She closed the laptop and stood, pretending to be busy elsewhere. "What's wrong, hon?" he asked, his hair a wet tangle on his head, an impossibly plush towel around his waist.

June didn't know what to say. In her hesitation, she spotted the envelope at the edge of the table and picked it up for David to see.

"Oh, shit, June. *Shit.*" Wet footprints trailed from the bathroom to where he stopped, dripping on the carpet. "Where *was* it?"

"Under the table."

"*Under* the table," he said, as if it had been the only place he hadn't checked. "Well, I'll have to go down and apologize."

"They've already fired her."

"Fuck," he said, genuinely bummed. "I knew I shouldn't have said anything."

I told you not to say anything, she thought. She glanced at her watch. "And since you spent so much time in there, I don't have time to get showered."

"Sorry, hon. Had to wash the sick off. Speaking of which, I'm all clean now..." He unwrapped the towel, exposing his neatly trimmed genitals, and tossed it on the back of a chair. "Care to get freaky, madam?"

"Put your clothes on, dork," she said, and threw the towel back at him.

DARREN SHINGLE STOOD ALONE at the altar for a good twenty minutes, looking elegant as usual in a classic black Gucci suit, wearing a newly whitened smile until finally he could smile no more. The gatherers had begun to talk among themselves, whispering concerns that Max had left him at the altar, and it was difficult for June not to suspect it herself.

Of course, Max could have been late for many reasons. The idea that he'd left Darren at the altar (the man for whom Maximo Morales had professed his undying love on at least a dozen occasions where June herself had been present, with whom he shared a home in the Western Addition and not simply his bed, who had virtually planned their entire life together from marriage until they would die together as old men) was about the least likely scenario June could imagine.

Darren passed words with the minister, a woman with the round and smiling face of a Buddha, who nodded, and said something conciliatory. He approached his parents, sitting front row left, speaking with them in hushed tones. Their mannerisms were diplomatic, cautiously optimistic. But Darren began to lose his temper, and waved his hands frantically.

David belched, attracting June's attention, the couple sitting next to them peering over. The worst of his illness had passed, but a few symptoms still lingered. June had suspected food poisoning—and worse, last night—but she hadn't felt the slightest bit ill herself.

Americo Morales took out his cell phone and dialed, stepping away from Darren and his wife to speak with whomever he'd called. When he hung up and shrugged at his wife, it was the final nail in the coffin of this blessed union. Darren plucked a champagne glass from the tower and sauntered off through the dewy grass toward the gardens, downing it as he walked. The country club—not quite as stuffy as the ones June had been dragged to as a child—had everything required of a wedding, including a view of the ocean beyond an archway smothered in impossibly green, blue-tinted gardenias. The only thing it didn't offer was a discreet exit. Darren's wilted form shrank into the distance, his polished Stefano Bemer shoes cutting two dark trails in the damp grass until finally he disappeared behind a squared hedge.

"Such a shame," the woman next to David said.

Americo Morales took a glass from the tower and clinked his car keys against it a few times. The guests hushed their speculations and faced the front, awaiting word.

"Ladies and gentlemen," he announced, "I'm sorry to be the bearer of bad news on such a beautiful day, but... it would appear that my son won't be attending. He's not answering his phone." There were murmurs of discontent, though June suspected most of them were contrived. "I'm not going to speculate as to his reasons. He's a grown man, even if he doesn't always act like it. It would have been nice of him to explain himself in person, of course, for Darren's sake, if not for the rest of us."

He placed the filled champagne flute back on the table. "You're welcome to stay. Eat, drink and make merry." Mrs. Morales winced. "Sorry," he said. "Poor choice of words."

While Americo wandered off toward the reception hall, guests began to gather their belongings. Once the first person—one of the groomsmen—snagged a glass of champagne, the tower descended faster than the fall of Babel. David snagged two before they disappeared and brought one back to June, who stood with two of Darren's groomsmaids and a groomsman, his brother, Charlie.

"I just can't see Max doing this," the girl in her early twenties said grimly, though the smile in her eyes betrayed a twinge of Schadenfreude as she adjusted the hem of her dress self-consciously. The dress looked great, even if she fit into it as well as a sausage fit its casing. Darren had picked them out; had it been up to Max, he would have put them all in pink crinoline, merely so they wouldn't upstage him.

Charlie Shingle shook his head grimly. "Little shit," he muttered. His wife, the other groomsmaid, swatted him on the lapel, not at all playfully. He turned to her with gentle reproach. "Don't tell me you didn't see this coming, Gretchen."

"Oh, please, tell me: why should I have seen this coming, Charles?"

David swooped in with the champagne just in time. June sipped at hers, if only to avoid eye contact with the happy couple. Their six-year-old twins, a boy and a girl, scurried around the archway, screeching and laughing, perfect little examples of why June didn't want children. Gretchen Shingle looked haggard, beginning to show at six months pregnant. Charlie Shingle was shitfaced.

"Well, I mean, if it's good enough for us, it's good enough for them, right?"

"*Them*?" David inquired.

Charlie glanced around himself. "Look, I'm not a homophobe. He's my brother, for Christ sakes. I just mean, they can get married now, so they should have all the problems that come with it, right?" His wife gave him a reproachful look that was far from gentle, her white Lee Press-On nails resting like talons on her round belly. "It only makes sense they should leave each other at the altar now, too, am I right?"

"I guess so," David said, and slugged down his champagne. *Ever the diplomat*, June thought with a smile. "Hey, uh, you two been to any restaurants yet? There's this nice little out-of-the-way joint—"

"Where he got food poisoning," June chimed in.

David flashed her a glare. "You don't know that. It could have been anything. Besides, you didn't get sick, and we ate the same things."

She shrugged. "It *was* great, though."

"Oh yeah?" Charlie said, not really interested. He would have been happy eating prepackaged sandwiches from a gas station. "What's it called?"

"Ambrosia," they both said at once. David squeezed her hip, amused by the jinx.

"Sounds a little..." Charlie said, and shrugged. "You know."

Gretchen shook her head, exasperated. The other groomsmaid chuckled to herself, took a large gulp of champagne, and peered around for single men.

"Expensive?" David suggested.

"Exactly." Charlie extended a finger beyond his beer bottle to point at David. "*This guy* gets it."

"It wasn't too expensive. Probably not the best place for kids. Spanish tapas."

Charlie pulled a face. "Can't eat Spanish. Gives me gas somethin' awful."

"*Everything* gives you gas," his loving wife said.

Charlie laughed. "Everything *she* cooks, anyway."

June made eye contact with David, who made a subtle motion with his head to skip away from the younger Shingles. "I should see how Darren's doing," June said, spotting his signal. "It was good to catch up with you."

"Oh yeah, real good," Charlie said. "Catcha later, Dave."

"David," he corrected.

"Yup."

Gretchen shook June's hand. "Really nice to see you again, June. You should come out to the house when the baby comes, hey?"

"Wouldn't miss it," June said with a warm smile. And she wouldn't, if she happened to be scouting locations in the Reno area sometime in the next year. The chance of that happening was unlikely, but it wasn't a direct lie. She waved at the sausage girl. "Nice to meet you, Dakota."

"Yeah, mm-hmm," the girl said, flashing June a glance before returning to the hunt.

David took her hand and they wandered off. "Well, that was awkward," he said under his breath.

"Oh? I didn't notice."

He laughed, then bent to kiss her cheek. "Did you see the smile on that blonde girl? You couldn't wipe it off with a chisel."

"No kidding," June said with a laugh.

"Hey, you don't really mean to try and comfort Darren, do you? I think I saw Max's sister head off that way. Weren't they friends before Max and Darren?"

"Good memory." She shook her head. "I've got a feeling he'll be pretty inconsolable, anyway. We'll talk later, I'm sure. I've got those photos for him to look at, anyway. I think outside the Mission would be perfect for the love scene in *Just Swell*."

The two lead actors were fossils, and the thought made David shudder theatrically. She laughed again, but the laugh died when she realized they had stopped under the flowered archway. He looked up at it. She followed his gaze, and an awkward smile passed between them, like strangers under the mistletoe. "Fifty percent of marriages end in divorce," David said, breaking the silence. "At least Max and Darren beat the odds."

June laughed, a little anxious. For a moment, she'd thought David might spontaneously drop down on one knee and pop the question. And would it be that terrible to get married? Just because her parents' marriage had been a train wreck didn't mean *hers* would be. David's parents had been together for 36 years, longer than she and David had been alive.

Would it be that terrible?

A horrible cackle shook her from her thoughts. June and David turned to its source: Gretchen Shingle's braying laughter at her husband, who was wiping the beer he'd spilled down the front of his rented suit with a mortified look as the children circled, circled.

It could always be worse, she thought.

———

JUNE PARKED OUTSIDE Ambrosia's stone gateposts and stepped out. Somewhere distant, a chainsaw roared—somebody felling trees or cleaning up a mess in the road, she couldn't quite tell by where the sound arose from. She snapped a few photos with the Nikon: of the mossy stones, silhouetted against knife blades of sunlight through the clouds, the blood-red AMBROSIA on the signpost. She switched to a wide-angle lens, and snapped a few shots of the restaurant and the hills beyond. Smoke rising from its little thatched roof, Ambrosia looked more surreal in the daytime than it had last night. The clouds had broken, giving the scene a golden, godlike tint, one she could easily punch up in Photoshop.

The air had turned brisk, but with the sun shining and the view so spectacular, she decided to shirk the car and walk down, to get some better angles of the cottage. Aside from the chainsaw, and the gravel crunching underfoot, the afternoon was silent. Not a bug, not a bird. June sauntered down the hill, snapping shots, when something struck her, and suddenly she stopped in her tracks, her heartbeat quickening.

Barely ten feet from where she'd stopped, a deer was grazing. June raised her camera, ever so slowly, as the animal flittered its tail, and continued nibbling at the dry grass. They'd seen deer the other day at the cove, but not this close, and not alone. It seemed as though everything had come together to create this special moment between June and the deer, and she wanted—*needed*—to capture the feeling with a photograph.

Click! She snapped a shot off from her chest and wound the film forward. The deer rose from its business in the dirt to regard her, hobbling slightly on its left front leg, which appeared to be an old break, gnarled like an old tree branch, but long-since healed. June brought the camera up to her eye—

The deer stumbled off, bobbing up and down on its crippled leg as it hurled itself toward the darkened woods.

"Shit," she muttered, the magic dispelled. The chainsaw grew louder as she approached Ambrosia. Someone cutting wood out back to keep the fire burning, no doubt. *Must go through a lot of it*, she thought, *burning day and night like that.*

She stood in front of the door and used the knocker. As she waited, she saw an old stone well she hadn't noticed last night, its cover mossy, the gray wood bucket swaying in a light breeze from its frayed rope.

Click! Click!

Nobody came to the door.

June jiggled the handle. It turned in her hand, startling her, and the door swung inward.

The vague scent of last night's meal hit her nostrils, making her salivate—until she detected an unpleasant sour smell beneath it, reminding her of David puking in the car. She gagged and covered her nose. The chainsaw doubled in volume once the door fell shut behind her, as if the back door were open, focusing the sound through the kitchen.

"Hello?"

The saw revved and roared. June stepped further into the room. Her reflection in the warped mirror was pale and stretched; she looked like a gaunt giant as she moved past toward the tables, toward the kitchen, and all the while, the roar of the chainsaw grew louder, as though someone was using it inside.

Ice sculpting, she thought. *Don't ice sculptors use saws sometimes? Probably carving a swan for someone's wedding.*

Leftover food in pots and pans at the chef's station between the tables coagulated, going to rot. A fly lighted on a thin slice of rolled white meat and buzzed off toward the kitchen. She snapped a photo.

Health code violations all over the place. This is turning out to be more of an exposé than a photo essay.

The chainsaw growling, June stepped through the darkened vestibule and into the kitchen.

Her heart stopped.

The head waiter, the Frenchman, stood with his shirt off, his pale skin glistening with sweat and spattered blood. He held the chainsaw in both hands, poised to make another cut. And what he was carving... June staggered back in unimaginable horror.

The Frenchman raised his eyes from his work and caught sight of her. For a long moment, he stood as frozen as June. She kept staring, unable to look away from the plump, naked woman strung above the table, her flesh hanging in ragged strips, yellow clumps of fat oozing from chainsaw cuts in her belly and hips and breasts. *Josefina*. Even with her damp black hair stringing down in her face, and the gag tied in her mouth, June knew it was the maid from the Seaside Inn & Gardens. This was her punishment, for the crime of being in the wrong place at the wrong time.

Eyes closed, breathing slow and ragged, Josefina still appeared to be alive after all the cuts and the spilled blood, had only passed out from the pain.

The chainsaw rumbled. A fly buzzed on Josefina's nose and another in her hair.

Unconsciously, as if in a dream, June snapped a photo.

The effect was immediate: the waiter's eyes came alight, his thin mustache curled upward in a snarl, and he stepped around the galvanized steel tub filled with Josefina's fats and juices.

June turned and ran, screaming through the darkened hall. Behind her, impossibly close, the chainsaw roared back to life, and as she stumbled out into the dining hall the front door burst open, Jörg tromping in with his hands full of bulky grocery bags.

"Armand," he called out, "whose car is that parked out front?" The large chef's head rose, and he took in the sight of June sweating and breathing heavily in the kitchen doorway. "What are you doing here?"

The chainsaw shrieked against something—stone or drywall— rattling the objects on the walls, and a grin spread across Jörg's unshaven face. "Looks like we have a guest for dinner, Armand!" he said, delighted.

Running past the tables, the Nikon beat and bounced forgotten against her breasts, she saw there was nowhere to go. *Nowhere*.

Wrong. A third doorway lay beyond the fireplace, across the large room from Jörg, who dropped his groceries and stepped away from the front door to meet her. If she could make it to the door before he did—

Her darting eyes fell on the pitchfork. She stopped to grab it, trying to tear it from the wall. But it wouldn't budge. She saw the grin widen on Jörg's fat face, the snarl spreading on the Frenchman's, and June placed a foot against the wall, pulling with all of her strength.

The rusted clamps holding it in place snapped, and June stumbled back, the pitchfork held in a death grip. Once she regained her balance, she spun on her heels, swinging the weapon toward Armand, who halted his approach, letting the chainsaw rumble. She swung it in Jörg's direction. Rather than stop, he stepped closer to her with his hands raised.

"Look at her!" the chef said. "The tenacity!"

The waiter only snarled.

"Put the fucking chainsaw down, asshole!"

"You heard her," Jörg said. "Put it away. It is unnecessary. Isn't it, dear lady?"

June panted heavily as Jörg crept closer. "Don't you fucking move another step!"

He stopped, the smile disappearing from his face, and his bristly wattle fell slack. "Dear lady, you have absolutely no idea what you are doing," he said soothingly. "Please, put down the trident. You look as though you've just seen Frankenstein's monster!"

Armand snickered, and in her peripherals, June saw he was moving forward again. She jabbed the tines at him. He stepped back, the pointed ends missing him by mere inches, clanking instead against the stilled saw blade.

Jörg scowled. "This has gone on quite long enough." He nodded at Armand, jowls quivering. "You may kill her. But leave the head untouched."

Armand flashed the chef a sneer, then took another step toward June. She swung out once more, grunting with effort—

—and bolted for the door by the fireplace.

Behind her, Jörg laughed. "Oh that's lovely, isn't it? Perhaps she'll—"

But June had jerked open the door and slipped into the darkness beyond, cutting off his words as she pulled the heavy door shut behind her. The sound of her breathing filled her ears, the hurried beat of her heart. She kept moving forward, swinging the pitchfork in front of her like a blind man's cane. Behind her, the chainsaw screamed against something metallic, and sparks brightened the long, stone hallway in which she'd found herself. In the brief illumination, June glimpsed a wooden door at the far end, with no obstacles in between. She ran for it, and when she reached it, she slammed against it headlong.

Locked.

Armand scraped the whirring blade against the walls, more sparks lighting the hall as June threw herself against the door again. On her third try, the lock gave with a groaning snap, and she hurtled forward into a small, candlelit chamber.

Pushing the door shut, she scoured the room for something to block the way and found nothing but an altar decorated with cream-colored candles melted down to the nubs. They lighted a glass jar containing a lock of silver-gray hair tied in a yellow ribbon, a desiccated finger bone, and something brown and gnarled which she recognized as a human tongue. Stood against the face of the altar was a photo of a glowering, robed Father Merced, and beside this lay an amorphous sculpture, a million-eyed, bulbous creature in place of a crucifix, or a Buddha—and as she puzzled at these bizarre religious artifacts, she realized she had stumbled into a shrine, but could just as easily have stepped into the foyer of Hell.

The chainsaw bellowed, echoing down the hall and in her skull. She moved alongside the shrine and shoved it forward. Grunting with the effort, she pushed back against the wall and the altar tipped. June watching it hover precariously in mid-air with her heart in her throat. Then it toppled over with an impossibly loud crash, smashing up against the door.

The candles snuffed out—*ssshhhhhh!* Darkness again, black as pitch. The chainsaw rumbled outside the room. The door rattled. The altar had barred the way.

"Go 'round the back," Jörg said, his voice echoing. "Mrs. Addison? That is your name, isn't it?"

"Fuck you!"

"Dear dear," the man clucked. "Would you prefer I call you June?"

June said nothing, only felt along the floor for the pitchfork, crawling on her hands and knees in the small room, six feet at its widest. Her fingers touched stone and mortar, sifted through every grain of sand and smoothed over every hardened drop of wax. Still, the pitchfork was missing. Desperation squeezed her insides, making her panic.

He knows my name. How could he know my name?

But he didn't, did he? He'd called her Mrs. Addison, and that was worse, because it meant he'd likely called the front desk at the Seaside Inn & Gardens, since she and David had checked in under Addison. The two men could easily have sent somebody to the room to kidnap David—

God, no...

"What is *wrong* with you people?" she cried.

"Wrong?" Jörg wondered. "There is nothing wrong with me, Mrs. Addison—"

"That's not my fucking name!"

He paused for only a moment. "—something is wrong with *society.*"

"You're a fucking monster. *Cannibals!* You made me—" She gagged at the thought of it, the delicious cured and salted meats, the *confit*, the tartar... No wonder David had gotten sick. How much of that meat was what it appeared to be? *Any* of it? How much of it was *human*?

At long last, she threw up, vomit splashing on her hands and the thighs of her capris. While she retched, she heard Jörg chuckle. She wanted to burst through the door and plunge the pitchfork right through his ribcage. She wanted to twist it and throw herself against it and tear his goddamned innards out, to shove them back down his throat so he choked on them. Buoyed by the spirit of revenge, she wiped the puke from her chin with the arm of her sweater, and felt again for the weapon.

"Cannibalism is such a detestable term," the chef was saying. "The Chinese eat everything from the trees to the oceans, and yet we do not fault them for it. We do not call them names such as *cannibal.*"

"They aren't eating people, you maniac!"

Her roaming fingers grasped a stone in the wall. It seemed to have dimension, not just a bumpy flat surface. It had *depth*. She slid her hand up to the rocks above it, found the same depth there. And suddenly she felt a cool breath of air, dank and musty and somewhat salty.

Around the back, he'd told Armand.

It was an *opening*.

She traced the contours. The passage rose maybe three feet from the floor, two or more feet across—the altar had hidden it, but now it was exposed. An exit. Freedom.

"June? What are you doing in there?"

"*Jakobi Uzh Ep a'Hethqa Est!*" she said, trying to divert his attention, hoping she'd pronounced it right. "That's your credo, isn't it?"

She sensed him smiling beyond the darkness, and, having distracted him, crawled into the opening. The passage seemed to slant downward at a shallow angle.

"Your pronunciation's a tad off, June," Jörg said, his voice beginning to recede. "Would you like to know what it means?" Without waiting for her to answer, he told her: "It's written in an auxiliary language the priest Antonioni Merced created to speak with the Yuman Indians—a little joke, really. It means 'We are what we eat, we eat what we are.'" The chef chuckled to himself. "You know, I sincerely believe you and your husband would make excellent Associates to the Order. And why not? You've already gorged yourselves on the forbidden fruit. There is nothing left to..."

His words were finally lost to the darkness. The further she crawled inside the cavern, the louder her own hurried breath and thrumming heartbeat became, but soon these were drowned out by heavy, constant drips from the cold ceiling and walls, and a rush of wind from somewhere deeper inside the passage.

Then: a great thump echoed from the altar chamber. She pictured Jörg throwing himself against the door, and hurried her descent, beginning to smell brackish water, suggesting sea caves or underground pools. Her throat felt incredibly dry, so parched she considered slurping the cold liquid pooled beneath her hands and knees... and somehow, despite everything she'd seen and eaten in the past day, June realized she was *hungry*.

An eerie greenish glow shimmered ahead of her, not far from where she crawled. She hurried onward, ignoring the pain in her knees, until finally the passage opened above her head, and cool air washed brushed her cheeks.

She stood with difficulty in a large chamber, her joints throbbing. Neon green phosphorescence illuminated the cave walls, and the glistening columns of rock like the rotted teeth of an enormous beast. A few feet from where she'd emerged from the stone passage was the source of the salty smell: a brackish pool of water, abnormally round, as if it had been bored by someone... or some*thing*. However it had come to be here, it was at least twenty feet wide, its depth impossible to determine in the gloom.

A growl arose from deep inside the belly of the beast. It grew and then quieted again, the snarl of a gigantic, yellow-skinned troll: Saturn, the titan, uprooted from June's nightmare and transplanted into reality. She shivered, wrapping her arms over her chest to stay warm. The temperature had lowered by several degrees the further she'd gone into the hole; now, it was practically freezing.

The noise steadied, fell again to a low grumble.

Soon, she realized the growl didn't belong to a monster; the *real* monster held the growling thing in his hands. As June peered down into the black water, looking for an opening below, Armand emerged from a passage across the pool with the roaring chainsaw in his hands, and a helmet strapped on his head, its light shining into the cavern. The beam hovered over June, momentarily blinding her. She threw her arms up to shade her eyes.

"Now I've got you, you bitch!" Armand shouted, his face greenish and alien-like from the phosphor, his green teeth visible in a snarl as he revved the saw. Its teeth whirred in the light from his helmet, sharp and hungry, and she knew she had nowhere left to run. If she crawled back into the hole, he'd catch her for certain—and if not him, then Jörg. He'd carve her into rough slices while she screamed and sweated and bled, and finally, mercifully, passed out from the sheer agony of it, the same as he'd done to the poor maid.

The beam of Armand's flashlight twinkled against the black water, causing tiny glints of light like stars set against the vast black emptiness of space.

June sucked in a deep breath, held it, and jumped. She had a moment to consider the possible consequences of such an impulsive act, and then she struck the frigid water, and something slithered about her head, her arms stinging with nettles. Pain slashed across the side of her head, a lightning bolt shooting down through her body to her feet, and then darkness.

IV—An Epicurean's Delight

VOICES ROUSED HER. June blinked at the harsh light, and looked around herself. Movement was difficult. Her head throbbed steadily, felt sticky and itched like hell.

David sat beside her, wearing a look of terror and concern, thick ropes wound around his arms and torso, securing him to a Queen Anne chair. Two huge silver platters lay on the giant, carved slab dining table before them, blanketed with stalks of dark green romaine, beet-red radicchio, and sprigs of holly. Fat orange-pink prawns nestled on melting ice cubes over the greens, and placed among the crustaceans in front of June was a man's severed head. His milky green eyes stared directly at her, accusingly, a juicy violet plum placed in his mouth. His flesh had been roasted to a glistening, crispy golden brown, the scalp and face entirely devoid of hair (June considered, gruesomely, that it had *cooked* off), yet still she recognized him as the Mission gardener, whose innocent, unfortunate mistake had cost him his life. On the tray in front of David stood Josefina's head, her dark brown eyes widened in horror. The maid had been kept raw, her flesh turned blue-gray, a fresh apricot nestled between her lips. David stared at her with a mixture of guilt, revulsion and horror.

"David," June groaned. Speaking hurt her head. Her throat was dry, her lungs sore. *What happened to me in that pool?* she wondered. *Did I hit something... or did something hit me?* "Where are we?"

"I don't know. I was asleep, and then..." He squeezed his eyes closed. "...it felt like I was being smothered. Then I was here, tied to this fucking —" He struggled a moment, then gave up and blinked at her. "Are you hurt? You're bleeding."

"I'm okay," she lied, and struggled with her own ropes. Not an inch of give. "We have to get out of here."

"Tell me about it."

His sarcasm annoyed her. It was *his* fault they were in this mess, wasn't it? If he hadn't made a point of tattling on Josefina—

But she couldn't avoid blame. It was her curiosity that had brought them to this table. Her impertinence, for daring to mess with the Association... whoever the hell they might be.

"You're awake," came a male voice from behind them. June twisted to look, but the back of her chair was too high. She saw nothing but her own hair, matted with blood, staining the rococo fabric.

"Where are we?" David said immediately. "Why are you doing this to us?"

"Tut-tut, Mr. Addison," the voice said. "All in good time."

A rumbling approached from outside the dining hall. Beyond flocked wallpaper and portraits of cheerless old white men—each under their own brass lamp, as portraits of the Old Guard always seemed to be —something moved toward the darkened doorway.

Not the chainsaw. Please.

"Ah, our special guest has arrived," the man said at their ears. June swung her head, fireworks shooting through her vision—and saw nothing of the man holding them captive but an arm draped in white silk.

June's heart sank as Armand wheeled in a dolly, their situation so much bleaker than she'd dared to imagine. Strapped to the dolly was Maximo Morales, naked and unconscious, quite possibly *dead*, and hairless but for the shiny black curls on his head. Armand had washed the blood from himself, and dressed neatly in a black tuxedo and bow tie. He stood the dolly up vertically, leaving Maximo prone and unconscious, with only a strap to conceal his nudity, and joined the man in the white suit, moving out of June's field of vision.

"Max!" David shouted. He twisted his head to look at their captor. "Let him go, you bastards! What did he ever do to you?"

A soft chuckle met his plea. "He was *born*," the man in the white suit seethed. "He crossed through our border and into our *home*. Like a goddamn *cockroach*."

"He was *born* here," June said, not that it mattered one way or the other. Reasoning with these monsters was futile, but someone had to speak for Max. "His family's from *Spain*."

"His father's Americo Morales," David added, hoping it meant something to these maniacs.

"*Dagos*," Armand spat. "I don't know what's worse."

The man in the white suit ignored them, kept plodding forward. "Build a bigger wall, they'll find other ways around it. Under it. *Through* it. The only reason we tolerate them is because they're *so fucking good* at what they do, and they do it with *aplomb*!"

Armand picked up a metal bucket from the floor and tossed its contents at Max's face, painting him in crimson. David sank back against his chair, turning from the sight. *Whose blood is it?* June wondered. *His or hers?* That didn't matter, either. It was the blood of every immigrant, legal and illegal, who had dared to cross these people.

Max roused, shook the blood from his hair and blinked it from his eyes. He sucked in a massive breath, his broad, skinny ribcage expanding, and let it out in a scream.

"Max!" June called. "Max, it's us! June and David!"

He blinked. The blood had dripped into his eyes, making the whites pink. "Where—the fuck—*am I*?" He looked beyond them, at their captors, the Associates. "You fucking pricks, *what are you doing to us*?"

"We're going to get out of this, Max," David said, though it was clear from his tone he didn't believe it himself.

"Like fuck you are," Armand said, and Max began to weep.

"This one," the man in the white suit said, "mincing around like a schoolgirl. Do you believe he was hoping to get married in *my* town? To another *man*? You see? This is what they bring to us—the *Europeans*." He said the word with purest contempt, as if his own ancestors were a somehow nobler breed. "Shitty pop music and queerdom. And the Mexicans. Christ, what's to do with the Mexicans when they outlive their usefulness? I ask you this, Mr. and Mrs. Addison."

When they didn't respond, he slammed his fist on the table between them, rattling the cutlery, stubby fingers with clean, square nails. The white cuff held a gold cufflink in the shape of some kind of sigil. His face remained out of sight. "Why not make a nice meal out of them, hmm?"

He indicated the heads before them with a sweep of his hand, palm up. "Eating is a ritual, after all."

Off to the right, Armand began sharpening a large kitchen knife —*shhhick shhhick shhhick*—wearing a look of fixed concentration as he stepped between them, still sharpening, and plucked a carving fork from the table. He jabbed it at an angle into the gardener's cheek. The blade carved flesh, a smell arising from the steaming meat: something like roast pork, but slightly tangy and acidic. The meat was white, and clear juices dripped down to the gardener's chin.

June felt a pang of hunger and turned away in disgust. She hadn't eaten since breakfast, and the strenuous afternoon had depleted her energy. Despite the type of meat now prickling her nostrils, she found it difficult not to salivate—and the thought that she'd partaken of Jörg's "forbidden fruit" the night before and still felt fine, while David had vomited up every last bit, made her wonder what kind of monster she was herself, to not only have enjoyed it but *kept it down.*

"Mmm! Num-num!" The man in the white suit smacked his lips. "Looks scrumptious, doesn't it? Well, *bon appétit,* as the French say— right, Armand?" he added with a chuckle, and suddenly his chest exploded outward in a spray of blood, spattering against June and David's cheeks, while from the doorway came a seemingly simultaneous explosion. The man gasped and slumped over the table, one hand scattering the shrimp on Josefina's platter, and tipping her head at an unsettling angle. His hat, white straw, had settled brim-up beside the gardener.

Armand brandished the knife and the sharpener, stepping into a defensive stance. Two more reports flashed from the darkness in the hall, and he shook like a ragdoll before falling back on the chair at the head of the table. The chair tipped, and Armand crashing down beside it on the floor. The man in the white suit, a small man with thinning silver hair and a tanned, lined neck, whimpered. His scrawny buttocks began to slide downward, the suit jacket pulling up, exposing a nest of fine silver hairs on his back. His weight tugged the tablecloth before he fell sideways, clunking his head on the arm of June's chair. He crumpled to the floor with an agonized exhale.

"Son!" the intruder's gruff voice said, stepping into the light from the chandelier, handsome and muscular and slightly frazzled. Americo Morales wore a loose blue chambray shirt, white slacks and hiking boots. In his right hand, he held a silver, long-barreled gun. In that moment, he couldn't have looked more heroic.

"Oh, thank God!" David gasped.

Americo approached his son, tucking the pistol into the back of his pants. Max Morales had passed out again, his chin resting on his clavicle, a little runner of blood-tinged drool hanging from his open mouth. "Is he okay? Is he hurt?"

"He's fine," June said. "Just pretty shaken up."

"They were going to kill him," David said. "They thought he was Mexican," he added, and laughed somewhat deliriously. Americo gave David an odd look, then began to unstrap his son from the dolly. The boyish man fell into his father's arm. Americo hugged him to his chest, and began to weep.

The man in the white suit groaned.

"Sir?" David said. "Sir!"

Americo blinked away tears, and peered back at them.

"This one's still alive."

Americo narrowed his eyes, and laid his son on the floor. Max curled immediately into the fetal position and put a thumb in his mouth, fully regressed in his terror. His father stood, jerking the gun from his slacks, and he stepped over to David's side and shot the man twice, point-blank. The shots were satisfyingly loud.

"Fucking old-money prick," Americo grunted, and spat on the dead man at his feet. He laid the gun (wood-handled, with PYTHON 357 etched into the barrel) on the table between them, took in the sight of Josefina and the gardener, and swallowed something distasteful. "*Jesus*," he said. "To think I'd hired these people to cater my party."

He began to untie June. The ropes slackened, and she struggled with them. "Hold on, sweetheart. It's June, right? You're going to be okay, June. Looks like you put up one hell of a fight."

June nodded, smiling gratefully. A tear dropped; she felt it prickle a trail down the blood coagulating on her cheek.

The ropes fell. June wriggled out and stood, freed—*delighted*. She swayed on her feet, woozy from the blow to her head whatever had caused it (she remembered, vaguely, a large and unseen *thing* writhing in the dark, some squirming, natatorial creature with stinging nettles), and she grasped the table.

Americo was untying David. "Anything you need me to do, just ask," David said. "*Anything.*"

Meanwhile, June stood over the man in the white suit, which was now almost entirely red. She hauled back and kicked him as hard as she could. His body shifted, but he uttered no sound. The toe of her dock shoe came back bloody.

"—how did you *find* us, though?" David was obsessing about details, as was his custom. "It just seems... I don't know. Kind of well-timed."

"Son, have you ever heard the expression 'Don't look a gift horse in the mouth'?" Americo asked this with a stern look, and David stopped talking. In a moment he was freed, and rubbing at his wrists. His boss went down to one knee beside Armand's lifeless body. He threw a look back over his shoulder. "I want you kids to get as far away from here as possible," he said, and unbuckled Armand's belt.

"Shouldn't we call the police?" David asked.

"He *is* the police," Americo said, indicating the man in white. "That's Sheriff Cooper I just put three hollow-points through."

"That's not good."

"No, it is not. Leave town. Don't pack up. If you get a phone call from any unknown numbers in the next couple of days, I suggest you don't answer it."

"What about you? What will you do?" June asked, as the man slid the waiter's pants down to the knees. The Frenchman wore silk briefs over his deeply-tanned legs, the exposed buttocks pale.

"Well, first I'm going to dress my son, and take him back to his mother and fiancé." He jerked the pants over Armand's bare feet, and brought them to Max. Pausing there for a moment, he eyed the two of them sharply. "And then I'm going to move Heaven and Earth to turn this whole goddamn town into a parking lot."

June took David's hand, and they ran. Lifeless, musty unfurnished rooms seemed to go on forever: the great halls, the dusty libraries, the swollen antechambers. It was a mausoleum; nobody lived here but the dead. They lost themselves twice, had to turn and circle back, only to head through another dark doorway, another bare, enormous room. Finally, they came to a solid door set in a gothic arch, much wider and sturdier than the others. June let go of David's hand to throw the bolt back, and tore it open.

A bitter wind whipped up at them from the yawning cliff at their feet, the smell of salt water strong. Its rocky face crumbled into the ocean far below as they stood gripping the smooth stone arch. The mansion had been built by the ocean; erosion had brought the cliff to its walls.

"Honey?" David said, his voice small, frightened. June turned to him, saw that he was looking down—not just looking but *staring*. She followed his gaze, and saw frenzied movement in the shadows along the rocky shore. *Crabs*, she thought; *there must be hundreds of them*. But her eyes adjusted, seeing it now for what it was: a behemoth cloaked in darkness, a slithering, crawling leviathan dragging itself up from the churning tide. She saw eyes, a glimpse of its hide, and legs, and *claws*, but all of these quickly vanished, swirling away into its dark shroud.

June scrabbled back out of the doorway, terrified into action. David stood where he was, fixated on the grotesque thing rising from the depths. She tore his fingers from the door, and he rocked on his feet, a stunned look in his eyes. She shook him, and the blank look cleared. He seemed to realize what was happening, and stepped back from the abyss.

"What... what *is* that thing?"

June said nothing, only slammed the door on it.

Hurrying back the way they'd come, he stopped suddenly and stared straight ahead, appearing confused. June tugged him forward by the hand, and they ran past the dining hall again, where the dead remained dead, and Americo and Max had departed.

Out on the front lawn, its grounds gone to ruin, the toothless cadaver of a mansion receded into the dark. A sudden wave of dizziness struck her as they passed through its moldering gardens, and she stopped only for a moment, catching her breath, letting the oxygen flow to her swimming head. Then they took to the hill, damp grass licking at her bare calves, and when they finally broke through the woods, June and David found themselves in a clearing behind Ambrosia.

No smoke arose from the chimney. Its fire had finally guttered out.

Once in the car, David drove as if the Devil were at their back wheels, but it seemed as though the thing draped in shadow hadn't followed. Driving gave him something to focus on, and June's head hurt too much to look at anything but the mirrors, searching for frantic movement in the dark.

"How are we going to get past this?" he asked her, with another nervous glance at the rearview as they turned onto the highway. "Knowing what we know... everything we've seen... Can we just forget it ever happened? Is that even *possible*?"

"We have to try," she said. June felt him gazing at her, not looking at the road, so she tore her eyes from the mirror to look back at him. His eyes were pleading, requiring something more from her, which she didn't have to give. She forced a smile, put a hand on his thigh, and squeezed.

Strengthened by her perceived courage, David pressed his foot on the accelerator, and the road sign disappeared behind them: YOU ARE LEAVING MONTE VERDE.

Thank God, she thought. *Thank* Americo.

What was he doing there? she found herself wondering.

The truth didn't matter. *Don't look a gift horse in the mouth*, Americo had said, and she didn't intend to. It didn't matter how incredibly timely his intervention had been. What mattered was they were *free*.

Maybe he had Max micro-chipped? she thought. *He seems like the kind of guy who'd protect an investment—especially his child.*

But her mother had a different opinion: *What if he'd come for dinner, Juniper? That's something to consider, don't you think?*

She racked her brain for something to take her mind off the useless speculation. There was a secondary camera in the glove compartment. June took it out: a small, virtually useless thing, a backup camera for touristy-type photos. Now that her good camera was gone, she supposed it would have to do. She brought it to her eye, and turned to look back at the retreating town through the viewfinder.

In her mind's eye, she saw beachfront houses topple into the black froth of the ocean. She envisioned the Mission set ablaze in the dead of night, burning against the moonless desert. She saw gardeners, maids, chauffeurs, construction workers and janitors stalk through the streets, using the tools of their trades against their exploiters. She saw the mesas crumble and the forests burn, as if now that outsiders knew its secrets, the town of Monte Verde were being obliterated from the earth, like a Biblical city by the hand of God—or Americo Morales.

Good riddance, she thought, and snapped another photo.

Scavengers

A Novella

1

TWO DAYS BEFORE the first of those murders you may have heard about on the news, I saw Jim Taymor stapling a poster to the utility pole between his yard and mine. I'd been mowing my lawn, and I stopped the mower to ask him what was up. I recall thinking it was for a special event at the restaurant, but the look on his face told me I was wrong. Jim had been my neighbor and my friend long enough for me to know the not-so-subtle working of his jaw meant he was jazzed up about something. A glimpse at the poster he'd half tacked up told me what it was before he spoke.

LOST DOG

had been printed in large computer letters up top. Below this was a picture of their rat terrier, Rosco. I happen to know his show name was Rosco P. Coltrane, after the idiot deputy in *The Dukes of Hazzard*, which I believe Jim or his wife, Leanne, had thought was funny. Like the character, the dog was perpetually terrified, and the photo, with its downward-pointing wide angle, had captured this look just fine. Below that were a few details: black and white coloration, that he'd been wearing a red collar around his neck, that he was "very friendly" (a fact I cannot attest to, having known Rosco intimately for the six years they'd had him), and that he had a "slightly crooked" tail.

I don't suppose I have to tell you I'd never been fond of the Taymors' dog. He was loud, rambunctious, and somewhat feral—if there was ever a dog so different from its owners, Rosco was it. But upon witnessing the look of woe on Jim's face that morning, the sympathy I offered was honest. I said I hoped he'd find it (a lie), and that I'd keep my eye out for Rosco myself and be sure to contact Jim or Leanne the second I heard or saw anything. To be frank, I had my doubts the little mutt would ever be seen or heard from again.

What I'd been thinking of were the cougars reputed to be in the area. Family pets had gone missing more often than usual that spring and summer—outdoor cats in particular, but gates were sometimes left open, and runaway dogs had not escaped the fate of their feline brothers and sisters. It was not unheard of to see mangled raccoons splayed out far from the closest road, nor carcasses of squirrels that were little more than fur and bone scattered on someone's lawn. I'm certain the thought of those damn cougars hadn't escaped Jim and Leanne Taymor, either. Hell, Jim's LOST DOG announcement remained half-tacked between a new one for a missing orange tabby, and a weathered one for a black Lab named Chico, its PLEASE CALL tabs flapping hopelessly in a light spring breeze.

If only it had been the work of cougars, life in our little village of Knee High would have gone on as it always had—not quite *simply* (I am not so delusional—at least not *yet*—as to believe life anywhere can be altogether simple), but less hurried, perhaps. And certainly we would not be on the map, as we are now, resting uneasily in the collective fore-brain of the country at large, already weary from the previous *tragedy du jour*.

Would things have happened differently if Rosco the trained rat terrier had shown up shivering and hungry at their doorstep that night, or any subsequent night leading up to the dreadful culmination of their crimes? I can't say for certain. It is difficult for me to believe Jim would have done what he had over the death of a dog, no matter how he felt about Rosco. What I can say is that Jim and Leanne Taymor were two of the finest people I have ever met, yet their crimes, of which they are most certainly guilty, remain among the most heinous things I have ever heard. I believe they call that a dichotomy. It's a word I've considered quite a bit since Jim and Leanne dropped in on my wife and me, little over half a year ago now, and revealed to us their terrible secret.

If you watch the news (and who can avoid it these days, what with round-the-clock footage of all the late-breaking celebrity scandals and puff pieces your brain can handle), you might think you know all there is to know about what the news took to calling "The Taymor Murders." Even if you'd hung on every word of that damned media circus throughout the fall and winter of 2011/12, questions remain. Their motivations seemed to defy logic, their impenitence was harder to swallow. If they had pled insanity, we might have understood; if they'd *appeared* insane, even, rather than how we'd seen them as they were hauled off toward prison and sitting in court, both wearing identical expressions of happy-pill serenity, it might have made some sense. If they hadn't looked like the typical small-town White America couple with the minivan and the 2.5 children, we might have been able to scratch the itch in our subconscious, the one which reminds us we all walk a tightrope between sanity and madness, a rope that is both slippery and barbed. The odds are not stacked in our favor.

Before the murders, Jim and Leanne had been what folks would call "people people," and if you leafed through either of their high school yearbooks (they hadn't met until university, having grown up on either side of the state), you'd see they always had been, though they didn't care for the term and surely would never have applied it to themselves. Jim and Leanne weren't the type to toot their own horns, blessed with a knack for remaining humble even while receiving well-deserved praise. Friends and neighbors had been quick to assure the frenzy of newshounds that the Taymors were "friendly, caring people," "a happy and loving couple," and "two of the finest people you could ever meet."

I've always thought one of the sadder aspects of the whole mess— aside from all those dead folks, which is unquestionably tragic—was that every single good thing those people had to say about the Taymors was the God's honest truth. They say it's the quiet ones, the nice ones, who commit some of the worst crimes. I don't know how true that is;

what, for instance, would Hitler's neighbors have said about him? Likely nothing pleasant. But it was certainly true in their case.

How could such a happy, generous couple commit the horrible acts of violence they showed on the news, you ask? How could two peace-loving, human-rights-touting Democrats—who'd voted for *Gore*, I should add, before anyone had cared a lick for that tiresome old fool—murder six innocent men and women, a young boy and a dog... *in cold blood*, and with all the ease and indifference of a child trampling an ant hill?

Well, I happen to be privy to that information, much as I often wish I weren't. I was their neighbor throughout the whole mess, and I remain their friend. I am the only one who did not abandon them after they were sentenced to seven consecutive life-sentences each, with zero chance of parole. Whether that makes me a fool or not I'll leave up to you. Even my Virginia, who sat with me during their entire confession, gripping my hand under the table as the more appalling details were revealed, had been shrewd enough to jump ship when it seemed there was no redemption in sight.

From what they told me, during and after the incident, and from what I've pieced together myself through detective work and bald assumption, I'd like to tell you that story, if you'll hear it. You can make up your mind as to what's true and what isn't. I'm not even sure I have myself, to tell the truth.

And like I said, I was there.

2

THOUGH THEIR DOG was missing and presumed (by me, at least) to be dead, the so-called Taymor Murders began with the trash. It happened quite regular that Jim or Leanne would open up shop mid-morning to discover raccoons had gotten into the Dumpsters in the alley out back of La Costina again. "La Costina" in Knee High, Nebraska—can you imagine it? The name of that place was about the only whiff of pretension I'd ever gotten from them, otherwise we likely wouldn't have been as close as we'd become over the years.

It's all boarded up now. Nobody wants to eat at a place where people were murdered, and so far no one's been foolhardy enough to rent it out in the wake of it, even though they could for a song. Tragedies leave their imprints—not just on the bereaved, but on the community at large. I'm sure the good folks in Sandy Hook could tell you that. Or Sanford, Florida. Or Centennial, Colorado. Or any number of small towns across this great nation of ours. That particular piece of property is a black stain on the incorporated village of Knee High, and will be, I suspect, long after I'm gone.

When Jim came to me with his idea—it was Leanne's idea, in truth —to quit a perfectly good career as a geologist and open an *Italian restaurant* in a town with a population of roughly 2500 (this during the summer months, when migrant workers fill up the empty rentals and campgrounds), with virtually no tourism and the economy heading into the crapper, I told him flat-out he was crazy. As his best friend and his accountant, I felt I had the right.

That restaurant was meant to be their retirement fund; now their golden years will be on Uncle Sam's dime. Nobody ever expected it to do well. In actual fact most people thought it would go bust in less than a year's time. But word of its old-world charm and inventive take on traditional dishes carried to the city, and while other businesses fell into dissolution around it, La Costina drew in crowds every night.

Most of this had to do with Leanne's cooking. She'd started taking classes in the Big O as a lark after the fall of the Towers, to "take her mind off the tragedy," as she'd put it, though I suspect the tragedy she meant was one of a more personal nature, one which had been on her mind for some time by then. Pretty soon she was in charge of the cooking for all sorts of events around town. Knee High Collegiate's bake sale in the spring of 2002 paid for an entire class to go to Ecuador (God knows what they'd wanted to do down there, aside from muling cocaine back across the border), along with all brand-new equipment for a football team that had never done well in the rankings and probably never would. I doubt any of those kids had any delusions about being scouted by the Huskers, but hell if they didn't look sharp in those new uniforms.

Even so, nobody thought the restaurant stood a chance. People thought the both of them had gone crazy, an idea that came to haunt some of these folks just lately. Not only did the Taymors and La Costina prove our assumptions wrong, they did us one better and brought several small businesses back from the brink of extinction, with the help of some much-needed tourist bucks. No one could begrudge them their inexplicable success when said success restored hope to a town struggling to stay afloat like so many others, while the government fat cats gave handouts to corporations that had overspent their means.

Five years later they were still doing a fine business. The only trouble was with the raccoons, and for the self-employed, that was very little trouble indeed. *At first.* When it became big trouble, Jim came to me on the evening of May 1st while I sat on the veranda with a sweating bottle of O'Douls (which tasted like cold piss to me, but my blossoming love of the alcoholic kind in that first year of the Great Recession had almost cost me the love of my wife of thirty years), watching a storm gather on the outskirts of town. He nodded and sat beside me. Like the day before, when I'd seen him tacking up the LOST DOG sign, I could tell there was something on his mind; his eyes had a storm of their own brewing in them, an odd look for Jim Taymor. The only other time I'd seen him with a look like that, prior to that night in May, was when Leanne had had her miscarriage in '98.

It was not just the dog, missing three days by then, weighing on his mind.

Our own kids had grown and left the nest, Jim and Leanne being twenty-some years our juniors. But Virginia and I had kept pace with them in '98—Gin sometimes joked the Lewinsky scandal had been planting dirty thoughts in her head—and with our bedroom windows practically side-by-side, some nights it seemed like a competition. Jim and Leanne won. They had had a name chosen (Olivia) before Leanne had even started to show, which any fool could tell you is bad luck. As a professional accountant for forty-two years, and a retired one for six, I believe less in luck than in numbers. For instance, the chance of a woman in her mid-to-late-thirties losing a child is much higher than the odds of winning the $2 Powerball. Life is a Ponzi scheme, I tell you; you only get back what you put in, and more than likely you'll lose your shirt.

Jim sat in the Adirondack chair next to mine, where Gin would have been sitting with a cup of iced tea if she hadn't been visiting our eldest in North Dakota. When he planted his hands on the armrests, I realized with dismay I could see the bone of every knuckle, emblazoned white against his tanned skin. This was not good news I was about to be treated to, and I took another swig in preparation for it, hoping for the sweet sting of alcohol and getting nothing but bitter. I was expecting word of another miscarriage, or of financial crisis: the town's predictions of failure finally coming 'round the bend. Hell, even learning that Leanne had up and left him in the night would have been less bewildering than what he did say.

Less *disconcerting*.

"Have you ever heard of Frugaltarians?" he said after a time. There was a noisome whiff of trash on him, but that was nothing new; he often got his hands dirty at the restaurant, and some of the stink wouldn't wash off until his morning shower. I loathe to imagine what his side of the bed must have smelled like.

Right then he was eying the tract houses across the way. Not many had lights on, despite the growing dark. This was as much to do with the economy as with the fact that there was not much for the modern American family to do in Knee High on a rainy weekend evening. Children don't spend long nights playing board games with their folks like they did when Jessa and Tim were growing up, except for maybe the Mormons. These days they drove into the city to sit in darkened theaters and the Dave & Busters, their zombified faces tinted blue by the screens of their intelligent telephones.

I knew of them, the Frugaltarians. I'd heard of them from the news, where I suspect most people who don't have the internet hear of things like that. Dumpster divers, or so it was said. It had seemed like a reaction to the recession to me, but the Frugaltarians themselves said it was about social responsibility and an opposition to corporate greed, and I suppose that's a reaction to economic decline of a sort. These weren't homeless people, I should stress. The Frugaltarians were hard-working Americans, rooting through the trash for edibles *by choice*, taking food from the mouths of vagrants. At least, that was what I had gleaned from the story.

"If we don't eat it," one woman in a smart business suit and tortoise-shell glasses told the reporter, "it'll go to waste."

"I guess the thrill of boycotting the Walmart must have lost its luster," Gin had said, shaking her head the way she always does when something goes beyond her comprehension.

I told Jim that I had.

He nodded. It was the sort of nod you might expect of a man who'd just been told he had cancer of the rectum. Then he said: "They're not what they seem." His eyes remained unwavering on the black windows of the empty subdivision, finger bones chalk-white on the armrest.

I guessed he was going to elaborate, but he never did. What he did shook me more than anything he'd done since he had risen the creaky stairs to my porch: he stood up and walked right back down to the sidewalk, without even a fond farewell. Right then I had an inkling Jim was in deeper trouble than I'd imagined, and I should have mentioned it to Gin when she returned from Jessa's dormitory that Wednesday.

Like Jim Taymor departing my porch, his head hung low while God bowled a perfect game in the distance, I said nothing. If I had told Virginia, she would undoubtedly have gone to Leanne. A woman should be spared her man's darkest moments, that's what I've always believed. This moment was surely the darkest side of Jim I'd seen since they'd moved into the house beside us in September of '96.

The darkest by far.

3

I *DIDN'T* TELL Gin, and that's on me.

If I'd told her, could I have stopped events from progressing the way they had? I often wonder that now, particularly on those nights with a storm threatening in the east. More than likely the two of us would have been drawn into it ourselves, and that would have been good for no one. The same government who bailed out Merrill Lynch and Citibank, in spite of the massive bonuses provided to upper management, would have been handing out meals and accommodations, meager as they might be, to four lifers instead of two. And although I've always thought Virginia looked damned fine in orange, it would do me no good being halfway across the state in the men's institution and her in the women's. Distance is one problem those little blue pills cannot solve, with the exception of a few meager inches.

The next time I saw Jim, he was out mowing his front lawn, wearing that silly, sweaty blue bandana he always tied around his head while doing chores, although he was not so much *mowing* the lawn as running the push mower in a zigzag pattern around the center of it, counter to his usual methodical rows. Only a few days had passed between then and that night on the porch, but Jim's hair was unkempt and I could see cheekbones where he'd had a bit of pudginess since his high school days.

I didn't find out until many months later what had happened to cause such a drastic change in the interim. I'll spare you the wait.

That night on my porch was the first time he'd seen them, *really* seen them for what they were. It was a Sunday, and as was typical for a Sunday, they'd closed up shop early. It was Leanne's night off. Only Jim was there, along with a few of the young wait-staff, Arnie Jacobs the sous-chef, and the Latino fella who ran the big ugly Hobart dishwasher. I don't remember his name, having only spoken to him a couple of times in his broken English—it might be Javier. Something with a J that's pronounced like a Y; I suppose with only that to go by it could be anything, really. Anyway, Javier or whatever his name was had to leave early—wife had had an accident at the leather mill, so the story went, cutting up her hand pretty badly in one of those deadly machines—and so Jim was left with the last of the dishes and cleanup duty.

He didn't mind the job, said it was where he'd started in the food industry a long way back: bussing tables and running the dishwasher to pay his way through school. It was a Zen thing, he said, something he could do on autopilot, switching off his thoughts for a time. I guess I knew what he meant. In those days before the troubles had come, peace and tranquility hadn't been strangers to me, having been retired a handful of years already. I did a fair bit of work during tax season, to pay for the things Gin and I hadn't saved for, the trips out to see the kids, hospital bills, repairs on the house, etc. But mostly I just puttered about, not doing or thinking much of anything. Peace of mind is something you don't often notice until you've lost it, and it's a luxury no amount of spring tax work has afforded me since our little town of Knee High became a household name.

Jim stepped out into the darkened alley, lugging a stuffed garbage bag in each hand. The mouth of that alley was just wide enough for the garbage truck to pass through with a man hanging off the side, but it opened wider from there, allowing room for two, maybe three cars, two large trash bins and one for recycling. There were three doors. One led to La Costina; the other two were for the army-navy store (in the middle) and a video store. This last was empty (and still is), its windows barred and its doors chained—much like La Costina's and the army-navy's are today.

The single yellow light above the surplus store provided meager illumination for the entire lot. It was triggered by motion, and didn't work the way it was meant: it'd go off with a sudden gust of wind, yet wouldn't when you were standing right below it, waving your hands like a spastic air-traffic controller. This layout is fresh in my mind because I've been there recently, after the police no longer considered it a crime scene and the tape had been cleared away.

Call it morbid curiosity. I needed to see for myself where my friends had lost their innocence. That may sound foolish to you—the mawkish behavior of a washed-up old fart, perhaps. I wanted to see if it held the same dark power over me as they had seemed to hold over the psyche of my fellow Kneeites (a peculiar, vaguely Biblical demonym voted into being some ten years back, which few self-respecting Knee High residents, outside of town council, ever use when referring to themselves). After La Costina's back lot, I hobbled out to the place where the Schultz house once stood, leaning heavily on the brass-tipped cane Gin had bought for me when my knee (of all things) had gone bad a while back.

The oddest thing about these spots was how normal they felt. Nothing at all appeared to be sinister about them. Seven people had been murdered, and the earth itself seemed to know no difference. The ground was dry in places, wet in others; spongy with rotting leaves, hard with packed dirt and stones. In the parking lot, a patch of dandelions now grew where the pavement had cracked, the green paint had flaked from metal doors, the mortar between bricks crumbled here and there. The garbage bins were a little rusted but otherwise serviceable. These were typical post-recession American settings—something you'd see in just about any town from Portland, Oregon to Portland, Maine.

I'm not sure what I had expected to find, precisely. I suppose I thought I might feel an imprint of those murders—the *aftershock*, so to speak. Like those women on the boob tube who, upon entering even the most cookie-cutter of suburban homes, become tearful, grasping whatever medallion worn around her neck and declaring, "I sense a tremendous amount of suffering here." I felt none of this. Horrific things had happened; the world went on, despite them.

What I did feel was an end to that profound sense of loss with which I'd been burdened since the night of their confession. Leanne had picked up the telephone in the kitchen and dialed 911, and Jim had watched her with a strange hybrid of resignation and regret on his face, as she asked the police to come and arrest them. Sitting there, I felt as though the neighbors I knew and, yes, had grown to love, had been murdered before my very eyes. Trudging over the Schultz property, running my fingers over nearly every square inch of the alley behind La Costina, it felt as if I were standing at the graveside of Jim and Leanne Taymor.

I felt—for the moment—at peace.

Nearly a year before, I had stood in the alley, touching things indiscriminately, as if to be certain of their corporeality, and Jim had stepped through the back door with trash in hand, his shadow drawn long over the scale of dried slime on the concrete you often saw out the back of a busy restaurant: the shriveled bits of lettuce and potato shavings, the fish scales and egg shells, the soap suds. The first bag had landed true; the second one had thudded off the edge of the bin. The sound which accompanied it—a "low sort of mewling growl," was the way he described it—had arisen from somewhere in the darkness of the back lot. It was, he said, the sound of an animal either in pain or in heat, and made the hackles on his neck stand at attention for "The Star-Spangled Banner."

The garbage bag had split open, oozing filth onto the pavement. If he left it overnight, raccoons would get to it, or skunks, and spread it all over the damn place. They'd have an even bigger problem to deal with when the maggots and flies set in. Leanne was a fine woman, but she didn't tolerate half-assedness; the spic-and-span, "a place for everything and everything in its place" condition of their home was a testament to that. The animal—whatever it was—suddenly the furthest thing from his mind, Jim approached the shredded bag, preparing to scoop the raw food up with his hands, since there was no shovel handy, and slop it into the bin. Leave it for the guy with the truck to deal with; Lord knows they paid him enough.

As he got down on his haunches and scooped up a handful of filth, there came a scratching behind the bin. Startled, Jim peered around it.

There, clawing at the rusted corner of the bin, was a fat orange tabby. It yowled at him, its eyes shining in the half-light from the kitchen.

"Here, puss puss puss," Jim cooed, and made kissing sounds he would have been embarrassed about in public. He was certain this was the lost cat from the posters. It did not scurry away, merely yowled again, a plaintive sound, nothing at all pleasant about it. It reminded Jim of the time he'd accidentally closed the sliding door at his grandmother's house on the tail of her vicious Siamese. Not the sound it had made immediately, that had been a cry much like a wailing baby, but after the initial pain had subsided. It had lain beside Grandma, glaring resentfully at eight-year-old Jim, yowling every so often, just like the cat behind the bin did now.

Jim waddled toward her on his haunches, making his kissy sounds.

The tabby shied away, the little blue bell on its collar jingling against the tag, and suddenly he saw the reason for its wails. Someone had left the cat tethered to the bike rack on the far wall by a length of chain. They'd been feeding it by the look of her, but a few dishes of 9 Lives didn't excuse the mistreatment.

The cat squalled again. Jim looked at his watch face, slimed with the juicy innards of some vegetable. The minute hand was closing on midnight. His eyes scoured the lot, gazing into every dark nook and cranny, waiting for a shape to present itself, for someone to emerge from the shadows. He'd only seen the man who ran Knee High Surplus once or twice: a pleasant enough older fella, military haircut, dressed not in the camo he would have expected, but in a shiny red tracksuit with an emblem on the left breast.

He didn't look the type to chain household pets to walls as a form of torture, but Jim knew the old notion that *No man is an island* was pure claptrap. Every man, woman and child on God's green earth is an island unto him or herself, with oceans of inscrutability between them. We tell ourselves we know someone, even those who are closest to us: our neighbors, or those who share our beds. But how much do we really know? I ask you that in all sincerity. *How much do we know?* In truth, Jim Taymor knew his neighbor at La Costina's no more than I, apparently, knew my own. He could have been a ritual animal abuser just as easily as a saint.

Fear clutched suddenly and coldly at Jim's midsection. He was thinking of Rosco P. Coltrane. The poor little mutt was on his own out there, defenseless against the animal savagery of the world outside his backyard. Had Rosco spent a night at the end of this same chain?

A sucking, clucking sort of sound startled him. He recognized it as human, even before he turned to see its maker—and what he did see made him reconsider.

The woman, naked as Eve before the serpent, was climbing down the brick side of the building. This in itself did not make his heart perform an awkward triple-somersault beneath his scuzzy apron. What troubled him was that she was climbing down *face-first*, hand over hand, foot over foot. Her flesh, under the motion-sensing light, was gray-black and cracked like the basin of a dried lakebed.

There was a wet double-slap of bare feet as the woman landed, just outside the slanted rectangle of fluorescent light from La Costina's kitchen. She perched there like a toad, knees perpendicular with her shoulders, hands planted on the ground before her, and in the vague light it seemed as if her eyes were *glowing* like those of an animal. But her shape was distinctly human. Of that, Jim was dead certain.

He was certain of another thing, too: he *knew* this person. He'd seen her jogging by the house just about every morning. *She lived in our neighborhood*. It was Cordelia Moone, who made a living wage fashioning clay pots and trinkets out of her home. He recognized her, even with her graying blonde hair hanging in dirty strands in her face, instead of tied up in its usual neat little ponytail. I'm not inclined to doubt him; Jim has always had a preternatural recognition of faces, which is perhaps one of the reasons La Costina had fared so well. Even out-of-towners he'd remember by name, if he saw them more than once. If he says it was Cordelia Moone he saw under all that muck, as opposed to some wild-eyed transient merely passing through town, I would be apt to take him at his word.

It made the mystery of what happened the following week a fair bit less mysterious, in retrospect.

Jim said he heard Cordelia Moone make a low mewling growl, a sound he'd never heard uttered so authentically from a human mouth. It sounded, in truth, like the cat chained to the bike rack. While Jim scuttled out of sight behind the Dumpster, Cordelia Moone stood on her haunches and yowled. The cat repeated the sound, and it turned in a tight circle toward her, its little blue bell jingling. And as the Moone woman crept into the kitchen's light, her eyes began to glow like a wolf's in a pair of headlamps.

Eyeshine in animals is caused by what they call the "bright tapestry," a layer of tissue directly behind the retina. (The red-eye effect you see in photos is blood illuminated by the flash, an entirely different phenomenon.) The closest a human eye can approximate that animal shine is something called "white shine," caused by cataracts or cataract surgery, cancer, etc.

I looked this up the morning Jim told me everything, while he and Leanne were getting processed at Knee High's Sheriff's station—trying to convince myself, I suppose, that there didn't have to be a *supernatural* explanation for the glow in the Moone woman's eyes. That the story they told Gin and me wasn't quite as batshit-crazy as it sounded. That *they* weren't as crazy as I believed them to be. But it was also to re-inter the corpse of childhood superstition their tale had dug up in me, whose shadow had crept up on me during their confession, drawing its claws around my throat. If what they'd said was even *half* true, my little bubble of a worldview was set to burst.

Only Cordelia's doctor would know for sure, I thought.

And the coroner. He would know too.

Jim told us Cordelia Moone had approached the tabby cautiously, crawling on all fours with her mud-caked tits swaying beneath her, flecks of earth shedding off her like dried skin or insects from a neglected animal. Even from where he was, crouched behind the Dumpster ten feet away, he could smell her: a rancid, musky sort of odor that seemed to radiate from her in hot, fetid waves. He had pinched his nose shut, feeling the prickle in his nostrils that signaled an oncoming sneeze, and watched.

The cat had mewled, like a kitten calling to its mother.

The woman had stroked its fur. Her lips peeled back in a gentle smile, dirt crackling in the wrinkles on her face.

Then she had gripped the cat by all four legs, and while it yelped and jerked in her hands, plunged her face into its soft, furry belly.

There was a crunchy squelch, Jim said, as her teeth tore into its flesh. Jim felt revulsion curdle the contents of his stomach. Her face came up with a Velcro rip, glistening innards and orange fur hanging from her lips, dripping fluids. The cat hung loose in her hands, its glassy marble eyes seeming to stare at Jim with the same accusing look Grandma Taymor's Siamese had given him.

Cordelia swallowed, wiped her mouth in the dirty crook of her elbow, and bowed her head for another bite.

I don't believe Jim would have lied about that, particularly after having admitted to seven murders—eight, if you included the accidental death of the dog. Cordelia Moone was the first, but not that night. Jim stood up slowly, letting the egg yolk and peeled carrot drip through his fingers onto the cement at his feet. I imagine the cold, chunky egg must have felt sickening in his hands right then, like vomit or innards.

Cordelia's nostrils flared suddenly. She lowered her meal, seemed to sniff the air for a moment, and then her shining eyes fell upon her observer. She mirrored his action, rising up on her—I almost wrote "hind legs" there, as if she weren't a woman at all. But of course she was a woman, or at least *had been*. If she wasn't, the actions Jim and Leanne took from that point on would have been justified. Maybe even *lauded*.

Her dinner discarded, the Moone woman's blood-streaked arms hung loose at her sides, her shoulders hunched "like an ape," as Jim described her posture to us at our kitchen table. She was swaying back and forth, into the light and out of it, and as she did the flicker in her eyes waxed and waned like... well, like the moon. And when she made that low growl again, he saw her blood-pinked teeth had been whetted down to fangs.

It seemed to Jim she was sizing him up, measuring whether the tasty treat she'd found was worth snapping his neck, or if the risk of killing him was worth the meal Jim himself would make. And while she mulled this over, Jim stood immobile, so terrified by this woman he'd seen puttering in the vegetable garden out front of her bungalow, where most folks had a lawn (or rusted car parts and the like), or sweeping her walkway, or up on a ladder cleaning out her gutters, her face now virtually unrecognizable beneath its coat of grime and her filthy hair. So terrified was he, he admitted freely enough, for a moment he was certain he had wet himself. But it was only the slop from the trash bag, oozing a cold wet trail down his leg.

His attention momentarily diverted by the stain on his pants, Cordelia Moone vaulted over the fence, disappearing into the night.

Why she returned the following night, I couldn't say. Perhaps it's like that song about the cat said, and she just couldn't stay away. All I know for certain is the next night, which was a Monday, Jim came prepared.

Cordelia Moone's sister, who lived in a neighboring town, reported her missing two days later. The hunt was on. MISSING posters were tacked up all over town (by whom I do not know; I never saw anyone putting them up, they had simply appeared one morning, as if the job had been done in the skulk of night) alongside those for Rosco, the Taymors's dog, the orange tabby (that Cordelia had half devoured), and the dozens of other pets who'd vanished from backyards that year. Rumors spread, as they tend to in small towns, like a California wildfire.

And though her body had not been found, the local rag suggested that perhaps our resident cougar had acquired a taste for human meat.

I thought nothing much of the disappearance, aside from your typical neighborly concern. Well, not entirely. Because I knew Cordelia Moone was a Frugaltarian. Or at least, *suspected* I knew. Jim's words that night on my porch, while I choked down my bitter brew—*They're not what they seem*—had been planted in my brain, and they grew a poison plant in my heart like the rhubarb Jim had killed her with. And what could I do, even if I had been certain? Go to the police with a hunch? With Jim's reputation around town, they would have laughed me out of the station.

Of course, by then she was only "missing." When Cordelia failed to surface after several months, the case, like her corpse, grew cold.

4

JIM LAY AWAKE in bed that night he'd come to my porch smelling of trash, while Leanne's breath came slow and steady beside him, much as I would lay awake beside my Virginia when the absurd idea occurred that Jim Taymor might have had something to do with the Moone woman's disappearance. And it *was* a silly notion. If you had known Jim Taymor—the *old* Jim Taymor, not the shell of a man I'd since gone to visit each Friday at the State Penitentiary—if you knew him like I did, you would have laughed the thought away without a moment's hesitation. But it was *because* I knew him so well that the thought wouldn't shake so easily. Because that night on my porch, I had seen a different man—or rather, a glimpse of the man he had only just started to become. A man who'd been lurking under the surface, waiting to come out from hiding.

He lay awake that night, stewing in the certainty he could never tell the woman he loved anything about what he'd seen behind the restaurant, despite the promise they'd made after the miscarriage to share everything. Most men know a promise like that is conditional; no woman wants to know every dirty little secret about her husband, just like no man wanted to know how many men his darling wife had taken behind the bleachers before he had met her. Just the same, I think Jim was the rare type of man who *wanted* to know, not out of jealousy but because he was genuinely interested, and the promise they'd made was something he had aimed to follow to the letter. Until that very night, I believe he had honestly thought he could keep it.

While Leanne slept, Jim replayed the scene on the darkened stucco of the bedroom ceiling: Cordelia's glowing eyes, the grime on her face and in her straggly hair, the way she'd mollified the cat by mimicking its own sounds, before tearing out its raw guts with her teeth. Her nudity, bizarre and somewhat grotesque at the time, aroused something primal within him as his wife snored softly beside him. Cordelia was old enough to be his mother (she may even have taught him how to bake clay pots in a kiln when he was a boy, when they had taken classes to her studio), but he found his mind now returning to the dark, mud-slicked place where her muscled legs came together, and felt himself stiffening under the sheet. This was the sort of dark detail a man's wife should be spared, as I've said. I only relate it to you because it illustrates Jim's chaotic state of mind—and certainly body—as he contemplated what he'd do, if anything, the next time he saw Cordelia Moone.

She's killed him, too, you know, he thought, and the erection immediately began to subside. It hadn't just been Cordelia. Whoever had left the cat chained to the bike rack behind the restaurant, like a treat left for a larger, far more dangerous pet, was equally, if not more, responsible. *You've given Rosco his last Snausage. He's pissing on the carpets in doggy heaven now, the little rascal.*

He thought of Rosco—shivering and yelping in the dark, chewing obsessively at his paws as he sometimes did, his cries met with nothing but anger from apartment dwellers trying to sleep—and was reminded of the Golden Retriever he'd had as a child, a dog named Rufus. Jim swallowed a hard lump and held back his tears. They weren't Jim the adult's tears, anyhow; they belonged to the boy he'd been. The rat terrier had been Leanne's idea, and Rosco had loved her most, perhaps sensing Jim hadn't liked him much. Rosco was too wimpy, too yappy, too disobedient—Jim and I had the same complaints, it seemed. Mostly, he had reminded Jim of Rufus, despite their obvious differences, and looking at Rosco had called up happy childhood memories poisoned by Rufus's miserable demise.

He would not cry for Rosco, whom he liked but could not love.

Somebody, somewhere, cried for their fat orange tabby. A young girl, maybe, who'd smiled each time she'd heard the jingle of its little blue bell as it scampered through the tall grass in their yard, who'd watched it toy with a ball of yarn for hours at a time, squealing with delight as it did. (I was thinking of my youngest, Jessa, as I wrote that. Her Maine Coon, whom she'd named Mr. Muggins for reasons neither Gin nor I could gather, had played a mean string ball.) Somebody somewhere wept for their black Lab named Chico, their ferret, or their pair of long-haired Peruvian guinea pigs.

And if Cordelia Moone had eaten these defenseless animals, was it much of a leap to think she might *eat a child*? If you scraped away the morality, if you slathered it over with animal feces (judging by the smell), and transformed yourself into the savage she-beast he'd seen in the back lot, if you crossed the rather rational line between keeping household pets and *eating them alive*, would enough humanity remain to think in terms of morality and mortality?

Of course, nobody would believe him if he told them. If he'd said *Cordelia Moone rubs shit on herself at night and hunts pets for dinner*. If he'd said, *The Frugaltarians cannot be trusted*. He'd tried it out on me, and I'd looked at him—rightly—as if he'd gone mad. Leanne herself wouldn't believe him, even if he'd wanted to keep up his end of the promise they'd made in the fall of '98. Oh, she might *want* to believe him, if only so she didn't have to think her husband was insane. But sooner or later she'd suggest, as passive-aggressively as she could manage (and Leanne Taymor was anything but passive), that he visit that quack shrink at the Medical Center who walked to work each day with a metal lunchbox and still clung to the few scraps of hair he had left on his scalp, suffering from the delusional belief that nobody had noticed he was bald.

If he hadn't seen Cordelia with his own eyes, he wouldn't have believed it himself.

What's to stop her from eating a child?

What is she, anyway? Is she even human at all anymore?

These were the thoughts that plagued him, while Leanne rode out her NyQuil coma beside him.

If he'd been planning murder from the get-go, he could easily have visited her at her home and strangled her or stabbed her, then messed up the place a bit to look like a hot burglary. They say this type of robbery has been on the rise since the recession hit. With businesses taking more extreme preventative measures, private residences have become easier targets, despite the higher likelihood of casualties. Nobody would have blinked an eye over it, I suspect, and perhaps Jim and Leanne and all of those others they put to death would have been spared the fates they got.

But Jim didn't go to her home, nor did he follow behind her in his car on her morning run. What he did was drive to the empty lot on Mulligan Avenue, where there had once been a profitable Chrysler dealership. It's all gravel and weeds, the remains of the showroom foundation crumbled and sprouting dandelions, strewn with cigarette butts and broken beer bottles. Among the weeds each year grows a particularly ample crop of rhubarb. Jim clipped them at the stem, using a pair of Leanne's gardening gloves to stuff them in a trash bag so as not to touch the leaves directly.

He was counting on the idea that, whatever she may be at night, Cordelia still believed in the Frugaltarian movement. Short of house pets chained mysteriously to bike racks, perhaps she'd resort to scavenging.

As a restaurateur, he knew all about the sorts of foods you could and couldn't eat. He must have known the amount of rhubarb a woman of her weight would have to consume to reach a lethal dose of oxalic acid was approximately seven to eight pounds. No one, even a morbidly obese vegan, could possibly eat that amount of leafy greens. He would have known, as I now do, that cooking the leaves with soda bicarbonate dramatically increased the plant's toxicity. These are facts you can easily divine on the internet, as I've come to learn, ever since Gin persuaded me to chip away at our retirement fund for its low-low monthly fee so she could keep in touch with out-of-town friends and relatives, in particular Jessa and Tim.

Jim knew the leaves were poisonous, but for fear that it wouldn't be enough, he added a healthy dose of rat poison. I believe they call that "overkill."

He closed shop early, much to the discontent of his wealthier customers, and cleared the staff. Leanne still felt ill, and Jim had pulled double duty for Javier, whose own wife was still in the hospital (Lord knows how they afforded the medical bills on their meager salaries; perhaps my neighbors had footed the bill there, too). Sweating in front of the stove in the darkened kitchen, he prepared a few special dishes for his nighttime visitor. The extra ingredient was not *love* but *poison*. He cooled them in the walk-in, scraped them into the trash. A small part of him mourned the loss of so much good food as he hauled the bag to the Dumpsters.

No animals chained out back tonight. Good for him. Not so good for the creature calling itself Cordelia Moone.

Jim sat at the mouth of the alley behind the wheel of his Suburban, waiting. One of those maddening talk shows on public radio played low in the background, but he wasn't paying attention. If he had been, he might have heard that the man responsible for the attacks on September 11 had been killed. A bit of good news like that might have changed his mind, but Jim wouldn't hear about it until the next morning, and by then the deed was already done.

In actual fact, I don't believe he expected anyone to show. A part of him, he told me, had come to think he'd imagined the whole experience. It has always been difficult for me to believe that. The details he'd given were so vivid, names and faces withal, that if he had imagined it all he surely would have seen the signs much earlier. A man doesn't acquire schizophrenia overnight, not without benefit of drug or alcohol dependency, a tumor or lesions in the brain. Court-appointed neurologists and psychologists had him checked for these and found nothing. In any case, the trap was set. If things ended up with a family of dead raccoons in the bins, they'd go out with the trash on Wednesday. No harm, no foul.

He was about to give up when he heard rattling somewhere near the far end of the alley, a hubcap's clatter and scrape as it rolled to the ground. Then the lid of the furthest Dumpster swung open so violently it slammed against the back. Jim leaped up in the driver's seat, jerking his collarbone against the seatbelt. In his agitated state, he must have buckled himself in, though he didn't remember having done so.

Cordelia Moone crawled onto the lip of the Dumpster and perched there. She remained motionless for some time, perhaps sensing for predators. Finally, she began plucking out a single piece of trash at a time. She brought each item close to her face to sniff at it, and tossed what was spoiled over her shoulder. What hadn't begun to rot she nibbled at with both hands held to her mouth like a rodent, and Jim watched with cold captivation for her to reach the bait bag. He didn't think she would suspect poison, especially when you factored in the treat that had been left without it the night before. She would see its contents, virtually devoid of the plastics and scraps which constituted real garbage, as the motherlode.

As Jim sat there, with news of bin Laden's assassination going unheard in the background, he could think of only two things. One was that she would see him. Nocturnal animals can see in the dark, and it appeared to Jim that whatever Cordelia was during the day, she was surely a creature of the night now. Something had *changed* her. He held a vague idea that the Frugaltarian movement (these things were always "movements"; one couldn't simply *do* anything these days without belonging to one group or another, so eager we human animals are to be placed into our little labeled boxes) was some kind of cult. But the notion they could have somehow *altered* her into the subhuman creature he saw before him... It wasn't just difficult to believe, it was outright preposterous.

The other thought was that if she did happen to see him, he'd have to be quick about it: start the Suburban, drop it into Forward and step on the accelerator, before Cordelia Moone had a chance to react. If she was still on the Dumpster, so be it. He'd ram the bin and Cordelia so hard into the back wall of the building that even if it didn't kill her, she'd be too broken to get up. And if she came at him, if she was running full steam by the time he got the car going, he'd plow her down like roadkill. Then he'd simply back out into the street, leave the door open and the keys in the ignition, and walk home.

He'd tell the police the car had been stolen—with any luck, it would be—and they'd assume it had been a joyride gone bad. Cars were stolen all the time, particularly in the current economic climate. Besides, what motive would Jim Taymor have to kill her, aside from her rooting through his trash? If she really was no longer human, as Jim truly believed, the unidentified carjackers would be hailed as accidental heroes.

Fortunately, Cordelia did not see him, and Jim never had to lie about it. That was one thing he never did: *lie*. Everything he said to the police, to Leanne, and to Gin and me was the truth, at least as far as he saw it. The polygraph they'd administered proved it. I suppose that's a pretty decent reason why they aren't admissible evidence in court.

What Cordelia did do was find the goodie bag Jim had left for her. Her eyes lighted, quite literally, as she tore it open to poke through its contents: spinach lasagna, sautéed spinach with garlic butter, spinach and salmon mousse. She must have thought she'd died and gone to Frugaltarian heaven. Except what looked like spinach to her was actually leaf rhubarb, and in addition to the nutrients you'd expect to find in your leafy greens, your vitamins A and C, your potassium and dietary fiber, these were loaded with oxalates, cooked in soda bicarbonate, and sauced with the rat poison kept under the sinks as a just-in-case, which he'd never had occasion to use until just then.

She sniffed at the handful she'd scooped out, like a kid with a handful of pumpkin guts. In the moonlight, Jim was close enough to see her nostrils flare.

A creeping certainty grew in him then: *she'd smell the poison*. Or *taste* it. She nibbled a bit, and waited, like a rat would. Waiting for the onset of stomach cramps that would tell her to avoid the brown acid.

A minute passed on the dashboard clock.

Two.

Cordelia sniffed the cloudless night air. In the distance came terrible squawks and screeches: raccoons fighting over a tasty morsel in some poor bugger's yard. Her head twitched to the left, the gold eyeshine vanishing momentarily, leaving only black. It seemed to Jim that black had spread from eyelid to eyelid, as if she were no longer human at all. It took all of his strength not to run her down right then and there.

Then he thought of Leanne, sitting on the living room sofa surrounded by crumpled tissues, something mindless on the boob tube, and the thought of her discovering what he'd been doing out here, when he should have been serving steak in mushroom béchamel sauce and lobster ravioli to a house full of salivating customers, gave him the strength to hold out. He chuckled softly to himself as a dark thought occurred to him: *I'm still serving food... at least technically.* It made him feel like a homicidal chef in some dime-store detective novel, and he stopped cold, looking at the dashboard clock. Four whole minutes had passed. Finally, Cordelia returned her attentions, and her *snout*, to her supper.

People may tell you warfarin poisoning is a painless, more humane death, but I tell you this: Cordelia's death was far from painless. She'd eaten roughly an entire helping of rhubarb lasagna laced with rat poison, when her fingers clutched suddenly at her belly. The expression on her face, which Jim neither relished nor entirely abhorred, was that of pure agony. She toppled from her perch to the cold concrete, crying out like a wounded animal. Had she loosed a human cry from her conspicuously human lips instead of that monstrous howl, she might have caused alarm. Someone might have called the cops, and the paramedics might have arrived just in time to save her life. As it happened, the sounds of her death were lost in the din of the raccoon skirmish maybe a block away. No one had ever considered that a woman lay dying in the back alley of Jim and Leanne Taymor's Italian family eatery. Good for Jim. Not quite so good for the thing calling itself Cordelia Moone.

Jim sat in the comfortable cab of his Suburban and watched her die. Rufus, the dog Jim had when he was a boy, had gotten sick, suffering multiple seizures near the end that had terrified eleven-year-old Jimmy's father as much as they had Jimmy. In the waiting room, while the vet put down old Rufus, Jimmy had wept the whole time. Adult Jim remembered this while Cordelia Moone twisted and moaned at the foot of the bins. Rain pattered in through the sunroof, falling on Jim's cheeks and tracking warmth down to his chin. But it wasn't rain—the sky was clear, full of stars, and the sunroof was closed, anyhow. These were tears streaming down his face, just like the little boy who'd lost his dog.

He looked up from wiping his face, in time to see shadows skulking into the back lot, perched on the fence and on the rooftop. Terror rattled through his bones; curiosity held him there, the same sort of reckless curiosity that would cause a man to stick his head into a darkened hole to see what lay beyond. He peered up through the tinted portion of the windshield, then the sunroof, counting heads: six of them in all, mere silhouettes against the moonlit sky. Cordelia's caterwauling had summoned them. They whimpered and howled and lay down on their stomachs, their chins resting on their hands like a pack of wolves grieving its Alpha. Jim couldn't see their faces throughout this performance, just the eyes, and the same glow fading from Cordelia's life-lamps burned brightly in theirs.

Jim waited for them to leave, but as time ticked away, he grew ever more nervous. There was, after all, a dead woman in the alley, or some manner of thing with the *look* of a woman, which would amount to the same thing when the police showed up. He needed to be gone when they did. He had a successful restaurant to worry about. A reputation. A *wife*—

The moment he thought of Leanne, his cell phone began to ring. As I recall, it was some classical piece or another and high-pitched as all get-out, the sort of thing they use to deter teenagers from loitering at some shopping centers. Naturally, it was Leanne. Speak of the Devil and he (or she, in this case) doth ring. This was especially true when you had your phone surgically attached at the hip (or ear) like most everyone seemed to these days.

It was after midnight, and she'd be worried. Jim scanned the fence, the rooftops, certain they'd heard. Night animals had heightened senses, he knew; whether that extended to hearing for these creatures, only human in appearance... Well, he was about to find out firsthand.

One head turned toward the sound, atop a smallish body that might have belonged to a child. Another, large and distinctly male, crouched at the edge of the roof of the surplus store directly across from where Jim was a sitting duck, and turned toward the Suburban.

He scrambled to get the phone out of its holster. In that moment— a moment that seemed to draw out longer than the time it had taken for Cordelia to die—the smallest of the pack leaped down from the fence, landing on all fours, its knees drawn up higher than its shoulders. It was no human posture, and even from the relatively low height of the ten-foot fence any normal human child would have been injured in the drop. Like Cordelia, the boy was naked, encrusted with dried muck and animal scat. Judging by his little winky (that's Virginia's word, not mine, and it pains me some to see that I've written it, but for this to be an authentic account, I feel I should censor myself as little as possible), a hairless knot below his abdomen, he had yet to reach puberty. Maybe eleven or twelve at the most, just about the age when Jimmy Taymor had wept for his dead dog.

On the third ring, Jim fumbled the worthless thing out and thumbed it off. It was already too late. The others had heard, shining their mutant eyes in his direction. The big male climbed a pipe down the side of the building, nimble as a monkey and big as a gorilla. A female bounded from rooftop to awning to the ground below, with the speed and grace of a house cat, though she was heavy-breasted and thick in the waist and bottom.

The boy-thing crawled foot over hand toward Jim, like some jittering specter from one of those Japanese horror movies Jessa liked to watch on her visits. Jim saw its face as it crept into the light from the kitchen, and he realized—with genuine despair—it was the son of an old friend from junior school. *Do his parents know he's been drawn into this?* Jim wondered. *Are they there with him, lurking somewhere in the dark beyond the rooftops?*

He turned the key in the ignition, forgetting it was already half-turned, even with the radio "personalities" buzzing like know-it-all bees in the background. The engine whinnied. The largest of the creatures closed the distance, prowling toward him; there was no doubting the murder in his—I should say *its*, if I'm to fairly represent Jim's state of mind—eyes. He eased back on the key, and the engine roared to life. The gas gauge flittered and the tachometer shot straight up to 1000 RPM.

The brights came on in that same moment, blasting cold white halogen over the entire scene. The effect was like flicking on the kitchen lights at a cockroach party. Before he could see any of their faces, they threw their arms up over their eyes—he had a sudden foreboding feeling the others would be disfigured somehow, twisted into shapes too horrible for the human mind to comprehend—and drew back a step at a time, their shadows thrown long and black against the far wall.

Emboldened, Jim laid on the horn: one long blast. Two. On the third, the pack began to scatter, crawling back the way they'd come. The big one threw one last baleful look over its shoulder. It was a bear of a man, muscular as well as fat in the gut, and prematurely bald (most of the hair had migrated to the torso, including the back, and poked through the cracks in the layer of filth, like grass sprouting from dry ground). It was the type of guy with an overabundance of testosterone, probably working some hands-on, outdoors job, like road work or forestry, maybe farming, with a healthy thirst for the wobbly pop. Jim didn't recognize him, but it didn't mean he was a stranger. In a town of a little over 2000 souls, it wasn't possible to know everyone, despite what television might have you believe.

Then the creature scaled the wall, getting fingers and footholds in the small chinks between bricks.

Alone now, Jim allowed himself a chance to breathe. He gave his phone a contemptuous look (or so I imagine; were I in his position, it would have ended up in the trash alongside Cordelia's leftovers). Simple concern had almost cost Leanne a husband: death by cell phone. Had she been widowed that night instead of being greeted by Jim's cold, distracted look at the door, she would never have known the horrors her husband was soon to show her. She would never have known how it felt to have human blood on her hands. *Child* blood.

But she would have known heartache. In this case, I believe, such grief would have been a kindness.

Not that I believe my friend should have been set upon by those things, torn apart limb from limb, or whatever they might have done to him for murdering one of their own. I do not wish that at all, except the Jim I knew is long gone. If he'd died on that warm, clear night in May, instead of the other six innocent folks he put to death (and the dog, lest we forget him), would the world have been better off?

I have to think it would.

Jim *had* lived, though, and because he'd lived, Leanne got to hear the whole unspeakable story, straight from the horse's mouth. How Cordelia had had a kind of foam clotted on her lips and chin, pink with her own blood. How putrid she'd smelled when he'd folded her body into the gazebo tent they kept for charity events, like pungent, musky animal feces. Like *rot*. How he'd carried her inside and through the kitchen, where La Costina's staff had worked and laughed and danced along with silly songs on the radio, and how her head had thumped against every stair on their way to the basement cold-storage. How she'd looked when the tent had slipped away, frost growing on her pitch-black eyes, as mist from the deep freeze rose around her, like it had off Stevens Lake in the early morning sun, back when they were still in school.

Jim spared Leanne no detail, no matter how gruesome. ("It was the only way," he later told us, as the two of them sat at our kitchen table, holding hands through it all. Leanne gave his hand, which was trembling, a little squeeze. "It was the only way I could live with myself after what I'd done.")

He told her everything that very night, and when he had finished, he closed her hand over something cold and flat.

It was a key, the key to the basement freezer, only to Jim, it was more than that. She held his life in her hand, small and metallic though it was. "Keep it," he told her, still holding her hand in both of his. He gave her an unsmiling look. "Or hand it over to the police. You do whatever feels right, sweetheart."

What felt right to Leanne was to sleep on it.

5

I CANNOT IMAGINE how Leanne must have felt, lying awake beside her husband of over twenty years, a man she thought she'd known, while Jim slept like the dead.

I lay awake myself that night, wondering what had gotten into my friend and neighbor, yes, but also worrying about our youngest, Jessa. I finally fell asleep in the wee hours, and woke some time later from a nightmare I cannot fully recall, in which I'd become lost in grass the height of a man as it was cut down by the blades of some God-sized lawnmower. I woke with a gasp, my hand held out before me as if to stop God's thunderous John Deere from mowing me down. Gin, my sweet Virginia, took me by the wrist and kissed the back of my hand. I took hers in both of mine and kissed back, still cold from my dream.

At the Taymor house, Jim woke to find Leanne's side of the bed empty. Her half of the comforter lay flat, meaning she'd made her side of the bed when she got up. In those few moments between sleep and fully awake, he thought for sure she had left him. The worst of it was that he couldn't fault her for it. She'd stuck with him through tragedy and triumph, but nowhere in their vows had murder been among them. She would have been well within her rights to pack a bag and slip out during the night, with or without leaving a Dear John (as well as the John Deere sitting in their garage).

Hell, she would have been *smart* to.

So it was with mingled regret and relief that he found her in the kitchen, looking like the illness she'd had was gone, scrubbing the stove in a frenzy. The room was already gleaming—it was *always* gleaming—yet still she spritzed cleaner and scoured away like a madwoman. I suppose in that moment she might have been a bit mad, and with good reason. To discover the man whose bed she shared was capable of such a horrendous undertaking... I think we'd all go a little crazy burdened with such knowledge.

Jim stepped around Rosco's bowls, as he did every morning before he realized they were missing from their mat on the floor—the mat itself was gone, too. A good sign for his case, or so he thought. It meant Leanne had believed at least a portion of his story.

I do not know how Jim talked her down from her manic state, I only know neither of them had much interest in the coffee she'd scalded. Knowing Leanne as I do, I don't believe she would have acted as if nothing had happened, nor would she have given him the silent treatment. She would have been moody, almost surely, and who could blame her? She might even have given him the cold shoulder for a while. But at the restaurant, it would be business as usual. She would put on her game face, and no one outside of the two of them would be the wiser.

Spinach, however, would be off the menu for quite some time.

I'm not sure Jim could have said anything to sway her in his direction, frankly. Had the large man not come into La Costina that night, she might be paying her husband conjugal visits now, instead of wearing a matching orange jumper. She might even have kept his secret, sparing him his fate, but the weight of it would have driven a wedge between them that the miscarriage hadn't. Spinach might not have been on the menu, but divorce surely would have been.

The large man stood just inside the doors, looking through the pass-through at the busy kitchen and gnawing on his fingernails, as if they might provide him the sustenance he'd been denied in La Costina's back lot. Jenny Meyer, the hostess on duty, scurried away from her station to approach Jim, who was offering a young couple on their honeymoon a complimentary dessert.

He took Jenny aside. "What's the trouble?"

Jenny looked off in trepidation, and Jim followed her gaze. If he hadn't recognized the face straight away (and of course, he did—I've already mentioned his recollection of faces), the man's build would have been a dead giveaway.

"He's giving me the charlies," Jenny said with a cold shiver. (For the record, "charlies" was the word Jim told us Jenny had used. I am not overlaying my own unhip old-timer version of teenaged slang over her words, though I suppose Jim could have done so himself.) Jim agreed, not taking his eyes off the man. He was used to making quick decisions on the job, yet none of them had been life-and-death until now. "I'll take care of him," he said, laying a hand briefly on Jenny's shoulder. "Why don't you go have your break?"

Jenny eyed the large man suspiciously before wandering back to the kitchen, beyond which the break room, and her cell phone (with probably more than a dozen text messages; Jenny was a pretty girl, and popular), awaited.

Jim spared a look into the kitchen, where Leanne was plating food with the same frenzied expression she'd worn in their home kitchen that morning. She glanced up from her work, caught the frightened look in Jim's eyes, and knew, the way a spouse instinctually understands the geography of his or her marriage, her husband's fear had been caused by the large man at the door, chewing the ends of his fingers. There was nothing very menacing about the man, aside from his monstrous size. He *was* a behemoth: six-eight if he was an inch, possibly taller, broad in the shoulders and heavy in the gut.

Jim gave her a troubled nod, but she didn't need it to know this was the one he'd told her about: the man-thing who'd scrabbled down and then scaled back up the brick wall, as sprightly as a child climbing the playground monkey bars.

Jim pasted on a smile and headed for the front of the house.

The large man had to duck under the hanging lamp at the host station as the two men approached each other. They met in front of the bar. Jim stuck out a hand. The large man left it suspended, and Jim lowered it to his side unshook. He had a prominent brow, the sort of forehead that folds down over the eyes like a hood, giving the appearance of brooding—or idiocy—when the face is slack. The eyes themselves, though... intelligence shone in them, as brightly as they had shined in the dark.

"Can I offer you a drink?" Jim said, aware he was stalling. Business such as this was best handled in the back office, behind a closed door, but Jim's desire for a stiff drink came on sudden and strong, a sentiment I understand fully but don't currently endorse.

"I don't drink," the large man said. His acrid sweat filled Jim's nostrils: a musky, nostril-stinging sort of smell, barely concealed by a liberal application of Brut aftershave. His voice was as deep as Jim had expected. Not Jolly Green Giant deep, but the sort of baritone that commanded attention, if not respect.

"No," Jim said, visibly shaken, "I don't suppose you do." He threw a glance back at Leanne, wondering just how much this man knew about them. Did he know they were married? Where they *lived*? "Step into my office," he said, thinking, *Said the spider to the fly*. Only he was the fly now, wasn't he? Never in his life had he wanted to be elsewhere —*anywhere*—so badly.

The large man, who did not introduce himself then and never would, followed Jim through the kitchen. I happen to know his name was Richard Holland, with the benefit of Jim and Leanne's confession, not to mention the endless news coverage. He answered to the nickname "Dutch." I'm sure you can guess why.

A man his size does not pass through a crowd without being gawked at and, though this was their busiest time, tonight was no exception. Every single eye in the back of the house looked up as he lumbered through, ducking his head to miss the pots hanging on the rack. Even Arnie Jacobs, sweat dripping out from under the bandana on his bald, coffee-colored scalp, turned to gape, and Arnie stands at least six-four himself.

"Let's keep focused, guys!" Leanne said, clapping her hands to get their attention.

Work resumed. Jim opened the office door. Dutch had to duck again to step inside. Leanne shot her husband another look—one that said, *Shout if you need me in there*—and Jim closed the door between them.

Sitting behind his desk, Jim said, "Have a seat." He gestured toward the chair he used for interviews and one-on-ones with the staff, the same one I sometimes sat in when the two of us were going over the annuals. The chair was clearly too small for Dutch. He didn't even regard it.

"I'll stand."

"Of course you will," Jim said, the large man towering over him. "Well, I suppose I should just come out and say it—"

"Cordelia and I weren't close," Dutch said. "Simple fact is, I hated the bitch."

Jim made to say something, but Dutch held out a hand large enough to crush his head like an egg, palm first, to silence him.

"But she was one of us," he continued. And whatever the "us" was, be they Frugaltarians or members of some peculiar, cat-eating religious sect, whatever Jim had thought he'd seen in the alley the night before, this was certainly a man standing before him now. No nictitating eyes, no scales or unusual birthmarks. Not a monster—a man. A decidedly *large* man, make no mistake. But nothing more.

"She was family, and that's gotta stand for something."

"Uh-huh." Jim didn't know how to respond.

"So here's what I think we should do." He'd begun to chew his fingernails again, already inflamed from biting. Jim couldn't get a good enough look at those teeth to see if they were as sharp as Cordelia's had been: the teeth of a *carnivore*. "You forget what you saw," he suggested, "and we got no truck with you. You go on with your life, we go on with ours."

"You killed my dog," Jim said, surprising himself with the outburst. "All those lost pets, you killed them and ate them."

"That's one of the things the bitch and I disagreed about." Dutch took his paw out of his mouth long enough to make a swishing gesture with it, then planted it right back between his eager jaws. "Certain principles and tenets of the organization, you might say, including but not limited to the consumption of living meat."

"You're against it, I suppose," Jim said, feeling rather sickened by the man's flippant use of the word, *meat*. As if anything with flesh was by definition edible, and anything a man could eat should not be excluded from the menu without consensus.

"*We're* against it."

"*We*?"

Dutch ignored the question, began looking at the framed photo of Jim and Leanne on the desk, from their Missouri University days. Jim had no gut and sideburns and Leanne's hair was still a shock of platinum-blonde curls with dark roots, hanging loose over her stonewashed jean jacket with the sleeves rolled up. They had made quite a pair: Jim the shy geology student, eager to bust out of his shell, and Leanne the English Lit. major, hoping to shut down the party and settle into life as an adult.

Jim flipped the photograph face down. "You can't expect me to believe you won't turn me in. I *poisoned* a woman. A woman is dead because of me, and you people are gonna let me walk away *scot-free*?"

Jim had never been the type to disregard the dental hygiene of the horse he'd been presented with. I know this from my many years preparing his taxes. All the little tricks where I could save him some cash, he'd say, *This can't be legal*, knowing full well the kind of man I am, and of course that it was not only legal but *required*.

"Not exactly," Dutch said, with a sly tilt of his big round head and a nibble on the red-raw index finger of his right hand. "There's still the matter of Cordelia's remains."

This was the twist of the blade Jim had been waiting for, though he'd never imagined he would be bargaining over her corpse like a couple of fellas haggling over the price of cukes at a roadside stand. "I see," he said.

"If it was up to me," the large man said, "you could grind her up and feed her to those *wasters* out front. Unfortunately, it's not up to me."

He spit a bit of nail out. Jim saw where it landed, on the L-key of his computer, and made a note to wipe it up the moment the man left his office.

"The others feel we should give her a proper send-off. It's tradition. Me? I say, fuck tradition. Cordelia Moone didn't give a squirt of piss for tradition, pigging out on all those kitties and pups. Worse than that, she was *stupid*, too stupid to smell a trap when it's already clamped down on her leg. If it'd been up to her, we'd all have eaten that shit out of your Dumpster, and you'd have had one hell of a mess to explain to the cops."

Jim considered the idea for a moment. Already his mind was working, you see. If he handed over the Moone woman's remains, what was to stop Dutch and "the others" from turning him in to the police? One body or seven bodies—murder was murder in the eyes of the law. And whether he'd serve one life sentence or multiple consecutives, they'd amount to the same: the rest of his life spent behind bars, without his wife. Probably he'd be filling the role of wife himself in the Big House.

"What would happen if I didn't hand her over?" Jim said. "Hypothetically. Say her body was no longer intact? What would you do to me?"

The large man squeezed his hands into fists, the knuckles cracking, and relaxed them. His dull expression never changed. "It's not me you'd have to worry about," he said finally.

"The others?"

Dutch nodded ominously. "They would split you apart at the joints."

Jim didn't for a second think the man was exaggerating, but he decided to push a little harder. "Well then I guess I'm in a bit of a bind. But you seem like a reasonable man." He spat out the word—not *reasonable* but *man*. "Maybe we can come to some kind of understanding?"

The idea seemed to pique the large man's interest. A finger hovered for a moment in the empty air near his lips. "How much of an understanding are we talking about?"

"Ten?"

A thoughtful nibble on his left pinky finger, palm-out "Make it fifteen," the man said.

"Fifteen thousand is a lot of money."

"So is ten. Fifteen grand, Mr. Taymor, and I personally guarantee you, nobody comes to your house in the middle of the night and takes a pair of hedge clippers to you." He tipped his head toward the photograph lying face down on the desk. "Or your pretty wife."

"*Hedge clippers!*" Jim repeated to us as he later related all of this. It seemed to him much too specific not to be a grim reality. I have to say I agree.

"Fifteen it is," Jim said, and swallowed hard. "Only, that amount of money, I'm going to have to shift a few things around, talk to my accountant..."

"Friday afternoon. Out back of here. *Cash.*"

Jim nodded and stuck out his hand again. This time, the large man took it. A deal was made. His giant fingers, chewed to rat shit, crushed Jim's average-sized hand with only the slightest of pressure. *Hands that big could do a man's job with a pair of hedge clippers*, Jim thought, and shook away the pain the moment his hand was set free. He opened the door with the other hand. The large man ducked to go.

"We never settled on a time," Jim said.

"Before dark," Richard Holland told him without hesitation, hovering in the doorway.

"How about six?"

The large man nodded. "Six is good."

6

J IM NEVER CAME to me to ask about money. If he had, I would have told him it was readily available, and we didn't need an Acid-test to know it.

The money was a stall. Leanne knew that, too. What Leanne also knew was that if they *did* pay the man, they'd be paying for the rest of their lives. A few thousand here, a few thousand there, until their entire nest egg vanished into the wind. Every single dime that came out of La Costina not already earmarked for the restaurant itself would go into Richard "Dutch" Holland's double-XL pockets. They wouldn't be giving him any fifteen-thousand on Friday at six P.M. or ever, because they'd never see the end of it.

With that settled, Jim and Leanne put their heads together to figure out what they *would* do. They knew they could clean out their accounts quite easily between then and Friday (it was late Tuesday they discussed this, after Richard Holland had left, with their customers cleared out and the staff gone away home). They could walk away with all the cash they could liquidate, a tidy sum, and live out the rest of their days in Belize, or somewhere else extradition laws to the United States were lax.

They *could* do that... but by then their little Italian eatery had become no longer just their retirement fund, but their *lifeline*. It had occurred to both of them at some point or another that La Costina was the baby they'd never been able to have, and to give it up would be like little Olivia dying all over again. My Virginia had long suspected they'd begun to drift apart after the miscarriage; that restaurant of theirs had breathed fresh life into their marriage, where since the autumn of '98 there'd been only death.

Jim and Leanne stood in the door of the basement walk-in, weighing their options. Cordelia Moone's flesh was gray-blue, with little white snowflakes of frost in her hair and scaled over her eyes, which seemed to have returned to their original brown. Her breasts remained flat, even after they'd stood her up in the corner, though not from gravity; Jim had left her on the floor overnight, and they'd frozen that way. (It was a morbid reminder of the erection he'd gotten the night before, a detail he did spare Leanne, only telling me via the visitor's phone at Nebraska State Pen.)

Earlier, before the staff had arrived, Jim had turned the basement lights off and shined a flashlight in the Moone woman's face for Leanne to see. At first it hadn't worked. There'd been too much frost in her eyes. But when Jim scratched enough of it off—a sickening task if there ever was one (he told me later he tried to think of her like a side of beef, an image that would have just made it harder for me to look at beef)— sure enough, two golden flickers of light appeared.

It wasn't enough to convince Leanne just then, but when the large man had lowered his head to duck under the pot rack, she'd seen it in his eyes too. That animal shine. And the condition of his fingers had sealed the deal. He'd chewed them raw, like Rosco had sometimes chewed obsessively at his own paws.

"Jim... what *are* they?"

"Pandas are carnivores," Jim said. "Did you know that?"

"No." She wasn't sure where this was going, but she was willing to follow along. *For now*, she told herself. She'd come this far without turning him in. Already she'd be considered an accomplice, so she might as well hear what he had to say and hope it didn't sound as crazy as she feared he'd become.

"Well, they are. They have all the characteristics of a carnivore. Carnivore genes, carnivorous digestive tract, ursine teeth. That's bear."

"I know what *ursine* means," Leanne said, annoyed by his unintentional patronization.

"Right. They even belong to the order *Carnivora*. But for some reason, they only eat bamboo. Maybe twenty percent of the 30 to 40 pounds they eat gives them nutrition. Carnivorous animals get sixty percent or more. The rest of that bamboo is waste."

"So why do they eat it?"

"They eat it *by choice*, not necessity. They're the vegans of the animal kingdom." Leanne let the obvious mistake slide, because it seemed he was on a tear. It was easy enough to forget humans were part of the animal kingdom, despite our higher level of consciousness. We put a robot on Mars, for Pete's sake—when was the last time you saw a chimp do that? "Whether that's because they've evolved to be too, let's say *hefty*, to hunt," Jim went on, "or they're conscientious objectors, nobody knows. All we know for sure is that they *were* hunters, once."

"You mean these, these *things*," she said, nodding toward Cordelia's frozen corpse, uncertain just what to call it, "they eat our leftovers so they don't have to hunt?"

Jim shrugged. "I'm not sure why they do it. But I know these—people? Whatever the heck they are—I know they have the teeth and the strength to eat *us*, if they wanted."

Leanne took a step toward Cordelia Moone's stiffened corpse. The freezer was empty, aside from the few boxes on some of the shelves, freezer-burnt breadsticks and various foodstuffs whose Best Befores were long behind them, things they'd meant to get rid of so they could shut off the freezer for good. She was glad they hadn't now. What would they have done with Cordelia, otherwise?

Leanne reached out, meaning to touch her.

"What are you doing?"

Jim's voice startled her. She'd forgotten he was there. Without answering, she peeled back Cordelia's upper lip. When she let it go, it relaxed slowly, then stiffened in an Elvis-like sneer.

She stepped back in absolute terror, her breath expelled in a frosty cloud. The front teeth—the *glamor teeth*, her dentist called them—were perfectly normal.

But Cordelia's molars were as sharp as razors.

7

I T WAS LEANNE who suggested their next move. In the two-and-a-half days between late Tuesday night and their Friday evening deadline, the Taymors gave as much time as they could spare to finding out who the large man was, where he lived, how he spent his days, and with whom, if anyone, he had relationships.

As it happened, Richard Holland ran a carpentry shop on the south end of town. Leanne had almost contracted him to do work on La Costina's interior, back when it was still a dream on the horizon, but Dutch's company had rescinded their bid at the last minute without explanation. She had only spoken to him over the phone, or she surely would have recognized him. Though her recall of faces wasn't quite as finely tuned as her husband's, there was no mistaking a man of his size and stature.

So while Jim took care of business at the restaurant, Leanne followed Richard Holland from the carpentry shop to his home, a smart little split-level on the east side, close to the old mill. She drove the sedan, so as not to arouse suspicion. If he'd looked out his window and seen the Suburban, he would have gone out to investigate. She couldn't chance that.

As the sun sank in the west, Dutch's home darkened along with the sky. He didn't turn on any inside lights, even after the streetlamps came on overhead, and Leanne began to think he'd slipped out unnoticed through the backdoor, or worse, that he'd seen her parked out front, recognized her from the restaurant, and was presently slinking around back to pounce on her, to use those unusually sharp molars to strip the flesh and gristle right off her shivering bones.

Leanne thought of those pandas, who had the equipment and refused to use it. Though Dutch had told Jim they were against the consumption of what he'd called "living meat," did she believe they would not they lash out, if cornered? There was no doubt in her mind. Even a rat is smart enough to attack when afforded no other option.

Still she waited, as Jim had waited, in a different car in a different part of town, both of them choked by the very same fear.

It was perhaps an hour later—the same radio voices droning on and on about President Obama's military might—when the front door opened and a great shadow emerged. He didn't need to duck; he'd retro-fitted the otherwise small house to be giant-proof.

Instead of heading for his car as she'd hoped he would, Dutch turned and crossed the street, taking up on the sidewalk and lumbering like an ogre *right past her car*. She ducked, cold terror flooding her insides, turning them to acid, certain he had seen her, *would* see her. She waited for the knock of his meaty fist on the window.

Or the shattering of glass.

But the monster that was Richard Holland passed by without inci-dent, leaving Leanne, when she'd finally caught her breath, with three options as she saw it. Following by car would attract too much atten-tion, not to mention the trouble she might run into if Dutch slipped down an alley or into a back lot, as seemed to be his custom. She'd be less likely to be spotted if she followed by foot, but she'd worn heels (*Stupid girl!* she cursed herself), so she'd have to do it barefoot.

The third option, which she gave short shrift, was to give up: to head back to the restaurant and tell Jim she was through; to gather up the money and await their back alley meeting with bated breath (though not *baited*, as Cordelia's had been), hoping that first $15,000 would also be the last.

The thought of those glimmering eyes, those pointed teeth... *all the better to eat you with, my dear...* These images arose in her mind, as clear as the dried-out strawberry air freshener swaying from the rearview, as her own harrowed reflection staring back at her from the mirror, as the dulled gold wedding band and the permanent indent it had made on her finger.

Lying awake the night of the murder (Leanne began thinking of it more as an *extermination*; it gave the death a more humane slant in her mind, much like using the warfarin had for Jim), the idea of turning her husband in had grown awfully tempting. With the key to the old basement walk-in on the bedside table, within her view, and Jim snoring contentedly beside her, the thought of him locked away safely behind bars—this man she'd lain beside for 26 good years, who had turned out to be a cold-blooded killer, or so she'd considered it at the time—began to feel like the only sane decision, the *right* decision.

The moment she realized this, she'd gotten up, made her side of the bed, and started cleaning. It wouldn't do to have a filthy house when the police showed up, let alone those newspeople with their immaculate hairdos, and their hot lights and cameras that could pick out every spot of grime and dust-bunny in brilliant high-definition.

(These were thoughts a wife should spare her husband, yet later on, Leanne Taymor spoke them. In front of me, and in front of Gin. In front of God too, I suppose.)

She hadn't made up her mind entirely about sparing Jim until she was sitting outside the Holland Woodwork & Joinery. She'd been watching the large man through the big front windows as he glad-handed clients and pored over blueprints with employees, all the while smiling that toothy, hooded-eye smile. At just past noon, she tucked into the Hammental sandwich she'd made that morning, consisting of maple-glazed ham, Emmental cheese, lettuce, tomato, Dijon mustard and a few sprigs of dill. Over time, it had become a favorite, but now it occurred to her she hadn't made one in quite some time. Not until that morning.

She remembered the first time she'd made this sandwich—two of them, actually: one for herself, and one for Jim. Back then she had been Leanne Wexler, and Jim had been a boy she'd seen around campus every so often, with his few friends or by himself on his way to class. She'd smiled at him in the hall once, and he'd turned away shyly, blood rising in his neck all the way to his fluffy, tawny sideburns. After that day she'd decided the next time she saw him, she would strike up a conversation herself.

She couldn't remember exactly what they'd talked about. Their talk had been brief, she remembered that much. He'd been sitting on one of the stone benches in The Quad, in front of Jesse Hall and the four columns left over from the old Academic Hall that had burned to the ground in the early '80s. He was eating a Big Mac and flipping through a thick geology text, something with the incomprehensible name *Quantitative Seismology: Theory and Methods Volume II.*

Leanne had sat down beside him. He'd pretended not to notice her until she'd leaned in between his eyes and the dense text and said, "As an English major, I have to say, I find your taste in literature deplorable." He grinned, still not daring to meet her eyes. "Although any guy interested in making the earth move is okay by me."

His cheeks had flushed with color at this. The rest of the conversation had been rushed, following the nervous pace of a young man who hadn't spoken to many girls. He asked her out, more as a reflex than at his own behest. The details were nailed down, a few delicate innuendos made, and Jim was up on his feet with his giant book and ugly yellow Styrofoam sandwich package, ostensibly heading off toward his next class.

They picnicked at Stevens Lake on Saturday, walking the trails and feeding the ducks. She'd filled a thermos with sparkling wine and they'd drunk it out of paper Dixie cups: Jim sipping, Leanne taking healthy gulps, enjoying the feel of the bubbles filling her mouth and prickling down to her belly. Despite the blanket Leanne had brought to sit on, Jim held a napkin under his sandwich—which he'd named "Hammental"—while he ate. At the time, she thought it was just about the most absurdly adorable thing she'd ever seen. He complimented her sandwich-making skills, and when she joked "All that's missing is the special sauce and a sesame seed bun," he'd laughed so hard champagne spurted from his nose.

After lunch, heading back to Jim's car (he drove a Plymouth Acclaim back then, its wheel wells growing so much rust the once-white rocker panels had turned a deep brown), he had stepped back suddenly, startled. At his feet, a baby bird lay shivering and wet in the grass. From the branches of a redbud, its sweet, wild-smelling purple canopy shading them from the sun, came the frantic squawks and chirps of its family.

"Poor little guy," Leanne said, and continued on, certain the mother would fly down to pluck it from the ground to deposit it safely back in the nest.

"We can't just leave it."

Leanne turned back, saw Jim looking down at the poor thing, and felt her heart swell with affection. Before she could say anything—about fleas, about the Avian flu she'd heard them describe on the news just lately, about the poor thing's *mother*—Jim scooped it up from the grass and tucked it into the pocket of his surfer hoodie.

Mama Bird immediately went wild, swooping down from her high branch with a violent chirrup and dive-bombing Jim's head like a kamikaze pilot. Jim paid it no mind except to duck out of its way as he pulled himself up into the low branches of the redbud tree. Petals fell around Leanne in a violet snowstorm. She stood below him, laughing fretfully, praying for his safety. With perfect mental clarity, she saw the image of Jim laid out on a hospital gurney, the baby bird a squashed mess of blood and tiny broken bones in his pocket.

Over the edge of the nest, the hatchlings stretched their little orange beaks to Jim, as if he were their mother returning with a worm. He placed their sister back among them, and beamed a big pleased smile down at Leanne, a job well done.

"Now get your butt down here," she said. She'd been about to call him "hero" when Mama Bird swooped in and struck the base of his skull with her beak. The sound was like a baseball dinged into the crowd. He fell.

A moment later, Jim was lying on his back at the base of the tree, legs in the air, laughing at the ridiculousness of it all.

Get a good look, Leanne, she'd told herself, before rushing over to help him to his feet. *That's the man you're going to marry.*

She laughed now, remembering it. She must have had the memory at the back of her mind while making her lunch that morning. And since she'd been thinking only of what Jim had done the night before, and the key he'd given her, putting his life in her hands, she thought she must have made her decision without even being consciously aware of it. The sandwich was her answer. Jim's Hammental.

And speaking of food, not once did she see big Dutch Holland eat something, not even sitting alone in his office. She supposed he could have been on a diet, considering his size. But as the afternoon went on, and Leanne grew hungry yet again, she was seized by the certainty Dutch was saving his appetite for the delicacies of the evening. The moment this idea occurred to her, she knew she could no longer share the world with *things* like Richard Holland, inhuman creatures wearing human skin like children wore costumes on Hallowe'en. She understood then that Jim had done right by poisoning Cordelia Moone.

By *exterminating* her.

Knowing what they knew, there could be no turning back. Not for Leanne, and not for Jim.

Not ever.

8

I FEEL I should backtrack a tad here. Remember me? Why would you? I am the nameless narrator whose voice you have likely been imagining all wrong: a folksy yet slightly prissy tone, due to my profession, my age bracket, my background. I have never offered my name, just my wife's—though I suppose the sharper among you could deduce, given what you already know about the Taymor Murders, who I am: Retired accountant, mid-to-late 50s, fiscal Republican (during the Bush Jr. administration, this was often difficult to admit), husband of Virginia, father of Jessa and Timothy, next-door neighbor to Jim and Leanne Taymor. The sharper among you might also have deduced I could easily have "changed the names to protect the innocent," as the true crime shows claim. It might be of interest to the ghoulish types who need to know every morbid, minuscule detail surrounding a murder case that I enjoy puzzle books and have a mole on my right ass-cheek that looks somewhat like the state of Florida. The journalists have left these last two details out, but I'm sure, had they known, it would be household news. *Neighbor of convicted Frugaltarian Killers has a mole on his buttock! More at eleven.* That sort of thing.

I've said I was there during the time of the murders, but the truth is,

I both was and wasn't. Gin and I had troubles of our own to deal with: Jessa, our youngest, was in and out of the hospital, for symptoms which seemed at the time to be related to multiple sclerosis. It wasn't, thank God, but it *was* quite a scare, and Jessa had almost lost her entire first year of college over it (we had her in our early-40s, if you're wondering about the age-discrepancy, an accident but a blessing). She managed to make up some credits here and there, but I was less troubled by her missing classes, or even by those bewildering symptoms: chronic headaches, oversensitivity to light, confusion, and spastic muscle movements which felt to her as if she no longer owned her own body—all of which seemed to dissipate in a little over two to three weeks. What worried me most was the thought of my little angel passing away before me. This was the thought which caused most of those sleepless nights the week of the murders, as I'm sure you can imagine.

By June, when she came back home for the summer, the scare had mostly passed. When Gin and I picked her up from the bus depot, she wore a black t-shirt, cut off above her navel, MEAT IS MURDER printed in blood-streaked letters over her chest. She fairly reeked of marijuana. Gin, who had never smoked it in her life (had perhaps never even *seen* it being smoked), had commented on Jessa's "nice perfume," and I caught a glimmer of a smirk in our daughter's eyes in the rearview.

If it is difficult for any man to truly know what lurks inside the mind of a teenaged girl, it is even more true when the girl is the man's daughter—and that goes double if said father is edging toward sixty, I suspect. I did my best to cut her slack, in light of her recent health scare, but I found it hard not to lose my patience in those few months between semesters. She was moody that summer, all too often snarky with her mother. She wouldn't eat much of what we put in front of her, preferring instead to get food with her high school friends. I kept my suspicions, that one or more of her professors had been filling her head full of liberal propaganda, to myself. A child's mind is easy prey, even a child of college age. Give them a free beer cooler, promise them no payments, tell them what they want to hear, and they'll be yours to mold.

Jessa was far from the perfect little girl I remembered, but *she was alive*. I was grateful for that much, at least.

And like they say after those oh-so important news breaks, which Jim and Leanne have starred in many a time: *We now return to our regularly scheduled program...*

9

PARKED OUT FRONT of Richard Holland's house, Leanne slipped out of her heels and left them on the driver's seat. She stepped out, eyeballing the man's large shadow as it turned the corner onto Flint Street, where it disappeared behind a hedge.

Those first few steps were the worst. Barefoot, it felt like she stepped on every single stone and twig and upturned bottle cap between her sedan and the corner, struggling not to cry out as they bit into her heels, the calloused pads, cursing herself silently every step of the way.

From Flint Street, the large man turned onto Genoa. Where the two streets come together, the Elementary School stands behind a chain-link fence. Both Jessa and Tim went to that school, ten years apart. That night Leanne paid no mind to the SLOW CHILDREN sign, which had always caused her distress; what she wouldn't have given to have been blessed with *any* child, even a slow one. Her thoughts were on the chase; the pain in each step reminded her of the potential cost if she lost sight of Richard Holland. And by the time she had hobbled and limped past the schoolyard, she'd gotten used to the pain anyway. The soles of her feet would be bloody and raw when she finally got back to the car, worse even than the skin surrounding Dutch's fingernails. But the *gains*—the gains of this venture could prove to be very fruitful indeed.

From Genoa Avenue to Devlin, past her friend Paulette Chamblee's four-star B&B overlooking a woody ravine. From Devlin to Sammon. On Sammon, which dead-ended at the edge of those same woods (*Lord help me if he goes in there*), the large man strode heavily down the center of the potholed road to the foot of the Schultz house, where he stood on its sagging porch for a long moment, until the crooked front door swung inward onto darkness, and he ducked inside.

Anyone born or at least raised in Knee High should be quite familiar with the Schultz house and its sinister aura. To call it an *eyesore* would be too kind. It was a *blight*, and had been, for much longer than the Taymors were my neighbors. With wallboards as gray as ash, the crumbled slate-shingle roof sagging in the middle, its porch nothing but a broken heap of old lumber, its staircase sunken, its cobblestone walk and front yard (to call it a *yard* was flattery) a wilderness of jimson and hogweed and wild ficus, the Schultz house had been known by children to be haunted, long before Tim and Jessa had attended Knee High Elementary.

Old Lady Schultz had been rumored by kids to be a witch. If you'd ever seen her out there on her porch, you might have been hard-pressed to contest it. In her youth, she'd been a librarian—Lord knows why; it was obvious she loathed children. Perhaps she'd found sadistic pleasure in shushing them, in squeezing every last nickel of their allowances out of them for their overdue books throughout the years.

I knew Old Lady Schultz, though when I was in school she'd been called Dotty, and Dotty Schultz had been just as mean in her twenties as she'd been in her decrepitude. When she finally kicked the bucket in the early aughts, you can bet there were cries of *Ding-dong, the witch is dead* from many a mouth.

It was thought that when she died her house would be demolished by the bank, but when news of her death arose, lo and behold, the rats crawled out from the woodwork! The rats in this case were long-lost relatives—"long-lost" meaning those relations who could not tolerate her when she was alive, and were only too happy to snatch her property (including about fifty acres of the woods behind and to the left of it) from her cold, dead hands.

Her great-nephew, as chance would have it, was a land developer. I have no clue if he'd held this job *before* laying claim to his great-aunt's property, but just three weeks after Dotty Schultz keeled over, a sign went up out front, in the same surreptitious manner as those MISSING posters had:

LAND RESERVED FOR FUTURE DEVELOPMENT

I suppose Great-Nephew Schultz suspected Knee High might be soon to expand, what with the new addition to the highway, perhaps incorporating with nearby towns across the Platte and finally, to the great city of Omaha. Commuters and retirees would need condos and townhouses, and what better place to put them than a quaint little valley town with low property taxes and little to no pretensions?

These days they call that sort of market speculation "hope value." Whatever young Mr. Schultz's hopes had been, the house (and sign) remained until the recession hit, and by then any hope of future value had sunk, along with the rest of the housing market. That the same sign stood for Leanne to hide behind some ten years later—albeit with the thoughtful addition of *BARACK SUCKS COCK* Sharpied across it on a diagonal by some semi-literate *artiste*—was a testament to the failures of economic recovery, debt ceiling be damned. One of Jim's **LOST DOG** posters was stapled haphazardly to the utility pole nearby, dampened by the other night's rain. As her eyes adjusted to the dark, Leanne made her numbed, barefoot approach and peered inside a darkened window.

They were cross-legged on the floor, amid stacks of yellowed—a slightly darker shade of gray in the gloaming—newspapers, all six of them just as naked as Jim had told her, though they lacked the crust of filth he'd mentioned. The night sky was just bright enough through the dead trees outside the Schultz house for her to make out their faces, and the horror of recognition widened her eyes.

There was Pete Wallin, who drove the resurfacer at the public ice-skating rink in the winter and, come spring, a big lawn tractor (though not as big as his Zamboni) at the fairgrounds on the other side of the woods. He was as skinny as a rake with his long, Ichabod Crane face, and every single rib visible in his hairless—save for a few stragglers around the nipples—chest. His spine stood out like alligator spikes.

She remembered the heavyset woman from the checkout counter at the Food 4 Less in Lincoln, mouthing numbers as she counted the food stamps of a customer ahead of Leanne. *Tara or Tina*, she thought, trying to conjure up a mental image of the woman's nametag, before realizing it would be worse if she knew her name. Bad enough she knew their faces, let alone their names.

The kid Jim had recognized belonged to George and Helena Lannegan. She thought his name was Kyle, and knew he was enrolled in the same school up the road that Tim and Jessa had attended. Neither parent was among the adults seated around him. He was a stray, it seemed, like the others—but *how*? If they truly were no longer human, as it appeared from everything she'd seen herself and all that Jim had told her, how could Kyle Lannegan be one of them if his parents weren't? She supposed it could have been a recessive gene or a mutation, like dwarf parents siring a child of normal height. Or—and the thought of this caused her to shudder uncontrollably—he could have been *changed*.

Richard Holland's head twitched suddenly on its tree trunk neck, his nostrils flaring in her direction. She ducked, certain he'd caught her scent. *Like a dog*, she thought. *Like my Rosco.* Fear and anger pumped volcanic adrenaline into her veins, her breath quickening. Surely they'd hear her, she thought, if they hadn't smelled her already. She waited for Dutch's thick fingers to snatch her up by her hair, or the scruff of her neck, and for a moment it felt as though they'd actually slipped along her spine. But it was only a moth.

Typically, the very sight of them gave her the charlies, as Jenny Meyer might have said. ("It's the dust," she explained to Gin and me during that long night spent around our kitchen table. "Why do they have to be so *dusty*?"). But crouched outside the decrepit Schultz house she merely watched the moth flutter awkwardly away, counting out Mississippis as she slowed her breath, waiting for the hand to fall on her neck.

At thirty-Mississippi, she steeled herself to chance a peek over the window ledge.

They remained sitting in their ragged circle, all heads turned toward the heavyset woman, who plunged her hands into what looked at first to be a hole in the floor. The woman's gut folded over her crotch, yet pubic hair was still evident in the folds at her hips. Her hands came up streaked with black, and the smell—earthy and musky and sour, the smell of death and rotting cheese—was strong enough to make Leanne's eyes sting. She swallowed an involuntary gag, but the hot innards stench had already imprinted itself on her olfactory bulbs. It was a smell she would likely compare to every other stench, from that day forward: *Sure, it stinks, but it's not as bad as the time...*

This filth was black as tar, and Tina/Tara smeared it onto the naked torsos and necks of the others. They scraped it from their skin with their palms, not to fling it away in disgust but to rub it on their faces and in their hair, the way someone might attempt to conserve the suds of a single dried-out sliver of soap in the shower.

The delight Leanne saw in their glimmering eyes spoke of sacrament. Whatever they were, human or animal or something in between, Cordelia's Frugaltarianism had merely been a cover for this undreamed of private-interest group or secret society, who met not in the library basement or the Legion Hall, but at an abandoned house on the edge of the woods in the dead of night, providing neither coffee nor donuts, but a liberal application of animal shit on their naked bodies.

Once they'd entirely covered themselves, they raised their arms to the rotted ceiling and bent at the hips, slapping their open palms into the excrement with a wet sound and raising their blackened palms again to the sky. They did this perhaps a dozen times, uttering soft, animal grunts with each elevation.

Finally, each of them shook out their limbs like some post-meditation ritual, and lay down to dry out on the bare boards. Their chests rose and fell rapidly, the panting of desert wolves. Leanne stayed at the window, and while she watched them sleep she began to formulate the first inklings of a plan.

If the body-paint and bowing were parts of a ritual, surely the sleeping was a part of it, too.

A lot of things could happen while a person slept—that much had already been proven by the men and women (and child) sleeping fitfully in the Schultz house, who had gone skulking unnoticed through the streets and alleys of Knee High for God knew how long, while the rest of us slept.

Well, Leanne was awake now. She thought she might never sleep again until this business was done, but she was wide awake.

Her blood froze. The boy, who'd been asleep only moments ago, had gotten up while she was thinking and had begun sniffing at the air, staring directly at the window where she was crouched. She was frozen in place, caught by that innocent, terrible stare, the eyes shimmering out from his shit-streaked face like stars in the void of space.

He sniffed.

Did he smell her?

The short woman beside the Lannegan boy stirred in her sleep.

How could he not *see* her?

Sniff-sniff-sniff. Sniff-sniff-snifffff.

Kyle Lannegan squinted out at the dim night, the light in his eyes closing to slits. Then he turned away from the window and sank back to the floor, curling up beside the short woman and planting a grimy thumb in his mouth.

10

EANNE REMAINED MOTIONLESS at the window a while longer, wondering why the boy hadn't seen her when he'd been looking her right in the eyes, or if he had seen her, why he hadn't awakened the others.

They were still sleeping when she walked back to Davis Street, where the car was parked. Once there she gave the agony in her feet a rest, lying across both front seats with her poor tootsies hanging out the driver door, cooling them in the night breeze. She would bathe them in ice water once she got home, but for now they had work to do on the pedals. It had been just over an hour since Richard Holland had left his house. Ten more minutes of strain couldn't possibly hurt them worse than they'd already been.

When Jim got home from the restaurant, she was asleep, sitting up on their plush recliner, her feet soaking in a basin of lukewarm water, pink with her blood.

He woke her gently. Still, she was startled. She wrapped her arms around his neck as if she were clinging to a life-preserver, and he carried her to bed. He dressed her feet in gauze and bandages and ointment. She tried once, in a sleep-muttering sort of way, to tell him her plan, but he shushed her. When he slipped into bed himself a few minutes later, she was breathing soft and slow and steady.

Jim flicked off the light.

11

"JEWISH LIGHTNING," HE said, skeptical.

They sat in the kitchen, sipping their morning coffees—fair trade coffee, I suspect. Leanne normally liked hers black, but she took a little cream and sugar today, the color just too similar to the grime she'd seen at the Schultz house. Even dumping out the wet grinds she'd gagged a little, thinking back.

"Jim," she said with a disapproving squint.

He let out an exasperated sigh. "We're talking about roasting people alive here, Leanne, and you're concerned about an ethnic slur?"

"Those *things* aren't people," she quickly reminded him. "Just tell me what you think."

What Jim thought was that it wouldn't work. The outcome was too uncertain, and the possibility it could blow up in their faces—both literally and figuratively—was far too high.

"First of all," he said, "we don't know if it's a daily event, this..." He shook his head, not knowing just what to call the thing she'd witnessed. "And even if it is, how can we be sure we'll get all of them in one shot?"

Leanne let her shoulders sag. He was right, and she knew it. Her idea had been to throw a Molotov cocktail through one of the windows (though what she'd called it was "one of those bottles filled with gas and a wick thingy on the end"—Jim had provided her with its name), hoping there was enough methane in the feces to act as an accelerant and engulf the whole group of them in flames.

Even if it were a surefire plan, the idea of burning people alive felt not just morally but physically repugnant, a whole lot worse than letting an old, oft-used ethnic slur slip (a forgivable sin, perhaps, given the circumstances, though the B'nai B'rith might disagree). Jim didn't voice the opinion. Having poisoned a woman just two nights prior, he was hardly in a position to judge.

Leanne was right about one thing, though: they had to take out the whole group at once, and before the "Dutch" wolf came knocking at their door. If not arson, though, then what? Chances were pretty slim the lot of them would return to La Costina's Dumpsters, which meant another good dose of rat poison was out of the question. Besides, there was hardly enough free space in the old downstairs freezer for Cordelia and Dutch, let alone the rest of their clan. And the likelihood that on a few days' notice, either he or Leanne could get their hands on a legitimate assault weapon—*a bazooka*, Jim thought with childlike excitement —was slim to none.

"What if we slipped in earlier in the day and splashed around some gasoline? Or should I be concerned about wasting gas in this economic climate?" Jim asked with a sly wink.

She ignored the joke and gave it thought. "No, they'd smell gasoline. But the stench of that—" She didn't want to say it. *I don't believe I've ever heard Leanne utter a cussword in the twenty-five years I've known her. I've heard* sugar *quite a bit, though, and not in the context of asking to borrow some.*

"*Shit*," Jim said for her, and she gave him a nasty squint again.

"It *smelled* like natural gas, under all the other icky smells."

"If we were to make it look like J—" Not wanting to incur her full wrath, he reconsidered the phrase. "—like an *insurance scam*, it should seem accidental. If the Schultz kid was going to burn it down, he'd want it to look like an act of God. Maybe I'm wrong, but I doubt there's been propane in that house since Old Lady Schultz shuffled off to that dusty old library in the sky."

"Everyone thinks that place is a flophouse," Leanne said. "If we put a hotplate upstairs, they'll just think some hobo left it with the gas on."

She was onto something, he thought, but she was missing a key element. "They'd smell *us*, though. Even if they didn't notice the propane, they'd smell *us*. You said you thought they'd smelled you from *outside*. Cordelia smelled me from fifteen feet away. And I'm pretty sure animals can smell if a predator's been inside their den."

Leanne thought for a moment, rubbing absently at the bandages on the sole of a bare foot. "If they were camouflaging themselves with the—"

"Shit."

This time she dismissed him. He'd made a guess earlier that if Dutch and the others covered themselves in the eye-watering stench, they could move among whatever scavenger the excrement belonged to—he'd said skunk, though he supposed it could just as easily have been raccoon, wolf... or *cougar*. Aggressive mimicry, like what Cordelia had done with the cat, lulling it into a sense of security before tearing it to shreds. The dark color would also allow them to slip through the night, virtually unnoticed by human eyes.

She didn't want to consider it, but the idea was there for the picking. "What if we used their own tactic against them?"

"You mean...?"

She nodded.

"We don't even know if that's why they do it," he said. "It could be like you said, just a ritual."

"But if it *isn't*..."

"I'm not rubbing shit on myself, Leanne." Jim gave her a look of suspicion. "And you're not exactly volunteering, are you?"

"We've only got one shot at this, Jim," she said. "Don't you think we should do whatever it takes to get it done? And that means one of us has to go inside that house, and plant the propane tank. If they smell it, or *us*, then it's over. We'll pay the giant his toll and pray he doesn't get greedy for more."

Jim thought for a long moment, aware she was using the same not-so-subtle coaxing technique she'd employed when she had convinced him to quit his well-paying job and open an Italian restaurant in his rural hometown. She'd been right then, and she was right now.

Somewhere, a dog barked. And somewhere else, six people who weren't really people went about their lives in plain sight. Whether they were alien body snatchers or were-creatures or cultists didn't matter.

What mattered was what they *weren't*.

"Fine," he said. "I'll do it."

12

LEANNE CALLED THE wild animal sanctuary out on the county road Thursday morning, inquiring about the possible hazards of wild-animal manure. "For fertilizer," she explained, saying she'd hoped to use something local and sustainable, preferably not farm waste.

The woman on the phone advised against it. "Intestinal worms, rabies, you name it," she said. "Steer clear of raccoon latrines, especially, if you can help it. You'll be able to tell what kind of dung it is from the smell. Raccoon is probably the worst-smelling of all." There was a cheerful note to her voice when she added, "If it's unavoidable, we'd be glad to send someone out to disinfect your property. All proceeds go towards preservation and maintaining the sanctuary—"

Leanne hung up on the sales pitch. They wouldn't provide her with material goods, but they'd made up for it with information. Handling raccoon feces without protection was dangerous (and it was surely raccoon feces they wanted—what she'd smelled could only have been the foulest, worse even than the elephant exhibit at the Kansas City Zoo). The risk of infection too great. They'd need some sort of protective gear, and she knew exactly where to find it.

The crisscrossed bars in the video store window upset her almost as much as those SLOW CHILDREN signs did as she passed by. Of all the failing businesses their success had resuscitated, they could do nothing for Big Top Video. Robert "Red" Ritter had sold what he could in a fire sale (the Schultz house would never get the luxury, but it would burn, all right—you bet it would), and left town. Off to greener pastures, Leanne dared to hope, though I happen to know the authorities found Red dead in a small, virtually barren apartment in Lincoln barely a year after Big Top folded its tents. *Died suddenly*, the obits said, which I also happen to know is the polite term for suicide.

The bell above the door to the army-navy store dinged as she stepped in. *Ask not for whom the bells tolls*, Leanne thought, remembering the phrase from her English Lit. days, as recited by that professor who'd once asked her on a date. She had declined with some trepidation, hoping it wouldn't affect her grade, and happy when it hadn't.

"Be there in a minute," the proprietor called from the back. Funny how in all the years she'd had her business beside Knee High Surplus she'd never once seen its owner, just that beat-up maroon Volvo parked out front (of all possible automobile makers he'd gone with the Swedes, one of only a handful of neutral nations during WW-Eye-Eye), from sunrise to well beyond sunset with bullet-hole stickers on its rear window beside a Garfield suction toy, a wooden bead seat cover on the driver's side, and a back seat full of storage boxes.

Jim had suspected the man lived out of that car, and had considered having it towed several times. But Leanne had ixnayed the idea. "If he *is* living in that car," she'd said, "you'd be towing away a man's home. Haven't there been enough foreclosures around here, without the two of us adding to it?"

Inside were articulated mannequins wearing gas masks, camouflage and Kraut pickle-helmets. Military regalia hung from the walls, the shelves lined with folded uniforms, green, desert beige and orange. Though most of the items in the store had been used for violence at one point or another, the manner in which they were placed suggested collectible, not arsenal. The overall atmosphere was of dust and antiquity.

In the center of the room was a long table filled with swords and weaponry of the Orient, with grenades and mortars and oiled black

Lugers, and long rifles with dulled bayonets. Leanne suspected—she *hoped*—the explosives were no longer usable, although if they were live, it would make the task at hand a whole lot easier.

A short man with cropped gray hair and deep circles under his eyes materialized from the gloom in the back. He wore none of the green and brown both Jim and Leanne had expected, but a pristine white tracksuit with black stripes, and dock shoes on his sockless feet, though there is no water nearby and Memorial Day was still a few weeks away.

"Howdy, neighbor," he said.

"How—?" she started to say.

He smiled affably. "Just because we've never met, doesn't mean I don't know who you are. Buddy Ames," he said, sticking a hand out over the glass counter filled with sharp, shiny knives. He wore a fresh scent like Ivory soap, a pleasant counterpoint to the shop's musty odor.

"Nice to meet you, Mr. Ames."

"Buddy's fine. We're neighbors, after all."

Leanne nodded and smiled, knocked for a loop. She felt a twinge of guilt for thinking this man had been sleeping in his car. He was clearly doing fine or, at least, had regular access to a shower and a washing machine.

"What can I do you for, Leanne? You don't strike me as the Soldier of Fortune type, nor a collector, for that matter. So I presume you're looking for a gift of sorts." He smiled then—a crooked smile that set her immediately at ease and got her mind working again.

"Actually, I'm looking for protective clothing. We've got a bit of a raccoon problem at the house, and Jim, my husband, he's dead-set on cleaning it himself. We'd really rather not call an exterminator. Those chemical cleaners..." She shrugged, and Buddy Ames smiled again.

"Yup, can't say I blame you there. I suppose if you'll be handling the waste yourself you'll need something with a little more protection than coveralls and a dust mask, am I right?"

"Preferably. The animal sanctuary—"

"The chipmunk zoo," he offered.

"That's the place. They said there's a high chance of contamination?"

"And you're hoping I've got a hazmat suit among my wares."

Leanne smiled and nodded again. Such a shrewd businessman should have been selling something of value, she thought. Gold, or cell phones.

"Well, Leanne, it would seem you're in luck. I've just gotten a new shipment, and wouldn't you know it? It contains not one but two used Level B Tyveks, a large and a small. His and hers, you might say."

"That *is* lucky."

"Indeed." He fixed her with his shrewd gaze. "But I've got a feeling you'll need a lot more than luck with what you and your husband have in mind."

"Excuse me?"

"Please," he said, holding up a small, manicured hand. "We're neighbors."

"Meaning what, exactly?"

"Meaning they're *my* Dumpsters, too. And I know all about our... " He made quotes in the air: "...*visitors*."

13

LEANNE STOOD WITH Buddy Ames as he smoked his thin brown cigarette, surveying the small lot behind their businesses where Cordelia Moone had dined on Ms. Kitty and had breathed her last the following night. They'd gone through the large back room where it seemed Buddy slept, ate and bathed in a small military-style quarters, replete with bunk, hotplate and a shower, doubling as a breakfast nook when the curtain was thrown back and the white plastic table was raised on its hinges.

"I first saw them two years ago," Buddy said, "about the time the lurker next door skipped town." Next door meant Big Top Video; the "lurker" was Red (now deceased) Ritter.

"*Two years?*" Leanne said. "And you never told anyone?"

He favored her with a look through the haze of smoke. "What would I have said? 'Hey there, neighbors. Property taxes sure are taking a bite this year. Oh, and did you happen to notice the human Rodentia in our Dumpsters?'"

This surprised a laugh out of her. "I suppose you're right. I wouldn't have believed it myself if I didn't see it with my own eyes."

"And I wouldn't have had the guts to do what your husband did, though I've thought about it quite a bit."

"You—? You're the one who..."

Buddy blew out a cloud of smoke and looked her over. "I suppose he told you about the cat."

Leanne managed a sickly nod. "Was that the first animal you left out there for them? For bait?"

"Not bait." He gave her another of his shrewd glances. "And to answer your query, I didn't leave your... what was his name?"

"Rosco," she said, nearly choking it out.

"I did not leave your Rosco out for those monsters, I assure you."

She let out a breath of relief.

"That's not to say he isn't dead. Your husband's posters were one of the reasons I caught Ms. Kitty and left her for them."

Leanne didn't follow.

"I'm sure you've noticed the inflated amount of missing pets this past year. Rumor has it there's a cougar loose in the area." He lowered his head, looking up at her through the canopy of his eyebrows. "I assure you, Mrs. Taymor, as I believe your husband may have gathered when Cordelia Moone gobbled up Garfield's little sister, these missing pets are not the victims of a mountain lion."

"She *ate them all*?"

"Not *just* her, but yes. That's my belief. I left Ms. Kitty there because I had to be sure. Right now, they're predominantly scavengers. *Right now*. But it won't be long believe me, before meat is on the menu again. Your husband saw what Cordelia Moone did to that cat. That wasn't the first animal I'd left for her, either. I had to *know* before I agitated the nest. I had to be sure. And, Mrs. Taymor, I am absolutely certain now."

"Leanne," she said, distractedly, almost dreamily. "Buddy... you've known about these things for two years, and what? Sat back and waited for them to do something awful like this?" She shook her head, swimming with questions. "I just can't imagine living with that knowledge for so long, and not *doing* anything about it."

"That's why you're on their bad side, and I'm not even on their radar. I saw the big one the other night—"

"Richard Holland," Leanne said.

He exhaled a plume of smoke in surprise. "As in Holland Woodwork?"

"That's him. I followed him to the Schultz place—the old house on Sammon Circle?"

He nodded. "I know it."

"They were all there. I even *knew* some of them."

He looked at her in amazement and admiration. "You must have gotten close enough to touch them," he said. "Or for them to touch you."

Leanne shivered, picturing Kyle Lannegan's cold, blank stare through the window.

"And now you think you can get rid of them," he said. She turned away from his eyes, which gleamed with excitement. It was too grisly, all of this, and Buddy Ames's enthusiasm for this business was all too ghoulish. "Seven at one blow."

"Six," she corrected.

"Of course," he said, "now that Ms. Moone is on ice."

She was dumbfounded, unable to respond.

"I watched the whole thing as it happened," he explained, pointing to the eaves, where a small but obvious camera pointed toward the bins. "Smile. You're on *Candid Camera*."

That shiver ran up her spine again. How could she have missed *that*? Buddy Ames knew so much, but how much longer would he keep their secret? *Two years, Leanne,* she reminded herself. *You can see he's grateful. Good riddance to bad rubbish pickers.*

"Trouble is," he said, "you wipe out this hive, and another one's going to creep in and take its place."

"*Another one?* What do you mean? There are *more* of these things?"

"'Fraid so. The ones you followed to their home away from home, you might call them the Knee High Chapter."

Leanne shook her head, unable to believe the situation was so entirely hopeless.

"Or maybe," he said, that hopeful twinkle in his eyes again, "maybe you'll scare the livin' bejesus out of them. Let them know Knee High is not a lurker-friendly town."

"That's twice you've said that: lurker."

"What they call them," Buddy said with a nod. "On the internet. Whole chatrooms are devoted to 'em, alongside the *chupacabra* and

Bigfoot. They also call them coonies, though I don't use the term. Don't like the connotations."

It occurred to her that *lurker* was the perfect name for them: not that they crept, as such, though they did move on both hands and feet. But there was no doubting they lurked within the shadows, existing unobserved by society at large, their true nature concealed behind a human guise.

"Big Top Ritter was one of them, I'm almost certain of it. Do you remember, a little over two years ago, when that kid went missing? Danny... what was his name?"

"Danny Reynolds," Leanne said, remembering the Amber Alert all too clearly, the photo of the little blond-haired boy with glasses that had later shown up on the sides of milk cartons. "Nine years old. Last seen wearing a green parka and a red backpack." She considered what he was saying. "You don't think...?"

"There was a fight between Ritter and Ms. Moone, outside his shop one night shortly after the kid went missing. I heard her say something about 'that boy,' and the spooky way she'd said it, I knew right away Danny was the boy she meant. Big Top denied it, of course, but she kept at him. Then, just when it looked like it was just about to devolve into fisticuffs, they started screeching at each other."

"You're saying our former neighbor killed and ate that little boy?" she said. "And you saw Cordelia Moone confront him about it. How could I have missed all this?"

"You've got a successful business to run," Buddy said. "Meanwhile, I've got nothing but time. And free time, I'm sure you'll agree, is a building block of obsession."

14

I 'M GOING TO cut to the chase here, because this story is running a bit longer than I'd intended; it would seem I'm obsessing a bit myself. What I said about most of this being true—well, much of the preceding conversation was how I *imagine* it must have gone, based on what Leanne later told me. I hope you'll excuse the fiction. While I doubt it's true what they say about everyone having a novel in them, it would seem I've got one lurking inside me dying to get out. Though, as you've likely noticed, Steinbeck I am not.

Too much free time, I suppose. If it were April, you'd be getting the abridged version, and so much the better for it.

Buddy Ames was not available to corroborate their story, nor his part in progressing it along, when the authorities went by his shop. The morning after the Schultz house burned down—along with half the woods behind it, and the fairground's gazebo—his Volvo was no longer parked out front of Knee High Surplus, the store and all of its stock having been left abandoned. He was not, as Red before him, found dead in a barren apartment in Lincoln, NE. So far as I know, he was never found.

And when you consider the story Jim and Leanne had to peddle, who could blame him for running?

15

ACCORDING TO BUDDY (via Jim and Leanne, a broken telephone of pseudoscientific mumbo-jumbo), these things he called "lurkers" had once been hunters, just as Jim had suspected, but had given it up in favor of scavenging, around the turn of the last century. According to American frontier folklore (which you can easily find on the internet, as I have), it was decided—by some Lurker High Council, I presume, though the thought of it gives me shivers—that the consumption of human beings had become increasingly hazardous to their freedom, and with tuberculosis, cholera, influenza and typhus spreading like the legs of some diseased whore, it was hazardous to their health as well.

And so, sometime between 1890 and 1920, the lurkers had stopped eating meat.

Mostly.

There were still the odd transgressions, of course. Albert Fish, the Werewolf of Wysteria, had claimed he'd eaten close to 100 children. The ritualistic fashion in which he'd carved up his young victims was the work of a truly grotesque gourmand; he did not just enjoy his food, he *loved* it. "I never ate any roast turkey that tasted half as good as his fat little behind" was how he described the meal he'd made of one child. (I'd advise you not to look up the rest of his confessions. If you have any vestige of a soul, it would turn your stomach, as it did mine.)

Fish, *aka* the Brooklyn Vampire, *aka* the Gray Man, is not only one of America's first serial killers, he is considered by some to be the first known *lurker*, though he had never identified himself as such. I imagine they don't call themselves lurkers, anyhow. Likely, it's a pejorative term to them.

Before you ask, the Donner party was mentioned by at least two "experts" on the subject of lurker mythology. Likewise with Jeffery Dahmer, the so-called Master Butcher of Rotenburg, and the Miami Zombie (who'd attacked a man and eaten pieces of his face while under the influence of marijuana, and not "bath salts" as earlier reports had stated, and said man had still been quite alive). Some halfwit suggested Hannibal Lecter be added to the list, and was swiftly rebuked, proving the line between fiction and reality was at least somewhat intact among this gathering of internet delusionals.

Not all cannibals are lurkers, they say, but all lurkers are cannibals by nature. Big Top Video owner Robert Ritter proved that, if you believed Buddy Ames's suspicions. Given the opportunity, a lurker would eat your child, your mother, your *grandparents*—it was only by choice that they did not feed on us, as Jim had also suspected, and decisions, like leftovers, could be all too easily discarded. Just think of the last New Year's resolution you made, and you'll know what I mean. Not a day passes when I don't wish I could rescind the choice I made to trade in the hard stuff for the non-alcoholic beverage in my hand, as my rocker rocks and the sun sinks beyond the houses opposite. Particularly on those nights I think I've mentioned, with dark clouds gathering on the eastern horizon—east, toward where the Schultz house stood before Jim and Leanne Taymor razed it to the ground.

I suspect Leanne might feel the same about the decision she'd made to follow Jim from the frying pan into the fire, so to speak.

Many of the rumored victims of the Mexican *chupacabra* (roughly translated, it means "goat-sucker") are thought instead to be the work of the lurkers. When a few goats in a field lay disemboweled, most people —*sane* people—think wolf, or cougar. These people get out their torches and pitchforks and hunt down the monster.

The Algonquin Indian *wendigo*, if you're familiar with the legend, is thought to be the basis of lurker lore, or the first known example. These ghouls are eternally ravenous, no matter how much they eat. It is this bottomless hunger which drives them to eat humans. The Algonquins believe humans themselves become *wendigos*, should the flesh of their fellow man be consumed. In Canada, prior to his arrest in 1906, a shaman called Jack Fiddler put fourteen supposed *wendigos* to death. In some cases, it is said, the afflicted tribesmen turned themselves in to be euthanized.

Fourteen murders... and in his little community, Jack Fiddler was *celebrated*. Fiddler committed suicide before standing trial, for the record; just as Robert "Red" Ritter would, a little over ninety years later, for reasons unknown—unless you believed Buddy Ames. *Fourteen*. That's twice as many lurker exterminations as Jim and Leanne were soon to lay claim to, and in Knee High, as everywhere else, they would be *reviled*.

Rightly so, I have to say. Rightly so.

16

JIM COULD SMELL their shit right through his mask.

The stench was worse than the time he'd found his old dog Rufus wriggling on his back in the tall grass behind his old house. The Golden Retriever had positively *reeked*, worse than any animal had a right to. The dead coon Rufus had been rubbing his fur in, streaking himself with its scent, lay frozen among the gnarled roots of their giant oak, fangs bared and paws curled into claws. Its guts lay coiled beside it, red as raspberry jam. Ants climbed the sticky, glistening mountain for treasures to bring back to their Queen. There were more ants trudging in the brown, putrid ribbons of raccoon scat and gore in Rufus's fur.

Jim's father had given Rufus a good couple of swats with a rolled-up copy of the biweekly *Knee High Whistler*, and his mother had bathed the miserable mutt in V8. Despite the old wives' remedy, Rufus had carried on stinking for almost a week. Kids held their noses and made exaggerated retching sounds as he followed Jimmy to the school bus, no matter how hard he'd tried to send the dog back to the house.

Along with the two Tyvek suits and SCBA masks she bought, Buddy sold Leanne a flare gun at a good discount. I would have approved, even though I would not have approved of its intended use. Buddy also happened to have been storing up a good deal of thermite in the fallout shelter he'd created under his living quarters, enough thermite to take down a skyscraper, he'd told Leanne. The twinkle had returned to Buddy's eyes when he told her that, as if this might be first-hand knowledge.

The creek where Jim and Leanne stood, in the woods between the Schultz house and the fairgrounds, has no name. So far as I know, it never has, though during a particularly wet spring or fall it sometimes rises just about high enough to be considered a river. It is a distributary of the Missouri, I believe, perhaps the Platte. As a child I played near its banks with various groups of friends, most of whom have either moved away or passed on since. Those who are still with us, physically as well as in spirit, I see on occasion. A few of them live—if you want to call it *living*—at the seniors' home up on the hill, what Gin likes to call the Cripple Castle. We share a nod or a wave, but rarely do we speak. Back then, we'd had nothing but the exuberant curiosity of youth in common, though when you're a kid that seems like enough. Old age isn't quite the grand unifier childhood is, despite what the Castle's advertisements in the *Whistler* would like you to think.

"I wish I'd thought to bring Vaporub," Jim remarked as he zipped himself into the protective gear. Raccoons are a peculiar animal, obsessive about touch, and about washing their food before they dine. Conversely, they have no misgivings about shitting where they eat. Leanne stood back where the woods cleared for the creek, holding her nose as Jim shoveled scat into the red plastic bucket he used to wash the cars. He scooped up a shovelful of clear, cool water into the bucket next. Then he shook in a good amount of thermite from an emptied paint can. It rose in a gray-black cloud.

"Careful," Leanne said with a wince. She knew it wasn't necessary; Buddy Ames had assured her it was safe until it was ignited—and then *stand back, Jack!*—but she'd always felt it was best to err on the side of caution.

Jim ignored the warning, using a long branch to stir up the filth into a rich, black paste, indistinguishable from what Leanne had seen the lurkers smear onto their skin. As soon as she'd come within whiffing distance of the latrine, she'd been certain it was the same smell from the

Schultz house, though it seemed to Jim she would have said just about anything to step clear of its powerful stench.

"Get the bags ready?" he said over his shoulder, picking up the bucket full of lethal sludge. Leanne shook them out, gagging when he approached. "That's not the first time I've had that effect on a woman," he joked, though it was a pretty lame attempt at levity. Her reaction was somewhere between a laugh and a groan.

He lowered the stinking bucket into the doubled-up trash bags, then took the bundle from Leanne. She ran off to the trees immediately. The bran muffin and coffee she'd had that morning—more cream and sugar today—came up and splashed against the mossy earth, a few rebound droplets spattering her sneakers.

Jim tied the bags and set them down. "You okay?" he said. "I'd hold your hair, but my grip is like a lobster's with these gloves."

Leanne wiped her lips with the back of her hand. "I'll be fine." She rose from the bushes and regarded him with a probing look. "Jim... can we do this? I mean *really* do this?"

"It was your idea," he reminded her.

"Well," she said, "it looked good on paper."

Jim smiled wanly. As their pet phrase, it would normally garner at least a chuckle. He felt like doing a lot of things right then—*run* was very high on that list—but laughing was not one of them.

"This is the best way," he said. "The *only* way. Six in one blow."

There were other ways, of course. Buddy had suggested poisoning the feces, a contact poison that would slowly kill them as it seeped into their skin. He'd suggested pumping carbon monoxide in through the unused water pipes while they slept, essentially putting them to sleep for good. He'd suggested using a couple of propane flamethrowers to roast them alive, but it seemed to Leanne this mode of death would require some sort of clever one-liner, and she'd been fresh out.

"There's always thermite," Buddy had suggested, with an eyebrow raised and his eyes twinkling again.

Leanne had urged him to go on.

"Thermite burns fast and hot. It melts right through metal. If you pour water on it while its burning, you'll get hundreds, thousands of tiny little explosions from the superheated water, like dousing a grease fire only much, much worse. It's undetectable by explosive-sniffing dogs, so our lurkers wouldn't be likely to smell it either. You guys sprinkle it along the floorboards, in the ducts, and it looks and smells just like dirt and rust. Mix it with their war paint, camouflage, whatever you want to call it, and they'll become walking—*lurking*—thermite grenades." With his trade-marked shrewd look, he said, "If you're serious about doing this, and I believe that you are, thermite is the only way to fly."

She'd taken his word for it. The three other paint cans filled with thermite lay in the back of their Suburban, parked on Hammersmith Road at the other end of the fairgrounds. Jim had reasoned that if they were going to accidentally blow themselves up out there looking for turds, one can was sufficient.

It had occurred to her that the thermite squirreled away in Buddy's fallout shelter could easily have blown the entire building sky-high, including La Costina, but the man had seemed unconcerned. Below ground, his supply of assault rifles and handguns, unlike their surplus counterparts on the ground floor, were *very* functional. Along with the shelves of canned goods, toilet paper and cigarillos lining the walls, Buddy Ames was well prepared for an apocalypse, whatever its cause might be.

17

JIM SLIPPED OUT of his Tyvek and headed back to the car for the rest of the thermite, while Leanne sat on mossy rocks by the edge of that nameless creek (a good distance from the latrine), eating leftovers. They'd left Arnie Jacobs in charge of lunch at the restaurant, and would leave him again with dinner. The man had been at it long enough; in many ways, he was a better chef than Leanne.

"You don't take risks," Arnie had told her once, "*that's* your problem. You're a fine cook—you should trust yourself to improvise more."

If he could see me now, Leanne thought with grim humor.

The wild mushroom risotto he'd made two days ago was still delicious cold from a plastic container. It occurred to her this whole mess had started because of leftovers; if only Jim had never seen Cordelia Moone chowing down on that cat. If only he'd left it alone. Leanne had been quite happy until then, being blissfully unaware of the presence of the lurkers and their contribution to the town's dwindling pet population—not to mention little Danny Reynolds.

Had they come too far to change their minds?

She had no doubts what they were doing was right, but was the *motive* genuine? Were they doing it because they believed these were creatures that *should not be*? Was it because of the slaughtered animals,

271

because what Buddy Ames believed had happened to Danny Reynolds could happen to another child? Or was it simply to save their own hides?

Leanne dumped the last of Arnie's wonderful leftovers in the creek and rinsed the container. She'd lost her appetite. Second-guessing herself at every turn wasn't going to help, and neither was applying conventional morality to an unconventional situation. A distinction had to be made. These weren't *people* they were killing, after all—hadn't she said as much to Jim the day before?

They were *lurkers*.

A twig snapped behind her. She twisted round, scared out of her wits, certain *he'd* be standing there, Dutch Holland, with his massive paws and his glowering forehead.

But it was only Jim. She'd probably been as glad to see him before, though not by much.

"Phew! That's hot work," Jim said, setting down the cans (he'd carried two in one hand; anyone who's tried that knows the murder it can be on the fingers), and rubbing his sore hand. He'd sweated patches in the neck and armpits of his old MIZZOU t-shirt. He grew concerned as he approached Leanne.

"You okay?" he said. "You look like you've seen a ghost."

Leanne forced a smile. "I'm fine. Just thought you were someone else."

"Oh." His hand felt like a fat, heavy spider on her shoulder. "Honey, he's at work. You know that. We *saw* him there. The others, they have no idea what he's been up to."

"You can't know that."

"I *do*. If they knew, they'd be after more than money. That Dutch, whatever he isn't, he *is* a businessman."

"Okay," she said, sounding unconvinced.

"No one knows what we're planning except the two of us, hon."

And Buddy Ames, she thought but didn't say. *He could have given us up the second I left his store. Two years is a long time to keep their secret— you thought that yourself, remember? Certainly long enough to make a pact with the Devil.*

"Nobody's going to spring a trap on us," he assured her. Jim was just as worried as Leanne—hell, he was *terrified*. But sharing fear works like an echo chamber, one person's jitters playing off the other's until you're screaming at every sound and flit of shadow. "If that's what you're thinking," he hastily added.

"Okay," she said, and this time she made sure to sound persuaded.

18

THE HOUSE WAS cool and dark as they slipped in through the back door on an old kitchen filled with earthy, rusty, rotted smells.

Leanne's breath fogged the clear plastic screen of her mask as her eyes scoured the gloom. Cabinets opened, rotting from their hinges, wallpaper peeling, linoleum cracked and broken and bent up at the corners, rusted silverware scattered just about everywhere, broken plates and tea cups. It was surely her image of Hell, a nightmare version of her own home kitchen. Jim moved into the next room without much thought. After mourning the loss of so much good china, Leanne followed.

Here was more of the same, though it was phonebooks and framed photographs (and their accompanying shards of glass) littering the floors, along with newspapers, and small mountains of dirt and pine needles. It was difficult to tell if the wild patterns on the peeling wallpaper were mold stains or flocking.

The stench of raccoon feces was thick in here. At the far end of the room, Leanne saw the window she'd been looking through the night before. In the middle of the room the floor disappeared like a Wile E. Coyote illusion. Jim crossed to it. He set down the trash bag and paint can. Then he knelt beside it, a man-sized artist's well of rancid black paint, and dipped a gloved finger into the mess. It came up black.

"Still wet," he said as he rubbed the thumb and forefinger together.

"Great," Leanne said, too disgusted to show her enthusiasm.

"Why don't you start shaking that stuff around the room, and I'll get to work here."

"Any particular pattern?"

Jim gave a wearied look.

"Right," she said. She got to work, using the edge of the Suburban's key to pry open one of the cans while Jim untied the trash bag. Then she began shaking it out around the baseboards. She was three-quarters around the large room before the can was empty, and she returned for another. Jim, meanwhile, had dumped the bucket and smoothing out the smelly black sludge with the lid from a paint can.

"It's not a *cake*," Leanne said over her shoulder. "It doesn't have to be perfect."

"I think it was smoother before we started."

"It's *shit*, James," she said, startling Jim with her sudden bluntness. "They're not going to notice."

With a resigned nod, he dropped the bucket back into the bags. He tied them again as Leanne scattered the contents of the second can. "You've already emptied one? I can't even see it."

"That's the idea, isn't it?"

Jim didn't like her snarky tone, but he kept mum. "You know, I really think this might work," he said with a grunt as he opened the third can and began to distribute it around the room.

19

T HEY SAT UNDER the opened tailgate, waiting for the sun to go down and darkness to fall over Knee High. I imagine they thought back on that sunset quite a bit later on, when the lights were dimmed for the night in their respective correctional facilities. I imagine in their minds that orange ball of flame might have warped and distorted into the other fire, the one they were soon to set at the old Schultz place —those images that would burn themselves onto their retinas like the shadows of Hiroshima.

They'd made sure to kick away their footprints in the dust and dirt and thermite as they left the house. Now all they had to do was wait on Dutch and the others to arrive, and hope, when the time came, they'd have the guts to go through with it.

Leanne thought they would, but she wasn't the one holding the flare gun.

"I've been thinking about Olivia," Jim said suddenly.

Leanne turned away from him. "Don't," she said.

He sat silently for a time. But Jim had more to say on the subject, and he could hold his peace no more. "I keep thinking if she had lived..."

"*Jim.*"

"...we never would have opened the restaurant, and none of this would have happened."

"So this is *my* fault?" She wouldn't turn around; it meant she was probably crying. Leanne dealt with tears like a dog going off alone into the woods to die. Touch her now, and she was likely to bite back with hurtful words.

"I'm not saying..." He stopped, deciding on his approach. "It's nobody's *fault*, Leanne. I never blamed you for what happened. If that's what you think..."

Leanne turned on him then, eyes full of tears. "*You never had to.*"

"Honey..."

She got up and grabbed her Tyvek suit from the behind him. He put a hand on her shoulder—that heavy spider again, poisonous now—and she jerked away from his touch, glaring at him with ice cold, red-rimmed eyes. She stepped into the suit a leg at a time, got the wrong leg first and tried to yank herself free. It bunched around her shoe and she crumpled against the bumper, allowing herself to weep openly for the first time in years.

Jim risked another hand on her shoulders. She fell into his embrace, jerking beneath his arms with each shuddering, long-postponed sob. He held her, stroking her sweat-dampened hair, rocking her like a baby, waiting for her to speak. She said nothing. Finally, she wiped away her tears, and he let her go.

"Thank you," she said, the corners of her mouth quivering.

"Thank *you*."

She blinked the last traces of tears away. "For what?"

"For staying with me, after everything," Jim said. "I know how difficult a decision it must have been for you."

She said nothing, only smiled.

"I couldn't live without you," he said. "You know that, don't you?"

"You could."

"No. I can't."

Leanne thought about this for a moment. Then she spoke: "I used to think that, too. I thought if you died before me, I'd leap into your grave and let them bury me with you."

"And now...?"

"I love you, Jim. I'll always love you, no matter what. That's something I've decided, too." She traced the rough hair on his cheek with her fingers. "But I don't need you like I used to."

Jim nodded, the lump in the back of his throat a cork holding back tears of his own. He knew it could never be the same between them, but he was grateful for the years they'd had. Whatever came next, those damnable monsters couldn't take that away from them. He would hold on to that just as long as he could.

20

BY COMPARISON TO death by fire, Cordelia's rat poisoning was the rough equivalent of sending her a gift basket from FTD Flowers. It is believed that unconsciousness strikes the victims before the pain becomes too much to bear. More than likely this is something people say to comfort the bereaved. It certainly doesn't explain the Tibetan fellow in New Delhi, who ran a country mile while burning from head to foot, though I suppose he could have been an exception to the rule.

It is not a pretty death, despite the beauty inherent in fire. I have watched, horrified and amazed, as great arcs of burning napalm from Navy riverboats torched entire villages; I know more than a man ought to of the metaphorical shadows of the dead etched onto those walls in Hiroshima. Jim and Leanne discovered their shadows quite suddenly on that beautiful, summery night in May.

The heavyset checkout lady arrived first. They had parked the Suburban a few blocks from the fairgrounds, and sat watching from an old hunting blind they'd happened upon in a tree near the unnamed creek. (Leanne was no climber, and had had to be hauled half the way up.) They had donned their Tyveks to be safe, and the woman, Tess or Tina or maybe Tammy, didn't even raise her head as she passed under the blind.

The woman appeared to be in a daze, swinging her arms like a Bigfoot as she trod through the woods until she eventually disappeared among the trees. They gave it until full dark, and when nobody else appeared beneath them, Leanne figured it was a safe bet the others had come from the front, as Richard Holland had two nights prior. The Taymors climbed down one after the other, and weaved through the moonlit woods, only losing their way once before the trees opened up on the Schultz house.

The grunting chants Leanne had heard were already in progress, offering sound cover to sneak around to the front of the house. She threw a passing glance through an unevenly boarded side window, saw them slapping their hands in the excrement and raising them to the sky in exultation, the air already redolent with its nasty smell. Leanne thought she detected a hint of thermite, but it was probably her imagination; if the lurkers hadn't caught it, there likely wasn't anything to smell.

It had worked.

Don't get ahead of yourself, she thought. *There's still a chance it won't ignite.*

Jim crouch-walked ahead of her, the flare gun held out at his side, his Tyvek a crinkly white beacon under the moon. She saw the glow of her own suit in her peripherals, but it was already too late to turn back. Jim was under the window now, and as she crouched down beside him, he loaded a flare into the red plastic barrel. They could always turn around and run, she supposed, but if Buddy Ames was right, if there really were lurkers just about everywhere, in every *town*, they could find themselves running for the rest of their lives.

This was no time for indecision.

The grunts from inside stopped, and the night fell silent but for the sound of frogs chirping and the whine of mosquitoes. The lurkers would be resting soon, gathering their strength for a long night of scavenging... or a hunt. Jim rose up on his haunches. She wanted to cry out to him—*too soon!*—but didn't dare raise her voice, certain they would tear both of them apart, limb from limb, with or without the use of hedge clippers.

She wasn't about to become the first human meal of these particular lurkers because of her husband's poor timing.

Jim raised the flare gun, the index finger of his safety gloves creaking as it tightened on the trigger. But his right eye twitched behind the mask —and the finger relaxed.

He turned to her, his face twisted in a voiceless scream.

She saw it then, too: Pete Wallin holding a gentle hand on the checkout clerk's swelled, naked belly. The others shined their eyes toward the proud Mama and Papa as those Three Wise Men might have looked at Mary rocking Jesus in his manger.

The heavyset woman was pregnant.

Leanne snatched the flare gun from Jim's hand; he'd all but dropped it in his astonishment. Rage had overcome her, unsure if she was mad at Jim for hesitating, or at the two lurkers for being able to conceive, even if their spawn would be born a monster.

Whatever the reason, she did not hesitate to squeeze the trigger. A flare burst from the barrel, a red so bright that trails remained on her retinas for several minutes afterward. She watched it arc above the heads of the creatures inside, saw them look up from the heavyset woman's belly and follow its descent in shock and awe. Saw it overshoot them by a dozen feet or more, and land somewhere in the kitchen, where it fizzled out on the cruddy linoleum.

Eyes as bright as lamps flashed toward the window.

"*Flare*," she snapped. Jim sat in a daze, stunned into idiocy. "*Gimme the FLARES!*"

Jim's face alighted with awareness then, and he began to rummage through his pockets.

The lurkers rose on all fours. Flares fell from the pocket of his vest and scattered on the beige carpet of pine needles. Leanne darted for them.

Jim was still fixated on the window, the lurkers skulking toward them, orange cinders burning in their filth-blackened faces. Leanne scrabbled with a flare in the barrel, like trying to thread a needle with a poisonous snake in her lap. It kept scraping the edges and sliding out. She heard them in there, their animal screeches, their wet hands and feet slapping against the floorboards, closing the distance.

She heard a dull click. By some sort of miracle, the flare had struck home. She snapped it shut and stood. Richard Holland was ahead of the others, a lumbering giant, his mouth upturned in a snarl, his white, fanged molars visible even from a distance.

She squeezed the trigger.

The flare hit the floor behind Dutch's charging feet, igniting the thermite so suddenly and violently it was difficult to believe what she was seeing. One second there was a dingy old room, and the next they were looking through the window at the inside of the sun.

PHOOM!

Waves of heat blew Leanne's mask off her head and whiffled her hair back from her brow. She closed her eyes, for fear they'd bake in the hollows of her skull. When the ringing in her ears stopped, the lurkers' agonized screams rushed in to take its place. She opened her eyes again to see sparks flying from dancing white-hot pillars of flame. They were living sparklers, writhing and tearing at their charring flesh, human-shaped candles melting into fatty puddles on the floor.

Dutch had been thrown like a giant ragdoll with the force of the explosion. He lay huddled against the far wall near the stairs, virtually the only part of the first floor not yet ablaze. He rose to his feet, no crawling now, skirting the flames like some invincible movie monster rising from the ashes of his own death, barely giving a glance to his dead and dying companions, things he'd once referred to as "family," at first only striding and then running toward the open window.

Jim fell back from it, immobile with terror, certain now that this was how it would end: with husband and wife gored by the hands of the lumbering giant for a paltry $15,000.

But Leanne hadn't given up. Moving on autopilot, she plucked another flare from the pile. Her hands shook badly, her brain felt like it was on fire, but she managed to get it loaded just as Dutch reached the window, planting his hands on either side. The heat had burned the hair right off his head and baked the flesh from his skull—a decidedly *human* skull. Just two cavernous slits remained of his nose, between eyes glowing not with eyeshine now but with the reflection of the flames. All of Dutch's flesh hung in charred strips, yet still she could smell the fresh, cool scent of his aftershave: Brut for the brute. Sharp teeth bloodied, rows of molars stretching all the way up between his eyes and the oozing holes of his ears, the lurker grinned right in her face. Then his jaw opened wider than any human jaw had been meant, wide enough to gnaw off her head, and Leanne breathed a silent prayer.

The floor collapsed beneath Dutch with a belch of fire. He dropped, hanging onto the window ledge with hands that were no more than skeletal claws, fragile things, true terror registering on what was left of his face for scarcely a moment.

Then he plunged into the inferno.

Leanne fell back in utter exhaustion. Jim crawled over to her, put his arms around her. She let him hold her. It was over (*For now*, her strained mind added, but she thrust the useless thought away). As the great conflagration overtook the upper floors and that awful house burned to the ground, Leanne and Jim hugged each other, hot tears baking on their cheeks.

21

VOLUNTEER FIREFIGHTERS STRUGGLED all night to put out the fire. Once it spread to the woods, dry as bone from that long, hot first week of May, it was a losing battle. They had the knowhow, they just didn't have the tools. But rain came, mercifully, early that morning, a torrential downfall that filled the gutters and swelled the nameless creek from my childhood, flooding basements and smothering the blaze in under an hour.

People speculated that the Schultz kid had set the fire for the insurance money, just as Leanne had suspected they would; the bastard would have burned down all of Knee High if the wind had blown in the right direction, and the rain hadn't come when it had. Nothing was left of the house but coal, some of it still upright in blackened columns. Most of it lay in a heap in the cement pit that had been Dotty Schultz's basement, along with the charred remains of six people, burned so badly that dental records had to be used to identify those without families to miss them.

After the roof collapsed, sealing the Knee High Chapter's tomb for good, Leanne and Jim had tossed the Tyvek suits into the fire and left through the fairgrounds. Leanne placed an anonymous call to the fire department from the payphone at Daisy's Pantry. The convenience store had been closed. No one had seen them arrive or leave, and the store had no cameras.

In a tragic bit of irony, Jim and Leanne arrived at the restaurant Friday morning to find their rat terrier dead at the foot of the Dumpster. At first, neither of them could believe the wretched thing slumped on the cracked asphalt (where the orange cat had been less than a week ago) was their Rosco. He was scruffy, dirty, and possibly mange-ridden. He looked like the kind of creature you might see shuffling through the street in the background of those ads about children in some scorching, dirt-poor corner of the world. *Choose the child you want to adopt. Call now, operators are standing by.*

It wasn't until Leanne gasped and staggered back a step that Jim realized he was looking the same dog from the posters he'd tacked up all over town. Leanne fell to her knees beside Rosco, and wept.

One of the trash bags Jim had left for Cordelia had been dragged out of the bin. The dog lay among its contents, gathering flies. Probably a raccoon had done it, and had realized before it was too late that the food was bad. Surely Rosco hadn't; he had neither the smarts nor the stature to manage such maneuvers. Jim used a big spatula from the kitchen and oven gloves to peel the stiffened corpse off the concrete ("It sounded like peeling a Band-Aid off a hairy leg," Jim told me, with understandable distaste, from behind a glass partition at Nebraska State Penitentiary), while Leanne held open a trash bag, fresh tears running down her face.

Jim comforted his wife, but didn't join her in her tears, not as he had for his boyhood dog, Rufus, nor for Cordelia Moone. Not as he would when the County Sheriff's Department finally hauled off him and Leanne to their separate cells, either.

They tied the bag and tossed it in with the rest of the trash. I suppose we in the accounting trade would consider the death of Rosco the rat terrier a passive-activity loss. As I've said, I didn't much care for Rosco, but I would not will such a death on any creature, man or animal.

The following Monday, Jim mowed neat rows into his lawn with a smile. But the smile was forced. After what he'd seen, what he'd *done*, he might reach up to find his eyes leaking like bad plumbing every so often, but he didn't think he'd ever truly smile again.

Nobody suspected Jim and Leanne Taymor of the crime. Why would they? They'd been nothing but model citizens until the night Jim Taymor had stepped on the unstable precipice at the edge of sanity and tumbled headlong into the abyss. Days became weeks, months, as speculation grew and the investigations proved arson. The Schultz kid (who was in his mid-thirties, not much of a kid at all) was questioned and released. Residents petitioned for the State Fire Marshal's resignation. He stayed on another term, and is still in office at the time of this writing. All the while, Jim and Leanne lived with those death shadows on the walls of their minds, hiding in plain sight much as the lurkers had, living in fear of being discovered, and marveling when another day passed and the police hadn't come knocking at their door.

La Costina continued to thrive, but their hearts were no longer in it.

They came to us in early October, the trees in the woods surrounding the fire pit that had once been the Schultz house already bare, the black streaks on their trunks a physical representation of the marks the tragedy had painted on all our hearts. The guilt had gotten too much for them to bear. They spilled their guts, and Gin, after they'd told us everything they could remember, asked for them to confess.

They agreed almost at once, as if all they'd needed was our approval.

There was no trial. Had forensic psychologists been asked to testify, they might have pushed for psychiatric care. *Folie à deux*, the well-spoken interviewees said on those 24-hour news channels. The public would have none of it. They cried out for blood—for the life of the child, mostly, and for Rosco. It was 26 days before the sentence was handed down, during which time it was as if the entire town held its breath: seven consecutive counts each of life with no chance of parole. Overkill again: Neither Jim nor Leanne are immortal, so far as I know.

I cannot speak for the mortality of their Lurkers.

I went to see them quite a bit over the next six months. Their visitation days were staggered, and the drives gave me plenty of time to consider whether I believed any of it. And the thing of it is, the more they told me, the absolute *sincerity* of their words, the more I found myself *wanting* to believe them. The alternative is a far worse thing to contemplate: that Jim and Leanne Taymor, my two closest friends, had decided as a sort of a lark to murder seven innocent people, and if anyone found them out, they would simply pretend they had gone insane.

My rational mind refuses to believe their story, of course. But the primitive part of my brain has me checking the darkened corners of the house, quickening my step past the opened doorway to the basement, looking under the bed and behind the door before I settle down for the night. Primitive me jumps at the sound of raccoons fighting in some trash-strewn alley. Primitive me looks for that distinctive glow in the eyes of everyone I pass. He sees a flicker of lamplight in a man's glasses and shouts, *Lurker! There! Right there! Can't you see?! Can't you see it's only a mask?!*

Rational me, meanwhile, tightens his lips.

Leanne seemed to be doing well, the last I saw of her. She'd even signed up for the Second Chance Pups program, and had brought with her a Golden Retriever—who probably looked a lot like the dog Jim had loved as a boy—she was training to be a seeing-eye dog, of all things. I have to say, I find some pleasure in knowing she'll be okay, in spite of all that has happened. As long as I've known her, she's been a fighter. The dog sat pretty for a treat. Around his neck was the same blue bandana Jim had used to tie on his head for yardwork. Everything neat, and in its right place.

I'd like to say Jim Taymor held up in prison as well as his wife had, but I'd be lying. The last time I saw him, he was a hollow shell that had once contained a man. Sunken, jittering eyes, lips chapped and pursed, stubbly flesh hanging under his chin.

"Thanks for coming," he said.

"My pleasure," I told him, though it had never been much of a pleasure visiting either of them. It felt more like penance, like those non-alcoholic beers I drank less and less of these days. "You look good."

He shook his head, and said nothing for some time. Something on his mind, I suppose, but I didn't have all day. I'd been about to ask if he wanted to be left alone when he came out with it. "Can you do something for me? I know you've done enough just coming here to see me, but this is the last thing, I swear it." He looked at me imploringly. "I *swear*," he said again.

"Name it," I said, regretting the words before they'd entirely left my mouth. We'd discussed writing down their story, and I'd already begun the chore of it.

"I'm so sorry," he said, and snatched a glance over his shoulder. A burly guard about the size of Richard "Dutch" Holland stood expressionless behind him. Jim seemed unreasonably focused, fixed on the door he'd come through. I wondered, fleetingly, if he meant to escape. As it turned out, escape was precisely what he'd had in mind—though not as I'd imagined it.

"There are more of them, you know," he whispered. "*Much* more." He stole another frightened glance at the door. "There's a key, under the doormat of the gazebo behind the house," he told me. "Buddy put it there."

"Buddy Ames?" By then I'd come to the conclusion Buddy was either a ghost or a figment of his and Leanne's imaginations. "This key," I said, thinking of the key he'd given Leanne when the whole mess started, "what does it open?"

He told me. I asked him what he meant for me to do, and Jim just said, "You'll know when you see it." Then he apologized again, and let the guard take him away.

It was the last time I saw him. I still remember that haunted expression on his face as he was pulled roughly through the door into the darkened hallway beyond, and out of my life.

Haunted... yet somehow at peace.

22

I HAVEN'T GONE to visit Leanne in over a month. I can't bring myself to, not after opening Jim's lockbox in back of the Wells Fargo (procured under the pseudonym Ross Coltraine), and having read the document within.

Gin told me to leave it alone. The key was trouble, she said—trouble we couldn't afford. "We've already done all we can for those two," she said. "Can't you see how people act around us? How they hush when we enter a room?" Of course, I had. Particularly come April, when typically I'd do a decent business filing taxes. This year, my list of clients was less than half what it was before this whole mess happened.

I wish to God I had taken Gin's advice.

In the lockbox was a single sheet of foolscap. My fingers shook as I unfolded it. I'm not sure what I expected, but it certainly wasn't what I got.

On the foolscap was a list of names. A letter had arrived at the penitentiary with too many stamps and no return address, but the postmark said NEW MEXICO. Leanne might have recognized the handwriting as the same she'd seen scribbled in Buddy Ames's notes, but Leanne had received no similar letter. The letter revealed to Jim that a key had been placed under the gazebo, and the key belonged to a lockbox.

Inside would be a list of names.

Jim killed himself in the showers the night of my final visit, using the sharpened end of a toothbrush. It had taken him two good stabs to find the jugular. I have to admire the courage that second jab must have taken, to pull it out of the first wound and try, try again. But perhaps it was fear that did it. Those last words he said to me, *There are more of them, you know...* I think it's highly likely there are as many lurkers among the prison population as there are on the outside. If not more.

Prison officials claimed murder, of course. Said he must have had a run-in with one of several gangs. Why else would he have been found in the showers? I knew better. He'd done it in the showers for the same reason he stood over the kitchen stove every day eating his morning toast: Leanne had trained him well, and he hadn't wanted to make a mess.

We each have a decision to make, I believe, as to how much pain we can endure, how much loss and regret and unhappiness is too much for us to bear. We each must choose the horrors we can abide without collapsing under their weight.

Would Jim have done it, if Leanne's name was on that list? Could Leanne have, if his had been? If they'd had a child of their own, and that child's name were there among the others, people whose lives and faces were otherwise abstracts, could they have done what was required of them? Could they have lived saddled with such frightening knowledge, and done nothing, as I have?

I burned Jim's letter in the kitchen sink the moment I came home from the bank. I couldn't bear to look at it again. So far as I know, Jim had never seen the list with his own eyes. He had chosen me not because of what was on that list, but because I was the only one who would *listen*.

The last name on Buddy's list, you see, was hers.

Gin, my sweet Virginia. Lord help me, just last night, as I flicked off the bedside lamp, *I saw the shine in her eyes.*

I think I can bear it. Rational me knows it can't be true. I must think rationally. We've slept in the same bed, longer than we've been married. In that time, I've seen her get up for many a glass of water and cup of hot milk, for her headache powders, to relieve herself, and once, when she'd gotten quite drunk after Jessa was born, she got up to vomit with the door locked tight behind her.

Not once has she left the house in the skulk of night, so far as I know. Not once has she come back from those brief excursions from the warmth of our bed, wearing the noisome smell of animal excrement, or of trash. I must not succumb to fear, as Jim and Leanne had. My love for her is too strong to give in to that niggling voice in the dark. Love can conquer a great many things. But love, like fear, does not always respond to reason.

Rational me believes I would kill myself before I could harm a hair on her beautiful head.

Some nights though, with the sun sinking, and dark clouds gathering in the east, I find myself thinking what a lovely night it would be for a fire.

Video Nasties

Published 2017

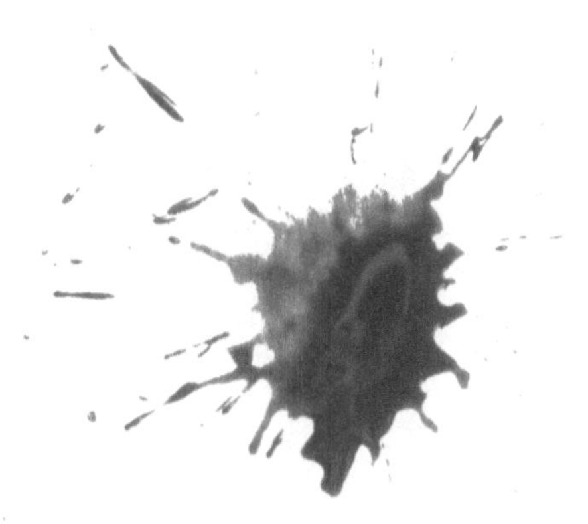

Cuttings

K ATIE WAS IN the kitchen when a low rumbling rattled the window. As she moved the curtain aside to peer out, a large off-white object filled her view, and the blast of a horn startled her away from the glass. Someone had pulled into the driveway.

Hanging half out the kitchen door, Katie took a cautious look at the back of an ugly old van spewing black exhaust into the carport. The tinted rear window was cracked, the bumper on a sharp cant, every inch covered in a layer of scum, even the small silver letters spelling out RAM.

"What the heck is this?"

The driver door opened as she spoke. Katie recognized her husband's designer jeans before he stepped down on the concrete slab, and she saw that he had clearly gone mad, because only a crazy person would have such a bright, goofy smile stepping out of such a filthy, run-down vehicle.

Gavin Leslie had only just recently lost his job and now he'd lost his mind.

"Honey, before you say it, I got a great deal."

"Unless you traded for magic beans, a great deal is still too much."

"Honey," he said again, in the tone he used when he knew he was in the wrong, "you're gonna love this van. And she was only twelve-hundred dollars."

"*Twelve-hun*—" Katie let go of the doorjamb and stepped out onto the cement porch. She *had* to, for fear of keeling over in shock. "Jesus, you really have lost your mind."

Gavin threw open the back doors, his biggest surprise saved for last. In the back stood a bathroom cabinet papered with faux wood, alongside a soiled mattress. Katie gaped at them. Gavin took her surprise for a favorable reaction and the smile returned to his scruffy face. "You love her, right? I knew you'd love her."

"I know times are tough, Gavin, but surely you don't expect us to live in that van." Trying for patience, her tone sounded more like measured anger. Had he really just called it *her*?

"I'll take out the mattress," he assured her. "And the cabinet. I guess the previous owner must have camped in it." He squinted into the back, a forlorn quality to his look Katie didn't quite like. Then his eyes lit up. "I forgot the best part. It's got a tape deck! You remember cassettes."

"Honey, we're the same age. Of course I remember them."

"I found a whole bunch of old cassettes in the cabinet. It's got Mr. Big. You remember Mr. Big."

Katie rolled her eyes, and Gavin drew himself away from the van to stand below her at the steps. "I bought her for us." He took her hand. "For the business."

"What business, Gavin?"

"The flower shop." Excitement crept back into his voice. "*Cuttings*," he added with a hopeful look, reminding her of the name he'd picked as a joke only the two of them and his dead stepmother would get.

Katie peered over her husband's newly balding head at the beaten-up van with its tape deck and '90s hair band cassettes and the moldering bedroom in the back. She knew what her sister would call it: she'd call it a rape van. Katie held a similar sentiment. Likely a previous owner had camped out of it, as Gavin suggested. *Or lived in it*, she thought uneasily.

But they could take out the mattress. They could take out the cabinet. The flower shop had been a pleasant dream when they'd first started dating, before bills and real life had gotten in the way. Before Gavin's stepmother, Deanie, who'd always filled the Leslie home with the colors and mingled fragrances of a hundred different blossoms, had passed away in a hospital room resembling a greenhouse with all the Get Well flowers.

"The flower shop," Katie said, warming to the idea. "I hate the name Cuttings, though. If we're going to go through with this, we really ought to call it Deanie's."

A smile crept onto Gavin's lips. He took her hand and kissed it gently.

SIX WEEKS LATER, Deanie's Flowers was a living, breathing thing eating up a good portion of their life. But it felt good to be doing something other than banging out her latest book, and even better to see Gavin working again. The layoff had been hard on him. Secretly, Katie thought he'd felt emasculated living off the meager royalties of his wife's crime novels.

With a view of the back gardens, the glassed-in conservatory made an excellent workshop. They'd removed all the furniture, filled the space with tables and covered them with asters and baby's breath and poinsettias and tulips. In the center of the room they'd erected a long counter with a stone finish where the two of them could work side-by-side.

Gavin was an expert with flowers, but arranging wasn't his strong point. Here, Katie discovered an untapped talent. So while he cut the flowers and groomed them, kept them fresh and vibrant, she performed magic with vases and pots and floral foam. While Katie placed orders and created the budgets, Gavin's experience in marketing gradually brought in new customers. He also drove the delivery van, which with its new paint job and Deanie's Flowers decal began to look somewhat respectable, despite its shabby past.

Together, Katie and Gavin Leslie made a perfect team, and as Deanie's Flowers began to bloom so did Gavin's libido. His hunger for her had waned after the layoff but now it roared like the engine of his ugly old van. The day they cleared out the workshop, high from the news of their loan approval, they'd fucked on the cool ceramic tiles in the middle of the glassed-in room, oblivious to potential stares from over the back fence. Gavin devoured her with an enthusiasm he rarely showed, even during their courtship. Secretly, Katie had often thought he felt inadequate, despite her reassurances. But that night and every day since, he'd pushed her to orgasm multiple times until her own cries grew so loud she embarrassed herself, and the two of them lay their sweaty heads together on the cool slab floor, laughing and panting.

The Leslies were happy, healthy and growing more successful by the day.

GAVIN SNAPPED AWAKE. He'd been sleeping in an awkward position and his legs felt numb, belonging to someone else. His chest was constricted. His first instinct was to struggle, bound to a familiar chair, though his hands were unrestricted.

Where am I?

He blinked into the dark. As his vision adjusted, he saw the black rectangle before him, a glimmer of glass. He thought of the conservatory, of his chair at the worktable, but here the glass was too close. Moreover, he didn't smell flowers and damp earth but a familiar musty vinyl.

Yellow light flooded the backyard, triggered by some creature of the night, and he recognized his surroundings: the van. The pressure on his chest was the belt in the driver's seat. Somehow he'd wandered out here in his underwear and buckled himself in behind the steering wheel.

The yard light dimmed, throwing him once again into darkness.

"How did I get out here?"

As he spoke he became aware of a presence at his side, the urge to turn both powerful and repellent. He unbuckled first, drawing his hand slowly across his lap, conspicuous of the erection tenting his boxers, the snap of the buckle like a dead twig to a prowler. When he was free, able to bolt if he needed to, Gavin stole a look at the pallid thing in the passenger seat.

The girl shivered in her flimsy bra and panties, bruised and beaten, rivers of mascara and saliva pooled in her sharp jugular notch. Someone —*Couldn't have been me*—had tied thick nylon rope under her conical breasts and around her ankles, the flesh red and angry beneath, as if she'd been struggling.

"Who—?" Gavin tried to ask, but the tape player came on abruptly with the dash lights, blaring the three-part harmony of Mr. Big's "To Be With You." At the sudden noise, the girl snapped her head toward him. Her eyes, dark brown and moist, bore the look of a beaten puppy.

She's afraid. Afraid of me.

Gripped by a fear of his own, Gavin snapped on the dome light.

The phantom girl vanished under its harsh white glow. The music stopped and the dash lights dimmed like the picture in an old TV set.

Shaken, Gavin staggered out, bare feet on cool concrete, wondering what the hell he'd just seen.

Was it a dream? Never had a lucid one before. Never sleepwalked before, either...

Crickets chirped in the night. Otherwise, Dayton Street was silent. As loud as the music had been, it hadn't woken the neighbors. Gavin let out a small sigh. He crept into the house through the kitchen, aware of every creak.

Katie rustled in her sleep when he returned to bed, but she didn't wake. Gavin was glad for it, despite the persistence of his erection. He wouldn't have been able to explain where he'd been if she was awake. He couldn't explain to himself what had happened, let alone his wife of seven years. The image of the abused girl—*whatever* that had been—had disturbed him terribly.

Despite his worries, Gavin eventually drifted back to sleep. When he awoke in the morning, he found it easy enough to convince himself what had happened in the night was just a very bad dream.

. . .

THE WOMAN BANGED on the glass while Katie was at the grocery store. Gavin looked up from spritzing aphids off the primroses to see her dark figure standing at the door.

He let her in. "Welcome to Deanie's Flowers. You must be Madison."

"Yes." Dressed in black from her cloche hat to her shoes, she sniffled as she slipped inside. "Thank you."

Madison Davis had called in an order for her husband's funeral two days prior. Katie had taken the order and later told him, "If you died, I wouldn't have the strength to make that call." Gavin directed Madison toward long-stemmed flowers, bunched tightly among white carnations into several slim glass vases and wicker baskets.

"They're lovely," the woman said, wiping her nose with a tissue.

"You can thank my wife for that."

"I will."

"You know, callas aren't true lilies. They're from the genus *zantedeschia*. They're mildly toxic."

"Why do they call them lilies?"

Gavin shrugged. "A rose by any other name..."

"Well, my husband always loved them," the grieving widow said, almost apologetically, shifting so their elbows met for a brief moment. Gavin stole a sideways glance at her round face. Her green eyes shimmered with tears, plump lips pouty, her thick, lined neck with the visible blue slash of her jugular. Her heavy breasts rose and fell under a cinched black trench coat ending at a knee-length wool skirt and black pantyhose. Beneath a light woody perfume Gavin smelled the mingled aroma of sweat and baby powder, and he involuntarily stiffened in his work jeans. He stepped away from her, blushing.

She turned her dewy eyes to him, so sad and broken—and suddenly Gavin wanted to swat everything off the work table and throw her down on the space he'd made, slamming the breath out of her in a terrified gasp, her fat tits popping the top buttons of her jacket. He wanted to jerk up her skirt and tear down her panties, thrust his face between her smooth white cheeks and savor the fragrant bouquet of her cunt.

Madison seemed to sense something wrong. She took a step away.

Gavin flustered. *Not now*, he told himself. *Please, not now.* "I'm sorry for your loss," he said, hoping to cover whatever his face had revealed.

She thanked him again with a wary look at his dirty hands.

"Let's ring these up, shall we?" He crossed the workshop. Madison hesitated only a moment before following. The cash register stood beside the doorway to the hall, the master bedroom mere feet away. Gavin knew he could snatch her by the throat and the belt of her jacket and push her inside easily. He could throw her down on his marital bed and dry fuck the bitch while her tears dampened the comforter and she cried out for her dead husband—

STOP IT!

His hand shook. His head swam with her sweat and perfume and his balls felt heavy. He caught her eye. Again, she looked down at his hand. "Sorry," he said, and forced a cough. "I think I'm coming down with something."

"It's been going around," she murmured.

"If you'd like, I could send you the bill?"

Madison nodded a little too emphatically, her red-rimmed eyes on the door now, longing for escape. "That would be nice."

"I'll just bring them to your car then."

Gavin juggled two tribute arrangements through the door. Madison carried the third herself, eager to get away. Under the carport the air was in motion, her scent not as potent, and the sudden terrible urge to violate her disappeared. She wasn't his type to begin with, and worse: her tears reminded him of the phantom girl from the van.

He threw a look toward the van now, its fresh white paint job shimmering in the cool autumn air.

I'll go for a drive, he thought. *Play some tunes. Calm the nerves.*

He stood the tributes up on the floor in the back of her Audi. Madison held the third out to him with an uneasy look. *She wants me to do it*, he thought. *So she won't have to turn her back on me.*

Gavin took the vase, eager to get her going and get behind the wheel himself. In his haste, his still-quivering fingers brushed hers. The widow snatched her hand away with such a look of fright he might have thought she'd caught a glimpse of his twisted fantasies.

"I'll get the last of them." He placed vase with the others and hurried back to the workshop.

Madison Davis was already in the driver's seat when Gavin returned. She'd started the car while he crouched for the last of the bouquets, a flower basket and the casket spray. He found the widow staring through the windshield at the back of the van, a troubled look in her eyes. Gavin loaded the last arrangements. She didn't acknowledge his presence until he said, "All done."

Only then did she shoot a brief, thin smile over her shoulder, flinching when he shut the door.

"Drive safe," he told her. The back tires squealed as she pulled out of the driveway.

The tape player blasted INXS when Gavin started the engine.

THE FIRST TIME he came to Almond Street, Gavin met the van's previous owner.

He'd taken a circuitous route through town, clearing away the stress of the day, listening to the tunes he loved in high school. When he emerged from under the dirty graffitied overpass, he found himself in a seedy neighborhood of potholes and brick-faced warehouses.

The street sign out front of a run-down convenience store said ALMOND in white letters on green. Gavin made the realization as if in a dream. He knew the area by reputation only: it was said a man could get almost any kind of woman he wanted here, even underage ones. He hadn't meant to drive here, had only been going by the feel of the road, subtle vibrations in the steering wheel causing him to twist the wheel this way and that. He wouldn't have driven to Almond Street if he'd been aware of his destination—if he'd entered it into the GPS on the dash. It had been entirely unconscious, almost as if the van had driven *him*.

Women in impossibly short skirts and heels of equally improbable length trolled the grimy sidewalk. Gavin pulled up to the curb, meaning to make a U-turn and go back home, but pair of hands with black lacquered nails grasped the window sill before he could pull away, and a young woman peered in, chopped black bangs framing a pale, eager face and junkie's eyes.

"Hey, hot stuff," the girl said, before squinting at him uncertainly. "You're not Tony."

Another woman sauntered over, dark nipples like saucers protruding from a white tube top, cut-off blue jeans so short the frayed edges hugged her crotch and a waistband swallowed by her stomach. "How 'bout a threesome?" this woman suggested.

"Fuck off, Indica," the first girl said over her shoulder, ushering her competition away with a flick of her wrist. Indica stayed put, while the junkie hooker looked over the interior of the van. "Tone let you borrow his baby?" She gave him a dubious look, absently flicking the piercing under her lower lip against her teeth.

Gavin's entire being screamed for him to leave. He jerked the wheel and stepped on the gas, peeling the girl's fingernails off the passenger window with a clack as the van squealed away from the curb. He drove home with his thoughts thudding in his ears as loud as his heartbeat. *What was I doing there? What the fuck is happening to me? I love Kate. I don't want anyone else. I love my wife. It wasn't my fault. I love her. I didn't mean to do it!*

But you didn't do *anything,* a stranger's voice assured him—a strangely *familiar* voice. *All you did was satisfy a little innocent male curiosity.*

The man's voice had a pleasant, gravely timber that felt like cinnamon candy melting in Gavin's head. As the van went over another pothole, the fuzzy dice Katie had begged him to throw out rustled from the rearview mirror.

Nothin wrong exercising your rights, the voice told him. *Nothin wrong with bein a man.*

"Nothing wrong at all," Gavin agreed. The voice seemed to come from everywhere, from the porous vinyl seats to the cold hard plastic of the dash. From the fuzzy dice. From the musty air. It was *the van* speaking to him, Gavin realized—and all this time he'd been calling it a "she."

"Who the fuck is Tony?" he wondered, recalling the look of recognition and confusion from the dark-haired prostitute.

At this, the van remained silent.

The owner of the storage facility, an old man by the name of Grosvenor, hadn't mentioned a Tony, a Tone, an Anthony or Antonio. The Ram had been gathering dust in a storage shed for six or seven years. When Grosvenor's brother Barrett died, the old man liquidated his assets, but the owner of that particular shed couldn't be found. "Old number, I guess," Grosvenor said. When Gavin asked if the owner would be upset, the old man answered, "Fuck 'im. I'm getting outta Dodge, no pun intended. Gonna buy me one of them mobile homes. Get while the gettin's good."

Get while the gettin's good, the voice agreed. *That's some excellent advice. There's a reason they call marriage an institution—it's a* correctional *institution. Marriage is a prison, and that brainy little wifey of yours is the warden.*

"You're wrong," Gavin said. "She *saved* me."

Saved you? The van chuckled derisively. *From what? Gettin too much* pussy?

Gavin flicked on the radio, trying to tune the voice out. He sang along with Tom Petty until the dial changed on its own.

Can't get rid of me that easy, compadre, the van said, speaking from the static between stations. *We're takin the long way home, and you an me are gonna pow-wow.*

Gavin flicked off the radio. Relief washed over him in the silence that followed. *Is this what it's like to lose your mind?* he wondered.

Laughter as sharp as razor blades answered the unspoken query.

You really are pathetic, you know that? Sorry excuse for a human being, let alone a man.

Gavin tried to turn at right at the next intersection, back toward home, and the wheel jerked out of his hands with a peel of tires. He tried to unbuckle, but the latch was stuck. "Why don't you leave me alone?" he cried. The man in the car beside them threw Gavin a queer look.

You an me are gonna get somethin straight. I'm runnin the show now, got it? So just shut up, sit back, and let the smooth grooves of WTNY All Tony All the Time wash over you.

The van drove straight. Gavin did as he was told—*Gonna hurt me more than it hurts you*, he thought inexplicably—but he didn't have to listen. So while Tony talked, driving him past ugly warehouses and rundown tenements, Gavin listed all the flower genera he could recall in his head: *Astragalus, Bulbophylium, Begonia, Centaurea...*

■■

"...GAV?"

KATIE STOOD at the top of the stairs, a towel around her midsection, the smaller one from the set perched atop her head. She called down the stairs again. "Gavin?"

No answer.

"Where is he?"

She'd popped in for a quick shower before bed, and had been in there a little longer than expected: having realized her legs were bristly, she'd taken the extra time to shave. She emerged, toweled and moisturized, hoping to find Gavin primed and ready on the duvet cover, but instead it seemed as though he wasn't in the house at all.

With her deadline quickly approaching, Katie played catchup, moonlighting in the flower shop while writing her novel by day—barely any time to breathe, let alone play. Tonight during dinner, eaten at the workshop counter, Gavin casually mentioned it had been two weeks since they'd spent any time together. Katie promised to rectify the injustice tonight, deadline be damned, but Gavin was nowhere to be found.

"That son of a bitch," she muttered, suddenly sure where to find him. Holding the towel to her breasts, she hurried downstairs. "*Son of a bitch*," she said again, bare feet stomping down the hall. She heard the engine rumbling even before she got to the kitchen door.

"Gavin!" Katie stepped out, moving toward the van while Mr. Big rattled its windows. She pounded on the back window before approaching the driver door.

Gavin sat in the driver's seat, staring off into the dark backyard. Several weeks back, he'd started going for long drives at night to God knows where while she worked on her novel. Secretly, Katie feared he was going through a midlife crisis, that the van's nostalgia had regressed him. Secretly, she worried he was having an affair.

He turned at the sound of her knuckles on the window, fixed on a proper loving smile, and rolled it down. The twangy ballad spilled out into the carport, four overgrown boys longing to date the cool chick in school.

"Hi, honey," Gavin shouted over the music, oblivious. He looked her over, eyes lingering on the valley between her breasts where the towel pushed them up.

"Could you turn that off, please?"

Gavin gave the tape deck a queer look, as if he'd been unaware it was on. "Sure thing, hon." He flicked off the music. "We were supposed to be doing something, weren't we?"

"You were supposed to be doing *me*. Instead, you're doing... whatever this is."

"Just letting off some steam. You know—unwinding."

"Well, I'm going to bed. Are you gonna come, or not?"

His grin was half snarl. "Oh, I'll come," he growled, stepping out. He shut the door gently behind himself and turned, standing so close the hot breath from his nostrils warmed her forehead. "I'm sorry, babe," he said, smiling down at her. "I know you're stressed about your deadline. How 'bout I make you a drink? Give you a nice back rub?"

He was already hard. It throbbed against her stomach as he drew her into his arms and kissed the crook of her neck. His tongue slid into the divot below her trachea, flicking up, down. Katie leaned in to him, getting wet. She wanted to be full of him—*needed* it.

The moment the door closed behind them, Gavin snatched off her towel. She yelped in surprise, rushing naked into the darkened hall, and he laughed as he chased her to the stairs. She laughed with him, couldn't help herself, bounding up two by two.

In the bedroom, Gavin whipped her around and pushed her down on the bed. Katie spread her legs, felt his fingers wedge into her, out and in, felt them pull out entirely and heard him suck them before the velvet head of his cock spread her wider. Delicious pain in a thousand nerve endings of her scalp made her cry out as he grabbed a handful of her hair, pushing deeper inside her. His hip bones smacked her ass, warm vibrations spreading up her spine.

His thrusts grew frantic. Suddenly he jerked her up from the bed, wheeling her around by her hair and hip to stand her against the wall, pressing her face and tits against its cool surface. She cried out, unsure if she meant it in pleasure or fear.

Gavin grasped her shoulder, mashing her further into the wall with each thrust until her tits throbbed and cheekbone ached. Then his fingers slipped around her throat—

"*No,*" she breathed.

But his fingers closed around her throat, dirty nails squeezing the thin veneer of flesh. Katie felt the airway close to a pinhole. Gasping now, she reached behind herself, throwing a blind fist at him, striking his thigh, his hip, feeling weak and very small. Gavin humped and humped until his body grew rigid, every muscle flexing but his fingers, which relaxed, a tender mercy. Before she had a chance to catch her breath he fell against her with a mighty groan, pinning her to the wall, cock spasming as it spewed his hot seed inside her.

Gavin drew away from her then, staggering back. She heard the springs creak as he flopped onto the bed, and stood there panting, feeling the dull ache of at least one skin tear in her vagina, maybe more, as his cold sperm trickled down the inside of her thigh. Gavin had never been like that before. *Never.* Katie couldn't begin to comprehend such a vast shift in behavior, so she didn't try. She merely held herself and wept against the wall until the pain and fear and confusion subsided and all she had left was anger.

When she finally turned, Gavin lay draped across the bed, staring up at the ceiling, still hard after several minutes untouched. "Never do that again," she told him. He turned to her with a look of wide-eyed innocence. "*Do you hear me?*" she said more forcefully.

Gavin nodded stupidly, looking like a hurt little boy.

This is going to hurt me more than it'll hurt you, Katie thought. *Isn't that what Deanie used to tell him?*

"I'm going to wash of." She gave him a measured look. "Sleep in the guest room, sleep on the couch, you can sleep in that fucking van of yours, if you want. But I don't want to see you in bed when I get out. You crossed a line. I don't want to look at you again tonight."

Again he nodded, lower lip pooched like a petulant child, impossible to tell if the words had sunk in. Katie held his gaze for a moment, then strode out of the room, to hell with the pain between her legs.

"I'm sorry!" he called after her, but she didn't return.

◼◼

IN THE WEEKS since his first visit to Almond Street, Gavin and Tony's "pow-wows," which mainly consisted of Tony speaking and Gavin listening, became more frequent. Picturing the man behind the voice, Gavin saw Tony as the type of guy who sits at the bar swallowing two fingers of Jack Daniels, dressed well but all in black, spouting off about all the shit straight white males are forced to endure at the hands of the demon Political Correctness—and despite Gavin's innate loathing of conservative pundits, it troubled him how much truth he began to see under all of Tony's bullshit.

Gavin sang "Urgent" along with Foreigner on the way to Almond Street, beating his palms against the steering wheel, glad for Tony's conspicuous absence on this particular drive. The cassette collection old man Grosvenor discovered in the cabinet had sold him on the van. Gavin owned some albums on vinyl and many more on CD, but his first love had been Memorex. As a kid, he would stay up late with a flashlight waiting for his latest favorite to play on the radio, RECORD and PLAY and PAUSE already pressed, just sitting on the floor with his legs crossed and a finger hovering over PAUSE, waiting for the DJ to announce his song coming up in the next row of hits, or to hear those first few telltale notes. Gavin had gotten so good at instant recognition he'd won a radio contest, although he hadn't been allowed to collect the prize because he'd been twelve.

"Those were the days, man," he told himself, wearing a goofy smile. He peered at his reflection in the rearview, brushing his dark hair out of his face. Crow's feet from his cold blue eyes betrayed his age, as did the lines on his forehead. Even the sides of his hair were starting to gray. Soon he'd be too old to fuck without taking a pill, and too ugly to find a decent piece of strange even if he did. Soon he'd be shitting and pissing in adult diapers, sucking all his meals through a straw.

Ain't that a bitch, Tony said. *Best to live while the living's good.*

Getting old *was* a bitch.

Katie could be a bitch, too, Gavin thought. The way she'd acted when he fucked her last night, after she practically *begged* him to fuck her, it was—

Uncalled-for, that's what it was, Tony told him. *Hysterical. Just like a fuckin woman.*

"Just like a woman," Gavin repeated, feeling Tony's influence like a thick finger probing in the steaming meat of his brain. "Maybe she was right about crossing the line, though. I mean, maybe I was a little too rough."

You just took what was yours, Tony assured him, the dead lights of the dash peering into Gavin's soul. *She's your wife. You wanna break off a piece, that's your right as a man.*

"My right as a man."

That's the undeniable truth.

"Undeniable," Gavin said, pulling up to the grimy curb at Almond Street. The woman named Indica clicked over on high cork-heeled sandals. A violet vinyl skirt hugged her thick thighs tonight, her lower stomach fold obliterating its waistline. Jade jewelry dangled from a raw hole in her navel. A flimsy piece of leopard-print fabric barely concealed her tits.

Gavin shut off the van.

"Back again, huh, sexy? You musta got your GPS set on speed-dial."

Having a smoke a few paces behind Indica, a young Asian in latex thigh-highs chuckled as she exhaled.

"Do you know a guy named Tony?" Gavin asked. The girl by the wall raised her penciled-in eyebrows and dragged eagerly on her smoke a few times, remaining quiet.

Don't go asking questions you don't want the answer to, Tony warned.

"That some kind of innuendo?" Indica smirked. "Like 'If You Seek Amy'?"

Gavin had no clue what she meant, and didn't care. "Where's the dark-haired girl? The one with the lip piercing."

I'm telling you, man, you don't wanna go asking about me or that girl.

"It's called a labret," the other woman said on a breath of smoke.

Indica sucked her teeth and looked off. "You mean Lola. She ain't workin tonight." She turned her thick eyelashes toward Gavin. "But I can help you forget alllll about that skinny-ass bitch."

"Thanks for the offer. I'm just looking for some information. Maybe your friend knows something?" he asked, indicating the smoker.

Indica threw a dismissive look over her shoulder. "Got a taste for the Orient, huh? All right. I can tell when I'm not wanted." Gavin relaxed when she stepped out of the window. She sashayed toward another vehicle and another john who'd pulled up behind the van, while the smoker held up the wall, giving Gavin a sidelong glare.

"You know who Tony is, don't you?" he asked.

"Everyone knows Tony." She took a quick drag and exhaled. "That's why the other girls are avoiding your van like it's got genital warts."

"Listen, would you mind...? I have money." He took out his wallet. "I just want to know who he is. I *need* to know."

You aren't gonna like what you hear, compadre.

"Put your wallet away." She came over, leaned her elbows on the window. Squinting into the darkened van, she saw the back filled with soil bags and hand tools and littered with dark earth. "You sure you don't know Tony? You aren't friends with him or anything?"

"I bought this van from an old guy at a storage facility. I swear I don't know anyone named Tony."

The girl nodded, still wary. "What's with all the dirt?"

"I'm a florist," he told her.

"I guess I shouldn't be afraid of a big bad flower man," she said, faux pouty, and opened the door. Sitting in the passenger seat, she flashed him a somewhat shy look, then held out her small right hand. "My name's Kitty."

Gavin shook it. "I'm sure you understand if I don't tell you mine."

Kitty smiled. She pushed Eject on the tape player and a cassette popped out. "Tom Petty and the Heartbreakers? What is that? Country music?"

Gavin started the van.

Well, hello, Kitty, Tony piped up a moment later. *You know, you're prob'ly just gonna get horny again in half an hour. You get it?*

Gavin ignored him.

"There's an alley where I take guys sometimes," Kitty said as they pulled away from the curb. "A few blocks over. It'll be more private there."

"I just want to talk," Gavin assured her.

Talk about the first thing that pops up, Tony quipped, and laughed uproariously.

"Sure. Talk. Fuck. Long as you've got cash, I'll walk on all fours and bark like a dog if you want."

"Now there's an idea." The words came out before Gavin could stop himself, Tony's thoughts from his mouth.

Atta boy! Guess you got a pair, after all!

Gavin flashed Kitty an apologetic look. She merely smiled.

I love a woman who knows her place, Tony mused.

"Pull over in here." Kitty pointed to the dark steaming mouth of an alley. Gavin pulled in cautiously, worried he might tear off the passenger side mirror in the narrow passage. Kitty rose to peer out her window. Her ass, a perfect heart caressed by black leather, was a distraction to driving. It was a distraction to *rational thought*, though rational thought had pretty much flown out the window the moment Gavin met Tony.

"You're good," she told him, and Gavin eased the van through.

Oh no, sister, Tony replied for him. *I'm far from good.*

"You know, you kinda look like Tony," Kitty said, scrutinizing Gavin's face in the dim light once he'd parked the van. "Cuter, though. Tony had a goatee."

Probably means a Van Dyke, Gavin thought. *Not many guys have true goatees these days.* He'd had a Van Dyke himself, in his younger days, but Katie had convinced him to shave it off a few months before the wedding. The clean-shaven look suited his face better, anyhow. Made him feel like a different man.

"You knew Tony well, did you?"

"We fucked a couple of times. Cheap asshole, though. Always trying to gyp me. Said I should be used to it since 'my people' bargain all the time. I'm third-generation American, I don't know what the fuck he was talking about." She flipped her sleek black hair with a hand. "He likes dark-haired girls. That chick you were asking about, with the labret? I haven't seen her around for a while."

"How long?"

"Like a month or so."

"And how long since you've seen Tony?"

"Six, maybe seven years." She shrugged. "Tony's the type of guy when he doesn't come around, you count yourself lucky. Why you wanna know so much about him, anyways? He owe you money or something?"

"I'm just curious who was in the driver's seat before me." Gavin patted the vinyl between his legs. Kitty took it for a cue and eased over onto his lap before he could stop her.

"You smell better than Tony did, too. I swear he must have bathed in Aqua Vulva." Straddling him, she leaned in to Gavin's ear. The heat of her breath prickled his spine as she nibbled on the lobe. "I'll call you Daddy," she told him, raising up on her knees and rubbing her small, hard tits over his dry lips. "I'll be your Mommy, if you want that, too," she whispered, tugging on his belt buckle.

The idea repulsed him, all of it, but when he searched his heart for a reason not to let her keep going he found it empty. *Already crossed the line*, he reasoned. *Katie said so herself.*

He helped her with his pants. His cock sprang up, and Kitty took him into her mouth. Her small, slender fingers matched the rhythm of her lips, mashing his balls against his bunched jeans. Kitty expertly reclined the seat without removing her lips from him and followed him down, taking him deep into her throat.

Gavin stretched out his limbs, ecstasy swallowing the whole world. But the feeling they were being watched nagged at him, and eventually he had to open his eyes. Tied up and gagged, the eyes of the dead girl in the passenger seat locked on his. She turned her gaze to the back where more bloodied, beaten women sat and kneeled, straight slash wounds festering on their skin, worms and beetles skittering and squirming in the moist earth.

Each woman was stripped to her panties and tied up with nylon rope. Each one as dead as Gavin's stepmother.

It was when he saw Madison Davis among them, the grieving widow, that everything fell into place.

Thaaaaat's right, the voice in his head purred—so obviously his own voice he wondered how he hadn't noticed until now. *You been tuned into WTNY longer than you care to admit. Now don't touch that dial, compadre. We're gonna play all your favorite hits tonight!*

Gavin stared into the bound girl's sorrowful eyes while the cold hands of the dead roamed his body, showing an eagerness no woman had ever displayed, not even Katie, and while Kitty sucked, a smile crept onto his lips. He grabbed the whore by the hair, thrusting her head down until she gagged, her eyes widening as he unburdened himself into her willing mouth.

His orgasm racking through him, Gavin felt free. He felt *powerful*. He felt like himself again, and he knew exactly what he had to do.

He didn't need his alter ego to tell him his next stop was home.

■■

EARLIER THAT NIGHT, Katie acknowledged Gavin's emergence from the workshop with a nod from behind her computer desk. Her book was speeding along at a good clip. Gavin ordered a pizza, giving her a wide berth since what she referred to as "the incident" the night before, and went upstairs to shower. He came back down smelling of fresh soap and the new cologne she'd bought him, and while the scent awakened her urges, she couldn't help but feel an undercurrent of disgust.

Katie ate her usual two slices in front of the screen with a desk lamp illuminating her corner of the open concept living room. Gavin polished off the rest watching the final season of *The Sopranos*, belching loudly when he was full.

"Could you turn it down a little?" She didn't want to be a bother but it was hard to concentrate with all the macho bullshit onscreen. Instead, Gavin turned the TV off entirely and got up from the couch.

"I'm going for a drive."

Katie watched him go. He'd never been as aggressive as he'd been last night, and she'd already decided to forgive him. She knew he didn't have the balls to try it again after what she'd said. They needed to put an end to the subtle hostility, to spend some time hashing it out—all night, if that was what it took—but her deadline loomed, and she returned to the incessant blink of the cursor. In her current state of mind, Katie found it difficult not to make her protagonist seem too put-upon.

That sort of behavior doesn't just happen out of the blue, she thought, the words on the screen blurring as she chewed the ragged left temple of her glasses. *He must have been thinking about it for a long time.*

She thought of how gentle he'd been before, almost timid, and had to admit that until last night she preferred the new Gavin's assertiveness, at least in the bedroom. She could do without the mood swings, the late night drives, the blaring music from that awful van, and the all-around acting like a sullen, spoiled teenager.

I guess that would make me his mother, Katie thought dourly.

"That's not even the least bit funny," she told herself, and slipped her glasses back on, wondering what her editors would think if her straight-laced detective protagonist suddenly and brutally murdered her husband halfway through the book.

The words wouldn't come. The truth nagged at her. *Did he* rape *me? Was it* rape?

She'd said the word "no," that much was clear. She'd told him *no* and still he'd choked her until he finished, using her like a fuck doll and leaving her to clean herself off. It didn't sit well.

I can't sit well, she thought, shifting painfully in her chair. *I'm all cut up inside.*

Thinking this brought a conversation with Gavin's stepmother to mind, in which Deanie revealed a long-kept secret, describing Gavin's adoption in a florist's metaphor. "He's a cutting, dear," Deanie had told her. "Snipped from his birth mother's garden, and transplanted into wonderful new soil. You have to be delicate with a cutting. They take patience, and nurturing. They're more fragile. They have to grow new roots, you see. They have to *hold the soil*." With this Deanie had leaned in, her breath smelling of the cinnamon candy she favored, which Katie had sneaked in to the hospital room. "But a hard wood cutting must be totally *submerged*. That's why Julian and I never told Gavin what I've told you today. And why he must *never* know, my dear..."

Naturally Katie had told Gavin soon after Deanie passed, and he hadn't seemed at all surprised. It had seemed to her that he'd already known, though he never seemed to show any interest in looking up his birth parents. He'd loved his stepparents dearly, but it was clear from what little he'd told her that they had been strict. When his mother was still living, he recalled phrases like "Spare the rod, spoil the child," and "This is going to hurt me more than it'll hurt you." After her death, it was easier to remember the good times, the loving times.

Why did I think of that just now? she wondered.

Katie eyed the photo of the two of them at Machu Picchu, snapped at the summit overlooking the ruins. Gavin's smile, partially obscured by that silly goatee he'd finally shaved off before the engagement photos, reminded her of better days, happier days. He told her she had saved him on that trip. She hadn't understood, and he'd never explained. She supposed she should have asked, but she'd assumed he had meant it metaphorically.

How could he hide so much anger?

She remembered thinking he seemed like a different person the night she'd sat on the cold floor of the workshop, the night his appetite became ravenous.

He was acting strange well before that, Katie reminded herself. *Ever since he brought home that fucking van.*

Katie flicked the word processor aside on a whim, and brought up the web browser. She typed in "vehicle registration lookup," and clicked the first link. She entered everything she knew about the van: make, model, year, license plates. When it asked for her credit card information, she provided it.

She drummed her fingers on the desk, awaiting the results.

What it revealed drew the breath out of her.

Before Gavin, the van was registered to a Tony Gleeson—but the address provided was 223 Dayton Street—*this* house, *their* house. Before that, Tony Gleeson had been living at the Leslies' bungalow with Gavin and Deanie and Julian, who had died when Gavin was twelve. The registry listed no prior owners.

"Who the hell is Tony?" she wondered. It didn't take long to realize Tony was a fake name, that her husband had been hiding a lot more than just the anger he'd shown in the bedroom the night before. That at one point in his life before her, he'd slept in a dirty van and from the look of that old, stained mattress had done a lot worse.

Headlights swept across the living room. A moment later the van rumbled into the driveway. Katie closed the browser hastily and brought up her manuscript. Minutes passed while she chewed her glasses, waiting for Gavin to come in through the kitchen door.

She got up, tired of waiting.

Katie called out his name as she stepped out into the carport. The van idled there, thick exhaust eddying around it like mist the color of graphite. Someone sat in the passenger seat, and though she could tell it wasn't Gavin, in the dim evening light and the haze of exhaust she couldn't make out who it was—but from the small, slim figure, Katie thought it was a woman.

She crept toward the van. "Gav?"

Cold metal struck the back of her head. Blinding white pain shot across her vision. Katie cried out and fell forward, darkness overtaking her as she reached out blindly toward the van to catch herself before she hit the concrete floor.

THE BITCH WOKE with blood clotted in her hair.

His cuttings had whispered a warning in his ear, pawing at his chest, groping him, running their hands through his hair: the bitch wanted to take them away from him, and they wanted to be with him forever. There had been many flowers before but these were his only *cuttings*, snipped from the hard soil of prostitution and drug abuse and transplanted into Tony's Eternal Garden. They were his for all eternity, freed from the burden of lives filled with nothing but pain and misery. His birth mother had named him Tony and they were his cuttings.

This was his van.

This was his legacy.

A seventh flower had joined their Garden tonight: Kitty's cooling remains still graced the passenger seat, the wimp's sperm congealed in her esophagus. Tony had been obliged to strangle her himself because the wimp still had cold feet, and the bound girl—not one of his victims but his birth mother, the young prostitute Julian and Deanie Leslie had adopted him from shortly before her untimely death—had howled in agony, but Tony had made the wimp silence the filthy cooze with the back of his hand.

Soon his Garden would welcome an eighth—but first, the bitch had to bend to his will. She had to *tremble* in fear of his power like a flower before the hurricane.

Gavin was kneeling before her when Katie's eyes snapped open. He looked insane, a wild man stripped down to nothing but a pair of argyle socks, fingernail scratches marking his chest and stomach. He was erect, the head of his cock crusted with dead sperm. In his left hand he held a pair of gardening shears. A small, olive-skinned hand and wrist dangled from the passenger seat, ugly jewelry and painted nails, the first two torn at the quick. Katie saw this and struggled against the ropes binding her bare arms to her ribs, wondering what had happened to the man she loved, wondering where her clothes were, crying out with all of her breath as she tried to tongue away the gag from her mouth.

Tony made Gavin's free hand pop in the cassette. A dark smile came over him as Mr. Big muted the bitch's cries. *Great fucking tune,* Gavin thought in Tony's voice, because he was Tony and Tony was him: he was turned on and tuned in: *WTNY, All Tony All the Time.*

Katie watched Gavin grasp the large shears in both hands, his wild, incredibly vacant blue eyes burning holes in her. "This is going to hurt me more than it'll hurt you," he promised, chuckling softly, because that was what Deanie used to tell him when she gave him the belt. Katie shook her head wildly, screaming through the gag, praying for the neighbors to investigate the loud music. But they wouldn't. They'd had plenty of opportunity to complain in the months before and said nothing.

Gavin opened the shears. Had the music not been so loud, she would have heard a squeal of rust. She cringed away as he moved toward her on his knees. His dirty hands quivered. He hesitated, and for a moment the burning hatred fell away and he fixed her with a look of pure sympathy.

The rusted blades located his target—and *snipped*.

The vile things plopped to the floor before the explosion reached Gavin's pain receptors. The shears fell from his hands and he reeled, staring down at the wet, oozing cavity he'd made at his groin.

His still-hard prick lay like a fat, wet slug in the loose soil. His testicles had oozed out of his scrotum, a pair of glistening pinkorbs beside it. But Tony's cuttings were free—*Gavin* was free. The station had changed, and Tony Gleeson had left the airwaves for good.

Gavin looked up at Katie, and through her tears she saw him laugh, causing blood to spurt from the raw red and yellow meat where his genitals had been.

"Tony's gone now," he said, before his eyes rolled back in his head, and he collapsed against the back of the driver's seat.

When the song ended, Katie's screams filled the silence.

CHOMPERS

DR. BARRERA—IF he was a real doctor—worked out of an abandoned warehouse in the factory district. Shipping containers stood empty amid slats of dust-swirling lamplight, scattered like broken teeth after a bar fight. Dim light poured in through holes in its painted-over windows. Shreds of wiring hung loose from high catwalks, where metal staircases had rusted and toppled. Somewhere deep inside, a generator grumbled.

At the far end of the warehouse, one shipping container had been set up with a dentist's chair, a small sink, a white cabinet, and an instruments table. Long orange cables snaked from its insides to the rattling power supply. A garden hose led off into the darkness beyond the container, toward a source of water. The contents of the container were pristine white and shimmering steel under large halogen lamps strung from its corrugated top. A mid-fifties Hispanic man dressed in white, dark hair with silver-gray wings at the sides, and an older woman with curly hair and large tinted glasses on a lanyard—clearly his assistant, possibly also his *madre*—stood on either side of the dentist's chair. They both smiled, showing off perfect white teeth in their tanned brown faces.

Ray Havers thought of a tropical spa in the desert.

How Ray had ended up here was simple: his teeth hurt like heck. Several wiggled painfully when he ate, and his gums had months ago turned an angry crimson. Since he couldn't afford the insurance, he'd already put off going to the dentist for several years. With a wedding to pay for, with a fiancée too timid to get a job, and a temperamental diabetic cat who required two daily shots of insulin, he just couldn't afford to get any sort of dental work done on his meager salary working night security at the West Midland Mall... especially so close to Christmas.

Ray turned to his friend and coworker Santiago Tinto. The older, slimmer security guard had suggested visiting Dr. Barrera—a possibly illegal dentist he'd heard spoken of through friends of friends—but now that they stood here, he seemed to think better of it. Ray shrugged, and Santiago said something in Spanish to the dentist. Dr. Barrera replied with a single word Ray recognized: "*Si.*"

"*Bueno,*" Santiago said, and to Ray: "Go on."

Pausing at the heavy steel doors, thoughts of cartel death squads and organ harvesting squirmed through the spongy gray tissue of Ray's brain. He knew Santiago would never have deliberately led him into a trap, but his entire adult life until this moment had taught him to expect the worst.

He might actually have turned and gone back the way they'd come, sparing himself the trouble that followed, had his teeth not suddenly felt like the keys of a badly tuned piano slammed discordantly by an angry student. The agony doubled him over, grasping at his jaw before quickly withdrawing his hand with a wince. In that moment, he made up his mind to do whatever Dr. Barrera said, no matter where the man had received his diploma... if he'd gotten one at all.

Ray's hard soles made hollow clanking sounds as he staggered into the container. "What? No magazines?" he said, joking to cover his nervousness.

The dentist gave Santiago a quizzical look. Santiago translated, but neither the dentist nor his assistant appeared to get it.

"You have money?" Dr. Barrera struggled with his English. "Jes?"

"Yeah, I've got money."

"Show me."

Slightly irritated, Ray pulled out a wad of bills, a good chunk of his wedding fund. He displayed them for the dentist and his assistant with his eyebrows raised challengingly.

"Hokay. Seet. Please."

Ray stuffed the money back in his wallet, and sat in the chair. The assistant put a bib around his neck with an ingratiating smile, and Dr. Barrera leaned over him. The man's breath smelled like cinnamon and cigars when he said, "Ahhhhh," sticking out his tongue like a wizened brown lizard.

Ray mimicked the action, opening his jaw until it hurt.

Dr. Barrera picked up the scraper and pressed it into a molar. Pain erupted on the lower right side of Ray's mouth, white explosions blooming behind his eyes. When the dentist removed the instrument, Ray felt a tackiness, as if the molar itself were gummy. Spanish was muttered to his assistant. Out of the corner of his eye, Ray saw Santiago recoil at whatever Dr. Barrera had said. The dentist did the same with ten more teeth, poking them and—Ray assumed—naming them to his assistant, who scrawled them in a chart while Ray tried not to squirm in the chair.

Finally, Dr. Barrera withdrew from Ray's open mouth. He lowered his green facemask with a sour look, and shook his head.

"What? What does that mean?"

Santiago repeated the question to the dentist. Dr. Barrera spoke hurriedly.

"What? *What did he say?*"

"He says that you're gonna need *denturadas*. Dentures."

"Dentures?"

"He says your gums have receded, and the nerves of many teeth are very dead. Either you can get dentures—"

Dr. Barrera spoke again. His assistant agreed with a solemn nod.

"—or transplants, he says."

"I can't afford transplants. Heck, Santiago, I can't afford *dentures*."

Santiago said something to the dentist (Ray recognized the word *dinero*), and the dentist replied, animatedly waving his hands.

"He says it won't cost much. Five-hundred dollars."

"Five-hundred—!"

Dr. Barrera spat out a reply.

"He says he could do it for three-hundred and fifty."

Ray considered it. Not much to lose, just some rotten teeth. If he cheaped-out and went for the dentures, he'd have to clean them in a glass of Polident at night, and Nora would wonder where he'd gotten the money. "Can I look at the teeth?"

Santiago translated. The dentist nodded, and the old woman opened one of the low cabinet doors. Inside were an array of teeth set in molded gray plastic gums. Oddly, not a single pair looked the same. Tiny square teeth, and long straight teeth. Teeth with too-long incisors, and teeth that all ended in a neat, straight row like a movie star's. Even a set of snaggleteeth lay on the bottommost shelf, though Ray found it difficult to believe anyone would choose them, let alone that any company would have manufactured them. He supposed they might have been defective, pulled from the production line to end up here, in a storage container doubling as a dentist's office.

Dr. Barrera spoke.

"Dr. Barrera... he says he wants you to choose," Santiago began translating.

The dentist spoke again, insistent. Santiago squinted, as if he didn't quite understand.

"He says... 'You must choose the teeth which *sing* to you.'" He shrugged. "That's creepy, right? That's kinda creepy."

"That *sing* to me, huh?" Ray looked them over again. Aside from the ugly ones, nothing really jumped out at him, not at first—certainly, nothing *sang*. It felt like when he tried to pick scratch tickets at the bodega, going by juju, hoping something would call out to him *Pick me!*

And then he found them: the perfect set. They didn't quite *sing*, but Ray had always admired his grandfather's long, straight teeth, so he chose the teeth on the top right. Dr. Barrera's assistant took them down for him to inspect. Ray thought they looked handsome. Distinguished. They also looked very realistic. Not quite what he'd expected implants to look like at all, although they were shorter than real teeth, ending in a smooth semicircle, without roots.

Dr. Barrera spoke to Santiago. "Okay, he says they're going to give you the gas, and then they'll put in your new teeth. You'll be..." He listened to the dentist. "He says you'll be good as new."

Ray nodded.

Santiago said, "I'll be right here if you need me."

"Thanks, Saint. You're a good friend."

Santiago waved the compliment away, going red in the cheeks. "Aw, shush."

The assistant brought over the nasal mask. She pointed at Ray's head, clearly embarrassed by her lack of English. "I need..." she began.

Ray lifted his head. The woman gave him a grateful smile, and tugged the strap over, settling the mask snugly on his nose. Before she could bend to turn on the nitrous, he said, "Wait!"

Startled, Santiago and the dentist turned to look quizzically at Ray.

"Will I... dream?" Ray asked, a little embarrassed by the question.

Santiago passed the question on to the dentist. In stilted English Dr. Barrera said, "No. No dreams."

"Okay." Ray nodded. "I'm ready."

The dental assistant twisted the nozzle.

Squeak. Squeeeak—

■■

WHEN THEY ASK Mickey what he wants for his last meal, he says, "Chocolate. Lots of it."

The two hacks look at each other like it's the strangest request they've ever gotten, but Mickey Dunn knows the last guy they gassed in cell block C asked for pussy, and rumor has it the guy before him asked for world fucking peace. They bring Mickey his chocolate without question, just some stuff one or the other of them picked up at the Safeway on break: a box of maraschinos, a couple of Charleston Chews, a 3 Musketeers and a Butterfinger. He eats them all, relishing the sweet chocolate liquor oozing down his throat, and when they strap him down on the gurney two hours later, he's still licking bits of it out of his long, straight teeth.

Here in Oklahoma they use nitrogen asphyxiation instead of lethal injection. They call it "killing with kindness," and Mickey figures it must beat the shit out of riding the lightning. Killing with kindness is a far cry from how he'd cut up those girls in Tulsa, and Stillwater and Broken Arrow, and the irony of it makes him chuckle.

The pastor asks if he has any lasts words, and Mickey says, "Yeah. I wish I ate more of 'em," meaning the chocolate, but he realizes the victims' families probably think he means their daughters and sisters and wives, and even though it wasn't what he meant, he smiles at the memory of their blood on his tongue and oozing through his teeth, and the taste is far sweeter than chocolate. As the pastor does his little pantomime, the nurse reaches out to draws a clear plastic mask over Mickey's head—he sees the glint of the pretty young thing's wedding ring and snaps out at her fingers with a snarl, but the strap across his chest prevents him from rising, and his teeth miss her by mere inches. He laughs as she hesitates, and one of the hacks—Mickey can't see which one—holds him back by his hair so she can secure the mask over his nose and clenched smile.

Mickey says, "Gas me, Doc," and the doctor does, turning it on with a prolonged squeeeak.

It's not long before Mickey's head feels like a partially deflated birthday balloon some kid rubbed against his corduroys and stuck to the wall. The faces of his victims' families swim beyond the safety glass in the gallery. He can't make out their expressions, but he feels their bitterness, their rage. He gets drunk on it.

"Shit, man, I'm high as a kite," he laughs, but the mask makes his words sound hollow, even to his own ears.

He struggles to keep his eyes open, to remain conscious. He knows if he closes them, he'll never wake up. If he drifts off now, it'll be into death, and his limbs are numb, and he can't feel himself breathing, and the numbness is crawling up his chest to his neck, to his mouth, he can't even smile, show them he's still cool as Hell, he's still fuckin' invincible, but soon the cold gray numbness will reach his eyes and they'll shut on him whether he lets them or not, like the steel door to the cell he'd spent the last six years of his—

WHEN RAY SWAM UP OUT of the darkness, the entire lower half of his face felt like it was missing. He had to reach up and touch it to make sure it was still there.

Numb.

He felt dislocated, like waking up in a strange hotel. Blinking at the harsh light, he searched his surroundings: the shiny steel, the pristine white. Santiago stood nearby with worry in his eyes and crumbs in his black beard. Sometime during the operation, he'd obviously gone to get his sandwich from the car. The dentist stood looking over Santiago's shoulder. Behind the two men, the assistant cleaned what looked like blood off the porcelain sink.

"Heyyy, man." Santiago smiled. "How you feelin'?"

"Could be better," Ray tried to say, but his tongue couldn't quite form the words. "How do I look?"

"'Ow ooh...'? Oh, how do you *look*? Great, man. Never better. I mean, you've got a little Bell's palsy thing going on there, but Dr. Barrera says that'll clear up once the freezing wears off." He flashed Ray a wan smile, then gave him a queer look.

"What?"

"Nothing, man. Nothing. Hey, let's give him a look at those chompers, huh, Doc?"

Dr. Barrera handed Santiago the mirror. Santiago held it out for Ray to have a look, and Ray saw what he'd meant: the right side of his face hung entirely slack. He couldn't quite get the hang of moving his lips, and when he tried to smile, they peeled back from his new teeth like a dog bearing fangs, startling himself. He looked the same, only the teeth were different... but the teeth changed everything. It was as if his face had always been waiting for them. Like the last piece of a complicated jigsaw, Ray's new teeth completed his face.

Gradually, his lips formed a smile.

∎

STILL UNDER THE effects of the gas, Ray got a lift home from Santiago. The bungalow he and Nora shared with a nice elderly couple was dark, aside from the small basement window out front, where the blue light of the television flickered. Nora had likely fallen asleep on the couch with Mr. Muggins in her lap, as she often did when he worked. Since he'd told her he was working a half shift tonight (as opposed to telling her the truth, which he had to admit he might not have believed himself), she'd just gone with the routine, waiting for him to come home and tuck her into bed.

Drifting in and out of consciousness, Ray had noticed Santiago giving him weird looks a couple of times on the way to the house. As he opened the door and the dome light came on, he decided to ask what in the hell was wrong.

"That was some really sick shit watching Dr. Barrera drill into your jawbone. I never seen anyone get so many teeth pulled before. Probably won't ever be able to eat again."

"You got some crumbs in your beard."

Santiago ran a hand over his salt-and-pepper facial hair. "I mean, I was hungry, so..." He shrugged up his shoulders. "Hey, don't forget to drop by Stanford's office this afternoon. Pick up your bonus."

"Oh crap, I would've forgotten. Thanks, Santiago. And thanks again. You know, for everything. I owe you one."

"No worries. You got your pills?"

Ray shook his jacket pocket, rattling the pills in their container. The Oxis had cost him a little extra, but he thought he might regret not having them if his new teeth started singing—wasn't that what Dr. Barrera had said? —like the old ones had. Surprisingly, though his gums were a little sore now the freezing had mostly worn off, his new teeth didn't hurt at all. He supposed it made sense, since the teeth themselves weren't connected to any nerves, just abutments screwed into his jaw.

Ray said his goodbyes and crept down the stairs. The sound was off, but the TV still flickered. He turned it off, and knelt in front of Nora.

Mr. Muggins, resting on the bunched-up afghan in her lap, opened a single green eye to glare at him, then stumbled off to the floor.

Nora woke. She blinked at him, her own green eyes looking dark in the gloom. "Mmmhi, honey. What time is it?"

"It's late."

She held out her hand for him to kiss, something he'd done the day they met, a dorky sort of accident that became one of those "cute couple things," as Santiago called it. He pressed his lips against her knuckles just below the small diamond he'd saved six months to buy. She'd told him she loved it the night he'd slipped it onto her finger, but he'd always felt she deserved better.

"How was work?"

"It was okay. You ready for bed?"

"Mm-hmm."

Ray helped her off the couch and into bed. Before he followed her, he stood in front of the bedroom mirror, admiring his new teeth. Already it felt like his gums were less angry. The pain was minimal when he bit down, just a dull ache—a memory of pain. He considered brushing them, but since he hadn't had anything to eat since the procedure, he thought it might be a little redundant, maybe even vain. Instead, he turned out the light, and crept into bed. He kissed Nora on the forehead, and drifted off to sleep.

■■

IN THE KITCHEN the electric can opener buzzed. "Hon, where's the cat?"

Ray stood in front of the bathroom mirror, waiting for the shower to heat up. "Huh?"

"Mr. Muggins?" Nora said sleepily. "He didn't come to bed last night."

Ray wiped a circle of steam off the mirror and bared his teeth at his reflection. They looked better in the light of day. A little pink he assumed was blood had stained the white, but no sign of infection Dr. Barrera had warned about. They felt better than they had in years—like finally being able to scratch an itch after months of being in a cast.

"That's weird," Ray called over the running water. He sniffed his armpits. Still smelled relatively clean, although he supposed he wouldn't have sweated much since he hadn't actually gone to work last night. He drew the curtain and stepped in.

Once he'd given his hair a good lather, he turned to rinse out the shampoo. Blinking water out of his eyes, he saw the bloody handprint caked on the tiles. Worried, he checked himself for wounds, thinking the cat might have clawed him while he slept. Finding his skin without injury, he splashed and scrubbed the handprint off the wall. Pink water ran into the drain.

Nora's scream startled him. He dried himself hastily, enough so he wouldn't track on the carpet, and hurried toward where she stood calling his name. "What? What's the matter?"

"Look," she said sullenly, pointing at a dark stain behind the furnace.

"Flooding again?"

"That's not water..."

Ray took a step closer, barefoot on the cold cement. The smell hit him then—cat urine. His watering eyes adjusted to the dimness and he realized Mr. Muggins lay in a pool of coagulated blood, his innards spilling out, his little pink tongue lolled between his fangs, his big green eyes already turning milky white.

"Oh, jeez," he muttered.

Nora threw herself on him, weeping. He took her hand, brought it to his lips to kiss, but the idea overcame him to bite the finger that held her ring—and not just nibble it but tear the goddamn thing off with his new teeth. He pictured separating flesh from bone, suckling on the gnawed end like a kitten at its mother's teat, and the image disgusted him so thoroughly he thrust her hand back at her. It struck her in the chest, and she staggered back in shock, looking up at him with tears in her eyes.

"I'm sorry," he choked, suddenly nauseous. "I feel sick..."

Ray stumbled off to the toilet, and fell to his knees, a violent red torrent splashing against the toilet lid, chunks of undigested meat splattering in the bowl. His mind processed what he saw, and another torrent of red and purple chunks came hurtling up from his gullet, tearing his throat as he groaned.

"Ray...?"

Nora stood in the doorway, her face ghostly white, eyes bulging at what he'd unleashed into the toilet. *"Go away!"* he cried, kicking the door shut in her face. He spat a thick string of syrupy red into the bowl, and slammed the lid, flushing the contents out of sight—

The bloody handprint. Blood in his teeth. Could he have sleepwalked?

Had he just thrown up everything the dentist's suction tool hadn't managed to slurp up from the procedure... or had he done that terrible thing to poor Mr. Muggins, their diabetic cat? Had he done it with his *teeth*?

His gums itched, crawling under the skin like insects. He shook a pill from the container, staring at his pallid face in the mirror, a streak of blood staining lip to chin. He chewed the pill dry, bitter, numbing. Shook out two more and did the same.

■■

MR. STANFORD'S OFFICE door was open when Ray headed into the back of the mall in a drugged-out haze. The water and air conditioning pipes hummed and rattled pleasantly. Kitchen sounds echoed from the opened back doors of food court restaurants, and the smells made his stomach growl, despite his earlier bout of vomiting. A day shift security guard Ray knew only as Dino stepped out of Stanford's office, tearing open an envelope. He blew into it, then pulled out the contents.

"Shit, man... A Midland Mall gift card."

Ray parsed the comment. "How much?" he asked, feeling his words vibrate his teeth.

"Fifty bucks. But you gotta spend a hundred bucks to get it. Can't even use it in the food court. I mean, shit, they coulda just mailed the fuckin thing."

"Yeah. Guess I should've just stayed in bed."

"Story of my life, bro," Dino huffed. "See ya on the flipside."

Ray knocked lightly, then entered. Mr. Stanford had wedged himself in between his desk and the wall, where his diploma in Business Management hung askew beside a picture of his pudgy, apple-cheeked self with the late Ronald Reagan.

"Ray, come on in."

"Hey, hi, Mr. Stanford," Ray said, too mellow from the Oxi to feel his normal awkward self in the presence of his boss's boss.

"Have a seat."

Ray plunked down into the offered chair.

"Ray, in the ten years I've known you, you've been an exemplary employee. A real credit to the West Midland Mall, and to your uniform. But times are tight. I'd love to say the old gal is doing better, but the fact is, our profits are far lower than in Q3, and it's almost Christmas."

Ray wasn't sure what to say. Odd, this talk of money concerns, considering the "old gal" was currently elbow-to-elbow with shoppers.

"What I mean to say is, if there were more in the coffers, I'd be happy to offer you a better bonus. As it is, please accept this gift certificate, and a sincere thank you from myself on behalf of Terrace Green Holdings and W.M.M. LLC."

"Thank you, Mr. Stanford," Ray said, pocketing the envelope. "Sir, you're not obligated to give a bonus, are you?"

Stanford's eyes narrowed. Ray hadn't ever dared question him before, but the pills had numbed his fear—and the teeth were pulsing, making his jaw open and shut, a motion he felt the need to fill with words. *Singing* to him, he supposed, like the dentist had said. Ray plucked a pencil off the table and put it between his teeth to stop their restless movement. Heard the wood crunch between his grinding teeth.

"The company offers bonuses this time of year as a gratuity for its employees," Stanford said. The phrase sounded more like a question as he stared in mildly angered bafflement at his pencil between Ray's teeth.

"Right," Ray said, "but if times are tight, like you say, why not just do away with the bonus, instead of giving us the same gift certificates you offer customers?"

"I don't—" Stanford's mouth hung open. Ray felt his teeth wanting to gnaw off the man's plump lower lip. "*What?*"

A rap on the door startled Mr. Stanford from his stunned gaze. "What is it?" he demanded.

One of Santa's elves, a pretty young blonde, leaned half through the door. Ray's gaze flashed on the shiny crucifix swinging between her small breasts and the pencil snapped between his teeth.

"Mr. Ellison just puked all over Santa's Village," the girl said.

"Who in the hell is Mr. Ellison?"

"*Santa*, sir."

"Oh, jeez..." Tapping his plump fingers meditatively on the desk, he caught Ray's narrow-eyed gaze at his hand and stopped, withdrawing it, hiding it under his desk. "Get one of the food court janitors in to clean up the puke. Where's Santa now?"

"Mrs. Claus sent him home."

"Christ, you gotta be kidding me! It's nearly Christmas and we've got no Santa Claus..." His gaze fell on Ray. "Did—Ellison, was it? Did he puke on the suit?"

"There's a little on the lapel. Should clean up easy."

"Good. Ray, what are you doing this afternoon?"

Ray looked from Stanford to the elf and back. "Mr. Stanford, I can't play Santa Claus..."

"It pays a hundred an hour."

He did need the money. Refill the coffers, as Mr. Stanford might say. "But, sir, I really don't do well with children."

"Don't like 'em?"

"More like they don't like me."

Stanford laughed, his belly jostling like the jolly old fat man's. "*Nobody* doesn't like Santa Claus."

▉▉

RAY PLOPPED DOWN in Santa's chair. Already the beard was itching, the extra stuffing inside the bright red coat made him sweat, and the line outside Santa's house was mind-bogglingly long. Kids crying, pulling each other's hair, tugging on their mothers' sleeves. He nodded to Kelly, who opened the gate, and he waved the first kid up. Kelly lifted the child onto his lap.

"Hel-*low*, little boy," Ray said, making his voice deep, thanking God for the Oxis. "What would you like for Christmas?"

"Um, um... I want um, a nucular weapond so I can blow up my sister!"

Ray couldn't help but laugh. "That's very naughty... but I suppose we all want to blow someone up every once in a while. I could use one of those to blow up my boss, come to think of it—*ho ho ho!*"

Kelly gave him a queer look, and Ray lifted the boy off his lap.

"Merry Christmas!" he bellowed, already certain it was going to be a long day.

A dozen kids later, he'd been peed on, gotten a sucked-on candy cane stuck in his beard—which Kelly had patiently trimmed out with scissors—and a child's size shoe in the balls twice. His patience beginning to wear thin and the drugs wearing off, the urge to tear off the whole costume and spoil the mystery of Santa Claus for everyone was pretty strong. Kelly hoisted a skinny kid with brown smears on his freckled face onto Ray's lap. The boy was sucking on the end of a chocolate Santa. Ray's stomach growled. He'd never much liked chocolate... but the kid kept waving it in his face when Ray asked what he wanted for Christmas.

All Ray ever wanted was a mouth full of teeth that didn't feel like shards of glass. He'd been granted his wish, but it seemed like every treat he'd ever gotten in life came with a trick.

The kid leaned in to whisper in Ray's ear, breath sweet. The Santa, its head sucked to a round brown nub, hovered close to Ray's bushy beard as the boy's hot breath tickled his ear. "I want my mommy and daddy to be nice to each other." Not the first time he'd heard something like that in the hour or so since Ellison left sick, but Ray's hunger overcame him, and he leaned forward to bite the top off the kid's treat.

"What are you doing?" his mother screeched.

"What?" Ray said, mouth full.

"I saw what you did! You ate his chocolate!"

The boy saw the demolished treat, and his face twisted up in misery. Before he could start bawling, his mother yanked him off Ray's lap by the arm. The damn busted then, tears virtually squirting out of the kid's eyes. Ray used the moment to chew. The sugary liquor oozed between his teeth and down his throat, so sweet it made him gag.

"Santa wouldn't do that, ma'am," Kelly assured the woman, but her eyes showed she knew the truth.

"I *saw* him do it!" The boy's mother pushed her son behind her back to approach Santa's chair. "Spit it out," she told him, holding out her hand palm-up like a school teacher to a loud gum-chewer.

Ray wanted nothing more than to spit the excessively sweet saliva into her waiting palm. But the teeth gnashed out, as they'd nearly done to Nora that morning, and his mouth filled with the salty tang of her blood.

The woman screamed blue murder. Ray spit the meaty part of her palm into her hand before she closed it into a quivering fist. A shower of red ran down his beard and spattered the coat's white fur trim as she hugged her injured hand to her breast. Kids began crying, screaming, parents shielding their eyes and drawing them away from Santa's Village. Kelly hugged the freckled boy, who stood in stunned silence with tears rolling down his cheeks while his mother caterwauled, blood painting her fur jacket like an animal rights protest.

Ray fell back against the chair, stunned at what he'd done. The chair toppled, smashing into Santa's gingerbread house, splitting the wall and breaking the plastic "icing" window frame. He lurched off, tripping over the Rudolph and the candy cane fence, and ran headlong, the stuffing shaking loose from inside his blood-stained coat, pushing through the crowd of sudden goggle-eyed onlookers. He barreled through the hardware store turnstile, rushing past a slack-jawed greeter, knocking the flyers from his hands.

"Sir! Sir!"

Ray recognized the voice: Dino, the day security guard. Someone had radioed him. Now he was at Ray's heels. But Ray had one more thing he needed to do. Tearing off the beard as he ran down the tool aisle, he scoured the shelves, hunting, hunting—there! He grabbed the plastic packaging and hurried to the back of the store as Dino rounded the corner, the former football player's beefy shoulder slamming into the shelf, rattling tools and shaking screwdrivers and hammers and wrenches to the floor.

Ray tore the clear plastic open with his teeth, amazed by their strength, their sturdiness. He pulled the tool from the wreckage and slammed into the men's room. Wheeling round, he pushed the door shut against Dino's football tackle, and locked it.

"*What the hell*, Ray?" Dino said as Ray brought the pliers to the mirror. "I'm mad about the gift certificate too, but you don't have to go nuts."

Ray stared himself down, looking like a demented elf with the baggy red velvet pants and big brass belt buckle. This was going to hurt like hell...

He opened his mouth wide, and reached inside with the pliers. The teeth bit down on it, clacking hard against the metal, pain reverberating in his jaw. "Huck!" he cursed, his tongue depressed by the cold metal, and yanked it free, the bolt scraping against the two front teeth. They clacked shut on each other, refusing to open.

"C'mon, Ray, open the door. You won't like it if I have to bust it down..."

"You don't want to come in here, Dino," Ray said through clenched teeth, then squeezed his eyes shut and swung the pliers at his mouth. The tool rattled off them, bolts of pain shooting up into his temples and exploding behind his eyes. When he flashed his gums in the mirror, the teeth remained unharmed. He yanked on his lower jaw, trying to pry open his mouth, but the teeth held fast.

"You goha be hucking kidding ee..."

Seizing on an idea, he grabbed a fistful of hair and yanked his head back. His mouth opened involuntarily, and before the teeth could shut again he dove in with the pliers, attacking a molar. He yanked. At first he felt no give, was merely pulling his head along by the metal grips, painfully stretching out the tendons in his neck. He would have killed for those Oxis now, possibly *literally*. And suddenly the tooth tore free from his gums. Blood streaked the mirror, and the tooth rattled into the sink.

Ray dropped the pliers, staring down at the *thing* in the porcelain bowl.

The tooth had grown *roots*.

Even more inexplicably, tiny red nerves wriggled and trashed like the tentacles of a dying squid. Ray had a moment to realize the other teeth lining his gums had likely grown similar appendages—that they'd laid down roots, making themselves a home in his unsuspecting mouth.

Behind him, the door frame splintered inward.

Ray saw Dino's eyes widen as the Taser came out. He cried out, "Wait!" through gritted teeth, throwing up a hand as the larger man pulled the trigger. One dart struck Ray in the chest. The other hit him in the jaw. His whole body seized as the electricity passed through him.

Falling unconscious to the floor, his mouth fell slack.

TWO OFFICERS THREW Ray into a small, dank cell. His whole body ached from the Taser and the beating Dino had laid upon him before the cops showed up, when he saw what Ray had done to the poor woman at Santa's Village—all but his teeth, which felt, aside from the constant squirming beneath his gums, perfectly fine.

In the silence that followed the heavy metal bars clanking shut, Ray sat on the bunk, and thought he could finally hear his teeth singing.

He stood, and went to the window. Grasped the bars and pulled himself up. Not a far drop to the ground below. Two stories. Maybe three.

Ray stood on the seatless toilet and twisted his head to bite down on a cold steel bar. He ground his teeth against it, moving them forward and back like a saw, tasting flecks of metal shavings on his tongue.

Oh, the teeth were singing, all right. And they wanted one thing: *blood*.

MENTAL

I CAN TELL they're getting close by the ringing in my ears.

They'll find me soon. Find me and lock me up in a small white room with a hard white bed and stark white walls. I know because I've been there. Nothing to look at, nothing to do but submit myself to their experiments, their mind games. Poking me with needles, pushing me to exhaustion, forcing me to my limits, *beyond* my limits, clouding my conscious mind with experimental drugs to tap into the basement levels, the subconscious... where the killer lies sleeping.

I have to leave this room. If they've sent a low-level Empath, hoping to get the drop on me, I'm already caught. I doubt they'd risk it. They know how powerful I've become. Their training made me the Mental I am now. In a duel of minds, I'd pop a low-level Empath's neural net like frying a circuit board and be out of here before the trench coats have even gotten close.

Still, I shouldn't stay. Just leave this message, and go. I know where that ringing in the ears leads. I've seen it. I've *caused* it.

They can't use me anymore. I'm a liability. I understand that. They'd happily erase me from the world. Redact me.

I just need to think.

Think about what to do next.

Think about what came before, and how it might be able to help me now...

■■

AS A KID, all I knew about my power was that people didn't want to be around me for very long.

My parents abandoned me at the hospital. The other kids at my foster home never wanted me to play with them. Nobody ever picked me for anything. In a big old farmhouse with eleven kids all under the age of sixteen, I was lonely but rarely alone. Our foster mother hated the others, was only keeping us for the monthly checks, and I suppose it's why she took a special liking to me. While she beat and scolded the other children, she taught me how to read and write. She taught me to be strong. To conceal my emotions. To guard my thoughts. She was a cold woman, and she was vengeful. She never married, and to my knowledge, she'd never been in a relationship of any kind.

Mary O'Shaughnessy loathed people. And since people had always taken an unconscious disliking to me, I suppose she must have felt we were somehow similar. Kindred spirits.

The night everything came crashing down around me—the night Billy died—I was up in my room in the attic, the only bedroom not shared by more than one dirty, underfed and undereducated child. I was reading Orwell's *Nineteen Eighty-Four*, and I'd just gotten to the scene where Big Brother's agents capture Winston and Julia when little Billy came bolting into my room, torn shirt, dull brown eyes wide with fear, his face red from crying.

Ms. O'Shaughnessy shouted up after him. By the sound, her voice slightly tinny from echoing off metal pots and pans hung above the stove, she was still in the kitchen. Billy locked eyes with me. I could almost feel his fear turn to calculation, like flicking on a table saw, the blade cold and sharp. In an instant he was scurrying over on his hands and knees so our foster mother wouldn't hear his footsteps. Those dull eyes never left me, his little red mouth twisted into a snarl.

Billy was two years younger than me. Small, but vicious. Even the older boys, like Parker and Jeb, were wary of him. He could slip out of their chokeholds. He could climb onto their backs and jam his thumbs into their eyes while pummeling their kidneys with his dirty little feet. I saw him do it a dozen times. Nobody messed with Billy, and by luck of being in the spot Billy had chosen to hide, I'd stumbled onto his bad side.

Without a word of warning, he leaped onto my bed, swatting the book from my hands, and before I could scream for help, a wiry arm slipped painfully around my neck while his other hand, smelling like sweat and chicken grease, slapped hard over my mouth.

We stayed that way for what seemed like forever, but I knew from the clock on the wall had been no more than a few minutes. During that time, Billy kept whispering to me, "It wasn't my fault. I didn't do it on purpose. Always picking on me. Not fair, is what it is. Anyway, it wasn't my—"

My heart beat sluggishly, as if time had slowed. My imagination still swarming with Orwell's Thought Crimes and doublespeak, I thought if I could get inside Billy's head somehow, I just might be able to *make* him let me go. Even then I knew it was a silly thought, but fear had its cold claws in me, and I was grasping at straws.

I thought of myself as a small insect, an earwig—no, a *spider*—and I crawled into the warm, fleshy shell of Billy's ear. My weightless legs navigated daintily through the dark, smelly maze of tiny hairs and brown wax until I reached his ear drum. My abdomen distended, I pushed and pushed until the pale pink orb squeezed out of my shimmering black carapace. I danced over the egg sac, spinning my wriggling, squirming children into a silken cocoon, and scurried out of Billy's ear just moments before he dug a finger into it, feeling nothing but a slight itch.

"—didn't do it on purpose. Always picking on m—"

A low-pitched drone rose to a crescendo in my ears—you know how kids used to say if you hear a ringing in your ears, it means someone is talking about you? Like that, only stronger. *Louder.* The whole time I imagined myself as an evil little spider crawling into Billy's ear, my own ears burned.

In my imagination the egg sac split open, spilling hundreds of little versions of me into his ear. We broke through the barrier into the spongey, wet tissue of his brain, and *bit*.

"Ow," Billy groaned. "*Ow OW!*"

His hand slipped from my neck. I heard it slap against his head. The other came free of my lips and I fell off the bed onto the floor, rolling and crab-walking back until my head struck a rafter. Billy had been holding his head, but his arms fell slack to his sides as the pain at the back of my skull rattled him from my thoughts.

"*My ears—*" he cried, and that's when blood started spilling down his cheeks from those smelly orifices, as if the imaginary bugs I'd filled his head with had gobbled up all the meat inside. Billy's eyes rolled back to the whites and he slumped over, flopping like a fish onto my bedspread—arms flailing, legs kicking out spastically. I watched him in growing horror, certain he was dying, unable to move from where I sat with my back against the wall. Finally, he rolled off the bed onto the floor, where his head struck a raised nail, and he stopped moving.

Blood trickled into his eyes and he still didn't blink. His body remained motionless. Not even a breath. Somehow, my thoughts had done that to him. Somehow, I'd killed him with my mind.

Ms. O'Shaughnessy's head rose through the attic opening in that same moment. I suppose the first thing she saw was Billy lying there dead, blood oozing from his ears onto the oval rug. She looked up at me and held my gaze.

"You did this to him." It wasn't a question. She could always tell when I was lying, so I nodded.

"He came up here, and you—what? Hit him with something?"

I shook my head.

"You made it so he couldn't hurt you."

I agreed with a tearful nod.

With a nod of her own, very business-like, she came up the rest of the way. She pulled the folding stairs up, the coils *twang-twang-twang*ing against my nerves. Already it seemed like what I'd done wasn't real—but the evidence still lay on the floor, bleeding into the multicolored wool. Hunched so she wouldn't hit the ceiling, she approached me cautiously, like I was a wild animal trapped in the attic, and she seemed to be undecided on what to do next.

"Whatever you did, we'll tell them he fell."

She nodded as if to solidify the notion, and held out her hand. I took it reluctantly. She gripped mine tight, her fingers dead cold.

"Promise me," she said. "Whatever it is you've done, promise me you'll never do it again."

I promised her. She'd never really meant much to me, our foster mother, and I understood she was not a good person, even though she'd treated me well for the most part. But the promise wasn't for her, it was for myself. Watching Billy squirm, even though just moments before I'd hated him to the core of me, with every firing synapse, even though when he'd had me trapped I'd wanted him dead more than anything I'd ever prayed for in my short, miserable existence, I could never forgive myself for what I'd done. I never wanted to do something like that again.

But it was a promise I wouldn't keep. Not because I couldn't, not because I ever wanted to harm another person after that night...

Because *they* made me.

The police never arrived. Two men came in their place. Men with sharp, smooth faces, wearing gray trench coats. The other children gathered around in the front hall—their hatred made my skin crawl. My foster mother spoke with the men in hushed tones, then turned to me with wet fear in her eyes. She addressed the others with a forced smile.

"Your sister has been invited to join a gifted program. These men will be taking her with them."

The others, my "brothers" and "sisters" (though Ms. O'Shaughnessy had never referred to us as siblings before), looked at me with pure malice. I'd been chosen. They hadn't. There was always the possibility one of us would be chosen before the rest, but none of them would ever have imagined it would be me.

It was Parker who offered me the tiniest of smiles as the men led me away. He'd never shown me kindness before, unless ignoring me when it came time to dole out punishments toward his younger "siblings" could be considered compassion, but I would remember that smile fondly, until the men and women in white coats warped even that memory into something terrible.

The men were pleasant as they led me to their car, not forceful. They wouldn't answer questions: I suppose they didn't know much themselves. I discovered, much later, these men had found me because of the ringing, reported by dozens of households for several blocks around our foster home. For over a decade, they'd passed it off as electromagnetic hypersensitivity caused by the nearby power lines, but they never stopped watching, hoping to pinpoint it with an incident like what I'd done to Billy.

"The cause is *you*, Marigold," the man I knew only as Lex told me in my cold white room the following morning. The men and women in white coats became my new family, the white room my home and my prison for the next five years.

THEY'RE GETTING CLOSER. Can you feel it?

The ringing in the ears is just the first sign. It's how you can tell one of them—one of *us*—is thinking about you. This is not a good thing, to be thought about by a Mental. Even a low-level Empath could scramble your emotions enough to give you a nervous breakdown.

Next comes a sensation of being very close to powerful electricity. You've probably felt it. Your hair might stand on end, like you've just rubbed it against a balloon. If you hear ringing and static electricity snaps your fingers when you touch something—doesn't matter what it is, metal, plastic, fabric, whatever. The best thing for you to do is run. Don't hesitate, don't pick a direction, just go, as fast as you can. If the ringing gets louder, that feeling of electricity so strong your teeth start to feel like you've just stuck a battery against an old silver filling, turn around and run faster.

Don't stop until the ringing goes away. Even then, keep running if you can.

Because it means we're thinking about you.

One of us. A Mental.

Please trust me when I tell you: *you do not want to be in our thoughts.*

I WAS THIRTEEN when they brought me to The Eye, their secret compound. One of the White Coats, a woman with a long scar down the side of her face, told me abilities such as mine often presented themselves during puberty. I had my first period in that room, in the white pajamas they'd given me—as if getting my period in front of a bunch of strange adults watching me via closed-circuit cameras wasn't embarrassing enough in a room as white as a detergent commercial T-shirt. They must have had other girls there concurrent to me, since maxi-pads had been readily available. The scarred woman, whose name I never learned during my time at The Eye, taught me how to use them.

It was Lex who taught me how to harness my powers.

On the afternoon of the first day, he brought me *Nineteen-Eighty Four*, still marked where I'd hastily dog-eared the page when Billy stormed into my room. He was skinny and pale, shaved bald, with thick, wormy veins at his temples. "You're just about at my favorite part," Lex told me, grinning as he placed electrodes on my temples. "Room 101 terrified me when I was your age."

"It scared you?"

He nodded. "Will you raise your shirt for me, please?"

Dutifully, I pulled the back of my shirt up. I had no reason not to trust them at that point. They had been nothing but pleasant. In that first night, aside from the oddness of the accommodations, I felt as though I'd been treated to a stay at a luxury hotel. The food—chicken Kiev with scalloped potatoes and crunchy green string beans—was better than I'd had in all my years living under our foster mother's roof. They'd even rolled in a television and let me watch *The Craft* on the VCR, and made microwave popcorn for me to snack on. Ms. O'Shaughnessy never would have let us watch a movie like that, with curse words and witchcraft. She certainly never let us have treats like popcorn or candy, confiscating them if she'd caught us with them in our rooms.

Lex reached over my shoulder and stuck two electrodes already cold with lubricant to my skin under the shoulder blades.

"But you still like it?" I asked him, referring to the book.

"Mm-hmm," he said. When he stood before me again, he wore an earnest smile. "It's good to be scared, Marigold. Fear reminds us of the importance of life."

I thought about that as Lex left the room. A moment later, his voice boomed over the loudspeaker set up in a high corner of the room.

"Marigold, I want to ask you about William."

"William?" The question confused me.

"Billy," he clarified. "I want you to tell me what you did."

I shut my mouth tight. My lower lip quivered as the image of blood dripping into his vacant, unblinking eyes flashed in my mind.

"Marigold...?"

A tear tracked an itchy trail down my cheek.

"I know it's difficult to talk about, Marigold. But the reason we've brought you here to stay with us is to find out a little bit about why you are what you are."

The word stung me, calling me a *what* as opposed to a *who*. I suppose I must have flinched, because I heard a bassy rattle followed by a flurry of muffled, hollow-sounding voices, like listening through the inside of a shell, and I guessed that Lex had cupped the microphone with his hand. After a moment, the voices ceased, and the rattle of Lex removing his hand brought crispness back to his voice.

"Marigold... you are not like other children. You are special. Your parents saw that in you, but they lacked the strength to raise someone as special as you. Your siblings at Ms. O'Shaughnessy's home saw it, but it made them scared, and jealous. We see it, too. We want to help you live up to your potential, Marigold. We only want what's best for you.

"Nobody here will judge you for what happened. You may think what happened to Billy was your fault, but it wasn't. It *wasn't*. If Superman tried to open a jar and he didn't know his own strength, no one could blame him if the jar broke. What happened to Billy..." He paused briefly. "What happened to Billy is the same thing. You didn't know what would happen, and you broke the jar. But it was an *accident*, Marigold. We forgive you."

Tears had been streaming throughout his monologue, but something in his words reached me. I suppose I must have been seeking forgiveness. Or maybe it was what he'd said about my parents. Whatever the reason, I told them everything then: the fear, the spider, the egg sac, the fall. They asked me about my relationship with the other children, and I unburdened myself. I'd had no one to talk to for so long, aside from Ms. O'Shaughnessy, who mostly just lectured, it felt good to be able to talk to a sympathetic ear. I told them about my loneliness, how I somehow both loved my parents and hated them for abandoning me, how I escaped into books, how the only one who'd ever shown me kindness was my older "brother" Parker.

I had no idea I had offered up every little detail they required to shape me into a killer.

The following week, they brought in two gerbils and told me they were to be my new friends. I asked Lex why they hadn't brought me rats, and he grinned slyly. He nodded at the book on my nightstand. "Did you like the part in Room 101?"

"Uh-huh. Only..."

"Only what?"

"Well, I didn't so much like it when he told them to torture Julia instead. He loved her, so why would he want her to get hurt? It really wasn't very nice."

Lex thought about it. "I don't think Winston wanted her to get hurt. He only knew he didn't want to be hurt himself. Do you remember, earlier in the book, how they say Room 101 is 'the worst thing in the world'?"

I nodded.

"Well, the way I see it, the worst thing in the world wasn't the rats chewing off his face," Lex said. "The worst thing in the world was that Big Brother made him betray the only person he ever loved."

I nodded again, thinking I understood it. "You were right, though. The scary parts made me glad I wasn't in Room 101, too."

His smile was halfhearted. Changing the subject quickly, he pointed to the little tawny gerbil. "This is Nibbles. And this is Chewie," he said of the dark brown one. "You can do whatever you like with them."

Hesitantly, I asked, "I can take them out of the cage?"

"Uh-huh. If you want to."

"I can feed them?"

His eyes flashed with an emotion I couldn't make out, but something about it disturbed me. I understood later that he must have known the outcome of their little experiment long before they even knew who I was. I supposed they must have gone through many gerbils with silly names from the other boys and girls living at The Eye before they'd found me.

"Yes, you can feed them, too," he said, and left the room.

I stood over the gerbil cage as soon as the door closed behind Lex. It smelled like sawdust and the slightly acidic tang of urine. Aside from the wood shavings covering the floor, the dish filled with little greenish brown food pellets and a bottle of water attached to the metal bars, it looked like a child's playground, with colored plastic tubes to run through, a slide, and a translucent blue den where Nibbles cowered, chewing his paws. Chewie got into the wheel and started it spinning. It rattled lightly as he scurried up and down, up and down.

I wanted to take them out and pet them, but I didn't find the courage to do so for a few hours. The only rodents I'd known were the rats and mice that chewed our cereal boxes and left turds on the counters and next to our beds. After lunch, I removed the lid and reached out to Nibbles.

His sharp little teeth snagged onto the end of my finger, and he hung on tight as I pulled my finger from the cage. Nibbles plopped down onto the floor, and I managed to grab him before he could scurry under the bed. I held him cupped in my palms, and sat cross-legged on the floor.

"No wonder they call you Nibbles." The gerbil had curled into itself, chewing on its paws, peering up at me with little black dewdrop eyes. "Aw, you're just scared, aren't you? You didn't mean to hurt—"

Suddenly, I understood why they'd given me the gerbils, or at least thought I did. They wanted me to know that even innocent little animals will fight back anyway they knew how when frightened enough.

I stroked his soft fur, and put him back into the cage. Immediately he scurried over to his den, and dug a pit into the wood shavings. Chewie had grown bored with the wheel and was eating from the dish. I watched them a while longer, then picked up a book Lex had left for me, *We Have Always Lived in the Castle* by Shirley Jackson. The book had a sort of hypnotic hold on me. I felt bad for the girl, Merricat, because she was ostracized like I was, but also because she was so strange and seemed to have no idea how odd her behavior was.

Over the next two days, I read and ate and watched my new pets play. In the afternoon of the second day, after waiting patiently with a kibble between my thumb and forefinger for several minutes, I got Nibbles to finally scurry out of his den and approach my hand to take the food. His little claws pawed delicately on my fingertips. He didn't even bite me. It made me smile. We'd become friends.

I'd almost finished the whole book by the time I noticed supper had gone by without a visit from Lex. My stomach growled. Nibbles had emerged from his den again to gnaw on a kibble. I assumed they must have just been late with it, and I read the end of the book. I remember taking away a lot from it, but mostly the idea that change is a good thing. Merricat and her sister had always lived in the castle, and they would always live there, in its crumbling, dirty, waterlogged rooms, because they refused to change. The castle was a ruin, and they were its ghosts.

I'm still not sure if Lex was trying to tell me something by giving me the book, but I suppose he must have been. He'd always been subtly manipulating me, even though I didn't know it at the time. I would find out soon enough.

There was no clock in my room, no windows to judge whether it was day or night. I knew it was late because my stomach hurt from hunger, and the nocturnal gerbils skittered restlessly around their cage. I flicked off the light, pulled the covers over myself, and tried to sleep. I woke up sometime later, shivering from hunger. I flicked on the light, padded barefoot to the camera in the upper corner near the door, and waved my hands at it.

"Hello! I'm hungry!"

Nothing. Not even the telltale rattle of Lex's microphone.

"Hey! *Hey!* I'm starving in here!"

I felt a bit like when I used to pray for my parents to come and rescue me from Ms. O'Shaughnessy's house. Just like God, the White Coats ignored my appeals.

I returned to my bed. I watched Chewie eat a kibble, feeling a twinge of jealousy as sharp as the pangs in my stomach. Finally, I drifted off to sleep again. When I awoke, I was drenched in sweat and felt feverish. The tip of my finger where Nibbles had bit me two days prior had swelled to an angry white welt surrounded by red. I was convinced he'd given me rabies.

I spent the next several hours alternately shivering under the covers, and pacing my cage. I shouted to my captors that I needed food, that I was sick, but they didn't respond. I cursed them. Begged for Lex to save me. For the first time in my life, I swore aloud, calling them every rotten thing I'd ever heard the boys call each other.

I was lucky to have a bathroom attached to my little cell, where I could at least satisfy my thirst and cool my sweltering head under the tap. I considered eating the soap, trying to decide if filling my gut would be worth suffering through its awful taste. Eventually I settled down on my bed again, and tried to sleep. The pain in my stomach was too much to bear.

The hollow clatter of hard pellets against ceramic and tinny rattle of ceramic against metal wire drew my attention to the gerbil cage. Nibbles was eating from the overstuff dish. I wondered what gerbil food tasted like.

I couldn't read. I couldn't *think*. I was angry. Frightened. I wondered what would happen to me if they'd all just gone home, and left me in my room. If they'd forgotten about me, I knew I would die.

I tore the blankets off my bed. I threw my pillow at the camera. I began to shred the sheet in strips, desperately hoping that if I acted out they could no longer ignore me.

The gerbil wheel rattled. Chewie ran, up and down, up and down, while Nibbles stuffed his furry fat face with food.

I was a parasite living in the kibble. Nibbles chewed up my home and swallowed me, unaware of my presence in his food. I sat in his guts, gestating, then burrowed into his bloodstream, like a gerbil in a plastic tunnel. I swam the tight canals of his veins, passing through into his little gerbil head and gnawing into his pea-sized brain.

A high-pitched whine in my ears built in intensity during all this until Nibbles squeaked. He dropped his food and tumbled into the wood shavings. His back legs twitched, his tail squirmed. Then he stopped moving altogether, and the whine in my ears stopped.

When I broke down in tears, it wasn't for Nibbles and it certainly wasn't for Billy. I cried for myself. For everything I'd been neglected throughout my worthless life, for all the pain and suffering at the hands of bullies and careless social workers. For all the times people threw me away, my parents especially.

Exhausted, I collapsed on the bare mattress.

The door came open with a heavy clunk, waking me. I had no idea how long I'd been passed out. It could have been minutes or hours. Lex stepped in with a tray of food in Styrofoam dishes. I smelled chicken noodle soup and sweet tea. My stomach churned with hunger, but for a moment, I thought I'd dreamed the whole thing. That I hadn't torn up the bed and poor innocent Nibbles was still alive.

I sat up groggily. Nibbles remained in the wood shavings beside the bowl, stiffened. Chewie spun the wheel, oblivious. My bedding lay on the floor, scattered and torn.

Lex smiled at me as he laid my food on the nightstand.

"What the heck are you smiling about?" I snapped at him.

"You passed your first test, Marigold. You got an A."

Ignoring him, I dove for the food before he could take it away from me. Lex paid me no mind, just removed the gerbil cage from my room and locked the door behind him. I ate until my stomach began to hurt again, then soothed it with tea.

I slept again. When I woke it must have been morning, because Lex had left breakfast for me where the gerbil cage had been. I ate the scrambled eggs and buttered toast, the cantaloupe wedge and grapes. I guzzled down the carton of milk, and the plastic cup of orange juice. When I finished I burped pleasingly.

"Good morning, Marigold," Lex said over the loudspeaker. "Did you enjoy your breakfast?"

I sat down on my bed, crossed my legs, and folded my arms across my chest.

"I'm sorry about Nibbles. You understand I have superiors. If it were up to me, none of that unpleasant business would have happened."

I picked up my book and pretended to read.

"So... what did you think of Merricat? Did you feel sorry for her?"

I flipped a page, trying my best to ignore him, though it was getting difficult, his voice penetrating my thoughts.

"If you like that book, I could bring you more. You're old enough for a real scary book, I think."

I glanced up at the speaker and became electricity, surging through the wires and out the other end. As Lex reached out to touch the microphone, I jolted him with a shock. The thousand-watt charge traveled up his arm to his heart, cooking it like a frog in a pot.

"I think you'd like that, wouldn't you?" Lex said, his voice unwavering, seemingly impervious to the murderous effects of my imagination. I gave him nothing back, though his books were all I had. Without them, I was alone.

"I don't *have* to bring you books, you know," he whined. "Maybe I'll just take them all back to the library."

"No," I blurted out, my voice very small. "Please. I want you to."

"Mm, nah. It doesn't sound like you *really* want them."

I got up out of bed and stood under the camera, looking up. Wearing my biggest pout. I clasped my hands tightly against my chest like some kid beseeching the angels to bring her father back safe from the war. "Please, Lex? I'm really sorry. I didn't mean to get mad. It was just... it was dumb. *I* was dumb. Please, bring me more books."

The microphone muffled voices in the background. A moment later, Lex came back on, clear as day. "Okay, Marigold. You've convinced me."

I smiled, much wider than if it had been all about the books. Because even though I apparently couldn't harm Lex while he was outside of my room, he was no longer the only one manipulating people around here. I didn't need his books, but I did need him to *believe* I needed them, to think he held this power over me.

What I took away from the Gerbil Test was that the White Coats,

Lex included, and whoever he was accountable to, they would push me to the brink of death to get what they wanted from me. They might even kill me, if I refused them.

So I would give them what they wanted. I would betray myself and the promise I'd made. But I wouldn't let them get inside my head.

This was *my* Room 101 now but I wouldn't be their victim, not any longer.

I'd be the rat.

THEY PUSHED ME to limits and beyond over the next few months. During that time, my "brother" Parker had always been a ghost in my thoughts, whispering in the halls of my mind, smiling at me from darkening recesses of memory. I dreamed about him often. Aside from Ms. O'Shaughnessy, he was the only real person I ever dreamed of—unless you counted my parents, who sometimes showed up in my dreams in various incarnations even though I didn't know what they looked like. I suppose those dreams of Parker, where he would show me kindness, where we would hold hands and sometimes kiss, had solidified our relationship long before I ever saw him again. I often woke up wondering if he dreamed of me the same nights I'd dreamt of him. If somehow we had shared the experience.

One day the scarred woman injected me with something that made me groggy and giggly before she brought me to a room so tall it could have been an old missile silo. At the center of the tall white room was a school desk, the kind made of chrome and orange fiberglass and wood laminate. It stood under a great big skylight, with a view of the perfect blue sky way, way up top.

"This is The Eye," the woman told me, and left me there to wander. We'd passed no one in the halls as we traveled there. It seemed as though, aside from Lex and me and the woman with the scar, the place was deserted.

I ran a hand along the smooth, circular wall, feeling cold where it must have been its outer edge, on the opposite curve of the wide room from the door we'd entered. Seeing the sky above got me really thinking of escape, though I'd been vaguely plotting it since the Gerbil Test. I wanted to work on a map in my head of what places might potentially lead outside, and how I might get out there. Aside from the single door and skylight, The Eye itself seemed to be impenetrable.

"Hello, Marigold," Lex said over a loudspeaker, his voice strained. He cleared his throat. I heard a small squeak I assumed to be his chair as he situated himself.

"Hiya, Lex," I replied brightly, feeling what I would later discover was very similar to drunkenness.

He chuckled. "You're sounding very chipper today."

"Why wouldn't I be? It's a beautiful day."

I heard the smile in his voice. "It is, isn't it? Marigold, why don't you have a seat at the desk so we can begin our lesson."

I sat obediently. He thanked me.

On the desktop were several sheets of blank beige drawing paper and three black Crayola crayons.

"Do you like to draw, Marigold?"

I shrugged. "I kinda suck at drawing."

"Well, that's not really the point of drawing, now is it?"

"I don't know." I was deliberately argumentative at that point. I couldn't let them have everything they wanted without a fight, or it would look suspicious.

"Could you do me a favor?"

I nodded.

"Pick up a crayon and just start drawing. Whatever pops into your head. A tree, a pony—"

"A pony?" I said, rolling my eyes.

"Right, you're too old for ponies. Well, why don't you draw something you dream about?"

Immediately Parker came to mind, and my cheeks flushed red. The camera pointing at my face buzzed. I felt their eyes on me, and it only made my face and neck hotter.

"Marigold?"

I cleared my throat. "Mm-hmm, yes?"

"Might be better to draw something you've never seen before, okay?"

I picked up a crayon, put the tip to the paper, no idea what I would draw, certain it would all end up looking like stick figures even if I force my imagination to play nice.

The walls began to rumble, as if the air conditioning had come on. The temperature didn't change, but I did feel a rising vibration in the legs of the desk. I hummed along with it, trying to find the right pitch, until my voice melded with the sound of the walls.

Feeling a tremendous pressure just to start something, whether from the White Coats or myself, I just started scribbling. The scribbles came together, darker in places, lighter in others. Eventually almond-shaped eyes begin to take shape. A sharp nose. A narrow mouth with tight lips. The crayon snapped and I kept going, wearing it down to a nub. Small ears with slight elfish upper curves. Angled eyebrows, one raised slightly higher in a look of suspicion. A square jaw and dimpled chin.

Finally, I set the crayon nub down on the page and looked at the woman I'd drawn. My own skill surprised me. I'd never drawn anything as realistic in my life. Whoever she was, I was certain I'd never seen her before.

The air conditioning died down, the hum giving way to silence.

"You're finished?" Lex's voice startled me. I held it up for him to see. I heard clapping in the background before he covered the mic. "That's good, Marigold. That's *very* good."

"Who is she?"

"I'm sure I don't know that. She came from your imagination, I suspect."

The woman with no name came to collect me and my drawing, and brought me back to my room. They gave me a chocolate popsicle with lunch, and we never spoke of the woman I drew again.

Over the next few months they asked me to draw more things, like men I'd never met, whose faces seemed to jump into my head full-born like the woman with the dimpled chin had the first time, and a bus, and black stretch limousines. During the second session I noticed the air conditioning or whatever it was began to hum again just before I started to draw, only it was a different tone from the first. I drew an angry-looking man with a small head, narrow eyes and a curled goatee. Again, he looked like no one I knew or had even dreamed.

Over the months, I began to see the pattern. The hum, the seemingly automatic drawing, the praise from Lex and the nameless woman. I never really got any better. All of my drawings remained scribbles, only vague impressions of what I supposed they were meant to be. And the tone of the hum changed every time. I began to understand it wasn't air conditioning at all. *They* were making the walls vibrate, controlling the sound. And something about that sound was connected to the scribbly people I drew for them.

One day the woman and I entered The Eye to find a standup piano set up where the desk used to be, its back to the door. Lex stood beside it, smiling, a hand on its gleaming wood surface. He was dressed in his typical white jumper, but I half-expected him to be wearing a topcoat and tails.

"Good morning, Mary."

"Morning," I said as I approached him. "I hope you don't expect me to play that thing."

A smile crept onto his lips. He sat down behind it, an old red chestnut-stained Steinway, and ruffled the cuffs of his white coat before playing the high notes of "Heart and Soul"—and not very well.

"You *stink*," I told him.

"It's really a duet." He shifted on the seat, and patted its surface. Reluctantly, I sat with him. I noticed in the interim the nameless woman had made her exit.

Lex shifted his knees toward me. "I thought maybe you were ready to know a little bit about why you're here."

"Okay..."

He pressed down on what I now know was Middle C, but then I just saw it as a white key near the middle. The note rang out in the wide, tall room. "I'm sure you know what we hear as notes are actually vibrations. The way we perceive pitch or frequency is through the oscillation of thousands of tiny hairs on our tympanic membrane, or ear drum. They convert the sound to electrical impulses that travel directly to our brains. You know this, right?"

I shrugged. I don't recall Ms. O'Shaughnessy ever teaching me that, but it seemed to make sense.

"What if I told you, each of our brains works on its own frequency? And that frequency is as unique to us as our fingerprints."

I folded my arms across my chest. "That sounds a little farfetched, honestly."

Lex laughed. "Well, for the sake of argument, let's say it's true. Now, you can see the piano has a wide range of notes, or frequencies..." He thumbed the lowest key, which rumbled out into the spacious room. For some reason those low notes on the piano have always given me the creeps, and I was glad when the sound faded away. He did the same with the highest key, reaching over me. His elbow brushed against my left breast, which was still no more than a nub, but it made my cheeks feel hot. Lex didn't seem to notice. The note he'd played was so high it didn't resonate long.

"But it doesn't have quite the same range as the human ear, or the human brain, which can *sense* far more frequencies than the ears can perceive. Those lower frequency vibrations, lower than 20Hz, are practically *ghosts* of sounds. And anything higher than about 20,000Hz can damage our ears even if they don't perceive it. There are studies now that are looking into ultrasound—higher than the human range—and *infra*sound—lower—that are producing excellent results which may lead in the future to acoustic weaponry."

"Great," I said sarcastically.

Lex flashed a grin. "Anyway, as you can tell, the human limit of hearing is not anywhere near the limit of sounds that can be produced. Even just within the range of human perception, there are nineteen-thousand nine-hundred and eighty different frequencies *that we know of*. There may even be frequencies *in between* those frequencies that we've yet to discover!"

His eyes twinkled at the thought of it. "I can see your eyes are glazing over. To the point then. Think of these frequencies as radio waves. On a simple radio, you have your FM band and your AM band. There are millions of stations around the world, but since these waves travel over the air, we're only able to hear a certain number of them in any one place, and the rest of the dial is filled with static. Now think of each radio station as a person, or more specifically, a person's thoughts. That's seven billion radio stations! Instead of the latest Beyoncé chart-topper, or the local weather in Kazakhstan, as you turn the dial you're hearing *thoughts*. There's absolutely no static on the dial, because there's barely enough room to contain the stations we've got. Some children can tap into those thoughts like they're listening to the radio. We call them Psychs, which is short for psychic. Others can tap into only the emotions. Here at The Eye we call them Empaths.

"You, Mary—" He'd started calling me Mary a few months into our drawing sessions. While I didn't so much like the name, it meant he was feeling more familiar with me, which was to my advantage. "—we don't have a name for children like you yet, because there *are* no children like you. You've been able to mimic just about every frequency we've thrown at you, with or without your drawings. And when you tap into the frequency of someone's thoughts, you tap into their *mind*. You may not be able to hear their thoughts, or sense their emotions..." His eyes twinkled with unknown possibilities. "But you can tinker with their brains, and that's *far* more powerful. Those other abilities are parlor tricks compared to what you can do—especially when we boost your signal here in The Eye."

I considered this. Somewhere along the line I'd figured out what they had me doing here was far less innocent than mere doodling. But the exact nature of their experiments, considering I hadn't been able to "tap" into Lex's mind when he was sitting in the next room from me, didn't quite fall into place. Now it all clicked. I felt a hollowness in the pit of my chest, and swallowed hard.

"All those people you had me draw..."

"Criminals, gangsters, killers," he said. "Evil men and women, every one of them."

My head was spinning, but I struggled to gain control of myself, on the verge of blacking out. I stood up from the chair, needing air. The faces I'd drawn over the months and days rose in my rapidly grayed-out vision. I grabbed the piano to stay upright, heard the wires hum discordantly at my touch.

"I never wanted to hurt anyone," I choked out.

Lex had stood up and took my shoulder, but I shrugged it off violently. He stepped away, looking wounded. I paced the room, getting my sight back, gaining more control with each step away from the piano and Lex.

I thought of the limousine. The bus. How many people...? Surely I couldn't have crashed a *whole bus* to kill a single victim?

I wiped tears and snot from my face, and looked up clearly, as fiercely as I could, at Lex. He shrank from my gaze. The walls began to hum at a very low frequency.

"Marigold..." Lex pressed a finger against his right ear. "Mary, you don't want to do that now—"

The walls rumbled. The piano began to match its resonance with a deep twang.

I had found Lex's frequency: a very low minor chord.

He stood and staggered to the door. I saw blood trickling down from his ear as he pushed past me.

The sound ceased immediately as the door slammed behind him. I sat cross legged on the floor, staring up at the camera.

Eventually, I began to laugh.

■■

I FIRST NOTICED Lex's lingering looks—jeepers, there's a mouthful—the year I turned sixteen. That was the year the girl I saw in the mirror begin to change into the woman she would become. My button nose straightened out. I lost the baby fat in my cheeks, my cheekbones becoming more prominent. My blonde eyebrows darkened, and my lips grew plump. I wouldn't exactly say I was pretty, but I was definitely not what people would consider ugly.

At first I thought it was fear in his eyes from our encounter in The Eye, but soon I realized I was mistaken. The day I found Lex's frequency—not to kill him, I don't think, just to assure them I wasn't quite as helpless as they might've imagined I was, that I still held some power in our arrangement—that happened so long ago I could barely recall what had started it by then, but the consequences of that day remained. Lex never entered The Eye with me again, and I never saw the woman again. I suspect she must have quit, thinking her life might be in danger. Lex came to my room to present me with food and clear the tray, but we never talked like we had. From that day on, we only spoke with the loudspeaker and camera between us. On those brief visits, and while he walked me to the silo, I noticed an addition to his wardrobe: a small black earpiece.

They were jamming my signal.

The day I discovered Lex's feelings for me, I'd just gotten out of the shower as he brought me my lunch. I'd put on the T-shirt I'd worn the day before, and was changing into a fresh one when the door opened. I turned to find Lex's mouth agape, the tray of food just about forgotten in his hand. When he closed his mouth his teeth clacked together.

I stood there with my not-so-small-anymore breasts exposed beneath the rumpled shirt, my elbows still in the air, marveling at his reaction.

"I... sorry, Mary, I... here's your lunch." He set the tray down and scurried out, his cheeks revealing the embarrassment if his stammering hadn't already.

He waited until I'd sat down to eat before addressing me again, but by then a vague plan was in motion. He'd pulled the lever himself, and the rats had moved into the front compartment. With a little bit of coaxing from me, I would chew off his face.

"Mary." He cleared his throat. "I've got a special surprise for you."

I chewed silently, not reacting until I'd swallowed. Then I looked up at the camera. "Oh?" I said.

"You have a visitor."

The news caused me to drop the spoon into my tomato soup, tipping the bowl. A splatter of red stained my white shirt as I stood abruptly, rattling the kitchenware.

"You've spoken quite a bit about this person recently, I thought maybe you might like to see him."

I scurried to my drawers and put on a second fresh T-shirt, thinking it could be only one person. In all the years I'd thought about meeting him, I'd never thought it would be here. I'd expected to be out in the world by then, living on my own somewhere in a nice-sized condo, working a job I didn't care about just to pay the rent while I... well, that was where the fantasy ended. I had no idea what I would do out in the Big World, aside from be relatively free and *live*.

I didn't know then I would end up running for my life.

We met outside in the yard, which was just a long stretch of concrete that may have once been a runway. Lex hung back at the door, within earshot. Parker stood under the silo's shadow, and when he turned to me I saw just how much he'd changed since I last saw him at Ms. O'Shaughnessy's.

"Hello, Marigold." Parker twiddled his fingers in a wave. He wore a tweed jacket and tight blue jeans, not skinny like people wear them these days, but form-fitting enough that I got a good look at the shape of his ass.

"Parker," I said, trying my best to play it cool. The teenage scruff he'd had on his chin had spread, thickening to a dark day's growth of stubble. His blue eyes took me in with intense curiosity.

"So... this is where you live?"

I looked back at the enormous, windowless facility and shrugged. "Beats Ms. O'Shaughnessy's."

Parker laughed. "Yeah, I suppose it does." He scowled, the sun in his eyes. "Are you happy here?"

"Is anybody really happy these days?"

This got another chuckle out of him, before he looked at me seriously. "They say you're doing good work here. That you're helping the government with a top secret project."

I glanced back at Lex, who shook his head so subtly I might have imagined it.

"Yeah. It's interesting work," I said. "Experiments and stuff. Mostly I just spend my time reading."

"Same old Mary." He smirked. The diminutive didn't bother me so much when Parker said it.

I asked the question that had been on my mind since Lex had told me about my visitor. "What are you doing here, Parker?"

"It's funny." He laughed awkwardly. "You probably wouldn't believe me if I told you."

"You'd be surprised at what I can believe."

"Well, okay," he said. "Can we walk and talk?"

I looked over my shoulder. Lex nodded. We walked, Parker and I side by side. He was taller than me and when I looked up, once we got out from under the silo's shadow, his face was silhouetted by the sun. Lex followed a little ways behind us, always within earshot.

"I've thought about you a fair bit since you left the house," he began. "I know that sounds weird, you were only twelve—"

"Thirteen."

"Which would make you, what now?"

"I turned sixteen in September" I told him, desperately wishing I was older.

He nodded soberly. "Right. But... but it wasn't like I thought of you that way, you know? At first I think I was just happy for you. And I wished you would do great things, because it was hope for the rest of us. Or me, at least. Do you ever think about m—" He stopped himself, squinting off at the buildings on the horizon. "—about *us*? The other foster kids?"

I nodded, unable to stop my cheeks from turning red. A sly grin briefly crossed his lips.

"Okay. Okay, good. But here's the weird thing: I started to notice every time I thought about you, my ears would start ringing. You know how they say 'your ears are burning,' and it's supposed to mean someone's talking trash about you?"

"I kind of always thought it meant you were thinking about each other at the same time," I told him. "Like when you go to call someone and they're already on the other end."

Parker smiled. "I like that. Let's go with that." The smile faded. "Well, after a while I started to notice the ringing in my ears would be louder, and sometimes it would be quieter, like that game you play where you're looking for something and they tell you whether you're hot or cold? I'd be on my way to work on the subway and the ringing would get so intense I couldn't hear the music on my phone. It kinda drove me nuts," he said, chuckling a little. "But eventually I realized it always happened when I passed this place. So this morning I rode my bike out here, and the ringing all of the sudden just stopped. I went up to the security booth and the security guard told me to go away, but when I told him what happened, you know, why I was here, pretty much desperate for someone to believe me, he didn't laugh at me like I expected. He called up to the main building, and your friend Lex came to talk to me." We both looked back at Lex, who pretended to be studying the clouds. "I thought he was going to send me home, but when he asked me where I grew up and I told him about Ms. O'Shaughnessy, he brought me inside."

"I'm glad you came," I said, not knowing quite how to respond, since he obviously hadn't known he'd been drawn here by me, nor who or what he would find when he got here. He hadn't come here to visit, in other words, which was what I'd been hoping to hear.

"I'm not disappointed, if that's what you were wondering. It's real good to see you, Mary." When he put a hand on my shoulder I felt warmth spread from his fingers and radiate through my body. "I'm glad you're okay." He offered a smile, and in that moment I truly was okay.

Lex had approached us from behind, spoiling the moment. Parker withdrew his hand from me, as if embarrassed. "Marigold, it's time for your lessons," Lex said.

Parker nodded. "I guess this is goodbye."

"I guess," I nodded.

He leaned down and kissed my cheek. "Stay well."

I said, "Mm-hmm," and frankly it was all I could say. To have him swirl into my life only to be whisked away so quickly, it was startling, to say the least. But as Lex led him back to the door and came to collect me, standing in the sunshine, I thought I understood why they had let me see him.

"Well, that was a nice visit."

"Strange," I agreed.

"How do you think that happened?"

I shrugged. I had a theory but I wasn't about to let Lex in on it. I wanted Parker out there in the world, to live for both of us. If they'd realized what I had, that Parker must have had some vague empathic abilities even he was unaware of, I was certain they would have locked him up, too. Lex had assumed I'd called him to me somehow, I thought, but his next words made me wonder.

"You know you can't think about him anymore, don't you." Not a question—it was an imperative. "I don't have to remind you of the danger in that."

I nodded, glad Lex had his own theory. Let him believe Parker was merely picking up my signal if it spared him from harm. "He won't come back again," I assured him.

"He'd better not." Lex gave me a dark look. "But just to be sure, I've told Garrison to give him a ride home."

"That was nice of you," I said, painfully aware the sentiment was far from "nice." They would learn where Parker lived, and I would be forced to do whatever they told me to do from then on, no matter how grievous.

That afternoon in The Eye, before I knew what I was doing and could stop myself, I'd drawn an airliner. The terrified faces of passengers stared out at me from hastily scribbled windows.

THE RINGING STOPPED. I know you can't hear it, not over the webcam, but it's gone now. Maybe I was wrong. Maybe I've got time after all. Maybe they haven't found me.

It's stupid to hope I've gotten away. I know that. All the months I've spent running, they've been so close behind me all along, like shadows. Like an echo.

I'll never get away from them. With all that I've done, maybe I don't deserve to be free. I am a killer. I've *killed*. And I will do it again, without hesitation. Nibbles the gerbil bit me because he was cornered. All of their training at The Eye taught me how to bite so hard no one would be stupid enough to bite back.

But they have to contain me. Not because they're worried I'll go to the papers, not because I'd reveal everything they did to me at The Eye. They have to contain me now because I'm a danger. I'm a wolf in the henhouse. A terror cell in a hoodie and black jeans.

The government distanced themselves when Project Blue Sky became declassified. You probably heard about it on the news. "A modern-day MK Ultra," CNN said. "Our Nation's children subjected to Guantanamo-like conditions," the headline said in the Washington Post. And my personal favorite, "An Orwellian nightmare," from some newspaper in Canada. The other kids were released back into the world, like domesticated animals into the wild. I read an article recently about one of the older boys having committed suicide, and another who'd tried to kill the couple who'd adopted her. She's currently locked up in a mental hospital. Post-traumatic stress, her court-appointed psychologist claimed.

Lex disappeared. I'd love to believe he's given up on me but I've felt his frequency too close and far too often not to know he's still on my trail.

Project Blue Sky didn't end, it just went underground. Off the grid. It's a science experiment beyond the petty concerns of limitations and government sanctions.

If I hadn't escaped, if I'd waited it out a few more months—and honestly, what's a few months when you've been locked up for five years?—they might have let me go. My participation in Blue Sky might have been explained away as another attempt to awaken dormant psychic and/or empathic abilities in children. They might have forced me to sign non-disclosure agreement in exchange for a massive payoff. They might have threatened my life, and the lives of everyone I cared about—a list growing smaller by the minute.

But Lex made waiting it out impossible, and I ran the first chance I got. Those black lines in the declassified documents, they're hiding *me*. I've been redacted.

I'm just an inconvenient mess to sweep under the rug.

■■

ON NEW YEAR'S EVE, 2013, Lex staggered into my room after dinner holding a bottle of champagne. I'd just turned eighteen years old.

"Maaaaary," he sang, and flopped down drunkenly on my squeaky mattress. Unconsciously, he'd managed to replicate his own frequency on the low note. Or maybe he knew. Another game. Another tease.

"The girl already collected my tray," I told him.

"I'm not here to clean up after you," he said with a long, heaved sigh. He took a pull from the bottle. The sound of his lips withdrawing from the rim reminded me of when he used to muffle the microphone, back when the White Coats weren't quite sure how to deal with me yet. Some of the champagne spattered on my pillow.

"Celebrating all by yourself?" I asked, standing by the door. I sensed something was wrong, more than just Lex's unrestrained drunkenness, and it made me wary, like a wolf when the zookeeper's come to clean its cage.

"I'm not by myself," he slurred. "*You're* here."

"But I'm not drinking."

Lex rose groggily from the dampened pillow. He squinted at me drunkenly, and made a come-here gesture with his index finger.

I glanced up at the camera then. Lex followed my look and grinned stupidly.

It came to me then, what was wrong. The camera's ever-present whine I'd grown so accustomed to in all the years I'd spent in my small white room—it wasn't there.

Lex had turned the camera off.

He studied the soft rise of my belly beneath my T-shirt, visible because I'd taken to cutting the midriffs out of them, mimicking a style I'd grown up seeing on television and in movies. His ogling made me tug at the frayed edge, pulling it down to the waistband of my pants.

"You're a shy one, aren't you? Coy." I shrugged, feeling suddenly very vulnerable. With the camera off and the door mag-locked, I was at his mercy. He swung his feet over the edge of the bed. "The government's cut our funding, you know. We're done here. Finished. *Kaputnik.*"

"Where is everyone?"

"Big party in the silo," he said, flashing me a cruel look. "One last hurrah on the government's dime."

He caught my look back at the card reader lock, and laughed. "Cheer up, Marigold. It's New Year's Eve!" Slowly, he staggered to his feet, champagne sloshing in the bottle. "Oh, and guess what. I've made a resolution..." He swallowed an apparently sour burp as he approached me. "Mary. I've decided... that I'm going to kiss you."

I crossed my arms over my breasts. "What if I don't want to be kissed?"

"You're a tease," he said, his smile twisting down in a grimace. "You think I don't see you putting on a show for me in front of the camera? You think I don't know when you've been naughty?"

His implication made me sick. I fell back against the door, reaching back to prop myself up. Lex stopped barely a foot from me, and took another swig from the bottle before offering it to me. "C'mon, Mary. Be *nice* for me. It's just you and me here. Nobody has to know."

"They won't see?" I asked, as innocently as I could muster.

The stupid grin returned. "I shut off the camera."

I smiled and took the bottle from him. Swigging from it, I let most of the sour, fizzy liquid spill down my chin. His greedy eyes followed the white froth down my throat to my T-shirt, where it soaked to the skin. While he stared at the nipple it revealed, I took a deliberate step toward him.

My eyes lingered on his small, angry mouth, then shot up to his eyes. His gaze moved from my chest to my parted lips as I pressed myself against him. A little moan escaped him. I felt him begin to stiffen in his jumper, and that's when my teeth clamped down hard on his nose.

Lex screamed, staggering back, stymieing the flow of blood with his hands. Behind his fingers his eyes were wide with surprise, but anger quickly followed. "You bitch!" he said, his voice muffled by his hands, reminding me again of our first meeting, when he'd referred to me as a *what* instead of a *who*. I hoped my teeth had stung him as badly as he'd stung me that day. But just to make sure, I gave him back the bottle.

It struck him solidly above the ear, making a hollow note as it connected with his skull. The black earpiece fell to the floor and skittered over near the bathroom door. Stunned, bleeding now from his nose and the gash at his temple, Lex scrambled for it on his hands and knees, but I was quicker. I crushed it under my sole before he could snatch for it.

His eyes grew wide with fear.

No need to imagine anymore, no need to draw. I simply let the anger flow from me. For all the times he'd tricked me. For all the times he'd gotten the upper hand. For his leering. For Nibbles. For the people he'd made me kill. For the five years of my life he'd kept me locked up in that tiny room, a place I hope I'll never see again.

On the floor, the emptied bottle resonated a pitch-perfect match to Lex's frequency. The digital bedside clock flashed all 8s. The desk and bed began to rattle, the overhead lights flickering.

"Mary, don't—" he gasped, his lips drenched in blood from his nose.

I reached down and tore the keycard from the lanyard around his neck. "What's the code?"

Lex fell over on his side, grasping at his ears.

"Tell me the code, or swear to God I'll fucking kill you!"

"Two-two-five," he sighed, squeezing his eyes tight as a wave of agony struck him. "Two-two-five."

I punched in the six digit code, giving him points for the reference.

"You know they won't let you get out of here," he groaned, looking up at me from the floor. "Even if you do make it, you'll be looking over your shoulder the rest of your short, miserable life."

"Maybe," I said, swiping the card over the reader. The maglock clicked, and the door opened with a gasp of air. "But at least I'll never have to see your ugly face again."

I backed into the hall.

"Don't count on it!" he shouted after me as the door locked between us.

The hall was empty. As quiet as a museum. I ran, passing more doors like mine, wondering how many children like me were behind those doors, praying for escape. I thought about letting them all go, taking them with me... but the risk was too great. What if they drank the punch? What if they were perfect little obedient killers?

The rest happened in a blur. Doors flew by, corners, dead ends. The alarm began to blare, flashing red on white. My heart beat so heavily in my ears I could barely hear it. Finally I stood in front of a door, knowing this was the end.

"GET ON THE GROUND!"

I turned, a cornered rat. A guard in full body armor had taken up a stance at the bend in the corridor, aiming a huge black machinegun at me. I found his frequency in seconds. The gun began to quiver, its parts rattling. He gritted his teeth, struggling to maintain his grip. Finally the resonance was too much for his tiny mind and his finger flew open, and the gun clattered to the floor as he brought his hands to his ears with a cry of agony, falling to his knees with a heavy thud of armor and gear.

I swiped the card. The maglock clicked.

The door opened with a sigh of fresh air.

I took one last look at those white walls, and stepped out into the clear, crisp night.

▌▌

I'VE BEEN RUNNING EVER since. For the first few days, I was terrified of being caught. For about a week after that, when no one seemed to be following me, I was sure I'd gotten away.

The news broke during the second week. The President came on TV to address the scandal, claiming Project Blue Sky had been officially terminated. The children were freed, some sent back to their parents, others to foster homes. No one seemed to be aware of my participation. He revealed nothing about assassinations, bus accidents or plane crashes.

Those first few weeks were the most difficult. I'd never lived on my own. I'd never had to fend for myself. I spent two nights on the street, shivering in an ATM vestibule under a blanket I'd salvaged from a dumpster. Once I'd decided I didn't have to worry about Lex anymore, I moved to a women's shelter. I told them I was an orphan, that my husband was abusive and probably looking for me, that he was in law enforcement so I couldn't tell the police. The woman in charge of The

Healing Place, a shelter run out of her rambling ranch-style home, was sympathetic when I said I hadn't been able to get at my ID before I ran. She assured me no information would be shared with the police or the public. My "husband" would never find me, she said, despite the resources he would have at his disposal as an officer of the law.

Unfortunately, Lex had been granted far greater power to find me.

I was provided clean clothes and the basics: toothbrush, toothpaste, hair brush, shower gel. They cooked for us and we kept our own small rooms clean. It was The Eye all over again, in that respect. All of these women were running from someone. They had all been through horrific trauma. But none of them had suffered quite the same experience I had. Once again I found myself lonely but never alone. I listened to their stories, and kept tightlipped about mine, only offering a few fake details when it felt necessary to maintain someone's trust. I felt more kinship with their children, and spent much of my time there reading stories to them, babysitting when they weren't in school or daycare and while their mothers attended group sessions, counselling, and social assistance appointments.

The night the news showed the remaining children escorted by police from The Eye, their faces blurred, I was reading *Where the Wild Things Are* to the little wide-eyed survivors of abuse and addiction, acting out the voices the way I thought a mother might have to her children. I stopped to listen to the broadcast.

"Those poor kids," a woman named Elana said, her prematurely gray hair a reminder of the years of physical and mental abuse she'd suffered at the hands of her husband. I saw tears standing in the eyes of some of the other women. It amazed me how much they could feel for someone they didn't know, when their own lives were in such disarray.

I'd read somewhere that suffering breeds compassion. A Buddhist thing, maybe. I thought about my own life, how selfish I'd been when I'd lived at Ms. O'Shaughnessy's, how all I'd ever cared about was my own little interior world, and whether or not I would ever find someone to love me, to accept me for who—not *what*—I am.

At The Eye, all of Lex's training had backfired. I'd actually learned how to care about others while they forced me to kill. Without compassion, I wouldn't have spared his life the night I escaped, to the detriment of my own. As my eyes filled with tears watching the other kids being led out of The Eye with coats and blankets covering their identities from the press, I thought that was something, at least.

I think I'd finally learned my lesson.

ME AGAIN. I'M back.

Did you think about me while I was gone? No, of course you didn't. I'd know it if you had.

Sorry I took so long, but a lot has happened since that first message. A few minutes after I stopped recording the last video, someone knocked on my door. My first thought was to run, but I knew if I did it would be just like Lex said, I'd have to keep looking over my shoulder for the rest of my life.

I'd had enough of running.

So I made a choice. I opened the door.

It wasn't Lex. It was her: the woman with the scarred face. The woman from The Eye.

But it wasn't *just* her. Behind her, the hallway was filled with children, teenagers, and young adults. Their faces showed fatigue, but they didn't have the malnourished look of Ms. O'Shaughnessy's kids. I wasn't sure how to react until the young crowd parted, and Parker stepped out from among them.

"Hello, Mary," he said.

They all smiled then, as if on cue, mimicking his words like hopeful students addressing their new teacher.

"Hello again, Marigold. I'm Dr. Nadine Maven," the woman without a name introduced herself, and stuck out her hand.

I shook it.

She told me we had very little time. We were going underground. Off the grid. Project Blue Sky was meant to be about understanding the limits of the human mind, but Lex—she called him Dr. Lexington, which I thought was funny—and the military higher-ups had warped it into a killing machine. He'd lied to me when he said there was no one like me. There were others. Dr. Maven needed my help to round them up.

We had work to do, she told me. I packed up the few pairs of shirts and pants I'd gotten from The Healing Place, my laptop, and a copy of *Nineteen Eighty-Four*, both stolen from the public library a few blocks from my motel room, and followed them outside.

In the yellow school bus with tinted windows that drove us toward our final destination, an old Victorian asylum somewhere deep in the woods, Parker sat down beside me.

"Bet you thought you'd never see me again."

"I had a feeling," I told him with a grin.

"You were thinking about me."

I shook my head. "We were thinking about each other."

I put my hand on Parker's knee. He smiled, covering my hand with his. I tucked my head into the hollow of his shoulder and we sat that way in silence, watching the world flit past in the windows.

We each have our own rooms. We're free to come and go as we please, and the people in the small town nearby think we're students and teachers at a special school, which I suppose we are, but not the same kind of special they believe. Some of us provide therapy for drug addicts, veterans, people suffering from mental illness, and victims of abuse. Some help authorities track down murderers and missing persons. Others teach new recruits how to harness their own gifts.

The truth is I finally feel accepted. I finally feel like I'm a part of something bigger than myself. We are the children of The Eye. We can manipulate your thoughts and emotions. We can make you reveal your darkest secrets. We can cook your brain like a microwaved potato, but we can heal it if it's broken.

We use our powers for the Greater Good.

We are the Mentals.

How to Kill a Celebrity

A HOT WIND swept up from the Mississippi as Annie Watkins entered Channel 5 through the employee entrance. Barely a year out of school, she hadn't expected to hear back from "NOLA's Favorite News" at all, let alone in the same week as her interview. The job hunt had been arduous, but with any luck it was finally over. Annie thought, and not for the first time, about destiny.

After a wait of a few minutes a man named Ray Smart met her in the foyer, introducing himself as her supervisor. She laughed aloud, elated by the news, before rushing to apologize for the outburst. After so long working at the City Park Muffuletta stand while looking for a job in her field, she could finally tell them she was done—unless, of course, she screwed it up acting crazy on her first day.

Ray gave her a tour of the station. She'd been to several TV facilities the past year, almost literally begging for unpaid work, but had never gotten the full tour. When Holly Weathers—a fitting name for a meteorologist or an adult film star—strode past them in the hall, beaming her sunny smile on them, Annie found herself a little star-struck, but she managed to conceal it well.

Ray was friendly in a business-like way, chatty about colleagues and staff, but never offering gossip. Annie, with a pad and pen, took notes of things he seemed to feel the need to stress. Rotating shifts, days and afternoons, with overtime as required.

Annie came back on Monday to meet the man who'd be training her. Scrawny, hunched-over, wearing prescription sunglasses, a Rush 2112 t-shirt and cargo shorts with gray tube socks pulled up to his virtually hairless shins, the man reminded her of a grimy '80s record producer. His brown hair was thick and wild, skin like tallowed leather and teeth so clean and straight they could only be dentures.

"I'm Burt Ellis," he said, offering a scrawny hand with too-long fingernails. Annie took it, zapping him with static. She pulled back, shaking out her hand in pain and embarrassment.

"Sorry," she told Burt, who stared, mouth agape, in something like horror. "Must be the carpet."

Burt's dentures clacked shut, and he gave her a measured look. "Musta been," he agreed. He didn't appear to be pleased to have her beside him in the cramped editing suite, but he did as Ray asked, showing her the ropes in a mechanical, droning way as they recut a digitized version of the Rod Serling obituary Burt had edited on 2-inch quadruplex videotape in 1975. Annie was too young to remember *The Twilight Zone*, but she recognized the theme song.

She found Burt's tobacco smell unpleasant, and his stolen half-smiling glances were vaguely disconcerting, but she learned a fair bit, and made copious notes. During lunch, the two of them sat side by side in the cafeteria, eating without conversation. After lunch, more of the same: a methodical recitation of information and demonstration, after which Annie showed him what she'd learned.

"Close enough for cable," Burt said at five minutes to six, pushing out of his chair. "That's enough for today. *Hasta mañana*. I need a fuckin' drink."

The following day, Annie returned to work to discover Burt Ellis had retired.

"You're on your own," Ray told her.

"But... but I'm not ready."

"Burt told me you have a gift. He said... what was it he said? Was it 'Practice makes perfect'? You'll do fine. It's just standbys." The telephone rang. Ray gave it a look of annoyance. "Let's touch base at the end of the week, huh?"

"Wait a minute, sir, what are—" The door closed behind him. "—standbys?" she finished with a resigned sigh.

▐▐

"STANDBYS," KYRA NG told her over lunch. "Obituaries of famous people. Say the Queen dies, or, I dunno, Steven Tyler. You need an edited package for a live hit. You've seen them. The more famous the celebrity, the more unstable, the older or sicker they are, we've got their life stories on hand, ready to tweak the second the news of their deaths comes down the wire."

The cafeteria was noisy, every seat packed with techies, office workers, and on-air talent. The sports team took up the table next to them, chatting and guffawing in the phony-sounding way they did during color commentary. Annie found it difficult to hear.

"That's pretty morbid, don't you think?" she asked, leaning in close, taking the opportunity to spear a crouton from her colleague's Caesar salad.

Kyra raised her eyebrows by way of reaction while she chewed and swallowed. "Morbid?" She sipped from her water bottle. "Welcome to 24-hour news."

Annie and Kyra, who worked in the edit suite across the narrow hall, had made fast friends. A little older, a little more cynical, a few too many animal sweaters in her wardrobe, Kyra edited hard news pieces: terrorism, murders, arson, gang violence.

As for Burt, he had edited the standbys for as long as Kyra could remember, and she'd been at Channel 5 for twelve years. Word was he had started in the Telecine days, when they shot programs on film and transferred them to tape for air. "It was weird that he retired like that," she said. "He musta had his foot halfway out the door, just waiting for you to get here."

Annie nodded. "Maybe." She recalled his strange sidelong glances. At the time she thought he'd been ogling her, but now she had to wonder.

"Anyway, you'll do fine."

"That's what Mr. Smart said."

Kyra laughed. "'*Mister* Smart'!" She shook her head. "It's Ray, hon. Just Ray."

After lunch, Annie sat in Burt's old editing suite—considering it as her own would jinx it, she felt—and waited for an assignment. The whole day long, no one had entered the room after Ray had left her with Burt. She hadn't thought anything of it then, but after hours of twiddling her thumbs in front of the identical wavy backgrounds on the two computer monitors, she started to wonder if she'd entered the Twilight Zone herself.

Peering across the hall, she waited until Kyra looked up from her work and caught her eye.

"What's wrong?"

"Should I be doing something? It feels like I should be doing something."

From down the hall a deep male voice Annie recognized as one of the *Live @ 5 News* anchors shouted, "Kyra, how's that ISIS piece coming?"

Kyra threw an annoyed look at the wall. "Keep your pants on, Phil!" She turned back to Annie, looking frazzled. "When they need you, they'll let you know."

"But what do I do until then?"

Kyra provided a brief look of sympathy. "You've got the internet, don't you?"

Annie faced the Mac's desktop, found the browser icon. "Uh-huh."

"Well, there's a whole world wide web there just waiting to be discovered," Kyra told her, and swiveled her chair back toward her desk.

Annie stared at the icon a moment, then clicked it. The browser opened. She watched the cursor blink in the search bar. She hadn't signed on for this. She craved action. She wanted hard deadlines, she wanted Phil Macready yelling at her for the ISIS piece. Sitting all day facing two monitors each with empty edit windows—they were *paying* her for this?

At six PM, after what seemed like endless hours surfing the internet, Annie grabbed her purse and stood up from the desk. "Close enough for cable," she muttered to herself, and stepped into the hall. "See you tomorrow, Kyra?"

Kyra looked up, still frazzled despite having handed off her piece. "You bet."

Annie made a weak attempt at a smile. "Have a good night."

Kyra saluted her, and returned to the screens.

■■

IT WAS A week before Annie's first original standby obituary.

The second day on her own, a young blonde Production Assistant with hipster glasses and a wallet chain told her to update a few older standbys: a hip hop artist with a notoriously dangerous lifestyle, an actor with a degenerative disease, a famously inflammatory politician facing a handful of death threats.

Then... nothing.

Several days, staring at the monitors. On the fourth day, she brought in some home videos to practice cutting. Her father having passed two years prior, she thought she'd put together a little tribute to him for her parents' anniversary this year. Not sure if such a thing would be appropriate, she'd asked for her aunt's blessing before proceeding. It was difficult for her to watch, at first. Eventually, she grew accustomed to seeing her father's face again: the way his bright smile rose all the way to his eyes, the way he often swept a hand across the top of his head, as if brushing away non-existent dandruff from his close-cropped hair, how he'd sweep Annie and her mother up in giant hugs and twirl them from the kitchen, passing under the creaky bannister, to the front room.

Orville Watkins had been a defense attorney before taking up the gavel, though his closest friends had been calling him "Judge" since grade school. He'd been a good father, had called Annie from the office when putting in extra hours, and when he finally attained the chair he'd been born to fill, he'd spent long evenings in the backyard, tooling in the garden while the sun sank over the lake. She'd bring out a tall glass of bitter iced tea, the way he liked it, and he would beam his big smile up at her.

All the while, all those years, an invisible noose had dangled over his head, poised for the right moment to tighten.

At noon, with a good amount of footage digitized and some clips dragged in a rough edit on the timeline, Annie broke for lunch.

How did Burt deal with so much boredom? she wondered, slinking off alone to the cafeteria. With Kyra on days off, she had no one to sit with. Other people in her department were pleasant enough but seemed to be too busy or too into their own cliques to offer much more than a nod and smile.

"This seat taken?"

Startled, Annie looked up to see the creepy old Camera Operator from *Live @ 5*, though she'd already identified him by the aura of cheap Scotch. He stuffed an apple in his mouth like a cooked pig as he sat, setting his cafeteria tray down on the table. She thought his name was Walt or Wilt, though it didn't matter. She wasn't so desperate for company as to consider making conversation with a career alcoholic.

"Burt asked how you're doing," he said, crunching the apple between words.

She wasn't sure if he was talking to her or the news anchor across from them, but the newscaster—a term Annie always liked, as if they created the news through magic—dressed in a pinstriped suit, didn't look up from the sports pages.

"Excuse me?"

"Burt Ellis," Walt—it was Walt, she remembered, Walt Brenner— said. "The guy whose shoes you filled?"

"Oh." Some people thought Burt had come into money, but it didn't look to Annie like the guy had ever seen real money in his life. He'd retired early, apparently. No golden handshake, just a reduced pension. And no one knew why.

"Never did occur to you why they let you jump the book to get that position, did it?"

"'Jump the book'?"

"Whole ass-load of union members lookin for editing gigs," he said by way of explaining, "not to mention freeloaders—I mean free*lancers*, excuse me—and they give the job to you, fresh out of college." He crunched his apple, breathing loudly through his nose. "You couldn't *give* that job away, sugar. Then here you come, fresh-faced and innocent, ready to take on the whole goddamn world." He swallowed just as noisily as he breathed. "Burt knew right away, you were the one."

Annie sipped her vegetable cocktail, playing nonchalant. "What does that mean, 'the one'?"

"He woulda felt a whole lot better if it'd gone to someone who deserved it, you know? *Really* deserved it. Like that little twerp who does Chyron. I'd love to smack that kid in the chops."

Walt gnawed off a chunk of apple, looking off while he chewed, likely imagining how the scene would play out. "I don't want you to blame Burt in this, okay? He didn't choose you any more than he was chosen. Just bad luck, I guess. Some of that N'awlins juju. But he asked me to tell you, the burden is yours now. And practice makes perfect." He set the apple core down, already beginning to go brown. "I'm real sorry this had to happen to you, kiddo. That's me saying that part, not him."

The last bite of chocolate croissant stuck in her throat and wouldn't go down. She took a big gulp of juice, swallowing hard to dislodge it. "Sorry for what?" She tried not to gasp for breath. "There's nothing to be sorry about. I love my job."

Walt Brenner gave her a look, his tired gray eyes jittery. "Suit your-self." He shrugged up his skinny shoulders and slid his tray away from her, moving himself to the next seat.

A half hour later Annie returned from the tape library with an armload of yellow Betacam boxes. Not sure what she was hunting for, Annie came across a movie she hadn't seen since she was a kid, which started her on a hunt for more of Eddie Bing's comedies, talk show appearances, and standup specials. She made herself stop at the seven tapes she could carry without mishap, hoping to find more footage in the digital archives.

Kyra stopped what she was doing to give Annie a funny look.

"Anyone come by while I was gone?"

"Just some tumbleweed." Kyra smirked. "Looks like you got your work cut out for you."

Annie shuffled the tapes awkwardly. "Yup. That'll be the time someone gives me an assignment, right?"

"Don't count on it."

She stacked the boxes beside the old VTR, and, one by one, began racking through the tapes, looking for the best clips to digitize. With headphones on, her laughter at Bing's antics drew the attention of Kyra.

"You all right in there?"

"Remember that movie *Cool Feet*?"

Kyra sneered. "Ugh! I hate Eddie Bing. So corny."

Annie shrugged. "I like it." She caught Bing hamming it up as he tried to remove his foot from a toilet, and laughed a little quieter, self-conscious. Kyra shook her head, while Bing ended up slipping out of his shoe and fishing it out of the toilet, only to be caught by his fiancée's father with the dripping loafer in his hand.

Annie cut the footage together into what felt like a fitting tribute, a good mix of Bing's comedy performances and dramatic roles, with sound-ups in all the right places, ending on a slow-mo clip of his famously awkward smile, and fade to black.

Something jingled down the hall toward the edit suites. Shuffling feet on the carpet stopped at her doorway. The P.A.'s wallet chain jingled once more, then quieted as she stopped in the doorway.

"We need a new standby, ASAP."

Annie rose in her chair, brightening... It took her a moment to realize a more respectful expression was required. This was, after all, someone's life. "Who is it?"

The P.A.—Hilary, Annie recalled from her first-day notes—caught a look at the monitors and staggered back a step. "*God—*" She gave Annie a look of horror. "How did you...?"

Annie followed her wide-eyed gaze. "What? It isn't...?"

"It's Eddie Bing." Hilary shook her head in incredulity. Behind her

Kyra peered out of her suite with concern. "Suicide, they think. Dead in a hotel room, that's all I know." She tore her eyes off the screens to look at Annie again. "How did you *know*?"

Annie felt accused. "Me? I didn't know. It's just a coincidence."

The P.A. took another step out of the room, shaking her head. "Just... I'll get a reporter... for the voiceover." She backed away until the doorway was empty. Her jingle-shuffle disappeared back down the hall. Kyra remained in the door to her own suite, eyeing her queerly.

"Annie? You okay?"

"Yeah." Annie was shaken by the coincidence—at least she *hoped* that was all it was. She felt like she'd stepped on a live wire plugged directly into the macabre machinery of the universe. "Yeah," she said. "Just a little weirded out, that's all."

"No doubt." Kyra was clearly a little freaked herself. "Let's get a drink tonight, huh? Just you and me."

Annie nodded, turning back to Bing in the dual monitors. Looking at it now, she recognized how haunted it appeared. Unlike her father's, the smile never reached Bing's eyes.

"I think that would be good."

■■

THEY SAT AT THE BAR, drinking too-sweet Sazeracs, watching KBNO's sister 24-hour news channel. Annie's pony tail had come undone, sticking out from the purple elastic like frayed wires. Beside her perspiring Old Fashioned glass, she'd ground a small pile of peanuts into the scuffed, dark wood. She plucked another nut from the bowl, cracked it open, and smashed its insides under her glass.

Eddie Bing's death occurred two weeks before the theater premiere of his latest comedy special. A dramatic series had just been greenlit with him in the lead role, he'd been reuniting with his ex-wife, and communicating with his estranged children again. All signs pointed toward a renaissance in Bing's career, in his life, until—

"*Suicide.*" Kyra shook her head at the big screen TV over the bar. "No one could have predicted that. Just a whole lot of bad luck, Annie."

"It happened at the *same time...*"

A troubled look crossed Kyra's face before settling on a sympathetic smile. "Coincidence."

"Hung himself, just like—"

"Like?"

Annie simply shook her head and crushed another peanut. The anchor repeated that more would be revealed about Eddie Bing as it was discovered, then threw to the 11P.M. news. Annie's standby was the first piece.

"Turn this up," Kyra told the muscular bartender. When the segment ended, she turned to Annie, their faces washed in blue light from the TVs. "No matter how you feel about it, that's a hell of a package you cut." Annie said nothing, merely sipped her drink. "Hey, it took me eight years to make the top story," Kyra told her. "You did it in *six days.*"

"Are you trying to make me feel better, or worse?"

Kyra shrugged. "Little of both, maybe. I'm totally jelly."

Annie allowed herself a grin. Her companion nudged her with an elbow.

"There's that smile." She turned toward the bartender's gleaming bald head. "Bartender!" When he turned, she shook her glass. "Another two Sazeracs, *por favor.*"

"It really is good, isn't it?" Annie asked when her companion's attention wandered back from the bartender's tight jeans.

"*Too* good," Kyra agreed with narrowed eyes. "I better watch out. You might make a standby of me, and take *my* job."

Annie slugged her in the shoulder. Kyra cackled, rubbing her arm.

"I'm totally kidding!"

"It's *not* funny." Dead serious, Annie scowled until Kyra could no longer keep a straight face, and the two of them busted out laughing. The bartender gave them a peculiar look, only making them laugh harder.

∎∎

ANNIE CAME IN hungover the next morning, the licorice taste of absinthe still on her tongue.

She stood in the doorway to her edit suite—it was *hers* now, no denying it—and peered in at the equipment. Green lights flickered in the dim room, lighted by the overheads in the hall. Nothing particularly menacing about anything. And yet...

A groan from behind shook her from the edge of psychic distress. Krya shambled toward her, baggy eyes and hair a mess. "I am so tired."

"Me too."

Kyra stepped past her into the dim room and flopped down in Annie's chair. Annie imagined latches clamping down on Kyra's wrists, the chair swooping her toward the desk, the twin monitors turning themselves on like the eyes of a malevolent animal rousing from sleep. But the monitors remained dark. Kyra looked up at her in mild curiosity. "Whatcha doin'?" she asked, drawing out the words in singsong.

Annie shook her head, temples throbbing. "Nothing."

She following Annie's gaze toward the monitors. "Annie, it was a *coincidence*. It's just a bunch of—" She plucked the mouse off the table, set it back down. "—*harmless* junk." She flicked on the monitors, one after another. They brightened to their wavy backgrounds and tiny icons, not malicious eyes, not a cackling malevolent demon trapped behind the twin screens.

Annie nodded. Of course it was a coincidence. *Of course.* She hummed the *Twilight Zone* theme. Kyra squeezed her aching temples while the two of them laughed.

A metallic jingle moved toward them. They both turned with identical looks of dulled shock.

"Annie, we need a standby for Eleanor Harrison," Hillary said, not daring to meet Annie's eyes. "You guys look like shit."

"What happened?" This was Kyra. Annie couldn't speak.

"You guys didn't hear? She's on the news right now."

Kyra changed the input on the small monitor beside the VTR.

Without sound, all they saw was a black man in his mid- to late-fifties speaking somberly from behind a podium. Behind him was Eleanor herself, fifty-three, a tad overweight but otherwise healthy, hugging her grown children, who in turn hugged her grandkids. The story swept along the bottom of the screen: **PASTOR AND CIVIL RIGHTS LEADER ELEANOR HARRISON CANCER DIAGNOSIS SHOCKS FAMILY AND FRIENDS, CELEBRITIES LEND SUPPORT...**

Shocked into action, Annie got to work, scouring old library tapes for clips of Harrison in sermons, interviews and debates, protesting another black youth gunned down by white police officers, shaking hands with Maya Angelou and Queen Elizabeth. Watching the highlights of this uncompromising woman's life, Annie couldn't help but feel genuine sorrow. Harrison was one of her parents' heroes and her own. She cut a suitable tribute for the woman, "sweetened" it with somber music, and had Phil Macready sit for a voiceover, all the while bothered by the look on Hilary the P.A.'s face when Annie handed the Bing standby to her.

After work, she puttered around the apartment for hours, trying to get the Harrison standby off her mind. *Couldn't happen twice*, she told herself, a mantra on repeat. Inevitably, she ended up opening one of a stack of photo albums. A photo of her parents made her smile, young and in love in the '80s, Orville with his short jheri curl, her mother's blonde hair in Bo Derek cornrows that dangled over her dashiki dress. Exhausted, Annie finally fell asleep on the sofa with the book in her hands, missing the 11P.M. news by eleven minutes.

She woke early the next morning, but still had to rush to get to work on time. Driving in dense traffic with the news on and a cool breeze coming from the open windows, the words "Eleanor Harrison was found dead..." shocked her so badly she stepped on the brakes in the middle of the road. Horns bleated by on either side, vehicles swerving to avoid collision. Annie sat rigid behind the wheel, breathing shallowly, unable to think beyond those terrible words—*found dead*—let alone make the movements required to signal and pull off onto the soft shoulder of the road.

She couldn't go back to work. Couldn't face that room, those monitors. Fear got her moving again. She pulled into the Raising Cane's lot, told the on-call scheduler she was ill and wouldn't be able to make it in for her shift the next day, then speed-dialed Kyra's cell.

"Hey, sweetie." There was compassion Kyra's in her voice. Still at work, she'd obviously heard the news. "You okay?"

"I'm fine," Annie said. "You wouldn't happen to know Burt Ellis's home address, would you?"

"That old creepazoid? Oh yeah, me and him were tight."

"Kyra, I'm serious."

A moment's silence. "There's a master list in Scheduling. Let me go see if he's still on it."

"Call me back."

"I *will*," Kyra said, responding to the urgency in Annie's voice. "Are you coming in today?" Annie told her she wasn't. "Probably a good idea. People are really creeped out about that standby, especially after Bing's. Although I think most of them are just jealous you made top story twice in two days."

Annie sat in the car, peering out at the red and white blur of passing traffic. *Twice could still be a coincidence*, she told herself. *Couldn't happen again.*

Her ringtone startled her. "Got it." Kyra rhymed off Burt's address. "Be careful, Annie. He's one odd duck. I'm not entirely sure he's not a serial killer."

I'm not entirely sure I'm *not one*, Annie thought. She offered thanks instead of voicing her concern.

Burt Ellis lived in a boathouse in the West End. The next morning, Annie parked beside his truck in the small lot up the road, gold metallic paint with a cap on the bed and a bumper sticker declaring EDITORS DO IT ON A TIMELINE.

Burt's twiggy mail-order and/or stripper girlfriend answered the door in a kimono. She shouted into the dim house in a thick eastern European accent—as if the couple lived in a multi-story house rather than what was essentially a double-wide trailer on the water—then lit a cigarette and slinked away inside, but not before shooting Annie a scathing look.

Burt came to the door in a grimy robe he was still tying over boxer shorts and scrawny, hairless legs, blinking rapidly before putting on his prescription sunglasses. "Well, I can't say I'm surprised to see you, except for maybe that it took you so long to show up."

Dishes clanged in the sink inside, deliberately loud. Burt peered toward the kitchenette. Annie couldn't see from where she stood, but she could imagine his girlfriend or wife doing the dishes in a fit of jealousy. "Guess we should pro'ly take this outside. Let me get some pants on."

A few minutes later they sat down at a picnic bench in Breakwater Park, overlooking Lake Pontchartrain. The dark scudding clouds from earlier had moved off toward the east without rain. In hurricane season, the city would surely have felt their wrath. Nearby, children shouted and scurried while their mothers gabbed.

"You're scared, aren't you?" He stuck an unlit smoke between his lips with a sheepish grin.

"Why did you leave so suddenly?"

"I take it you're not ready to talk about this."

Annie held her tongue while Burt lit his smoke. "It was the '70s when I started at Channel 5," Burt told her, "back before all that *Five Means Live* bullshit, when we still called it KBNO. We were still smoking in the studios, and everybody, I mean *everybody*, was on coke." He dragged on his smoke. "That's what I passed it off as, at first: some paranoid dope fantasy."

Annie didn't ask what he meant. There seemed to be no point in pretending she wasn't scared out of her wits.

"The Serling standby, the one we worked on last week? That's the one that really got under my skin. The first handful, it was easy enough to pass them off as coincidence. With Serling's, I couldn't shake that feeling—"

"Like standing on a live wire," Annie said.

Burt agreed with a solemn nod, blowing smoke as he squinted out at the clear, flat water. "How are you sleeping? Any nightmares?"

"I don't sleep well."

"No, I wouldn't imagine. That'll change. You'll get used to it."

"I don't want to get used to it." Annie watched a little girl in a polka-dot dress chase two boys around the swing set. "I keep thinking it can't be real, it couldn't be me causing this to happen..."

"Except for that feeling." Burt butted out his cigarette on the picnic table. "I used to think the film caused it. When Serling died, KBNO still had a lot of old footage on film. We had to transfer to video with a process called Telecine before we could cut it for air. They probably taught you about it in school. They did? Good. I thought maybe it was the silver gelatin—you know, silver's been thought to have magical properties for centuries. Personally, I think it's a bunch of bullshit, but back then I was grasping at straws. And hell, this was *Rod Serling* we're talking about. The guy practically *invented* shit like this.

"June 26th I cut that obituary. Serling was my third standby. We knew he had heart troubles. By then he was already in the hospital. Docs were talking about open heart surgery. These days that's nothing, but in those days, it was a huge risk. It took him two days to die from that last heart attack on the operating table, but I knew... I mean I *knew*...that last one was because of me."

"But you must have done hundreds of obituaries since then. Every one of them died?"

"Only the completed standbys seem to do it. Think of it like casting a spell. It ain't gonna work without reading the last few words, will it?"

"But you did it again?"

Burt raised his t-shirt—Meatloaf's *Bat Out of Hell*—to reveal a long white scar from his right hip to the middle rib on his left side.

"*Ouch.*"

"You said it. I flew the coop after Serling died." He mimed a plane taking off with his right hand, an unlit cigarette poised between his fingers. "I wanted to get as far away from the Big Easy as possible, but I knew I couldn't stand those New England winters. Miami seemed like a good start. Took the Airlift flight from New Orl'ns International—this was long before they changed the name—on a rickety old DC-8."

Annie didn't know where to begin. She couldn't imagine why he would have come back, burdened with the curse she now bore herself, and told him so.

He grinned. "Guess you never heard about Airlift International Flight 208."

Annie admitted she hadn't, but she was starting to feel as though she knew what happened.

"I swore to myself I wouldn't do another standby. Not a single one. I mean I quit without a day's notice, just up and left. Packed a bag, high-tailed it. I got on that plane feeling... *blessed relief.* About as close to whatever you want to call a religious experience as I'd ever felt. I mean, I was twenty years old. I didn't know shit about God. But when that plane took off, I felt like I could join the seminary and be perfectly content for the rest of my life."

He lit the cigarette. Took a long drag, long enough for the ash to curl. "Weren't up in the air ten minutes before the trouble started. There was this loud *boom*, and suddenly the plane is leaning on its side. Not just women and children screaming but grown men. Hell, *I* was scream-ing. Those of us who hadn't fell into the lap of their neighbor or into the aisle were hangin from our seat belts. They told us later that an engine blew. But I knew different." He narrowed his eyes at her. "*It* was pulling me back. *It* wouldn't let me leave until I was done."

Annie merely shook her head.

"I prayed, I mean I *prayed* like I never have in my life. I promised I'd go right back to work if whoever was in charge of all this would spare my life. I meant it, too. And just about the time I'd finished promising, the pilot managed to get that bastard horizontal again by some force of sheer luck, and we water-landed in the Gulf just past Chandeleur Sound. If we'd been any closer to shore, no doubt the gators woulda been eatin leftovers for weeks. Out of a hundred and twenty-seven passengers fifty-three of us made it, including two stewardesses, without whom we all woulda drowned. Everyone in the cockpit died. Everyone in the front of the plane died. Miserable, groveling excuse for a sack of shit me made it out alive to kill again. And God help me if I didn't think that someone like me had already cut the story for the late news. That someone had, through the same sort of magic or what-have-you that made me cut the Serling obituary, caused that DC-8 to drop out of the sky."

"That's..." Annie didn't know how to describe what he'd told her so she merely said, "*Wow.*"

Burt uttered a morose chuckle. "Honey, that is the understatement of the goddamn century. And you know, there isn't a day goes by I don't wish I'd died in that crash. That it ended, whatever the hell it is, with me on that plane in 1975."

"Cut to forty years later," Annie said sardonically.

"More like a long cross-dissolve. All told I've killed thirty-eight people. I wish like hell I'd had the guts to kill *myself*."

Annie's father might have *Amen*-ed to that. Of course having sent an innocent man to the chair in 1990, and having later discovered the deceased's innocence through DNA evidence linking the murder-rapes to a man already doing time for aggravated assault, Judge Orville Watkins had hung himself from the bannister in the Watkins family home.

Executioner was her family legacy.

"Why me, Burt? Why did it have to be me?"

"It's a dirty job, but someone's gotta do it." He favored her with a dour smile, crushing another smelly butt on the table. "I wish I knew. I'm sorry, but I didn't choose you anymore than I was chosen."

"That's what Walt said. I think there's more to it than that."

Burt shifted uncomfortably, wiping away bits of cut grass that had blown up onto the table. "It wasn't a choice, you gotta understand that. You ever see someone for the first time and swear you've met before? It's like that. First time I saw you, day you brought in your resume, I passed you in the foyer and knew—*I knew*—you were the one. I gave my notice that same day. Then when we shook hands..."

"The spark."

"Passing on the torch. Old Jewish fella by the name of Ham Gottlieb ended up blowing his brains out with an antique Ruger after passing on the hex or whatever it is to me. I mean this guy survived the Holocaust, and he couldn't hold another week with what he'd done."

"You think it's a curse?"

"Annie, I wish I knew. This is powerful shit you're dealing with. I mean, this thing survived film, videotape, all the way into the digital age. Who knows, it could have existed before film, maybe the guy who passed it on to Gottlieb wrote obits for the *Times-Picayune*. All I know for sure is you don't just quit on it. I learned that the hard way."

He slipped the end of a cigarette out of the pack.

"Not another one," Annie said. "Please."

Burt shrugged, tapping the butt back inside. She thanked him. Her *lungs* thanked him.

"I still don't get how you knew they'd pick me. They could've picked anybody for the job."

"Same way I knew my time was up, and for the same reason old Ham Gottlieb picked me out of every kid who put in an application, I suppose." He traced out the symbol for infinity with a finger on the table. After a moment, he looked up at Annie again. "Way I figure, they don't know they're doing it. Probably think the decision was theirs, when they hired you. When they hired *me*. But it's not. They're just playing into the hands of fate."

Annie shook her head. "So there's nothing I can do. I just have to— what? Wait thirty years for that feeling to hit *me*? Pass it on to the next poor kid who drops off her resume?"

"I honestly don't know." Burt smoothed his mustache. "I feel for you, kid, sincerely, I do. But... and this might sound insensitive... but have you considered keeping the balance?"

"Like what? Yoga? Fucking *meditation*?"

Burt snickered. "Hell no! I mean, you make a standby for someone who might actually deserve it. Maybe get some serial killer's death penalty put on the fast-track." He shrugged. "Make some scumbag scam-artist like Madoff get his just desserts."

She thought of her father's gray face. The noose. The creak of the bannister. Annie had been the first one home that night. If Lydia Watkins hadn't stopped for groceries on the way from work, she might have spared her daughter a lifetime of questions, of *nightmares*. "I couldn't do that," she said, her voice weak. "Play God like that."

"Aren't you already? I mean, I don't know if you noticed, but it seems to me like God's been on extended sick leave, don't it, sugar?"

"Don't call me that. All you old-timers call me *sweetie* and *sugar* and it drives me up the fucking wall."

"Annie it is." Burt grinned sarcastically, holding up his hands in mock surrender. "Wouldn't want to upset you. You might wind up making a standby for *me*."

"That's not fucking funny. And I wouldn't. I *can't*. I can't do it again. Not ever."

"Suit yourself," Burt said. "Sooner or later fate or destiny or whatever it is makes you and me and Gottlieb do what we've done is gonna force your hand. All I know is, when I hated my job, my *life*, I did everything I could to make it as painless as possible."

He plucked the twisted butts off the table, and pushed himself up with a groan, both from himself and the aging wood. "I wish you all the best, Annie Watkins. Sincerely, I do. But if I spend any longer out here shooting the breeze with you, the wife'll be fixin' to Bobbit my ass."

Annie watched him go, shrinking into the distance across the long expanse of grass, the weight of helplessness pressing down on her, stopping her from chasing after him and screaming at him until her throat was raw.

The table creaked as she stood herself, creaking like the bannister, like the noose around her father's neck. She wondered, and not for the first time, if suicide was her legacy, too.

MAXINE WATKINS KEPT shop in Bywater, selling Central African-inspired art and sculpture out of her home. Fat little terra cotta heads with bug eyes and fish-like mouths were her biggest seller—one even graced the Contemporary Louisiana Art exhibit at NOMA. As a child, they'd always reminded Annie of the illustration from the books of Roald Dahl.

Maxine poured her niece a glass of iced tea, then sat on a small stool at the worktable. She did good business with her art, good enough to move into a larger home in Algiers or the Garden District, but she'd lived in the "Sliver by the River" long before her name became known in the local scene. She had her studio, her kiln out back, and a small living quarters in the camelback upstairs, and that was all she required.

Annie sipped her tea. Bitter, the way she liked it.

"What's on your mind, child?" Maxine asked, kneading a large hunk of clay. "You didn't come all the way out here to drink my tea."

A ghost of a smile crossed Annie's lips. "No, I didn't. But I would, you know. It's that good."

Maxine waved the compliment away. "Is this about your job? I never did congratulate you, did I?"

"No. Thank you, Auntie Maxie."

"Well? Are you going to tell me or would you have me drag it out of you?"

Maxine wore her hair in a scarf, and her overlarge, brightly colored shirt couldn't hide the many paint stains and smudges of dried clay. Annie had always admired her aunt's artistic abilities, but she'd never envied her wardrobe. In snug blue jeans and a white t-shirt, Annie felt underdressed. She told Maxine everything.

"Well that's quite the tale," Maxine said, pushing aside another fat little head ready for the kiln. "If you weren't your father's daughter, I wouldn't believe a word of it."

"You believe me?"

"I've never known you to lie, even when you should have. You didn't come to tell me a story, though, now did you? You came to see if I could speak to the Loa on your behalf."

Maxine was the only family member who practiced what Annie thought of as "authentic Louisiana Voodoo." Annie's father had disavowed it, ashamed of the commercialization and skeptical of the religious aspects, although her grandparents had been traditionalists, like Maxine. Annie had loved Maxie's sculptures and paintings, but the Hoodoo charms, the dolls and Gris-Gris in her aunt's bedroom, had always intrigued her most. She'd often wondered if they were merely decorative, or if Maxie had ever used them.

Tears stood in Annie's eyes. "*Please*," she said. They fell, moistening the clay in two spots on the table. "I can't live like this."

Maxine took her niece's hands. The dried clay felt chalky against Annie's skin. Maxine held them firmly, glittering green eyes fixed on the deep brown of Annie's. "Though it works through modern tools, this evil is *old*, Annie. Make no mistake."

Annie shivered. Despite the late-spring heat, the warmth from her aunt's hands was just about the only place she didn't feel cold. "Can you help me...?"

Maxine kissed her fingertips. The warmth spread to Annie's wrists.

"I can try."

THE HALLS OF CHANNEL 5 were virtually empty when Annie brought Maxine through. The security guard on duty looked up from whatever he was watching behind the big desk and gave them a nod. Annie used her card on the door, and held it open for her aunt.

"He's cute," Maxine said once they were safely behind the door. "For you, I mean."

Annie shook her head, proceeding down the main hall. Maxine followed, lugging the cloth bag onto her shoulder, glass clinking inside. A spiral staircase took them down toward the newsroom. As short as the two of them were, they still had to duck under the ceiling. The overheads came on as they entered the carpeted hall leading toward the edit suites, startling them both into an embrace.

Maxine clucked her tongue. "Look at us. Scared of the lights."

They chuckled nervously and let go of each other. Annie continued to her suite, flicking on the light before entering. Maxine settled her bag on the chair.

"I expected something more ominous. This..."

"Is it cursed?" Annie wondered.

"We'll find out, won't we?" Auntie Maxie opened up her bag of tricks. She brought out the candles first, white and black, a half dozen of each. "To send the evil back from where it came," she'd said while taking them off the shelf and packing them into the bag. Next came the checkered cloth in red and white, which she laid on the chair, setting the fat candles atop it. "Red and white. Those are Papa Legba's colors," she explained.

Annie repeated the name as a question.

"You'll see, Annie-dear." Maxine began marking out a large circle on the carpet, a cross in the circle. "Can't do this without the cosmogram," Maxine explained, reacting to Annie's mortified gasp. She laid the cloth over the center of the cross, placed candles at the ends of each line. She removed two tall wine glasses from the bag, a bottle of water, a bottle of white rum, and a clay pot painted red, then placed them on the cloth. She poured water into one glass and stood it in one of the pie-shaped areas she'd chalked, and the contents of the rum bottle into the second. Into the bowl, she placed a handful of salt water taffy, a cigar and a tea candle. She scattered some coins beside it.

"For the offering," she explained.

Maxine poured water into a rag, and held it out to her niece. "You might want to cover the smoke detector." Annie did so, wrapping it with the dampened fabric. The two of them lit the candles together, then Maxine stood in the circle, holding out a hand to Annie.

Annie took it. Stepped into the circle.

In the silence, the hall lights went out. They turned to each other, momentarily frightened. "Somebody ought to do something about those lights," Maxine said. Annie agreed with a nod.

Maxine led Annie in reciting The Lord's Prayer, Hail Mary, and the Apostle's Creed. Once finished, she let go of Annie's hand, got down to her haunches, and raised the bowl. "Odu Legba!" she cried, holding out the bowl to the four directions. "Papa Legba, open the door! Open the door for me, so that I may pass!"

Annie listened to the dull hum of electricity, watched their flickering shadows on the wall. There was no live wire feeling tonight, senses dulled by too much crying, too much worrying.

"Open the door, your children await!"

The monitors flickered on. Annie sucked in a nervous breath.

"We wish to speak with the Loa! We wish to speak to Baron Cimetière!"

Video was already playing in on the twin monitors. Watkins family home movies. The two women shared an anxious look. "That wasn't you, was it?" Maxine asked, an edge of fear in her voice. Annie merely shook her head. Something about the videos troubled her. Something was different, but she couldn't put her finger on what it was.

The hall lights buzzed on.

Both women turned, expecting the Baron's dark figure to enter the room.

Suddenly it hit her: Orville and Lydia Watkins weren't present in the video. All the time she'd spent cutting it, making it just right, and someone had removed all the clips of her parents, leaving only herself and Aunt Maxine.

Boots clomped down the hall toward them. Maxine clasped Annie's hands tightly in her own as a tall figure stepped into the doorway, candlelight flickering over the figure's brute features. She recognized him immediately. Not a supernatural presence, but the night security guard, the one Auntie Maxie called "cute."

"You ladies can't be burning candles in here," he said, eyes wide to take in everything. "You can't be doing Voodoo in here, neither."

"*Hoodoo*," Maxine corrected, before apologizing and hurriedly blowing out the candles. Annie joined her, fear still gnawing at her like animals chewing on electrical cables. The videos had played by themselves, for one. For another, they seemed only to feature herself and her aunt.

The security guard stood out in the hall while Annie and her aunt gathered everything back up into the bag. "You know, you could get into a lot of trouble bringing alcohol onto the premises," he warned Annie.

"We'll keep that in mind," Maxine said for her. "Have a good night."

A light rain had slicked the pavement as they made their way to the car. "You felt it in there, didn't you?" Maxine asked. "An evil presence... reaching out from beyond?"

"I don't know."

"Those videos... playing by themselves... Did you make those?"

Annie got in behind the wheel. "It was the video for Mom."

"I thought you said it was a tribute. I didn't see your father in them at all. Didn't see your mother, either, come to think of it."

Annie started the car, drove out of the empty lot, her mind still on the videos. She pulled out into oncoming traffic without looking—

"*Watch out!*"

Annie jerked the wheel, swerving a hair too late to avoid the oncoming car. The sedan clipped the driver's side and Annie's car spun out, skidding over the slick street, leaping over the opposite sidewalk. It struck a tall hydrant head on.

Shattered glass silenced Maxine's rising scream. The air bag exploded in a cloud of talcum, bursting Annie's nose, the pain dulled by the agony in her lower back as the seat belt jerked her backward. Stars flooded her vision. The horn bleated out into the night.

She came around a moment or minutes later. No one had come across the accident yet, so she assumed it was the former. The airbag had deflated. Blood smeared over its silver surface, her own blood. The windshield lay in pieces on the crumpled hood.

What she at first took for rain pattered on the roof and fell in through the window frame. Even in her semiconscious state, she understood the collision had popped the hydrant.

With immense strain, she turned toward Maxine.

Rain fell into her eyes. Her vision blurred, went pink, as she stared at the empty passenger seat. Blinking away blood, it struck her: Auntie Maxie had gone through the windshield.

Please, she thought, as a queasy wave of oblivion washed over her. *I'll do whatever you want... just please... don't let us die...*

The promise echoed in her ears as her world faded to black.

■■

GETTING BACK TO health took time. She'd suffered fractured discs, had broken two ribs and fractured two more. The surgeons had straightened her nose, stitched gashes in her forehead and cheeks. After weeks of healing and physiotherapy, Annie once again sat in front of the editing monitors in her eight-by-ten cell, a sentence she would serve forty hours a week until her time came to pass the torch.

Ray Smart welcomed her back, told her he'd "touch base" with her at the end of the week. For the constant pain in her back, he'd brought her an orthopedic chair.

Maxine had survived the crash with extensive internal injuries.

Blood was drained from her skull, her punctured spleen removed. Due to compound fractures in her left leg, she walked with a cane. Walt Brenner, drunk and speeding toward an overtime shift, had passed away in the second ambulance.

Annie eased into her new chair, gazed for a moment down at the indistinct chalk marks left on the carpet between her feet. The pain wasn't so bad with her pills. She'd been taking too many, but the haze was navigable. She settled in behind the monitors, and got back to work.

On the streetcar ride to work, she'd read about Congressman Lassiter, a staunch homophobe and segregationist currently suffering from heart troubles. When the P.A. jingled down the hall, dragging her feet on the carpet, Annie was ready.

"How did you—?" Hilary began. But of course she knew. *They all* knew.

"Just keeping the balance," Annie said with a morose chuckle, handing it over.

Kyra peered over from across the hall, and for a moment, their eyes locked. She turned away quickly without expression, and the P.A. crept out of the room, standby in hand, glancing back at Annie until she was gone.

DEAD MEN WALKING

PALOMINO WORKED THE night shift for the peace and quiet.

There were only two problems with this: one was his work partner, Jim Friedkin, just about the biggest class-A asshole you'd be likely to meet. The other was that executions at Alamosa County—or "Alamo," as they called it around here—were scheduled for the break of dawn, a tradition dating back to its early days, which meant he'd have to serve on just about every one of them.

According to a handful of old-timers Palomino talked to—those who *would* talk—when they used to fry Death Row prisoners at midnight the breakers would trip pretty regular, poor wiring being the likeliest culprit, plunging the entire prison into a Hell of pitchest black, subjecting anyone present to a horrific display of light and *smells* and *sounds* as the remaining electricity in the condemned's body made him dance a jig that would haunt any sane individual until his dying day.

Those same old-timers told Palomino about an inmate who'd caught fire in the chair back in 1921 or '22. It happened a handful of times but this particular instance had been the worst, according to consensus. The man's name was Harvey Jessop, a farmer convicted of killing half a dozen migrant farmhands in a rampage with a pitchfork.

Because Jessop was a pig farmer, the press had bestowed upon him the unfortunate nickname "The Pig-Man," though less imaginative writers had called him "The Pitchfork Killer," and less often, the more esoteric "Devil's Hand." They could have called Jessop "mud" for all the difference it made once the fire started, his agonized screams filling the execution chamber as thick as the black, choking stench of his charring flesh. According to Jeb Watson, a CO during those days, the human body smelled a lot like salted pork when it burned, and Harvey Jessop, aka the Pig-Man, had been no exception. It was an anecdote Palomino tried not to remember on the mornings Jenny cooked bacon and eggs for him and the kids.

With the lights out, civilians and officials scurried and screamed, trampling and vomiting on each other and themselves in their combined revulsion and panic, unable to escape the putrid-smelling smoke until someone managed to get to the breaker and the overhead lights were restored. Those old-timers said that had been the last straw. A few men had even quit over it and Palomino couldn't say he blamed them. From that day on, Retired Navy Col. Hap Shetland, the warden at the time, decided it would be best to wait until sunrise to fry up some cons.

Most of Alamo's people thought the Warden's decision had been purely practical. Citizens and politicians failed to appreciate the macabre, and it was in Warden Col. Shetland's best interest to play the game, his position being elected. Some claimed superstition: that Shetland believed killing a man so close to the witching hour was bound to create angry and vengeful spirits—and Alamo already had enough of these among the living. Whatever the reason, this new tradition stuck long after Alamosa County and the rest of the state gave up the electric chair in favor of lethal injection.

They called it a more humane death. George Palomino hadn't been around in those days, but he'd seen a few men ride Old Sparky. And since not one single prisoner in Florida (where electrocution was still on the menu) had chosen to ride the lightning since 2000, when the State had switched to the three-drug protocol, Palomino had to figure they believed it, too.

Given the choice, Palomino had to agree. At least that was how he'd felt before the execution of José Vasquez, when just about everything changed.

. . .

▌▌

JOSÉ VASQUEZ WAS a lifelong sinner who met Jesus Christ somewhere between two consecutive life sentences and the death penalty. Corrections Officers Jim Friedkin and George Palomino led the three-time murderer from his Death Watch cell through Z Block—where José's old cell remained empty, until the new prisoner was scheduled to arrive, not long after José shuffled off his mortal coil—and to the death chamber.

Palomino's peace and quiet had come and gone. Though the inmates watched quietly from their bunks, painfully aware they would soon be walking bowlegged in these same shackles toward their own end, it was difficult to stay Zen leading a man to his death, be he cold-blooded killer or not.

Seemed a little like overkill giving José The Ride the way things were going on the outside, at least to Palomino: the war, the economy in the shitter, the various epidemics, famine and AIDS and all our heroes caught doping or cheating on their wives. Sending José back to Jesus felt like more of a mercy these days than any sort of justice. José's Biblical horsemen were saddled up and ready to ride, and they would all face their own judgment soon enough. They were all dead men walking on Z Block (that was the reason for the name, after all—the signage and forms were labeled "BLOCK C"), whether they'd come to terms with the fact or not. It was only a matter of time.

Palomino didn't believe in the Rapture but he did believe in the law, and as an officer of said same his duty was to uphold it, no matter what his own morality said about them on a case-per-case basis. José's God required an eye for an eye, a life for a life. The good people at Alamosa County Prison were happy enough to oblige.

A shadow leapt up from the bunk in cell 7B and grabbed the bars with the speed of an animal in a cage. It was Mozey. His dark skin, lined with tattoos even on his shaved skull, glistened under the halogen lamps.

"Hey, Vasquez," he hissed, "pass dis along to Jesus when you see him, uh?"

José, rail-skinny and so pale his skin just about looked yellow—he'd sicked up Red Vines all night, puking and shitting the color of fresh blood—cocked his bowed head to an angle as they passed. Mozey's horker caught him right between his dazed eyes.

That old dog Friedkin was unnaturally quick with a baton despite, or because of, his age. The hollow *thock* and crunch startled Palomino. Friedkin had freed the baton and slammed it across the fingers of Mozey's left hand before Palomino saw it coming. Mozey yelped and fell back into the darkness of his cell.

"That'll teach ya to blaspheme, faggot," Friedkin growled.

Mozey held his hand in his lap, rocking back and forth on his mattress. "Broke my fingers, cocksucker," he whimpered. With Mozey's accent it sounded more like *Coke-suckah*, which wasn't an insult as far as Friedkin was concerned. The veteran CO was a sugar junkie as much as some of these cons were just plain junkies, and he sucked down two medium-sized bottles of cola per shift.

Palomino—known to some as "Pal-o-mine"—knew a fair bit about most of the men on the Block and Mozey was no exception. Mozey wasn't his real name, for one: it was short for Mozambique, where his family had emigrated from when he was a child, since his real name was unpronounceable to most—Hell, *Mozambique* was a tongue twister to some of these halfwits. Mozey'd been caught stealing a car when he was fourteen. He'd killed the cop, and because he'd killed one of their own, the State had tried him as an adult. He claimed self-defense, that Officer Mike Daniels, a rookie cop with a wife and two kids at home, had used excessive force. Mozey had beaten Officer Daniels into a coma with the steering wheel lock, what they used to sell on TV as "The Club." The charge of aggravated assault became Murder One when Officer Daniels died in the hospital a few weeks later. When they'd transferred Mozey here, his skin was so thoroughly cut and bruised he looked like an extra from *Roots*, aside from the tattoos.

Same old story. Whether it was sad or a fine example of the law protecting upstanding citizens from harm was up to the individual. Palomino figured it lay in the gray area between: as a law enforcement officer, he thought it was in his best interest to give the good guys the benefit of the doubt.

Still, he didn't think Mozey deserved to have his hand broken for what amounted to a minor beef, and he planned to tell Friedkin so as soon as they were done shift. A power struggle between two hacks still on the Block would only make one or the other of them look weak in front of the inmates, and that was never a good idea.

"What's the hold-up?" Captain Jepson said, leaning her head out the guard station window.

Rather than answer, Palomino nudged Vasquez along, and Friedkin followed with a final snarl at Mozey's cell that told of more coming if Mozey dared made a stink to the higher-ups.

The three of them reached the gate, and Donna Jepson buzzed them through. She was heavyset with short-cropped hair, skin as dark as most of the men on the Block. Palomino had always thought it must be tough for her being a woman in this job, tougher still being African-American knowing what she must about the skewed correctional system. It was hard not to admire her, particularly with the way she was treated by the inmates, as a piece of meat for masturbation material despite—or because of—her reputation as a hardass. Married, no kids. Kids or not, Palomino couldn't imagine letting his own wife work here. This was no job for a woman. No job for a man, really, short of options. Palomino himself had pretty much been railroaded into it. In Jasper, FLA, without a college degree, it was either work the prison or in the steel mill, and his asthma had ixnayed that.

Z Block's gate slammed closed behind them. Palomino and Friedkin turned Vasquez to face that long, dim hallway in which he had spent much of the last thirteen years of his life. He didn't appear to be homesick. His expression was entirely blank. Made his peace, Palomino guessed. Either that or his mind had shut down from fear. It did that to some of them: their eyes just glazed over, their faces slack and devoid of emotion, like deer caught in a set of onrushing headlights.

Donna came out of the station to give José a thorough pat-down, her duty as Death Watch Supervisor for Vasquez. Some of the COs on Z Block figured it was a PR move by Warden Cole, putting a woman in charge. It wasn't like she was any more or less capable than the rest of them. Palomino and Friedkin had already checked José before removing him from his cell, but this was procedure. *Measure twice, cut once*, Palomino's dad used to say. The last thing the Warden needed was a prisoner slashing his own throat with a sharpened toothbrush or a knife fashioned out of reinforced glass that he'd somehow managed to hoop up his ass crack, especially in front of a live studio audience.

Palomino considered José Vasquez's pitiful life as they strapped him onto the gurney. Grown up dirt poor, seventh child of migrant workers, never knowing a home for longer than a season at a time. He told Palomino he'd lived in Alamosa longer than anywhere, making it the closest thing he'd ever had to a home. At the time it had struck Palomino as one of the saddest things he'd ever heard. He'd been a rookie then, and had heard a lot of sob stories since, not many of them sadder than that. For some reason the men on Z Block felt they could confide in him. It was why they called him "Pal-o-mine." Dale McKittrick, the closest CO George had to a friend, said it was because Palomino had an honest face. Friedkin told him it was more likely they knew how to spot a sucker.

Even José's last meal was pitiful: three McRib sandwiches, two super-sized French fries, a large Pibb Xtra, and a big bag of Red Vines. He'd eaten the entire meal, sucking a finger to stick to the grains of salt at the bottom of the fry box, licking the leftover barbeque sauce straight off the greasy cardboard. It had cost more than the twenty dollars allotted for the condemned's last meal—the delivery charge was five bucks, plus a buck for a tip—but Palomino had paid the extra three dollars and fifty-eight cents out of pocket. Maybe he was a sucker after all, but the way Palomino figured, if he was about to be put to death he would have wanted someone to do the same for him.

He and Friedkin wheeled José into the execution chamber, Donna walking heavily just steps behind. Once inside, a pleasant-looking female EMT and a grim specter of a man in doctor's whites went about the business of unbuttoning José's pale blue shirt and attaching electrodes to his smooth, jaundiced chest. They found a fat juicy vein in the crook of José's left elbow—Palomino'd always considered that a strange phrase, *the crook of the elbow*, up there in the category of Strange Phrasings with *a murder of crows* and *bite the bullet*—which the nurse swabbed with alcohol.

José stared at the ceiling while they worked on him, never once looking at his executioners. He didn't so much as flinch as the needle penetrated his flesh. Was he still too dazed by his approaching death to notice, Palomino wondered, or did the pain of a little prick pale in comparison to whatever bug had hit him during the night, making him puke up his last meal, and giving his skin that waxy yellowish appearance, like a man carved from margarine?

Palomino didn't know. What he did know was the sight of blood filling the flash chamber had always made him queasy. He looked away, accidentally catching the eye of Deputy Warden Adams. The nasty little pissant had dressed him down for a minor uniform violation last week, and of course he'd had to stand there and take it, Friedkin snickering to Donna in the guard station and Donna staring at her feet, just waiting for the situation to end. Palomino couldn't afford to lose this job, not with the way things were on the outside, not with Jenny and the boys to take care of and a baby on the way, but he didn't have to *like* it.

Adams gave him a slight, expressionless nod. Palomino looked off, pretended he didn't see, a snub that would likely put him further in the doghouse. Fuck it. All he had to do was win this week's lottery and he'd be free and clear. No more taking orders from self-important prigs like Adams, no more making excuses for mean little tyrants like Jim Friedkin.

How did that jingle go? *Just Six Little Numbers Could Change Your Life?*

Where the hell was the Warden anyhow, leaving Adams in charge? Most likely Vasquez's case wasn't enough of a PR win for him to show. Nobody cared whether José lived or died except the usual die-hard Liberal zealots, the witnesses, and the few illegals who'd heard about the case on the six o'clock news. Palomino had arrived last night expecting the usual picketing that came with these events, but he'd driven through without any trouble.

Deputy Warden Adams checked the restraints, dress shirt buttoned so tight around his throat Palomino could see the arteries throbbing under the stubble on his neck. He nodded to the doctor, to Donna, then went and opened the blinds to the witness room.

Behind the window men and women sat muttering to each other, sweating through their clothes and fanning themselves even though the sun had just barely risen. The air conditioning in this part of the building always seemed to be on the fritz, the whole damn wing as hot as the Devil's nutsack. As the blinds rose a reverent sort of silence fell over the room, as before a sermon.

The faces he met once the blind went up had always bothered Palomino. The stabbing looks of hatred had never troubled him, they were expected. It wasn't the keen interest of the morbidly curious (the ghouls), or the press, either. It was the *hope* on the faces of family and friends of the victims, hope that bearing witness as the murderer of their loved one was put to death would offer a sense that *justice had been done*, a closure this monster's imprisonment had failed to bring. Yet more often than not they would leave disappointed, disillusioned, heads hung low, ashamed of their own desperate hunger for vengeance.

Hope is the slowest poison, Palomino had always thought. Pessimism isn't the antidote, but a healthy dose did the heart a lot of good.

In the execution chamber José said something to the Chaplain, and the young priest—far too young to have acquired much life experience outside the three years he'd spent at Alamosa County—smiled beatifically, offered the Sign of the Cross, and began his prayer.

"My Jesus, by the sorrows Thou didst suffer in Thine agony in the Garden, in Thy scourging and crowning with thorns..."

While the others in the execution chamber bowed their heads for the Chaplain's benedictions, Palomino scanned their faces. He saw the EMT turn to whisper something into the doctor's ear. The doctor nodded but not before throwing a worried glance at Deputy Adams, who was closest them. Palomino saw all of this, and wondered what she'd said that Doctor Death was concerned Adams would overhear? Had she noticed the subtle quiver of the doctor's hands as they went about their business, as Palomino had, and the sweat glistening on his brow? Or had she declared she couldn't wait to get this execution in the bucket so she could put his limp uncircumcised dick between her lips?

Palomino sneered at the idea. Thoughts like this were Friedkin's influence. He'd worked side-by-side with the racist, sexist bully far too long. Captain Milton was stepping down in a month, and Palomino had talked with Jenny about putting his name in for the position. It would get him off the night shift (he would miss those early morning Zen moments, but he could live without them), and allow him more time with Jenny and the boys, the new baby they hoped would be a girl. It would also get him away from Friedkin, and nothing bad could come of that. Of course it would put him closer to Adams, but he supposed kissing a little pucker was the price one had to pay for ambition.

Deputy Warden Adams spoke briefly to the Commissioner, voice hushed. He nodded once, and cradled the phone. "José Vasquez," he announced, and at the sound of his name being spoken José rolled his eyes in the Deputy Warden's direction. "You have been condemned to die by lethal injection by a jury of your peers, a sentence imposed by a judge of good standing in the State of Florida, and to be carried out by the staff and officials of Alamosa County Prison. Do you have anything you wish to say before the sentence is carried out?"

José's eyes rolled toward the witness room window, regarded the people sitting there for a moment. Palomino expected a final dramatic statement, a *May God have mercy on your souls* to turn the table on his executioners, or something more befitting of his newly Christianized state of mind, like the confession he'd never offered. A turning of the other cheek. Tears. Blubbering. Christ, *anything* really.

What José Vasquez did was shake his head and lay back to await his fate, a pitiful end to a pitiful life.

Adams covered his surprise well. If nothing else, the man was a PR machine. "Very well." He tipped a nod toward the executioner's room, where the doctor stood alongside Donna Jepson, soundproof, bullet-resistant glass between themselves and the condemned.

Doctor Death opened the IV clamp. Sodium chloride began to drip down the tube. Palomino imagined its ice-cold fingers creeping through José's veins. The doctor then administered the Nembutal into the IV port. This was a slow, methodical process that in reality Palomino had only seen a handful of times in his seven years on Z Block. There were eleven syringes in all: four 50cc injections of pentobarbital to put the convict to sleep, followed by a saline flush to clear the line; two 50cc injections of pancuronium bromide to paralyze the inmate, so as to prevent any inconvenient muscle twitches or dancing limbs during the final set of injections, and a second saline flush; two syringes of potassium chloride, 50cc in each, to stop the heart.

Another saline flush would be administered, but by then the inmate would already be dead. This last injection was simply to clear the poison from the tubes.

It was during the second flush that Palomino grew concerned. He'd been staring at the fluid bubbling its way down the tubing when he spotted the pinky finger on Vasquez's left hand twitch once, twice. The self-inflicted tattoo on its first knuckle was a crooked cross of tiny dark blue pinpricks.

Palomino studied the faces in the death room to see if anyone else had noticed. He met only impassive looks, expressions they'd practiced once a month in Day Four simulations with volunteers in place of inmate and physician. Friedkin caught his eye and gave him a brief scowl, and Palomino was suddenly sure.

Not a single soul had noticed the movement but him.

Well, so what? he thought, hoping to calm the strange cold creeping into his own veins. The worst that could happen was José might do a little hop and jiggle on the table when the potassium chloride hit his heart, a Mexican hat dance without the hat. And anyway, it was too late to stop the process now. The final chemicals were already coursing down the tube toward José's prostrate body.

The only thing Palomino could do now was wait and watch, both things he was being paid to do anyhow.

Watch the fingers for twitches. Watch the eyelids for a flutter. Watch the chest for a slow rise and fall.

Palomino's heart beat heavily against his uniform shirt.

Nothing.

Thirty seconds passed without movement, and he finally allowed himself to breathe a hushed sigh of relief. Involuntary muscle spasm, he figured, and the moment he thought this, the heart monitor began its steady drone, signifying José Vasquez's life had ended.

The doctor gave a somber nod to Adams.

"The sentence of José Vasquez has been carried out." Deputy Warden Adams adopted a suitably gloomy tone. "Thank you for your attendance, and please ex—"

The creak and pop of the restraints stopped him from finishing, from saying *exit*, but that final word would not be necessary. Somehow José's right arm had come free. The dead man lashed out with it, untrimmed fingernails slashing across the Deputy Warden's cheek, tearing it open, before anyone could react.

In the witness room, a woman shrieked: high-pitched and tremulous, as if she were consciously trying to break the glass separating herself from the horror show.

José was still attached to the heart monitor—he was still *flatlining* —but somehow, despite the poison they'd filled him with, his left hand snapped from the second restraint and he sat up, arms pin-wheeling, clawing out mindlessly at his captors as a long, rattling cry of rage arose from his snarled lips, his eyes rolling wildly like an animal at the slaughterhouse, feet kicking at the restraints like a child crying out for a toy.

Palomino thought: *Something's wrong with the monitor.*

Friedkin's hand went to his baton. He fumbled with the clasp and couldn't manage to free it for probably the first time in his twenty-eight years on the job. The Deputy Warden had fallen to his knees in the corner, holding a blood-soaked handkerchief to his cheek, probably some sort of Italian silk, as he wept. In the witness room a mass exodus had begun with the scream: chairs overturned, purses forgotten, hats knocked off. A behemoth of a man wearing khaki shorts up over his belly button and a fat woman in a sundress had lodged themselves in the doorway, and neither would back down. The rest of them pressed these two through the doorway until finally they popped out into the hallway, the others spilling out behind them, a human levee breaking.

Behind the soundproof glass, Donna had the doctor in a headlock. The execution hadn't gone very well, and Death Watch Supervisor Donna Jepson was far from pleased. José Vasquez wasn't dead—or *was* dead, but his body refused to admit it. Dead/not-dead José had nearly beheaded Deputy Warden Adams with his fingernails. He had the nurse by the hair while she screamed for help, running in place, the soft soles of her Crocs squeaking on linoleum, her head wrenched back as she struggled to flee the monster's grip, her lime green scrunchie unraveling.

Palomino was in shock. His limbs refused to move, as if he, instead of José, had been given the near-lethal dose of pancuronium bromide.

Thankfully, Friedkin got his baton free and brought it down in a swift arc onto José's forehead. The flesh split open like a ripe melon. Blood spilled down into the maniac's white eyes, and the pain didn't even cause him to flinch.

"Kill it!" Adams shouted, still on the floor. "For God's sake, *kill it*!"

Palomino watched impassively as Friedkin gave it his best shot, strike after strike on the dead man's skull, neck, spine—*thock, thud, thump.* And though it was probably a slip of the tongue, Adams was right. José was no longer a *he*. This mindless creature, still strapped at the ankles to the gurney, was officially a *thing*, no more conscious of its own life than an insect. A man suffered no moral quandaries putting an insect to death. He just smashed and smashed and smashed until the goddamned thing was dead.

And Friedkin would have, except the thing on the gurney unexpectedly struck back. It let go of the nurse and grabbed the baton in the same motion. The poor woman, still running full-tilt away from José and screaming at the top of her lungs, slammed headfirst into the witness room window.

Whatever mindless instinct controlled José's body, it was fine-tuned. The dead man's hand fought with Friedkin's grip for only a moment. What Friedkin had with his baton was speed, and the element of surprise. The José-thing had *ferocity*. It wrenched the baton from Friedkin's hands and tossed it casually aside before turning José's face and rage toward its tormentor. José's pupils were no longer visible at all, trying to get a look at its own prefrontal lobe.

Friedkin's head twisted between José's hands with a kind of *pop! pop!* like bubble wrap, and in the moment before the CO realized he was dead, he looked straight at Palomino with a strange muddle of shock and anger. Then he fell to the floor.

It was only after his long-time partner was dead that Palomino noticed the electrodes were no longer attached to José's chest. They'd come detached when he'd torn out of the straps. He was *still alive*. He *wasn't dead*, let alone *undead*. Once this sunk in, Palomino found himself able to move again. A shotgun was racked on the wall for just such moments. Not moments *exactly* like this—moments like this didn't come up often, if at all, Palomino figured—but it would do. He ran for it.

Behind him, José lurched off the gurney. Still strapped in at the legs, the condemned toppled with a clang and a crash, his hips twisted sharply. The slap of his palms on the floor, the metallic drag of the gurney across the execution chamber's chipped tile floor.

Palomino fumbled with the shotgun, tried to pull it from the wall.

The nurse screamed again, waking from unconsciousness, and in the same instant as Palomino felt José's cold grip on his ankle, the latch opened and the shotgun all but fell into his hand. The thing was loaded, but still required cocking.

José clawed at his leg. Palomino's white sock, red stripes mismatched from the left's blue, slipped down to his boot as he turned to look into the whites of José's eyes. His hand, icy with fear, somehow managed to squeeze the forestock and jerk it back. *Clack-clack! Body's gon' stack!* as the "gangstas" in George Jr.'s rap songs said.

It was not customary for the executioner to speak. Palomino knew that. But José clawed at his leg with inhuman strength, threatening to pull Palomino to the floor, where the condemned could easily perform a repeat of Friedkin's fate on him, or something even more gruesome, and he found himself shouting—

"GAH!"

—as he pulled the trigger.

José's head exploded like chunky, wet red streamers, splashing on Palomino's uniform. A chunk of something, brain or bone or cartilage, struck his throat and unstuck when he swallowed, spattering on the linoleum floor by the gloppy, stringy remains of José's head. What was left looked a lot like what José had puked up overnight. Vasquez slumped to the floor. He did not move again.

Tendrils of cobalt gray smoke issued from the shotgun barrel.

Palomino stood for a moment, regarding the scene. That perfect dead quiet had fallen over Z Block again. His guts turned over suddenly, spoiling it. His dinner, a Tupperware of Jenny's leftover chili, came up on his shoes, fitting quite nicely with what was leftover of José.

The door to the executioner's room opened and Donna Jepson charged in, Doctor Death—*Doctor Fuckup, more like*, Palomino thought, and he liked that so much he laughed—running in on her heels.

"Oh shit," Donna said, wide-eyed, surveying the carnage. "What the fuck, George? What the *fuck*?"

Instead of replying—did she even *want* an answer?—Palomino looked through his tears, past José's headless corpse and Friedkin's twisted remains, beyond the upturned gurney, and several feet above the Deputy Warden still cradling his face with his bloodied handkerchief was the clock on the wall, showing a quarter to seven. Fifteen minutes until shift change. Gina Stavros was probably toweling off in the change rooms right about now, maybe having one last smoke before she came in to relieve him for the day.

I better get overtime for this, Palomino thought, tossing the shotgun aside. Donna knelt down beside the Deputy Warden, and while she helped him to his feet, Doctor Dipshit stood looking over the corpse of José Vasquez.

Palomino knew that look. He'd seen it from coworkers, when the punishment for some minor violation of the rules had somehow spiraled out of control. When a prisoner lay unconscious and swollen, bloody and bruised. Or dead, like José. The look on the doctor's face mirrored Donna Jepson's words. The look said *Oh shit*.

Regarding the gooey chunks of José he wiped from himself, Palomino decided this would be his final execution. José Vasquez had been a model prisoner, it was a shame for him to die like this. (Jim Friedkin, however, wasn't likely to be missed.) He would put in his name in for Captain by the end of the week. The way the Deputy Warden was looking at him, with a combination of amazement and fear, he'd be likely to get whatever goddamn job he wanted.

Even if he didn't—if Donna got it instead, though after today's debacle her chance of seeing any career advancement was about as likely as Jenny being able to get the bloodstains out of this goddamn shirt— he'd make sure he was out before the next con was hauled down to the

Death Watch cell. He'd transfer off the goddamn Block if that was what it would take.

Who was next, anyhow? Mozey? That chickenhawk creep, Jim Lee Allen?

It didn't matter. They were all dead men on Z Block. Even Palomino would someday be a wet splat on a funeral director's shirt, he figured.

Just a matter of time, really.

In the meantime, there was the lottery. He decided to buy two tickets tonight, instead of the usual one. After today's shift, he felt like his luck just might be heading for a change.

THE EYE AT THE DOOR

TODD PENDLETON HAD always felt like a poseur in the world of PR consulting, and the thought of his colleagues at Savvicorp knowing how he felt gave him stomach troubles.

While the Big Dogs power-lunched at Hy's Steakhouse or Canoe, at the top of the TD Centre, Todd would wolf down what he half-jokingly called a "powerless lunch" at one of the cheaper places in the mall. He and Darlene had just bought a house, and he'd always said it paid to save where he could. Darlene had offered plenty of times to pack up a lunch of leftovers, but Todd wasn't about to eat from a Tupperware container at his desk.

"Why not just put a big old sign on my head?" he'd asked her, miming the flashing sign by splaying his fingers out from his forehead. *"Loser! Loser! Not meant to be here!"*

Darlene had smiled patiently. After seven years of marriage she knew when her husband was just blowing off steam. Todd knew that she knew, and was glad when she permitted it. He kissed her on the forehead. "Sorry, Apple." He'd been calling her *Apple* for years now, and neither of them could remember why. "You're just looking out for me. And you know I love your cooking. But they're gunning for me down there, that's something *I* know. So far as they're concerned I've been

"

meeting you for lunch, and while it's not optimal—what kind of weirdo meets his wife every day for lunch?—it's *worked*. At least the women around the office respect me for it."

Today was Casual Friday. Some of the others wore jeans, but Todd wore his favored suit—one of two he'd picked up at Tom's Place. They fit nice and looked twice as expensive as they'd been—afraid that if the others saw him in jeans, they'd spot how out of place he felt right away. Todd was rarely, if ever, casual at the office. Casual implied comfort, an easement with one's surroundings. Todd Pendleton was perpetually aware of the eyes at his back. A man like that was only ever comfortable with a door closed firmly behind him.

Kenneth Pratchett, the office wildcard, shot finger guns and/or winked at everyone as they stepped into the boardroom for their big Friday morning meeting. When Todd sauntered in, taking up the rear as usual, Kenneth simply nodded. "Todd," he said, not meeting his eyes.

The meeting didn't go well. The boss was as irritable as Todd's bowels. Work on the Raleigh's account was a slog, but it *was* progressing. The problem was they'd undershot the amount of time required to complete the job to guarantee they'd be the ones handling it.

Then they pawned it off on me, Todd thought miserably, sitting at his desk. *Raleigh's Industrial Lubricant. Sheesh.* What the heck was he supposed to do with a company that sells petroleum-based oils for machinery? If it was cooking oil, he could slap a pretty face on it. Hell, if it was *sex oils* he could do something with it. *Raleigh's Personal Lubricant: perfect for lubing up and taking it in the old poop chute from your superiors!*

He sighed heavily and glanced at the clock beside his framed photo of Darl. Looking at her picture always made him smile, but the smile would quickly fade. He didn't deserve to be with someone so perfect. Not that she would make a man jealous of him. She was, he hated to admit it, awfully plain (he wasn't so hot in the looks department either, particularly in recent years, with the growing paunch and his once magnificent auburn hair retreating from his eyebrows like Allied soldiers during the Battle of Mons). But intelligence and personality radiated from her. The two of them had married straight out of high school —"plucked her right off the vine," as his dad had once described their pairing—and as a result, he often thought she must have felt like she'd missed out on some of the more exciting aspects of life.

Lunchtime came, though he wasn't very hungry. He'd eat, of course. He *always* ate, even when he didn't feel like eating. He opened his brief-case, gathered a few things from the Raleigh's account—the pretense was that he and his wife worked together over lunch, Darlene grading papers—and tucked them in neatly with the Pepto Bismol and antacids, perfect companions for the National Post he kept for bathroom excursions.

Vic Reagan peeked around the cubicle wall, startling Todd, who snatched up his briefcase and held it against his chest protectively.

"Ted," the boss always called him *Ted*, not Todd, "lemme see you in my office after lunch, 'kay, Big Guy?"

Big Guy. Was that a crack on his weight? Todd wondered. Sure he'd put on a few pounds since he'd started five years ago, but he was by no means heavy, and most of that weight gain was stress-related.

The rest, he supposed, was related to lunches at the food court in the mall.

Todd felt the eyes of the whole office on his back as he lowered his briefcase. He made sure to plaster on a smile before turning to face them, saw Kenneth Pratchett leering, savoring his humiliation. Guys like Pratchett would always be at the top of the food chain, unlike Todd, who swam in the wake of the apex predators.

Todd had read that the unattractive earned significantly less than conventionally good-looking people. They called it the *plainness penalty*. Todd had been seated on that bench for most of his life.

"Sure thing, sir," Todd said, as Vic Reagan—who prided himself on his namesake as if he'd been the one to tell Gorbachev to tear down the Wall—breezed past without awaiting his reply.

Todd's mind reeled with awful uncertainties. Office after lunch. On a Friday. Vic Reagan was notorious for firing off little Friday hand-slap emails to the entire office, not blaming anyone in particular, but refer-encing a specific incident so the intended target would still know they were being blamed, albeit unofficially. Then the coward would head out early for the weekend before anyone could offer their two cents. Seeing someone *in his office* on a Friday... that was an entirely different beast, and in Todd's imagination, the beast had horns and shark's teeth still pink with its previous meal.

They terminated people on Fridays. Todd had once read that if they fired someone earlier in the week there was a statistically higher chance of an "incident." What the incident might be was never specifically stated, but he'd seen enough movies to hazard a guess.

■■

TODD WAS ON his way to the mall parking lot after lunch when the basket of deep fried calamari hit his colon like a freight train heading for the end of a long, dark tunnel. *Good God, not now!* The stomach cramps had been getting worse over the past few months, with the mortgage, the bills, the guys at work eyeballing him, and Darl hoping to conceive.

The wolf wasn't exactly at the door, but he was getting his pipes ready to blow down *Chez Petit Cochon*.

Todd squeezed his cheeks and power-walked back to the washrooms, head swimming with the nausea pushing at the back of his throat. He knew exactly where they were and he should, considering he'd passed them five afternoons a week. The problem was that he hated —absolutely *loathed*—using public toilets. The few times he'd had to go to the john at work, after one coffee too many, or a particularly heavy dinner the night before, he'd try to use the washrooms on another floor, in another office. And still he'd startled with every squeak of a fart, pinched his legs closed around the space above the bowl where his meager genitals dangled over the filthy water, courtesy flushing to waft away the smell before wiping.

Insanely enough, he'd feared his colleagues, Big Dogs that they were, would sniff out his fear of them in his excrement.

If he thought he could have made it home, he would have. At home, the bathroom was a refuge from his daily stresses. It was his castle, as his father used to say—as in, "A man's crapper is his castle." It was where he came up with his best pitches, like the one that had landed him the job he held now, and the campaign that had gotten he and Darlene out of the sticks and into a nice new semi-detached in High Park.

But he had no choice in the matter. It felt like everything he'd eaten over the past two days was about to drop out of him like the flush of an airplane toilet, whether he was hovering uncomfortably over the well-used bowl or still hurrying on his way to it.

A toilet flushed behind the closed door, and a man stepped out of one of the stalls just as Todd stepped in. He pressed past Todd, eyes on the floor—surprisingly clean for a public restroom—and on through the door. Todd watched him go, then glanced at the unused sinks, shaking his head in slight disgust. Some people.

With a quick scan of his surroundings, he saw no feet under any of the three stalls. No one stood at the urinals, either. At 12:30 on a Friday, this was about as close to a miracle as Todd had ever experienced.

Sweat beading on his brow, he slipped off his pants and cotton Jockeys just in time—Darlene had pressured him to wear boxers in order to increase his sperm production, but they just didn't keep the boys together the way he liked, and sperm production was the opposite of what he needed now—booting the stall door closed behind him.

Wouldn't that have been great, he thought, *shitting my pants before a meeting with Reagan.* He supposed he would have been all right, seeing as he was already at the mall. Just throw his crappy underwear in the trash and buy a few new pairs at the cheapest department store he could find. But the stink wouldn't wash off. He'd feel it sticking between his cheeks, itching, while sitting across the big desk from his tormentor. *What's that aroma, Big Guy?*

Someone was peering in at him, through the half-inch crack between the post and the door.

At first, Todd thought he'd imagined it. He hadn't even *heard anyone come in.* But someone *was* there: a single silver-gray eye scrutinized the place where Todd's legs came together. A blistered, pink tongue poked out to lick whitened, cracked lips. Wiry facial hair sprouted from nostrils like a tangled mass of tentacles, spreading out in a full mustache and beard. Under the door, Todd saw the dirty, paint-spattered coveralls and scuffed work boots that left a black rubber streak on the tiles.

Todd had a moment to think, *It's my imagination. No one's looking in, he's just waiting to use the toilet. Bad calamari, that's all. I'm sick and I'm seeing things.*

He tried to blink it away, to forget about the fact that there were *three* stalls, and all of them had been free when he'd come in. It wasn't even as though he'd gone into the wheelchair access stall by mistake. Whoever this person was, he was deliberately standing outside the door to the throne Todd occupied. This was no minor, excusable invasion of privacy, like taking the seat right next to someone on the train when there were dozens of empty seats. This wasn't just a minor violation of social convention. This was an infringement on a *basic human right*, to be able to shit without fear of harassment. If public toilets had been around in Moses's day, *Thou shalt not loiter outside the toilet while thy neighbor is shitting* would surely have been carved on one of those tablets.

Todd focused again on the crack in the door.

The pitch black pupil in the center of the silver-gray eye constricted. Todd had once read that pupils were sphincters. He pushed the useless thought away, noticing with rising horror a faint movement at the man's mid-section, but he couldn't see (nor did he want to imagine) what the man was doing to himself. It was all too much for his fragile mind to handle... that he was being spied on while defecating, and worse, that the voyeur might be *pleasuring himself* to the sight (smell?). Todd pulled his legs together tightly and cupped his hands over his genitals, unsure how he should respond to this violation... what he should say, if anything.

Please, God, make him go away!

Todd made to say, *Excuse me,* but immediately knew how it would sound. It was a problem he'd experienced often with colleagues: sounding meek. They'd swing their big dicks around the office—"Vaginas, with the women," he'd add for the benefit of Darlene—and Todd would still be scrabbling at his zipper like a nervous kid on Prom Night.

It was only then that he noticed the graffiti on the walls. There were the usual tags, the crude jokes and drawings. What commanded Todd's attention had been etched in rigid letters with a key or, he supposed, a jackknife:

SEE "ReSULTS" BELOW

But Todd didn't want to see *anything* below. In fact, he'd already seen a lot more "below" than he'd ever wanted.

The man's breath came quicker, in tandem with the rustling at his crotch, the metallic clack of his zipper, and Todd felt suddenly sicker than he had after eating the calamari. What kind of man would do such a thing, in plain sight of anyone?

What kind of man *allowed it to happen?*

But he was completely vulnerable. He'd realized it the moment this perverse dance had begun. His pants were loose around his ankles, his privates exposed, excrement smeared between his buttocks. If he did say something—if he was to shout at this pervert to *Leave me alone,* to *Let me shit in piece for Christ's sake!*—he could neither prevent an attack nor make an escape should the fecophiliac take offence and stop pleasuring himself just long enough to kick in the door.

What could he do to defend himself if the silver-eyed man *attacked* him? If the smell was no longer enough, and the freak wanted a *taste?* What if he wanted to *play with it,* like a rotten little boy plunging his fists into his dirty diaper, to smear it over the walls and on himself and on its maker? What could he do besides sit there and let the terrible man do whatever terrible things he wanted, to wait until the man had finished with him—with him and his *shit*—then pull up his pants and wash off his shame in the sink?

Todd considered in that long, excruciating moment—with his help-less brown eyes pinned in place by the single scrutinizing gray one—that he was a sitting duck, one which had been stripped of its feathers and splayed out naked, about to get its most private of orifices crammed with a fistful of bread and onions.

The man was grunting now, a vile, ululating groan of pain or plea-sure—*uh-ruh-ruggh! uh-ruh-ruggh! uh-ruh-ruggh!*—as though he'd already rubbed himself raw in a prior affront and was gritting his teeth through the discomfort. The eye opened wider, the tongue sliding back and forth like a blind, desiccated worm feeling its way along dried concrete after a storm. One work boot shuddered and kicked out, the

way a dog's leg might jerk when scratched in just the right place, thudding softly against the post.

Todd realized, as he watched the boot kick out, that it wasn't *paint*
on the man's pants at all. Or, if it was, it was the thickest paint he'd ever
seen, great globs of it like giant white slugs.

Oh, please, Todd thought pitifully, *why don't you leave me alone?!*

Todd heard the *clack* of someone pushing at a locked door, and his
heart leapt. The relief that it wasn't the door before him was short-lived
upon realizing it was the *outside* door, the door separating them from
the food court. Somebody had tried to enter the bathroom and was
foiled by the lock. Someone who could have potentially spared him
further indignity at the hands of this maniac.

His thwarted savior.

Todd Pendleton was locked in and alone, trapped by the nasty silver-
eyed man.

Why does this have to happen to me? Todd wanted to scream. But he
knew why. It was the perfect metaphor for his impotence: both figura-
tive and literal. He'd bitten off more than he could chew with the
Raleigh's account, and everyone knew it. Meanwhile, Darlene wanted a
baby—preferably a boy, but she'd be happy with either sex "just as long
as it's healthy"—and Todd didn't have the guts, so to speak, to tell her he
wasn't ready for such responsibility. His unrequited need to talk her out
of it, at least temporarily, had just last week presented itself in erectile
difficulty.

The man at the door had no trouble achieving an erection, unfortunately. All at once the silver eye widened, and the man began to sputter
out breath after breath like a braying horse, sucking in through snot-
sticky nostrils, the hairs in there writhing like tentacles—*Goddamn you,
vile food court calamari!*—after each stinking discharge of cabbage and
sulfur and a sickeningly sweet smell—*Maple syrup?*—from his lungs. It
brought with it thoughts of death and rot and the fiery cauldrons of
Hell and childhood trips to Pioneer Village where Todd had invariably
gotten his face pushed into the snow by one of the Big Kids.

A gob of the man's cold, wet spunk landed on Todd's knee. Todd
cried out. It was the first sound he'd made since he'd seen the man in the
crack of the door, and its echo in his tiny metal death chamber startled

him further. He wanted so desperately to wipe the sperm from his leg, but the libertine's cold, silver eye held him in place, daring him to move. Another spurt struck between the door and post, and oozed its way to the floor like a gleaming, pearly snail.

Then, as if Todd had nothing more to show him, the scatologist let out a pained grunt—*uuurrruunnghh!*—and shambled off, dragging his feet with each belabored step. Hunching down over his naked midsection, Todd watched the dirty boots scuffle away. The bathroom door unlatched and creaked open. The boots stepped out. The door hung silently in space for a moment, then slammed shut.

Todd heard himself whimper with relief. He wiped his ass and the jism from his knee—there was toilet paper at least, thank God for small mercies—and left the stall, grimacing in disgust as the man's semen plunked to the scuffed tile at his feet. He washed his hands, peering at himself in the mirror. His face was ghostly pale, sickeningly gaunt. His were the haunted eyes of a victim.

What he wondered was: had the man been lying in wait for just anyone to enter the toilets? Or had he picked out something in Todd, a vulnerability he could exploit? Todd sometimes used this toilet, so it was likely the man had seen him in this stall before. And the idea that the man had chosen *him*, of all people—*For what? Because I look like a wimp? A sucker? Someone who would sit there and take it and wouldn't make a peep in his own defense, exactly like I just did?*—made him more angry than the assault itself.

Strangely, the anger was not directed at his assailant but at the mortified face staring back at him in the mirror.

The door creaked open. Todd startled, watching its reflection as it swung open. A teenage boy in a black toque and a tight, ribbed under-shirt stepped up beside him, began primping himself, swiping his hands through the scruffy hair above his ears and slicking back his eyebrows with the index and little finger of a single hand—the Devil's sign, Todd noted—all before spotting Todd standing beside him. The kid took one look, pulled a disturbed face, and walked out.

As Todd rubbed his hands together under the dryer, he glanced at the stall he'd been sitting in, indistinguishable from the others except for a pearly splotch still trickling down the door handle. He had an impulse to wipe it off, to spare the next person from the indignity of getting it smeared it on their palm, but an insidious, selfish little thought wormed its way into his head, surprising him into sudden, delirious laughter:

Fuck 'em.

He stood in front of the row of mirrors, laughing, *cackling* at his own reflection.

What would someone say, he thought, *if they walked in and caught me guffawing like this—like a genuine nutjob?*

The laughter died in his throat.

He went back to the stall, wound a good bunch of toilet paper around his hand, then tentatively wiped away the spunk from the door. He did the same with the spot on the floor, glistening under the fluorescents, then chucked the sticky wad into the bowl and flushed it away. Todd had been raised to clean up after himself, and though it hadn't been him who'd made this gloppy mess, he felt at least partly responsible.

It occurred to him that feeling personal responsibility for being victimized was unhealthy, but he pushed it out of his mind. He wasn't a victim. He'd just been in the wrong place at the wrong time. It could have happened to anyone.

Yes, but would anyone have let it go on *happening?*

Again, he pushed the thought away.

He washed his hands a second time before leaving the washroom for good.

As he scurried through the food court, he scanned the patrons surreptitiously, looking for the man in the white-stained coveralls. Not to confront him—*Heavens,* no—but to *avoid* him. To identify him, so he could steer clear of him in the future.

A few customers caught his furtive looks. A teenager scowled over her taco salad and cell phone and an elderly gentleman smiled and ruffled his newspaper. There were no coveralls, there was no man with a beard and silver-gray eyes. If not for the mess he'd cleaned from the door, he might have been able to convince himself he'd imagined the entire ordeal.

Whether imagined or incredibly, horribly real, Todd never wanted to see those silver-gray eyes again in his life, if he could help it. And he'd certainly never go into that bathroom again, not even to wash his hands before eating. Maybe he'd drive to another mall on Monday, a little further if need be, to get his lunch.

If I've still got a job come Monday, he thought, launching into the parking lot elevator just as the doors began to close.

TODD DUCKED UNDER the scaffolding and back into the lobby of 323 Bay Street. They'd been doing renovations on the building for months now, caulking around the exteriors of the windows, painting the halls, and the inconvenience was bordering on intrusive. The living wall they'd installed when the renos began trickled pleasantly as always, but today it reminded Todd of urination, and urination reminded him of the washroom at the mall.

He hurried by to the elevators.

Hurrying to my own execution, he thought, and pushed the thought away. As a skill, he thought he'd just about gotten the hang of it.

All eyes fell on him when he stepped into the office, like wolves on their prey. Kenneth Pratchett nodded up at him from his chair as Todd passed by toward Reagan's corner office, the kind of nod you gave people at a funeral, with slightly downcast eyes.

Todd gave a hesitant knock on the door, opened just a crack so Vic Reagan could say "My door's always open" and mean it literally as well as figuratively. "*Come*," Reagan shouted, which had always reminded Todd of Captain Jean-Luc Picard of the Starship Enterprise (he and Darlene were closet Trekkers), but today made him think of the eye between the crack in the door, the silver-gray iris jerking up and down as he—

Todd pushed the thought away. In a way, ignoring the truth was an inherent component of working in PR.

"You wanted to see me, sir?" He cursed himself silently, remembering the promise he'd made to himself not to phrase everything as a question around his superiors. He'd read once that it made the speaker sound weak.

"Have a seat, Ted."

Todd, he thought but did not say. It was much too late to correct Reagan on that. He made to close the door.

"Leave it open," the boss said. Todd sighed inwardly, imagining Kenneth Pratchett pressing his ear against the crack, giving a hushed play-by-play to the rest of the office. Imagining the silver-gray eye at the office door, and its grunting, self-pleasuring possessor.

He sat. Vic Reagan lingered by the windows, taking in the impressive penthouse view of the city, the Harbourfront. His masculine figure, maintained at his personal gym by a fitness trainer who worked with visiting celebrities, silhouetted by the empty sky over the lake. "Ted, I've worked here fifteen years," he said, not turning. "I used to do copy when I started, did you know that?" Todd had heard it countless times, like everyone else in the office, but Reagan pressed on, not requiring a response. "In all my years at Savvicorp, I have never seen such potential as you had when you started here... just *squandered*."

Todd felt his cheeks flushing, and could do nothing. He shifted uncomfortably in his chair and glanced in the direction of the door.

"I took a chance when I hired you." Reagan finally turned. His silver gray hair shone in a halo of sunlight. "I looked past your cheap suits, both of them, and your not-quite-close shave, and that *cologne*," he pulled a face, "do you know what people say about your cologne, Ted? Look, I don't mean to sound like I'm berating you—"

Oh no? Todd thought but would never dare say. *You could've fooled me.*

"—honestly, Big Guy, I was pulling for you. I wanted you to succeed. Sincerely, I did."

Sincerely. The same complimentary close Reagan used in all of his emails, as if he were writing a personal letter. With Vic Reagan, sincerity was the equivalent of a liar saying *Trust me*. About as genuine as a politician in the midst of a sex scandal.

If you wanted me to succeed, he thought, *you wouldn't have stuck me with the damn Raleigh's account.*

Todd said nothing.

At the window behind Reagan, while the man pontificated—sincerely—a work platform lowered into view.

"I mean, we're a *consulting firm*, Ted," Vic Reagan was saying, "we're certainly not being paid to consult with our wives over Big Macs at the mall."

Behind him, the platform blotted out the sun.

Todd watched as the worker shuffled his feet, his legs the only part of him in view, silhouetted against the sky. Could Todd push away the thought that those were work boots scuffling on the platform? Could he push away the thought that those were *coveralls*?

The ability escaped him.

Caulking, he thought. *The little white slugs were* caulking.

Todd considered how apropos it was that the sicko had caulk on his pants as the boss continued his spiel. "It's a dog-eat-dog world, Big Guy. Either you're the dog," Vic Reagan said, "or you're the bone."

Bone... Like the one the pervert at the mall tried to give me.

The sun highlighted straggly whiskers below the man's chin and on his cheeks. The caulking gun held in both hands at his groin. The silver-gray eyes staring with hunger, the shriveled tongue dragging across sun-chapped lips.

Todd could hold his tongue no longer.

"*AHHHYEEEAAGGHHHH!*" he shouted, leaping from his chair. He lifted it into the air, all sixty pounds of it, while Vic Reagan, he of the mixed metaphor, sat flabbergasted.

"Ted? What the heck are you doing, Big Guy?"

Todd rushed headlong at the window like a Spartan with a battering ram. He launched the chair, all sixty pounds of it, at the tempered glass.

Vic Reagan said "*Shit!*" as he leaped from his chair, shielding his immaculate salt-and-pepper hairdo from the imminent explosion.

The window shattered outward in a million tiny pieces. Todd stepped back, hit by the shock of impact, the *sound* of it, like a depressurizing airplane cabin at 32,000-feet. Recycled air rushed past him, ruffling his hair and the panels of his six-hundred-dollar suit, sucking out papers from Reagan's desk—his pink slip along with them, Todd hoped—which fluttered like doves into the pure blue sky as a rain of glass pattered against the polished hardwood floor.

Todd took another step back, sucking in a gasp like a man waking from sleepwalking, and surveyed the damage he'd done. A golf ball rattled to the edge and over, where the entire pane from floor to ceiling had disappeared.

So had the work platform.

Oh no, Todd thought. *Oh God no, please.*

He put a hand on the frame and peered over the edge of slick wooden flooring. Wind whipped his suit, his tie fluttering, slapping at his chin and cheeks.

Todd craned his neck upward first, certain the silver-eyed man from the bathroom had pulled the apparatus up in time to avoid the chair that would certainly have killed him. His gaze found nothing but glass and sky. Above them the rooftop was green, an innovative addition that had garnered them national attention at the time. There were no wires, nor anything to suspend them with. Anyone looking up would see the mirrored surface of 323 Bay, the reflection of the buildings along the Harbourfront, the blue of sky and water, unmarred but for the single black gap where a man stood, his mouth agape, his tie flickering in the wind.

They would assume he'd be soon to follow the chair out the window. It was just the sort of incident managers strived to avoid by firing on Fridays.

His first instinct was to apologize, to beg for Vic Reagan's forgiveness. But his boss had hidden behind the big desk. And anyway, he should at least see what sort of damage he'd done before he made his excuses. He might be better off saving his apologies for the jury.

Beneath the scuffed tips of his orthopedic dress shoes, colorful ants scurried about, huddling around a bright orange taxi in the street where Todd's chair had landed. The miniature cab driver stepped out of the car. It was difficult to tell whether or not he'd been injured. From the way the cabbie was moving, it appeared as though Todd had dodged a bullet.

"Whoops," Todd said, and cackled madly.

Behind him came a brief knock at the door and Kenneth Pratchett's smug voice saying "Everything okay in here, Vic—? *Ho*-lee *shit!*"

Todd turned and met Pratchett's eye. They stood in silence, the spacious room separating them. Todd on the other side of the desk now, Pratchett peering in with a look of shock, like a frightened animal caught in the headlights of Todd's wild-eyed gaze. Todd could think of nothing to do but shoot Pratchett with his own trademarked finger gun. Startled by the implication, the handsome weasel slinked back out of the room.

Todd stretched around, his right hand still on the window frame, to look for his boss.

Vic Reagan was kneeling alongside his desk like a kid practicing Duck and Cover during the Cold War. There were tiny square chunks of glass in his hair and on the shoulders of his Gucci double-breasted suit. He shook them off and stared at Todd with fearful fascination for a long moment. He didn't get up off the floor.

Todd held his gaze, until his so-called superior looked past him at the gaping mouth of the window.

"Todd? You know, you could have killed someone down there, Big Guy."

He knew it. And although it must surely have been his intention to kill someone at the time, he hoped—*sincerely*—nobody was hurt now.

"Maybe you should take a vacation," Vic Reagan suggested. "Relax for a bit, come back with a fresh outlook."

Come back? How could he come back? These people would think he was a crazy man. You don't "come back" from an assumed nervous breakdown.

"That's a good idea, Vic," Todd said, looking at the open space where the window had once been. Had he imagined the man in the window? He was certainly nowhere in sight—which was good, Todd considered, because if he *had* been in the window when the chair went out, Todd would be worrying about how to shit in the toilet of a two-man prison cell instead of considering a vacation.

"A *very* good idea. But what about the Raleigh's account?"

"The lubricant guys? Oh Christ, Kenneth can handle that," Vic said with a dismissive wave of his manicured, unnaturally tanned hand.

That was good. Kenneth deserved it. That handsome little weasel deserved everything his good looks would afford him.

The telephone rang. Vic stood to answer it, still eyeing Todd cautiously. "Vic Reagan." As he spoke he never took his eyes off of Todd, until Todd turned his way. Then, blessedly, he lowered them. "Is anyone hurt? Oh thank God. Yes, it was an accident. The damn thing just slipped out from under my ass." Todd had to hand it to him. The man knew how to spin. Not the best maybe, but he could sell a line of bull with a straight face. Vic squinted at the window. "Okay, thank you very much. Yeah, bye."

Todd stepped away from the window. "I'm going to go now," he said.

Vic's face told him it was a wonderful idea. "Sure thing, Big Guy. Whatever you like."

Whatever he liked. Todd thought about this as he strode through the cubicles, everyone watching him until he turned to face them, then looking away, to their desks, to their computers, to their feet, anywhere but *at* him. It seemed as though looking at Todd Pendleton as he beamed through the office had suddenly become like looking directly at the sun.

They were seeing him for the first time. Oh, they'd looked a lot before, but they had never really *seen* him.

He was one of the Big Dogs now. Big Dogs did whatever they liked, and what he wanted right now was to go home, eat some supper, watch *Jeopardy!* and make love to his wife. He had a good feeling he'd see "results" below tonight... and an even stronger feeling he'd have the confidence to tell Darlene he wasn't ready to have kids just yet, particularly with a vacation in their future.

Maybe he'd swing by the mall first. Head into the men's room. See if the silver-eyed man with the bushy beard and filthy coveralls was in there, exposing himself to some other poor schmo. Todd wanted to thank him for inspiring his newfound courage.

Or smash his head into a door, he really hadn't decided yet.

Bus Driver Man
A Dark Pines Story

THE LITTLE SHIT was at it again and Mr. McAllister figured someone oughta teach him a lesson.

Not me, though, he thought, pulling the big yellow bus away from the curb out front of Josie Stafford's house. *Hell if I'm gonna do jail time just so some lunkhead kid gets his just desserts. The world don't favor heroes.*

No, Mr. McAllister would play it by the book like he always did. He always followed bus routes outlined by the School Board, except during roadwork, in which case he'd notify them of any delay longer than ten minutes. He always kept his vehicle clean enough to cook a steak off the rad, and free of hazards, going so far as to file down sharp screw heads on the seats where the shop mechanic had stripped them. Always kept his class B driver's license up to date, and bathed and flossed daily. This last didn't matter so much to the School Board, but Mr. McAllister knew what it was like to sit for half an hour or more in someone else's stench, and so he made sure his breath was minty and his farts smelled like roses.

Mr. McAllister glanced in the rearview mirror. Only a few cars on the dirt road behind him. One of them, the maroon wagon, belonged to Dora Strathcomb. She followed behind the bus, and her son on it, every

426

day. Crazy as a soup sandwich, but she had a tight little bod Mr. McAllister had taken pleasure in checking out once or twice. God only knew why she didn't drive the kid herself. Probably wanted to be sure he integrated well with the other kids, since the government had stepped in to stop her from home-schooling when they figured out he tested at a second grade level, a twelve-year-old kid. Not that slinking around while the kids took the bus to school helped get him situated among his peers. Probably got him beaten up more often than it didn't.

Somebody oughta teach Jessie Kinsmen a lesson, but it sure wasn't going to be Dora's son. *Pipsqueak* is what they used to call kids like him, and that was when they were playing *nice*.

"Oh, that little diaper-stain cocksucker Jessie Kinsmen," Mr. McAllister would tell the boys down at The Tap. "That little smoldering lunch sack of dogshit Jessie." He'd swallow a mouthful of Labatt's and add, "Did I say 'little'? That 'little' shit's bigger'n me. His poor mother must be looser than a landslide havin crapped that thing out her babymaker."

The boys knew this diatribe well enough not to interrupt. They'd just chuckle to themselves and nod their heads, sipping on their own wobbly pops. But there'd always be some bystander, some Tap tourist, who'd want to chime in with something like, "Yeah, but he's the *Mayor's* kid. So whaddaya gonna do?"

What am I gonna do? *Good question, Mr. Knowitall. Mr. Nosey-Parker, prob'ly hyphenated with your wife's last name 'cause you're so goddamn progressive.* He couldn't let that little—that *big*—dicksmear Jessie Kinsmen get away with the things he'd done just because he was the son of the most prominent person in town. *Hell, I didn't even* vote *for Kinsmen. He can suck my dirty dick if he thinks he can tell* me *what to do.*

Jessie Kinsmen was six-foot tall if he was an inch, and built like a fortified shitter. His fists were the size of ham hocks, and probably felt like it when they struck any kid on the back of the head who dared to sit in front of him. The one satisfaction Mr. McAllister got was when Jessie's big ginger melon would hit the roof of the bus going over the bigger bumps on Shiner and Dewlapp, the worst roads on their route with macadam older than Mr. McAllister himself. He'd slow down a little just so the big yellow bus wouldn't glide smoothly over the potholes, and grin wide in the rearview, savoring the sight of that big ginger head getting a solid thwack on the aluminum, Jessie himself screwing his eyes up against the pain so the other kids wouldn't get the idea he wasn't invincible and maybe they could defeat the giant.

Mr. McAllister would chuckle satisfactorily to himself, seeing that. But it was hardly enough.

Now Jessie was ragging on Mrs. Plimpton, the bus chaperone. Sure, she smelled a bit like baby powder and cat pee, and she dressed like a nurse on night duty with all those loose, flowery tops and her dirty yellow plastic shoes, the kind with the holes in them like peek-a-boo playground equipment, but she'd outlived probably everyone she would have seen in the early days of television, even plenty of folks she grew up hearing on the radio. She'd been around for the invention of nylons, and for the beginning of the Second World War. And this little—this *big*— heap of rat dumps scattered amongst little bitty grainy pellets of warfarin, who hadn't even been living when the goddamn digital watch was invented, thought he could shit all over her?

Huh-uh. No way, pal. Not on my Timex timepiece.

Problem was, you couldn't get away with anything these days. Last time Mr. McAllister had scolded a boy for kicking the back of the Freely kid's seat, one of the others had been videotaping with their phone (old Mrs. Plimpton had been alive when barely anyone had telephones in their *homes*, let alone their *pockets*), and had conveniently only caught Mr. McAllister's reaction to the abuse. He'd been written up for it, the School Board telling him they understood discipline had to be meted out, but if they didn't make an example of his, Mr. McAllister's, behavior, the PTA would shit a Brampton Brick.

That had been just fine with Mr. McAllister. The boys down at The Tap had joked he'd had to eat a hot bowl of shit, but what the hell did they know, working the pit—a *union* job. Sad fact of life is everyone wants to feed you shit, and you're gonna have to smile and choke it down at least some of the time.

And some Tap tourist, some nosey parker, had chimed in, "Why don't you do what that fella in Cleveland done? Kidnap the big dumb sumabitch and tour him around a few hours. Scare the pants off'm."

Of course, this had been before the "fella in Cleveland" was discovered to have been a mental fuckwit who kidnapped those poor girls. For a while there, Mr. McAllister had sort of looked up to the guy, being brave enough to attempt something so daring. Not that the kid likely deserved it, when you considered new evidence. But if any kid *did* deserve to be driven around against his will, it was Jessie Kinsmen. Hell, Mr. McAllister might be *applauded.*

But the incident with the Cleveland fella, who'd offed himself in prison since, had happened in the days before bus chaperones like Mrs. Plimpton, who was just now doing an admirable job ignoring that diaper-stain—*Oh fuck me, did I already use that one?*—that *fucktard* Jessie Kinsmen.

Mr. McAllister pulled the bus up to the corner of Groonie Road and Van de Meer, where the Freely kid waited, backpack in hand. Janey Freely was one of the good ones, which probably meant she took holy hell at school. "Good morning, Mr. McAllister," she said cheerily, with a wide smile that showed all of her braces.

"Ain't it, Janey?" Mr. McAllister said. She smiled again, a shining million-dollar smile, and took a seat near the front while Mr. McAllister closed the door and pulled away from the curb.

Mr. McAllister had no delusions any of these kids respected him. Not like they were taking up a chorus of "Hail to the Bus Driver" back there. But most of them were friendly, and that was something. He'd heard horror stories from other drivers at the annual NTSA meetings, stories about fruit kicked deliberately under pedals, about wads of spit-covered paper shot at the back of their heads while they made sharp turns on a road with poor visibility, about curses and pulled hair and snot rubbed into their clothes. *Jeezus Please-us lemon-squeeze-us*, Mr. McAllister thought, *if the kids on this bus tried to pull any of that bullpucky on me, I'da gone ballistic for sure.*

"Mrs. Plump-ton!" Jessie Kinsmen said in singsong, emphasizing both *plump* and *ton* to be sure she knew it was a measurement of weight. Some of the others giggled at that, with an edge of fear to their laughter. "Missus Plummmmmpton!"

Christ! He's grating on my last nerve. Lord, grant me strength...

"Why'nchta stop picking on her?" said a kid near the back of the bus, a voice so meek at first Mr. McAllister thought he'd imagined it. He glanced at the rearview, saw the Strathcomb pipsqueak sitting up with his slender fingers gripping the back of the seat in front of him, and Jessie Kinsmen wrenched his big freckled neck around to fix the small blond boy with a look of death.

Aw, kid, you gone and done it now, Mr. McAllister thought, though he had to admire the kid's courage, even if he'd signed his own death warrant. He'd keep an eye on the two of them on the way in to school, but after that he couldn't do much for the kid aside from pray the fat shit-stain didn't thump him too hard. The world didn't fare well for heroes these days. There were policies and shareholders to think about, parents who refused to parent their own children to appease. Every action micromanaged and disciplined and Twittered about and shamed on the internet so you couldn't squeeze out a fart without having to issue an official fuckin apology.

The children all scurried off the bus, favoring the Strathcomb kid with looks of sympathy, and eyeing Kinsmen like a wild dog as they passed. Finally it was just the four of them left on the bus, Mr. McAllister, Mrs. Plumpto—*Plimpt*on—and Jessie Kinsmen and the Strathcomb boy, who both refused to leave until the other went first.

"You boys are gonna miss first bell if you don't skedaddle," Mr. McAllister warned them, trying to be as diplomatic as possible so as not to incur the wrath of the School Board.

When Jessie scowled, his fat face wrinkled up just like a sharpie dog, and Mr. McAllister had to wonder what sort of upbringing would make a Cujo like him. Probably got a good beating or two himself, with any luck. Ken Kinsmen looked like the type of guy who would beat a kid stupid, with his barrel chest and his perpetually rosy cheeks and his military-style hairdo.

"This isn't over," Jessie told the smaller boy.

Mrs. Plimpton harrumphed, watching the two boys through her thick, tinted spectacles, her whiskered lower lip eating the bottom half of her face.

"Go on to class, Jessie," Mr. McAllister said, causing Jessie Kinsmen's frown to deepen. He hauled himself out of his seat, shot another look of death at the boy in the back, then shuffled up the aisle toward the front. "What about *him*?"

"He'll be comin along soon enough, don't you worry." *And don't make me put my foot in your ass on the way down those steps*, Mr. McAllister thought, grinning wide at the notion. Jessie Kinsmen gave the smile a queer look, then he slumped down the stairs, one by one, the bus rocking slightly with each deliberately heavy step.

"Thanks, Mr. McAllister," the Strathcomb boy said, shuffling up with a hangdog expression.

"Thanks nothin. You lookin to get yourself killed, kiddo?"

The boy's eyes bugged out as if the idea hadn't even occurred to him. He peered out Mrs. Plimpton's window at Jessie, who threw one last baleful look at the bus before trudging up the cement steps to school. "I just couldn't take it anymore, is all. Why's he gotta be such a dick? Sorry, Mrs. Plimpton."

"Don't you worry yourself," Mrs. Plimpton said. "It was brave of you to stand up for me. Brave, and terribly stupid."

And wouldn't you know it, here was the widow Strathcomb, knocking on the folding door with a look of deep concern.

"Better not tell your mother," Mr. McAllister warned him. "Got a feelin she'll go ballistic."

The boy's eyes bugged out again, cobalt blue like his dad's had been.

Mr. McAllister put on his most charming smile and opened the door. "Why hello there, Dora. Aren't you a sight for sore eyes."

Dora Strathcomb stepped onto the bus without an invite. "Where's my son? Why isn't he in school?" She saw him then, her concern softening. "Dennie, sweetie, are you okay? What's the matter?"

Dennie Strathcomb gulped. "Nothing, Mom. We was just talking."

"*Were* talking," his mother said, then glanced at the two adults to see if they'd caught the mistake. After the government had forced her son out of home-schooling, Dora Strathcomb was very particular about how the two of them spoke in public. "He hasn't been any trouble, I hope," she said to Mr. McAllister, with a look that required a single answer Mr. McAllister was happy to supply.

"Go on to class now, Dennie," Mr. McAllister told him. "And don't you take any wooden pickles."

Dora gave him a weary smile before ushering her son off the bus.

Mr. McAllister and Mrs. Plimpton watched Dora walk her son to the doors. Even after they closed behind him the distraught mother seemed undecided whether or not her boy was safe, whether or not she'd done enough. She took a hesitant step up the stairs, then back down again. Another half-step and down. Finally she scurried off to her station wagon.

"She can't watch him forever," Mrs. Plimpton remarked unhappily.

No, she couldn't. And Mr. McAllister sure as shit wasn't going to step in.

THE BUS PULLED up to the Gunny Street stop on another gorgeous day, the morning sun baking the black vinyl seats. Aaron Lesley, a gangly looking kid with a bad case of acne and the dirtiest, holiest t-shirt you ever saw on a kid outside of a PSA about Third World children, shuffled onto the bus with his head down like usual.

"Where's the Strathcomb kid?" Mr. McAllister said. "Where's Dennie?"

The tall boy shrugged, continuing on to his regular seat near the middle, far enough away from the front where the goodie-goods sat, and not too close to the back where the hotshots ruled their domain with an iron fist. Mr. McAllister decided to wait at the stop a minute. A peek in the rearview confirmed his suspicion: Dora Stathcomb's maroon wagon wasn't around, either.

"Maybe he's sick," Laura Engval suggested. What was funny about this kid was how close her name was to the woman who wrote *Little House*, which Mr. McAllister use to watch as a kid, and her resemblance to the little pig-tailed girl was pretty uncanny, too.

Maybe he *was* sick. That would explain why neither mother nor son were at the bus stop. Mr. McAllister glanced in the rearview again and happened to catch Jessie Kinsmen staring back at him with a big grin spread across his freckled face. Little piss squirt didn't even try to hide it.

Mrs. Plimpton raised a wrinkled arm to show Mr. McAllister her watch—digital, he noted—and Mr. McAllister nodded. He looked again at Jessie in the rear view, but Jessie was peering out his own window, aiming his smile at the sun.

"All right, then," Mr. McAllister grunted. "Can't wait forever." He dropped the transmission into gear and pulled the door shut, then drove on to the next stop and the next, greeting the kids with a smile as he always did, glancing every so often at Jessie Kinsmen's big ginger head in the mirror. But the boy never returned his look, only beamed his contented smile out the window, like a Buddhist.

Troubled by that smile, Mr. McAllister hurried home after he'd dropped Mrs. Plimpton safely back to the retirement castle (she said nothing on the ride home, merely gummed the bottom of her face to death), and checked in briefly on his father while he was there (still a vegetable? check). He skipped his usual Rueben sandwich and crinkle-cut fries at the Rodeo Diner (which the owner, Sara Chutley, strangely pronounced *Roh-DAY-Oh*, like the street in Beverly Hills), climbed on his computer even before he had his boots kicked off, and looked up Strathcomb in the White Pages.

"Nothin," he said to himself, leaning back in the old desk chair with a fart of faux leather.

Well, what the hell was he going to do, anyway? Place a call to the kid's mother? Ask her if her boy was doing all right or if he'd run into any doors lately? Maybe the kid really had gotten sick. Or maybe—and this was more likely—maybe the kid was *playing* sick to stay home from school, worried that if he'd attended today he might have had to contend with Jessie Kinsmen after school let out. The kid probably figured if he could wait it out a day or so, the big red-headed dummy would forget all about five-foot-nothin Dennie Strathcomb and set his sights on some other runny-nosed brat.

"Ah, hell," Mr. McAllister said, getting up from the chair with another fart of leather. He threw on his jacket, stepped into his boots, and went out to the car. The phone book might not have their number, but he knew their *address*. He could check out the house, at the very least. See if the boy was anywhere in sight. If he felt adventurous, he might even go knock on the door. It would be nice to see Dora outside of the school bus, anyhow.

Why do you care so much about this squirt all of a sudden? he asked himself as he climbed behind the wheel of the old Datsun. *Why him?*

He thought about it for a moment. "'Cause the world don't favor a hero, for one," he answered aloud—but there was more to it than that, he just wasn't sure what it was. Maybe it was that the little pipsqueak reminded him of himself when he was a boy. Maybe he just wanted to get into Dora Strathcomb's pants.

Mr. McAllister silenced these thoughts by doing what he did best: he threw the transmission into drive and Christ-alive *drove*. Traffic was light, and he didn't hit a red all the way to Dark Pines Estates. Dora Strathcomb's maroon wagon wasn't in her gravel drive. The attendant, whom Mr. McAllister had gone to school with forty years ago, and whose better days were about that far behind her, looked up from reading *Better Homes and Gardens* and regarded him with suspicion.

"What c'n I do for ya, Pip?" she said, referring to him by his grade school nickname, Pip as in *Philip*, not Pip*squeak*, though he had surely been that. The silly sweater and bucket hat she wore—*Didn't she wear that style of hat when we were kids?* Mr. McAllister wondered—made her look even older than their fifty(-ish) years, and from her expression she would have preferred him to do something for her, and get the hell out of her mobile court.

Out among the trailers, a grungy fella in tighty whites and construction boots tromped through the muck from one trailer to the next with his hound on a leash, sucking down a tallboy. *There goes trouble*, Mr. McAllister thought, recognizing the guy's face from The Tap. "Dora Strathcomb around?" he said to Rosie Ferguson, whose attention had wandered back to her magazine.

Her suspicion grew as she looked up again. *Musta been hopin I'da disappeared*, he thought. "Now what business would you have with her?"

"Well, Rosie, I'd have to say that's nunya. As in *nunya* business." With this, Mr. McAllister showed her his teeth. Rosie flinched, as if she'd seen gristle in between them, though Mr. McAllister knew they were just as minty fresh as always.

"Well," she said, adding, "*Pip*," with emphasis, "tough titty said the kitty but the milk's still good. We haven't seen her since yesterday." When Rosie said we she meant *we at Dark Pines Estates*, not we as in her and a suckling tabby cat. "Dora blew out of here in a tizzy to take that boy of hers over to the hospital."

"Hospital?" That giant hemorrhoid pain-in-the-ass Jessie. That fat lump of yesterday's trash.

"Uh-huh." Rosie didn't look too concerned about it. "Poor kid had an eye black as the ace of spades, jaw all swelled up like a punkin. Not that that's *any-ya* business," she added, riffing on his earlier joke, but he was too annoyed to laugh.

"Thanks, Rosie." He patted the counter. "You always were a peach."

She gave him the bird as he got back in his car. He drove the hour to Peterborough right away, figuring they would have had to take Dennie to Peterpatch Regional, being the closest hospital to Dark Pines. The nurse at the station directed him to the right room, and there was Dennie, his jaw wired shut, beaten and bruised as all get-out, the right eye closed up to a blood orange slit. Dora sat beside him, holding his hand. When Mr. McAllister stepped in she began to rise from her seat.

"Mr. McAllister?"

He held up a hand. "Don't get up. I just dropped by 'cause I heard what happened to Dennie. Jesus, I'm sorry, Dora. Is he gonna be okay?"

"The doctor said he'll be fine." Her eyes met his with suspicion.

"Why are you sorry?"

"That's good," he said, ignoring the question. *Can't a guy do something decent without everyone wondering what he's sellin?* Mr. McAllister wondered.

"Why are you sorry, Mr. McAllister?"

For a moment he considered telling her the truth, but he thought against it. "I'm just real sorry it had to happen, that's all. Nobody deserves that, not least of all your boy. Dennie's a good kid. He's—" He'd almost given himself away, about to call the boy a hero for standing up against Jessie when the fat asshole was ragging on Mrs. Plump—*Plimp*ton.

Goddamn it, now I'm callin her that, Mr. McAllister thought, and smiled down at Dora Strathcomb.

"Thank you." She smiled herself, her eyes damp, and turned to her son, squeezing his small hand in hers. "And thank you for coming, Mr. McAllister."

"Phil," he said. "You can call me Phil."

"Thank you, Phil."

Mr. McAllister stood a moment longer, looking at mother and son —his face like mashed potatoes with the skin on—and began to feel like he'd overstayed his welcome. "Well, I'm glad he'll be okay. Lookin forward to seeing the two of you back in my rearview, Dora."

She nodded. Mr. McAllister crept out into the hall, feeling deceptive, wishing he'd had the guts to tell her what had gone down the other day. But the world didn't favor a hero—Jessie Kinsmen had proved that true when he broke Dennie Strathcomb's jaw. There were more Jessie Kinsmens in the world than Dennies, as far as Mr. McAllister saw it, and that was the real shame of the world. And those who were neither a Jessie nor a Dennie, most times they'd turn a blind eye when the shit hit the fan, when the Jessies of the world spat their poison and hate on all the Dennies and Mrs. Plimptons. They'd look away or hurry past, they'd turn up the music on their headphones or absorb themselves in their cell phones, pretending they saw nothing, hoping the "nothing" would end before they felt even more like a coward for ignoring it.

The world didn't favor a hero, but it didn't mean Mr. McAllister had to turn a blind eye. He vowed, as he left Dora and Dennie Strathcomb behind, to stop playing it by the book just this once, whether the School Board liked it or not. He was through towing the line. If standing up for what was good and right cost him his job, so be it. *Something* had to be done, once and for all, about that lousy scum-sucking Jessie Kinsmen and all the other Jessies of the world, and this time, Mr. McAllister would have to be the one to do it.

The question, as some Tap tourist might have asked, was *how*?

He found the answer later that night. There was a time, a few years back, when Mayor Kinsmen had petitioned to get peanut butter removed from the schools. Mr. McAllister looked it up, and sure enough, there were several articles in the Dark Pines *Signpost* about what had been considered a scandal at the time. Parents had been up in arms. How dare he tell them how to raise their children? What were they supposed to give their kids for lunch? *Sushi*? Not everyone in town could afford fifteen-dollar a pound steak like the kind Mayor Kinsmen bought to feed his Dobermans. Not everyone ran a chain—not one but a *half dozen* throughout Peterborough and Haliburton counties—of successful used car lots like Mayor Kinsmen.

Kinsmen's soapboxing had won out, as everyone had expected it would, and both schools in Dark Pines adopted the new nut-free policy. Mr. McAllister had joked, down at The Tap, that the School Board already had a nut-free policy, kowtowing to the PTA whenever an issue came up they were too chickenshit to fight over. "That's nuts as in co-*ho*-nays, fellas," he'd added with a grin, and the boys had chuckled genially and guzzled their beers. They never did appreciate the comedic genius in their midst.

The point of all his research was that he remembered hearing Kinsmen had only started the campaign because his son, Jessie, was an anaphylactic. Big old bully Jessie Kinsmen was afraid of an itty bitty peanut. If he'd ever met Jimmy Carter and shook the man's hand, he'd have swollen up worse than Dennie Strathcomb's jaw and had himself a popleptic seizure.

He might even die, Mr. McAllister thought, and strangely the notion didn't bother him much at all. *You don't feel sorry for a rabid dog when he bites*, he told himself. *You just pull up your big-boy pants and put the damn thing down.*

Jessie Kinsmen was a rabid dog. He'd just bit his last kid.

■■

MONDAY CAME AND the trap was set. He'd spent the entire weekend mulling over the finer points, but the gist of it was simple. He'd leave a peanut butter sandwich under the seat, half-eaten (this proved to be the hardest part of the job, since Mr. McAllister thought peanut butter tasted like salted shit), and the epinephrine injector the School Board had made mandatory on all buses—after serious lobbying from the PTA—would have disappeared. "Couldn't say," Mr. McAllister practiced saying in front of the mirror, watching for the tell-tale facial tics of a liar, "I s'pose it musta fell and got trampled off the bus when the kids rushed off to school. You know how kids are with trash, always wanna kick it 'stead of puttin it where it belongs."

When he was satisfied with his confused yet tormented expression, he raided the cabinets at the old house on Greenbury Street. He'd had to put his father in the convalescent home recently, after the old man had fallen down the stairs and couldn't stop shitting himself. His visits to casa del McAllister, the old homestead, were far less frequent these days, mainly to make sure the roof hadn't caved in and the lawn wasn't going to pot. Having power of attorney, he could have sold it if he'd wanted. He just couldn't bear to get rid of the house he'd grown up in, not with all the photographs of his mother on the walls, who'd passed on when he was still quite young.

The peanut butter was in the cabinet. He opened the jar, sniffed it, and gagged. It was oily and smelled worse than normal—chemically. He'd bought a loaf of white at the Hometown Proud, aware there was a crusted jar of blueberry jam in the fridgerator he could use. He'd only have to take a few bites.

So he poured himself a tall, cold glass of milk, and he slathered the bread with salted shit and jam. Looking down at the sandwich, cut in half on a diagonal and laid out nice on a plate beside the milk, brought back memories of his mother. His dad had never been the same after she passed. Never cracked a smile or joked with him anymore. Never taught him how to ride a bike. Never spent a night without a six-pack in front of the boob tube. The shell of a man Mr. McAllister visited twice weekly, who pissed and shat in his semi-electric bed at the Castle, was just showing on the outside how he'd felt on the inside since Florence McAllister passed through the Pearly Gates in the summer of 1969.

He bit into the sickly sweet, gooey sandwich and chewed until it was doughy and gritty and swallowed it down before he could puke it with a big gulp of milk. Then he did it again, just so it would look authentic. He didn't even have to swallow, but it felt like eating a few bites of shit sandwich would be a minor penance for the crime he was about to commit. Even if the kid just got a small allergic reaction, it could still be considered assault in the court of public opinion. These days, that was just about the only court that mattered.

What happened, as far as he could figure, was that the mechanic who worked on the buses on weekends, idiot that he was, had been tightening the bolts under Jessie Kinsmen's seat while eating a PB&J. The sammie fell out of his hand, and forgot about the 5-second rule. He must have bumped his head or something, because he left it laying on the floor to rot instead of throwing it in the trash.

If the kid really was as allergic as they said and not just faking it for attention, all the Dennie Strathcombs of the world might breathe a little easier knowing Jessie Kinsmen had a kryptonite.

He tried to hide his smile pulling up the curb in front of the Kinsmen house. The kid had the stop all to himself, that's how you could tell he was King Shit among all the little floaters. Other kids who lived closer to the Kinsmen stop walked several blocks out of their way to get on before or after Jessie, and Mr. McAllister couldn't blame them. What kid in their right mind would want to stand around without supervision in the company of a rabid dog?

"Jessie," Mr. McAllister said, biting his cheeks so he wouldn't grin, as the boy's weight depressed the right front shocks.

The kid wore a smile of his own, probably feeling pretty fine about the job he'd done to the Strathcomb boy, not seeing Dora's car idling behind the bus, nor the kid himself in his regular seat. The downcast eyes as Jessie passed made Mr. McAllister feel pretty good himself about the job he was about to do on Jessie Kinsmen's immune system.

But Jessie walked right past his seat, where he'd sat day after day for as long as Mr. McAllister could remember, right past his kryptonite, right past any chance Mr. McAllister had of getting even on the fat squirt.

Sweet fancy molasses! Where the shit is he going?

Jessie tromped on to the empty seat near the back, where Dennie Strathcomb would sit if it wasn't already occupied by one of the cool kids. The boy wedged himself into the seat and turned to face the front.

He beamed his smile at Mr. McAllister, the proud smile of a boy who'd won a trophy, if only in his own mind.

Fuckity-fuck!

Mr. McAllister angrily threw the tranny into gear and pulled off from the curb, the whole plan foiled.

The whole plan! What now what NOW...

For a split second he considered slamming his foot on the accelerator, taking the corners at high speed in the desperate hope the sandwich in its plastic baggie would skitter across the dirty floor and somehow come to rest near Jessie's feet, a fucking *impossibility*, not fucking likely at all, Pip old chum, old chap, and even if it *was* possible he'd take hell from that, the PB&J wouldn't be the only shit sandwich he'd have to eat, and this time the School Board might just suspend him, or worse. He'd end up working the limestone pit with the boys from The Tap, choking up rock dust while sucking down their wobbly pops.

"Fuck that," Mr. McAllister said to himself. He looked in the rearview to see if anyone had caught it, but the only one looking at him was Jessie, his green eyes wide like he was gawping at a carnival freak.

Mr. McAllister squeezed the wheel and focused on his driving. It was all he could do to keep from pulling over to the side of the gravel road, stepping off the bus and just keep on walking all the way back to town, to The Tap, which hadn't even yet opened for breakfast, let alone for boozing. He'd sunk all of his hopes into this Hail Mary pass, a desperate clutch at his last scraps of humanity, and nobody was in the end zone to catch the damn ball.

Feeling more depressed than he'd ever felt in his life, except for those first few months after his mother passed, Mr. McAllister pulled the bus up to the corner of Groonie Road and Van de Meer, where Janey Freely stood, backpack in hand. "Good morning, Mr. McAllister," she said cheerily, as she always did, her braces glimmering in the sun.

"Ain't it, Janey?" Mr. McAllister managed to spit out. She smiled again, though she stopped suddenly as she turned toward her seat near the front, and her backpack slipped from her hand to the floor with a jangle of pencils and three-ring binders.

"What's the—?" Mr. McAllister turned as he spoke and caught sight of Jessie Kinsmen, his fat neck and round face much redder than normal, just about as red as a beet.

"...Mr. McAllister?" Janey said.

Jessie was choking, and not just on a sip of water that went down the wrong tube—Jessie Kinsmen choking *to death*.

"Cripes," Mr. McAllister gasped, looking around himself desperately. Mrs. Plimpton shifted in her seat to look back. She removed her glasses and held them out from her face like binoculars to get a good look.

"Somethin's wrong with Jessie," Barclay Robbins shouted.

"He's not breathing," said a girl whose voice Mr. McAllister didn't recognize.

Everyone stood up in their seats, but nobody moved. No one made to help. They were frozen, transfixed, as Jessie's pink hands came up to claw at his throat.

"Christ Jesus," Mrs. Plimpton muttered, blinking hard with her beady chipmunk eyes. She turned to Mr. McAllister. "What do we do?"

"The EpiPen," Janey said, both she and Mr. McAllister turning to it at once. But it was gone, of course. He'd made sure of that this morning. The hope visibly drained from Janey's face.

Mr. McAllister hurried back to where Jessie sat, clawing at his own throat, eyes bugged out of his fat head. All the kids gawped. *What are they thinking?* Mr. McAllister had a moment to wonder. "Jessie," he said. Jessie stared straight ahead, his fingers clawing at his WWE t-shirt like they belonged to someone else. Mr. McAllister took hold of the boy's shoulder. "Jessie, look at me."

The boy's eyes rolled in the direction of Mr. McAllister's voice. "Jessie, have you got an inhaler? An EpiPen?"

Jessie shook his head more vehemently than it had already been shaking. Tears broke free from his eyes and streamed down his freckled cheeks. Pink froth began accruing in the creases between his lips. Pink froth. It brought back images of Mr. McAllister's father, dying slowly in a hospital bed. They'd asked him about pulling the plug last week. There wasn't much they could do for him, they'd said. He likely wasn't conscious at all, they'd assured him.

He said he'd think about it.

More pink froth spilled from Jessie's mouth, dripping down his chin and gathering on the collar of his shirt.

Think about it, Mr. McAllister told himself. Had he really *thought* about what would happen before he'd started this, or had he been moving on autopilot, as unconscious of what he was doing as his driving had always been? Did he even consider the fact that this was *murder*?

Mr. McAllister threw a look over his shoulder at Mrs. Plimpton, whose bug eyes looked even more insect-like with her glasses held out from her face. He caught the eye of Barclay Robbins, a handsome kid, like his father. The boy seemed to shake his head. Tanner Jones seemed to do the same. Even Janey, hugging herself at the front of the bus, seemed unsure.

They don't want *me to save him*, Mr. McAllister realized then, to his growing horror. *They've seen their chance. They'd let him die here, gladly, and that's on me. They'd smile and wave bye-bye but Christ-alive they'd regret it once he's gone. Can't put that on them. They're just mixed-up kids, they don't know what they want.*

"Fuck," he said, and nobody seemed to care. They just kept staring at him, at Jessie—who was just a boy, after all, not a rabid dog, not a monster—and praying for it to be over soon.

Mr. McAllister dropped to his knees before the dying boy. He peeked under the seat, pretending to look for the missing EpiPen. There was the sandwich, right where he'd left it. It hadn't moved an inch and still Jesse spazzed-out.

Guess he really is allergic, after all, Mr. McAllister mused as he surreptitiously slipped the EpiPen out of his pocket. "Found it," he shouted, popping up from the floor with the epinephrine in hand. He bit the top off and, hesitating for only a moment, jammed the needle into Jessie's leg.

Jessie began to cough immediately, his hands falling limp to his sides. His freckly pallor returned as he coughed and coughed. When he had the breath to speak, he said, "That hurt, you dick."

Then he allowed the ghost of a grateful smile to creep onto his lips.

Mr. McAllister patted the boy's back as a smattering of applause began in the back of the bus, Barclay Robbins furiously clapping, the others following suit, adding, "Way to go, Mr. McAllister," and "You da man," and slapping him genially on the shoulder as he made his way to the front of the bus.

"Atta boy!" Mrs. Plimpton said, her smile eating the bottom of her face.

Janey picked up her backpack, and looked up at him as he approached the front of the bus. "Where was it?"

"What's that, Janey?"

"Where was the EpiPen?"

The suspicion in her eyes made him flinch. "Well, Janey, I s'pose it musta fell and got trampled to the back of the bus when you kids rushed off to school."

"It was on the floor then?"

Mr. McAllister laughed. "Where else would it have been, Janey?"

She squinted past him, where Jessie was getting his own shoulder claps and praise, the boy smiling like a kid who'd won a trophy, as if he finally fit in. Janey's eyes softened, and she favored her bus driver with a brace-faced smile. She said nothing to him, only nodded, as if she understood exactly what had happened here, and she approved of the outcome, whatever he'd been planning.

Well, the world don't favor heroes, Mr. McAllister thought, driving the kids toward school just like he'd always done, *but liars seem to do okay.*

In the Shadow of the Masters

— - ALBRECHT DÜRER

YANNICK TREMAINE HAD never come across a painting he couldn't copy, and Abrecht Dürer's *Self-Portrait* was no exception. Still, the forgery had troubled him since he'd begun it, and he often half-jokingly mused that the so-called Forger's Curse might be responsible, not that he believed in such things.

Tremaine's Kraków studio was quite large, with a spectacular view of the old synagogues and the flat, cool waters of the Vistula River, beyond which the Jewish Ghetto once stood. The apartment itself lay above a Turkish-run fabric store in a crumbling relic built long before the Great War, like most of the buildings surrounding it. With his considerable wealth, he'd converted his suite to suit his needs. Here, he painted Vermeers and Caravaggios and Monets—sometimes from memory, sometimes from books, often from stolen originals his benefactor kept hidden in temperature-controlled basement vaults, large humidors, and abandoned salt mines, like Göring had before him.

The day Mr. Ziminski came to check on his investment a final time, Tremaine snapped out of a trance at the sound of the doorbell, feeling like he'd run a marathon. Sweating, his mouth dry, eyes red from not blinking, from staring transfixed into Albrecht Dürer's haunting golden eyes, he blinked the haze from his own eyes and plopped the brush he'd been using into a Dripol fruit cocktail can he kept half-filled with linseed oil. Once again, he found it difficult to draw himself away from the long-dead painter's gaze. It troubled Tremaine how few people outside of the art community seem to know Dürer's *Self-Portrait*, also called *Self-Portrait at Twenty-Eight Years Old Wearing a Coat with Fur Collar*. Like many painters, he considered the piece worthy of the *Mona Lisa*'s fame. The stark interplay of light and dark, with a black void behind him, as if Dürer had deliberately painted himself adrift in time and space. A metaphor? Tremaine would leave it for the scholars to decide. Dürer's hand, slightly raised to handle the fur of his collar, thought to mirror portraits of Christ. But it was the eyes that held him in their sway—always the eyes. He lit a cigarette from a pack of Sobieski Premiums with a quivering hand, and took a long drag, consciously avoiding eye contact with the painting.

The nicotine calmed him enough to chuckle at his foolishness. *Does anyone believe in curses anymore?* he wondered as he crossed his flat to the door.

Through the peephole he was greeted by the mashed nose of his benefactor's beefy Russian bodyguard. He muttered "*Fuck*" under his breath—quiet enough, he thought, but the ex-Spetsnaz raised his eyebrows and peered back into the dim hall.

"He hear hims," Vladimir said to his employer, lurking somewhere in the shadows beyond Tremaine's sight.

"I'm coming!" Tremaine called over his own shoulder, attempting to throw his voice. He unlocked the latch and chain barring the behemoth from entry, and Vladimir—Ziminski's very muscular, very ex-Russian paramilitary bodyguard—barged in. He eyeballed the large room with a hand held over the Desert Eagle Mark 1 carried in a leather sling holster over his black turtleneck, as if expecting a Navy Seal team crouched behind the kitchen counter, ready to get the drop on him.

"Is clear," he said to the open door.

Ziminski buzzed in then, his motorized wheelchair tracking dirt all over Tremaine's new floors, like the tracks of Nazi Panzers through the streets of Kraków. And like the city officials of the time, there wasn't much Tremaine could do but accept it.

Parked in the living room, his employer looked up with cold blue eyes, a colorful shawl holding in what little warmth his elderly body still created. "Well, Tremaine? Aren't you going to offer us a drink?" he asked, his accent faint—Americanized.

"Where are my manners?"

He would have offered Ziminski a can of turpentine if he hadn't switched to linseed oil to keep his brushes clean. Just looking at the old man's pale, yellowed-parchment skin always made his own flesh crawl... but Ziminski's money had paid for the flat and all its renovations. It kept the pimps from pounding down his door. And it was Ziminski's money that allowed Tremaine to paint for a living, which was all he'd ever wanted to do for as long as he could remember.

Reminding himself of this, he poured the evil man an American whiskey, and cracked a Tyskie for the Russian. Vladimir blew foam off the top of the can before taking a healthy swig.

"So what brings you here, Mr. Ziminski?"

"I've come to see my Dossi," Ziminski said, speaking of the reproduction Tremaine had been working on concurrent to the Dürer: Dosso Dossi's *Triumph of Bacchus*. "Coming along nicely, I hope?"

"It's getting there."

In truth, he hadn't been able to focus on it since he'd started the *Self-Portrait*. He'd been having trouble getting Dossi's depiction of the god Bacchus right, and he realized why just then: the nude minions hoisting him up in that throne, carrying him toward the endless after-party, reminded him too much of Vladimir lugging Ziminski and his wheelchair up the apartment stairs. He'd been subconsciously painting the youthful god as a decrepit old ghoul in effigy of his benefactor.

"Let's take a look, shall we?" Without waiting for his say-so,

Ziminski zipped past him, over the fucking Berber shag—*mercifully* without dirtying it—and into the daylight bright studio.

"*Mój Boże...*" Ziminski breathed before Tremaine had even caught up, and he understood instantly the old man was looking at the Dürer and not the Dossi. He'd been so astounded by its likeness, he reverted to his mother tongue to say, *My God*.

When Tremaine laid a hand on the old man's bony shoulder, the bald, scabrous head jerked upward. The look of shame in his eyes—at least Tremaine *thought* it was shame—almost made him feel sorry for the old man. Ziminski brought his shawl up to his lips with a quivering hand and wiped away a runner of drool. Ice cubes tinkled in the glass in his other claw.

"Here's the Dossi," Tremaine said, directing his attention to the other painting.

"Lovely, lovely," Ziminski remarked dismissively. Then he clucked his tongue in disapproval, as something caught his eye—the Dürer forgotten now his critic's hat was on. "The breast is wrong. Too full. You've been sleeping with too many whores, Tremaine. Forgotten what a real tit looks like, hey?"

"It's still a work in progress," Tremaine said, barely hiding his annoyance. Worse than the insult, Ziminski had been able to see with his deteriorating eyesight what Tremaine himself couldn't, being too close to the work. The breast in Dossi's original was plump but not full, the nipple pointing downward. The breast Tremaine had painted could have belonged to an American stripper, a hard-rock thing with its nipple aimed toward the heavens.

Tremaine had always been a skilled technical painter. His teachers, back in art school, had said this of his work all the time. What he *lacked*, they had told him, was that creative spark the da Vincis and Picassos of the world seemed born with. A good painting drew you toward it, you could *feel* its meaning like an ache in your chest. You could *hear* it, whispering its untold secrets in your ear. An exceptional piece of art could move you to tears with its tale—it *lived*. A masterpiece, like Dürer's woefully underrated efforts, could make the work and its artist *immortal*.

Tremaine's own paintings had always been derivative of someone else's, even artists he'd never before seen, let alone glimpsed their body of work—this according to men and women whose own landscapes and portraits and bowls of fruit were so middle of the road they'd had to resort to teaching middle-class suburban children the Golden Ratio and color theory just to make a living. And how he could copy something he hadn't known existed had always eluded Tremaine, up until the day he'd taken their criticism to heart and decided to try his hand at forgery.

Eventually he became grateful for their criticism. Aside from having to paint at the literal barrel of a gun, he'd lived a decent life, and the thing he'd come to learn in his late-twenties that he hadn't been able to accept during school was that his teachers had been *right*. He'd never had that spark. Never would. His mind was a blank canvas, never to be filled with an image of his own design. Tremaine and his work would forever be left standing in the shadow of the Masters.

Ziminski had seen that in him. When Tremaine was still trying to make a name for himself, pimping his derivative art in as many galleries as would allow him, the old man saw a hunger in Tremaine's work, in *him*, that spoke of someone with big dreams—if only he hadn't lacked the "spark." And so Tremaine had appealed to Ziminski's vanity, as an artist must do with a potential patron. He professed admiration of the old man's appreciation and indisputable knowledge of art.

The first time he met Miłogost Ziminski, the old man had been standing with a group of glitterati, entertaining them with his critiques. This was before the wheelchair. Ziminski had once had dreams of his own to be a painter, in his youth. Even with the wealth he'd amassed since, he knew he couldn't sell a single watercolor, not without critics accusing him of using his money to buy acclaim. His skill had been middling at best long before the accident that had made his hands clumsy with a brush.

Ziminski liked to keep desirable things for himself, particularly, but not limited to, artwork. Back when he'd been married, Ziminski would only trot his wife Magda out during big gala occasions. This buxom blonde thing—and he'd criticized Tremaine's taste for whores—who wore furs and glittery dresses and offered her hand for strangers to kiss like she was royalty, Ziminski would parade her around at all the big parties, but when the event was over she'd vanish. He'd tuck her away in a closet somewhere in his hundred-room mansion. He'd lock her back up in her gilded cage.

Always wanting things he couldn't have, Tremaine had taken her in one of Ziminski's toilets during one of Ziminski's events. He'd fucked her again in the old man's vault, and had wondered more than a few times what had happened to her since the last time he'd seen her. He didn't have the nerve to ask the old man, knowing how easy it would have been to erase her from his life. Everyone would simply have assumed she'd left him for a younger man, gone to live on the French Riviera on the old man's dime.

Ziminski stroked his wispy Fu Manchu beard, admiring the texture of the Dürer. "Look at the *craquelure*," he marveled. "So much like the real thing."

Tremaine agreed the aging process was coming along nicely, despite having done most of it in a trance, applying layers of umber and water he'd snuffed cigarette butts out in to simulate centuries of wear.

Ziminski reached out to touch it with one shriveled, liver-spotted claw, causing Tremaine to shout "*Don't!*" The old man peered back with sullen ferocity, like a bad kid who'd had his hand slapped away from the cookie jar, and wetted his lips with his cankered tongue.

"It's still drying," Tremaine explained hastily, catching a darker disapproving glare from Vladimir, who cracked his knuckles in response. Cold sweat dripped from his armpits as he awaited Ziminski's reaction, imagining his ribs would make a similar sound caught in one of Vladimir's big Russian bear hugs.

The old man nodded at his monstrous companion. "Stand down, Igor," he said, blithely mocking a man who could crush him like a Soviet brand cigarette underfoot. "The man values his art more than his life. If that's not a quality worth admiring, I don't know what is."

Vladimir merely sipped his beer, eyeballing the artist over the rim.

"It will be ready in a week, I presume?"

"The Dürer? I thought the deadline was two?"

"The *dead*line—" Ziminski seemed to savor the word. "—is whenever I say it is. I've lined up another job for our technician in Munich a month from now. She'll need time to prepare."

"*I* need time, Mr. Ziminski."

"*Tosh*," the old man scoffed. "Fix the breast on the Dossi and keep up with that *craquelure*. Honestly, Tremaine, you're such a perfectionist. It doesn't have to fool them very long."

█▌

IN TREMAINE'S DREAM Dürer stepped out of the painting, his gaze unwavering, as undying as the colors in which he'd painted himself, his golden eyes focused on Tremaine through the darkened bedroom doorway. The man from the painting crept across the studio floor in the moonlight, bare feet padding over Tremaine's Berber shag, and entered the room.

Standing over the bed while Tremaine slept, fingering the fur of his collar, eyes glimmering in the gloomy abyss of night, Tremaine couldn't get a clear look at him in the darkness of his dream, but he was able to see Dürer whispering—staring at him and whispering. Cursing him in German. The Forger's Curse. Tremaine tried to wake up, to defend himself, to defend his work, but he couldn't move. Eventually, he woke up screaming: "I have to! It's all I can do!" Sweating, heart beating hard, he looked around, the sun already high above the Vistula, shimmering on its glassy surface.

Catching his breath, he padded out barefoot to the studio, following the path of Dürer's ghost, and found the dead painter still where he should be, still in the painting, those golden eyes challenging Tremaine to continue his day's work.

Fraud, they said. *Forger*.

Tremaine threw a drop cloth over the painter's head, and went to work on the Dossi. *Forger*. He could feel the young Master's stare through the fabric, couldn't fool himself into believing the eyes had closed, that they'd turned away. *Fraud*. Judging him. Watching him paint.

Tremaine dropped his brush in the Dripol can, threw on a jacket, and hurried out of the flat. He walked for miles, trying to clear his head.

He ate brunch in the Rynek. Downed shots at a vodka bar in Old Town. When he returned, he was sufficiently drunk to finish the Dossi untroubled by thoughts of Dürer's judgment. The curse made him laugh aloud, and he eyed the pale drop cloth with reproach.

Returning to his Dossi, a little yelp escaped him, and he backed into the table, spilling his liquor and the contents of the Dripol can all over the floor. *Somehow* he'd painted the eyes of Bacchus to look like Dürer's. Tremaine got down on his knees to wipe up the spill, grabbing a cloth and patting the stain down, worried it would spread to his Berber shag rug. Finally satisfied he'd soaked it all up, he stood and turned to fix the Dossi—

His heart leapt. "*Where is it?*" The drop cloth was gone and Dürer stared into his soul. Tremaine scoured the studio, cursing himself, cursing the painting. Finally, he stopped moving around in angry endless circles, and found he'd used it to mop up the spill.

"Idiot!" He smacked himself on the forehead, hard enough to cause stars in front of his eyes. "Fucking *idiot!*"

Tremaine turned to the painting, his *curse*, throwing all of his anger and frustration toward it. Dürer returned the glare with a frozen smirk.

Burn it, he thought. *Burn it and be done with it.*

"And then what? Ziminski would have me killed."

Flee the country. Go back home.

"*Home...*" he said mockingly. "There's nothing for me there."

At least you'd be alive. Put the drop cloth back, and push it a scooch closer to the ashtray... you could say it was an accident. Left a cigarette burning.

"He'd never believe me."

It would buy you some time...

Tremaine gave Dürer a baleful look. The Master said nothing.

A perfect forgery. His *best.*

An idea occurred.

"I'm not going to burn you," he cooed, approaching the painting. He picked up his brush, dipped it into a brownish yellow blot of paint on his palette. It was the only way, his drunken mind told him. The only way to break the curse.

A counter-spell. An *incantation.*

By the time he'd blended the words into Dürer's fur collar to be almost indistinguishable, it began to seem a little less crazy.

"YOU KNOW WHAT Dürer said about forgers, don't you?" the thief asked as they approached Wawel Castle from Kazimierz. In the distance Tremaine heard the *hejnał mariacki*, the historical call of a lone bugler atop St. Mary's Cathedral. The trumpeting stopped abruptly, as it always did, the same note left hanging in the cool night air as legend said it had during the Mongol invasion, when the bugler signaling the horde's approach had been shot in the throat by an arrow.

Tremaine wondered how the trumpeter must have felt, his life's work ended with a sudden realization his throat no longer held the breath to produce sound. He'd always believed his own need to create would only ever end with his death. Break his hands, and he would have found a way to paint without them, like Christy Brown, the painter born with cerebral palsy. Hell, he would have painted with his *cock* if it came down to it.

"Huh?" Tremaine said, only now realizing the woman he'd been walking with in silence for the last twenty minutes had finally spoken.

"Don't you ever worry about the Forger's Curse?" she asked him.

Tremaine sputtered. "Silly superstition."

The thief shrugged and carried on down the cobblestone street.

Wawel Castle, built for Casimir II the Great in the early-1300s, was even more beautiful at dusk, and Ziminski's "technician" stopped in the sidewalk on Dragon Street, gawking up at its lighted walls and turrets. Tourists milled below, snapping blurry evening photos and selfies. One of the largest museums in Kraków, Wawel housed an art gallery in rooms where 700 years of royalty ruled and prayed and fucked and shat, and its armories presented some of the finest examples of warfare, from the earliest broadswords to ship-mounted cannons. Tremaine had been many times, as new exhibits came and went between its walls, but he'd never grown immune to its beauty. Ziminski's technician, who'd just arrived from Sweden (a country not lacking in castles), managed to catch her breath before continuing on toward the front gate.

She stopped again in front of the bronze dragon. Some teenagers, drunk or high and chattering in Polish, had just sent it a text message that would cause it to breathe fire. When it finally did, the thief startled, her pale oval face blazing orange in the firelight, her choppy bangs as red as a Titian beauty's. Tremaine's initial loathing of her, for the simple fact that her presence required him to rush his work, lifted a little as the kids raised a cheer around them. In the firelight, under the hem of her black hoodie, he saw Vermeer's Girl with the Pearl Earring, Botticelli's Venus, Caravaggio's Salome.

Tremaine sneered at the fantasy. She reminded him of America, that was all. Her Midwestern accent, rough around the edges, dredged up bittersweet memories of his wasted small town youth. Thinking of home made him remember snippets of his drunken evening spent painting the Dossi. He thought of the incantation he'd painted into the fur collar, and smiled again. No one would be the wiser until he'd gotten his money and left Poland.

The flames died. "C'mon, Tremaine," she said, calling him by his last name, the only name he or Ziminski had ever given her. He knew her as Archer, which made him think of the dead man and his trumpet. Ziminski had him meet her at the airport in one of his cars, like he wasn't the best fine art forger in the world but a common chauffeur. He'd claimed he wanted the first face Archer saw to be a pleasant one, but really it was to prove how thoroughly he owned Tremaine, so Tremaine drove the living hell out of Ziminski's Bentley like he'd rode Ziminski's estranged wife.

Holding up a sign he'd hastily penned "ARCHER" in the front seat of the car, he got more than a handful of smartasses miming a bow and arrow at him as they left baggage claim. Tremaine didn't even give her a second glance until she was standing right in front of him, telling him her name—or at least her *codename*—was Archer. His surprise must have been evident, because she'd said, "You were expecting Hudson Hawk?"

Tremaine was a regular visitor of the gallery. The technician required time and silence to "case" the building, and with him at her side, her furtive glances at cameras and other security measures would likely go overlooked.

Tremaine enjoyed traveling to the galleries in other countries, as well. He loved to be steeped in art. But one of the great benefits of his job was being able to *touch* the works of the masters, not just gawk, once the technicians had swapped them for his forgeries.

"Imagine touching the *Mona Lisa*," he told Archer as they entered the castle. "Running your fingers over every brush stroke. Feeling the contours, the *impasto*, and understanding exactly what brush shape da Vinci used for each stroke, what type of bristle, which pigments he'd mixed to make each color and shade, what organic materials and metals and semi-precious stones were used to derive its natural pigments." He sensed her losing interest, as she gazed at gates and darkened, hidden recesses in the walls. "*Knowing* the secret in her smile and her eyes, that if she were able to move she would seal it with a finger placed upon her lips. Imagine, for a moment, stepping into the shoes of Munch as he composed *The Scream*, or van Gogh dotting his *Night* with stars. Imagine stretching up to the ceiling of the Sistine Chapel and touching the finger of God as He passes the gift of life to Adam. Imagine standing in front of the rough sketch of *Guernica* and choosing, with all of the colors in the spectrum at your disposal, to paint it instead in stark black and white monochrome."

Archer gave him a look then, as if he'd gone mad.

Thinking of the curse and his counter-spell, Tremaine believed maybe he had.

Upstairs in the State Rooms, the galleries, the halls quiet as a tomb, but the walls would not stay quieted. The chorus of a thousand voices followed them through chambers and antechambers, bedrooms and banquet halls, from tapestries and paintings on wood, on canvas, and directly on the wrought leather walls. The forger and the thief slipped silently past a thousand years of art history, and he suspected Archer cared little, if at all, about any of it. This was a job to her, nothing more. He saw it in her eyes, flitting past Madonnas and Sabine women, chubby cherubs, muscular angels and fussy royalty without a second look.

They moved into the Royal Audience Hall, where stone floors glimmered. Above, eyes met his gaze from Biblical scenes woven into tapestries, and from the coffered ceiling, where carved and painted wooden heads that once watched over Kraków's royalty watched over them, the art thief and the painter. The forger. The *fraud*. Never had a lick of talent. Never would amount to anything. Their gaze, with hollowed-out irises, full of silent reproach.

"Tremaine?"

Archer stood in the next room, a look of curiosity visible under her hood. Tremaine studied the faces above him a moment longer, then followed. She stood before two paintings hung side-by-side: Dossi's *Jupiter, Mercury and Virtue* and Dürer's *Self-Portrait at Twenty-Eight Years Old Wearing a Coat with Fur Collar*, on loan from the Alte Pinakothek in Munich. *Jupiter* was a sort of painters' painting Tremaine had never particularly responded to, though he generally liked Dossi's work. But the Dürer had what art appreciators called "wall power." It drew the eye. It *spoke* to him, even more so than his own replica. It *commanded* his attention.

"Jesus..." Archer muttered. "Those *eyes*..."

Tremaine could tell she had no eye for art. Nothing had moved her to waver from her business, not a single painting had spoken to her until just then. If that didn't speak of the power of Dürer's painting, Tremaine thought, then nothing did.

While Archer stared, open-mouthed, Tremaine noted that aside from a few minor differences in brush strokes and *craquelure*, his forgery and the original were virtually identical. Even the best experts, the people Sotheby's called when there was a question of authenticity, or the agents who worked fine art forgery cases in the FBI and Scotland Yard, or conspiracy theorists who would spend hours poring over alleged ciphers in Dürer's work—even they would have been hard-pressed to tell the two paintings apart.

Only Tremaine knew about the flaw, his incantation warding against evil... just two simple words he hoped would protect him long enough to get far away from the painting and his forgery.

No matter what happened, this would be his last.

██

TWO DAYS LATER, pleased the theft had gone unnoticed—or at least unreported—Ziminski and Tremaine shared a drink in the old man's study. Tremaine peered through the glass of amber liquid at a roaring fire, pleased Ziminski hadn't invited his bodyguard to drink with them. When a knot popped in the fire, he simply shifted in the large leather chair, and sipped his Scotch. With the Russian nearby, he might have flinched, or twisted round to make sure Vladimir wasn't looming over his shoulder, cracking the knuckles of his massive fingers.

"*Na zdrowie*," Ziminski said, raising his glass in a toast. Tremaine sat up and clinked his glass against the old man's. Ziminski eyed him queerly over the glass as he drank, as Tremaine settled back into the groaning chair, sipping his Scotch. "Your work's improved these last few months. I've noticed a sense of pride not present in previous works, particularly in your Dossi, and of course, the Dürer."

"Thank you, Mr. Ziminski," Tremaine said. "As much as it's about the money, it really is a labor of love." The old man nodded thoughtfully. "Say, where's Vladimir tonight? You give him the night off?"

"The Mad Russian? He's making room in the vault. We have a new acquisition, as you know. It requires a place of prominence." Ziminski's thin lips curled in a smirk. "You've... never seen the vault, have you?"

"No sir," Tremaine lied. Magda had lured him there during a soiree, her breasts heaving as she dragged him through the house, and the both of them out of breath they'd proceeded to fuck on top of Ziminski's large antique safe. Since he hadn't had much of a chance to look at the paintings stored there, he felt the lie was more of a stretching of truth.

"Let's you and I go have a look at my Dürer, hey?"

Tremaine swallowed the last of his drink in one gulp. He leaned forward to place the glass on a coaster on Ziminski's black granite table. "I'd like that," he said.

Ziminski buzzed down the hall, turning left toward the east wing where the gallery lay, and beyond it, the vault. Inside, paintings much too valuable, not to mention illegally procured, to display to the general public lay. Tremaine had gotten a fleeting glance during his stolen moment with Magda, enough to know much of what lay inside had been painted long before he'd met the old man. There were paintings and statuettes long thought lost to looting and war. There were portions of frescos chipped and pulled from church walls, ornate capitals from the columns and pilasters of unprotected ruins, portraits of wealthy families thought stolen by jealous relatives excised from their wills.

Ziminski zipped into the gallery. Tremaine heard grunting up ahead —only Vladimir hauling sculptures and display cases to make room for the Dürer, he knew, but it still unnerved him. He'd been feeling mellow, certain he'd gotten away with painting his little flaw into the forgery. As they approached the far room, the certainty dwindled.

"Do you mind if I use the loo before we...?"

"It can wait," Ziminski said over his shoulder, his wheels rumbling over bare wood buffed to a high sheen.

"I'd rather not," Tremaine said, lagging a bit. "My back teeth are floating."

Ahead of them, Vladimir stepped into the doorway. He wore a t-shirt and his shoulder holster, his hard muscles gleaming with sweat, his wide chest pounding from exhaustion. His brow furrowed as he looked up at Tremaine. The painter had no doubts even though Vladimir had tired himself, the Russian would outrun him before he could reach the stairs. Either that, or put a bullet between the shoulder blades.

Ziminski zipped around to face him. "If it hadn't been for Archer, I might never have noticed. She's got a good eye, that one."

"Noticed?" Tremaine tried hard to swallow. He'd misjudged Archer: she'd had an eye for art, after all.

"Don't play games, Tremaine. I always knew your ego would be your undoing. You couldn't just let it be. It's just like with Magda. You couldn't stand that an old man like me had a woman like her, and so you had to have her for yourself."

"I would never do that, Mr. Ziminski—"

"Oh, *tosh*. She told me everything." He smirked. "You're a scoundrel, Tremaine. I knew you couldn't keep it in your pants, but I had hoped you'd had enough pride of purpose to *not fuck with my painting*!"

Ziminski's words resounded off the silent walls. Vladimir cracked his knuckles, stepping out of the gallery and into the hall.

Tremaine threw up his hands, backing away. "Mr. Ziminski, Milo, please—"

"Oh, Milo nothing." The old man's face twisted into an approximation of disappointment. "You've failed me, boy. But worse than that, you *betrayed* me."

Much too late, Tremaine turned to run. Vladimir grabbed him fiercely by the shoulders and spun him round. Tremaine saw the old man look away in disgust as Vladimir slammed a fist into his face and painted the world black.

▐▐

THUNDER ROARED IN Tremaine's skull.

He knew where he was from the smell before his eyes grew accustomed to the harsh light. Oil paint, dust, canvas, parchment. Tremaine blinked away a crust of blood and peered blearily at the empty insides of Miłogost Ziminski's vault.

Ziminski sat in the doorway. Vladimir stood over his shoulder, smiling darkly.

"You know, this vault is air-tight," Ziminski said. "I've thought a lot about what I would do with you when Archer pointed out your folly, and the solution was simple. What better place to kill you, than in the very place you first betrayed me."

"Milo, just listen to me," Tremaine groaned.

"Oh I think I've listened to you long enough. It's all bullshit, Tremaine. You're a fraud. Everything you do, everything you say, none of it *means* anything."

Tremaine said nothing.

"Funny thing." The old man licked spittle from the corner of his lips. "Magda gave me the same look you're fixing me with now, when she was where you are. It didn't take her quite as long to die as I suspect it will take you. You want to know why, Tremaine?"

Tremaine only looked at him.

"It's because you're full of hot air," Ziminski blurted with a laugh. "How long did it take, Vladimir? For Magda to die. Half an hour?"

"Forty-three minutes," the large man said.

"You see, after Magda told me about your little sexcapades, I installed a hidden camera in the vault."

Tremaine glanced at the bare steel walls.

"She never knew it was there, but Vladimir and I had a wonderful time watching her die. Gulping like a goldfish out of its bowl." The old man smiled at Tremaine. "We shared a bottle and toasted to the little slut's death."

Tremaine cleared his throat to speak.

"How long do you wager Tremaine will take to die? An hour?"

Vladimir shrugged. "Maybe less. If he's lucky."

Ziminski's smile grew wider. "'If he's lucky.' I rather like that." The old man backed up his wheelchair. His bodyguard grabbed the thick steel door. Behind them, the Dürer stood leaning against the wall. Tremaine locked eyes with the Master and chuckled morosely.

"Goodbye, Yannick," Ziminski said, as Vladimir slammed the door shut.

The painter threw himself to his feet, scouring the walls for indents, for loose screws, for seams. He fell to his knees and slid his palms along the floor, feeling for grooves, rivets, knocking and listening for hollow spots. The metal had bent in a small place on the edge of the door. He tore his fingernails on it, cursing, shouting at it, goading himself on through the pain, all to no avail. Exasperated, his raw fingers left a smear of blood on the door and he returned to where he'd started to begin again, his breath short, heart beating hard. After what felt like hours, he plopped down on the floor and wept with exhaustion. Nothing. All seams smoothed down. All rivets firmly in place. The vault solid and thick all the way through.

The air felt thick. Soupy. Difficult to breathe.

He thought of the trumpeter, bleating out his final note as the arrow pierced his throat. Dying doing what he did best. Not locked in a vault, breathing his own dead air, left with nothing to paint with and no canvas in sight.

Tremaine regarded his quivering hands, soiled black with grease from the floor and red with blood from his fingertips. Hands that had forged so many masterpieces. Fingers that had spread and smeared and scraped. A thought occurred to him. He pushed himself raggedly to his feet, his head swimming, on the verge of unconsciousness. Not much time left, really. He vaguely wondered who would win the bet: Ziminski or Vladimir.

The painter staggered to the door.

Peeling the skin of his fingers on the sharp curl of metal. Carving into the pads of flesh. His hands dripped crimson as he turned to the wide, blank wall.

He began to paint, laughing wildly.

Drunk on creativity, Tremaine stepped back to admire his final masterpiece, his coda, his dying words. He'd painted a hand flipping the camera the middle finger and signed it with his name, a counter-spell painted in bold, bloody capitals:

YANNICK TREMAINE

Yannick stumbled out of the way, falling back against the door, hoping Ziminski and his bodyguard had an unimpeded view of his *pièce de résistance*.

Outside the vault, something toppled. Glass shattered.

Tremaine perked up, pressing his ear against the cold metal. Breathing shallow. Another great crash startled him, the sound of concrete or plaster crumbling. Heavy footsteps. Canvas tearing, wood splintering. For a moment, the painter thought he might be hallucinating the sounds. Wishful thinking, as the air grew thin and the last colors of his life bled away to white.

A horrific *BOOM* pierced the silence. Another. And again. Vladimir's Desert Eagle, firing at—*what?*

The man himself let out a blood-curdling shriek, cut off as it reached its crescendo like the final note of the trumpeter of St. Mary's.

Muffled, he heard Ziminski cry out, "No! *No, this can't be—*" before he was silenced, too.

In the quiet that followed, the world around Tremaine began to wash gray.

A squall of metal on metal drew him from soupy oblivion. Gears clattered, the door fell open, and Tremaine spilled out into the gallery. Sprawling face-first with his blood-smeared hands spread on the cool wood floor, he gasped for air. Slowly his vision returned, color bleeding back into the world. Blurry white snowflakes fell around him. He saw Ziminski's chair toppled, the man himself curled into a fetal ball, his head smashed on the floorboards like an overripe melon. What he'd thought was snow came into focus, shreds of parchment and canvas falling delicately around them.

Shakily, Tremaine rose on his hands and knees.

Behind Ziminski and his fallen wheelchair, the rest of the gallery was in ruin. Vladimir lay twisted and broken against the far wall. Paintings shredded, frames snapped into kindling, sculptures and idols smashed to sharp bits of gray and white and clay brown, display cases shattered into jagged, shimmering glints, wallpaper torn, floorboards splintered.

The only undamaged art in the room, Dürer's *Self-Portrait* regarded him without expression. In a loose pattern around it, three bullet holes still smoldered.

Tremaine held Dürer's gaze a moment longer, waiting. The air seemed electric, though he supposed it could have been his starved lungs. He watched for movement, and noticed the light from the vault had caused a dim shadow of himself to fall on the painting.

When nothing happened for several minutes, Tremaine decided it was time to go. He did not know why the Master's curse had spared him, although he recalled something Ziminski had said to the Mad Russian: *The man values his art more than his life. If that's not a quality worth admiring, I don't know what is.* Tremaine thought perhaps that might be the reason but he supposed he'd never know for sure.

He pushed himself to his feet, stumbled, righted himself, and staggered toward the door.

The Master's eyes remained fixed on the empty vault, and what his pupil had painted there. They did not follow Tremaine as he left the gallery.

SANCTUARY

THE EAST TEXAS sun beat down on my head as I jogged the marsh trail through the animal sanctuary. Sweat poured down my back, matting my hair to my scalp. Togo, the four-year-old mutt my ex-wife stuck me with in the divorce, panted heavily as he ran along beside me.

The ex used to say—before the divorce made anything she'd said fall on deaf ears—I should exercise more. Exercise is fine, but the gravel crunching under my feet is a meditation thing for me, hypnotic. It cleared the head. The sanctuary was one of my favorite spots in the area, and just about the only place nearby you could go to get away from the trucks and bustle of the city.

A bird chirped high on an electrical pole, repetitive, trying to get my attention. "Robins are active today," I told Togo. He looked up at me, tongue lolling to one side—thirsty already, but we'd only just started running. I promised myself to stop once we got to the next intersection in the trails.

Up ahead, black smoke rose over the trees. A hunting cabin, most likely. The sound of rifle fire cut through the wind filling my ears, confirming my suspicion. Some yahoo gun nuts firing off automatic weapons. Something I hear a lot these days is, "Go big or go home." The expression doesn't just apply to pickups, or the portions at your local Tex-Mex.

Never was one for guns, particularly after having one pointed in my face where I tend bar. At least with open carry laws you know where you stand. It's the ones who've got them tucked into the back of their pants or under their jacket you have to worry about. When a fight breaks out in a bar where open carry is the norm, things either escalate quick—usually one dipshit or another ends up shooting himself in the foot trying to pry the thing out of its holster, Billy the Kid-style—or people calm down in a hurry, not wanting to be the object of some psycho's target practice.

Alligators lurk in the marsh out here. With Togo by my side, I had to keep an eye out that one of them hadn't slinked out of the muck to warm itself on the gravel trails. Part terrier, Togo would make a nice light snack.

I was in a sort of trance when he yelped behind me.

I spun around, still moving along the trail, running backward. Togo had gotten down on his haunches, quivering and looking up at the sky. Up in the haze of blue and white, a bird circled. As I looked, it dove toward us with a familiar cry.

The gull swooped down, its beady yellow eyes locked right on mine. I ducked out of the way, but it was Togo the bird wanted. The poor little mutt rolled over backward as it landed in the dust, squawking at him, dancing toward him. Togo reared back and growled, but the bird kept coming, squalling, calling out for the feeding frenzy.

Scouring the tall grass where the marsh reached the ditch, wary of gators, I grabbed a fat black branch and hauled back with it to pitch at the gull before realizing my error. The stick wriggled in my hand, cool and fleshy to the touch.

Startled, I dropped the coachwhip, crying out in fear and disgust. I've seen those snakes eat mice whole before, but they're incredibly wary of humans. Rather than slither off into the brush though, the snake came right at me, and with a moment to react, I stomped down hard on the thing, feeling its insides crunch and squirt out from under my shoe.

Togo, meanwhile, bared his teeth at the gull. More cries came from nearby as two others landed near the first, the three birds menacing my poor dog. I moved to shoo them when something hard and sharp struck the back of my head.

I turned to a flutter of wings, a familiar chirp. As I rubbed the spot where the robin had hit me, feeling the wet warmth of blood, it dove in for another strike.

I ducked, swatting out blindly. The bird fluttered over my head. Somehow my wrist managed to penetrate its flapping wings and struck its fragile body. The bird chirped—whether in pain or out of anger, I had no idea, but I suspected the latter—then flew up to its perch on the pole.

Nature's gone haywire, I thought. *So much for sanctuary...*

Togo barked, frantic as the birds flanked him.

"Get the hell out of here, shithawks!" I shouted, kicking gravel at them. They stepped back, raising their wings defensively. Pleased, I stomped toward them, waving my arms like the biggest bird around. They waddled back, spreading out. Their yellow eyes, somewhat reptilian, watched me without betraying their intentions.

Togo screeched then, a tremulous sound that rattled my nerves. I wheeled, ready to kick some avian ass, but it was already too late. A gator had lurched up from the marsh, still shimmering, and had caught Togo in its jaws. Togo's front legs danced, his wet brown eyes looking up at me for assistance. I had none to offer. The gator snapped its head back, revealing a sickening glimpse of the steaming insides of my poor dog, and swallowed the rest of him whole.

I ran.

The birds parted for me, trilling cries. Out in the marsh, three fat gators splashed into the black water. The eyes of another rose from the reeds, locking on me. The one that had eaten Togo bypassed the gulls, as if unaware of them, and ran headlong at my heels. If you've never seen a gator run, be glad. It's probably the most terrifyingly hilarious thing you'll ever see, like a man-eating mudskipper.

As I thought it, glad I'd worn runners, glad to be in the best shape of my life after the divorce, the goddamn robin swooped into view and struck me on the bridge of my nose, shooting stars across my vision. I batted it out of the air, but the damage was done. The gator had gained precious feet. I was lunch.

Rifle fire made me jump. In the next moment, the alligator's head exploded in a shower of meat and gore. Its momentum kept propelling it forward, the legs still pumping, until the huge rugged beast slopped down at my feet, spilling its insides on my shoes.

It was then that I heard the growl of trucks. I'd never been so happy to hear axle-back exhaust and see a set of Bumper Nuts in my life.

A portly guy with mutton chops stood in the back, brandishing some sort of rifle. "Just about made yerself a horsie doover there, buddy!"

I looked back at the trail. The robin fluttered on the hot gravel. I'd somehow managed to break its wing. But the gulls were still coming, and more gators crept up from the marsh on either side.

The driver smacked the door. "Don't just stand there pissin' your panties. Hop on in!"

Another truck met the first, carrying two more guys I wouldn't want to meet in the woods on any other day, every one of them packing.

I didn't hesitate, just climbed into the passenger seat.

Peeling away, we left the gators in a cloud of dust.

The driver turned to me, chewing on a mouthful of tobacco. "When the animals rise up against their masters, the whole G.D. world's gone snafu, ain't it?"

"Yeah," I said, peering in the rearview.

The fat guy in the bed had taken up a stance on one knee, the rifle sight at eye level. He squeezed off a round, a trail of gray smoke rising from the weapon. "Missed 'em!"

"No shit, you moron," the driver shouted over his shoulder, jumping up and down in his seat. "We're bouncin' all over the damn road. Save your ammo!" He spat a wad of tobacco juice out the open window.

"Gotta get to the city," I said, knowing the birds circling overhead would follow us, but at least we'd be safe from the gators, the snakes— for a while, anyhow. "Get to a high rise, and wait this out. Whatever it is."

The driver turned with a slimy brown grin. "You're in good hands, fella." He patted the Dirty Harry gun holstered on his hip. He was loving this, had probably been waiting for any excuse to kill every damned animal on the planet, and now he would get his chance.

Kill or be killed. Eat or be eaten.

I looked beyond the insane grin and out through the window. I saw the black smoke rising above the trees, and knew we were doomed. It wasn't a hunting cabin—I was wrong about that. The *city* was that way. We were too late.

When the animals rise up against their masters...

The driver yelped, and shielded his eyes, too late to even attempt to swerve out of the large buck's path.

The front end crumpled. The truck swerved, grinding hard into the gravel, and Mutton Chops standing in the truck bed pitched over the roof, crying out. The beast's head shattered the windshield, shards of glass pattering down around me, its antlers gouging up through the driver's throat and pinning him to the ceiling. His glassy eyes bugged out and his tobacco-browned tongue stuck out between his teeth.

The second truck braked, raising dust that swirled around us in a churning wind.

I sat there stunned, covered in glass. The buck snorted, breathing heavily, its face so close I could smell its rank breath and musky hide, see the feathered lashes on its glossy black eyes.

Slow as I could, I reached down for the belt buckle. The eye followed my progress. The animal was stunned, likely just as pinned as its victim. Its bulk had crushed the hood, and one leg was badly broken, jagged bone poking out through flesh.

The belt clicked, releasing me from the driver's chrome tomb.

The buck's head shifted. It blinked, moaning pitifully.

"Good," I said, and jerked the door handle, propelling myself out into the road.

Mutton Chops rose from the dirt, groaning. His rifle had skittered away from him. I thought if I ran I could get to it before he could. Dog eat dog, and all that.

Poor fucking Togo...

Behind me, the other two had gotten out of their truck, rifles at the ready. "Jesus Pleasus! That's a twenty-point buck right there," the second driver remarked, dressed in full military camo.

"Like hell it is," his skinny partner shot back. "Eighteen at the most."

"When we tell the story, it's a twenty." Warning in the driver's eyes. "Teevo would have been honored to die by the hand of that sucker."

"Hoof," the other guy corrected him. "Bucks don't have hands."

"Would you shut the—" His eyes widened. "Oh, my shit..."

I looked where he was looking. A dozen gators had crawled out of the muck and stood poised to strike barely fifteen feet from the truck. Snakes had filled in their ranks, a battalion of Kings, pit vipers, coachwhips, corals and hognoses. Behind them, the rats, voles, moles, and hedgehogs clambered over each other to reach their next meal.

I ran.

Gunfire erupted behind me, and I bolted past Mutton Chops and his rifle. As the reports died out and the cries of immense pleasure became screams of intense fear, of agony, I kept on running. My lungs burning, my legs already beginning to tire, head swimming with thoughts of home, of a city teeming with killer animals, with nature gone amok, I sprinted down the sanctuary trail, evolution's last cruel joke clawing at my heels.

My Protector

"The state of those young boys..." the Principal lamented. "You understand, I'm sure, why it behooves me to have your daughter expelled."

Jenny's mother understood. The two boys outside Principal Villeneuve's office had been viciously attacked, barely able to sit in the hard plastic chairs without squirming for the pain. She turned to her little girl, whose eighth birthday they had recently celebrated with a tea party and pony rides. Jenny's green eyes, wet with shame, refused to leave her patent leather shoes, hovering inches above the gray carpet. Her freckled face twisted in a pout, her little red pigtails rested on the shoulders of a pale blue smock dress, Jenny might have looked the part of innocence were it not for the obvious spatters of blood. Whatever had happened, Mrs. Cooper couldn't imagine her little girl possessing the strength to do such horrid things to a single ten-year-old boy, let alone two of them—especially considering how much bigger they were. But shame had sealed the boys' split lips. And all Jenny seemed able to say was, "It wasn't me."

The shock of it, for Jenny's father, was dulled by a glimmer of pride. He fought to hold back a smile when he looked at his daughter, thinking she just might manage middle school all right on her own. The thought reminded him of the empty seat at the dinner table, of the room that would no longer carry loud music or laughter, only gather dust. He no longer felt the urge to smile.

"Mr. and Mrs. Cooper, I truly am sorry. But you see, I'm sure, how her actions left us with no choice. The parents have threatened to sue, and they have yet to see the damage she's done to their children!"

Jenny could no longer hold her peace. Her voice was so small, so meek, her father had to ask her to repeat it. "It wasn't me," she whimpered again, with a beseeching look toward her parents. "It was *Aaron.*"

Jenny's mother and father shared an anxious look, and Principal Villeneuve's face lost all color. When Mr. Cooper looked at his daughter again, his heart nearly burst with compassion.

Only then did he notice she bore no wounds on her hands. They were, in fact, entirely free of blood: the boys' or her own.

▌▌

WITH HEAVY HEARTS, Jenny's mother and father dropped her off at Camp Broken Wings. Bereavement camp was Principal Villeneuve's idea, and Jenny's parents had agreed spending time off school with other children of her age, who had suffered similar trauma, would be beneficial.

For her part, Jenny had been silent during the trip, and had yet to apologize for what she'd done. Her mother was still trying to wrap her mind around what Jenny had told them, that it hadn't been her who'd hurt the boys but her older brother. She tried to put herself in her daughter's shoes, to fathom why she would have made up such an obvious lie after doing something so despicable, when she could have simply blamed it on another student. She must have known no one would believe her. But the fact that she'd lied to them without a trace of guilt made Mrs. Cooper angry, particularly since it had been her brother she'd pointed to as a culprit, knowing full well it was impossible for

470

Aaron to have hurt those boys. He'd protected her from bullies before the accident, but now...

Mrs. Cooper shied away from the thought. In the same moment, she looked up to catch her daughter's eye, and was surprised to find a glimmer of hatred behind the sullen pout. Hatred burning toward *her*.

The camp looked decent enough. Freshly-painted log cabins bordered the parking lot, surrounded on all sides by fragrant pines, spruce and cedars. Beyond them children laughed and squealed, and the faint smell of fresh water reminded her of the small lake, where boys and girls ages 8 – 16 could swim, paddle and play. Other activities included rope-climbing, scavenger hunts, soccer, and many more—at least according to the brochure Principal Villeneuve had given them.

Two counsellors dressed in red t-shirts and shorts approached from down a wooded trail, a teenaged boy and girl. Once they were nearer, Mrs. Cooper realized the white emblem on their shirts wasn't an ink blot—her first thought, and a peculiar one at that—but a bird with one wing twisted at an angle, the name of the camp spelled out in letters made to look like carved wood. She eyed the tanned, muscular thighs of the brunette, late teens, as the girl bent to address Jenny, pleased to note that her husband's eyes remained scanning the trees.

"Hi there. You must be Jennifer. I'm Brooke."

"Say 'hi,' honey," Mr. Cooper urged.

Jenny looked back at her father, then turned to face the counsellor with a sullen, "Hi."

"You're gonna have a lot of fun with us, Jennifer. Isn't she, Jonas?"

Jonas, the young man regarding Mrs. Cooper with his hands behind his back, snapped to and nodded. "Huh? Oh, you bet."

Jenny shifted her knapsack onto her shoulders. Above them, the red maple leaf strung from the end of the flagpole fluttered limply in a light breeze.

"You be good, okay?" Mr. Cooper told her with a hand placed gently on her head. His little girl nodded. "Your mother and I will be back to pick you up on Monday."

Jenny looked sullenly at her mother, who tried her damnedest to smile with tears welling in her eyes. This would be Jenny's first time away from home, and despite what had happened to bring them here, Mrs. Cooper couldn't help but feel a little saddened.

The tanned girl, Brooke, stood and held out a slender hand for Jenny. Reluctantly, Jenny took it. As the two counsellors led her away, she turned back in the direction of the car. Mrs. Cooper hitched a breath, waiting to meet her daughter's eyes, to leave her with one last hopeful smile. But Jenny seemed to find something interesting in the empty space between them and the car, and smiled anyhow.

■■

JONAS AND BROOKE showed Jenny to her cabin, where she'd be spending the night with nine other girls of similar age, then introduced her to a group of young boys and girls on the soccer field. They played Red Rover. They paddled canoes. They made wallets out of duct tape, and friendship bracelets. They changed into swim trunks to play Marco Polo in the shallows of Lake Caribou. The counsellors tired the children out, and try as she might, Jenny couldn't manage to hold onto her sadness for long. She started to enjoy herself. She opened up to other kids. They found a baby turtle, and showed it to their counsellors. Brooke told them to wash their hands so they wouldn't get salmonella, and a little boy with a bowl-cut asked, "Don't you mean *turtle*-monella?" The children all laughed. The day wound down, the evening filling with cries of joy and laughter as they played tag and caught fireflies. For lunch, they'd had tacos. For dinner, it was chicken fingers and French fries. No bone-dry chicken and couscous like her mother made her eat at home. No cauliflower "steak" and Brussels sprouts.

After dinner when darkness fell, the children and counsellors all gathered on wooden pews circled around the big fire pit, reminding Jenny of paintings she'd seen about the mysterious Druids. Soon a tall fire crackled, and mosquitoes buzzed around their ears. Trees whose color had faded now glowed orange, their pointed tops stark black against a sky filled with more stars than Jenny, a city girl, had ever seen in her life. The counsellors roasted marshmallows for s'mores, and passed the finished treats around. Soon everyone's fingers were sticky, their mouths tingly from sugar, and their bellies full.

"Who has a story they'd like to share?"

Several children put up their hands. Jenny sat beside a chubby girl with short dark hair named Colleen. The girl, whose older sister had passed a few weeks before Jenny's brother had his accident, had given her a friendship bracelet. The two of them had stuck together during free time at the lake and had sat side by side at dinner. Neither girl put her hand up.

Darius, a bearded counsellor older than both Jonas and Brooke (and much too handsome to have a beard, in Jenny's opinion), pointed to a tween boy.

"W-what kind of story?" the boy asked, unfortunate enough to have both a lisp and braces which flashed with firelight when he spoke. "Like... a ghost story?"

A ripple of excitement followed this. Darius motioned for the children to quiet down. "We don't tell ghost stories at Camp Broken Wings," he said. "You know that."

"Yeah, but why not?" a girl called out.

"Well, it's just our policy. Now does anyone have a story that's a little more pleasant? Maybe a story about something funny. Or heroic."

The children looked at each other. Nobody wanted to say anything, or had anything to say. Jenny felt frustrated. The suggestion of ghost story had stirred something in her and the others, but the camp's stupid "policy" wouldn't allow them to be told. But he had asked for a story of heroism, and the only hero she'd ever known was her big brother.

Jenny put up her hand.

"Yes." Darius pointed out a young boy in the front row he then called Timmy.

"My big brother tried to fart on my head once, but he pooped himself instead."

The kids all laughed, even the older ones. Everyone except Jenny, who wanted to tell her story and felt only anger toward the dull boy.

"I'm sure that wasn't funny for your brother, or your mom," the counsellor said, and scuffed his sandals in the dirt. "Anybody else have a story that doesn't involve poo?"

Jenny's hand fired up again. She twiddled her fingers so he'd see her first.

"Yes, uh..." Brooke leaned and whispered something to Darius. "Jennifer," he said.

"My brother is a hero," Jenny told him.

"Okay. That sounds like a nice story. Why don't you tell us a little bit about him?"

Jenny struggled to describe him, though his face was as clear as day, even at night. They both had the same freckles and red hair, the same green eyes. They both had dimples when they laughed, though presently he wore a scowl, shaking his head 'no.'

"Well... he's got one wonky ear and one normal one. My mom calls it his elf ear, but Aaron told me a while ago it was a defect he got in the womb. He's really really tall, but not as tall as my dad. Dad always said he'd grow up taller than him, but that was before. We don't talk about Aaron since the accident, an' if I forget and say something about him, Mom cries and Dad looks all worried."

"*Oh.*" The bearded counsellor turned to his fellow counsellors, who seemed at a loss. "Jennifer, I'm sorry, but we're not supposed to talk about... those who've passed."

Her nose wrinkled. "What's 'passed'?"

"He means died," Colleen explained in a whisper.

"Aaron's not dead." She turned to the empty seat between her and the small boy to her right, a cold place where the boy had first sat and then immediately shifted away from. "He's sitting right *beside* me."

Colleen reached out and clutched Jenny's arm.

The small boy looked at Jenny, fear registering on his face in the flicker of firelight. He hesitated a moment, scowling at Jenny, before pushing his friend over and scooching further away. Someone made a ghostly "*Woo-oo-ooh!*"

"Jennifer, that's not funny," Darius said.

Children craned their necks and stood up in their seats to get a look at her brother. An older boy sang the *Twilight Zone* theme tunelessly, and some of the children laughed.

Darius waited for the children to settle with a look of concern. "Your brother's not here, Jennifer. There's *no one* sitting beside you."

Jenny felt small and weak, her cheeks growing hot from all the attention suddenly focused on her, from the handsome counsellor with the stupid beard not believing her. She looked to the place where her brother had just been. "He *was*," she said, "until all your stupid jokes scared him away."

The children all tittered nervously, and the counsellors, apparently eager to change the subject, launched into a silly song about a camel named Alice and her many humps. Everyone seemed to know the words but Jenny, and her embarrassment deepened. She pretended to sing along to *On Top of Spaghetti* and *The Log Driver's Waltz*, but the counsellor had made her angry, and she was no longer enjoying herself.

Colleen turned to her as they all sang *Michael, Row Your Boat Ashore*, and whispered, "You can tell me about him, if you want. When we get back to the cabin."

Jenny turned to her, genuinely pleased. The two girls smiled conspiratorially, and began to sing along.

██

AFTER LIGHTS-OUT, the girls gathered at the foot of their bunks where they could see each other in the dim cone of light from a flashlight cupped in an older girl's hand. The oldest girl, Shondra, had directed them to tie their blankets around the beds to block the light from reaching the windows, "so the counsellors won't see we're awake." In the dark outside the cabin, frogs and night bugs chirped, but inside all was quiet.

"Nice one at the campfire, kid," Shondra said as she tucked the corner of a blanket into her bunk to act as the roof of the tent. "You broke the cardinal rule on your first day. Thou shalt not talk about the dead."

Jenny stirred on the bottom bunk closest the door, the word upsetting her. "I *told* you, Aaron's not dead. He got in a bike accident with a car on my street. When we got to the hop-spital, I heard the doctor say he died on the operating table but then they brought him back, an' after that, they let me in to see him. He had all these tubes and junk coming out of him, but I could tell he was still alive because sometimes he blinked. My mom said he's in a cona."

The older girls giggled. Jenny felt her cheeks grow red again. She didn't like to be laughed at.

"It's *coma*," Shondra told her, with the patience of a friendly older sibling. "So he's in a coma. You said he was sitting beside you at the fire."

"He... comes and visits me. Sometimes."

The other girls shared a look. Doubtful, worried—Jenny couldn't tell.

"V-visits?" Colleen asked.

"Uh-huh. Like the day before yesterday, these two boys were pickin' on me, pulling my hair and stuff when I was just trying to walk down the stairs, calling me 'ginger' and 'freckle-face,' so I told 'em to stop, but they didn't care." She shook her head, as if the boys should have known better. "They just kept on doing it. But I told them, 'I wouldn't do that if I were you,' because I knew what my brother would do to them if he found out."

Jenny took a deep breath. She saw the eager looks on their faces, wide eyes in deep shadow thrown by their cheeks from the flashlight. She hadn't been able to tell anyone what had happened that day. Nobody had wanted to hear the truth—not the principal, not her parents. But these girls were eager to listen. And technically, she wouldn't be doing wrong, since what she was telling them wasn't a ghost story.

"But they *still* didn't listen," she continued. "They kept teasing me even worse. They pinched my bum and stepped on the back of my shoes." The girls shook their heads in disgust. "And then after that they chased me under the stairs, but I bet they didn't expect my brother was gonna be waiting there. Right away, he hit 'em with a hammer from the art room. *Bop bop bop.*" She made a striking gesture, the girls flinching as if she'd hit them. The flashlight beam flickered, causing their shadows to flutter on the blankets. "They ran crying to the Principal's office and lied and said I was the one that hit 'em."

Jenny looked at the others, saw the fear in their eyes mingled with delight, because the bad boys had been punished.

"But it was Aaron that did it," she finished. "Aaron's my protector."

In the shocked silence that followed the blanket closest to Jenny came down violently, and all the girls screamed, even Jenny herself. The girl called Delia who had a lazy eye dropped the flashlight, and when it settled on the dusty floorboards, the intruder's giant shadow fell on the wall by the open door, the blanket rumpled at his feet. They crawled to the ends of their beds, hugging their knees, eyes widened in fear of the man whose face still lay in darkness. But Jenny held her ground because she knew he wasn't her brother. This man was slimmer and wore sandals.

"I told you, *no ghost stories*," Darius said, bending into the light to grab her roughly by the wrist and yank her out of bed. "You're coming to the office."

Jenny allowed herself to be pulled along quietly, sullenly. Colleen reached out to her, and the other girls protested. Shondra merely shook her head.

"Wonder if her brother will protect her now," she muttered sarcastically.

■■

DARIUS SAT ACROSS the desk from Jenny, who swung her feet from the tall chair. On the wall were photos of children at play, along with several framed newspaper articles touting the healing power of Broken Wings. A clock made from a flat piece of driftwood ticked away the seconds above two canoe paddles in the shape of an X.

The counsellor put his feet up on the desk, rattling a big metal flashlight with the words HEAVY METAL stenciled on its side, which rested beside a desk tray labelled IN and OUT, filled with various files. This was not Darius's office. The camp director, he'd informed Jenny, was away at a conference, and had put him in charge for the weekend.

"Whatever I say goes," he said with what looked like glee, "and I say we have to call your parents."

Jenny muttered something under her breath, her feet still swinging.

"Beg pardon?"

"I *said*," Jenny seethed, "'I wouldn't do that if I were you.'"

Darius's smile broadened. "Oh you wouldn't, would you?"

Jenny shook her head with a look of warning. Her feet stopped swinging.

The counsellor held her gaze a moment, then shook his head, chuckling derisively, and picked up the phone. He smirked at her while she stared daggers at him. In a moment, Jenny heard the dull sound of the telephone beginning to ring at his ear.

"Yes, hi, Mr. Cooper? I'm sorry to disrupt you so late in the evening. It's about your daughter." Darius stuck out his tongue at her. Jenny felt her brother's presence, very near. A sly smile crept onto her freckled face. The young man's smile vanished, and he swiveled his chair to face the wall. "Yes, that's right. I'm afraid she's been acting up. Well, we have a policy—"

Oh yes, Aaron was close now. She could feel him, and his presence emboldened her. Made her weakness solidify into raw animal strength. Made her grow armor. Made her *invincible*.

"Absolutely," Darius told her father on the phone. "No, that's no trouble. Tomorrow. That's fine. All right, see you then."

With a toothy grin, he swiveled back to cradle the phone. Surprise registered on his face when he saw Jenny standing over him.

"Pick on someone your own size!" She thrust the heavy flashlight down with both hands. "Pick on someone your own size!" The base struck his head with a metallic ping, stripping flesh from bone in a ragged flap. "Pick on someone your own size!" It obliterated his eye. Shattered finger bones when he raised his hand to protect his face. Cracked the top of his skull. Pulverized the gelatinous meat inside. He pitched forward, dropping the receiver, landing solidly on the floor.

Jenny panted heavily, standing over the counsellor's corpse as his blood soaked into the carpet. She dropped the flashlight beside him, then casually bent to pick up the phone.

"Dad...?"

The crackle of distance filled the long pause. "Jenny?"

She sighed heavily. "Can you come pick us up?"

Her father said nothing... but she knew he would come. He'd have to, if he'd heard what Aaron had done to the mean old camp counsellor. She cradled the phone then, and sat with her brother, who smiled silently from the seat beside her, waiting for their parents to arrive.

Do Not Shake or Rattle

G*RACE REALLY OUTDID herself this year*, Donald thought from his armchair, looking at the heaping pile of shiny gift-wrapped boxes under the sparkling tree. *I told her, Mara and Donnie Junior's spoiled little brats'll tear up all that pretty wrapping of yours in oh, about 5.3 seconds, and it'll be my job to clean it up just like last year. Like every year. But does she listen? About as close as a deaf dog.*

A knot popped in the fireplace as Donald rocked in his chair, thinking about his wife of 46 years. Met after his first tour in Vietnam. *Gracie sure blew the doors off all the chicks the other fellas went home with that night. A real foxy mama. 'Course that was before that Viet Kong land mine took my leg. Before the job and the kids and the grandkids and Gracie's "many-paws," like she calls it. Now she's gone weird in the head, hot flashes and cold flashes and running around afraid of her own damn shadow.* Had Mara while he was in a rice paddy shooting zips for Uncle Sam, and Donnie Jr. once he'd got sent home in two pieces—*Well, they probably didn't keep the* rest *of my leg, lucky the damn thing was a dud*— just before he started work at the plant. Overall their marriage had been fine, when the kids were in the house, when he'd been working —*Worked my way up from lubing the machines to district manager*— but now that the kids had families of their own, and he'd retired—*Not that I wanted to, damn government*—she'd been grating on his nerves. Always checking up on him in the garage. Always peeking in while he sat reading the paper on the shitter. *Dunno what the hell's wrong with that woman. It's like she expects I'll drop dead any minute!*

A solitary green light flickered on the tree, spoiling his reverie, blinking like a dying star. The others—red, white and blue—shone uninterrupted. *Thank God I took those damn bulbs Grace got back to the store and traded 'em for parallels. Came with extra bulbs, too. A deal is a deal, but you don't go getting cheaply made China crap just because it's on sale. I told her, "You get what you pay for," but does she listen? Like a deaf dog.*

Donald eased himself out of the ratty chair, resting the bulk of his weight on his cane. Leaving the chair squeaking behind him like his Vaseline-greased stump in the new prosthetic Donnie Junior had gotten him made special last year, he made his way to the tree. He'd kept the extra bulbs in a baggie garbage-tied to the mass of plugs around back of it. He stopped a moment and warmed his hands in front of the fire —*Damn woman's got the temp so low I could freeze to death. Maybe that's what she wants*—then shuffled his weary bones to the big Scotch pine. Beautiful tree. Not spindly and sparse like the white pines Grace's Ma and Pop had in their house back when he and Gracie used to bring the kids to their place Christmas morning. Smelled good, too. Taking in a good strong whiff, Donald thought they should make bathroom deodorizers smell like this. *Make every poop smell like Christmas morn for just a dollar ninety-nine!*

Something caught Donald's eye as he reached around the tree. *Was that there before?* A new gift, about the size and shape of a shoebox. He squinted down at it. "To Donald from Grace'? I told her we're on a fixed income, she doesn't need to be getting me anything fancy."

Donald bent, leaning over his cane, to read the note taped to the side of the box.

DO NOT SHAKE OR RATTLE

"'Do not shake or rattle'? What does she think I am?"

After 46 years you think she doesn't have your number? Even when you were a kid you used to shake the gifts under the tree. Gotta give it a good rattle to figure out what's inside, right?

Donald peered over his shoulder. The house was pleasantly empty. Grace was at her sister's house, bringing her some "Christmas cheer." That meant more alcohol for the alcoholic. Donald could never stand Gracie's sister Diane, and the feeling was so evidently mutual. Never been married, just her alone with a fat tabby cat, Donald had a sneaking suspicion the woman was a card-carrying lesbo. *Flying the pink flag*, he thought amusedly.

He bent down over his cane, and picked up the box. "Oof!" He hadn't expected it to be heavy. *Damn woman nearly put out my back. What's she put in here? A brick?*

Turning it from side to side, Donald noted the usual meticulous Grace wrapping job. He watched her sometimes from his chair, where she sat at the dining room table. Everything just so. Tape here, bow there. The corners folded delicately like those easy peasy Japanesey paper swans. Fold and fold and fold. Watching her tear off just the right amount of Scotch tape, he could picture her wearing a jeweler's loupe around her neck like some Hebrew pawnbroker.

DO NOT SHAKE OR RATTLE

My ass, he thought, and gave it a good shake.

He heard a solid *CLICK!* and the sound was so familiar he might have been able to place it if the gift hadn't erupted in hand, bits of Grace's delicate wrapping paper burning to ash as shards of superheated metal threw him back into his ratty old chair, where he smoldered.

GRACE HEARD THE explosion from Diane's kitchen, two blocks south and one block east, where she sat drinking cold Baby Duck with her little sister. The antique land mine she'd purchased from the back of a van filled with an array of assault weapons, handguns and antiques, had worked as Buddy had promised. She would stay in Diane's spare bedroom until the crime scene folks finished cleaning bits of Donald off the living room furniture and walls. The house would require some repairs, of course. But with Donald's life insurance, the home insurance, she thought she'd make out just fine. And she would tell the police it was an antique. She would caterwaul. She would play the fragile house-wife, the dotty senior citizen, the way she had for Donald.

"What was that?" Diane wondered. She placed the bottle of chilled sparkling wine—*So bubbly!*—on the table to go to the window. In her absence, Grace topped up her glass, then raised it in a mock cheer. After 46 years, she was finally free. No more bitter looks. No more complaining about her cooking, or his leg, or the government, immigrants, her sister, the "spoiled" grandkids, and all his ignorant racial stereotyping. This was a new world, and Grace wanted to be a part of it. There was no room for miserable old men like Donald.

"You get what you pay for, Donnie," she muttered, and downed the glass.

"Beg pardon?" Diane asked, still looking out the window.

"I said 'Merry Christmas.'"

Diane smiled, much too drunk. "Merry Christmas," she agreed.

STRAY

MAX AWOKE FROM an uncomfortable dream, vaguely aware of a wet, prickly thing sliming the palm of his left hand. He tore the hand away, shrinking back against the seat, clutching the duffel bag handle in his right.

A dog—a husky or malamute, Max couldn't tell which, and the breed didn't matter so much as the fact of its presence here at all—looked up at him with sad ice-blue eyes, peeling its lips back in a yawn or a snarl. Max couldn't decide which, and again, didn't care.

Looking up and down the car, hoping to find its owner, he found no one. The dog was on its own. *Max* was alone with *it*.

"Go on," he said, anxious. "Get out of here."

The animal didn't move, only panted, staring.

"Get lost!"

The dog whimpered, shrinking back, then sat on its haunches in front of the doors with a jingle—a sound signifying ownership, though Max saw no collar around its thick neck. Instead, a small loop of bathtub chain and silvery tags peeked out from its fur, reminiscent of another kind of dog tag. Its big pink tongue came out to lick its chops, as it eyeballed him with that *I-know-something* look.

Could it smell the rising fear in his sweat? Could it hear the increase in his heartbeat?

What was it doing on the train, anyway? Was it a stray?

Max had read an article once about abandoned dogs in Moscow that had learned to take the Metro into the city. Street dogs worked in packs there, using the smallest and cutest to beg for food and share amongst them. They stood behind people and barked, startling feckless humans into dropping their food so the dogs could eat it from the ground. The pack leaders were not the biggest and strongest, as in other species, but the *smartest*. The dogs with the most cunning.

What had occurred to Max from reading the article (and further research, including several videos) was that dogs, as a species, were growing smarter. But were they *evolving*, he'd wondered, or was it just a natural response to their environment, a "societal" change? Being a History major, Max wasn't scientifically inclined enough to say one way or the other, but history told him to be wary. And it was history— History *class*, in fact—that had put him on the train so early this morning, long before the other commuters. He'd needed to get to school before his fellow teachers, before Principal Anders, and before Don McTavish, the security officer. The janitors, who arrived early, would let him in without trouble, but Anders and the others would wonder what he was doing at school, and what exactly he had in his duffel bag.

■■

"... CLAUBERG TOLD THE women he'd artificially inseminated them with animal sperm, and while it's unclear whether this is true or not, it's yet another example of the Nazis employing torture under the guise of scientific advancement."

Silence drew out in the small classroom. A few students fiddled with their cell phones, one or two girls twisted their hair around pencils or chewed it. Others doodled. The kids in the front row wore looks of disgust, which had been his intent. He'd wanted to shock them out of their apathy. What he hadn't known at the time was that this lesson would get him a six-week suspension. The school board would go on to cite some of his extra-curricular activities as being "red flags," in particular the small bit of enjoyment he got from playing General Custer in the Battle of Little Bighorn reenactments. They had wondered why he would "celebrate" such an atrocious period in America's history, acting as if he flew the Confederate flag and wore white sheets in the night. Even his brief tour of duty in the Iraq Conflict had raised suspicions at West Brinkley High. The fact that his left arm was barely functional due to shrapnel from an IED had been the subject of much speculation during his three years teaching History to students who for the most part couldn't remember beyond their last keg party.

One of the football players in the back shot up his hand. Max held his right hand palm-up toward him, as Principal Anders had deemed pointing "too confrontational."

"Yes, Michael."

"So, like, all that stuff happened a long time ago?"

"During the Second World War," Max said, nodding genially, though he suspected Michael had something tricky up his sleeve.

"So, like, I mean, why should I care about what happened before I was *born*?"

A handful of others nodded, muttering their agreement.

"Well, Michael, a wise person once wrote, 'Those who cannot remember the past are condemned to repeat it.'"

"And was that wise man you, Mr. Ellis?" Michael inquired with a shrewd smirk, garnering a few chuckles.

"No, Michael, it was George Santayana." He smiled as Michael's grin faded. "So what do you think it means?"

"Huh?"

"The phrase, Michael. Let me put it another way. When Churchill misquoted it, he said, 'Those who fail to learn from history are doomed to repeat it.' What do you think that means?"

Michael stared blankly for a moment, his mouth hung open, his shaggy hair hanging in his face. "Like... you're gonna fail me if I can't answer the question?"

"No, Michael. You'll fail *life*. History is the most important subject."

"Not for me. I'm gonna go pro." Michael flashed his straight white teeth. "Gotta get *paid*," he said, and held his hand out so his friends could slap it.

"I'm going to be an entrepreneur," a girl in one of the middle seats said. "Why do I need to know all this gross stuff?"

Emphatic agreement met this. Even the burnouts perked up to join in.

These kids don't want to be teachers, or thinkers, or cure disease, Max despaired. *They all want to be Kardashians.*

"If you don't know this 'gross stuff,' you won't see the signs of it happening again under your nose, Larissa. Just as it's our responsibility to leave the environment in a good state for our children's children, we're also responsible for the state of *society*. We have to be wary, and *speak up* against what we feel is wrong, no matter the consequences. And when they come to silence you, when they force you into the shadows, remember what Edmund Burke said... 'The only thing necessary for the triumph of evil is for good men to do nothing.'"

This drew blank looks from almost half the class. The others appeared to ruminate on it, even the class entrepreneur, even a few of the burnouts.

Perhaps there's hope for the world after all, Max thought.

But someone had reported the lesson to their parents, and the parents had informed Principal Anders. Within a week, Max was out on his ass, his pleas for sanity unanswered. And during those first few weeks sitting alone in his apartment, pondering his place in the world, he wondered if he'd been wrong about there being any hope at all.

He began to think about the contents of his duffel bag.

■■

HE'D PLANNED IT all out so carefully in the following weeks, allowing for several possible contingencies. Not even the greatest military strategists—Carl von Clausewitz, Hannibal Barca, Julian Corbett —could have foreseen the dog.

Max watched as the it splayed its legs and began licking its genitals, dispelling any myth of higher intelligence.

How many times did it do that before licking my hand? he wondered, letting himself relax against the seat back. Releasing the handle of his duffel bag from his white-knuckle grip, the zipper tab clinked against its metallic teeth. It was a comforting sound, like the tinkle of wind chimes he remembered from summer nights at his parents' farmhouse when he was a kid, drinking lemonade on the porch after a long day's work as cicadas droned in the fields.

The doors opened with a discordant chime, sounding like an elevator arriving at the basement of Hell. A woman in a sharp business suit made to enter, looking up from her Blackberry just in time to see the dog. She leaped back, startled, then composed herself and scowled at Max, as if he owned the dog. When the doors closed, she was still glowering at him.

In the blink of an eye, the dog darted forward and bit his hand.

Pain splintered up Max's arm in hot waves. Crying out in surprise, he grasped his hand at the wrist, blood oozing from the jagged gash along the second and third knuckles, splashing against his work boots. Slashes of brilliant white bone peeked through the wounds on his numbing fingers. As he clenched his hand into a fist, tendons pulled taut in the exposed meat.

"Bit me!" he bellowed, incredulous. "You *bit* me!"

The dog reared back and bared its teeth, pink with blood. Max tucked into a quick roll as the dog charged again, slamming its full weight against the seatback he'd vacated. It staggered back, legs spread out to stop itself from slip 'n sliding across the slick tiles, then shook its head vigorously, spittle flying from its lips.

Max yanked the duffel bag off the seat and pulled it to his chest, using it as a shield as the dog attacked again, its powerful jaws tearing off a ragged swatch of oiled canvas.

With his left hand, Max tore at the zipper, shooting pain up his muscles from his old combat injury. The zipper slid easily partway, then caught. Momentarily fazed, he watched the dog spit out the grimy fabric, hacking at the taste. Grinning, Max reached into the bag and rummaged with his left hand. Pushing aside the Colt 1911—he'd trained himself to know each weapon by feel and weight, even with the backs of his fingers—he found the FN Five-SeveN easily, the same weapon used by Mexican drug cartels and the Fort Hood shooter. He jerked it free with a quick draw that would have made Cherokee Bill proud.

The dog registered almost human surprise as Max racked back the slide with the wrist of his injured hand, the hand itself still oozing crimson, and aimed with his left.

The dog bounded at him, snarling.

A deafening report filled in the cramped car. The Five-SeveN fired as smooth as—well, there really were no comparisons, in Max's mind, and if he'd done the firing with his right hand, it would have hit its mark. Instead, the bullet struck one of the safety glass windows and blew it outward. Hot morning wind blasted in, the sound of the elevated tracks clickety-clacking suddenly as loud as the gunshot.

The dog startled. Max fired a second shot, striking the dog in the leg, flipping the feral beast back with an arcing sprinkler spray of blood, Technicolor red under florescent lights. It rolled and slid all the way to the doors, where it slumped, eyes closed, bleeding on the shiny tiles.

Max stayed put, pressed against the seat, using the duffel in his lap to keep his aim steady. He wasn't stupid enough to think the thing was dead, to fall for that horror movie trick. Nor was he about to get up and check, like a kid approaching a firecracker that had fizzled out just before the explosion.

The dog shook its head, the chain around its muscular neck jingling. It lurched to its feet, eyeing him with its head lowered, and moved shakily toward him. A flap of grisly meat hung from its left hind leg, though the shot had merely grazed the flesh.

Max pulled the trigger, the kill shot, but the train began its herky-jerky entrance to the station and the small-caliber hollow-point went wild, carving a fist-sized hole in the ceiling that whistled as the train slowed to a jerky stop.

His right hand was scorched earth, the crotch of his jeans and the front of his plaid shirt black and gleaming with his blood. He could *smell* it, that acrid copper smell, and if *he* could smell his own blood, chances were pretty high the dog could, too.

Gravy Train makes real meat gravy, he thought humorlessly as the train stopped.

The shrill, unmusical chime stabbed his throbbing skull, and with the pain came a difficult decision. He could stay and fight, hoping he had it in him to go hand-to-teeth should the situation take a drastic turn —if the wounded dog managed to somehow gain the upper paw, ha ha so funny. Or... he could get off this Helltrain right this fucking second.

A man has to choose his own path, someone who'd never made the history books once told him. *Courage comes not from following the path others have chosen for you, but by* straying *from it.*

Max hauled the bag into his arms and as the doors began to close, he heeded the advice of his father, a Montana wheat farmer, by bolting off the train into the empty station.

A sound somewhere between a bark and a snarl told him the blood-crazed dog had followed.

The doors shut. The train began to move. No chance to turn back.

Max considered jumping down onto the tracks, but he couldn't count on the dog not following him down there. And he worried about that third rail. The knowledge of it might give him the upper hand, but even if he was able to shove the dog onto the electrified rail, he didn't know enough about electric current to be sure he wouldn't fry along with it.

Running for the stairs with the sluggishness of a nightmare, the duffel bag weighed him down. If he tossed it, everything went with it. All of his planning. All of his goals.

He chanced a look back, saw the dog slobbering at his heels, and heaved the duffel at it. The mutt yelped and skittered off toward the edge of the platform—

A breadcrumb trail of blood led from where he'd gotten off the train to the place he now stood, watching for a hopeful moment as the dog skittered and slid on the smooth tile. But the stubborn mutt struggled to its feet, undoing his attempt to make headway by throwing the bag in the first place. Now he was short a dozen maga-zines, the Colt 1911, a change of clothes—he would need it now, drenched as he was in his own blood—and he'd barely gotten a foot ahead.

Blasting off a few blind shots over his shoulder, he shortened the distance between himself and the stairs. Granite tile burst behind him in jagged gray clouds. The escalator stood not twenty feet ahead—blocked by a cage, CLOSED FOR REPAIRS. The stairs led down beside it. With a sudden burst of energy, like the last headlong rush to the toilet of the man who could hold it no longer, Max bolted ahead. He reached the stairs and bounded down two at a time. He hit the floor running in a bone-jarring crouch, saw the entrance, saw the fare collector sitting in his booth. Max got to his feet and waved his arms, running at full-speed.

"Help! *HELP!*"

But the man was asleep. *Oh, that's great! Hope you're having pleasant dreams, you asshole*, Max thought as his lungs grew tight and his muscles cramped. He dared a look over his shoulder, saw the dog still descending the stairs, squatting and moving down one step at a time, squatting and moving down, a look of fixed concentration in its wild blue eyes, its tongue lolled to one side.

"Ha!" Max cried ecstatically. "Ha-ha!"

Running for the turnstiles with renewed confidence, he smelled fresh air beyond them, summer rain and freedom just up the other set of stairs. Moist dirt and damp concrete. The sun would be up soon. All the little kiddies getting ready for school...

Behind him, all four of the dog's paws clacked down on the tiles. It had conquered the stairs, and now it would run full-bore toward him, treating the seat of his pants like a greyhound's rabbit.

Max used his gun hand to leap the turnstile.

"Hey! Hey, sir!"

Now the guy woke up. And he was concerned about the fare.

Max wanted to shout back at him, *Open your eyes, pal!* But he was short on breath and shorter on time. The dog skirted under the turnstile like a Marine under barbed wire, and now it was chasing, chasing, slobber dribbling back from its mouth, its fur rippling, and soon it would catch up to him...

"Hey, bud—" the fare collector said, then: "*Jesus!*" Max wasn't sure if the exclamation was about the bloodthirsty dog or the gun.

With a snarl, the dog bit into his Achilles tendon.

Max fell back, crying out in anguished surprise. He felt the flesh tear all the way up to the back of his knee, heard it tear like Velcro, yanking him back as the dog shook its monstrous jaws. His right foot slid forward on the newly buffed floor and the flesh tore free, like ripping off the world's largest Band-Aid, every nerve bursting, *pop-pop-popping* on his pain receptors, white-hot flecks of agony dancing in front of his eyes. The gun slipped from his grip and flew, clattering near the stairs to the outside, to freedom, and he lost his balance, arms pin-wheeling as he fell backward, slumping over the startled mutt.

The slashes on his hand had burst open, spraying fresh blood, and the back of his shin had been bitten entirely off, the torn scrap of flesh and tendon a joke-shop splat on the floor by the dog's hind paws.

The fare collector was on the phone. Max kicked the dog in the ribs with the boot heel of his uninjured right foot. It skittered back with a gurgling howl, teeth pink with his blood. Max pushed up onto his butt as the dog got to its feet and whipped around to snarl at him.

He snarled back, baring bloodied teeth of his own.

Max slipped the knife from his boot. The dog backpedaled, arching its back and lowering its head, watching as Max swished the blade back and forth, cutting the air, following the knife edge like a piece of meat.

Max darted forward with the Grohmann in hand. Its blade parted the fur on the dog's flank, slashing the grayish flesh beneath, finishing its arc bloodied.

The dog howled.

"Sir, the police have been called," came the fare collector's jerky voice over the loudspeaker.

"Fuck the police, call Huckleberry Hound!" Max shouted back with a crazed laugh. He turned back to the dog just in time to see its tartar-stained teeth clamp down on his face. They tore through his left eyebrow and eyelid, pressing like sharpened vice grips against the eyeball itself. Max's nostrils filled with the smell of dog breath, his entire face clamped between the dog's strong jaws, and he screamed into the wet, ridged cavern of a mouth as the dog jerked his head back and forth in its teeth, the straining in his neck muscles less worrying now than the sound like a popped cork—virtually painless—and the trail of something cold slime oozing down the cheek below his obliterated eye.

Reaching up, he grasped through tufts of fur for the dog's throat and clamped his fingers around its esophagus. The dog reared back suddenly, pulling its fangs from his flesh with a sucking sound and a metallic snap. Max fell onto his back, gouts of blood splashing the faux granite tiles. He lay there stunned, gasping for breath as the torn shreds of his lips spilled over with his own blood. Alongside him, the dog had fallen, its face covered in his blood, its chest rose and fell slowly, as if it was unconscious.

Vaguely, he felt a cold hard shape in the palm of his left hand. He opened it to find the broken bathtub chain, looped through a military dog tag. Blinking away blood from his eyes, Max strained to turn his head and read it.

His bleeding lips opened wide in a laugh.

The dog's name was Custer.

Max laughed until the paramedics arrived to cart him away.

He Is Risen

FERTILE GREEN FIELDS rattled by the dirty window. Madison still hadn't gotten used to looking left out the passenger side as opposed to right. Thankfully, Colin had taken to seating himself on the right side of the car to drive quite quickly.

"Easy peasy lemon squeezy," he'd said as he downshifted with his left hand. They'd been in the English countryside a couple of days by then, sleeping overnight at quaint B&Bs, and Colin had already believed he'd picked up the lingo. Madison was sure the locals thought he was bananas, this silver-haired Canadian asking for a "cuppa" and "biscuits," but she supposed she should at least count herself lucky he hadn't started imitating the accent—*yet*.

The weather channel had called for rain this afternoon, but the sky had been blue since they'd arrived at Heathrow on Tuesday. Odd weather for April, the weatherman had mentioned, particularly considering the great dump of rain that had hammered most of the northern hemisphere during the winter. Madison was grateful for the respite. Rain depressed her, and the snow and "greige" in Toronto still hadn't let up by the time they'd left the city. When Colin suggested they travel up the Irish Sea coast to a fellow professor's country home near the Scottish

494

border during break, she'd been leery, but anxious to spend some time with him off-campus. They'd only been dating since the beginning of first semester, and she thought this time together—away from the pressures of school and the prying eyes of the few students who knew of their pairing and found it questionable, Madison being Colin's T.A. (as opposed to his *T and A*, an insult she'd heard from several students)—just might push their relationship to the next level.

The weather had been a nice surprise. The sea air was crisp, but the sun felt good on her pale face. Colin was smiling at the road ahead, the small hatchback rumbling along a single lane of macadam carved out of the green as he slapped the wheel to an old Clash song on the radio.

"Hey, check it out," he said, his smile fading.

Madison followed his gaze. Among the green three—or was it *four*?—sharp gray stones jutted up from the earth like ancient claws. "Stonehenge?" she asked him.

Colin shook his head. "We're nowhere near there. The 'Henge is south of where we started. They've got standing stones all over the countryside out here, though. Nobody knows who left them, or why."

"*Nobody* knows?"

Colin gave her a curious look. "Well, I'm sure *somebody* knows. Spinal Tap, maybe."

He grinned at her, awaiting her reaction. Not getting the reference, Madison narrowed her eyes at him. The gap in their ages often showed itself in little things like this. She told her friends age didn't matter, and usually she tried not to let it get to her, but the more these differences piled on the more she felt the gap grow wider, until someday it would yawn like the mouth of a canyon, and one or both of them would stumble in reeling.

"Speaking of hard things..." Madison reached over with a grin and squeezed the crotch of his jeans. She felt for his cock, and began to massage it to life. Colin gave her an odd look. He took her hand, squeezed her cold fingers a moment, and placed it on her lap.

"Not while I'm driving, luv," he said.

Madison looked left out the window as they passed the standing stones, sulking for several minutes, as "London Calling" gave way to "A

Whiter Shade of Pale," and the gray slabs of rock disappeared in the mirror. Colin began to whistle along to the organ. Though Madison liked many modern artists, and he enjoyed a fair bit of jazz—a genre completely lost on her—a love of classic rock was something they both shared. She turned to him and smiled, his shaggy silver hair riffling in the breeze from his window, open a crack.

A road sign caught her eye then, written in an incomprehensible jumble of black letters she supposed must be Welsh or Gaelic:

Drws Marwolaeth

"Is that the name of a town?"

Colin squinted at the sign as they passed. "That, or one of the Elder Gods." He grinned at her and once again, the reference flew over her head.

Moments later, the town rose out of the fields. First there was nothing but green, and then pitched rooftops with smoking chimneys became visible, and windows bright with sunlight, and proper roads zigzagging, where people strolled cheerily and cars drove slowly, all seemingly moving toward the same place, the northern—if her directions were correct—end of town.

Colin followed the flow of traffic—not that he could have done otherwise even if they hadn't already been heading in that direction. Men and women walked hand-in-hand. Children scurried ahead, dressed in their Sunday best, some holding bunches of yellow flowers. Store owners flipped signs to CLOSED in the windows of stone shops, put on their caps and joined their fellow citizens marching down the main thoroughfare.

"It's Easter," Madison realized.

"Oh, right," Colin said, peering around edgily like a man in a shark cage. "Well, I guess that tells us where they're all heading."

A little girl wearing a pink bonnet waved at Madison, who smiled and waved back. The girl blew into a homemade pinwheel, making it spin. "What a friendly little town," Madison thought aloud.

"Too friendly, if you ask me."

"Why do you always have to be so suspicious of everything?"

"Comes with the territory," he said, grinning at her, and she managed to get that one: he'd meant because he was a philosophy professor. "You're a Catholic girl, aren't you? When's the last time you went to mass?"

"I'm a C & E Catholic." Colin raised an eyebrow at her. She grinned, having stumped him for once. "Christmas and Easter," she explained. "I totally forgot this year. Usually I'm at home over Easter, and my parents would take us."

"Doesn't say much for your devotion to the faith."

Madison scowled at him. Colin had often teased her about her religion. She'd never been devout, and didn't mind his jabs so much in the abstract, but in the midst of so many seemingly dedicated worshippers headed joyfully toward church, it irked her, felt somehow *profane*.

"How about we have a look at how Easter is celebrated in the picturesque town of Derwiss Marwo... *whatever*?"

"You just want to go so you can poke fun."

"No," he laughed. "I'm serious. I am honestly interested, Madison." Colin bit down a wicked smile, crossing his index and middle fingers. "Scout's honor."

Madison chuckled. "Who even says that anymore?"

Smirking out the window, Colin honked the horn, startling an old woman before waving innocently at her as she scowled down at him from under her frilly purple Derby.

"*Colin*," Madison scolded, grabbing him by the shoulder and swatting his leg.

"Just trying to get to get the giggles out before we enter the Holy Place."

"If you laugh in that church, you won't be seeing *my* Holy Place the rest of the trip."

Colin laughed. "That's what I love about you. You're not afraid to blackmail me with sex."

Madison's smile never faltered, though neither of them had ever spoken of love before, and she wasn't sure she felt it herself. She took a moment to ponder it, and by the time she'd settled on a response, Colin had already shifted focus to the massive church up the hill.

Hewn out of stone, like most of the edifices in town, the Gothic church towered over all that stood beneath it, casting its long shadow down the lush green hillside. The churches they'd seen here had dust older than most surviving parishes in Toronto, where few buildings predated the mid- to late-1800s. The sense of history in a place like this, of *life*, was far richer than in much of the Commonwealth.

Families left cars parked along the long gravel drive and in muddy tracks carved into the grass like at a rock concert, and ascended the rest of the way on foot. Colin pulled over into a tight space on the grass, muttering, "When in Rome," and the two of them climbed out together under the church's cool, dark shadow.

"Are you sure about this?"

"It's Easter," Colin said. "I'm sure God wouldn't approve of one of His children missing the day His only begotten Son rose from the dead," he added, rolling the *R* in *rose*.

"Don't start with the accents," she muttered, peering around to see if any of the townsfolk had heard him. "*Please.*"

"I shall make no promises," Colin said in passible posh English.

Madison elbowed him in the ribs, and he slipped his arm around hers. As she leaned into his shoulder, they caught up with the group.

"Welcome, welcome," a hunched elderly man with a shiny liver-spotted pate wheezed, his green jacket emblazoned with various medals.

"Did you see that?" Colin asked in hushed awe as they left him shuffling slowly behind them. "The two crossed swords. He was wearing a medal from World War I!"

"Is that weird?"

"Well, considering the last World War I veteran died in 2012 or so, I'd say it's a bit weird, innit?"

Madison removed her head from Colin's shoulder to study the faces of those around them, hoping no one had heard his Britishism. Everyone seemed focused on themselves or each other, wearing smiles as they trudged the gravel drive to church. A little boy in black short pants with a jacket and tie wound his way between moving legs, somehow managing to not get trampled as he hurried to the front of the line.

"Maybe it's his father's," Madison said, having lost the old man in the crowd.

Colin shrugged up his shoulders. "I suppose you're right."

Hard soles hoofed up the church stairs toward the arched doors, opened on a gloomy vestibule. The line seemed to take forever to progress, and as she and Colin rose the stairs themselves, she saw the priest or pastor shaking the hands of every adult as they entered, and greeting the children warmly. A sign at the front announced it to be The Church of St. Francis.

"Not too late to change your mind," Colin offered.

"You're the one that should be worried. Just don't touch the baptismal water, you'll probably get scalded."

Colin showed his white teeth in a grin.

As the husband and wife ahead of them shook the pastor's hand, the pastor caught Madison's eye and smiled.

"Welcome, welcome," the pastor—preacher?—said with a slight Welsh lilt to his voice. Tall and broad, dressed entirely in black save for the white collar, his pale face stood out starkly from under black, slicked-back hair. He held out a long-fingered hand, and Colin took it. The man rested his other hand on Colin's shoulder, which Colin glanced at without expression. "Welcome to our little church and our little town."

"Little?" Colin remarked. "I'd hate to see the big one."

The religious man smiled patiently, then focused his attention on Madison.

"We do so enjoy visitors." The reverend took her hand, his palm oddly cold. "But we'd love for you to stay a spell. Our little town has plenty to offer."

"Thank you, Reverend," Madison said as he let go of her hand.

"'Jack' is just fine." His gaze drifted to the people behind them, and she and Colin moved ahead.

"He seems nice," Madison whispered as they entered the knave.

"*Everyone* seems nice," Colin said. "It's a little eerie."

"You're so cynical, Colin." They sat in an empty pew near the back, Madison craning her neck to get a look at the vaulted ceiling high above, painted with scowling angels and morose saints, as more townsfolk piled in and took their seats. Finally, Reverend Jack entered and strode to the front. He took his place behind the pulpit, and the crowd quieted.

"Easter is a celebration of the Risen Christ... these days, it's difficult for some to believe in the Resurrection, and even more difficult to believe that Jesus brought a common man back from the dead, a man named Lazarus."

Murmurs rippled through the gatherers. Some shook their heads. "Of course, we here in Drws Marwolaeth know it to be true, as true as the rest of the Good Book. Jesus spent several days and nights in the earth—it's never quite clear how many days and nights He spent in His tomb, and nor does it matter. What matters is, crucifixion on Good Friday," he held out his right hand, palm up, "risen on Easter Monday," and he did the same with his left. "Jesus died to absolve us of our sins, and He rose again to prove that only He who created life has the power to *bring it back*."

His parishioners nodded. Colin turned to Madison with a quizzical frown, as if being used to this sort of rhetoric she might know where the reverend was leading.

"Man has always aspired to be like Him. It was our own St. Francis of Assisi who said, 'I want to *know* Christ—to know the power of His resurrection and participate in His sufferings, *becoming like Him in His death*,'" Reverend Jack emphasized, gaze sweeping from right to left. "Of course, there will always be doubters. Thomas couldn't believe the other Apostles when they told him—"

Several pews closer to the front, the little girl Madison had seen in the street turned and slumped her elbows over the chair. She raised the pinwheel and blew into it, its spokes reflecting bright colors as it spun. Madison waved, but the girl's mother tugged on her daughter's sleeve, and the little girl slumped back in her seat.

"And now," the reverend went on, "I'd like to ask that you all go outside, and join me in clipping our fair church, in the hopes that the Good Lord will bestow upon our church, and our town, new life."

The parishioners rose. Colin peered skeptically around at them. "That's it?" He shrugged. "I guess that's it."

"What's 'clipping'?" Madison wondered.

"Never heard of it. Likely just some folk tradition they trot out to creep out the heathens. And what was all that about the 'power of resurrection'?"

"Christ's Resurrection is very important to the church," Madison said, the two of them remaining seated for the time being while the parishioners marched outside. "Easter's much more important than Christmas for Catholics."

"Are these people Catholics, you think?"

Madison shrugged. "If they are, it's very different from what I grew up with. No bells and smells. Not even a Eucharist."

"Ah yes, the Holy Cracker," Colin jibed, and Madison elbowed him again. "You'd better stop doing that to me, or it'll become a fetish," he said, and kissed her neck below the ear. A chill ran up her spine and she giggled.

The little girl with the pinwheel passed by then, holding her mother's hand, and the girl waved timidly as Madison wriggled out of Colin's embrace to twiddle her fingers, feeling slightly ashamed.

"We would be honored if you would join us for the clipping," Reverend Jack said as he approached their pew.

Madison and Colin rose to their feet respectfully. "We'd love to join you, Rev— Jack," Colin said. "What is clipping, exactly?"

A smile flashed across the reverend's pale face. "Come and see." He ushered them into the aisle with an open palm. "We won't bite, I assure you."

Madison stepped out. Colin followed behind her, and the reverend led the two of them out into the gloomy vestibule.

"We use Easter as a time to reflect on our own mortality," Reverend Jack was saying. "And also to encourage a *renewal* of life. You've likely noticed there are many lovely young children in Drws Marwolaeth, but our hope is always for more children, to carry on our way a life." He smiled over his shoulder as they stepped out into the sunshine. "If I may be so bold, do you plan to have children?"

Madison and Colin shared a brief look, shielding the sun from their eyes. "We haven't discussed it yet, Jack," she said.

"I see. Well, plenty of time, I suppose. Time." He smiled, seeming to reflect. "This is a very old town. Our traditions predate that of many communities in the North West. We're one of the only towns to continue the practice of clipping, a very old tradition—and certainly the only church to do it on Easter Monday, in honor of our namesake. Clipping derives from the Old English word *clyppan*, you see, which roughly translated means embrace, or circle."

He directed their attention to the townsfolk who had gathered outside, not in a group but in a line, each holding the hand of those on either side of them as the queue began to stretch around the church. It reminded Madison of "Ring Around the Rosie," and the image troubled her somewhat as she recalled a time where she'd played the game with her friends, and when they all fell *down*, the other girls had pretended to be dead. She'd gone around shaking them, trying to wake them up, but nobody moved or spoke until Loren Ainsley broke into giggles and the rest of them rose around her in a chorus of damning laughter.

"What we do," the reverend said, "as you see now, is we all join hands and circle the church. Once we've all linked hands and the circle is unbroken, we round the church once clockwise, and once anticlockwise. There must always be enough of us to completely encircle the church, otherwise the point is lost."

"And what *is* the point?" Colin asked.

The reverend squinted at him. "Like many rituals, its intended purpose has been lost to time. However, we like to believe it protects us, and protects our way of life. There's something to be said for a bit of mystery though, no?"

"Some might say it's the spice of life," Colin agreed, and slipped his arm around Madison's.

A woman approached the reverend, holding out something slate gray and globular. As Jack took it, Madison saw it was a rabbit mask, though it was far cry from the Easter Bunny, so devoid of cutesy as to be sinister. The reverend placed the mask on his head, tugged the strap behind it and turned to them, only his clear blue eyes and mouth visible. "For the benefit of the children," he explained, shrugging up his broad shoulders.

Reverend Jack the Bunny trotted down the stairs, chasing behind a few straggling boys and girls, who scurried to meet the end of the line. "Run!" he cried, laughing heartily. "Run, little children! We mustn't dally or the Easter Hare shan't leave his eggs!"

Colin turned to her. "Well, what do you think?"

Madison shrugged. "It's bizarre. But it's kind of sweet."

Colin embraced her and kissed her temple. She hugged him back, then started down the stairs to catch up to the others as the head of the line emerged around the other side of the church. Colin took the hand of a young dark-haired woman with high Irish cheekbones at the end of the clipping circle, and Madison took the hand left over. The old veteran took her free hand, smiling warmly at her from what had been the head of the line as they continued their stroll. Jealousy tweaked at Madison's nerves as the fair-skinned woman smiled back at Colin, but she trusted him. He could sleep with just about any woman in school, and he'd chosen her. If he'd been in the mood to sleep around, he'd have suggested it by now, and he certainly wouldn't have dragged her all the way out to the other side of the pond to do it.

She let the cheerful townsfolk merry-go-round her to the side of the church, where the crumbled, mossy gray stones of an old graveyard became visible on a green hill, the flat gray sea beyond it. Madison looked up at the steeple and bell tower, meeting the googly eyes of a gargoyle made to look like a monkey sticking out its tongue. Ahead of Colin and the dark-haired seductress, the pinwheel spun in the girl's limp pale hand as the wind took it, the girl herself hidden behind trudging legs.

Reverend Jack the Rabbit sprung from a doorway, throwing up his hands, and several people screamed, including the dark-haired woman, who smiled embarrassedly over her shoulder at Colin. They all laughed when the reverend raised the mask, and he smiled down on Madison as she passed.

"I hope we don't ruddy go 'round for very much longer," the old veteran said to Madison as they marched around the back of the church.

Madison smiled politely. She considered asking him about the medal Colin had pointed out earlier, but a woman's voice called out, "Now, round and round anticlockwise!" It took a bit of fumbling, laughter and apologies for people to get themselves turned around and traveling in the other direction. They passed the doorway where the reverend had jumped out and scared them, and for a moment, she felt Colin's hand slip from hers before snatching it again.

"Do you have the time?" the old man asked over his shoulder.

Madison twisted the hand he held to look at her watch. "It's quarter to two."

"Quarter of two, already? *Cor*, I'll need my kip in an hour!"

Madison didn't know what a "kip" was, but she smiled in sympathy. Colin's cold fingers grasped hers tighter, and she turned to smile back at him, startling when she saw a freckled young man with thick, dark eyebrows held her hand instead of Colin. "Where's my boyfriend?" The young man scowled at her. She called out Colin's name, prying her hand loose from the young man's, who held tight. "Have you seen my... my boyfriend?"

The young man continued forward, shoving her brusquely out of the way. Men and women gawked at her, suddenly not so friendly. The fields were empty. Gray clouds scudded across the sky. "Colin!" she cried, hurrying along in the other direction, disoriented by the blur of townsfolk trudging forward. "*COLIN!*"

The little girl's pinwheel stood alone in the grass, spinning in the wind. A simian-like gargoyle stood on its perch displaying its genitals, mocking her.

Madison stopped running when she reached the doorway, a part of her already certain Colin had slipped off with the dark-haired woman into some dark corner of the church. Everyone was out here, mindlessly circling. Inside, they would have privacy. She had to get in. The queue kept moving forward, blank stares meeting her frightened eyes, no one kind enough to break the circle and let her through.

"Excuse me!" The townsfolk gave her bewildered looks. "Get out of my way!" she shouted, ducking to squeak in under the arms of an elderly couple, pulling their hands apart and temporarily breaking the circle. She stood in the alcove where the reverend had hidden, hugging the door in bewildered terror as the glowering eyes of the crowd still circled.

Nervous to turn her back on them, Madison kept an eye on the clipping circle and tried the doors. She spilled into a small dark vestibule as they opened. She closed them behind her, cold eyes peering in at her as the doors came together.

"*Colin!*" Her own voice echoed in reply. Madison pressed her palms against her eyes, adjusting them to the darkness. The small, round chamber contained a door and a winding set of stone stairs. She tried the door, found it locked. Upstairs then, or back outside with the insane people and their poor, oblivious little children.

Madison called out his name once more on the stairs. The damp walls were cold to the touch, but the height made her nervous. She felt her way up to the top, where another door muffled voices in whatever room lay beyond. She pressed her ear against it, not ready to get caught by surprise, worried she might die if she saw Colin with another woman. Difficult to identify the sounds beyond the door: moaning or talking or some kind of rhythmic chanting.

Only one way to find out, she thought, and twisted the knob.

She saw Reverend Jack Rabbit first, standing at the far end of the bell tower, reading from a book he held out in one long-fingered hand. Candles burned and smoldered from crevasses in the walls. Below the old brass bell, Colin lay shirtless on a stone slab. The dark-haired woman lifted his head by his beautiful silver hair and before Madison could raise her voice in alarm, she dragged a curved blade across his throat.

The blood came in gouts, splashing the dark-haired woman's coat and showering Colin's chest as his tongue wriggled in strangled chokes, his warm brown eyes locked on Madison. She stumbled back, reaching out to grab hold of the arch, only vaguely aware of the steep drop behind her. Cold hands snatched her from behind and forced her roughly into the room.

The reverend pulled up his mask with a grin. "Ah... you've arrived just in time, my dear child, to bear witness to the conclusion of the ritual."

Madison struggled against the hands. "Let me go! *What the fuck is wrong with you people?*"

"Wrong?" He closed the book. "There is nothing *wrong* with us, dear. You see, this town is quite old and so are we. A handful of us are older than this church, aren't we, Carwen?"

Carwen, the dark-haired woman, winked and smiled, allowing Colin's head to strike the stone while his gurgling abruptly ceased. As the reverend crossed to Madison, Carwen unbuttoned her long red coat, revealing her pale, freckled body, small breasts with puffy, perky nipples, a triangle of dark hair in the crease below her jutting hipbones.

"What's she doing?" Madison wanted to know.

"Never mind her. Listen to me, my dear. If we're to prosper, this town needs children. You could live with us, the two of you."

Behind him, Carwen unzipped Colin's jeans and jerked them and his white briefs down to his knees. Colin's penis, slightly crooked in its thatch of salt-and-pepper pubic hair, sagged over his tightened balls while his lifeblood trickled down the slab to the cold stone floor, and his dead eyes stared vacantly at the interior of the bell above his head.

"You ki— you *killed* him..." Madison wept as the reality of it sunk in. "*You killed my Colin!*"

"Ah yes, but the power of resurrection!" Reverend Jack said. "St. Francis was right... it is possible to know the power of resurrection! To become like Him in death. He will *rise again*, my dear. We have *all* risen again."

"This is insane!" She struggled against the cold hands, hot tears streaming down her face. "*You're insane!*"

The reverend unbuttoned and removed his collar, revealing a jagged pink scar across his throat. "Do not doubt me, Thomas," he said to her calmly. He nodded to whomever still held her tight. "Show her."

The hands let her go, and she twisted round, face to face with the young man with thick eyebrows. He pulled up his shirt and she turned away, not wanting to see.

"Look at him, dear."

She didn't want to look, but the reverend wore the rabbit mask again, and Carwen had straddled Colin's body, crouching over his hips and thrusting herself back and forth on his limp cock, now glistening with her juices. She'd always thought she would die if she saw Colin with another woman, but here she was still alive and Colin dead. Reluctantly, Madison turned. The young man smiled at her, fingering a large open wound like a fish gill under his ribs.

"The same wound Pontius Pilate gave to Jesus," Reverend Jack said. "Do you still doubt?"

Madison shuddered. "What is this...?" she managed to groan.

"We need more children," the reverend told her. "Only the dead can impregnate the dead."

"But... but he's..." She turned to her lover, tears filling her eyes, causing her vision to blur. She blinked them away, startling as Colin's prick began to stiffen, rising like a snake from the bushes. Carwen grasped it and slipped it into her dark, wet tomb.

"He is risen!" the reverend said with a pleased smile, and as Colin's bloodied hands rose from the stone slab to grasp the woman's buttocks, Madison fainted dead away.

Squirm

T HE SUN WAKES me, the sound of sparrows outside the open window. A summer breeze blows in, cooling the sweat on my bare skin where I've kicked off the sheet during the night.

I find it difficult to sleep in the summer. The heat makes me uncomfortable in my own skin. Erratic breeze from the fan startles me awake as it blows past, fluttering my hair in my face. Noises outside rouse me too easily with the window open: raccoons rattling garbage cans, distant sirens, drunken partiers. I've always been a light sleeper, but so much more so since the children came. Bill could sleep through the Apocalypse...

I lie there for half an hour, just listening to him breathe and watching the birds outside our window. I've always envied his ability to turn off his brain and recharge for eight hours a night. The boys don't wake him, creaking their way down the hall to pee or get a drink of water. When they were babies, it was always me who would wake first to shake Bill awake for his turn to change them or shush them back to sleep. Even now, I'd be lucky to get a few hours uninterrupted before my brain started circling around things that didn't bear thinking about so late at night.

I roll over to watch Bill sleep. In the dead of night, I may begrudge him, but watching him like this in the morning makes me smile. I think of how lucky I am to have such a perfect family, a perfect *life*, and the thought makes my heart swell with joy, bringing me close to tears. Few better ways to start the day.

The alarm clock on his side of the bed tells me it's still too early yet to wake him. I consider creeping out of bed and heading downstairs to read a little of my book, but a tiny twitch in Bill's cheek concerns me—something like a facial tic. I've never seen him do that before. He usually sleeps so peacefully, never shifting, eyelids barely fluttering, just lying there on his back like a man in his grave. The tic is something different. I don't do well with different.

He rouses a moment later to find me watching him. His lips upturn in a smile as he takes in a deep breath of morning air through his nose. "Mmm morning, honeybear."

"Morning," I say. He kisses my closed lips briefly, before I pull back, not wanting to give him a face full of morning breath.

Bill leans in again and kisses me deeper. Watching me. *Wanting* me. I let my lips part, despite my breath issues. I watch him as his eyes close, getting into it. I imagine him getting hard in his boxers, and the thought turns me on.

It's been weeks since we've had alone time (it's hard for me not to think of it as "Mommy-Daddy time," despite how fully it kills the mood), with the kids in bed, at their grandparents, or sleeping over at one of their friend's houses. I feel a deep urge to be with him, to have him inside me, his hands roaming over my skin. Then my mind starts circling. Stupid things. It's so hard for me to just be in the moment sometimes.

Should shower first. Brush my teeth. But then the kids will wake...

Bill's eyes open. A hand slips over my clavicle, down to my breast. All thoughts dissolve. His eyes follow the progress of his fingers, widening in hunger as the rough pad of his thumb circles my areola, bringing blood to the surface.

He blinks then, but his eyes don't close. He's too engrossed in his stroking, fingers tracing my freckles, the mole above my nipple. He blinks, but a translucent film closes over his eyes instead, shuttering over them from side to side, like an animal's, keeping them moist but wide open.

This is not my husband.

I tear my lips away from him, certain I must have imagined it. Pulling back in horror, I try to blink the image away, to look at him from a distance. To *study* him.

"What?" he whispers. "The kids won't be up for another half hour..."

Even if I knew what to say, I can't speak. It's impossible. My lips won't form words.

Bill pouts like a little boy, his typical reaction when he feels scorned. No evidence of anything different in his eyes now. Of anything *other*. But I can't forget I'd seen it. The facial tic while he slept... had that been part of it? I'd been stressing myself out lately, looking for full-time work now that the boys were older, still doing my regular duties as a wife and mother. Trying to be the Supermom society expects of me. Compounded with the lack of good, solid sleep... is it possible I'd imagined it?

As I lie there considering how to reply, the boys come bursting into the room in their pajamas, all smiles, giving me the opportunity to separate from Bill without making it something to fight over.

"Mommydaddymommydaddymommydaddy!"

They leap onto the bed and climb in between us. Bill play-wrestles Dylan over his shoulder, making a monstrous growl. Dylan giggles uproariously, his laughter high-pitched, almost a squeal. Ryan climbs over Bill's legs and snuggles up between mine. Any other time I might have found the scene cute, but the image of Bill's eyes closing without closing has filled me with such confusion and dread I can't enjoy our morning routine like I normally would, his playful growl—the Mattress Monster, the kids call him—now vaguely sinister. Ryan crawls up my legs and cuddles into my lap, wrapping his little arms around my waist. He looks up at me with a wide smile.

"G'morning, Mommy," he says.

He sticks out his lower lip to blow shaggy brown hair out of his eyes, and translucent shutters close over them, just like his father's.

Ice cold fingers run up the nerves in my spine, despite the summer heat. I so desperately want to jump out of bed, to run screaming head-long down the hall and into the street, but then they'll know that I've seen them, that I know what they are. So I force myself to sit perfectly still, and it takes a concentrated effort of every nerve in my face to return the smile.

"Morning, honeybear," I say to the creature that used to be my youngest son.

■|

NICTITATING—THAT'S WHAT it's called. Translucent membranes below the eyelids that protect the eyes and keep them moist. Birds have it, snakes have it. Some mammals. I spent most of the morning on the internet after dropping the kids off at school, looking it up, hoping it was possible for humans to have it. Some sort of vestigial thing. A holdover from our ancient ancestors.

After kissing Bill perfunctorily on the lips—with my eyes open to watch *his*—and whisking him out the door, I'd packed the boys' lunches into their backpacks and their backpacks over their shoulders, and hustled them off to the car. Driving behind the school bus with them sitting in the back seat, I found myself sneaking peeks in the rear view, worried they'd blink their membranes while I wasn't looking—or *worse*. I'd made sure they were buckled in tight, knowing I would hear the *click* if one or both of them decided to climb over the seat for a concerted attack while I had my hands on the wheel and couldn't defend myself without crashing the car.

I assured myself I was being crazy, a mantra I repeated in my head, one I hoped they couldn't somehow overhear. Thinking this, that they could possibly be able to hear my thoughts, I peered at them in the mirror again. Their brown eyes met mine instantly, as if they'd only been waiting for me to look. Their pale, gentle faces wore broad, inno-cent smiles. *Loving* smiles.

But when I looked away, I caught them turning their smiles on each other in my peripheral vision. And the smiles twisted into something menacing. *Knowing*. Their nictitating membranes flicked closed, and I swear I could almost hear a dry click, like a camera shutter.

It took all of my strength not to jerk the car into oncoming traffic.

I spent a lot of the day looking up postpartum psychosis, using terms like "delayed onset" and "late life" to narrow the search. Hoping desperately that what I'd seen was just a hallucination, something I could possibly suppress with pills or alcohol. I read that most sufferers experienced symptoms within the first six months after childbirth. Since Ryan, my youngest, was now five, postpartum didn't fit as a diagnosis.

Clearly I was hallucinating, though. You don't just wake up one morning to find your husband and kids have been replaced by humanoid reptiles. Things like that don't happen. This isn't Kafka. This is reality. There are rules.

Humans don't have nictitating eyes. That's something I *know*.

I look at the clock on the computer, and realize I've spent the whole morning sitting here fretting. My coffee cold, a skim of clotted cream on the surface. I erase the browsing history, and close the laptop. It's time to pick up Ryan from school.

He kisses me on the cheek, and I buckle him in. No evidence of the creature I saw this morning, he's the perfect little angel he's always been. We drive in silence, while he holds a toy car up to the window, pretending to be driving alongside us. Shame twists my insides, making me queasy. How could I have ever believed he wasn't my son?

Ryan flops down and watches cartoons for an hour before I tell him to go out back and play. I can't think with the sound of the TV, and I need to think, to hold on to the notion that everything I'd seen wasn't real. My gaze falls upon an opened bottle of red on the counter while prepping for dinner.

Wine before dinner? Why not?

When Dylan arrives home, he looks at me sitting at the table in front of an empty bottle of wine and a stained wineglass, and scowls in confusion. I realize I haven't greeted him like usual, and smile. It's much easier to force a smile after two glasses of wine. "Hi, honeybear. How was school?"

He cocks his head, unsure of me. Then he shrugs. "School was school. Where's Ryan?"

"Out back."

He sets his bag down on the floor, and heads past me to the backyard. I watch the boys through billowing curtains. They stand very close together near the shed, speaking to each other. Then, as if they'd been talking about me, they turn to the window.

I wave cheerily. It's easier to cover my increasing sense of panic now that I'm slightly drunk.

The boys turn to each other, confused. As if *I'm* the one acting strangely, and they've been perfectly normal. Perfectly *themselves*. Then they separate and throw the ball back and forth.

██

BILL WATCHES ME floss through the bathroom mirror. I can tell he's been wanting to ask me about the wine all night, and I've been preparing myself for it.

"Are you all right?" he asks finally.

"Uh-huh," I say, running the dental pick between my incisors, putting too much force against the gums.

"It's just..." He hesitates, trying to think of the most delicate way to put it to avoid an argument. "You don't seem yourself today."

You don't seem yourself today either, honeybear.

"I'm fine. Maybe a little stressed. Job-hunting and all that."

Bill nods, seemingly understanding. He watches me a few seconds longer, then picks up his Robert Ludlum from the bedside table and opens it, settling into the pillows.

I spit a mouthful of blood into the sink. Looking at myself in the mirror, I stare until my eyes blur from dryness, until I can't hold them open any longer and involuntarily blink.

I look at the dental pick in my hand.

Eyeing Bill, I gently close then lock the door.

I return to the mirror, hold my left eye open with thumb and forefinger, and bring the sharp end of the pick toward it. I've never been able to touch my eyes. Can't even put in drops without blinking furiously like I've been splashed in the face with acid. Just watching someone else deal with their contact lenses makes me cringe.

The pick end blurs it's so close to my eyeball.

Ohgodohgodohgod—

The mint green plastic barely grazes the spongey lens of my eye and I blink it away hard. Feels like I've scratched the cornea, even though I know it wasn't enough pressure to injure me. Tears already streaming down my cheeks, I bend over the sink and splash warm water on my face. Blink blink blink away the pain.

All I wanted was to see the membrane. To see if I'm one of them.

Now I'm sure I'll never know.

■■

MORNING, AND I'VE been awake all night. I look a mess. I feel like a train wreck. I laid there beside Bill watching him sleep while the sirens wailed and the raccoons rummaged. He didn't move all night, but his skin did. The tic I'd noticed the previous morning had spread, his whole face suddenly doing the jitterbug. That's what I'd thought for the first hour or so as I lay there in the semi-dark, our bedroom illuminated by the fingernail moon. Over time, I realized it wasn't his skin moving at all, nor was it nerves. It was something *under the skin.* The flesh moved in ripples and waves, as if parasites were living inside him. Or an alien presence had dressed itself in his skin.

It *squirmed* under his face, flesh rippling.

Tentatively, my own heart beating so hard I could hardly breathe, I laid my head on his chest and I couldn't hear his heart. There was no heart to hear. I couldn't feel it, pulsing below his ribs. But I felt the creature under his flesh move, like snakes in a burlap sack. A living thing in a dead body.

I wondered what might happen if Bill's skin could no longer contain the thing beneath. If it suddenly split open and peeled back while I laid there, revealing its true form, blood and extraterrestrial goo soaking into the good sheets.

After a while, I realized I could smell him. Not his usual scent. Not the sharp tang of man sweat under a light breezy cologne, and the flat smell of clean hair. He reeked of cloves, like how I imagine a mummy might smell, and the salty smell of mucous as he breathed in and out deeply through his nose, so cloying it made me gag and I had to turn away.

I laid there beside that awful thing all night, knowing I'd have to kiss it in the morning. Knowing the creatures wearing my boys' skin would scurry in once the sun was up, and expect me to hug them and tell them good morning. Bizarre, once-impossible thoughts circled my mind like sharks, terrifyingly plausible now.

I slipped out of bed as the sun rose so I wouldn't have to reenact our morning routine. After the night I had, I knew I couldn't have possibly dealt with it.

I drank a vodka and cranberry juice before they came shuffling downstairs wearing my family's pajamas over my family's skin, appearing bewildered and even a little upset, hair a mess. The vodka took the edge off, but I'm still jittery. Jumping at any sudden movement.

Somehow I manage to get breakfast made. Pancakes. Still their favorite, though I'm certain the things they've become are only eating to appear normal. To avoid detection, conflict. I'm watching the two smaller creatures eat, cutting up the food I've made into bite-sized chunks with their forks and spooning it into their toothy orifices. I'm frozen with the milk jug extended in my hand, and when the thing wearing Bill's skin asks me to pass the syrup, I snap out of it, but I still can't seem to make my hand pour the milk.

My limp hand quivers, milk splashing against the inside of the jug.

"Honeybear?" it says.

The two smaller creatures look up at me, forks poised before their opened mouth-holes. Their eyes nictitate, unblinking. The creature wearing my husband's skin cocks its head to the side and watches me, as if I'm the one who's abnormal.

I can't take any more of this. This can't be my life. Only yesterday I was reflecting on how perfect it was, and now...

Now. Have to act fast.

Instead of the syrup, I calmly pick up the knife. I don't even excuse myself as I stand with it clenched in a fist and leave the table. The things wearing Bill and the kids stare up at me with their mouths open, not sure how to react. It's not until I've bypassed the counter and left the kitchen that the Bill-creature's concern becomes evident. I hear his chair squawk as he gets up quickly to follow me, but by then I'm already running down the hall.

I'm in the en suite bathroom with the door locked when the creature raps gently on the door.

"Hon, what are you doing?"

I need to know.

"Honeybear, why did you bring that knife into the bathroom?"

I wonder, if I was one of them, would I even know it? Would I act any differently? Would I feel the same?

If my skin was a jacket, how could I be certain? If my insides squirmed, would I see it? *Feel* it?

He pounds on the door with his fist, but I know he's too cautious to break it down. I have time.

I need *to know.*

"I know what you are!" I shout at the door, moving in close to the mirror to study my reflection.

"*What?* Libby, what's *wrong* with you? What the hell are you *talking* about?

His fist on the door rattles the toothbrushes in their cup.

"Open the door!"

"Mom?" Dylan cries. "Mom, open the door!"

Ryan is weeping. I can picture the two of them, holding hands just outside the door. They sound so much like my family, but I know it's a trick. They're trying to lull me into a false sense of security, and when I open the door they'll spring their attack. They'll drag me back to their mothership or their underground lair to begin the change, to become one of them.

If I'm not already.

I grab my hair and pull it back, exposing my face to the naked white light of the vanity bulbs. I haven't looked at myself this closely in months, ever since I noticed the frown lines expanding between my eyebrows, and saw how large my pores looked in the makeup mirror. Aging is the least of my worries now.

I wonder if they age—the creatures? Do they mate? Procreate? Or do they just steal our bodies, using us like cuckoos use the nests of other birds?

I raise the knife to my face. Just below the scalp. This is where surgeons would cut me to erase the signs of having lived. Peel down the skin and sew it back together, tighter. The knife quivers in my hand, the edge of the blade resting against my forehead.

"Libby, open this goddamn door!"

It clatters against the jam. I've never heard Bill raise his voice like that before, and it startles me. I need to move fast. I need to finish this.

Cutting yourself deliberately takes much more force than you'd think. The first cut I make merely brings blood to the surface, leaving a raised pink welt that burns like a stinging swarm of bees. The second cut is deeper. The flesh blossoms open and blood trickles down my forehead, pain bursting in white stars before my eyes. The vodka I drank before preparing breakfast barely dulls it, but instead of making me stop, it's galvanizing. I cut deeper, dragging the blade, tracing an upside-down smile below my hairline, opening my flesh to the bone. I cry out in pain and frustration, finally allowing myself to grieve the loss of my family, blood spilling in rivers down my furrowed brow and into my wide, wet eyes. The creatures just outside the bathroom, faking tears, using Bill's fists to pound on the door.

"*Lib!*"

"*Leave me alone, you freaks!*" I scream at him, my face painted red like a woman warrior. The blood-drenched knife clatters into the sink, and I reach up with both hands to grasp the ragged edge of flesh I've carved. It feels like warm, raw chicken, but the mental image makes it no easier to pull apart flesh from bone. I watch my fingers peel my skin, the pain so far beyond anything I've experienced that I'm now mentally detached from it, as if I'm watching it being done to someone else's body, through someone else's eyes. This flesh is no longer mine. This body is merely a vessel. A husk.

The door frame splinters.

I watch Bill's shoulder smash against the door through the wide, angled crack. Behind him, I catch glimpses of the little ones, the boys who were once mine. Then the flap of skin falls over my eyes with a wet slap like a damp hood.

For a moment, I see nothing, blinded by flesh. Fingers peel away the darkness to bright white. The lids pull away from my eyes with a terrible sucking sound.

I can see.

In the mirror I see a woman, thirty-five years old, blonde hair. The beginnings of laugh lines and crow's feet obscured by a jagged, curved flap of glistening, angry red flesh draped over her nose. The eyes now perpetually widened in horror or fascination. The mouth open, smiling, whitened teeth stained pink as she laughs.

Glimpsing bone amid the raw meat of her forehead, she's unable to blink away the sight of her insides squirming as the door smashes inward and her husband stumbles in, his own eyes widening in revulsion, terror, stupefaction. The boys behind him, *her* boys, now screaming and huddling against each other.

Bill staggers back, a hand over his mouth. "Oh, dear God... *Libby!*"

A gauzy film draws over her eyes like curtains, moistening them. Nictitating.

I see the woman leave the mirror. She moves toward the creatures in the hall. No longer fearing them. She drops to one knee, and Bill and the children fall into her arms, weeping, afraid, relieved.

Creatures, like her, dressed in hand-me-down flesh.

"*We are family,*" I say, and the body I wear hugs them tightly.

Sharp

A PARCEL TRUCK the color of dried blood crept through the neighborhood, the sunny suburban quiet pierced by the incessant ringing of its bell.

No children scurried from their houses to chase it down. The ring had more in common with a plague-cart driver's death knell than an ice cream truck's jaunty jingle, and this 1950 Ford Step-N-Serve with **JERRY'S GRINDING SERVICE** hand-lettered on the delivery door side provided no treats, only tricks.

Below the name, smaller block letters spelled out, **KNIVES SCISSORS GARDEN TOOLS MOWER BLADES**. Larger, and in the same font, the word **SHARPENING** caught a shard of sunlight, bright enough to stab the eyes of anyone unlucky enough to be caught looking. Every letter had peeled to the point of being nearly illegible. Metal corners bent up under rivets, jagged and rusted. Black smoke plumed from its exhaust and the holes in its sagging muffler. The interior smelled of oil and foul chemicals, the walls adorned with sharpened tools that rattled and swung from hooks.

This truck was a rolling machine of death. Fitting, considering the man who sat behind its wheel ringing the bell was the man the newspapers had taken to calling "The Ken Doll Killer."

A diminutive man, Jerry drove with wooden blocks attached to the pedals so his feet could reach them. They hadn't called him "Ken Doll" because he was handsome. His victims had all been tall, slim and blonde, resembling the impossible standard of beauty set by Ken's sometime girlfriend, Barbie.

Without witnesses to his crimes, the papers weren't aware of his ugliness, which coupled with his lack of height made him self-conscious. Being called a "Doll" by the local news organizations gave him stabbing pains in his stomach that wouldn't go away with antacids.

"Sharp," Jerry muttered to himself, and tugged on the weathered string, clanging his bell.

Jerry eased the truck around the corner onto Hayworth Street, where he often idled to eat his lunch before turning in the cul-de-sac and weaving his way through streets named after dead celebrities. As he drove toward the end of the street, a woman in a bright sundress hurried down the steps of her colonial home. A look of disquiet pinched her attractive features as her heels clicked and clacked toward the sidewalk on the cobblestone path. The same sun that brightened the remnants of Jerry's sign shimmered in her springy cornsilk hair.

Jerry's instincts for spotting women in distress being nearly preternatural, he'd seen her long before she reached the street. She hadn't needed to wave her arms to flag him down, but he appreciated the glimpse of her jostled breasts as he slowed his already crawling truck to a stop.

"Ma'am?" He caught her eye for the briefest of moments before averting his gaze to the dirty floor of the truck and the wooden blocks he hoped she wouldn't notice. Always, Jerry outwardly deferred to women, while within the darkened, twisted caverns of his mind he stood before them tall and naked and proud—a *juggernaut*.

"Oh, thank God you're here," the blonde woman all but gasped. In his glance, Jerry had seen milky white flesh draped over her fine angular frame, and wondered fleetingly what her bones would sound like hollowed out and hung from his porch as wind chimes. He imagined their music might sound like Heaven.

"Thank God, indeed." He gave her an unforced smile. "What can I help you with today?"

"It's my good knives." The pout was audible in her voice. "The blades are too dull to cut butter, and I'm having a guest for dinner!"

"Just let me get my tools," he said in a tone he'd hoped sounded reassuring.

Rummaging in the back, Jerry attempted to control his breathing. He'd never seen this woman on Hayworth Street before. She must have kept herself busy inside the house, or in the backyard, during the many times he'd lunched here. Wherever she'd been, he felt grateful for his good luck finding her here today.

With his equipment gathered up, an awful certainty struck him: the woman had gone back inside and locked the door behind her, suddenly afraid of this small man with small fingers, small toes, and even smaller prick. Jerry hurried back out with his grinder, his breathing frantic again, only to find her still standing by the curb. The look of worry in her eyes became a strained smile when she saw his grinder: a hefty little thing with the look of a vacuum cleaner, the black grinding wheel cradled in its side like film on a projector.

"All set," he told her, leaping down onto the sidewalk, noticing as she lowered her chin to take in his small stature. Jerry didn't let it bother him. Now that he held his tools, he felt strong. When he got her in the house, his lack of height would not be an issue. When he stood over her prostrate body, breathing hard into the cleft of her bosom while hot, sticky blood oozed from her wounds, he would seem *enormous*.

"Follow me, please," she said, her sundress flipping up delightfully to reveal a muscular thigh as she turned on her heels. Jerry followed, taking small looks as her buttocks rose and fell, rose and fell like fleshy counter-weights, well aware that anyone could be watching from their windows, wondering why the statuesque beauty next door would stoop to consort with such an ugly little man.

"That's quite an impressive tool you've got," the blonde woman said, peering over her shoulder. She might have caught his look at her sublime posterior had he not averted his gaze to the cobblestones.

Still, Jerry felt his cheeks grow red at the—possibly unintended?—double-entendre. "It was my f-father's," he choked out. His father had been the original Jerry, the man whose truck Jerry Jr. drove up and down nice, quiet residential streets like this one, day after day, in search of blades to sharpen. Jerry's father was long dead, as was his mother. She'd cut her wrists with the sharpest knife in the drawer when she'd learned, from the nice old lady next door, that her husband had been cheating on her with a tall, blonde woman named Sandra.

Another thing the papers got wrong: his victims weren't Barbies. They were *Sandras*.

"Sorry about the mess," this Sandra said as she opened the door.

"I-I'm sure it's fine," Jerry stammered, having focused most of his mental energy on stemming the flow of blood to his penis. However small his erection might be (and Sandra had made it plain how incredibly small it was), he didn't want the stubby protrusion alerting her to his intent before the woman let him into her home.

Stepping inside, her heels clicked on tile as Jerry followed, and he noticed what she'd meant by "the mess" right away. End tables and glass vases and the corners of walls had been smothered in bubble wrap and clear tape. The sofa, the fabric on the dining room chairs... it was almost as if she'd been attempting to seal off anything of value. To protect it from the incessant gnawing of some feral animal, maybe: a miniature hell hound in a fancy dog sweater. Or to spare them from being humped.

The woman ushered Jerry past all of this to the kitchen, where she indicated with an elegant swishing gesture the knives laid out on the counter. "You see?"

"Oh, they're dull, all right," Jerry said, clucking his disapproval. "I can help with that."

Jerry looked around himself at the counter island stools, the appliances, and the windows all taped over with bubble wrap. Even her fancy kitchen gadgets had been wrapped neatly in bloated clear plastic. It reminded Jerry of the padded cell they had put him in when he was still a boy. The hefty tool in his hands no longer made him feel strong. He felt uneasy. He felt that stabbing pain in his stomach again.

"Moving, are you?" he ventured, and licked the roof of his suddenly dry mouth.

The woman shook her head and offered nothing further.

Jerry gestured to a stool. "May I?"

"Be my guest," she said, then smirked as if her words had amused her.

Jerry dragged a stool to the counter, where he'd laid down his grinder. The layers of bubble wrap squeaked as he sat, the sound of a clown twisting balloons. He thought maybe the woman might not have wanted his sharpening equipment to damage anything in the kitchen, but it wouldn't explain why she'd wrapped the rest of the house. Thinking about it set his teeth grinding. Best to get this done, then—the whole nasty, messy business—and be out of here quickly.

But once Jerry got started, he savored the grinding and the sparks that were always a prelude to the work ahead. Gradually, his anxieties floated away. While he sharpened her knives, he drank little sips of the woman as she crossed and uncrossed her long legs from her perch on a second bubble-wrapped stool, smoothing down her lipstick-red nails with a pointed nail file.

Aside from her height and her hair color, this woman looked nothing like Sandra. Sandra had been street trash. Jerry's father had met her at a bar after a long day, and judging by the stories she'd told to anyone who would listen, Jerry Sr.'s truck had been bouncing on its springs in the back lot within the hour. This woman had an elegance about her. A fragility that Sandra, who chain-smoked and spat and scratched her genitals in public, never had. Sandra wore Press-On nails, much longer than anyone needed, and all of Sandra's clothes had been form-fitting, to show off her hips and the roundness of her buttocks. And while the eyes of both women were blue, Sandra's had been cold and calculating. This woman's were soft. Kind. Sandra's whorishly painted lips had always twisted down, even when she'd been smiling. This woman's lips curled up at the corners, giving her the appearance of a smile even when she was frustrated.

Sandra was long dead now, murdered by Jerry's own hands. She'd moved into the house and into his father's bed barely a year after they had laid Jerry's mother in the ground. Sandra had toyed with young Jerry, both awakening and deterring his sexuality. The night she'd caught him masturbating at age twelve, Sandra had made him painfully aware of how small his penis was: "Stroking his little prick!" she'd called out to his father. Both father and son had been too mortified to look each other in the eye for days, though by then Jerry Sr. paid little attention to him anyhow, so enamored was he with his young new girlfriend.

And when he was thirteen, Jerry had heard his father grunting in the master bedroom. He had peeked in through a crack in the door to find his father lying face-down on the bed, his hairy ass in the air. The room smelled foul, like a soiled diaper. Sandra stood behind his father, her naked buttocks jiggling between the leather straps of some device, thrusting her hips toward Jerry Sr., grinding her hairy crotch—he could see the thick black thatch of her pubic hair between her legs—into his father's backside. Sandra's fleshy pink phallus—a dildo, Jerry knew now, though at the time he'd thought he understood why Sandra had mocked his penis, when her own penis was so large—plunged into his father's rectum and out, in and out, while his father grunted in pain and pleasure.

Cautiously, quietly, young Jerry had moved downstairs to the kitchen, ashamed by his erection, his young mind swimming with rage, jealousy, revenge. He opened the top drawer closest the sink, where the knife his mother had used to kill herself still lay, though cleaned, sharpened and unused since. He removed it from the drawer and crept back upstairs. He sneaked into the room as his father raised up on his knees and Sandra pulled on his father's hair like the reigns of a horse, his father's prick squirting milky fluid onto the fouled sheets.

Jerry Sr. had caught his eye just as Jerry brought the knife across Sandra's exposed throat. The mortification in his father's eyes could have been embarrassment of the act his son had caught him in as much as terror. Jerry would never know. As Sandra fell back, gurgling and clawing at her throat as gouts of blood spattered him and his father, the dildo popped out of his father's shit-smeared asshole with a wet plop and Jerry Sr. fell onto the soiled mattress.

Jerry had fallen upon him in an instant, the blade plunging in and out of him as the dildo had only moments before. His father's grunts were not of pleasure then, only pain. Sandra clawed the curtains down from the rod, the bright light of day cascading down on this grizzly scene. The smell of shit and blood had been so thick, Jerry's heart hammering so fast, that the world began to gray.

When Jerry awoke, he'd been in a padded off-white room. His

father, dead. Sandra, dead. The police hadn't wanted to go into details of how they'd been found—the embarrassment had been as plain on their faces as it had on his father's—but it was clear they knew that he'd been the culprit. He'd spent the rest of his childhood in the institution, released to a halfway house the year he turned eighteen. With good behavior, he'd eventually been allowed to return home. Since his father had been good about paying his bills, the house and truck now belonged to Jerry.

Finally, Jerry completed his work. He wiped his greasy fingers on a handkerchief and took his receipt book from the deep front pocket of his coveralls.

"That was quick," the blonde woman said, something she might be moved to say again later, though by then she would have neither the strength nor the breath—perhaps not even the *lips*—to voice the remark.

Jerry smiled his practiced smile. "May I ask... what your name is?" He wouldn't look up at her, intent on the pen scrawling on his pad. "For the bill," he added hastily.

All he required was her signature. Proof that she wasn't Sandra, that more blades needed sharpening, more work required doing.

One day, when there were no more Sandras left to skewer, he would reveal his dark Other to the world. His shadow self was *gargantuan*—it stretched out dark and monstrous behind him, particularly in the late afternoon. Jerry preferred to kill a few hours after lunchtime, so his shadow would draw out long behind him when he left his victims, a dark mirror to the giant inside.

When there were no more Sandras, the world would see just how BIG he was, so BIG their minds would struggle to see him all... and in their fear, and in their desperation, they would put him away for the rest of his life, with no chance of parole.

Over the years, lonely women would write to him in prison. They would proclaim his innocence, profess their love, send him their silky underwear, fragrant with their scent. They would *worship* him. Jerry The Giant, his minions would call him. Jerry the *Juggernaut*.

"I'm Rose Stark," his next victim said, picking up one of the blades and admiring its shiny edge under the florescent lights. He wanted to suck the fluid from her windpipe and use it as a flute. He wanted to sever her pelvis and use it as a sex toy. But he wouldn't do these things. Even when fully absorbed in his Other self, Jerry was no animal. He would only cut her major arteries, slowly and methodically, and let her pumping hot lifeblood be the lubricant to their sexual congress as he worked his little prick into her anus.

Out in the street, the bell in his father's truck tinkled softly.

"Oh, this is perfect," the woman—*Rose*—said, rotating the shiny-edged blade in her hand.

"Sharp," Jerry agreed, nodding hypnotically.

Behind her back, Jerry tugged his mother's kitchen knife—not the same knife, that was in a moldering evidence box at the police station, but its double, the same heft and blade—out of the homemade sheath in his coveralls.

As he brought the knife up, its shiny blade shimmering under the recessed lighting, Rose shrugged the flimsy dress from her shoulders. Its fabric caught for one loving moment on her hips, and she shimmied slightly, her taut breasts jostling before she slipped free of it, and it finally cascaded down to her ankles. She turned to him, naked and proud, though her body was not without its flaws. Her flesh was blemished with dozens of scars, paler than the rest of her: little inch-long nicks crisscrossing her hips, her legs, her breasts, her arms. He hadn't noticed them in the daylight, and though they were certainly *odd*, it didn't diminish Jerry's lust for her.

He swallowed hard. Everything about him felt hard, suddenly. No woman had come on to him before, aside from Sandra, who had used her sexuality like a carrot on a stick, flaunting her curves and taunting him, practically *forcing* him to strike out at her one way or the other.

This woman, Rose, she drew out her arms and bid him closer.

Jerry felt his mother's knife fall uselessly from his hand. The sound of its clatter on the tiles seemed far away, dulled by the pleasant thud of his own blood in his ears as he shuffled toward her, like a child taking his first steps to his mother.

Rose took him into a warm embrace. She drew his face to her bosom and cupped his head in her hand, stroking his greasy, shaggy hair. Jerry stood in her arms, pressed between her firm breasts, her heartbeat enveloping him the way his mother's once had when he was a boy. Tears welled up in his eyes, and he wept openly. She stroked his hair, shushing him, letting him weep, letting his tears smear on her breasts and drip down her belly.

"It's okay," she cooed. "It's okay."

And it *was* okay, Jerry realized. Suddenly nothing seemed to matter. The past was the past. Sandra, his father and mother were dead and buried. Her suicide and their murder, the abuses he'd suffered in the asylum in the years that followed their deaths, were nothing more than vague memories of someone else's bad dream. Jerry felt at peace, for the first time since he'd found his mother in the blossoming pool of blood on the kitchen tiles. He felt very small, a child in his mother's arms, and it was okay to be small.

It was okay.

Jerry heard a familiar sound like knives drawn across leather straps, only this was the sound of dozens simultaneously. As his mind processed this, he felt his flesh opening at his throat, his cheek, his chest, belly, arms and groin. Peeling open an eye, the one not pressed against this woman's hot flesh, he blinked away tears and got a good look at the breasts he'd been snuggling against. Only what he saw wasn't a breast at all... or, not quite. The flesh had parted, and from the nipple a long, sharp, ridged thing jutted out like a horn, slick with her blood.

Rose had grown *thorns*.

Terrified, Jerry squirmed, tearing his own flesh against her spiky protrusions. The more he wormed against her the more entangled he became. She held him close, shushing him, whispering *It's okay, it's okay*, and the thorn in his cheek popped through with a sound like the dildo springing from his father's anus, and it gouged the roof of his mouth, his tongue. The thorns in his abdomen and crotch had flayed him, his guts fell out like sauced spaghetti and his penis—just as small as Sandra had declared it—had been skewered like a cocktail weenie on a toothpick.

Jerry opened his mouth to speak, but the word gurgled out on a mouthful of blood. His heart stopped pumping, his limbs slackened, and his head dropped to the side, like a marionette on severed strings.

Rose let him go then. His lifeless body slipped from her sharp protrusions and fell to the floor in a bloody heap beside his grinder. And as her breathing slowed, Rose waited for the change to happen.

They came to her like flies to the spider, like moths to the flame: these monsters dressed as men, rotten little boys who still feared their mothers, their sisters, daughters and wives. Unconsciously they sought her out, and Rose held them and pacified them. Often she sang to them and often they prayed, and sometimes she slapped them and sometimes she let them suck and bite her at her nipples and once or twice, they had kissed. But always, *always*, she stroked their hair and told them it was okay. Because in the end it was all these monsters wanted: someone to comfort them and tell them they were forgiven.

The thorns drew back inside her with an epileptic shuddering. Already the flesh that covered them began to heal, and she wet a bunch of paper towels in the sink and daubed away the blood before stepping back into her dress, pulling it back up over the lightening dimples on her shoulders.

Rose opened the fridge, poured herself some lemonade, and brought it to the front porch, basking in the satisfaction of having pricked another slug in the garden. It really was shaping into a beautiful day. Sun shining, birds twittering. Next door, the Anders's wind chimes rattled pleasantly, like hollowed-out bones. Mrs. Bellows from across the street stood up from weeding her lawn and threw her a big friendly wave. "Hi, Rose!"

"Morning, Mrs. Bellows," Rose shouted back. She sipped her lemonade, sitting back with a contented sigh.

A fine, fine day on Hayworth Street. Nothing could spoil it, not even the sight of that ugly old truck and its gently rattling bell.

Video Nasties
A Novella

1 – NASTiES

EXTERIOR. STREET. NIGHT.

In the blur of driving rain, Harlan Wallis didn't see the box of old videotapes outside the fire-blackened factory until he'd just about walked into it. As an avid collector of old movies, his eyes immediately lighted on two rare video nasties resting upon the others—*Massacre at Central High* and *Nightkill*, both films only ever available on VHS. Like a man protecting a wounded animal, he dropped to his knees to spare the soggy box from further damage. Hurrying the rest of the way home hunched over the box, soaked to the skin, Harlan just hoped the tapes beneath the first layer might still be salvageable, if not the rest.

He supposed he owed his good fortune to Vicky, who'd thrust him out into the downpour despite his fear of being struck by lightning, telling him in a flurry of words she wished it would zap him straight to Hell. The storm had died down since, leaving only the rain to worry about—along with his battered ego. Vicky had really let him have it this time, facing him with the sad unalterable truth their relationship was definitely over.

They'd never been right for each other, he and Vicky, and it had never been more apparent than in their choice of entertainment. Harlan loved old horror movies, the cornier and nastier the better. He relished the feeling of superiority, knowing exactly what would jump out at him and when, being able to guess who would die and how within the first few minutes, and laughing derisively when his predictions came true.

Vicky, on the other hand, watched movies to be emotionally moved, and their argument tonight had related directly to this apparently irreconcilable difference. She had put on a horror movie in hope of bridging the gap, and he'd sniped about it the whole way through. After twenty minutes, Vicky had turned it off in frustration.

"You aren't even giving it a chance!" she'd cried.

"Oh, I did," he'd replied with a yawn. "It's just trying way too hard."

"And you think that's a bad thing? Maybe if you—"

She'd stopped there, but Harlan had seized on it like a piranha on a bikini-clad bimbo. "Maybe if I what? Tried harder?"

"No, that's not what I was going to say. You can't predict everything, you know."

Harlan had sputtered his objection, and Vicky, exasperated, had thrown a handful of popcorn at him.

"I'm sick of it, Harlan! Everything needs to be self-aware and snarky, or you won't give it a second look."

"That's not true," he'd said. "I love old movies."

And that was it: the phrase that ended their relationship. Moved to tears, Vicky said, "Sometimes I think you love those old movies more than you ever loved me."

For the first time in Harlan's twenty-six years, he hadn't been able to find the words to argue.

He loved her. Of course, he loved her. The question was if he loved her as much as he loved movies, and for that, he still didn't have an answer.

At the door to his apartment, Harlan held the dripping box awkwardly on one knee, and fumbled to get the key card from his pocket. He managed to heft the box into the living room just before the cardboard split at the seams, bursting open, tapes spreading across the rug like when he was little and would dump out his Lego blocks to build an army of original monsters.

Rows upon rows of old VHS tapes already lined the walls surrounding the television, but there was always room for new acquisitions. He slipped one out of its cover (*Peeping Tom*, once banned in Finland), shook water from it, and laid it on the carpet to dry. Thinking he'd better do the same for the rest, he rushed to the bathroom closet for towels. When they'd first started dating six years prior, Vicky had bought him a matching set of plush ones, having complained about the tattered and threadbare towels he'd scrounged from his family home after his parents had passed. The old towels were relics of his childhood —like his furniture, his posters, and much of his VHS collection.

Maybe what Vicky said is true, he thought now, looking over his newfound treasures. *Maybe I am living in the past.*

He didn't want to consider why.

Spreading the towels out on the floor and table, Harlan sat cross-legged on the rug and began removing tapes from their soggy covers, separating dry from wet. Classics like *Willlard* (the original, not the subpar remake with Crispen Glover) and Tod Browning's *Freaks*, a few Troma films, a handful of Hammer Horrors, the extremely rare *Snuff*. Looking over the vibrant, macabre, and often unintentionally humorous covers reminded him of those long-ago trips to the video store, his parents searching for what seemed like hours to find some-thing appropriate for the three of them to watch, while he marveled at demons sprung from toilets, buxom heroines clinging to muscular warriors, half-rotted skulls, switchblade hooligans, and muscle car grilles marred by streaks of blood. He'd felt most at home there among the oddities, with some horror movie flickering on the TVs overhead, the heady smell of stale popcorn filling his nostrils.

What kind of monster would throw these out in the street during a thunderstorm? Harlan wondered. Clearly someone who couldn't see value in old things. Someone who felt the past held little worth. *Someone like Vicky*, he thought, and quickly rebuked himself for thinking it. She'd always been kind and patient, open to new experiences. If anyone had played the villain in their relationship, it had been him.

Harlan absently picked up a videotape he'd surprisingly never heard of and read the tagline aloud, "'*NASTiES* will make your life a living Hell.'" He uttered a mocking chuckle.

The painting on the cover showed a VHS tape with a pentagram burned into it, glowing red and smoking. Above this, two teenagers in hooded cloaks held black candles, apparently in the midst of some kind of dark ceremony. A swirl of tentacles and greenish mist surrounded them. He'd seen this sort of un-ironically cheesy cover dozens of times during his visits to the only retro video store in the neighborhood, and much more often when he was young, at the old Blockbuster with his parents. Harlan grinned and turned it over to read the blurb.

The NASTiES *are just that: nasty, disgusting, rotten little tentacle demons hell-bent on nothing but destruction. High school student Troy Stark finds a possessed Betamax, and after reciting the ancient incantation in the accompanying instruction manual during a Halloween party at his parents' house—coinciding with a mysterious thunderstorm—he and his friends unwittingly unleash the* NASTiES. *One by one, they die in increasingly grue-some ways, while Troy and cheerleader Tina discover the terrible truth about his parents' involvement in the occult in their attempt to send the* NASTiES *back to Hell!*

"Sounds fucking awful." Harlan laughed. "I love it." He nearly dropped it when he read the credits on the back cover:

Co-Written, Directed & Edited
By Nicolo Funelli

"Holy shit! It's a *Funelli*?"

On his list of all-time favorite B-movie directors, Nicolo Funelli had always been among the top three. He firmly believed the old studio tagline, *Funelli puts the 'Fun' in schlock horror!* He'd seen every single piece of trash the deceased Italian director had put to film, even the lost "classic" *Ragers in Space*, all except this... and the fact he'd never heard of it only increased its worth in his eyes.

Harlan cracked a beer and sat in front of his laptop. He looked up Funelli's credits, but *NASTiES* wasn't among them. He searched for *NASTiES* specifically, with Nicolo Funelli in quotations—still *niente*, as they'd often said in Funelli's early films, when he'd still been working in Italy, and the subtitles would spell out "nothing."

"An undiscovered Funelli," he marveled. "I could make a fortune off this!"

The cover looked cheap, but still had the appearance of mass manufacturing, as opposed to something an industrious collector might have made for a one-off dubbed copy of a bootlegged film. The label was printed directly onto the cassette, not a sticker. Most of the names listed in the production credits had corresponding IMDB listings—Jack Emmerson, Funelli's frequent co-writer, and sometime collaborator Ham Gottlieb were among them—but Harlan found nothing about this film. Utterly baffling.

Maybe I've stumbled onto a rare one. Like, really *rare... NASTiES... wow!*

"Well, let's give 'er a run-through," he said to himself, and brought the tape to the VCR. Opening the gate, he eyed the physical tape to make sure it was free of debris and crinkles, so as not to damage the video heads. Giving it the okay, Harlan popped it into the machine. The player swallowed it with a hungry whir of machinery.

PLAY ▶ appeared on the black screen while Harlan sat on the floor amid the new tapes in his collection, eagerly waiting. The digital readout counted up:

00:00:00... 00:00:01... 00:00:02...

At **00:00:13** the VCR groaned. A horizontal line of video noise crackled down from the top of the screen. Harlan rose to his knees to adjust the tracking, or smack the top of the VCR, but the picture adjusted itself before he could do either.

00:01:32... 00:01:33...

Still nothing.

He pushed Fast Forward. The image warped, shuttling through nothing but black. His hopes sank.

"Someone must have erased it. Or left it next to a bulk eraser."

A flicker of light inside the machine caught his eye. Curious, Harlan pushed up the flap. He leaned over and peered inside. The tape dragged sluggishly over the video heads. Nothing out of the ordinary. As he closed the flap, a spark of electricity zapped his finger. Crying out in pain and surprise, he jerked his finger back. A whiff of burnt flesh and ozone stung his nostrils, the skin beneath his fingernail charred.

"Balls," he said through the finger in his mouth, hurrying to the bathroom to run it under the tap. The cold soothed his pain, but the running water made him need to urinate. *Not like there's anyone around to nag me about it*, he thought, relieving himself with the door open. The memory of his fight with Vicky made his heart hurt.

Life isn't all darkness and horror: her words from long ago echoed as he flushed the toilet. How long had it been since he'd thought of that night in her bed? Long enough he could barely remember it now. She'd helped him through that dark time, giving him six of the best years of her life, and he'd rewarded her with not-so-subtle insults, passive aggressive snarkiness, neglect. He deserved whatever fate lay in store for him.

Vicky had gotten him the job where she had worked since high school, a place much like a prison, each inmate with their own little 6'X6' laminate and fuzzy carpeted cell. But where Harlan saw only bars, Vicky saw the door, and while she rose in the ranks from Data Entry to HR Administrator, Harlan mindlessly entered data into his terminal, dreaming of one day becoming a famous movie director, each day getting one day further from realizing his dream.

ZAP!

A flash of blue flickered over his shoulder in the mirror.

ZZZZAP! ZZZAP!

A fork of lightning arced across the doorway. Harlan dried his hands quickly and hurried out, but what he saw in the living room made him launch himself back into the bathroom hall, pressing himself flat against the wall as his heart thumped. Blue flashes brightened B-movie posters on the plain white walls as he peered around the corner.

Lighting curled outward from the tape player, striking the tapes on the shelves and the ones laid out on the floor, reminding him of cheap film effects of the '80s, from *The Highlander*'s "Quickening" sequence to the clock tower scene in *Back to the Future*. Despite the very real danger of electrocution—hadn't Vicky wished he'd get struck by lightning?—Harlan scurried around to the power bar and yanked the plug with his foot before the machine could do any more damage to his collection. Surge protection would prevent errant electricity from frying his laptop, at least, but the tapes it had struck were likely toast. Dozens of them had rattled off the shelf and landed among the new tapes in his collection. Every one of them would need checking. It would take him hours. Maybe even *days*.

The VCR smoldered quietly on the shelf.

Harlan downed the rest of his beer, injured finger extended as he eyed the VCR. The tendrils of gray smoke had stopped oozing out of its mouth, but he supposed it still could catch fire.

"Better put it on the balcony, just in case."

A light mist fell. The air had cooled down considerably from the muggy, soup heat of the day. Harlan laid the VCR on a ratty old patio chair he'd salvaged from the Dumpsters, and laid a few dry newspapers from the recycle bin on top of it. He lit a cigarette butt from the ashtray, sucking the last few drags from it while gazing out at the purple bruise of sky above the apartment buildings.

He often watched miniaturized lives play out in lighted apartment windows while he smoked: people cooking dinner, having parties, playing with their children. Blue light flickered in many darkened apartment windows. After the electrical storm inside his apartment, the sight of those blue windows was vaguely sinister. He imagined arcs of lightning from cable boxes and satellite receivers zapping the zombified eyes of passive viewers, creating automatons who threw themselves down stairwells and off balconies, killing themselves to the soundtrack of some meaningless reality show.

The apocalypse will not be televised, he thought, and shuddered, crushing out the previously butted cigarette as he'd exhausted its nicotine supply.

Something clattered inside. As he peeked in through the doorway, the television came on with a high-frequency whine. He stepped in, curious and on edge despite the smoke, wondering how the TV could be on when he'd unplugged it from the wall along with the VCR.

On the TV was a dark attic, lit blue to look like moonlight. An actor meant to be high-school age—as evidenced by his letterman jacket—but clearly much older, read gibberish from an arcane tome: *"Shubish! Coitus! Interruptis!"* he cried with all the sincerity of a bad actor reading unintentionally horrible lines. Wind howled, blowing the actor's hair and flipping pages. The girl with a puffy pink sweater and teased wall of blonde bangs clung to his shoulder as cardboard boxes sprung open and dusty objects clattered off the shelves—

The image cut abruptly to the interior of a studio. A petite brunette sat tied to what looked like a director's chair in front of a green screen. Harlan recognized her pale blue monkey pajamas seconds before she turned her wet mask of terror in his direction—but it wasn't possible. This wasn't happening. Black lines of mascara ran down Vicky's cheeks as she tried to look everywhere at once, her small frame quivering in terror. Harlan stumbled over the coffee table and kicked through the cassettes on the floor, dropping to his knees in front of the screen.

"Vicky!" Harlan called, knowing she couldn't hear him through the television but too frightened not to try. "*Vicky, where are you?*"

She turned to him, her relief short-lived as she recalled her predicament. "*Harlan?* I don't know, I don't *know*, I was watching TV. I must have fallen asleep, but I woke up, I woke up *here*, and I, I don't know how I got here. Harlan, I'm *scared...*"

Clapping came from the side speakers of his old TV. Vicky's gaze followed the sound, struggling against the ropes as a man entered the frame, dressed in black with cowboy boots and a Stetson. From his tall, slim build and the loping way he walked, Harlan recognized him immediately. He'd seen him in hours of feverishly studied documentary footage.

It was Nicolo Funelli. Or a pretty damned good lookalike.

"Hello, Harlan," the long-deceased Italian director said, and his Dali moustache curled upward as he grinned. In one hand he held a Philips VHS Movie Camera, gray with a black shell. He raised it to his right eye, aiming it at Harlan through the screen. Behind Vicky and Funelli, the green screen filled with an image of Harlan's own terrified face. When he scowled, the face on the screen behind Vicky and Funelli scowled with him.

"What is this, some kind of sick joke?" Harlan said, searching the TV for a hidden camera. "You're a lookalike, right? Somebody hired you to mess with us? Tell me this a joke, Vick. Vicky?"

She merely whimpered, shaking her head softly.

"I assure you, Harlan, this is no joke," Funelli said, his accent heavy.

"We're going to have a little fun. If you play along, your lovely leading lady will be returned to you in one piece."

"If you touch her, I swear to—"

"Who? To *God*?" Funelli laughed haughtily. The green screen filled with a battle taking place in slow-motion through a spaceship's massive viewport, a scene from *Ragers in Space*. "If there is a God why am I here, talking to you, when I could be in heaven, drinking wine with Hitchcock and Kurosawa?"

For a second time, Harlan couldn't find the words to argue. This was no prank. Somehow, Nicolo Funelli had kidnapped his girlfriend.

Ex-girlfriend, Harlan reminded himself, as if the situation wasn't already bad enough.

"In here, Harlan, *I am God*."

The space battle cut to a close-up of Funelli, grinning down at himself.

"We're going to make a film, you and I," both Funellis said calmly. "In the movies, this is what they call the 'ticking clock.' You have until midnight to discover how to release me from this videotape, so make haste, my friend. If you don't, your leading lady dies."

He removed the video camera from his eye to nod in Vicky's direction. Her gaze flicked from the director to Harlan in unbridled terror.

"As you know, I have no compunctions about killing off my main characters, and that includes you." The director showed his teeth, and made a short bow. "Adieu," he said with a slight giggle, and the screen cut to black.

"Wait!" Harlan grabbed the sides of the television, shaking it on its shelf. "Wait! *How do I let you out? How do I let you out! Vicky! VICKY!*"

The screen remained dark. He plugged the television back in, and flicked uselessly through the channels. Blue screen... blue screen... blue screen.

"You're wasting your *time*," he told himself, glancing at his watch. 8:35. Midnight deadline. He had to do something, and fast. "Okay, I can do this. I just have to work it out in my head. I've seen every damn movie that motherfucker put on film, all except this one, I should be able to—"

Inspired, Harlan leaped to his feet and hurried out onto the balcony, where the VCR still lay under dampened newspapers. He brought it back to the living room, plugged it in, and ejected the tape. Staring down at the *NASTiES* cassette on the coffee table, trying to decide what the main character of a Funelli film would do, he lit a stubbed cigarette. He wanted to smash the cassette open with a hammer, but if Funelli really had been trapped inside the tape, like a genie in a bottle, he wasn't in there anymore. He'd gotten loose when Harlan played it, gotten into the cables—once Funelli's consciousness or whatever had kept the essence of him alive hit the optical cables, the fiberwire, he could literally move at the speed of light. There would be no stopping him...

"But he needs me to get out," Harlan said. "That doesn't make sense. He can pull people *in*, oh God, Vicky—but he can't get *out*."

Think about it for a minute. Stop and think. He's got her trapped in some kind of B-movie purgatory, but he's trapped there too. There's always some kind of curse or spell or demonic incantation to solve the problem, and somebody knows it, someone who knows a lot more about what's happened. A "guide." A Yoda. Who knows more than me about Funelli? The documentarian? No. No, she lives on the other side of the country, she's probably asleep by now, even if I could find her number...

"I've got it!" Harlan slipped the movie into its case, and tucked it into his jacket as he headed out.

2 – Funelli's Monster

So Hip Video was dark when Harlan arrived, but he knew the owner lived in one of the apartments upstairs. He thumbed all three buttons, hoping one of them belonged to Dave Lee. A light flicked on in the front apartment upstairs, and a slim silhouette stood by the window for a moment. A minute later, heavy soles trudged down the stairs to the paint-flecked door. With a rattle of locks and latches, it opened on Dave. He wore a black toque over his shaggy hair (dyed to a color Harlan had once heard him call "Asian orange"), and skinny pajamas tucked into Ugg boots.

"Harlan? Store's closed, bruh. Come back tomorrow," he said, already closing the door.

"Dave, wait, just listen for a minute."

"Okay, what? I just smoked a bowl, I'm trying to chill..."

"Do you know Funelli? Nicolo Funelli?"

"Funelli?" the store owner blinked sleep from his eyes. "Sure, sure, of course, he put the 'fun' in B-horror. That's a terrible tagline, by the way. Doesn't even sound the same. It's *Foon*elli not *Fun*elli, and two, Funelli's more like *D*-horror. Or *F*. Funelli puts the F in fail." He grinned proudly at the joke, scratching his sparse black goatee. "Did you wake me up just to ask me about Funelli?"

"No, Dave, I just really, really need your help. This is gonna sound crazy, but Funelli's trapped Vicky, my girlfriend. He's trapped her inside the TV or, or *something*... and I just need your help to get her out. *Please*. I'm desperate, man!"

Dave narrowed his eyes. "Are you doing a Vine?"

"This isn't a *Vine*, Dave," Harlan snapped. "This is *real life*."

"Dead directors don't drag girlfriends into the Phantom Zone, Harlan, not in IRL. You've been watching too much Funelli, and I am way too baked to talk movies with you right now, okay?"

Dave began to close the door. Desperate to make him believe, Harlan yanked the videotape out of his pocket and waved it at him. Dave's marijuana-addled brain took a moment to register what he saw, and then his eyes widened.

"Holy Tarantino! Where did you get that, dude? Wait, don't say anything!" He opened the door all the way and tugged Harlan inside by the jacket. The cramped entrance smelled like cabbage. Junk mail littered the floor. Red bled through the black walls where paint had faded and flaked off, the stairs grimy from years of trampled-in dirt and dotted with cigarette burns. The scene reminded him of the bathroom stairwell of a goth nightclub.

Before shutting and triple-locking the door, Dave peeped up and down the street. He turned to Harlan, inches from his face in the tight hallway. "Now, tell me everything from the start."

"I found the tape, and I played it—"

"No. *Dude*." He raised his hands to emphasize the mental stress Harlan had caused him. "Seriously, where did you find it? A garage sale? Scream Factory? The fucking *Twilight Zone*?"

"What are you talking about?"

Dave's eyes jittered as he tried to keep his stoned brain in focus, staring Harlan down. "This tape," he jabbed an accusatory finger at the offending object, "it was never manufactured, okay? This movie *does not exist*."

"But..." Harlan looked at the offending object. "But I'm holding it."

"No, dude, what you're holding is not *NASTiES*. It can't be *NASTiES*. You know why? Because Funelli *died* before that movie was finished, and all of the footage was lost in the fire."

"Fire? What fire?"

"You don't know about the fire? He doesn't know about the fire," Dave added to his imaginary audience. "Nicolo Funelli died in a studio fire shooting B-roll green screen footage for *NASTiES*. I mean this was some sick shit he was filming. Legend has it, he wanted this to be his version of *Hellraiser*. He'd really upped the full-frontal nudity and the gore, with just *buckets* of blood, but word is..." Dave stopped suddenly at the sound of creaking upstairs. "I'm hungry. Are you hungry?"

Harlan wasn't, but to be amiable he made a head gesture between a nod and a shake, and followed Dave up the stairs. At the top, a small landing led to three doors, each painted black, the peepholes, doorknobs and apartment numbers still rimmed with the previous sloppy red paintjob. Dave opened the door to their right, and disappeared inside.

The bachelor apartment reeked of weed. Dave had paused near the end of Dario Argento's *Suspiria* (some called Funelli a lesser Argento, but Harlan had always had a soft spot for the former, at least until very recently), and the blood-streaked woman hanging from a skylight stared at them from Dave's widescreen television. Every bit of floor space was covered in videotapes, dirty magazines, and dirty clothes, aside from a path of stained carpet leading from the door to the futon, futon to kitchenette, futon to bathroom. Harlan longed for the clean comfort of Vicky's small basement apartment. He kept his shoes on despite Dave's request to take them off at the door.

Dave walked the trail marked by '80s centerfolds and frayed tighty whities to the kitchenette, and opened a cupboard. He came back with a box of Fruit Loops and dug a hand inside, munching a handful of the sweet colorful cereal before offering the box to Harlan, who shook his head.

"Suit yourself." Dave flopped down on the futon, reclining against the arm with one foot up on the mattress, like a burnout's boudoir photograph. Considering all the skin mags on the floor, evidence of potential solo hand play on the futon, Harlan elected to gently kick some tapes out of the way and sit on a stool at the kitchen counter.

"You can sit over here, I won't bite," Dave said, his black goatee sprinkled with bright rainbow crumbs.

"Yeah, but I'm afraid your mattress might."

Dave snorted laughter. "Fair enough. Now where was I?"

"The, uh, the fire at Funelli's studio."

"Right. So..." He shoved another handful of cereal into his mouth, speaking as he chewed. "Legend has it, Funelli hired a bunch of non-union actors to shoot the cabal cutaways. If you listen to the tabloids, it was Satanists, but the word on the street is Funelli was into some really dark shit even Satanists wouldn't touch. I'm talking sex magick—that's magick with a *ck*, not with a *c*, and the extra *k* is for extra krazy. I'm talking ritualistic sacrifice. I'm talking summoning the Dark Lord Cthulhu type shit. I mean this stuff would make the Cenobites look like Jehovah's Witnesses."

In the brief silence, Harlan eyed the cassette case. "So you're saying... he was shooting some kind of ritual with these cult people when the studio burned down?"

"And Bingo was his name-o!" Dave grinned, his teeth stained purple-gray from artificial colors, BHT and God knew what else.

"Shit," Harlan said.

"Add to that the fact that the police never identified his body among the remains they found, and you've got yourself one helluva mysterious grand exit, Urban Legend-*stylee*."

Harlan considered it. Something in the story didn't follow, but he couldn't put his finger on it. The cabalists, the fire, the missing body. All of it was insane, but something felt wrong. "No, wait a second," he said, piecing it together. "I saw his funeral in those old documentaries. All of his ex-wives were there, crying and throwing themselves on the casket."

Dave shrugged. "They just buried his cowboy hat and boots."

"Jesus..."

Dave nodded. "And he's kidnapped your girlfriend."

Harlan nodded morosely.

"How?"

"I don't know. Vicky said she fell asleep in front of the TV and woke up in this studio... I saw her on the tape, tied up in front of a green screen, and Funelli was there with her. He told me I've got until—" He looked at his cell phone. The digital face read 9:04. "*Shit!* Less than three hours. He made a special point of reminding me he's not afraid to kill off main characters, and Vicky's a main character—"

"*Shit*, dude..." Dave sat up. "What does that make me? The Asian *sidekick*?" He got up from the futon and began pacing, trudging carelessly over cassette cases and magazines. "This is ridiculous, man. Just trying to smoke a bowl, watch a movie and chill, and some white dude I *barely even know*, by the way, comes knocking on *my* door and gets me caught up in a curse. I knew I shouldn't have answered the door but you're a good customer, and the customer's always right. The customer's always an *asshole* is more like it—"

Harlan stepped in front of Dave and grabbed him roughly by the shoulders. Dave snapped out of it, his gaze much more lucid than before. "Sorry, man," he said.

"No, *I'm* sorry. I shouldn't have got you caught up in all this but I'm in a lot of trouble here and you're the only person I know who knows more about bad movies than me. Also Vicky's mom is Chinese, so I don't think the 'Asian sidekick' thing really matters all that much."

"Oh, really? Where's she from?"

"Dave!"

"Sorry. Sorry."

"It's okay. Now what are we gonna do?"

"Well, okay," Dave said, gathering his thoughts. "I was thinking, Funelli's co-writer lives here in town. If anyone would know what to do in a Funelli movie, it'd be him."

"*Jack Emmerson* lives here?"

"I thought you were a Funelli *fanboy*, bro! They shot a lot of their movies here. If anyone would know how to help you, it's—" Dave paused, turning his head toward the TV in a slow motion move straight out of a demon possession film. "Wait a minute. You said Funelli zapped your half-Asian girlfriend into the television or something, right?"

"Dude, can you—?"

"What?"

"Well, what the fuck does her being half-Asian have to do with anything?"

Dave opened his mouth to reply, and seemed to think better of it. His mouth remained open, staring over Harlan's shoulder at the TV. Harlan turned to see the hanged woman break apart into digital blocks, warping and streaking across the screen, repeating the cascading motion of blocky smearing color like a digital waterfall until Funelli's face replaced her in close-up.

"*I heeeeear you!*" he said, speaking into a flopping, bloody severed ear with ragged flaps of torn flesh. Throwing the ear over his shoulder, he stepped back into a medium shot. Funelli's absence in the frame revealed Vicky tied up and unconscious on a dentist's chair. To Harlan's relief, both of her ears appeared intact. Behind them, Funelli had super-imposed a room filled with scientific equipment looted from the set of some '60s sci-fi series on the green screen. Harlan recognized it as the setting for a key scene in *The Quasar Conspiracy*, where the sadistic Lead Scientist used a laser to burn the protagonist's eyeball until it split open, oozing bubbling white goo.

The scientist stepped into shot behind Funelli with the laser in one oily gray mitt. The white coat had split in places, and a dentist's face mask barely concealed the bulbous alien features and slobbering, jagged-toothed sucker mouth of Funelli's Space Rager.

"You'd better not be trying to mess with me, Harlan. You have three hours. And then, I let my creations have some *real* fun." He flashed a smile. "Goodbye."

The screen went black.

Harlan hoped he could get to Vicky in time. He wished he'd been better to her. He wished he'd never found the box. Tears of helplessness welled in his eyes.

Dave grabbed him by his rain-dampened jacket. "Snap out of it, dude!" He dragged Harlan out of the apartment, locking the door behind them.

"We have to be careful," Dave whispered hoarsely. "Anywhere there's a TV, he can hear us. Probably even zap us from a cable connection, like that movie—" He peered around his feet, looking along the baseboards for outlets. "Okay, looks like we're safe. Here's the plan. We go to Emmerson's place, get him to help us figure out how to beat—"

CLAP!

Harlan and Dave turned to each other, both startled by the sound.

CLAP! CLAP-CLAP!

"What is that?" Harlan asked. The sound made him think of cartoon clams.

CLAPCLAPCLAPCLAPCLAPCLAPCLAP!

"It's coming from the store!" Dave bounded down the stairs. "Dammit, not again!"

"Not again what?" Harlan said, hurrying behind him.

An alarm sounded through the wall.

"I just got robbed last week, man!" Dave shouted over his shoulder, pulling his keys out of his PJs as he pushed through the front door. By the time Harlan got outside, Dave had already unlocked the door and stepped into So Hip. The alarm blared out into the street, cutting through the silence like a sawblade.

Dave cried out in anguish, swallowed by the blare of the alarm. Red light flashed over the darkened interior, throwing long shadows on the walls. Harlan thought it was all a bit much. The alarm likely did a good enough job deterring criminals on its own.

Dave snatched a baseball bat from behind the counter. Harlan barely heard him swearing at the top of his lungs for the intruder to *come out, motherfucker.* The door bumped Harlan in the ass, and he uttered a frightened little yelp, the alarm and lights making him nervous as the door swung shut behind him.

Dave crept toward the shelves, the bat slung against his shoulder. Harlan considered following, and when he'd finally made up his mind to go after his friend, a giant black limb grabbed Dave by the shoulders and picked him off his feet.

Dave's Ugg-booted feet dangled as the monstrous creature lumbered out from the shadows. Harlan saw it in red flashes: a heavy 21" television, one of the old wall monitors that would normally be playing some trashy film when the store was open, rested on the thick, clattering body of a massive humanoid beast made of plastic cassettes, wound together with shiny black sinews of magnetic videotape. The bat fell useless from Dave's hands. On the screen, Funelli's grinning face, bathed in ominous green light, stared directly into the video store owner's soul.

Harlan ducked behind the counter, breathing heavily as the alarm continued to wail. He had to help Dave, but Jack Emmerson's address was paramount. Dave could have been dead already, and Harlan wouldn't have heard his bones crack over the alarm. The little computer on the counter came to life as he reached up to grab the keyboard, bumping the mouse. Praying Funelli's Monster wouldn't notice the light from the monitor—praying the *monitor itself* had no connection to the same connection keeping Funelli alive—Harlan typed EMERSON into the search bar.

No hits.

Items on the counter and in the drawers behind him jittered as the Tape Monster shook the floor.

He tried again with two *S*s, fingers shaking uncontrollably, then again with two *M*s. With a sigh of relief, Harlan read the address that came up. He repeated it aloud several times before creeping up over the top of the counter.

Funelli's Monster held Dave up like a ragdoll to its flickering face, Funelli's teeth gnashing on the screen. Harlan made a decision to distract him, but he worried about Vicky. She was a pawn in all of this, a bargaining chip Funelli could use for Harlan to help him escape from his digital prison. He had to hope Funelli wouldn't harm her until midnight. He had to trust no matter how crazy being stuck in his own private Hell had made him, the director would stick to the logic of his script.

Harlan picked up the computer screen, hesitated briefly, then launched it as hard as he could. It snapped back on its cable and smashed against the front of the counter.

"Hey, Max Headroom!" Harlan shouted as he leaped out from behind the counter, waving this hands. *"C-c-c-come and g-g-g-get me, asshole!"*

The Funelli Monster's TV head twisted in his direction, Funelli's immortal rage visible on the screen.

Fear propelled Harlan toward the door. He came to an abrupt, painful halt against the frame, his conscious mind registering too late the door had opened inward. Funelli's Monster dropped Dave crumpled and unconscious to the floor, and lumbered forward like a massive practical-effect Transformer, its limbs clattering and shimmering in red flashes of black magnetic tape, rattling movies on the shelves.

Harlan fumbled with the door, his back still against it, trying to tear it open without moving closer to the creature's VHS claws. Finally, he managed to edge over far enough to get out of its way, but by then the

Monster was mere feet from him. Funelli's lips twisted into a sinister grin. Harlan yanked futilely on the handle. The director snarled, mere moments from his prey, reaching out with giant black plastic fingers when the cable at the back of his TV head pulled taut, jerking it back.

Funelli uttered a startled, strangled choke before the television tore off its body, smashing on the floor tiles. His face flickered with a buzz of static before the smoldering screen winked out, and the Monster's structure broke apart in a loose twisted heap of videotapes.

Harlan laughed aloud, short of breath. "Dave?" he called over the din. "You okay?"

Dave groaned in reply, rolling over onto a heap of scattered cassettes. "Dude... that thing literally killed my buzz."

The television fell off the wall so quickly Harlan was only able to shout a choked "*Dude!*" before it came crashing down over Dave's shocked face. The screen shattered and the tube exploded. Still plugged in to the wall, electricity jolted Dave's body in a morbid dance to the smell of burning circuitry and cooking flesh.

Police sirens neared, louder than the alarm. Too late to help his friend, Harlan rushed out the door and ran. He knew the writer's address, and it wasn't very far. He just hoped he could reach him in time to end this.

3 – The Writer

JACK EMMERSON LIVED in a crumbling townhouse in the gentrifying warehouse district. Harlan ran the eight blocks from So Hip Video, taking breathers while streetlights changed from red to green, wishing he'd quit smoking years ago and taken up jogging. Midnight loomed like the crescent moon that had parted the clouds above the city streets, flickering in puddles and storefront windows.

Harlan thumbed the doorbell, then knocked without waiting for a response. Jack Emmerson came to the door in a plush gray robe, and blinked out at Harlan. Bald head shimmering under the front light, he scratched his salt-and-pepper beard with the backs of his fingernails and grunted, "Somebody better have died."

Harlan didn't waste time with small talk. He simply showed the man the tape.

"*Dammit,*" Jack Emmerson grumbled, his whole body seeming to sag. "I guess it's worse. Someone *came back* from the dead." He narrowed his eyes, his crinkling face giving lie to the expression *black don't crack*—though to be fair, the man was in his 70s. "Well, you might as well come in, I won't be able to sleep tonight anyway. Not knowing *he's* out there."

Jack's townhouse was neat and clean, a tastefully furnished condo if it was still the 1980s, everything smooth, shiny blacks and whites. A brown wood stereo system with a record player stood alongside retro-futuristic shelves lined with colorful record jackets in the sunken living room. Harlan noticed with surprised relief the writer had no TV.

Jack pushed on the wall near the spiral staircase. A hidden door clicked open to reveal an astonishing array of booze. "Drink?" he asked.

"No thanks, I don't drink."

Jack arched an eyebrow as he poured himself a brandy. "You might want to start."

He stepped down into the sunken area, sat on the arm of a leather sofa, and directed Harlan to the chair. Harlan sat.

"I'm guessing time is of the essence. Nick always was a fan of the ticking clock. *Too much* for my taste, but what do I know, I just wrote the shit."

"Midnight," Harlan nodded.

"And he'll, what? Kill your boyfriend?"

"Girlfriend," Harlan said with a slight frown.

"Sorry. Don't mean to imply you look gay, whatever that means, but being in the business we are I figured I'd shoot for the odds. What are you? Movie critic, wannabe director, what?"

"Just a collector."

"A collector." Jack sipped his liquor thoughtfully. "And where did you find this... invaluable collector's item?"

"I was on my way home in the rain. Vicky and me got in a fight."

"Vicky and *I*."

Harlan gave him a flustered look.

"Sorry. Continue, please."

"We got in a big fight," Harlan said, choking up at the thought of never seeing her again. "I'm pretty sure we're broken up, but anyway... I was hurrying past the old factory in the rain when I saw this box of videotapes—"

Jack held up a hand. "Wait, wait. What factory?"

"The burned-up—" Realization struck him. In all his years passing by the burned-out shell on the way home from Vicky's apartment, he'd never put the two together. Now everything made sense. Somehow, Funelli had made it so the tapes had been out in the rain when Harlan walked past, leaving them as bait for someone who loved old video nasties enough to bring them home, to dry them out and put the tape—the only tape that mattered—into his or her VCR. "On Lexington and Rebar," he finished. "That's Funelli's studio, isn't it? The one that burned down?"

"You catch on quick. So you found the tape, and what? You put it in the tape player."

"Right."

"And when you did, it started to spark. All this blue lightning went just about everywhere, is that right?"

"Right..." Confused, Harlan asked, "How do you know all this, Mr. Emmerson?"

"Jack. And like I said—" He gestured with his fingers, wriggling them on an invisible typewriter, "—I wrote the shit."

"You..." Harlan shook his head in confusion.

Jack cocked his head at an angle, displaying annoyance. "Wrote. The shit. So I guess now we're at the Old Master scene. You've come to me to ask for my help, and that's when Funelli's Tapenstein monster shows up to kill me, and you escape by the skin of your lily-white nuts."

"You wrote all of this...?" Harlan muttered, sinking to the back of the sofa. He'd felt like a man living a nightmare before but the idea of living inside one of Funelli and Emmerson's screenplays made his skin crawl. If this was a Funelli film, they were all doomed. All of them. In Funelli films, things always ended badly for its stars.

"Funelli and I wrote this script while he was filming *NASTiES*," Jack explained. "The concept was Funelli, or a somewhat comically exaggerated version of Funelli, dies in a fire during an occult ritual because he's exactly what his critics have labeled him: he worships demons, he's a maniac, etcetera. Only Funelli's not really dead, he's trapped in a kind of Videolimbo, that's what we called it, where he can control video devices through the cable, basically like that Wes Craven movie with the dude sent to the electric chair."

"*Shocker.*"

"Right, *Shocker*. We called ours *Funelli's Back from the Dead*, sort of a play on the way they always put his name in front of the title because of his popularity: Funelli's *Last Stand*, Funelli's *Lake of the Damned*, Funelli's *Orgy of the Zombies*. Only, as you've probably guessed, the apostrophe wasn't possessive, it's a contraction: *Funelli IS Back from the Dead*. You dig?"

Harlan nodded. "Yeah, I... I do dig. But don't worry, that tape monster thing already showed up at the video store."

Jack chuckled dryly. "You went to a video store. That's clever, I wish I'd thought of that. Not a good idea when you're trying to escape a dead man trapped in a videotape, but as a story point..."

"So this... everything... you've already written it?"

The writer stood, shaking his head. "No. We never finished the script," he said over his shoulder as he moved toward the bar. "See, the fire happened the night we were supposed to work on the denouement, coincidentally." He shrugged. "Or not. A big climactic set piece. Main character figures out Funelli's got his girl trapped in the studio, so he sets out to find her."

"And then?"

"And then nothing, that's all we wrote. See, Nick hated to outline, and I never outlined unless I was getting *paid* to outline..." Jack spilled liquor into his glass. "You see where I'm going with this."

"The future's unwritten."

"That's a tad grandiloquent," Jack said with a shrug. He swigged from the glass, and poured more. "If this were my movie, and I suppose it is, I'd say something like..." He took another swig, lowered his voice an octave, and growled, *"Sounds like we gotta write ourselves a new ending."* Shrugging, he added, "Or something like that."

"I think I'll take that drink," Harlan said.

"I thought you might." Jack returned to the sofa with two glasses and a smirk. Harlan took his and sipped. The alcohol scalded on the way down, and he coughed.

"Bit of a lightweight, huh? Come with me. I've got something to show you."

Harlan followed Jack up the spiral staircase to his bedroom in the loft. He stayed by the stairs while Jack opened the closet, shifted some hangered clothes aside, moved some cardboard boxes behind them, and reached up to a shelf. When Jack returned, he held a pastel turquoise suitcase. He blew dust off it, and tossed it onto the water bed. The mattress rippled as he sat beside it to open the latches. Inside was a small blue-gray typewriter.

"This here's a Smith Corona Super Sterling manual typewriter," Jack said, pitching it like a professional salesman. "Now the purists will tell you, you want a vintage typewriter, you get yourself an Underwood, the kind Hitchcock and Heinlein and Orson Welles used. But for me, it's the Smith Corona. For one thing, I don't have to punch the keys as hard. This baby's smoother than Quiet Storm."

"What's 'quiet storm'?"

"It's a type of music. Now you want my help, kid, then don't interrupt me." He scowled down at the typewriter, seemingly looking for his train of thought. "The other reason I like it is, when I'm in the zone and I'm typing at 100-words a minute, I don't have time to dial back and X-out mistakes. This one self-corrects. Press a single button, it goes back and uses the correction tape to erase the previous letter. Press it again, it gets the one before that. Etcetera. Now that may not sound special to you, with your iPhone and your intelligent TV, but when I was your age *this...*" Lovingly, he removed the typewriter from the case and pushed the carriage return. "This was a godsend."

"I'll take your word for it."

"See, that's the problem with your generation. Always gotta shoot back with some snarky comment, always gotta be smug and look down your nose at the world. *Suspend your disbelief.* It's show business, baby!"

Jack's words, echoing the argument that had started all of this, shamed Harlan. He muttered an apology.

Jack brushed it off. "Forget it. Now we can make this happen, Harlan. We've got little less than two and a half hours to write the third act, and I've written entire films in less. So we bring this baby to the old studio, and we hammer out an ending where you get your girl back, you and I survive, and we send Funelli back to Hell where he belongs."

With a hoarse, triumphant laugh, Jack held out a hand.

"Right on!" Harlan said, inspired by the old writer's speech to slap him five.

Jack scowled down at his palm, and made a sour face, grasping at his lower back with his free hand. "I appreciate the sentiment but I really could use a hand getting up. Waterbeds are great for a man in his twenties, not so much when he's pushing seventy-five."

Discouraged—and even more embarrassed by his potential microaggression—Harlan helped the man to his feet.

4 – The Acolytes of Azathoth

JACK NEVER OUTLINED, but he and Harlan fleshed out a vague plan on the way to the old studio, the typewriter under his arm. He and Funelli had continued making video nasties while small budget auteurs like Soderberg and Tarantino, Smith and Rodriguez ushered in the New Wave of indie cinema in the early-'90s. If Funelli's career hadn't ended in the fire in 1993, he would have likely still been making B-movies today. Jack had seemed fine with retirement, with his dusty old typewriter and his lack of a television, but his eagerness to jump back into writing instead of suggesting Harlan take a walk into traffic spoke of a man who'd denied his true nature far too long.

The writer's bald head shined under the streetlamps, his shoulders slumped, his back hunched with age. Nicolo Funelli, who hadn't aged a day since 1993, had been 44 when his cowboy hat and boots were buried in an otherwise empty casket. Harlan hoped Jack's aged heart could handle whatever insanity Funelli had in store for the two of them.

"Your girl," Jack said, looking back over his shoulder. "Is she strong?"

"Strong?"

"Mentally. What I mean to say is, do you think she'll spring back from this, or will she end up in some nuthouse, blathering on and on about a 'world inside the movies'?"

Harlan thought it over. The idea had never occurred to him, but he supposed if anyone could come out of there unscathed, it was Vicky. "She's stronger than anyone I know," he said. "When my parents died, she got me back on my feet again. Got me a job, helped me settle my parents' estate. If it wasn't for her, I'd probably still be watching old movies on the top-loader VCR in their basement."

"Good. That's good character motivation."

"Speaking of movies, I think we need a video camera," Harlan said, spotting the yellow sign of a pawnshop ahead. "Something to record your ending."

Jack squinted back over his shoulder, considering it briefly before shaking his head. "That's Funelli's business. I'm a writer. I don't direct."

"But if we don't record it, it's just words on paper."

"It's *all* just words on paper, Harlan." He swept an arm out, indicating the totality of creation. "All of this. Now you got a keen sense of story, kid, but as Hitchcock once told me, your pacing is shit. We don't have time to go hunting down a VHS camera, and I'm sure as hell not stepping into a pawnshop likely to be full of TVs and television equipment where our undead Eye-talian friend could easily get the drop on us."

"I'll go in then. This is my movie—my *life*," Harlan corrected himself. "Whatever. Let me take the risk."

Jack's shoulders sagged as he looked back at the yellow storefront windows. "All right. But don't take too long in there, kid, it's nigh on ten o'clock. I'll get started on the script in the interim." He squinted up and down the empty street. "There's a park bench. Meet me over there when you're done."

"Thank you, Jack."

The writer smiled thinly, and shrugged. "Hey, it's what I do."

The bell above the pawnshop door jingled as Harlan stepped in. Jack squinted in at him through the barred windows, and gave him an encouraging nod. Harlan returned it. He watched Jack head across the street before stepping up to the counter.

The proprietor of Jiffy Pawn—or Yiffy Pawn, Harlan wasn't sure, as the *J* looked somewhat like a *Y*—eyed him with suspicion through thick-lensed glasses. Above the man, a sign read **YES! WE HAVE**

CLASSIC ARCAID MACHINES! An array of guns and complicated knives lay behind the counter's barred glass, holding far less potential danger than the black & white security monitor above the clerk's head.

Harlan studied it, making sure the split screen showing the store's exterior and back shelves didn't suddenly switch to Funelli and Emmerson's green-screened *Videolimbo*, as Jack had called it. He watched the old writer shrink in the exterior camera's view before Jack disappeared out of frame.

The proprietor scowled at Harlan. "Can I help you with something, or are you just gonna stand there gawking at my security monitor hoping something good'll come on?"

Harlan snapped out of it and focused on the clerk. The man stood framed by an *X-Files* **THE TRUTH IS OUT THERE** poster tacked-up alongside newspaper clippings about government conspiracies. A laptop lay opened on the counter to a website called *Society of Skeptics*, the post titled: **SPHERICAL EARTH: FACT, OR DISIN-FORMATION?**

"Yes. Sorry," Harlan said, taking it all in. "I need a video camera."

"Uh-huh. Camcorder, SLR, security, or action?"

"No, uh, none of those. I'm looking for an old one."

"I see. Would that be Super-8 or Betamax?"

Harlan shook his head, feeling like Jack had written this man a flimsy bit part, the thankless role of an expendable character created to serve a small story point and then die a very messy death.

I live in a movie now, he thought. Once upon a time it would have been fun to imagine, but with his every move watched by a psychotic deceased director, all he wanted now was for the credits to roll so he could finish his popcorn and go home.

"VHS," he said. "Philips, specifically."

The proprietor blinked at him without expression, his blue-gray eyes magnified to twice their size. "Don't have a Philips. Got a piece of crap RCA handheld in the back, if that's okay. Hasn't worked in ages."

"Could you just check?"

Frowning, the clerk said, "I know my own stock."

"Fine. The RCA is fine."

The bespectacled man unlatched the counter flap and stepped out. He took a step toward the back, then turned and blinked his giant eyes. "You're gonna buy this thing, right? I'm not going all the way back there and rootin' through all that junk just to come back and hear you tell me you don't want it 'cause it's broke?"

Harlan nodded enthusiastically. "I'll buy it. If it works, great. If not..." He shrugged. "And if you can find a tripod for it, I'll buy that too."

Big eyes blinked. "All right then," the proprietor said, and headed into the shelves. His reflection grew in a convex mirror placed strategically in the high far corner, near the darkened storeroom doorway, until he stepped under it and out of view. Harlan looked up at the monitor to see the strange man pass through the door.

Anxious, he checked the time. 9:55. Just over two hours until Funelli had his way with Vicky, no matter what Harlan and Jack did to try and put a stop to it. He wasn't even sure what they were attempting would work. All he could do was trust in Jack's screenplay, and their vague outline.

The image on the screen switched to a room filled with heaps of old junk, where the proprietor seemed to be hunting, moving boxes aside. The other side showed Harlan looking slightly off and to his right. To the left of the monitor, the main camera pointing down at him buzzed, and the picture zoomed in to a tight close-up of his eyes.

A loud electronic *BLAM!* filled them with fear, the sound something like the blast of a Space Rager's laser. The overhead fluorescents flickered as he turned from the monitor toward the once-darkened storage room doorway, flashing now with colorful lights.

"Sir?" Harlan called out.

His gaze fell again on the sign above the counter:

YES! WE HAVE CLASSIC ARCAID MACHINES!

On the security monitor, the proprietor moved cautiously toward the lambent screens of several old arcade games in the back. The other image cut to Jack typing up his screenplay at a park bench under a streetlight. One of the city cameras had linked to the monitor somehow —whether Funelli had done it or the proprietor had hardwired it due to his evident paranoia, Harlan didn't know, but he had a bad feeling this was the scene where he'd have to make a hard choice between saving the writer, and going back in there to find the camera.

"Shit..."

Hoping Jack could take care of himself for a few more minutes, he headed down the long, narrow aisle between shelves of broken dreams and lay-a-ways, guitars, game consoles and jewelry sold for rent and drugs and destination weddings. His reflection warped in the chipped convex mirror as he passed under it looking up, watching for movement at his back. The doorway flashed red, green and blue while the machines blared chiptune music, laser blasts, explosions and revving engines.

"Hello?" Harlan called into the otherwise darkened room.

A crackly 8-bit voice sample replied with deep booming laughter: *"MUHA-HAHA! MUHA-HAHA! MUHA-HAHA!"*

Harlan stepped through the doorway, his skin prickling at the sound. He'd never been big on video games when he was young, but he knew a bad omen when he heard it.

"Hello-ooh!"

"MUHA-HAHA! MUHA-HAHA!"

Dust permeated the air, the shelves jam-packed with old stock. The arcade games stood against the back wall. He recognized *Ninja Gaiden* and *Altered Beast* and *Cruisin' USA* from his infrequent visits to the arcade with friends, the one with the built-in car seat, but the fourth game was one he'd never heard of, something called *Acolytes of Azathoth*. The screen flashed **GAME OVER** again and again above three druids who stood over a man tied to a stone slab. The repetitive laughter came from its speakers: *"MUHA-HAHA!"*

Harlan approached cautiously. "Sir?" The clerk's hand slumped out from the replica car seat. "Are you okay?" he called out over the noise, even though Harlan was fairly certain he wasn't.

He peered over the headrest. The racing game displayed the same image as *Acolytes*: **GAME OVER** flashing above the three dark druids and the man fastened to the round stone altar. Adrenaline burned through his veins. *All of the screens showed the same image.* On the pixe-lated altar, the victim's eyes bulged behind bottle-thick glasses. Dressed in nothing but a pair of boxer shorts, the clerk's hands and feet were tied at four points of a dripping red pentagram, his head resting on the fifth.

"MUHA-HAHA!"

Each druid held a curved blade to their chests. They arced down swiftly in tandem, one blade piercing the man's heart, the second his groin, the third his throat. The middle Acolyte carved off the clerk's head with very little effort. In the driver's seat, the real clerk jittered like a man having a seizure. He uttered a strangled groan seconds before a huge red fountain splattered the screen. Drops spattered Harlan's face and shirt. He cringed at the salty copper tang, recognizing it as blood.

The clerk's severed head dropped onto the gear shift in his lap, and rolled off onto the floor, tacky blood picking up crumbs from the dirty tiles, where it stared wide-eyed and mouth agape at Harlan. On the screens, tinted a slick red, the middle druid held up his prize by the hair, blocky pixel droplets of gore spilling on the stone altar.

Harlan tripped over his own feet and fell hard on his hands and knees, his gorge rising. Before he could choke it back, he puked on the cement floor and into the drain.

"MUHA-HAHA!"

The laughter sounded closer, more human. The arcade machines had projected pixelated holograms of the three dark druids, and as Harlan crabwalked toward the door the images solidified, only their eyes visible in the shadows cast by their hoods, cackling as they raised their daggers, dripping with the pawnshop clerk's blood.

Harlan backed into something metallic and frail. It toppled with a clatter behind him. Glancing back, he found a camera already secured to a small tripod, **VHSmovie** stamped on its side. Rather than bask in his good luck, he snatched it with quivering hands and got to his feet. Steadying himself on the doorjamb, he took one last look at the evil druids before scurrying out into the aisles and running headlong toward the exit.

The bell dinged above the door as Harlan burst out into the street. He turned back, pausing to catch his breath. Jiffy Pawn stood empty, derelict, track lighting flickering. A gray ray of light burst from the security monitor, and the dark druids materialized behind the door.

"Oh, *shit...*"

The Acolytes stepped through the door. The bell dinged.

Harlan turned and ran across the street, shouting for Jack.

"Oh shit!" Jack growled, rising to his feet.

Harlan reached the sidewalk. "That's what I just said!"

"No, you don't understand, kid. Those are the Acolytes of Azathoth. They're the punks Funelli was running with on the night of the fire."

The Acolytes stood in the middle of the road. They peeled back their hoods in tandem. Despite their differences in height, all three wore Funelli's grin, his curled Dali mustache, and gleeful dark brown eyes. A chorus of voices said, "Hello, Jack. Lovely to see you."

"Can't say the feeling's mutual, Nick."

The dark druids shrugged. "You might want to scrap that draft, Jack. It's *boring.*"

Breathing heavily, Jack looked for his pages he'd written in Harlan's absence on the bench. His shoulders further slumped when he saw them in a puddle of brown water, the ink smeared and running. "*Son of a...*" he grunted.

"Midnight approaches, gentlemen," the Funelli Acolytes said playfully. "Release me..." With dramatic sweeping gestures, they added, "Or *everyone dies.*"

The Acolytes vanished in a swirl of mist.

"You all right?" Harlan asked.

The writer nodded a little too emphatically. "Yeah. Let's just get this over with." He lugged his typewriter up under his arm. "I see you found your camera."

"The guy didn't think he had one, either."

Jack narrowed his eyes at him.

"You don't think...?"

"Kid, if he can make *those things* appear out of nowhere, who knows what he can do that we haven't seen yet?"

Harlan nodded gravely. "Well, I guess we'd better do what he says."

"Now hold on, I didn't say that," Jack said bitterly. "This old dog's still got a few tricks up his sleeve. You just wait and see what I've got in store for you. And for *him*. Make me do a rewrite. Son of a bitch ain't even paying me."

Jack loped off down the damp street. Harlan gave one last look at Jiffy Pawn—or Yiffy Pawn—and followed.

5 – Videolimbo

FUNELLI'S OLD STUDIO ran with dripping rain from the gutters and still smelled charred after twenty-three years. The fire department had chained the front doors, but Jack led him down a darkened alleyway that reeked like piss and rotting vegetation. Finally, they arrived at a low window, where Jack pointed to a cinderblock that had come free of the structure and lay broken on the ground.

"Pick that up and throw it through the window."

Harlan heaved the block at the charred window. The muted sound was more like the breakaway glass they used in the movies than the sound of real glass shattering. He supposed it would have lost much of its integrity during the fire, but the thought was cut short as Jack told him to drag a crate under the window.

"You know, for someone who doesn't direct, you're doing a pretty good job bossing me around."

"Don't get lippy, kid. Now help me up."

Jack set down his typewriter and held out a hand, opening and closing it into a fist to get Harlan's attention. Jack grabbed his shoulder, using it to leverage himself up onto the box. He slipped through the window. A clatter of wood and metal arose from the darkened interior.

"You okay in there?"

Harlan peered into the gloomy silence just as Jack rose up from the darkness, startling him. "All good, kid. Just slipped is all. Hand me my typewriter and get your ass in here."

Harlan handed the case through. He passed the camera and tripod through after it, and climbed in. The charred smell was stronger inside, reminding him of the twisted jangle of metal and glass left of the family car after his parents' accident.

"Welcome to The Funhouse," Jack said with a sardonic grin.

Harlan looked around. The second floor sagged, resting hazardously on the burnt matchsticks of support columns. Cobwebs hung in places, broken boards and heaps of crumbled concrete littered the floor, glass and broken tile lay scattered elsewhere. Thieves had torn up the walls where the fire hadn't already destroyed them, and loose pipes and the frayed ends of copper wire stuck out everywhere. He felt the dead cold of this place in his bones, the epitome of every abandoned building in every horror movie and thriller he had ever seen.

"Probably should've brought a flashlight," Jack said.

Harlan tugged his phone from his pocket and punched up the flashlight. Jack sneered at it and headed off in a seemingly random direction. Harlan followed into the darkened recesses of the building, where dripping pipes and creaking floorboards gave the atmosphere a spooky Halloween effects vibe. The beam of his flashlight caught a fat, wet rat as it squeezed into a hole in the wall.

"Try not to step on any nails," Jack warned. "Probably get tetanus just from breathing in here."

A moment later the writer stopped in a nondescript corner. He genuflected to right an old plastic school desk and chair combo. Most of the plastic had melted, but the metal frame and pressed wood tabletop remained intact. "This is where the magic happened," he grunted, and set the typewriter up on the lopsided desk. He sat down in front of it, cracking his knuckles.

Harlan set the tripod up in front of the distinctive sloped green screen wall. Now what? "Need any inspiration?" he asked.

Jack glared back over his shoulder. "I need you to be quiet. Only thing I hate more than rewrites is a producer who thinks he's creative."

Harlan shut his mouth.

The writer ran a sheet of paper through the roller and began to type. Keystrokes echoed through the dripping ruin. The old man wrote seemingly in a trance state. Harlan crept up behind him so as not to disturb him and read over his shoulder.

<u>ACT III</u>

```
FADE IN:

INT. FUNELLI'S STUDIO - NIGHT

The blackened interior practically drips smoke as
JACK and THE KID enter. The Wordslinger swings his
trusty typewriter onto a beaten-up desk.

                    JACK
          This is where the magic happens.

JACK sits and rattles out a symphony on the old Corona.
His words shake soot off the walls and dripping pipes,
scaring rats from their nests and spiders from their
webs. JACK knows this tune by heart. He smiles as the
words flow out of him, from FADE IN to—
```

HARLAN STEPPED AWAY from the typewriter and began to pace like an imprisoned animal. Jack kept on typing, tearing out sheets of paper as he finished them, blowing on them to dry the ink, and laying them face down on the table beside the typewriter. He had a good four or five pages written by 11:30, and when Harlan looked over his shoulder again, Jack banged out the words

```
                                        FADE OUT.
```

THE OLD HACK cracked his knuckles and leaned back in the chair, stretching out his arms and wriggling his fingers. "Done. *Man*, I wish I had a stiff drink."

"Can I read it?"

"What good is a script if no one reads it?" He tapped the pages on the desk to straighten them, and handed them over his shoulder to Harlan.

Harlan read.

```
While JACK typed, he began to notice the music of the
old place. Pipes DRIPPED at a certain pitch. Floors
CREAKED at another. The WIND howled through cracks
and splits in the exterior walls—
```

A FETID GUST howled through the guts of the building. Harlan looked up, a chill running through him—whether from the coincidence or the howling of the wind, he wasn't sure, but anxiety leaned toward the former.

```
THE KID paced behind him, reading over his shoulder
and checking his watch every so often.

As THE KID remembers his girl, VICKY, we see her
tied to the dentist chair. Terror-stricken eyes.

FUNELLI himself paces, a caged tiger. His ACOLYTE
starts up the DRILL. Its BUZZ catches her attention.
The ACOLYTE grins at her from the shadow under his hood.

The CAMERA's red record light flashes, and VICKY turns
her terror toward the screen.

We PULL BACK to reveal the tiny B&W SCREEN of the VHS
camera.

THE KID watches the scene through the viewfinder.
```

HARLAN PUT a smoke in his mouth and lit it. He wandered over to the old camera and bent to peek at the viewfinder. The screen was black. He thumbed the ON button, hoping it still had some juice in it.

The camera buzzed to life. He peered through the viewfinder. The lens struggled to focus on the wall in the gloom.

"What are you doing?"

"Testing a theory."

"Kid, I don't know what you think is gonna happen. This ain't magic. This ain't the movies. This is real life."

"Now who's cynical? Whatever happened to 'suspend your disbelief'?"

"Look, I wrote you your happy ending. That's what you wanted, isn't it?"

"I want Vicky back!" Harlan spat. "I don't need more fantasy *bullshit*. I wanted you to *end this*!"

Jack's shoulders sagged as he sighed. "Kid... I'm just a writer. And not a very good one, if you ask the critics."

"Then *quiet on set*," Harlan said, and Jack's mouth shut audibly.

The lens autofocused.

Nothing.

Harlan stepped back, disheartened. "It's not working."

"You know, I've found sometimes it helps if you read back what you wrote aloud. Get back into the flow of the story."

Harlan nodded. He picked up the script and found his place. "Pull back to reveal the tiny black and white screen. The Kid watches the scene through the viewfinder. The tape whirs as it records—*Records*," he repeated. "That's it!"

Harlan opened the tape deck. He wadded up some foil from the cigarette package and jammed it into the empty write-protection slot in the *NASTiES* cassette. He inserted the tape, and pressed **RECORD**.

00:00:00... 00:00:01... 00:00:02...

"Funelli shoots the scene over-the-shoulder," Harlan read, "prancing around like a madman. His Acolyte steps closer with the whirring drill—"

Slowly, a blurry image formed in the viewfinder. Dark, ghostly shapes moved on the tiny monitor. Harlan squinted to bring them into focus. The lens whirred, twisting and turning, attempting to focus on the imaginary images.

"It's working," Jack stage-whispered. "Jesus, kid, it's *working*!"

Harlan looked up from the screen, expecting to see vague outlines, mere ghosts. But the scene before him solidified. Vicky lay in the dental chair, eyes wide and jaw tight in terror as the Acolyte stood near with a laser blaster. Funelli, oblivious to Harlan and Jack's presence in the studio, shot the scene over her shoulder, getting her POV as the weapon reached her open mouth. It was as like watching the scene through two-way glass, a window into an alternate dimension or, he supposed, from the undamaged appearance of the green screen area, a different time.

The fear on Vicky's face physically hurt his heart. His stupid obsession with old movies had gotten her into this mess, had almost gotten her killed. He'd taken their relationship for granted. If the both of them managed to make it out alive, he promised himself he wouldn't pressure her or trick her into taking him back, like he'd done before. He would let her decide whether his actions tonight merited forgiveness.

He looked at his phone. 11:48. Still time to make things right.

"*CUT!*" Harlan yelled.

The players froze, even Funelli. Tracking lines crackled up Funelli's slim, black-clad frame as Harlan stepped around the camera and reached out to touch them.

"Be careful," Jack said, rising from the desk.

"The Kid—*Harlan*," he corrected himself, "approached the scene cautiously."

He cast the script aside, no longer needing it. He'd seen enough movies to know what happened next. Pages fluttered to the grimy floor.

"Aww, kid," Jack said glumly. "Those were decent words."

"I'm sorry, Jack, but it needs a rewrite," Harlan said, moving forward. "Harlan approached the scene cautiously," he continued, "holding out his hand toward the Acolyte. A crackle of video noise rippled outward from his touch like a splash in a pond as Harlan gripped the Acolyte's weapon..."

The tips of his fingers vibrated with static electricity as he grabbed the Acolytes pale fingers and peeled them back. Even from an arm's length away all Harlan could see of its face beneath the hood were two blazing white eyes. The Acolyte flickered, like the beam of a dying flashlight. Harlan tore the weapon from the frozen fingers and aimed.

The trigger pulled easily. A green beam sputtered from the barrel and struck the Acolyte in the blink of an eye. The hood burst into flames in the instant before its head exploded, sending microwaved chunks of skull and gray matter and boiled blood every which way.

"Jesus, kid!" Jack groaned, wiping a hot chunk of earlobe from his shirt.

"Sorry." Sucking in a deep, ragged breath, Harlan aimed the laser blaster at the director. "Harlan realized these images couldn't harm him. He stood before Funelli, his former hero, ready to send him back to Videolimbo..."

Funelli came to life with sudden ferocity, swinging the video camera at Harlan's face. It struck his jaw, snapping his head back. He dropped the blaster, tasting blood. The director cast the broken camera aside and grabbed Harlan's wrist, twisting it behind his back. Harlan reached behind himself, fingers grasping for purchase. He managed to knock Funelli's Stetson from his head, revealing the scaled, bleeding flesh beneath.

"*You should not have fucked with me, Harlan.*" Harlan felt the director's hot breath on his ear as the man shoved him toward Vicky. He struggled to raise his head from between Vicky's breasts, as much as he longed to be there, while the director scrabbled with the instruments on the table. They settled on the scraper, and grasped it in a tight fist.

"*The director is always right!*" Funelli snarled.

Harlan caught a blur of movement in the small mouth mirror. Funelli's grip loosened with a loud jangle of metal coils and springs. He let out a cry of anguish, and Harlan sprawled over Vicky's unmoving legs. He rolled over in time to see Funelli raise a hand to protect himself from another attack.

"Eat my words, asshole!" Jack quipped, bringing the typewriter down on Funelli's already split skull. The director dropped to his knees. Blood spilled down his face, and he blinked twice in a daze. Then he fell sideways, raising a cloud of dust on the floor.

"Untie her," Jack ordered. "Quick!"

Harlan bent behind the chair, found the knot, and began working at it.

Funelli groaned. He tried to push himself up, and Jack kicked him back down. "That's for letting actors adlib over my dialogue," he growled, and kicked the dead man in the ribs. "And that's for ruining my career!"

Harlan worked the ropes free, but his delight was short-lived. He shook Vicky. Her body slumped lifelessly in the chair, teeth clacking together. "She's not moving..."

"You're the director," Jack said, panting over the broken typewriter. "Say the magic word."

Harlan couldn't seem to think beyond fear. He shook her again. Her dead stare jumpstarted his mind.

"Action!" he cried.

Vicky sprung from the chair and threw her arms over his shoulders, kissing his cheeks and his dry, cracked lips, moistening them with her vanilla lip balm. Harlan laughed and embraced her. He'd never liked vanilla before, but now it smelled like heaven.

"I love you," she said between kisses.

"I love you, too," he said, kissing her back, not caring that it hurt his injured jaw and lip. "Now let's get out of here before—"

BEEP! BEEP! BEEP! BEEP!

The red record light flashed. Out of tape. Harlan wasn't sure what would happen, but he squeezed Vicky as tight as he could, worried she would disappear again, sucked into the void.

The scene crackled and disappeared around them. He held her, closing his eyes tight, feeling her blood pulse against his neck. The camera stopped whirring. Jack had stopped gasping for breath. Even the wind had stopped.

Harlan opened his eyes.

Funelli's scene had vanished. No more dentist's office. No more *Funelli*. Harlan spun them around. Vicky's eyes widened as she came to the same conclusion.

The camera was gone. Jack was gone. All that remained was the damaged typewriter lying in the dust and debris.

"Oh no..." He let her go, running a hand through his hair. "*Shit shit shit!*"

"What?" she said. "What happened?"

"We're *trapped* in here! He got out!"

"*Trapped?*"

Harlan stepped up to the spot where the tripod had left marks in the dust. "Jack! *Jack! Action! ACTION!*"

The echo of his voice filled the silence.

"What do you mean we're trapped, Harlan? Trapped *where?*"

Harlan slumped down on the floor. "*Videolimbo,*" he panted. Frustration welled up in his throat, and he let his tears fall in the dust.

6 – A World Inside the Movies

HARLAN'S PARENTS DIED the year he'd headed off to film school. After hearing the terrible news of their car crash he'd dropped out, intending to take care of legal issues and clean up his childhood home to put on the market. What he'd done instead was sit in the basement his folks had converted into his bedroom and watched hours and hours of bad horror movies. He didn't bathe. He rarely ate. He'd just watched, remembering those long-ago trips to the video store, staring up in childish delight at all the exciting movie covers on the shelves.

Some good came of that time. He'd bumped into Vicky, an old friend from high school, and she'd helped him through his grief, lifting the dark fog of depression and pessimism that had fallen over his life since a young mother paying too much attention to the kids movie playing on the dashboard DVD player had T-boned Tom and Judy Wallis's hatchback on their way home from the movies.

Life isn't all horror and darkness, she'd told him, the night she'd first brought him to her bed. *There's paradise, too, if you want it.*

Somewhere along the line he'd forgotten that. Years of frittering away the hours behind a computer instead of working at his passion had worn down the magic of that night until nothing remained of it. Instead of being appreciative, he'd grown to resent her not just for getting him the job, but for letting him keep it now that she was effectively his employer. A part of him had thought of her as his jailor.

As they looked over the vast, empty wasteland beyond the crumbling walls of Funelli's studio, Vicky said, "Remember when you wanted to be the next great director?"

The dream was a bitter reminder of his failure. There'd always been an excuse not to try: he'd never had the time, he'd never had the money, he didn't have enough connections, the gates had been closed to him. But the truth was he'd been scared to put himself out there. He'd been too scared to take a risk.

"It was a stupid dream," he said.

"No, it wasn't. You proved it here, tonight." She left him ruminating that while she wandered back into the burned husk. When she returned, she carried Jack's typewriter with her.

"It's broken," he said.

"It's not too bad," Vicky told him, holding it up for him to see. "It just needs a little TLC."

"Don't we all."

Harlan spent the following hour working on the machine, setting coils and springs back into place, and returning the carriage to its cradle. When he'd finished, and all it missed of its former glory was the *U* key, he sat cross-legged in the dust, rolled a sheet of paper through, and began to type:

```
INT: F NELLI'S WAREHO SE - PERMANENT DARK

Harlan and Vicky stood side-by-side for a long beat,
taking one last look o t the door at the wastelands of
Jack's Videolimbo. Finally, Vicky t rned to him.

                    VICKY
          It's time to go.

Harlan nodded. He sat in front of Jack's typewriter and
rattled the keys.

O tside the light began to change, shifting from deep
orange to bright, s nny yellow.

                    VICKY
          Hon...? It's working!

Harlan typed in a fl rry. He saw a beach. A vast, blue
ocean. Palm trees. A cabana, stocked with everything
they'd ever wanted.
```

"HON...?" Vicky said. "It's *working*!"

Harlan stopped typing. He looked from the same words he'd typed to Vicky, who stood in the sun. *Coincidence*, he thought, and shook off the idea. He stood up to meet her at the door.

Outside a white sand beach stretched for miles in either direction. Vicky slipped her arm around his waist. She looked up at him and smiled.

He supposed he owed his good fortune to Funelli. The man had given them an ending he could have never predicted.

7 – Funelli's Revenge

HARLAN AND VICKY stayed on the beach for days, bathing themselves in the ocean, eating fruit from the trees, consuming a self-replenishing stock of cold beers and exotic food from the fridge in the small cabana. Vicky had been right. Life could be paradise, if they wanted it.

On the third perfect day, while they lay tanning under another perfectly unblemished blue sky, a small black and white television appeared between them and the beach. All dials and rabbit ears, it rested on a rickety-looking stand.

"Vick...?"

"Mmm?" she said, rolling over from tanning her back. She sat up abruptly, covering her breasts with an arm.

The TV flickered on.

"*Oh thank God,*" Jack said, peering at them through the screen. "Dr. Saunders, I see them!"

"Jack?"

Dr. Saunders appeared beside the writer, cramming into frame. She wore her graying dark hair in a bun, and squinted through her cat's eye glasses. Harlan recognized her as the film scholar who'd done several documentaries on the video nasties craze, and Funelli in particular.

"Where are they?" she asked Jack. "Is this your 'Videolimbo'?"

"I don't know where the hell they are," Jack replied. Tiny screams rose from the speakers. "Harlan, listen to me. Funelli's gotten *loose*. He's taken over *everything*. First he made them zombies, the ones who'd been watching when his broadcast went out on all the channels, *all over the goddamn world...*"

An explosion rocked the image, followed by more screams. A fireball erupted behind Dr. Saunders and Jack, who stumbled out of view as the window shattered inward and a rain of miscellaneous body parts thudded and squelched around them.

After considerable grunting, Jack stood the camera back up with agony in his tired eyes. Behind him, blurs of terrified people scurried past the window. For a moment Harlan was sure he saw giant squirming tentacles probing the debris in the background but the picture flickered to white noise and when the image returned they were gone.

"Harlan, please... we *need* you."

"*You're wasting time,*" Dr. Saunders snapped as she moved into shot. "Mr. Wallis, we need your assistance. Millions of people are going to die if you don't help us soon."

Harlan turned to Vicky. She watched the television impassively, as if she'd seen it all before. "What do you think?" he asked her.

Vicky turned to him. "What do *I* think?" A slow smile crept onto her face. "I think it's a repeat."

Jack's face crumpled. "No, Harlan..."

Harlan stood up, feeling the hot sand between his toes as he sauntered toward the television stand.

"Harlan, please don't do this. You've got to help us, dammit!"

Dr. Saunders shook her head. "It's no use."

"*You have to help us!*" Jack cried.

"I'm sorry, Jack."

Harlan reached out and turned off the TV.

In Every Dark
Corner

Published 2020

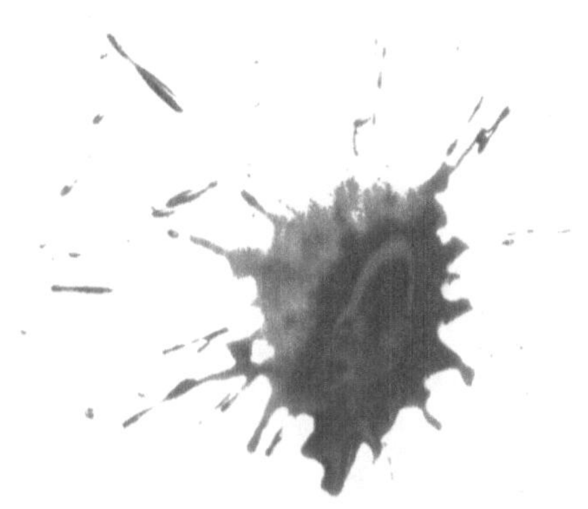

HEAD

Traeger tipped the driver and stepped out of the running courtesy car. He slung his overnight bag onto his shoulder to avoid eye contact as he passed a pair of Hare Krishnas offering their limp colorful flowers for a handful of change, and lugged the bowling bag to the airport doors. Lighting his last Chesterfield—Bogart's brand of choice—he took a drag as the building's air conditioning began to cool his face. The Big Apple in August was hot enough to fill a pie and Traeger welcomed the luxury.

Traffic had been murder and he was already running a bit late. He sidestepped a bank of life insurance kiosks inside but stopped briefly to pick up another package of Chesterfields from the cigarette machine for the flight. When he reached his gate, passengers had already begun boarding. The plane departed in twenty minutes.

Trips like this were typical in Traeger's line of work: a quick job, an overnight stay in some fleabag airport hotel with a coin-operated bed, jet back home in the morning. Often—like today—he would return with a souvenir in his overnight bag. He'd never check the bag, would always carry it onboard. After the latest unaccompanied suitcase bombings, Traeger suspected baggage handlers would be checking for explosives without permission.

Nobody ever gave him trouble at the gate, and he expected today to be no different. Still, it was a big risk, what he had in the bowling bag. Far riskier than the usual drugs, money or stolen items. How could he possibly explain the severed head of a notorious union boss, mummy-wrapped in tea towels and packing tape where the bowling ball should be?

The agent took his ticket and Traeger flashed his best I'm-a-normal-businessman's smile. He was still sweating from the drive over. He felt it on his brow and under his arms—he was practically swimming in his underpants. The AC unit in his hotel room had been on the fritz and the moment he'd stepped out of the shower he'd accumulated a fresh layer of perspiration. Under normal circumstances conspicuous sweating might draw suspicion. August in New York in the midst of a heatwave and even the ticket agent had noticeable stains under the arms of her blouse.

She returned his smile and ticket, gave his bags a quick, dismissive look and ushered him through.

As he descended the escalator to the runways a couple of air marshals stepped in from below. Heat from the tarmac blew in behind them like air from a cheap hotel hair dryer. His pulse, normally as perfectly timed as a Buddy Rich drum riff, suffered a momentary blip as their paths crossed. They returned the nod he offered.

A sweaty gym sock of muggy heat slapped him in the face when he stepped outside. Christ, he was glad to be getting out of this toxic waste dump of a city! The DC-10 pilot greeted a few stragglers climbing the stairs, mostly men in tweed or plaid suit jackets and pleated pants. A couple of black men loaded the remaining few pieces of luggage into the cargo hold, laughing and making easy jive talk. Elsewhere, mechanics worked on the underside of a 727. The buzz of an air wrench gave way to the shriek of a jet engine, and Traeger shaded his eyes against the sun to look out at the runway.

A big Concorde had reached takeoff speed and its tapered nose lifted off the ground.

Traeger blew an impressed whistle. He'd been fascinated by air travel since he was about six or seven. Gigantic hunks of metal hurtling themselves into the air, defying the laws of nature.

Back then, he'd been partial to Fokkers and Japanese Zeroes, the Supermarine Spitfire. These days it was the Concorde, for its impressive speed and sleek body. He hadn't had the opportunity to fly on one yet but one day he wanted to take the supersonic flight from New York to London. His job allowed no time for it, so it remained a retirement goal.

Unfortunately, retirement was looking less and less likely. These days hungry young kids willing to do the job for peanuts gobbled up all the smaller jobs that had kept Traeger afloat between larger paydays like this one. The Company trusted him with high-profile gigs now but how long would that last into his twilight years? Who would trust a contractor who dribbled while tying his sneakers?

Traeger dropped his cigarette on the tarmac among several discarded butts from other passengers and crushed it under the sole of a tassel loafer. Either the heat or the nicotine was starting to make him feel loopy. His sweat-slick palms slipped on the handrail as he pulled himself eagerly up the airstairs.

The pilot welcomed him and nodded toward the bowling bag. "What do you bowl? Ten-pin or five?"

Traeger sputtered. He didn't bowl at all but the pretense was important. "I haven't bowled five-pin since my eighth birthday, Cap."

"Good man," the pilot said. He snapped Traeger a salute. "Welcome aboard."

Traeger slipped into the cool, recycled atmosphere of the aircraft. Stewardesses were already slipping meal trays onto a cart. He winked at the busty older redhead. He would have preferred joining the Mile-High Club with the younger brunette but she didn't even glance in his direction. Probably for the best. Mixing business with pleasure was never wise, particularly 20,000 feet in the air.

"Could either of you lovely ladies bring me a boilermaker when you get a chance? I'm in B-15."

The brunette's eyes narrowed ever so slightly as she glanced at her partner. Even though the redhead smiled like she'd remember his order, Traeger was sure he'd have to remind her when they came around with the food.

The drink was inconsequential. What mattered again was the pretense. Act like a salesman, slightly aggressive but not disruptive.

These women expected a man like him to flirt. The pilot expected small talk. Not living up to these expectations was likelier to draw suspicion.

Traeger made his way to the middle of the plane, heading down the aisle to the left. He'd asked to be seated in the aisle, close to the wing. He liked to watch the flaps lower and rise, to see the ailerons vibrate from atmospheric pressure and watch the flow of air and cloud ripple over the top of the wing. It also gave him control of the overhead compartments, where he would store his overnight bag.

The plane was mostly full. Traeger passed three men sitting in the middle seats, all dressed in similar plaid suit jackets, a style he wished had died with the '70s, along with disco and casual cocaine use. In the row behind them sat an elderly lady with an oxygen tank, and a beleaguered-looking woman who could have been her much younger twin. Her young son flew a toy airplane over the back of his seat, reminding Traeger of himself when he was a boy. He had to resist the urge to tousle the kid's hair.

He stopped and waited for a portly bald man with beady dark eyes and large features to shove a suitcase into the overheads a row up from B. The guy made him think of Alfred Hitchcock in the old TV series. Hitch twisted and turned the suitcase several times, trying to cram a circular peg in a square hole. Out of patience, Traeger grabbed the bag and managed to fit it in lengthwise.

"Thanks," Hitch said, giving Traeger a brief once-over.

"No problem."

The man wedged into his row and began the process again, trying to fit his girthy hips into the narrow seat. Traeger moved on indifferently. He opened the overhead above his seat, found it empty but for a brown leather duffel and slipped his overnight bag in alongside it.

He sat down beside a black man in a three-piece suit, the jacket folded over his lap. The man looked up from an inflight magazine and smiled as Traeger tucked the bowling bag between his knees.

"No room in the overheads?" the man asked.

"Huh?"

The man gestured toward Traeger's bag.

"Oh. It's my medications."

"Yeah? I'm a diabetic. Got to prick my finger every few hours, check my glucose levels. Pain in my ass."

"You'd think it'd be a pain in your finger."

The man chuckled. Stuck out a hand. "Name's Voss. Henry Voss."

Traeger eyed the hand a moment, looking for pricks—reluctant to become accidental blood brothers with a stranger. He shook it. "Dennis Traeger."

"Good to meet you, Dennis Traeger. What business are you in, you don't mind me asking?"

"Insurance," Traeger replied, his go-to for derailing casual conversation. "Life, mostly. Some incidentals."

"You don't say." Henry Voss suddenly seemed very eager to return to the magazine. He pointed to a full-page ad, a well-dressed white couple in luxuriant, roomy airplane seats. The woman had a portable computer on the tabletop and the man seemed to be dictating to her while an attractive stewardess served champagne. The caption said *Welcome to the New Business Class*. "Is she supposed to be his wife or his secretary, you think?" Voss asked.

Traeger chuckled. "Does that look like the face of a guy who's getting laid? Gotta be his wife."

Voss laughed. Traeger lit a cigarette. He offered the pack to Voss, who shook his head.

"I quit. Doctor said it was bad for me, 'cause of the diabetes. You believe that?"

"The wonders of modern medicine." Traeger exhaled a fragrant cloud. "Christ, I don't know what I'd do if I couldn't smoke!"

"Calms the nerves," Voss said with a nod. "You know, Rod Serling smoked Chesterfields."

"Rod Serling? The actor?"

Voss smiled patiently, shaking his head. "You know the show *Twilight Zone*." He sang the theme, "Neener neener, neener neener."

"I'm not much for sci-fi. Listen, I'm gonna get some shut-eye—"

Voss held up a hand. "Say no more. I've gotta get caught up on my reading anyhow." He flipped a page to a piece about the Challenger space shuttle. "Hey, look at that. First woman in space. Only a matter of time before they put a black man up there, huh?"

"I think there's a colored—I mean a black guy—on the next launch."

"Oh yeah?" Voss smiled. "A brother in space. How about that?"

Voss returned to the article. Satisfied he would no longer be interrupted, Traeger leaned against the headrest and closed his eyes. A moment later the captain came on announcing the flight was about to take off. Five minutes later, they were in the air.

TRAEGER WOKE to a muddled voice whispering in his ear.

The plane hit turbulence and he jolted upright, worried about the bowling bag. It was still in his lap, still zipped. He breathed a sigh of relief and peered out he window. Dark already. He must have nodded off and slept right through dinner and drink service. His neck was stiff and he felt groggy enough to fall back to sleep.

He studied his seatmate, Voss, who lay with his head against his suit jacket pressed up against the wall and his eyes closed. Guy didn't even need a pillow, with his hairstyle—what did you call it? An Afro, that was it.

"Thought you got away with it, huh?"

Traeger startled at the voice. His seatmate's lips hadn't moved, though it was difficult to be sure in the dim light. He stared at Voss a long moment before deciding it couldn't have been him, even if the man was a trained ventriloquist. The shallow, steady breathing indicated sleep. To his left was a young couple. The guy was listening to music on a blue Walkman, staring at the back of the seat in front of him and bobbing his head. Traeger heard a vague tinny sound from the kid's goofy-looking headphones. The girl was reading a paperback copy of *Valley of the Dolls* with the overhead light on.

"Down here, asshole," the grim voice said from his lap.

Despite his better judgment, Traeger looked down. Somehow, the voice had come from between his legs—or, more accurately, from the head inside the bowling bag. From that goddamn commie union boss "Holy" Joe Hillier. From the head that had been until quite recently still attached to its body.

I'm still asleep, Traeger thought. *I'm having a nightmare.*

"*You're* having a nightmare?" Holy Joe said, his voice slightly muffled from within the leather bag. "I'm the one trapped in the dark. Smells like rental shoes and friggin' Hi Karate in here, you scum-sucking prick."

Traeger covered the bag with his jacket, looking around to see if anyone had heard. Of course, no one had. He might not have been dreaming but he was certain Hillier's voice was a product of his imagination. Which meant he'd lost his damn marbles.

"*Non compos mentis,*" Hillier agreed. "You ain't just lost your marbles, pal. You lost the whole stinkin' bag!"

Traeger stood abruptly, clutching the bag to his chest in an effort to keep the mouthy head quiet. The plane shuddered again, throwing him into the seat ahead. The guy who looked like Alfred Hitchcock glanced up with a scowl from a newspaper crossword he was filling in with a fountain pen in neat capital letters. Traeger apologized hurriedly and carried on to the restrooms, hoping like hell they were unoccupied.

The redhead stewardess stood up from the jump seat as he approached the restrooms. "Sir, we're experiencing turbulence, please return to your—"

"Urgent business," he said, tearing open the restroom door. He plopped down on the toilet seat lid, pulled the door shut and locked it. "Shit, shit, shit! Get yourself together, man."

He felt himself beginning to hyperventilate, sweating again despite coolness of the aircraft's interior. He heard the stewardesses discussing him behind the door, their sibilant whispers like fighting snakes.

"Yeah, get it together," Hillier said, making Traeger jump. "Wish I could do that. But I can't, 'cause you cut off my friggin' head and dumped my stiff in the East River!"

Shrieking like a sewer rat, Traeger cast the bag onto the sink and stared at it in the mirror. "You're not real," he said.

"Oh, I'm real," Hillier said. "I'm super-duper extra-primo real, my friend. And those folks out there, they're gonna start to notice me real soon. Go on and open up the bag, you don't believe me."

Traeger eyed the sealed zipper. He wouldn't entertain the thought. If he unzipped the bag he'd be giving himself over to his delusion. That way lay madness.

But if Hillier was right, if the tape had split and the towels had slipped off... if the head started to *stink*...

Christ! He had to know.

Slowly, Traeger stood and leaned over the sink. His reflection looked ghoulish under the overhead light: long shadows hooding his sunken eyes, salt-and-pepper five-o'clock shadow on his sharp cheekbones and chin. He unzipped the bag and drew it open. The pungent smell struck him immediately and he reeled back in disgust before peering down into the dark crevasse.

Hillier's head lay in an unholy halo of soiled tea towels, torn packing tape, cauliflower ears, and shaggy, sandy-blond hair flecked with blood. His neck had been severed at a clean angle just below his stubbly double chin, a wound Traeger had cauterized with the hotel iron to prevent blood from seeping into the bag during the flight.

The corpse's eyes snapped open.

Traeger dropped the bag in horror, staggering back until his calves struck the toilet. He plopped back down on the seat, his teeth clattering together painfully.

Holy Joe spat a strip of shredded tape and said, "Told ya."

"You can't talk," Traeger said.

"Tell it to your shrink."

Traeger shook his head. "I've lost my goddamn mind."

"Not yet, you haven't."

"Shhhh!" Traeger pressed the heels of his palms against his eyes until he saw stars. "You need to shut up."

"You can't hide from your conscience, Traeger. And you can't hide me in here much longer, either. I hate to admit it, but I am *fragrant*. They're gonna catch a whiff of me soon, like a ripe gorgonzola, and when they do, you're going down for a long time, believe you me. Head in a bag? You're looking at life in prison, that's if you're lucky—"

Traeger stood. He grabbed the cannister of lemon-scented disinfectant spray from the sink.

"Hey now wait a minute, pal—"

He pressed the trigger and emptied the contents of the cannister into the bag, ozone layer be damned.

"You think that's gonna shut me up?"

But it did. Hillier began to cough and spit and after a few seconds he fell silent. Traeger peered down at the head, now glistening with a thick layer of sticky, lemon-stinking deodorizer. The eyes were shut and the mouth closed the way they had been before he'd covered the head in rags.

Had he imagined it all?

A loud knock on the door startled him. He called out, "What?" trying to sound as calm as possible and failing miserably.

"Sir, the pilot has asked that you please return to your seat immediately."

The other stewardess this time, not the redhead. She sounded beyond aggravation.

"Much as I would love to, this one's gonna be a double-flusher, I think."

He could practically hear the woman cringe behind the door. He chuckled at the thought before Hillier suddenly began shouting: "*Help! Help! This psycho chopped my head off and stuffed me in a bowling bag!*"

Traeger zipped up the bag with a startled yelp and Hillier cackled with laughter. Desperate, Traeger swung the bag over the toilet, raised the lid and peered into the bowl.

"You wouldn't dare," Hillier said, apparently able to read his mind.

"I would!" Traeger shot back. But the pipe was only a few inches in diameter, and even if he could fit Hillier's fat head through the hole, he'd be returning home without his cargo. The Company would kill him for much less. Botching a high-profile job like this, Mr. Redman might even do it himself, with his bare hands.

There was only one option. He stared at the hinged fold in the door, reluctant to go back out there with the chatterbox severed head in his bag. How long could he stand listening to the damned thing? Judging by the time on his watch there was just over three hours left until they reached LAX. Three hours. Christ.

"Maybe you'll get the chair," Hillier suggested. "I guess it depends which state they arrest you in, huh? Hey, that reminds me of an old joke: if a plane crashes on the border between the U.S. and Canada, where do they bury the survivors?"

Ignoring him, Traeger kicked off his right loafer and slipped off the sock. Before Hillier could protest he crammed the sweaty thing into the man's fat gob. Quickly, he folded the tea towels back over Hiller's eyes and mouth and did his best to salvage the packing tape, sealing it with scraps. When he was satisfied with the job he zipped up the bag, pulled the latch from Occupied red to Vacant green, and drew open the door. The brunette stewardess rose from the jump seat with her eyebrows screwed together.

"I wouldn't go in there for a bit," Traeger said, pulling the door shut behind him. The stewardess made a sour face, and Traeger turned toward face cabin. He seemed to be free and clear, for the moment. Could he make it to his seat without incriminating himself further?

"Nowhere!" came Hillier's muffled punchline. "They don't bury survivors! You geddit?"

The plane hit turbulence and Traeger braced against the wall. The stewardess returned to her seat beside her partner, giving him a look like he'd just trailed out a cloud of shit from the can while Hillier laughed uproariously. Traeger clutched the bag close to his chest. The women eyed it with suspicion.

"I still want that boilermaker," Traeger snapped. He could feel them watching as he hurried back down the aisle. Hitchcock's lookalike had stopped filling in the crossword to goggle at him. Traeger flashed the man something between a snarl and a grin and glanced at the puzzle. He startled. The man had filled the word HEAD in the horizontal and the vertical. Had Hitch seen inside the bag somehow? Could he *smell* it? Traeger couldn't be sure but he thought so.

He hurried past and opened the overhead. The plane seemed to drop a frightening distance before steadying again and he fumbled and nearly dropped the bag. His hip struck the seat in front of him and Hitch looked up again with a pouty scowl. Traeger stuffed the bowling bag—*"Don't put me in there in the dark, c'mon, be a pal!"* the head pleaded—into the bin, slammed the door closed and dropped into his seat with a sigh.

"Feeling okay?"

Traeger turned his head. Voss was eyeing him cautiously.

"I'm fine, thanks."

"Took your meds, did you?"

Who the hell did this guy think he was? "That's right," Traeger snapped.

"What's your ailment, you don't mind me asking?"

Traeger gave the man an aggrieved look. "Mister, you don't wanna know."

Voss nodded. "Okay. That's fair." He leaned back against the headrest. "You know, I'm a psychologist." He turned to Traeger with a grin. "I know what you're thinking. You're thinking the average white man'd have to be really messed up to see a black psychologist. But the people I see don't have much of a choice. I'm a forensic psychologist. Most of my patients, if you could call them that, are either dead or in prison."

"Is that right?" Traeger said. The man's voice was calming. At least he didn't have to listen to that damned head anymore.

"Uh-huh," Voss said. "So I know the look."

Traeger turned so he was fully facing the man, intrigued. "What look is that?"

"The look of a man walking a tightrope between sanity and the abyss."

Above their heads, Hillier began to titter.

Traeger wiped sweat off his brow, fighting the urge to look up.

"He knows—hee-hee-hee... he knows, he knows he knows..."

"What are you on? Antidepressants? Barbiturates? Haloperidol?"

Traeger hadn't heard the question. He nodded, swallowing hard.

"Well, which one?"

"The uh, the last thing."

"Haldol." Voss nodded thoughtfully. "You must be going through hell right about now. Is it voices? Are they telling you to do things, Dennis?"

"You didn't tell him your name," Hillier whispered conspiratorially.

Didn't he? Yes. The psychologist had said his name was Voss—Something Voss—and Dennis had said 'Dennis Traeger,' like it meant nothing at all to tell a stranger his real name.

Traeger forced himself to nod.

"Are they telling you to hurt people, Dennis?"

"Yes!" the head shouted. "Hurt people! Rape the stewardess! Grab the pen and jab it through the crossword right into Alfie's groin!"

Traeger shook his head.

"Are they telling you to hurt yourself?"

"Slit your wrists! Open up your throat and spill your stinking guts on the shrink's lap! Take a flying fucking leap out the window, you scum-sucking prick!"

Traeger barely managed to shake his head again.

"Kill yourself! Guilty! Kill yourself kill yourself kill yourself!"

Traeger screamed and launched out of his chair. Voss's eyes opened comically wide as Traeger fumbled with the latch, tore open the overhead compartment, and grabbed the bag. Behind him the guy with the Walkman raised his headphones with a look of indifferent curiosity unique to the young. The elderly lady peered around the seatback and the kid stopped his toy airplane in mid-flight, gawping.

Traeger saw none of this. His eyes were on the bag in his hands. "Shut up!" he screamed down at it. "Shut up shut up shut up!"

Voss raised his hands, palms out. "It's okay, Dennis. The voices—they aren't real. They're just in your head."

"Head!" Traeger screamed.

That was it, the last straw. They all knew. They were all in on it, conspiring against him with Holy Joe's head. He had to get rid of the damned thing, but where?

Traeger spotted the EXIT sign. He turned for it and ran, clutching the bag like a fullback heading for the end zone. Hillier laughed as Traeger dashed past the restrooms and stopped in front of the door. He laughed as Traeger unzipped the bag and shoved the brunette stewardess back into her seat. He laughed as Traeger grabbed the emergency handle and jerked it all the way around.

"There!" Traeger shouted. "Who's laughing now, asshole?"

Voss shouted, "Dennis, please! You don't have to do this!"

"Oh no?"

Traeger pulled the head out by the hair and held it up. The jaw had fallen open and twisted in a horrible rictus. Bloodshot green eyes stared in vacant horror at the passengers. Voss cringed. The people closest to

Traeger, roused awake by the disturbance, gasped in terror. The old lady wilted into the aisle over the side of her chair and her oxygen tank rolled away from her limp body.

"Yeah," Traeger said. "Now you see."

Without another word he kicked the door open and shoved the head back in the bag. The door sucked outward with a thud and a huge rush of air and the bowling bag tore from his grip, shooting out into the cloudless night. Traeger laughed maniacally as loose newspaper pages and empty meal trays hurled passed him and out the gaping doorway.

For a moment he thought he was free—finally free—and then the atmospheric pressure grabbed him in a frigid fist and dragged him out into space.

Jet engines roaring over his head, Traeger hurtled back at a steep angle, caught for a moment in the slipstream... and then he was freefalling, watching the giant DC-10 grow smaller in the distance as the ground rose beneath him, his suit jacket billowing, hair whipping in his face.

There were worse ways to go. He could have been buried alive. He could have burned to death. He could have been eaten away by cancer or taken a shot in the gut and drowned in his own fluids. This wasn't so bad. In fact, now that he could no longer hear the engines it was almost serene.

He thought back to his youth, when he'd sat in the grass staring up at the sky as jet trails bloomed overhead and wondered what it might be like to be so far up in the air without a care in the world, sipping after-dinner cocktails like the ads he saw in magazines.

Out in the vast open darkness he heard laughter.

"No," he gasped. "No—God, no!"

He saw the bowling bag, a beige spot growing larger in the distance below his feet. It caught in the wind, opening like a parachute, and "Holy" Joe's head came tumbling out. The man was laughing.

"The head! The goddamned head!" Traeger screamed. The frigid wind stole the words from his lips, and he began to laugh himself until he cried.

Hillier's laughter followed Traeger until his body crashed to the earth. Every bone in Traeger's body crushed in a single agonizing moment, flesh, bone and organs sluicing across an open field.

When his remains were found the following morning, it was difficult to determine which head belonged with the body. The coroner placed both heads in the same bag.

The Boats

"Most folks think what makes the Everglades dangerous is the gators, but there are plenty of other things that can kill you in these beautiful blasted wetlands, Tolland.

"Snakes, for one. Did you know a Burmese python will wrap itself around a man and crush him to death in minutes? You didn't know that, did you? I'm a student of nature, Tolland. The animal kingdom fascinates me."

Xavier Tolland kept quiet, studying the cypress trees rising from placid dark water as the boats passed them by. Their wide gray trunks reminded him of the gowns young girls wore at their cotillions, which in turn got him thinking about the first time he'd found himself in over his head for a girl.

He'd met his first beau at her debutante ball when they were both fifteen and he'd slipped under her gown to eat her raw on her father's billiard table. After she'd come she'd yanked up her panties, thrust her petticoat down and scurried back to the party without returning the favor. Worse, she'd squealed to her father who'd had Tolland forcibly ejected from the premises with his pants around his ankles.

This brief encounter had set the tone for every relationship since until Charlotte Liddell. What he and Charlotte had was special, a love so strong it had swallowed him whole.

And still he'd ended up in deep water.

"You might want to listen to this, Tolland."

Straining, Tolland raised his head to look at the wooden boat towing him. Franklin Riley Liddell reclined in the backseat while his man, a brawny brainless Greek named Aristotle, rowed. Liddell held what Tolland had mockingly called a "dueling pistol" in one limp wrist draped over a cocked knee. He wore a boater hat, the kind popularized by barbershop quartets, and kept his short-sleeved white linen shirt unbuttoned to show his deep red tan and sparse golden chest hair.

The man was a Southern dandy of the worst kind, loathed by wife, children and employees. Tolland had worked for the company founded by Liddell's grandfather, Liddell Excavation, for thirteen years. Due more to charisma than skill he'd moved quickly through the ranks from heavy equipment operator to senior manager. As a laborer Tolland had suspected his superiors didn't give a damn for him or his coworkers. As Liddell's second-in-command he'd witnessed firsthand the man's ruthless contempt was not limited solely to employees.

It was for this reason he hadn't hesitated to lay the charm on Charlotte Liddell at a company barbecue on the Liddell estate, the former Bonnie Brae plantation, and the two had made time to see each other as often as possible in the seven months since. Five years his senior, Liddell's third wife had melted in his muscular arms and come buckets under the ministrations of his calloused hands.

"I'm long passed taking orders from you, Liddell," Tolland grunted.

Liddell shrugged. "Fair enough. I suppose I should satisfy myself with your present condition."

"You'll have to satisfy yourself plenty once Charlotte finds out about this."

The dandy chuckled lightly. "Oh don't flatter yourself, Tolland. Do you honestly think you're the first man she'd slinked around with behind my back? Charlotte has very little to do all day besides spend my money. You, my dear friend, were merely a chew toy for an anxious little bitch."

Tolland clenched his jaw, stewing in impotent rage. With his head, hands and feet fixed between two wooden boats similar to the one Aristotle rowed his movement was limited. The contraption held him almost like a medieval stockade, although he lay spread eagle and face-down across the wooden seats. The boat above held him firmly in place. Liddell, or more likely Aristotle, had constructed this torture device specific to his measurements.

Obviously letting Charlotte buy him a suit had been a bad call.

A stump dragged along the bottom of the boat. As it reached the stern the bow dipped, plunging Tolland's face into brackish water up to his nose. He got a mouthful of algae and scum before he could turn his head and spit, which reminded him of Charlotte's habit of letting him come in her mouth, spitting it into a tissue and flushing it down the toilet.

Isn't that how they got all those alligators in the New York sewers? he wondered.

"Speaking of big mouths," Liddell said. "If you're lucky a gator will come along swiftly and put you out of your misery. If you're *unlucky*, and all visible evidence points to that being likely, you'll experience what Aristotle's people were unfortunate enough to endure at the hands of the ancient Persians.

"The boats, or scaphism as it's also called, was used as a brutal form of torture and execution in the centuries leading up to the Christian era. They put Mithridates to death this way. I won't bore you with lurid details as you'll soon discover them yourself. Suffice to say your death will be a long, drawn-out and painful affair, much like my relationship with Charlotte has been."

A mosquito bit Tolland on his bare ass. The weirdest part about this business with the boats had been when they'd made him strip down in front of the Hummer before marching him into the water. He'd suspected Liddell or the Greek had just wanted to see him naked, maybe for sexual reasons, maybe to find what sort of tool had been operating on his wife.

"Hey, Liddell. Why don't you open this thing up and scratch my ass for me?"

The man pooched out his lower lip in aggravation and Tolland chuckled. He truly believed you had to take pleasure in the little things if you wanted to survive in this world.

Aristotle rowed the boat onto a small hammock surrounding a gigantic mangrove choked by strangling fig. He stepped out, sinking into the black water above his hip waders, and pulled the boat ashore.

Maybe they'll quit playing games and get this beating over and done with so I can go home already.

Liddell stood, balancing himself as the boat wobbled. For a delicious moment Tolland thought the man might plunge headfirst into the swamp, but Liddell steadied himself and Tolland swallowed bitter disappointment, watching his former superior return safely to dry land.

Aristotle returned to the boat. He unhooked the towrope from the back and dragged Tolland's floating torture device along the gunwale until he was close enough to shore to step out into the shallow water. Aristotle's groin came within inches of Tolland's face, and if he got close enough, Tolland promised himself he'd bite no matter what part of him was within reach.

Eat or be eaten, he thought.

But Aristotle held the rope high, wary of Tolland's exposed limbs and teeth. He waded in up to his chest and latched the towrope on a mooring ring secured to a cypress. Then he splashed a hand beneath the water and brought up a set of keys.

The Greek unlatched the padlocks at bow and stern and raised the boat off Tolland's back. It swung on its squeaky hinges and splashed down beside its twin, rocking the boat Tolland lay in.

With the weight off his back he tried to stretch out his limbs and spine, but since they'd tied his forearms and lower legs to the seats it didn't help much. If not for the ropes he would have risked escape despite Liddell's dueling pistol and the fifty pounds of muscle Aristotle had on him. Truthfully he hadn't expected Liddell's little game to get this far. A bit naïve on his part, especially since he'd seen firsthand the extremes to which Liddell would go when a client tried to fuck him over.

He'd thought the talk of torture and scaffolding—or whatever the fuck Liddell had called it—was just playacting. That at worst they'd bring him out here, rough him up a bit, and let him walk home naked through the swamp.

The boats rotated languidly. Tolland watched Aristotle return to the rowboat and lug a large white tub out of the back. It splashed down heavily into the water. Aristotle floated it to the boats by its handle.

Tolland noticed the cartoon bee on its label. Below were the words RAW HONEY.

Aristotle peeled off the lid and set it inside the boat. He reached into the tub, scooped out a handful of thick golden honey and began to smear it over Tolland's left arm.

"What the fuck is this, Liddell?"

The dandy chuckled. "As my lovely wife might have told you, Tolland, you attract more flies with honey than with vinegar."

Aristotle slathered the sticky honey over Tolland's shoulder blades and down his back. When his ass cheeks were coated the man cupped his balls and stabbed a thick finger into Tolland's asshole like he was giving him a veterinary exam. Tolland squealed in horror, trying to squirm away. Both Liddell and Aristotle laughed.

"He's a shy one, isn't he?" Liddell said.

Aristotle slopped his hand into the tub and slapped more honey onto Tolland's legs. He came back with the bucket and smeared gooey globs in Tolland's hair, over his face, and into his mouth.

Tolland spat the sickly sweet substance back at Aristotle but the man ignored the thick goober, snapped the lid on and returned it to the rowboat. He came back to Tolland with the padlock keys between his straight white teeth, waded around the stern and began raising the other from the water.

"No!" Tolland shouted, struggling against the ropes. "No, you can't do this, Liddell!"

"Oh but I can!" Liddell said as the boat slammed down hard on Tolland's back, a gasped breath exploding from Tolland's lungs. Aristotle snapped the padlocks into place while Tolland caught his breath and waded back to the hammock.

"I'll let you in on a little secret, Tolland." Liddell swatted a fly on his neck and flicked it away in distaste. "My Charlotte has had many affairs before you barked up her tree. She didn't fall apart when any of those men disappeared. And the woman truly is a creature of habit."

"You're wrong, Liddell. Charlotte and I love each other."

Liddell smiled amusedly. "I wish I could be here when you realize how wrong you are. Alas..." He made a sweeping gesture toward the rowboat. "I have a business to run, and Liddell Excavation is going to need a new senior manager."

Liddell returned to his boat and sat in the back. Aristotle pushed it from shore and jumped in soaking wet. His employer cringed away from him.

"Dammit, Ari! You're dripping on my trousers."

Without a word of apology Aristotle picked up the oars and began to row them away. As they passed, Liddell lazily raised a hand in farewell. "Ta-ta, Tolland. You treacherous snake."

"I'm gonna kill you, Liddell. I'm gonna get out of this fucking thing and I'm gonna tear your goddamn head off!"

"I very much doubt that."

Tolland couldn't see the man anymore but Liddell's tone had a smirking quality to it.

The sound of the oars splashing into the water and scraping the gunwale diminished until they were gone, and the only sounds were the creaks and groans of the trees, and the canopy swishing in a light summer wind.

He truly was alone.

The thought made him shiver despite the muggy heat inside the boats. Loneliness was one thing he could never abide. Since his mother abandoned him in his early teens he'd moved from one relationship to the next the way a roofer lay shingles. Women offered him temporary comfort. He'd thought his affair with Charlotte would be different, and yesterday he would have happily believed they might run away and grow old together. Now he knew it was a fool's fantasy. As much as she'd professed her love to him she never would have left her husband's money behind. Short of robbing Liddell blind Tolland would have had to be content with fucking another man's wife for the rest of his life, or at least until she'd grown tired of him and moved on.

Chew toy, Tolland thought bitterly. Was that really all she'd thought of him? Or was Liddell just kidding himself?

His joints ached, the limbs prickled with numbness. Pressed against divots carved into the gunwale his wrists, ankles and throat felt bruised. Gnats had swarmed around his head, green bottle flies and houseflies landed in his hair and whined in his ears and he couldn't swat them away. Mosquitoes and horseflies stung his neck and hands, his skin burned from the hot summer sun and starting to peel.

The boats thudded up against the cypress and scraped along its rough hide. Tolland grasped a chunk of protruding bark and held them still, hoping to gauge the lay of the land.

The hammock created by the roots of the mangrove and years of clotted gray muck lay maybe fifteen feet from what he'd come to think of as "his tree." Much too far to reach while trapped within the boats. Everywhere else was water, and more trees. No gators at least, but the Glades were teeming with them. Tolland didn't expect his luck to hold on that front much longer.

An ant crawled down his thumb and onto his wrist. He flicked it away, inadvertently letting go of the tree. Rocking gently on the still water, the boats drifted away until the towrope pulled taut.

The problem was he had no idea where they'd taken him. How far was he from the gulf? Had they brought him deep into the Glades or had Liddell been using the term generally, and actually stranded him somewhere within the Ten Thousand Islands? They'd driven him out from Naples with a bag over his head and the boats on a trailer hitch, but the rowboat they'd used to tow him out here had been waiting. Was there any private land out here or was it all parkland?

Never in his life had he felt so short on options. He could scream his throat raw hoping for someone to find him. He could keep working away at the ropes. He could try not to pass out from heat exhaustion or die of thirst.

If only he could scratch his goddamn itchy ass.

Tolland spat a mouthful of sticky-sweet saliva. A water strider kicked away from the frothy white glob, making tiny ripples on the surface.

Frogs chirped. High above a bald eagle shrieked. He heard a splash somewhere beyond the hammock and guessed the bird had found itself a meal.

Tolland had grown up dirt poor in a small town outside of Naples. When his father lost his job at the quarry, his mother had left them both behind. *Onward and upward*, as she'd often said. It had been a long time since he'd looked that far back but some good memories remained. Many of them involved heading out to the nearby swamp with his friends to catch frogs. Sometimes they'd use them to fish and sometimes they'd chuck them at a group of alligators—which his mother had told him was called a "congregation," as if they'd come to the swamp to worship—and they boys would marvel at the sudden feeding frenzy.

One time, he couldn't have been much older than ten, he'd been so thirsty he drank a bellyful of swamp water and ended up sick for days. His mother had told him he was lucky he didn't die. She'd said there were "microbes and such" in the water that could kill him.

Tolland knew the dangers of the Glades well.

Because of the mixture of salt water from Gulf of Mexico and fresh water from Florida Bay the Glades was home to both alligators and crocodiles. There were black bears. Poisonous snakes. Venomous spiders. Florida panthers. Wild boars. Fire ants. Vultures. At least most of these creatures couldn't swim, but there were still barracuda and gar to worry about, and even the cane toads were toxic.

And now he was trapped, alone and exposed to the elements, to all manner of hungry animal and insect, covered in honey and slowly dying of thirst.

"Fuck it," he groaned, and rocked the boat until his chin splashed into the water. He took a good mouthful, swished it around and spat it back out. The mix of salty and sweet reminded him of saltwater taffy he'd gotten from a shop on the boardwalk in Tampa when his dad had driven him out there to look for his mother. Turned out she hadn't been there, but he remembered that taffy and the trip back because his dad had gotten drunk as a skunk and Tolland had driven them back home without a license.

Tolland rocked the boat and took a huge gulp. He'd regret it later— if he lived that long. It was somewhat stagnant water but it seemed to cool off his body a few degrees inside the baking sauna of the boats.

His thirst slaked, at least temporarily, and his throat soothed, Tolland decided to put his voice to work rather than lie there like an invalid.

"HELLLLLLLLLLP!"

A flock of birds sprung from the top of the cypress, twittering excitedly as they fluttered away.

Cocking his head he listened for the concerned reply of a park ranger, an angler, a nature enthusiast—*anybody* with even a single functional ear and a pair of hands.

He waited.

His head swam from the heat. His eyes felt heavy.

Come on, you motherfucker...

Exhaustion strained every ligament, every muscle. Aristotle had kicked in the sliding glass door of Tolland's houseboat several hours before his alarm would have woken him. The man had punched him in the side of the head and kicked him in the ribs before dragging him along the dock by his hair to Liddell's idling Humvee. Then more than half an hour spent with a bag over his head in the backseat, breathing his own sweat and exhaled carbon monoxide. Then another hour or more pressed like a human Panini between the boats to get to this spot, and however long he'd already been lying here.

Tolland was exhausted but he knew he couldn't sleep.

Not like this.

Pain flared on his right foot like someone sticking a red-hot acupuncture needle into his heel and he jerked his leg, scraping the gunwale. It was far more painful than the mosquito bite. He supposed it might have been a horsefly but had nothing to gauge it against as he'd never been stung on the bottom of his foot before. Another sting came rapidly after the first and he realized he'd been holding onto a tree with this toes.

Oh fuck, not fire ants.

Tolland pushed off from the tree and used his weight to rock the boat. Water splashed his hands and feet but several ants had already crawled into the boats and bit his ankle, his Achilles' tendon, his lower leg. Scorching pain radiated from each bite and sting.

The honey had attracted them, but how many had crawled onto his foot before that first bite? Three? Four? A dozen? *Hundreds?* As they blazed an angry red trail up his leg he remembered Aristotle's finger attacking his asshole, and the honeyed palm cupping his balls.

Oh God. Maybe they'll be fill up on dessert and leave before they get to the buffet.

His entire lower leg was on fire but the ants kept gnashing their mandibles, stabbing him with their stingers, emptying their venom sacs into every inch of exposed flesh.

Tolland's violent cursing and writhing rocked the boats. Dirty, salty water splashed into his eyes and he blinked it away. His bladder unleashed a sudden hot torrent into the bottom of the boat. He hadn't even known he'd needed to piss.

The boats, the goddamn boats—I'll never get out of here, I'LL NEVER GET OUT!

He may have made a cuckold out of Liddell, but Liddell had fucked him in the end. And Charlotte would barely register his absence.

Without realizing it, he'd begun to weep.

Somewhere in the distance an egret squawked.

Despite his pain the steady drone of flies, the swish of the trees and the gentle rocking of the boats eventually lulled Xavier Tolland to sleep.

Tolland woke with a rumbling pressure swelling his intestines, aware he'd have to shit soon. Pissing had been easy lying on his front with his penis dangling. Shitting would be a very different animal, and judging by the pain churning through his bowels it was going to be nasty.

He hadn't slept long. A few hours at most, judging by the position of the sun directly above him. Inside the boats it was so hot Tolland thought they might spontaneously combust. The morbid pessimist in him wished they would.

Beneath the ropes his skin felt like raw, bloody meat. Where the ants had attacked him was one giant continuous itch but he could ignore it if he focused. He'd spent most of his life with an itch of a sort and had only ever noticed it once Charlotte had come around to scratch it.

"Charlotte," Tolland moaned. He repeated it twice more as if

invoking her name would make her appear. The thought that he'd never see her again, never fuck her again, was the worst thing imaginable.

Or it would have been before he'd ended up inside the boats.

A splash perked up his ears. The tendons in his neck creaked painfully as he craned to look, his bleary eyes scouring the knotted roots and low foliage surrounding his tree.

Then he saw it.

A snake—and not just any snake. Not your garden-variety garter or a water snake or even a rattler. No, this was the biggest goddamn python Tolland had ever laid eyes on outside of a zoo, its mottled green and brown body at least eight inches at its widest and as long as fifteen feet, twisting through the roots of the mangrove, only its head above the water.

"Jesus fuck!"

The snake tasted the air. Tolland had enough experience with rattlers on job sites to know the monster was searching for predators. But it also was also hunting for food.

Out here without a weapon, unable to defend himself, Tolland was the food.

His guts twisted in knots he eyed the colossal snake, willing it to move on and leave him be.

Come on, you big bastard... come onnnnnn...

The beast turned its flat head in his direction and Tolland felt his hopes dash like a man who'd lost everything on a hard eight. The python uncoiled itself from the roots and charged into the deeper water, tongue flicking, flicking.

Tolland recalled what Liddell had said about luck. If the python chomped down on his face or wrapped itself around his head and smothered him to death would it be a mercy? Could just lying here in the boats under the hot sun really be a fate worse than such a swift and brutal death?

The snake's massive length wriggled toward him like a leech, its hideous black eyes homing in on the boats.

As he waited for death Tolland noticed the insect drone had changed timbre as if in response to the presence of the slithering beast, though the flies themselves hadn't left the orbit of his head. Shifting his weight from side to side, he wobbled the boats, trying to steer them away from the giant predator—or at the very least get his head out of its reach. The water fought against him and he only managed to propel the boats backward until the towrope went taut, drawing out the agony by a few more seconds.

Literally at the end of his rope his mind suddenly seized on the buzzing.

It wasn't the flies. It was a *boat*.

Tolland began to scream, high and shrill and as loud as he could muster with his lungs compressed between the boats. He knew the vibrations would further attract the snake but he didn't care. He was dead already if he couldn't get the driver's attention. All he cared about now was getting out of the boats.

The engine roared and Tolland kept screaming as the airboat cut through the tall grass within his limited field of vision, just beyond the hammock of trees. From the corner of his eye Tolland saw the python dart away, heading back toward the mangrove. He didn't allow this small relief to quiet his cries. The tour boat was so close he could make out the individual faces of its ponchoed passengers and the white logo on the navy blue polo shirt of the driver riding high in the back.

Liddell must have left him near a tour route, the stupid rich fuck.

The airboat blew past, its propeller too loud to hear his screams, the day too bright to see into the comparatively dark cypress swamp. Even if someone had they would have seen nothing more than a pair of boats stacked one on top of each other and perhaps wondered why.

Still Tolland screamed himself hoarse at the retreating vessel.

Someone would hear him.

They would circle back. Break the padlocks. Get him out of these godforsaken boats.

Branches swished in the airboat's wake. Waves crashed against the far side of the hammock. The mangroves grumbled and swayed, unsettling birds from their branches. The sudden current upset lily pads and bent reeds on their way to the boats. The cloud of flies rose in a panicked swirl as he crashed into the big cypress, and resettled around his head when the rocking diminished.

Least it got rid of that fucking snake, he thought, swallowing a sickly-sweet mouthful of disappointment.

He knew the python would be back. It had already smelled lunch. Eventually it would come back for a taste.

Smell.

Would a snake care what its meal smelled like? If he shat himself inside the boats would the stench deter potential predators or attract them?

The pain in his guts was almost unbearable. As badly as he wanted to hold in the impending bowel movement—out of shame maybe, but mostly because he knew letting himself shit would make an already unpleasant experience even worse—Tolland had to give the idea serious consideration.

There had to be a reason, on an evolutionary level, for fear to instill a person with the urge to shit themselves.

One thing was certain, he wouldn't be able to concentrate on getting himself out of the boats with his stomach feeling like it did.

Bearing down, Tolland's innards rumbled. Maybe if he'd been lying on his back it would have been easier, or if he'd been able to raise a leg. He'd never tried to shit horizontally before. Obviously it wasn't conducive.

Before he knew it a geyser erupted from between his buttocks. It splattered against the floor of the upper boat and rained back down on him, hot and foul. Another explosive torrent oozed down between his legs, coating his dangling balls with filth. The stench wafted through the hole around his neck, prickling his nostrils. Eventually he would get used to the smell but smothered inside with the heat it would only get worse.

Only the most masochistic beast in the animal kingdom would attempt to eat him now.

He just hoped snakes could differentiate foul smells from delicious.

Already the skin between his buttocks and thighs itched. He vaguely wondered if he'd just made the biggest mistake of his life, leaving aside fucking his boss's wife. But the relief was almost glorious and he didn't intend to stick around for his excrement to attract flies and turn him into a floating maggot factory, and he certainly wouldn't hold onto the vain hope that another tour boat might pass by.

Tolland began to jerk at the ropes.

He heard a splash from the mangrove hammock and kept moving, desperate to loose his wrists. The boats were old. The wood was soft. If he could get one hand free, *just one hand*, Tolland was sure he could use the leverage to force this floating coffin apart.

The boats careened and battered against the cypress. The mooring ring jingled like a supper bell. In his periphery he saw the giant snake dart toward him. He hoped the violent movement of the boat would frighten it. And if it didn't he hoped his stink would make it think twice about eating him.

The snake inched closer, seemingly wary. Wake from the boats splashed over its head but the animal didn't retreat, it kept coming until its snout struck the side of the boat with a heavy thud between Tolland's head and his left hand.

Tolland was not a fearful man. He'd never experienced the sensation of having his heart in his throat until now. His entire body seized with terror. Adrenaline surged through his veins. The violent thrashing slowed to a gentle rock.

The snake reared back and flicked out its tongue, darted forward again and prodded the hull.

Tolland watched his fingers curl into an involuntary fist as the snake got closer and he jerked hand inward, not caring if he tore off every bit of skin and broke every bone, just wanting to get it out of reach.

The python hissed and struck.

Tolland howled in agony. Stars flooded his vision, his already limited view of the world fading to gray. Struggling to stay conscious he watched the giant reptile's tail curl under the boats.

He splayed his fingers. The reptile's head twisted back and forth as he dug his nails into the wet meat of its maw. He didn't expect the beast to choke. He merely wanted to cause it pain.

The python's tail flopped down over the side, wriggling in his face. Its massive body had curled around the boats. The devious fucker planned to break them open like a giant nut to get at the tasty morsel inside.

With an ear-splitting crunch the seats clamped down hard on his ribs, crushing the breath out of him. The hulls would split soon and he'd be free. But he'd have to fight a hungry two-hundred-pound Burmese python barehanded to get out of this goddamn swamp, and one of those hands was trapped inside the beast's mouth.

The floor of the boat split open. Stagnant water gushed in from below, splashing his chest and groin. Splintered wood gouged his thighs and exposed genitals.

Scouring the animal's mouth he found an opening and wormed his thumb inside.

Tail thrashing, slapping him in the face and beating against the hull, the snake widened and contracted its mouth around his hand but wouldn't let go. He'd plugged its airway. Hot breath whistled out around his thumb. The tail slapped down over his cheek and lay still just long enough for Tolland to gnash out and catch it in his mouth.

Bet I can swallow you before you swallow me, fucker.

With a massive crack the top of the boats caved in. Split planks tore into his back as the snake's cold, heavy body slumped over him. He felt his ankles slipped free. The tail snapped off between his teeth and he spat the raw hunk of salty meat into the swamp. The stump squirmed. Gore dripped into the water and smeared on the broken hull.

The boat sank rapidly at a sharp angle. In water up to his waist he jerked his legs against their bindings. The snake squeezed loose, splintered boards into his ribs and the gunwale tightened around his throat.

Drowned, strangled and eaten alive... They should make a Discovery Channel special about my death.

The hulls came apart and Tolland plunged into the swamp, gasping for breath. He kicked his legs free. Like a reversed crucifix the wooden seat was still lashed to his arms across his chest. Despite the fact that he'd plugged its airway the snake still tried to swallow his hand.

The python wriggled weakly around his legs, navigating jagged boards to wrap itself around him. Tolland wouldn't give it a chance. He stood on shaky limbs and waded toward his tree. Swinging himself at it with his arms outstretched, feeling like a human sprinkler, he bashed the snake's head against the cypress until its body stopped writhing and the pressure on his wrist lessened.

When the meaty pulp of the snake's head slipped off his fist and splashed lifelessly into the water, Tolland stood against the tree and tried to bring his arms together, like working the chest butterfly machine at the gym. He screamed from the exertion but the seat finally snapped in two and he stumbled forward, smashing his face into the tree.

The feeling of freedom eclipsed any pain.

He was going home.

And he wouldn't be going emptyhanded.

Tolland stood over Liddell in the dark while the man snored.

After her initial fright Charlotte had let Tolland in through the sliding glass door in the back. He'd slipped in quickly despite the extra weight on his shoulders. The walk along the tour route through the hammocks had been strenuous but once he'd reached a main road it wasn't long before an amused man in a pickup pulled over to marvel at him. When Tolland had told him what he'd planned the man had eagerly let him jump in the back and had driven him all the way back to Naples.

"Just keep that damn thing away from me," he'd said, and Tolland had.

Now he stood over Liddell while the swimming pool threw ripples of light over the art on the walls and the man himself snored, sleeping the sleep of a man at peace with the world.

"Hello, Liddell."

The man roused slowly. Finally he raised his head toward the intruder and drew up hurriedly on his elbows.

"*Tolland?* Is that you?"

Tolland couldn't see the man's expression in the dim light but the edge of fear was a treat. "Don't bother calling Aristotle. Charlotte woke him with that little dueling pistol of yours."

"What do you want? What is that awful *smell*?"

"You know, I thought about all the things I would do to you on the way back from the Glades. What do you get for the man who has everything?" Tolland asked in a jovial tone. "Then I remembered how much you like animals."

He let the python unfurl with a heavy thud onto Liddell's four-poster bed.

The man crawled back against the headboard with a squeak of fear, clutching the covers to his scrawny chest. *What is that?*

Grinning, Tolland slipped the kitchen knife Charlotte had handed him out from his belt and dragged it up the body of the snake. The reptile's stinking guts spilled out in cold wet clumps over Liddell's satin bedsheets. Immediately the man began to retch.

"Did you know a Burmese python will wrap itself around a boat and crack it like a nut?"

Tolland let the python drop into the bed. Its battered head flopped down between the white satin tents made by Liddell's legs.

"Jesus!" Liddell cried, kicking the thing away, but it was too heavy to budge. He retched again, bringing a hand up to cover his mouth. Puke spewed through his fingers, pattering on the bedsheets and a hundred pounds of snake guts.

Tolland laughed. "I guess I'm pretty lucky after all, huh, Liddell? And now you know how Charlotte felt sharing her bed with a snake like you."

He left the man vomiting.

PRICK

There was no escaping it: Zoey's date was a giant dick.

Within the span of an hour, he'd insulted their server, poked fun at Zoey's outfit, and shushed her to catch a baseball replay. Before the drinks arrived, he'd already oh-so-casually touched her shoulder three times in an obvious attempt to create intimacy, had set his phone down between them and regularly checked incoming text messages, and had talked over her twice to one-up her admittedly well-worn but still humorous anecdotes. Worse, he'd interrupted the answer to a question he himself had asked—as if he'd been checking it off a list—to tell her about his previous long-term girlfriend who was, according to him, a "certified crazy bitch."

Zoey Esprit knew his ploy. She'd experienced it in some form or another a dozen times, at least. Modern dating was a labyrinthine manscape riddled with trolls, bros, haters, and selfie-obsessed *divos*. It took a thick skin to find a good man swimming in an ocean of losers. Sometimes she felt like she'd been trying to find a specific needle in a *stack* of needles, where every attempt drew a potential prick.

Still, she had to put herself "out there." A girl could only Netflix and Chill by herself so much before friends and family started to think she must be frigid.

She'd met a few decent guys using dating apps, but more and more it seemed like dick pics had become a standard greeting. In the past month alone, she'd seen enough crooked, small, overly hairy, warted and/or ugly penises to make the publishers of *Playgirl* blush.

And then came Orson.

Zoey had been drunk, depressed, and maybe a little horny when they'd met on the elevator, after a night she'd spent dancing with the girls, and Orson had oh-so-casually slipped into her messy life like a Trojan horse with a slightly witty comment she no longer remembered. He'd been clever and intelligent and thoughtful during their brief conversations in the lobby and elevators since, and her defenses had fallen like the army of Troy.

She realized her error now, sitting at this sports bar across from this handsome yet socially repugnant man with Buffalo wing sauce smeared on his lips and chin, who bumped his cheap draft beer with an elbow, nearly spilling it as he made to cheer a homerun from whichever team was "his." She'd mistaken the fact that he'd been different from the pervs and assholes she'd encountered in her most recent experiences on social media with him being in a much higher echelon, when in reality he was likely far lower. At least those other men, sleazy as they were, were honest about it.

Attempting to slip out as casually as possible without causing a scene, Zoey grabbed her purse. It took a moment for Orson to snap his focus away from the game on the big screen behind her and notice she was slipping out of the booth.

"Where are you going?"

"Bathroom," she said, and flashed him an awkward smile.

Orson wiped his fingers on the stack of napkins. "You're taking your purse?"

Caught, Zoey shrugged and said the only thing she could think to diffuse the situation: "Tampons."

He glanced down at the splotches of red sauce on the napkins beside his plate. "That's cool," he said with a shrug. "I'm an enlightened guy. I also don't mind taking a ride down the Red River, if you know what I mean."

Zoey didn't bother concealing her disgust. "Good to know," she said, and wound through tables of sports fans toward the bathrooms.

The doors were in the other direction, but she'd already decided to head out the back, and while customers high-fived each other, raucously cheering another homerun—or something—no one heard the commotion in the kitchen as she hurried through on her way to the exit.

"No, don't stroke it," she told him. "I wanna feel it get hard in my mouth."

Orson cursed himself for calling Gina, but after he'd been ditched at the Wing Zone, none of his regular booty call fallbacks had answered any of his texts. Gina had messaged back immediately, almost as though she'd been *waiting* for him to text—despite the fact that he'd broken it off with her weeks ago.

Probably was, the crazy bitch.

Orson stopped tugging to let her slurp it into her mouth like a hot noodle. It thickened as she sucked, growing fat on her tongue, filling her mouth, and he began to forget about that bitch from the eighth floor sticking him with the bill for her appetizers and drinks. Losing himself to pre-orgasmic bliss.

He was only semi-erect when Gina's teeth grazed his flesh. Not hard, just playfully. Still, he yelped.

"Hey, watch the teeth!"

Her lips curled up in a smile around his fattened schlong, ice blue, heavy-lidded eyes wild with malevolent glee. She tossed her curly hair over her shoulder and took his cock in her hand to suck on his balls, a little harder than he liked.

Orson moaned—whether despite or because of the pain, he wasn't sure. His smooth ball popped from of her lips.

"Why do you sleep with all those whores?" she asked him, beginning to squeeze his wet cock between her tits.

"What whores? What are you talking about?"

"I've been watching you, Orson. All those women... do you *love* them? Do you love them like you loved me?" She let a runnel of spit dribble down onto the head of his prick.

Orson might have corrected her, might have told her he'd never loved her, had she not started stroking him between her perfect tits. Hard to concentrate. Difficult to focus on anything but the rhythm and the heat.

"*Fffffuck yeah!*" he moaned.

And she bit.

Hard.

Orson screamed, pushing against the top of her head, but Gina's teeth held him firm, like a dog on a bone. Something hot and wet splashed against his abdomen, and for a moment he thought it was spit or even vomit, but the pain was so enormous, so *all-encompassing* that he knew it must be blood, and he kicked at her, striking her flat stomach and smooth thighs with his knees, but her bite held, and he punched her temples and pounded on the top of her head, and still her teeth met in the middle with a pronounced *clack*, the blood vessels and urethra snapping, and she rose from his groin—he was blacking out now, thank fuck —smiling gleefully, her cheeks puffed out like a chipmunk's, the lower half of her face covered in his blood, before she strode stark naked to the open window and spat his cock out into the cool night air.

By the time she'd slammed the window, Orson was unconscious.

THE OLD MAN whom residents of Alton Towers called the T.P. Man, because his rickety shopping cart was always loaded with toilet paper, heard the screaming from above moments before something splashed into the puddle at his feet.

The T.P. Man grunted sleepily on the bench and looked down, peering into the shallow, gritty black water. Looked like a bird had fallen out of the sky, wings folded around its body. Or a fat, giant slug. Nothing of particular interest, until it *squirmed*.

He pulled his feet from the puddle, drawing his knees to his chest. The movement had startled him. Blinking his bleary eyes until it came into focus, he gave the object a closer look.

Some lady threw her vibrator out the window, the T.P. Man thought, watching the floppy pink thing splash.

"Bit small for a dildo," he remarked. "Must be for the backdoor. Or a junior Miss."

The T.P. Man chuckled, and began to push his shopping cart full of Charmin toward the above ground parking garage. In about an hour, security would be around to harass him, but he knew of a spot behind the garage where teenagers hung out to smoke their wacky weed during the day. A kind of clubhouse, where he could sleep until dawn.

Behind him, the splashes stopped.

He turned, expecting to see the vibrator in the still water, having run out its batteries. But the puddle was empty. The vibrator had disappeared.

"Some raccoon run away with it," he said. "Havin' himself a raccoon sex party."

He laughed again, pushing the cart down the roundabout. Damn back wheel was spinning again. Need to get that fixed or it'd get hard to push to the grocery store and back for his weekly stock of Charmin.

A tin can clattered in the gutter at his feet. The T.P. Man startled, looking down in time to see a small shape scurry into the bushes. Probably a rat. His nose wrinkled from the sour smell of urine. Drunk residents pissed in the bushes here sometimes on their way home from wherever, because they knew the Super would just blame it on old Rufus, the T.P. Man.

"Got more respect for myself than that," Rufus said haughtily. "Prob'ly pin all that dog shit on me too, if they could."

Rufus used the woods nearby when he needed to go. He'd built a small outhouse toilet out of scrap wood, and dug the pit himself.

"Good enough for the Pope, it's good enough for me," he said, and chuckled.

Low branches shook, leaves swishing as the rodent scurried on ahead of him.

Go on, little rat, Rufus thought as he wheeled the cart around the side of the garage, onto the dirt-floored "clubhouse." *You handle your business, I'll handle mine.*

"Speaking of 'business,'" the T.P. Man said, and grabbed a roll of toilet paper from the stack. Felt like it'd be a firm one today, which was good. The older he got, the runnier *they* got. Of course, his diet—or lack of it—didn't help firm things up much.

Rufus left his cart and trekked out into to the woods. He picked up a cigarette butt from the ditch on the way. The parkland was dark, at probably around one or two in the A.M., but not so dark he couldn't see. City dark never got much darker than a hospital ward, but the canopy of trees blocked out much of the moonlight, and his poor vision made it worse.

Unseen animals scurried in the underbrush. An occasional vehicle swished by along the highway. Otherwise, the night was still and quiet.

Rufus found his toilet. He untied his belt, pulled down his grimy, loose jeans and tattered undies, and squatted over the two weather-dampened planks that served as a seat, resting the toilet paper beside him. He straightened the stubbed cigarette, smeared with red lipstick, and lit it with a scratched pink Bic lighter.

Hard work tonight, more like birthing a baby. Just when he thought he'd never make and he'd have to go to sleep with an uncomfortable pain in his guts, his bowels loosened, and two fat turds fell into the pit with a crunch of dry leaves.

The T.P. Man tore off four squares of paper, folded them in two, and wiped. When he'd had a home, he'd liked to give himself what he'd called a "spray-lo," using the deodorizer to spray a halo around himself and his stink, but out here in the semi-wild the smell wafted itself away. He bunched up the used paper and tossed it into the hole.

He'd pulled his pants to his knees when the poop suddenly and violently squeezed through his anus, tearing at the delicate skin. Rufus cried out in surprise. He didn't like to be surprised, least of all by a sneak attack turd.

Only this turd seemed to be going *in*, and not *out*.

The T.P. Man leaped to his feet, feeling the shameful sting of sexual violation as whatever it was worked its way into his asshole. He'd been raped before, by two boys from the college who'd called him degrading names while they did it. It had taken plenty of rubbing alcohol to get beyond that trauma. Cost him most of his sight and probably half of his liver.

Rufus jerked around, looking for his attacker—but the woods around him were dark, and seemingly empty. Still, the fat thing wormed upward, like a shit that forgot the way. He felt it squirming inside him, while the pain in his anus lessened, though he felt blood—or shit—trickle down his inner thigh.

Meanwhile, he felt the thing—*L'il Miss's dildo? A rat?*—squeeze into his guts.

"Oh God, I'm gonna—"

Rufus puked, strings of bile splattering on his dusty jacket sleeve. He staggered forward, tripping on the pants around his ankles, sent sprawling headlong in the dirt. The thing was in his esophagus now—felt like a mouthful of food gone down the wrong way.

He swallowed hard, hoping to dislodge it, but it only worked its way further along, horizontal now, wriggling toward his throat.

Be over soon, at least. Damn thing prob'ly just wants out, and I ain't about stop it!

It stopped moving. Rufus made to gasp in relief, but it had plugged his airway. Couldn't breathe. Couldn't scream, the thing pressed against his vocal cords.

Tears streaming down his face, Rufus reached into his mouth, dirty fingernails scrabbling over his tongue, pushing past his uvula, scouring the back of his throat for the animal, whatever it was.

Without a voice to scream, the T.P. Man merely squirmed and moaned, rustling in the dead leaves at the foot of his makeshift toilet until he was dead.

On a torrent of shit and vomit, something small and plump oozed out of the T.P. Man's mouth, plopping softly onto a scattered pile of leaves.

A moment later, it was slithering through the woods toward the tall black pillar of sparkling golden lights where it was born.

Zoey had met Dan at a business event, and though she'd found him a tad posh, they had hit it off almost immediately.

It had been a month since her awful date with Orson Ladd, on a night the residents of Alton Towers now referred to as "The Night It Happened." Few would say aloud what "it" meant, but they all knew: a crazy woman had bitten off Orson's penis and spat it out the window of his fifteenth story apartment. The woman had fled, but police had caught her at her apartment, enjoying a glass of chilled Chablis. EMTs had earlier carted Orson off to the hospital, unconscious from shock and blood loss. And after an extensive search, the appendage was never found.

It.

Zoey felt a little guilty for what had happened to Orson, though she knew she wasn't to blame. If she hadn't skipped out on him—a cowardly act, admittedly—he might not have felt compelled to bring home the "certified crazy bitch" (Zoey had remembered her first name, Gina, which had corresponded with the name in the papers), and might still at this moment be intact.

Then Zoey had met Dan, and their blossoming relationship had taken her mind off of Orson Ladd and his missing piece.

She wasn't in love with Dan, no yet. But there had been an attraction there from the start. She supposed the accent had some to do with it; she'd always been a sucker for a sexy Englishmen.

At the end of their first date, he'd kissed her. For their third date, she'd brought him back to her apartment, and after cooking him dinner, they'd slept together.

"Fucking odd, isn't it?" Dan said over coffee—he had tea—at the shop across the street when they met the following Monday. "I mean, who would rape a homeless person? Can you imagine the *stench*?"

The homeless man who sometimes loitered in the foyer had been found dead in the woods nearby. The news said he'd been raped. The thought that it had happened so close to her apartment terrified Zoey.

"Can we talk about something else, please?"

Dan pushed the Jaffa Cake he'd brought around his plate, barely touched. "It's just so... *unsavory*. Honestly, I don't think I can eat." This seemed to tickle him. "That's rather ironic, isn't it? Being unable to eat because of a homeless man? Because of the starving thing, I mean."

"Yeah, I got it."

Dan gave her a look. "Are you angry, Zo?"

"I'm not angry, I'm upset."

"I don't understand the difference."

"I'm upset about that man," she said. "Rufus."

"Rufus!" Dan said, delighted. "On a first name basis with the Tee Pee Man, were you?"

Zoey threw her napkin on the table and gave him an icy glare as he leaned back in his chair, blowing on his tea. "You know, you can be really rude sometimes."

"Look, I'm sorry, Zoey. It's just that everyone is suddenly concerned with this guy when up until last week nobody gave a shit about him. I mean, did anyone go out of their way to find out why he was sleeping behind the garage? Did anyone offer him a hot meal or a bath?"

"That's not the point."

"I'd rather say that *is* the point. If he hadn't been squatting in the woods—*literally*, according to the news—he wouldn't have been in the woods that night for some deranged lunatic to rape and murder. God, I hope they used *protection*..." He pulled a disgusted face.

"You're being callous."

"Well, I don't see you out there, giving alms to the poor."

The bell dinged above the door before she could reply, and a man shuffled in, hunched and bedraggled, dressed in a baggy gray tracksuit. He walked with a hobble up to the counter, and ordered a grandé macchiato. Zoey recognized his drink before his voice, which was cracked, the hard edge softened.

"Orson?"

He half-glanced over his shoulder, keeping himself hidden under the hood.

"Orson, it's me." She went to his side. "Zoey."

Begrudgingly, he turned. His eyes were sunken, hollowed out. Like he'd dragged himself through hell and back.

"Hi, Zoey," he said, his voice small.

"Orson!" Dan giggled. "*The* Orson?" He approached them at the counter, chuckling as he stuck out a hand. "Zoey has told me a lot about you. How are you, then? You know... down there."

Orson looked down at the crotch of Dan's pants. "How are *you* down there? Or should I ask you?" he said, turning his inquiring look on Zoey.

"I just wanted to apologize—"

"*Don't,*" Orson said. "There's nothing to apologize for. In fact, the transplant's bigger than what I had before. I'm *happy* it happened."

His order came up. He took his drink, and shouldered past Dan. Dan watched him the whole way with an amused grin.

"D'you think that's true? You know, that it's bigger?"

Zoey left Dan standing at the counter.

She was still thinking about their tiff—Dan would call it a *row*—when the superintendent came into the mailroom, startling her.

"Yeah hi, Zoey, hi," he said over his bifocals. He had his tool bag with him, and like usual, he seemed busy and a little flustered. Zoey often wondered whether it was because his position was paid for by the tenants, that he was putting on a show to justify his paycheck.

"Hi, Mr. Popadopolous. Busy today?"

"I'll rest when I'm dead. Your pipes okay?"

"As far as I know. Is there a problem?"

Mr. Popadopolous leafed through his own mail. "Just some clogged toilets on the lowers floors. Real mess. You have any problems, you be sure and let me know," he said, and tossed the entire stack of mail in the recycle bin.

"I will, thank you."

As they waited for the elevators—the service one was out again, though she didn't mention this to Mr. Popadopolous—he turned to her briefly. "You don't happen to know anyone who owns a snake in the building, do you?"

"A snake?"

"You know..." The portly bald man flicked out his tongue and made a hissing sound between his teeth.

"I can think of a few men who'd fit that description, Mr. Popadopolous, but no, not the animal. Why do you ask?"

He shrugged. "Eh, no reason."

Elevator two opened. Mr. Popadopolous limped in. "Take care of yourself, Zoey."

"You too, Mr. Popadopolous."

As the doors closed behind him, elevator one opened, and she stepped inside.

Stavros Popadopolous, known as "Pop" to family and friends, stepped out of the elevator into the cool basement. "Snaaaake..." he called. "Oh, snaaaake!"

There was no reply. Not that a snake could reply even if it wanted to.

Two residents had claimed to have glimpsed a snake in the basement, and another had seen... *something*... in the parking garage. Pop hadn't let it bother him until he'd seen the LOST CAT poster on the message board in the lobby, and found the cat itself in the boiler room a few hours later, having lost a lot of blood from small bites all over its body.

Either it had been ganged up on by a pack of hungry rats, or there really was a snake loose in the building. Pop had seen *Snakes on a Plane* and had no interest in playing Samuel L. Jackson.

"Sna-*aaaaaake*?"

Mrs. Bartleby stepped out of the laundry room lugging an empty plastic hamper, and Pop nearly shit a brick.

"Oh! Jeez! You scared me, Mrs. Bartleby."

"You scare too easy, Stavros," the elderly woman said, and she gave him a good-natured slap on the shoulder. "Man up!"

"Ha ha, yeah, I guess I probably should. Have a good day, Mrs. Bartleby."

Truthfully, Pop was still shaken from what had happened in apartment 1303, the night he'd seen the door wide open and found Orson Ladd passed out naked on his bed in a puddle of blood, his "little Ladd" bitten off and spat out the window by some crazy woman.

Pop relaxed a little as he continued into the laundry room, and gaped at what he saw. The floor was covered in water. The drain in the center of the tiled floor gurgled.

"Dammit," he muttered, and searched for the source of the spill, cursing Mrs. Bartleby under his breath. Her laundry rattled in one of the dryers, the only one running this morning.

The spill had originated under the oldest of the frontload washing machines. Pop grabbed a dirty towel from the wash basin and laid it down, then knelt on it. The bottom of the tub was full of dingy water when he opened the door. He removed the drain panel with his socket wrench, and a small clump of gummy, wet pinkish gray lint oozed out from the hole. It made Pop think of afterbirth. Too small to have caused the mess though, whatever it looked like.

He scooped away the wet lint, and leaned his head into the tub, hoping to get a better look at the clog. Cavernous drips arose from the drainpipe, which lead straight back for a good three feet into the utility room, where it shot down into the ground, and to the sewers below, he assumed. He took out his flashlight and shined it into the dark hole.

Dingalingalingaling!

His cell phone rang in its hip holster, and Pop startled, banging his head on the inside of the washer with a giant *gongggg!*

He pulled his head out and rubbed his shiny scalp, thinking Mrs. Bartleby may have been right about "manning up."

One more scare like that and the old ticker's gonna give up the ghost, he thought, wondering if he'd remembered to take his blood thinners this morning. He was always forgetting since Muriel passed two years ago last spring.

Pop picked up the phone. It was the exterminator he'd called. The man was booked solid for the next two days, but he promised to come the following morning. Sounded like a stand-up guy, and he'd been recommended.

He put his phone on silent, holstered it, and reached into the drainpipe. Fingers roaming the width of the pipe, feeling damp, cool metal, and small clumps of lint, they finally came to rest on something warm and spongy.

Blood pumped under its flesh. It was *alive.*

The snake bit his finger before he could retract his hand, the pain more terrible than anything he'd felt before, even when he'd caught a chunk of shrapnel in the calf from a cluster bomb in Vietnam—which had been every bit as excruciating as it sounds.

Pop pulled back from the tub with a scream, blood dripping onto his lap. The end of his index finger had been bit clean off at the second knuckle, revealing pink muscle and white bone. He fell back on his ass in the puddle, holding his injured finger, staring into the small black hole at the back of the washing machine as he wrapped his hand with the damp towel.

The snake in the pipe launched at him. Pop's mouth opened wide in terror, and it lodged in his throat, silencing his scream. He grasped the fleshy thing with his uninjured hand, pull at the snake as it wriggled and squirmed, trying to slither down his throat and lay eggs in his stomach, like his grandmother had often warned him they would when he was a boy.

Pop jerked it from his mouth and gasped for breath, holding it away from his face as it thrashed in his hand.

His eyes went wide.

It wasn't a snake—it was a *penis*. A *human* penis, about ten inches in length and at least two wide, flopping in his hand like a dildo left too close to the radiator. He threw it at the wall—more out of disgust than fear—and tried to get to his feet.

His boots slipped in the puddle, and he fell on his back, cracking a rib, loosing his breath in a pained gasp. Pop lay there, stunned and terrified, unable to move without further damaging his rib, praying for someone, *anyone*, to come downstairs and help him up.

The buzzing dryer alarm snapped him back to reality. There was no penis, only a slightly large, very violent snake. He'd stunned it when it struck the wall, and hopefully it wouldn't risk another attack. But he couldn't count on it. Mrs. Bartleby's clothes tumbled as the drum rolled to a stop, and Pop tried to ease himself up.

The creature slapped wetly against his cheek. Pop reared back his head as far as he could, the pain in his ribs excruciating. He saw the thing—a penis, no doubting the wet slit in its mottled purple head, or the thick roll of foreskin—inch toward him out of the corner of his eye.

With the last of his strength, he cried out for "*HELLLLLLP!*"

The sentient penis plunged into the dark, hairy cove of his ear, and before Stavros Popadopolous could even *think* about shitting bricks, the monster penetrated his brain with a very loud *POP!*

Lana Mather sat in an uncomfortable chair the Sexual Health Clinic, nursing her sore stomach.

It had been hurting since yesterday morning, when she'd taken the walk of shame back home from the apartment of that guy she'd met on Tinder. She'd downed a few drinks to "get over herself" (heeding her girlfriend Trina's advice), and had taken an Uber to his building. She couldn't even remember his first name, let alone the last.

He was good-looking, at least, though with the lights dimmed she supposed he might not have been a stunner in the daylight. Not that his looks had mattered much. What had mattered was that he'd been slightly less disgusting than most of the men she and Trina had surveyed on her app, while downing tequila shots.

She'd never done anything like it before, but after Hunter had cheated on her, she'd felt like she needed to get a few bangs with randos out of her system, and Trina had agreed. Especially since Lana still planned on marrying Hunter in the spring.

"Miss Mather?"

Lana looked up from the magazine she'd been pretending to read. Other than her, two older women sat looking at their phones, trying to avoid looking at the pervy guy in the far corner, who wore sunglasses.

"The doctor will see you now," the secretary said. "Have a seat in room three, she'll be with you in a moment."

Lana stood, and made her way to the open examination room near the back of the building. She sat in the chair, and studied STD warning posters while she awaited the doctor.

Lana was surprised it was her stomach that hurt now and not her throat, battered and bruised by the guy's huge cock—way too big to take "balls deep" (another gem from Trina) into her petite pussy. Or her cervix, which he'd treated like a fat lady with a display shoe during a buy-one-get-one sale, causing her to shift uncomfortably on the subway and behind her desk at work all throughout the following day. She'd thought at first that was why she felt sick, since she'd swallowed his cum—a decision she'd immediately regretted, though she had only done it so he wouldn't cum in her hair, leaving traces for Hunter to find. But when she'd thrown up later that night, she'd known her problems were far worse.

She and Hunter had been snuggled under the covers watching Jimmy Fallon last night when a sudden wave of queasiness had overcome her. She'd flipped back the blanket and scurried to the en suite, where she'd thrown up as quietly as she did after a large meal, so Hunter wouldn't hear.

"Y'okay, beb?" Hunter had called.

Lana had cleared her throat, blinking tears away to look into the bowl. What she'd seen amid chunks of semi-digested sandwich made her throw up again.

Before she could explore the terrifying thoughts swimming through her mind, Lana had flushed the toilet, hoping she'd puked up the last of it. Still, she'd tossed and turned all night, barely getting a wink of sleep, and she'd gone to the clinic first thing in the morning, after Hunter had left for work.

The doctor entered, a small brown-haired woman in jeans, with a nametag on the breast of her t-shirt. She sat in the chair opposite, and gave poor miserable Lana a sympathetic look. "Hi... Lana, is it? What seems to be the problem?"

Lana swallowed hard—much like she wished she hadn't two nights ago. "I had unprotected sex," she said. "With a stranger. And now my stomach's sore."

"I see." The doctor drew her feet up onto the chair, holding the toes of her shoes in a childlike way. "Do you think you may be pregnant?"

"*Pregnant?* Oh God, no!" Lana chuckled nervously. "I mean, I *hope* not."

"Then why are you here, Lana?"

"I'm wondering... is it possible for sperm to have..." She felt lame asking, like an ignorant kid on WebMD. "... parasites?"

The doctor looked at her askance. "Parasites?"

"I swallowed," Lana said. Her mind flashed on what she'd seen in the toilet bowl last night. *Maggots.* Dozens of them. Little pink wriggly things with purple heads, worming through chewed bits of bread and cheese and lettuce and sliced ham.

Recalling the image made her nearly faint, and she stood abruptly, rushing to the sink, where she vomited again and again, hundreds of little pinkish parasites with purple heads squirming over each other in the flat bottom of the shiny metal sink.

She stood over it, catching her breath as she wiped her mouth, her throat raw.

The doctor gasped behind her, scaring her worse than the sink full of parasites.

"What's wrong with me...?" Lana cried, but the doctor was already backing away from her in horror.

MELISSA JOHNSON WAS SUFFERING through the worst cramps of her life.

She'd downed three Midol with a glass of vodka rocks, and still her ovaries kicked the shit out of her. Now the hangover was kicking in to boot, and her shoulders and head throbbed while her insides felt like a riding lawnmower was churning up her uterus and spewing it out of her vagina.

Melissa went to the toilet, certain her current tampon was no longer viable. She unzipped her jeans, slid down the old stained period panties, and sat on the toilet.

She planted her bare feet on the cold tile on either side of the toilet, and pulled the string.

The sodden tampon slid out, splashing drops of blood into the bowl that swirled into dark red whorls as they struck.

Melissa made to reach for the toilet paper when a painful, bloody torrent spewed from her, splashing into the cold water like a violent bout of diarrhea.

When the flood stopped, she ventured a mortified look into the bowl.

What she saw there, thrashing, splashing in the murky water, made her slip off the toilet as her vision grayed, and as she fell she tore down the shower curtain, striking her head on the porcelain tub.

***

ORSON SPAT into his hand and worked the goober over the bulbous head of his massive new prick.

Her asshole winked at him, a clean, tight pucker. He stuck in his moistened thumb, working it around inside as she moaned.

Orson thrust the penis into her and plowed away without much enthusiasm, his date moaning and writhing under his weight, pulling him down to the mattress. Sex would never be like it was before the Night It Happened.

Still, he'd learned over the past month to take pleasure in his partners' pleasure. He'd had to. Mentally, he was all there. "In the moment," as they say. Blood seemed to flow to it correctly and the penis stayed erect—much longer than it used to—but the feeling wasn't quite there. It was a foreign entity. Like using a strap-on dildo, or waving with a phantom arm.

The woman rolled over onto her back, rotating with it still inside of her. A move like that would have put him over the top before, but his new penis just craved more. When it finally did come, Orson only felt a ghost of what he would have felt before the injury. It was better than nothing, so he didn't complain. He just brought home more women, and let his penis have its way with them.

He no longer controlled himself. A slave to his prick, he merely did its bidding. At least before he'd been doing it for himself, or had lived under the pretense it was for himself, when really he'd been bound by his obsession.

He wished he'd never called Gina that night. And because he had, he wished Gina hadn't left the door open and Pop had never found him.

He wished he'd died instead.

She grabbed his hand and moved it toward her. Orson fishhooked two fingers into her pussy while his prick battered the inside of her colon, his thumb rubbing her clit, the pads of his fingers pressing against her g-spot until he felt the walls of her cunt contract, and as she cried out in ecstasy his monster cock spewed a huge load into her asshole like a kid puking off a rollercoaster.

He rolled off of her, the penis still rock hard.

"Oh my God, Orson," she breathed, lighting the joint she'd left on the bedside table. "Your big dick is amazing. *Ugly*—but amazing."

"The surgeon said it belonged to a serial killer," he said.

She blew smoke out of her nose in disbelief. "*What?*"

"Yeah. They said he was a real pussy slayer."

The woman laughed. He didn't even remember her name, just some professional-looking blonde woman he'd picked up at a nearby bar, who'd been so obviously craving a good fuck it was like he could smell her desire. Or his new cock could. It had started throbbing at the mere sight of her, full of Big Dick Energy, like a dowsing rod leading him toward water. Like a GPS homing in on her pussy, and finally, her ass.

He almost felt a sense of relief inside of her warm holes, that same feeling he'd been chasing ever since he'd gotten his first handjob when he was thirteen years old, from his best friend's mom behind the bleachers, while the other boys kicked a ball around like blissful idiots.

Like it was *home*.

***

REPORTS OF WOMEN experiencing unusually heavy periods over the past several weeks had gone mostly unnoticed by those in the medical community, and the string of deaths of menstruating women from heart attacks, car accidents, and severe internal bleeding—not to mention ulcers—were never linked by local news media.

Meanwhile, the incidents of clogged toilets around the city rose exponentially. Plumbers were glad for the extra business—all except one, who'd been splashed in the eye while snaking an elderly woman's shitter, and had waked in the night unable to see out of it. He'd gone to the bathroom to find a messy pulp of slime running down his cheek from his puckered eyelids, and stared at it in horror with his working eye.

When the small penis erupted from the eye socket, squirming out like a worm from an apple, Lorne Jameson suffered his third coronary, and his last thoughts as he writhed on the bathroom floor were to curse his wife, who'd often told him, "I swear to God, Lorne, you're gonna die in front of somebody's toilet!"

Which he did.

PRICK SLEPT in the ducts close to the boiler, where the air was warm and dry.

Life was difficult for the most part, ever since Fuck Yeah had bitten off its tail, separating it from God Orson. When Prick wasn't feeding, it spent most of its time lurking in the nooks and crannies and pipes and ductwork of the place where it was born, hiding from the bipedal giants and their furry minions.

This morning, several days after it had penetrated the old bald giant's ear and nested a while in the squishy warmth of his brain, Prick had spent hours worming through the water pipes, splashing up into urine bowls and trailing cold water onto the floors as it slithered into bedrooms, living rooms and kitchens, searching for food. Prick had been consuming a bowl half filled with soggy cereal when the sound of footsteps startled it, and Prick slithered away, spilling the bowl onto the table, and hid under the counter.

The female giant had screamed and chased Prick with a broom through an opened vent, into the next apartment.

Prick could sense God Orson's presence above, and had often communed with Him since they'd been separated. It was about the only pleasure Prick got now, aside from feeding, but its communions with God Orson, while miraculous, were also full of pain.

Prick had inched its way through the empty apartment, climbing counters and onto sofas, finding nothing of sustenance, and had finally slipped into an opened drawer full of bunched underwear, or what Prick had once called "prisons of cloth," until Prick had realized being nestled in the Groin of the Father had been a privilege, not a penance.

Prick had found a box of rubbers among the underwear, what female bipedal giants often called "protection," alongside a small plastic bottle, its cap removed, the blue candy contents spilled out on the bottom of the drawer. The candy had tasted bitter, but Prick had eaten every last one.

And now, as it molted inside the warm duct, shedding the dried-out husk of its too-small skin, Prick's belly grew fat once more.

God Orson the Creator did not know that Prick was female.

He did not know that she was *spawning*.

"I'm the exterminator. Sorry I'm late."

Acting as temporary Superintendent until someone was hired to take the place of the dearly departed, Mrs. Bartleby shook the man's hand and welcomed him to the building.

"What happened to Pop?" the small, slim man in baggy blue coveralls asked.

Mrs. Bartleby looked upwards, thumbing the crucifix around her neck. "He passed, God rest him."

"Oh. That sucks," the exterminator said.

Mrs. Bartleby leaned in close and whispered, "*The rats* got him. At least, that's what I suspect. Crawled right into his ear and chewed a hole in his brain." The exterminator gave her a disbelieving look, and she thumbed her crucifix once more. "So you see, the problem is quite urgent."

"Well, that's why I'm here. You got nothing to worry about, ma'am. I'll find your rats, and I'll kill 'em too. That's my motto," he added, showing her his toolkit, on which the motto was stenciled: I FIND YOUR PESTS AND I KILL THEM TOO!

"Wonderful," Mrs. Bartleby said, rubbing her hands together enthusiastically. "*When* they are dead, I'd like to see the corpses, if that isn't too much of a bother. Mr. Popadopolous—Aristotle—was a dear dear friend, and I'd very much like to know the creature responsible—or *creatures*—are disposed of in a most *in*humane manner."

"Well, that's why I'm here," the exterminator repeated.

"Thank you," Mrs. Bartleby said, touching his arm.

Alvin the Exterminator looked down at her wrinkled hand on his coverall sleeve with distaste until she removed it. "No trouble at all, ma'am," he said finally.

Mrs. Bartelby thanked him, gave him the master keys, and shuffled off to the elevators.

Once the crazy old bat was on her way up, Alvin got down on his hands and knees in front of the register in the foyer, listening to the *tick tick tick* of heat pumping through the duct, his hair blowing lightly in its warmth.

He detected no scent of urine in the air flow, and thumbed the down button for the elevators. Best to check the basement first, before dealing with the old lady again.

Chewed into his brain, he thought, remembering the old broad's words. That was nothing to Alvin. He'd seen a woman chewed to death by rats. He'd seen a man's flesh come alive, wriggling from an infestation of larvae under the skin. He'd seen a basement so filled with orb weavers and cobwebs it was like walking onto the set of a horror movie. He'd even seen a mythical "rat king," a pile of eighteen rats all knotted together at the tail, squeaking and tearing at each other to get free.

Nothing here he wouldn't have seen a hundred times before.

The basement was cool and dimly lit. No smell here, either. Alvin trusted his nose implicitly. If there were rats in the building, he'd have smelled them by now.

A teenaged girl wearing tight-fitting pink jogging pants with JUICY stenciled on the bum stood in the laundry room, tossing handfuls of frilly underwear in reds and blacks into a mesh hamper. He watched her bend to the dryer again, her buttocks jiggling pleasantly, before she popped up and caught him staring. He nodded at her, but she sneered, so Alvin moved on to the boiler room.

He smelled damp concrete, and a very faint sour smell that might have been rat piss, but it definitely wasn't fresh. As far as Alvin was concerned, there hadn't been a rat in this building for a few weeks, maybe even longer. He checked the corners, where dust and dirt and cobwebs had collected, looking for rat turds and finding nothing.

There were some dried insects, but otherwise, it was the cleanest building he'd ever encountered.

"Better check the ducts, just to be safe."

Alvin set his tool kit on the floor, opened it, and removed a multi-bit screwdriver. Too short to reach the ducts on foot, he returned to the hall where he'd seen a plastic milk crate. Standing on the crate, he removed the panel above his head, placed it aside, then stood on his tiptoes, sticking his head through the humming hole.

The inside was dark and littered with clumps of dust and hair and dead flies. Mustiness was the predominant smell, with a trace of copper, like pennies, which he supposed could have been whatever alloy the duct was made from. But a slight salty tang prickled his nostrils. He flashed his Maglite into the gloom.

No droppings here, either.

Alvin twisted around on the balls of his feet to check the other end of the pipe, and nearly jumped at the sight of a mottled purple fruit about the size of a watermelon, oozing clear slime from a smooth, intended gash.

The hole gurgled as more fluid oozed from it. Then it widened, exposing dozens of sharp little teeth. Its long body, at least a foot and a half wide, trailed down the shaft behind it, casting a shadow when his Maglite blasted white light on its eyeless face.

A lamprey? In an apartment building?

Whatever it was, Alvin wasn't about to stick around and find out. He ducked out of the duct so quickly the crate toppled below him, and he fell on his bony ass. The penis slithered through the shaft and dropped out of the vent, landing on him, its teeth gnashing.

Alvin caught it around the throat and hugged it, wrestling it like a gator, desperate to keep its mouth away from him. "Oh fuck! Oh fuck! Oh fuck!"

He rolled over the vicious thing, and if he didn't know better he'd have thought someone was pranking him with a robot movie replica of a giant floppy cock. But it was warm and fleshy, and it kept oozing the sticky clear fluid on his neck and face as he struggled, and he as he spit out a salty gob of it, the full weight of it stuck him like a dick slapped on his forehead.

It was *pre-cum*.

Alvin gagged.

The Juicy Girl stepped into the doorway and screamed, dropping her laundry in front of her on the cement floor.

"What?" Alvin said, struggling. "You never seen a grown man wrestle a giant pecker before?"

The girl's legs gave out, and Alvin took a moment to marvel at the sort of wobbly way she fell to the floor, like she was using an invisible hula hoop. The giant peckerhead jerked toward her as she hit the floor, and Alvin used the distraction to haul back and punch it. Its flesh was soft and clammy under his knuckles.

The pecker returned its attention to the struggle, foreskin fanning out like one of those screamy dinosaurs from *Jurassic Park* as it bared its fangs at Alvin.

Too bad it doesn't got any balls, he thought, gripping it around the throat—*Shaft? Whatever the fuck it is...*

He felt its lower half wrap around him before he could kick it away, and suddenly it began to squeeze, crushing his scrawny ribs. He gasped, his grip loosening from the pecker's throat. Its mouth opened impossibly wide, and the head darted at him, foreskin enveloping his head like an executioner's hood.

The last thing Alvin the Exterminator felt before he blacked out was those sharp little teeth grazing over his scalp.

Unfortunately, he regained consciousness a short time later with his flesh dissolving, his screams of agony muffled by the warm, thrumming insides of the giant mutant pecker.

His death was most assuredly not humane.

ZOEY OPENED the door to find Dan standing in the hall with a cooked chicken, a bottle of white, and a stack of DVDs.

"Movie night," he said with a boyish grin, and leaned in to kiss her.

She stepped aside to let him in, and he moved past toward the living room, where he planted himself on the couch. He set the food on the counter, the wine bottle on a coaster—he was learning—and the DVDs beside it.

Zoey went to the cupboard and got down two long-stemmed wine goblets. She held them crisscrossed in one hand while she grabbed the corkscrew, and brought them to the couch. The chicken smelled excellent, making her stomach rumble. "What did you bring?"

"Oh, just a handful of the greatest films in the history of moviedom," he said.

"Moviedom?"

He shrugged. "It's a work in progress."

She looked through them: *Aliens, Prometheus, Predator, Batman v Superman: The Director's Cut*. "I guess I'll go with the *Alien* one," she said with little enthusiasm.

"Actually, it's *Alien 2*, not one. Excellent choice, though. Ripley is one of my favorite characters of all time. You'll love it."

Dan got up, and while he put the DVD into the player, Zoey poured the wine. He came back, drew an arm over her shoulder, and sipped his chardonnay.

They split up the chicken and rice, and ate on the couch while the movie played. A good way through, during what Dan had twice referred to as "the chestburster scene," a knock at the door interrupted them.

Dan paused the movie and glanced at his watch. "It's half past nine. Who the hell could it be?"

Zoey shrugged and got up. The movie was decent, but she wasn't really invested, too worried about her big meeting at work tomorrow to focus. "I'll check." She crossed to the front door and peered through the peephole. "It's Orson Ladd," she whispered to him.

"What does he want?" Dan asked.

Zoey addressed the peephole. "What do you want, Orson?"

"I need help," he said. He sounded frightened. "Something is wr-wrong with me."

She couldn't imagine why he'd want to talk to her, of all people. Aside from that day at the coffee shop—the same day Mr. Popadopolous had been found dead in the laundry room, having slipped in a puddle and landed on one of his tools, which had apparently penetrated his ear canal—she hadn't even seen him at all. Some of their neighbors had speculated he'd been sleeping during the day, waking at night only for casual encounters with women, possibly even prostitutes. There was talk at the last condo board meeting of having him ejected, but so far no one could think of an actual violation he'd made to any of the charter rules.

Still, the guilt gnawed at her for ditching him that night. "Orson, it's past nine. Can't we talk tomorrow? At the coffee shop?"

"It can't wait 'til tomorrow!" he shouted, his voice breaking.

"She has a guest!" Dan shouted back.

Zoey winced. "Orson, Dan's here. We're watching a movie."

Orson pounded feebly on the door once more. Zoey peered out, and saw that he stood with both fists pressed against it, eyes squeezed shut as if he was in immense physical or psychic pain.

Then his eyes snapped open, dark and full of terror, and he jerked his head to his left. He slipped away from the door, staggering off toward the stairwell, hands held out to protect himself. Zoey squinted at the convex lens, looking for any sign of someone out there in the hall with him, but unless the person was crawling on the carpet, it appeared to be empty.

She heard the stairwell door open. Then the red bell alarm above her head went off, the sound drilling into her ears—*Like Mr. Popadopolous*, she thought—and she stepped away from the peephole, covering them.

She'd hated that sound ever since junior school, when someone had pulled the fire alarm right before recess, and they'd spent the entire fifteen minutes standing stupidly in lines of boys and girls when they should have been playing, and one of the boys had pulled faces at her from across the yard. Stuck in line, with Mrs. Winters watching the girls like a hawk, she hadn't been able to retaliate.

"What the hell?" Dan shouted, rising from the couch. "The bastard pulled the goddamn fire alarm! Right in the middle of the chestburster scene."

"Would you forget about the chestyburst thing?" Zoey said. "We have to leave the apartment!"

"It's not a fire! It's not even a drill!"

"We don't know he pulled the alarm..."

"Only one way to find out," Dan said, and moved past her to the door. He unlocked and unchained it, then opened it on an even louder rattling. He peered left and right before covering his ears and stepping out.

Zoey stood by the couch, watching the open door and the empty hall beyond, awaiting Dan's return.

The bell above the door kept jangling.

Dan stepped back into the doorway, startling her. "The alarm's been pulled." He turned to look down the opposite end of the hall. "Nothing to worry about," he said to Zoey's neighbors. "Some joker pulled the alarm." She heard a muffled reply. "I say, 'Some joker's pulled the alarm!' No, it wasn't me, you muppet. If it was me, why would I have said it? Go back to bed, for Pete's sake."

Dan stepped in and pulled the door closed behind himself.

"I tried to put the little handle thingy back, but it didn't work. Just have to wait it out, I guess." He peered out the peephole. "Cripes, they're still going. I told them it was a false alarm..."

"It's building policy. We should be going, too."

"Oh, Zo." He gave her a condescending pout. "Don't be so uptight, eh?"

"Maybe you should go home," she suggested, trying not to sound angry.

"I thought I was sleeping here tonight?" He winked. "Why do you think I got you all drunk and frightened?"

"I really wasn't in the mood tonight, anyway. And this—" She indicated the alarm, still being hammered by its clapper. "—this hasn't helped *get* me there."

"Orson Ladd strikes again," Dan said.

"What's that supposed to mean?"

"It means, he's been worming into your head for as long as I've known you. Messing with your mind. I *know* you still feel guilty about leaving him that night—"

"That's not fair..." she said, feeling small and ashamed. She slumped down on the couch, reaching for her glass of wine.

"He's playing on your sympathetic nature, don't you see? He knows you're a soft touch."

Something heavy fell against the outside of the door.

"Oh great! There he is again, right on time," Dan said, and twisted the door handle, jerking it open. "Right, I've had just about enough of—"

An enormous flesh-toned caterpillar rose up on its veiny belly, its purple head rearing back, its vertical, blood-red mouth opening wide. Dan stumbled back from the door, his voice rising in a scream of unadulterated terror as the creature vomited a thick, pearl-colored fluid onto him, and he held up his hands to shield himself from the violent onslaught, his scream ending in choking and gasps.

Zoey froze on the couch, unable to mentally process the sight of a giant penis spasming as it showered her boyfriend in sticky gobs of semen while the alarm still rattled above his head. It was like something out of a low-budget horror movie, only the penis creature was not a puppet, nor was it CGI. It was flesh and blood and jism, and it was standing in her doorway.

I have to do something...

Determined, Zoey grabbed the wine bottle, and thrust herself to her feet.

The penis had stopped spewing and slumped onto its belly in front of Dan, who dripped with its creamy filth, flicking his hands and spitting out a mouthful. Then the creature hunched up like an inchworm and dragged itself toward Dan, who sat in a very unfortunate position, with his legs splayed.

Zoey called his name, and he turned to her, looking confused and frightened. "Get out of the way!"

Dan drew his legs up and rolled to his side just as the creature's blunt, eyeless head began prodding the rug where he'd been sitting, like a blind man's cane. In the brief respite, Zoey launched the wine bottle, and it shattered on the creature's side. Its thin skin split open in several places, bleeding.

And they say pussies are fragile, Zoey thought.

The creature wobbled, seemingly stunned. She seized the opportunity to run for Dan. "Are you okay? It's not acid or anything, is it?"

He blinked painfully, wiping the milky fluid from his face. "No, it's just really fucking stinging my eyes!"

She grabbed his slimy hand, and hauled him to his feet.

"Where are we going?" he asked her, in a small voice reminiscent of a child's.

"To the balcony," she said, and he followed along behind her as she ran.

ORSON BOLTED UP seven flights of stairs, not daring to look down, fearing the beast was behind him, mere dick inches from his feet.

He never should have let it back into his apartment, he knew that now. He'd just been so overjoyed to have finally found it, after a long, desperate week without hope, that he hadn't been able to think straight. So he'd opened the door, and let the lonely, miserable thing crawl up under his bathrobe. It had fit like a glove against the open sore the surgeon had left for his eventual transplant, looking somewhat like a nasal cavity without the nose. Orson had closed the door gently, had locked it, and untied his robe to look down at himself.

"My beautiful prick," he'd said.

It had returned.

He'd washed it standing in the tub before the full-length mirror he'd had installed, admiring its heft and shape. The wound itself had mostly healed, the only evidence a small red-brown ring of scar tissue at the base of the shaft.

The prick itself had seemed larger somehow, and Orson hadn't questioned it at the time, just assumed it was an optical illusion caused by its absence. Now he knew better. It really *had* been growing—was *still* growing—because of the cancer inside it.

At the hospital, once he'd surfaced from unconsciousness, the surgeon had actually declared him lucky. Gina maiming him had saved him the trouble of going through chemotherapy, and the possible penectomy operation if chemo hadn't worked.

He would have gladly suffered months of radiation sickness, had he known the alternative.

When his prick hadn't been having its way with dozens of women over the past six weeks, returning to him nightly—God only knew where it spent its days—Orson had researched the symbiosis between parasites and their hosts. He'd read about the lancet liver fluke, a microorganism eaten by cows and humans, which laid eggs in their intestines. The eggs were excreted, eaten by snails, and the live flukes eaten again by ants. The fluke was so sophisticated in its programming that it was actually able, once it had burrowed into the brain of its ant host, to draw the ant to the top of a blade of grass to be eaten by cows, effectively committing suicide.

Orson found it humbling to know he was no more sophisticated than an ant.

In the meantime, he'd worried about his sperm. How many of those women had been on the pill? How many potential offspring did he now have growing inside their bellies? Or was his sperm even viable? Orson hoped to God it wasn't.

Meanwhile, his prick grew and grew. John Holmes would have been jealous.

Then, for an entire week, his prick hadn't visited him. He'd waited up, had even scheduled dates, but his dates had left unhappy, and Orson had drank himself to sleep. Seven days, feeling both hopeless and hope*ful*—wishing his prick would return while praying he'd never see it again.

And tonight, it came back.

As tall as a man and throbbing, leaving wet slime trails on his carpet, his prick had returned once more. Orson had taken one look at it and run terrified from the apartment, running to the only person in the building he'd thought might lend him a sympathetic ear: Zoey Esprit. She would help him if anyone would.

But she hadn't. Her posh British boy-toy had been there, and now Orson was running for his life, hurtling up the stairs two by two, hot breath tearing his lungs as his penis—a giant Freudian metaphor— chased him like something out of a childhood nightmare.

Orson burst through a door marked 23 and raced into the hall. He risked a glance behind himself as the door swung to a close, saw nothing lurking in the brightened stairwell, and carried on running.

His neighbors were leaving their apartments, heading his way. The fire alarm had drawn them from their slumber, or whatever they'd been doing. Most of them looked annoyed, but annoyed was a hell of a lot better than being dead.

Orson pushed through and hurried into his apartment, straight to the kitchen, and to the knife drawer. He took what he needed and returned to the door, catching a glimpse of himself in the foyer mirror. A madman in a bathrobe, holding an electric knife, hair damp with sweat and falling in his crazed eyes.

He hurried out, back to the stairs. A long line of aggravated people trudged slowly down to the first floor, the elevators stopped by the fire alarm. Orson buzzed the knife, startling the closest people to him.

A well-dressed Indian couple stepped aside with looks of undisguised terror.

"Out of the way! The dickless wonder's gone nuts!" some college bro shouted over the alarms, and his wonky-toothed girlfriend laughed at the play on words.

Orson zipped the cordless knife at him, and the kid fell back, bumping into the Indian couple behind him and dragging his girlfriend down by the hand. The way cleared then, as those in front looked up to see a lunatic in a bathrobe brandishing a weapon, and pressed themselves against the wall.

He bounded down the rest of the way, hoping he wasn't already too late to save Zoey and her boy-toy.

PRICK FELL into the sticky sludge of her own amniotic fluid, feeling the agony of loss for the millions of eggs crushed under her weight. Barely conscious, she lay there bleeding from her new flesh on her surviving brood, trying to muster up the will to carry on.

Prick blinked amnion from her eye and saw the bipedal not-so-giant female through a milky haze, dragging her companion out onto the balcony.

Prick burned with a single desire: the female had to pay.

She hunched up and dragged herself along the carpet, hunched and dragged.

In a moment, she would have them—both of them—close enough now to see the terror in their eyes. She would swallow them whole, digesting them over several hours as she had the exterminator, or immobilize them and eat them slowly, torturing them, savoring each bite.

Prick launched herself at the female, and slammed against an invisible barrier. She fell back, stunned, writhed in pain on the floor.

The female laughed.

Prick twisted to face her enemy, seething with rage at the heavy glass separating her from lunch.

She rose groggily, threw herself at the glass.

Both meals drew back from the door, casting nervous glances over their shoulders.

On Prick's third attempt, the glass began to crack.

⸻

ZOEY AND DAN stepped away from the balcony door, and looked over the ledge. A jump of eight floors might not kill them, but it wouldn't be pleasant. Especially now that the grass was milling with people. It wasn't as if they could crowd surf.

"Help!" Zoey shouted, waving her hands. Dan joined her. Over the blaring alarms, no one heard them, or at least made any indication they had. Sirens had joined the cacophony, making it even less likely they'd be heard.

"We could try to climb down to the next balcony," Dan suggested, but he didn't sound enthused.

The creature threw itself against the door a fourth time, streaking the glass with blood, making Dan jump up close to her, smearing the thing's vomit or semen on her favorite blouse.

The crack spider-webbed outward.

Soon, the glass would shatter.

A choice had to be made: certain death at the mouth of this... *thing*, or climb down to the next balcony, risking the fall?

The creature drew back, its blood-red urethra—mouth?—*eye?*—widening, and hurtled itself at the glass.

The cracked glass warped outward, held firm by the sheet of clear plastic on the outside. One more strike and the tiny square shards would fall onto the balcony and the creature would be upon them.

Dan grasped her hand. Together they watched as the thing began to dance behind the cracks, jerking back and forth like a puppet dancing on its strings.

Blood spattered the inside of the glass.

Vaguely, over the sound of the alarm, Zoey heard whining, or drilling.

A whirring blade tore through the front of the giant penis under its purple head—the frenulum, she supposed—and gouged downward, spewing blood and meat and flesh at the glass. Its urethra unleashed a horrible screech—*Mouth it is*, Zoey thought—and it began to topple sideways, smearing its insides down the door like a bug on a windshield.

Orson stood behind it, holding a bloodied electric knife, his arms and face and bathrobe drenched in gore.

"I told you it couldn't wait," he said.

"Is it dead?" Dan asked.

"I don't know, but I'm not waiting around to find out." He pulled on the door. With the broken glass pushed outward, it wouldn't budge beyond the bulge. "I'm gonna find something to smash it."

Orson disappeared into the apartment.

"He'll probably end up rooting through your sex drawer," Dan said.

Zoey flashed him an angry look, and eyed the creature for movement. It appeared to be breathing, its body rising and falling so slightly it could have been her imagination.

A moment later, Orson came back with her bedside drawer.

"What did I tell you," Dan said.

Zoey just rolled her eyes.

"Step back," Orson said as he prepared to launch the drawer. Zoey and Dan pressed back as far against the ledge as they could, while below the fire engines finallly arrived, their red lights flashing over the pebbled exterior wall.

The drawer punched through the glass, landing on a corner and splintering, spilling her contact lens solution, glasses case, lubricant, condoms, her little pink vibrator, and other nighttime things onto the balcony.

Both men stared at the vibrator.

"What?" she said. "Everyone has a vibrator, it's perfectly normal!"

Orson shrugged. "I have a vibrator," he said, and when Dan gave him a look, he added, "Don't you judge me."

Zoey flashed them an angry look, scooped her vibrator up into the pocket of her loose pants, and stepped over the mess into the apartment.

"What the hell is that thing?" Zoey asked, quickly stepping over the creature.

"That was my penis," Orson said.

She looked down at it from a cautious few steps away. "Why is it so..." There was no other way to describe it than, "...*huge*?"

"It's not *that* big," Dan scoffed, and jumped over the creature.

Orson looked his rival up and down. "What the hell happened to you?"

"I don't want to talk about it," Dan mumbled, swiping thick liquid from his shirt onto the carpet.

Zoey stopped suddenly on their way to the door, throwing her arms out wide to halt the men walking on either side of her. "Hang on a second," she said, turning back to the creature on the floor.

"What are you doing?" Dan asked.

"I'm gonna make sure that fucker's dead," she told him, approaching it cautiously.

The creature's body expanded and contracted, like the shallow breath of someone sleeping. She wondered, did it have organs? Lungs? A *brain*?

She would soon find out.

From the gaping wound Orson had carved with his turkey knife, she saw bits of bone: a ribcage, a spinal column. At first she thought it might be the creature's, that it had somehow *grown* a skeleton—which wasn't much crazier than the fact that Orson's severed penis had become sentient, and grown to the size of a human.

But as she drew nearer, she saw other bones among the gore of its innards: long with knobby ends, like human limbs, and smaller bones like fingers, and it dawned on her...

It had eaten someone alive.

Swallowing any pity that might have remained for the creature, she stepped down hard with her high heel on its bulbous head.

The men sucked in wincing breaths behind her.

"Oh grow up!" she said, wiping her shoe on the carpet.

Satisfied, she crossed the room to where Dan and Orson waited.

The kitchen faucet began to rumble and shake.

What now? she thought, glad her insurance would cover most of the damage to her apartment.

The three of them turned to each other, taking in one another's confused and frightened faces, and a violent splash arose from the bathroom.

PRICK WAS DYING.

Killed by the hands of her God. God Orson. The Creator.

She lay on the carpet in a puddle of her own blood and shards of glass, while the female and male followed God Orson to the exit.

And then she felt it: tremors in the floor arising from the pipes and the ducts.

They were coming.

As the female's foot squelched down on her head, ending Prick's short life, she found some comfort to ease her journey through that last long, dark, warm and wet tunnel toward death.

Her children had come home.

THE FAUCET ROCKETED UP from the sink with a clang, smashing a hole in Zoey's ceiling.

Zoey turned to watch as hundreds of fat pink larvae oozed out of the pipes, crawling over each other, their purple heads searching blindly.

Not larvae, she thought. *Penises. Its brood. Her* babies.

A wary glance down the hall confirmed there were more of them spilling out of the toilet, splatting wetly on the bathroom tile, and from the slots of the air vents, and from the cold air return... They swarmed the chicken carcass, devouring scraps of meat and leftover food on the plates.

She shook Dan, who stood immobile, gaping in horror at the sight before them.

"We have to get out of here!" she shouted.

Orson threw a final glance toward his giant cock, and nodded defiantly. He lead the way into the hall. Zoey and Dan followed him. He jerked down the remaining fire alarm as he passed, and threw a look over his shoulder. "So everyone doesn't come piling back in," he explained.

It seemed smart to Zoey, but when Orson opened the door to the stairwell and began going up instead of down, she wondered if he'd lost his mind.

Maybe his brain really was in his penis, she thought with bitter amusement.

"Where are you going?" Dan asked. "We've got to get out of here."

"I'm not leaving," Orson said, and a drop of gore fell from the electric knife onto his slipper. "Not until all of those wriggly little fuckers are dead."

"But *how*?" Zoey wondered.

Orson smiled darkly. "I'm going to call them back to Papa," he said, and nodded toward the ascending flights. "Go. You don't want to see this."

"No," Zoey said. "I'm staying to help."

He shook his head. "This is my fight."

"But what if your plan doesn't work?"

"It'll work," Orson said. "And if it doesn't... well, hopefully Mrs. Bartleby calls in some good fumigators. Now go on." He flashed them a smile. "Make lots of babies."

Zoey and Dan exchanged a brief look—an identical "Is he nuts?" expression on their faces—and started down the stairs.

Orson watched them go, catching a good glimpse of the last great ass he'd ever see—the last *two* of them, if he was to be honest—and turned to climb the stairs.

Five minutes later, Orson sat on the couch in front of his television. He'd set a tube of strawberry-flavored lubricant and a box of Kleenex on the table beside him, and he flicked on the cable box to his favorite channel. On the screen, two porn stars he knew by name violently scissored each other, sharing a long purple dildo between them, crying out *"Fuck yeah! Fuck yeah!"*

The stirrings of arousal had always brought his penis home.

He hoped it would bring her babies.

SOPHIE AND DAN mingled into the crowd of sleepy, annoyed apartment-dwellers, the lights of two fire engines flashing red over their faces. Some gave them strange looks, but most didn't paid no attention as they stood waiting for the alarms to stop.

"I'd like to take this opportunity to apologize on behalf of my gender," Dan said.

Zoey laughed and shook her head. She took his hand, and he gave her a quizzical look. "Don't be a dick," she said.

The two of them smiled and looked up, way up, hoping like hell Orson knew what he was doing.

ORSON LADD SAT WATCHING the women punch each other's cervixes with lubed fists, and thought back on his life.

He'd slept with hundreds of women in his thirty-one years, but he'd never accomplished much else in his life. He'd gotten his real estate license, sold some condos and homes to young couples starting their lives together, and that was fine, it had been rewarding, but he'd mostly done it for the money. He'd learned how to play guitar, brew his own beer, played on a coed baseball team, taken salsa and cooking lessons, but every one of those pastimes had been to impress women.

Orson drank the last gulp of lethal brown sludge. Swallowing, he heard the first rumblings from the pipes below.

"This is it, Orson..."

A moment later, the toilet erupted. The kitchen faucet exploded under the pressure, sending a shower of miniature penises splattering against the cabinetry, the counters and the tiles. When the heat kicked on, they began pouring out of the vents until the screws snapped and the vent covers popped off, spilling out onto the floor, crawling over each other in a writhing mass that swished and undulated like a pink and purple ocean, its surf teeming with tiny penis-shaped piranhas as the apartment slowly filled.

Orson shook violently, painful spasms gripping his innards. He'd drank half a box of rat poison, unsure how much would be lethal, only certain he'd need to consume a lot of it if he wanted to kill them all.

The first wave climbed up to his shins, dozens of the little maggot-like creatures sticking to his hairy legs, nibbling his flesh, crawling upwards. As the swarm overtook him, he untied his bathrobe, let it fall to his sides, and spread his arms wide to let all of his bastard creations come unto him.

His entire life had been consumed by thoughts of pussy, but it was pricks that consumed him in the end.

As the last of them plopped bloated and dead from his picked-clean bones, the alarms finally stopped ringing.

THE BURDEN

Amelia washed her father's trembling hands with a damp cloth, wrung it out into the bowl of cool water she'd set beside his wheelchair, and wiped sweat from his brow.

His sweat was not from exertion but from the heat in his upstairs bedroom. Her father never exerted himself anymore, and they had yet to begin their daily routine. Since Amelia had returned home to take care of him he existed in one of two states: sitting and resting. Sometimes she sat him in front of his bedroom window. Other times she sat him at the kitchen table or the back porch with a view of the bird feeders and the large maple her mother and father had planted when they'd bought the house several years before Amelia was born.

When she crouched beside him she could never tell if he saw exactly what she did. He could no longer communicate, except through simple eye movements, blinking once for *yes* and two for *no*. He couldn't feed himself, so he "ate" via an endoscopic tube. Couldn't bathe himself. Dress himself. Couldn't go to the bathroom without her help. She would often find she was already too late.

Not long ago her father had been strong, healthy, active. He'd eaten right. Hadn't smoked, never drank to excess. When her mother had been with them (*God rest her*, Amelia thought reflexively, though she no longer believed in God), her parents had hiked the nearby woods each morning after breakfast, and biked the dirt roads to and from the house at dusk. He'd exercised his minds as well as his body, completing puzzles, reading mystery novels, making woodworking projects by hand.

James Adam Corbel had done everything experts had suggested to stave off disease, dementia and the eventual wasting away of old age. And like a hijacked jet, amyotrophic lateral sclerosis had crashed into his body and demolished all of his progress. Medical experts called his current condition "locked-in," meaning her father was locked inside of his own mind.

Amelia placed the modified Brain-Computer Interface on her father's head and booted up her laptop. The software worked using subdural implants, converting electrical impulses from the limbic system to interact via transmitter with software on the computer. Researchers had already used the technology successfully to help ALS patients communicate with caregivers and loved ones but after months of daily attempts her father had yet to respond.

She'd known the process would take time. In the original study it had taken weeks for patients to type out a single letter using BCI tech-nology, and those results had been far better than previous attempts with locked-in patients. As far back as 1995, a journalist had written an entire book by blinking it to a transcriber. It had taken ten months and *two-hundred thousand blinks*, at an average of one word every two minutes, to finish the book.

Amelia had taken a sabbatical from her duties at the Academy. She had all the time in the world to work with her father. What she couldn't count on was how much time her father had left to live.

Just one letter and she would consider the day well spent.

"Come on, Dad... Let's make today a good one."

The software launched on her laptop, a combination word processor and image manipulation program she'd "borrowed" from the Academy. The cursor blinked on the white page. On the opposite side of the screen was a three-dimensional wireframe ball.

The idea was that her father could either type a word or move the ball, depending on his mood or mental landscape. Her thought was that just using a word processor might be too restricting. This way her father could work at his own level. She wondered though, if giving him too many choices had been the wrong way to go.

"How are you feeling today, Dad?"

His moist, jaundiced eyes twitched toward her. He blinked hard.

One for *yes*. Not exactly the response she was hoping for.

"Can you type it for me?"

He merely looked at her.

"Can you move the ball?"

The wireframe ball did not move.

Eventually he blinked, but she suspected it was involuntary.

Weeks of this.

Sweat had broken on his brow again. She dipped the washcloth and wiped it away.

"Not too much longer now, Dad. I'll take you downstairs to sit at the window when we're done. I think I saw the cardinal out there earlier."

He blinked.

The eyes themselves expressed no emotion. No sign of whether or not he wanted to continue, if he was finished with today's attempt or if he was done with the research altogether. He'd never given expressed permission to participate, aside from a blink for *yes*. For all she knew the whole process was torture to him—from the minor surgery to insert the subdural implants to the daily barrage of questions.

His body was already a prison, and his facial expression did seem to indicate anguish. The upward arch of his eyebrows and his angled, twisted lips made Helena, the caregiver who came in daily to help, once comment that it looked like he was perpetually going to the toilet.

It could have been far worse. At least he could still blink. Some patients couldn't even control that. Without her father's blinks for *yes* and *no* she might have given up on the experiment entirely. She might have put him in a hospital. Let him waste away to nothing.

Tears prickled her sinuses and she held them back, not wanting to cry in front of her dad, who couldn't help but cry in response despite his once-rugged exterior.

If only she could tell what he was thinking, but that was something she also hoped to achieve. Not only did she wish to communicate with her father, over time she hoped other researchers might be able to use similar the technology to map the human brain and bridge the gap between humans and AI.

Without the constraints of language and movement, Amelia saw virtually no limit to how much Humanity could achieve.

Without the burden of the body restricting the intellect.

But right now she couldn't even get him to push a goddamn ball or type a single letter.

"Just... push the ball, okay, Dad?"

The ball remained still.

"Can you push the ball? *Dad?*"

Blink blink.

She brought a fist down hard on the small table. *"Can you please push the goddamn ball?"*

The laptop rattled. Something thudded to the floor downstairs.

Amelia turned to the doorway and the stairwell beyond, thinking she must have shaken something loose.

Don't know my own strength.

She leaned down to stroke her father's wispy silvery hair and kissed his clammy liver-spotted forehead. "I'm sorry, Dad. I didn't mean to get mad. I'll be right back, okay? Then I'll bring you down to watch the birds."

Her father didn't blink.

Amelia left the room. The stairs of the old house creaked as she descended. Her great-grandfather's grandfather clock ticked away in the empty foyer. As she reached the first floor she could see into the living room. From where she stood at the bottom of the stairs nothing appeared to be out of place.

"Good morning, Ms. Amelia," Helena said behind her.

Amelia jumped, not expecting the caregiver to arrive for another hour. The woman held bags of groceries in her hands and must have let herself in from the garage with her spare key. Amelia helped the young woman, pleasingly plump in her pale blue nurse's scrubs, to unload the food into the fridge.

Later she brought her father downstairs on the chairlift and while he stared out the window at the birds fluttering around the feeders and the stone birdbath under the big maple she sat in the old wicker rocker beside him catching up on some research on the role endocannabinoids played on pathological anxiety.

Amelia's main field of study was cognitive science. She'd worked through her doctorate and had moved into the research field upon graduating. After nearly ten years she'd decided practically begging for grants was something she no longer wanted from life, and had taken an open position teaching specialized cognitive biology at the Academy of Modern Science in Boston.

When her father had called about his diagnosis she'd packed up at the Academy within the week and taken the train home to Toronto. The trip had taken her nearly a full day, and on the way she'd wondered how a university professor with no children and no nursing experience was going to take care of a man who'd responded to her scraped knees as a child with a brisk *Walk it off*.

When she'd arrived home her father had already been using a walker to get around. His limbs had shaken uncontrollably and his fingers had curled up into virtually useless fists. He'd fibbed about the progress of his illness. His specialist had given him between two and five years to live, but likely no more than three.

That was six months ago.

Amelia closed her computer and turned to him. Outside the cardinal was back, a bright red male with a crest on its head. It landed in the birdbath, startling the sparrows, and splashed its wings in the water.

It used to make her smile to see the joy those simple creatures brought to him, this old fashioned "man's man" who'd wanted a son but had been equally happy—if not more—with a girl. Who'd taught her how to hook a worm, play baseball, fight back against bullies, and never let a man treat her like a second-class citizen.

With his face twisted in an eternal rictus it was impossible to tell if the birds still made him happy. Was there joy in his tired green eyes? She couldn't tell. His disease had advanced so rapidly in the past six months he could no longer utter even a single laugh.

Amelia rolled her father into the kitchen. After dinner—Helena had prepared the blend of fruits and vegetables and nuts for her father's endoscopic meal—Amelia helped Helena clean up and wash dishes.

On her way upstairs she leaned into the living room and saw the baseball lying in the middle of the wooden floor.

"Helena?"

The woman came in from the kitchen, soap foam crackling on her yellow plastic gloves. "Yes, Ms. Amelia?"

"Did you dust my father's baseball?"

The woman gave her a confused look.

Amelia tried not to sound upset as she pointed at the ball on the floor. "That's his Jackie Mitchell baseball. It's a collector's item."

Helena shrugged. "I didn't dust today, Ms. Amelia."

Amelia watched the woman head back to the kitchen before bending to pick up the ball. She turned it over in her hand, reading the signature, chuckling bitterly at the irony.

Her father had gotten it when Amelia was young to remind her not to limit herself because of how the world might view her, that she could do anything she put her mind to with determination and strength. Jackie Mitchell had proved that by becoming one of the first female pitchers in professional baseball, and as her signature on the ball said she had beaten two legendary heavy hitters.

I struck out Babe Ruth and Lou Gehrig, it read.

That her father had picked this baseball of all the signed balls he could have gotten felt somewhat eerie.

ALS had also struck out Lou Gehrig; the disease itself had once been named after him.

Amelia wasn't sure she believed Helena hadn't knocked it down off the mantle, but she couldn't imagine why the woman would lie about it. If she *hadn't* moved the ball it had somehow managed to pop up out of its clear Lucite box stand, fall to the floor and roll to the center of the room of its own volition.

What was more unbelievable? That sweet trustworthy Helena had told a small fib for the first time since Amelia had known her? Or that an inanimate object had defied the laws of physics?

With a troubled frown, Amelia returned the ball to its stand.

It was time to face the truth, she decided: the experiment just wasn't working.

Despite all the coaxing over the past twenty-three weeks her father couldn't manage to type a single letter using the BCI, and she was beginning to fear they were better off when he was still just barely able to hold a pen, eking out two words a minute.

His health seemed to be deteriorating faster, as well. His crippled arms hung loose from his shoulders, lacking muscle, tired flesh sagging. Ribs clearly visible. Spine protruding like the back plates of a dinosaur. Sallow, sunken eyes. Teeth receding from his gums.

Dr. Jorgenson said her father wouldn't live much longer than six months in his current condition. He'd suggested she consider moving her father into a hospital for round-the-clock care.

Amelia had strongly opposed the idea.

The decision to keep him home was entirely selfish, she knew. Imagining her father wasting away in the hospital like her mother had after her stroke... she couldn't go through that again. Couldn't watch it happen to such a strong man as he'd been.

But the obsessive in her—a trait she'd gotten from her father—needed to continue their work here. She felt close to a breakthrough, in spite of all evidence to the contrary.

She knew they could always try communicating through eye movement, not through blinks but using the tracking software on her laptop. Her father might have taken to it quickly despite his misgivings but she didn't want him to get used to the ease of it.

By making the BCI his only method of communication she hoped it would force him to adapt or risk never speaking to his daughter again. Although she couldn't blame him if he chose the latter, after she'd treated him like a lab rat for so long.

"Come on, Dad." Amelia positioned the headset on his thinning scalp as her laptop fired up. "Today's the day, huh?"

She didn't believe a word of it.

Her modified interface converted several signals from the implants in her father's brain—EEG, iEEG, LFP, and other sensory input—into data her computer could process. It worked because the brain itself was essentially a computer, albeit far more complex than her laptop. With the addition of small implants on the medial prefrontal and medial posterior parietal cortexes, she hoped he might eventually be able to manipulate a 3-dimensional version of himself through self-recognition, a notion first attempted using virtual reality tech.

If only she could get him to type a single letter.

The air was sweltering in her father's room today. She brought a fan upstairs and set it in the window. It whirred distractingly as she sweated hunched over the computer but the cool breeze curbed her growing agitation.

After half an hour of watching him blink his bleary eyes she stood up.

"All right, Dad," she sighed, her spine popping as she stretched. "I guess we're done here."

As she moved to flick off the laptop the sound of the fan lowered in timbre, the blades slowing until they stopped altogether.

She bent to check the plug. It was loose but didn't appear to be the problem.

As she stood again she saw her father watching her in the big mirror on her mother's vanity. Off to his immediate left she saw the alarm clock no longer showed the time in its large red digital numbers.

"Power's out?"

Her father blinked once.

She put a comforting hand on his shoulder. "I'll be right back, okay, Dad?"

Leaving him in his wheelchair she hurried downstairs to check the electrical box. Helena wouldn't be in for another hour or so—her two young children had the day off school—and Amelia still retained a bit of childhood superstition about being alone in the big old empty family home despite having been back so long. She'd always felt that unease even more acutely in the basement, and although she wasn't imagining ghouls and beasties in every corner like she had as a child, the memory of her brief sojourns to the basement for a popsicle or an errand brought that childish fear back to the forefront of her brain.

The basement was bright enough she didn't require a flashlight. Sunlight streamed in through the two grimy windows on either side of the furnace with their view of the leaf-clogged cement wells. Even if it had been fully dark down here, what the eye couldn't see would have filled in by memory.

The mind is all-powerful, Amelia thought as she stepped off the creaky wood stairs, assaulted by smells, sights, sensations and memories. The smell of dust, wood and damp concrete. The drip of the washbasin faucet. The gurgle of the floor drain, a misplaced tennis ball nearby. Dust on her fingers from the stair railing. Rough wood of the stairs on her sock feet.

A computer couldn't process so much disparate information so quickly.

The burden of the body, she thought.

Cobwebs hung from the corners of the rafters, wood charred black in places by a fire that had happened long before the Corbels had moved in. As a little girl she'd often wondered if anyone had died in the fire but she'd never bothered to ask her parents or look into it herself. The walls were exposed down to the lath. The concrete cold on her sock feet as she crossed to the electrical box.

Her father had updated from fuses to circuit breakers when Amelia was young, worried the old knob and tube wiring might cause another house fire. She flicked the main switch down and back up.

As she did a blue tendril of electricity unfurled from the switch and as it struck her finger an image blossomed in her mind of her father lying upstairs in his bed. Not vague as if from memory or imagination but genuinely as though she were sitting right across from him. He was looking directly at her, though she realized she was not looking directly back at him but at his reflection in the vanity, made obvious by missing flecks of silver backing and the chip in the lower right corner Amelia herself had made when she'd tripped and fallen playing dress-up with her mother's jewelry.

It was almost as if she were *looking out through her father's eyes.*

In the mirror, her father blinked.

Yes.

The mirror cracked suddenly, fracturing his face down the middle. The pain of the shock finally reached her nerves and the vision disappeared as quickly as it had come, sending her reeling back from the electrical box.

Amelia fell down hard on her butt and her left hand struck the yellow-green tennis ball which rolled lazily toward the sports equipment bin.

Standing and rubbing her sore buttock, she wondered how to explain what had just happened. She'd never experienced anything like it before, never imagined anything with such clarity.

But it *was* her imagination, of that she was certain. It had to be.

Idly she surveyed the room. Her gaze fell on the tennis ball.

How did that get out of the bin?

Two weeks had passed since the incident with the Jackie Mitchell baseball, long enough that she'd forgotten about it until just then.

Was it possible the two were connected?

She recalled the vision of her father, blinking at her in the mirror.

Yes, Amelia.

Amelia crossed to the bin and picked up the tennis ball. She placed it carefully beside the drain where she'd found it when she'd first come down. Stood again and kept it under a watchful eye.

"Can you move the ball, Dad?"

The ball didn't even twitch.

"Dad? Move the ball for me, please."

Amelia stared at it. *Willed* it to move.

She was so focused on the ball the sudden buzz and rattle of the air conditioner firing up outside made her jump, and she laughed at herself as cool air began to hum through the duct above her head.

"You're a *scientist*, for God's sake. This is *ridiculous*."

She scooped up the ball, deposited it in the bin, and ascended the stairs.

Her father was still in his spot by the window when she returned to the bedroom he'd shared with her mother. He sat facing the mirror, unable to turn away from his reflection.

The chip was still there in the glass where her face had struck when she was eight, breaking in incisor. Otherwise the glass was unblemished, not cracked as it had been in her vision—or whatever it was that had happened to her in the basement.

Amelia didn't know what she would have done if the mirror *had* been broken.

Gone crazy, maybe, she thought, and the fan whirred by, prickling the flesh on her forearms and making her shiver.

Her father blinked.

<hr>

"YOU REALLY SHOULD GET someone out there to cut the lawn, Ms. Amelia." Helena stood at the kitchen sink washing the equipment she used to feed Amelia's father through the endoscopic tube. "My cousin, he owns a landscaping business. I could get you a family discount."

Amelia looked out over her father's shoulder at the backyard and saw Helena was right. The grass was shin deep. With the heatwave they'd experienced the past few weeks she was surprised the lawn hadn't just dried up and blown away on the wind.

"Thank you, Helena. But I can do it myself. It'll be good stress relief."

An hour later she'd forgotten the lawn, and sat again beside her father in the hot bedroom with the fan whirring.

A high-pitched grunt outside the window caught her attention.

Scowling at the interruption she went to the window. Her father hadn't made any progress since the day the power had gone out so it wasn't as if she would be missing anything at the computer anyhow.

Down below a young boy crept through the tall grass, hunting something. The grunt must have been from when he'd jumped over the tall wooden fence. He wore a backwards ball cap and a ball glove on his right hand, reminding her of herself when she was young, aside from the boy's lack of ponytail.

"I'll be right back, okay, Dad?"

Blink.

She hurried down the stairs and into the kitchen. Looking out through the glass in the backdoor she saw the kid shaking his head in apparent incredulity. Amelia opened the door and stepped out onto the porch.

"Can I help you with something?"

The tanned, freckle-faced boy looked up with worry in his eyes. His expression softened when he saw she wasn't mad. "I hit the ball. O-over the fence." With trepidation he looked at the surrounding grass. "*What is this?*"

"What is what?"

The boy blinked. "There must be like *a hundred balls* back here."

Amelia shook her head. "What?"

"In the grass. I can't even figure out which one is mine. You got like a dog or something?"

Amelia stepped off the porch onto the lawn. Immediately she spotted three balls within spitting distance: a racquetball, a tennis ball, a Nerf ball.

She took two further steps and saw more, each one nestled in the tall grass. It appeared to have grown around several of them. Others had rolled there recently, the tracks still visible.

Orange rubber balls, chewed pet balls, nicked croquet balls, dirty gray softballs, scuffed hardballs, stress balls, golf balls, even a pool ball. A whole neighborhood worth of missing balls, all of them somehow ending up here, in the Corbel backyard, under the shade of the maple.

What is this? she thought, unintentionally mirroring the boy's words.

Amelia shaded her eyes to look up at her father's window. The room was too dim to see inside but she could sense him looking down at her, and in her mind's eye he blinked *yes*.

"Take them," she said, heading back to the house.

"W-which one?" the boy stammered.

"All of them!"

Upstairs her father sat exactly where she'd left him. "Did you move those balls out there, Dad?" He eyed her blankly. She hunkered down in front of him, gripping the arms of the wheelchair. Not meaning to do it so violently. "*Did you?*"

Blink.

"How are you doing this?" Amelia knew how stupid it sounded but she couldn't shake the idea.

Blink blink.

"No. You don't know?" She frowned and stood, looking down at him. His tired green eyes tracked her movement. "I need you to work with me here, Dad. If this is... if this is *doing something* to you, I need to know."

He blinked hard twice.

"Do you want to stop?

No.

"What then? Why won't you meet me halfway here, Dad?"

He turned his eyes to the right and Amelia followed his gaze to the laptop. The screen had gone into sleep mode. Their reflections looked back from the glossy black plastic.

Her father had never liked computers. Never wanted to work learn how to use them, never written an email or used the Internet. A computer had run him out of his job at the factory. It was only natural he hadn't wanted to cooperate with her after having shunned the technology for so long.

Hand-craftsmanship, that's what you lose when robots start doing the job of men, he'd always said. *You wanna make something special you do it by hand.*

"It's the computer, isn't it?"

Yes.

"But how...?" She shook her head, realizing the question was useless. Occam's razor suggested her father must have unintentionally created some sort of energy field with the modified BCI, but with the amount of balls in the backyard the field would have had to be *enormous.*

It simply wasn't possible.

"This isn't possible, Dad." She shook her head, trying to convince herself. "This can't be happening."

He blinked once, hard.

Yes, Amelia.

"Okay." She began pacing the small room, mind racing. "Okay if it's real, Dad, maybe you can do something for me..."

Her gaze fell on the bookshelf. Stacked horizontally in front of her mother's old mystery novels were several crossword books. She brought one to the desk and opened it to where he'd clipped a pen as a bookmark before he'd lost the use of his hands. She removed it and flattened the fold, nearly set the pen down on the pages but hesitated at what she saw.

The puzzles on both sides were already filled in, a single word repeated over and over in the boxes.

Heart thudding in her temples she flipped through the book and found more of the same, every single box filled in with one of three letters.

Amelia held the book up for her father to see. "Did you do this?"

He didn't blink. Didn't need to.

He'd written the answer all over the pages:

E|S|Y|E   S|Y|E|S   Y|E|S|Y|E|S   Y|E|S|Y|E   S|Y|E|S|Y|E|S|Y E|S|Y|E|S

She set the book down on the desk beside the laptop and the pen on top.

"*Show* me."

He merely looked at her, eyebrows turned up, mouth turned down in a grimace.

Amelia let out an exasperated groan and flopped down onto the bed, holding her temples as she tried to piece it all together. "It's a joke then, isn't it? You... I don't know... what did you do, Dad? Did you fill it all in when you could still hold the pen? Did you get someone to put all those balls out there in the yard? Are you *messing* with me, Dad? Is this a *prank*?"

She looked down the length of her body from where she lay in the center of the bed and saw her father blink twice.

"I can't *do* this anymore, Dad. I love you, but I can't." A tear rolled down her cheekbone into her ear. Her vision blurred, looking at the ceiling because she couldn't bear to look at him as she said it. "You know I have to put you in the hospital, right? I have a *job* to get back to. People *need* me."

Yes.

"Is that what you want?"

No.

"Then what? Why won't you *show* me?"

That same anguished expression met her query.

Amelia wiped her tears and pushed herself up and off the bed. She grabbed the puzzle book and the pen from the desk and slapped them down angrily on the shelf.

His eyes followed her in the mirror as she left the room without saying another word.

AMELIA COULDN'T SLEEP EVEN though she was exhausted. After giving up on her father she'd finally mowed the lawn with the push mower, stooping to pick up all the balls the kid hadn't taken when he left. Still her body wouldn't relax. Her nerves were set on edge. Limbs full of energy.

Energy field, she thought. *Ridiculous.*

Rain pattered on the window.

Outside, a storm raged. Inside, the house stood silent.

Like Dad, except in reverse.

Amelia had made a decision today, and tomorrow she would place the call to Dr. Jorgenson. It meant an end to her pathetic "research." An end to her time with her father in this old house, holding on to memories of a life that no longer existed. Dad had always said he'd wanted to die in this house he'd made special for his family with his own two hands, and instead he would wink out of existence in a hospital bed just like Mom had.

She rolled to her side and watched the rain drizzle down the glass he'd replaced when she'd hit a homerun through it at age ten.

So much of this house was a part of him. Her mother had loved it just as much but had poured herself into the furniture, the wallpaper, the knickknacks and photographs. Her father had redone the upstairs walls when dry rot and mold ruined the lath and plaster. He'd replaced the ugly nicotine-stained stucco ceilings, built the kitchen cabinets by hand, remodeled the upstairs bathroom and added a second half bath on the first floor where there'd once been a closet.

This was his house more than it was anyone's.

The house *belonged* to her father. Her father *belonged* here, not in some hospital.

Lightning flashed, brightening the windowpane.

She counted Mississippis in her head, the way he'd taught her when she was little. Thunder rumbled after four. Less than a mile away.

Amelia rolled onto her back, closing her eyes, letting the pattering of rain lull her to sleep.

Lightning flashed over her eyelids.

One Mississippi. Two Mississippi. Three—

Noticing the blue light hadn't diminished Amelia opened her eyes and saw him standing at the foot of her bed.

No—*standing* wasn't the right word. He *floated*, several feet above the floor.

A man made entirely of light.

Not light. *Energy.* He was pure bright blue energy.

Like a spark. Like lightning.

Plasma, she thought.

Amelia stared at the plasma man until his bright silhouette had imprinted itself on her retinas. He stood—*floated*—near the foot of the bed with his feet stretched toward the floor and his hands held straight at his hips, palms out, like a diagram of the nervous system. White light traveled through each vein, every nerve ending crackling like static electricity.

She could see his heart pumping. See the light flooding his limbs and his brain.

Amelia sat up abruptly, gripping the sheet. "*Dad?*"

The plasma man blinked eyelids made of energy.

Then he winked away, casting her bedroom back into darkness.

She leaped out of bed and hurried for the hall, catching her toe on the doorjamb. Crying out she grasped her foot, squeezing it to dull the pain.

Eyes full of tears, as much from the sight of her father's transformation than the sudden injury, Amelia limped into the hallway.

By the time she reached his bedroom he was gone.

His body still lay under the tangled sheet, but the *essence* of him, the energy that made James Adam Corbel the man she called "Dad," had moved on.

Dispersed.

Glassy eyes stared at his own reflection in the mirror. When she followed his gaze she knew for certain he did not see what she did. He didn't see the mirror had split down the middle, fracturing his reflection just as it had in her vision.

The vision he'd *shown* her.

Her father's eyelids closed for the last time by her hand.

Amelia sat beside his body a long time, considering what she had accomplished.

What *he* had accomplished with her.

Whether through her modifications to the BCI technology, the sheer force of his will or some unknown spiritual method, her father had transcended his body, releasing himself from the burden of the physical world.

The first *plasma man*.

She would destroy the headset and purge all of the data in the morning but for now Amelia curled up beside what was left of her father, and slept.

The Passion of the Robertsons

I don't know any stories I'd call a *genuine* Christmas miracle, but since you asked I'd have to say the closest was when Harry Maitland met Mr. and Mrs. Robertson on the closing shift at the Hometown Hardware a couple of years back.

You've heard of this so-called "war on Christmas"? Well Eric and Jean Robertson had been fighting that battle on the front lines before the lines had even been drawn. From the day after Thanksgiving until just after New Year's they'd led a shock and awe campaign of charity work, door-to-door caroling and chants of "Merry Christmas" to just about everyone they met. Not "Happy Holidays," oh no. Not *ever*. Eric and Jean were "put the Christ back in Christmas" types. If you said to them, "Happy Holidays," you'd get a thousand-yard stare and hear them mutter under their breath, reminding themselves to cross you off their "Nice" list for next year.

And God help you if you wished them a "Happy Hanukah."

These people ate, shat and slept Jesus—and not just on Sundays when Reverend Davies passed around the collection plate. So when an atheist stumbled into their midst on the day the lady's true love gave her three French hens and a partridge in a pear tree, that is to say December 28th, the Robertsons felt a little "Christmas cheer" was in order.

When they came across Harry at the hardware store, it was just about quitting time. Beer o'clock for Harry, if the last few customers didn't dawdle. It had already been a "day from Hell," as Harry himself might have called it in those days, and he wasn't about to stand for their Bible-thumpery.

Come 9:05 the Robertsons finally gathered up their purchases at the front counter, having ignored both announcements over the P.A. that the store was closing. Harry grudgingly scanned the nylon rope, the rolls of duct tape and plastic wrap... and he couldn't stand by and say nothing any longer.

"Got a hot night planned, huh?"

Mr. and Mrs. Robertson just blinked at him.

"It was a joke," Harry mumbled. "You know, because of the..." He shrugged, his humor having flown over their heads. "Never mind."

He rang up their odd purchase and said nothing further until the couple hit him with their standard "Merry Christmas."

"It's not Christmas, anymore," he snapped, and it was the worst possible thing he could have said in that moment. "It hasn't been Christmas for like three days."

Mr. and Mrs. Robertson eyed him with suspicion, as if he'd admitted he belonged to one of those strange religions that handles snakes, or worships their ancestors. They snatched their bag from Harry's hand and stormed out into the snow.

"Have a good night," Harry called after them with heavy sarcasm. He'd already begun to count his till as the door swung shut.

At 9:38 Harry finally locked the front door and drew the security cage shut. As he crossed to the bike racks he spotted a station wagon sat at the far end of the darkened, otherwise empty lot, someone parked illegally overnight. If he'd noticed it before he'd closed the shop he might have called the cops and had it towed.

It was too late for that now. Harry had bigger fish to fry. A good few inches of snow had come down since he'd biked to work and he'd need to walk it across town to the Ram's Head here. After the day he'd had the call of the drink was strong. He'd planned to down a few shots with Marianne, his favorite bartender—she quit a few weeks after the incident in question, fancied herself an actress—before he got down to the good stuff.

Harry liked the dark beers, the kind so thick they were practically meals in a glass. Just perfect for when you hadn't eaten anything since lunch and also had an urge to get plastered. A beer like that fit the bill most days for Harry Maitland. The hardware store didn't pay him well enough to support both dinner takeout and his after-work proclivities, and he'd never been the kind of guy to brown-bag it.

Crouching in the dark beneath the busted streetlamp, Harry slipped a hand into his jeans pocket for the keys to his bike lock. He fumbled them out and jabbed one of the duplicates blindly for the keyhole.

That's not iiiit, he thought, mimicking the way his latest ex-girlfriend had teased him in singsong while he fumbled under the sheets.

Harry might have laughed it the sound of tires squealed hadn't startled him.

He dropped the keys on the ground and spent a tense moment sifting through the snow in the dark before he noticed the bike racks and the brick wall behind them had brightened considerably and were *still* brightening while he fumbled.

When he finally clued in that a car was speeding toward him, curiosity had him spin around when he should have been diving out of its way.

Behind the windshield of the advancing station wagon Mr. and Mrs. Robertson sat with matching halos of dome light, ferocious determination in their eyes. A moment later the bright white of the headlamps blotted them out of Harry's sight.

When the rust-flecked grill slammed into his pelvis, Harry saw nothing but black.

"—ON OUR NAUGHTY LIST," Harry heard Mrs. Robertson say as his world came back into sharp focus.

Under different circumstances waking to what he saw that night in the Robertsons's den might have filled him with nostalgia. The walls had been decked with tinsel and holly, stockings hung from the stone fireplace, a warming fire rumbling in the hearth. A plate of neatly iced gingerbreads and sugar cookies lay on a green-fringed table runner alongside a crystal dish filled with pinecones and fragrant potpourri, and three gold candles in polished silver sticks, one each—Harry suspected —for the Father, the Son and the Holy Ghost. A brass version of "Joy to the World" crackled from a record player while Mr. and Mrs. Robertson sat Indian-fashion on the carpet wrapping gifts and placing them under a gargantuan plastic tree held upright by a wire nailed to the wall near the ceiling. The plastic angel stood askew on the crown of the tree, its tiny hands clasped in prayer.

It was almost like Harry had fallen asleep on Christmas Eve during *It's a Wonderful Life* and woke to discover his parents hadn't put him to bed and he could watch—if he pretended to still be asleep—as they placed gifts from Saint Nicolas under the PVC tree.

Except for the pain, that is. The pain wouldn't let him wax nostalgic.

Struggling to move his limbs, Harry tried to look down but something constricted his head at the neck. A hazy memory recurred of Mr. Robertson slapping a roll of duct tape down onto the counter and finally Harry became truly horrified at his predicament.

"What is this? Why can't I move?"

Looking over his shoulder, Mr. Robertson stood abruptly, appearing both anxious and pleased, dressed in a ridiculous Christmas sweater with a shirt collar peeking out above the neckline. The man smiled. "You're awake. Welcome to our humble abode."

Looking like she'd just stepped out of a '50s television show in a checkered button-up dress with beige nylons, pearls and a plain white apron Mrs. Robertson plucked up a crystal goblet and a decanter filled with a creamy yellow-white liquid from the coffee table. "Would you care for some egg nog?"

"No, I don't want—" Harry remembered civility wasn't required of him. "*What are you doing to me?*"

Jean Robertson set down the decanter and offered him a pitying smile. "Relax, Mr. Maitland. You've been heavily sedated but you are very badly injured. Struggling wouldn't be in your best interest."

Eric gave his wife a look of concern. "Do you think I hit him too hard?"

Her response was curt. "He'll be fine."

"What if he's paralyzed?"

"He's not *paralyzed*, Eric. Are you paralyzed, Mr. Maitland?"

"I don't—" Harry swallowed a dry lump. "Why are you doing this to me?"

"Do you believe in God?"

Harry laughed in spite of his circumstances. Couldn't help himself, really. "*That's* what this is about? You fucking whackos—"

Mrs. Robertson slipped a delicate hand into the pocket of her apron and pulled out a dull black revolver. "Tut tut, Mr. Maitland. God is listening."

"Yeah? Well, God can *suck my fucking dick*!"

Pulling a face like he'd just sucked on a lemon, Mr. Robertson put a comforting hand on his wife's shoulder. Mrs. Robertson's naked lips rose in a sneer of disgust as she pointed the pistol at Harry.

"I don't *want* to shoot you, Mr. Maitland," she said. "But I cannot allow you to say such hurtful things about our Lord and Savior in this house."

Mr. Robertson dropped his hand to his side. "He's never going to believe, Jean."

"He'll *believe*, Eric. Did Thomas not believe when Jesus let him touch His wound?"

"What the fuck is going on here?" Harry demanded of his hosts.

"I'm glad you asked." Mrs. Robertson smiled like a teacher toward an attentive student. "Eric and I came to the realization many years ago that a man such as yourself—an *atheist*—would never truly appreciate the pain Jesus suffered *for our sins* . . . without suffering yourself. And you *will* suffer here tonight, Mr. Maitland. You'll suffer greatly."

The carol ended and the needle rose from the record.

Harry screamed to fill the silence.

Without missing a beat Mrs. Robertson fired the revolver at the ceiling. The bullet gouged a hole in the stucco above Harry's head and a sprinkle of plaster dust fell like snow on his face and chest.

"No one can hear you," Mr. Robertson said, slipping the old 78 back into its jacket. "Our closest neighbor is half a mile as the crow flies."

"It's just the three of us and God now," Mrs. Robertson agreed with a solemn nod. "And if He ignored the cries of His only begotten Son, I very much doubt He'll intervene for you. The next one's going in your chest," she added almost incidentally.

Harry had no doubt of the woman's sincerity. These people were lunatics. They were cuckoo for Christ. And if all they wanted was for him to believe in their Angry Man in the Sky, he had no qualms humoring them to save his own apostate ass.

No heretics would be burned at the stake tonight.

"Okay," Harry said, trying his damnedest to sound calmed. "Okay, you got me. I've just been pretending, okay?" He blinked a drop of sweat from his eye. "I *love* Jesus. Jesus is *my dude*, okay? Can I go now? That's what you want, right?"

A new record started with a fanfare of trumpets and cavalry drums. The chorus sang "Onward Christian Soldiers," and Mr. Robertson returned to his wife's side. They took each other by the hand and smiled beatifically down on Harry.

"Jesus Christ," Harry breathed, his teeth beginning to chatter. "You people are *insane*."

Mr. Robertson approached the chair and tore the tape off Harry's neck.

Harry screamed again. The first three layers of skin felt like they'd come off with the tape and he wouldn't be surprised to discover he was bleeding.

The pain cleared and he peered down at himself, at his hands taped around several times to the dark, rich wood arms of what looked like an antique chair to Harry's untrained eye, with plush red fabric and buttons. He figured if he couldn't break the tape he might be able to bust the chair itself.

But only if Mrs. Robertson was unarmed.

When he saw what lay to the left of the coffee table and the sofa under its clear plastic cover, all hope of escape blew away like chaff before the wind, and Harry began to shiver uncontrollably.

Two four-by-four inch slabs of pressure-treated lumber lay on the carpet by the supper table, fastened together to form a crude crucifix. At the foot of it were a mallet and railroad spikes, along with two lengths of bristly rope.

And even though Harry was an atheist, he had watched the torture scenes from *The Passion* on the internet.

He knew what came next.

"The people walking in darkness will see a great light," Mrs. Robertson said reverentially, gripping the pistol in both hands against her chest, like a holy man clutching the Good Book.

Mr. Robertson crossed to the hearth and drew an iron poker from the tool rack. He hefted its weight as he returned to Harry's side.

"Unfortunately we'll have to forgo the traditional flogging of Roman crucifixions," the man said, moving around behind Harry. "We wanted your experience to be as authentic as possible, but obviously we couldn't go into one of those *awful stores—*"

Mrs. Robertson shook her head, glaring at the floor.

"—and we couldn't have the postman thinking we'd ordered smut online," Mr. Robertson continued gravely. "So . . . we'll have to make due."

"No!" Harry cried, jerking forward, desperate to evade the man's reach. "You can't do this to me! Turn the other cheek! That's what Jesus said, isn't it? *Isn't it?*"

He searched the woman's eyes for mercy. Mrs. Robertson afforded Harry another pitying smile, and the poker came down across his back.

Cold hard metal slashed through skin and cracked the bone beneath. Harry's scream tore his throat raw, the taste of blood causing his stomach to rebel. When the pain finally lessened he found himself thanking God Mr. Robertson hadn't stuck the poker in the fire to heat it up, and the realization of what he'd done struck him as deeply as the poker had sunk into his flesh.

"I get it now!" Harry screamed as a chorus of horns filled the room. "No atheists in foxholes! That's what this is, right? Well, you win! Glory glory Hallelujah, I *believe!*" he shouted, and he would have thrown his hands toward the heavens in fraudulent jubilation had they not been taped to the chair.

The corners of Mrs. Robertson's smile turned down in doubt.

"I told you, Jean," Mr. Robertson said.

Harry twisted round as far as he could. "Shut the fuck up, Eric. You want me to pray? I'll pray. Please . . ." He imitated a booming parody of a preacher's voice. *"God, please* . . . forgive my wicked ways! Spare me from the rod of your righteous followers! I know not what I do, you see? I know that now!"

Mrs. Robertson nodded toward her husband.

Harry heard the whoosh of the poker a heartbeat before it cracked against his ribs. The air catapulted from his lungs and he hunched over himself, weeping and whimpering, an itchy stream of blood trickling onto his thighs.

"Please . . ." Every breath felt like a spear stabbing his lungs. ". . . I'm begging you, *please stop this.*"

"'He who began a good work in you will bring it to completion at the day of Jesus Christ,'" Mrs. Robertson said, and she nodded to her husband again.

"What does that mean?" Harry cried. "I don't even know what that—"

The poker came down across his fully exposed back, the pain so omnipresent he puked up chunks of chicken fingers and French fries undigested from lunch.

"Why won't you *stop*?"

"You still don't understand, Mr. Maitland," the woman said with a shake of her head. "We're not doing this to hurt you. We're doing this to *save* you."

Harry wept.

Mr. Robertson struck him three more times before Harry lost consciousness.

Thank goodness for small mercies.

When his eyes opened again Harry was lying on his back. Even through the pain he could tell they had spread him out on the makeshift crucifix. A choir pa-rum-pa-pum-pummed "The Little Drummer Boy" on the record player, and Mr. Robertson was on his knees tying Harry's left wrist to the horizontal board. Harry realized he couldn't move his arms even if they hadn't been tied down. He wasn't sure if it was the sedative or the injuries to his pelvis and back that had made movement below the neck impossible, but what he did know was that his hosts meant to drive nails into his hands and feet, and let him hang from their homemade cross until he was dead.

There would be no pleading with them. If there was one thing Harry had faith in, it was that. These two lunatics would not relent. He saw no mercy in their eyes, only the fervor of old-time religion.

The Passion of the Robertsons, he thought.

Blood trickled from the corners of Harry's lips when he laughed.

Eric Robertson gave Harry a queer look while picking up the mallet and spikes. With the tools in hand the man looked up at his wife. From his expression Harry could not tell if the look was for encouragement or in the hope she'd put a stop to this madness before it went so far they couldn't turn back. Mrs. Robertson was out of Harry's line of vision. But he didn't need to see her to know she'd nodded once more.

Mr. Robertson rested the narrow end of the spike on the meat of Harry's left palm, and poised the mallet above it to strike.

The sound rang in Harry's ears like the clang of a choir bell. Metal split flesh and separated bones like the parting of the Red Sea. Harry's agonized scream unintentionally harmonized with the choir of voices from the record player. Mr. Robertson muttered along to the music, and when he struck the spike again it was synchronous with the "ding" of their bell.

Harry had naively assumed the second strike would be less painful. It was not. The wrist contains eight bones, and each one detached further as the spike drove in, stretching outward so that his hand felt as though it might burst at the sides.

On the third strike, Robertson bashed his own thumb.

With a wincing intake of breath, the man brought his injured digit to his mouth and sucked on it. Harry managed a weak laugh through his tears.

"Give me that, you big baby," Mrs. Robertson snapped, as if she were talking to a child.

Through a blur of tears Harry watched Mrs. Robertson kneel at his side and snatch the mallet from her husband. He caught a glimpse of beige satin panties between her thighs and in some distant, painless galaxy Harry felt the stirrings of arousal.

The Last Temptation of Harry, he thought. *God, I really am going to Hell.*

Mrs. Robertson caught his eye and clucked her tongue in disapproval. But she wasted no time in scrounging up the other spike by tugging down her dress.

And while she drove the final nail, the pain blistering up his arm with each additional strike, Harry focused what little consciousness remained to him on the shimmering fabric between her legs, imagining himself hammering railroad spikes into the delicate, downy folds of her privates, before crushing her husband's testicles with the mallet.

When the job was done, and the choir sang "God Rest Ye Merry, Gentlemen," Mr. and Mrs. Robertson hoisted the crossbeam onto their shoulders and dragged Harry and his crucifix toward the kitchen doorway, where they laid it to rest against the arch.

And so it came to pass that Harry Maitland, atheist, bad boyfriend, Hometown Hardware employee and part-time alcoholic, was crucified in the year of our Lord 2015.

Hanging by his hands, his lungs felt constricted. He could barely get a breath. Blood oozed from his stigmata and pattered on the carpet. They'd made him a footrest, but it was of little comfort or joy.

He would not repent.

He would not accept Jesus as his Lord and personal Savior.

He would *not* let the Robertsons beat him.

Looking up at their handiwork with smiles of approval, the Robertsons took each other's hands, and though his agony reigned supreme Harry wondered if their little passion play had ever been an attempt to save his admittedly wretched soul, or if it had been an excuse from the very beginning for the couple to torture a man to his death.

As they watched their sacrificial lamb for signs he'd received the Holy Spirit, Harry found himself studying the angel atop the Christmas tree, placed at an odd angle, and thinking about how the words *angle* and *angel* were similar, wondering if the similarity held a deeper meaning.

He noticed the top of the tree had bent at the same angle, the wire pulled taut.

"You forgot . . . the crown of thorns," he gasped, and chuckled when the Christmas cheer dropped from their holier than thou faces.

A discordant twang interrupted "Silent Night." A heartbeat later a small metallic object struck the wall behind Harry's head and the tree sprang forward, launching the angel through the air. Bulbs and ornaments crashed to the floor.

And like Harry had turned toward his inevitable destruction rather than leap out of the way of approaching death, the Robertsons whipped round as the tree landed in the hearth and burst into flames.

Mrs. Robertson's nylons caught next. She dropped to the carpet and began to roll but the fire spread to her dress, the carpet, the red and green table runner, while Mr. Robertson stared down in horror, seemingly immobile.

The fire alarm began to blare as Mrs. Robertson writhed on the carpet. Bulbs burst like popcorn. Ornaments and plastic needles dripped into a black puddle on the floor. The record had warped, the choral voices rum-pa-pum-pumming became ghostly and surreal.

Already the sulfurous smell of Mrs. Robertson's burning hair filled Harry's nostrils. Her cooking flesh smelled something like burnt pork and the coppery tang of bubbling blood. This combined with the foul stench of burning plastic should have conspired to make Harry sick.

Instead he smiled.

Calm as can be, Mr. Robertson bent to pick up the revolver from the coffee table. He turned his back but Harry could still hear the man ask God for forgiveness before firing a single shot into his wife's head.

The woman stopped moving.

Mr. Robertson's arm rose and he put the pistol in his own mouth.

Realizing he was in direct line of fire should the bullet pass through Mr. Robertson's skull, Harry tried to move his head. He could not, and so he closed his eyes instead, awaiting the end.

The second shot rang out. Hot blood struck Harry's face like a splash of holy water on a newborn babe. He heard the thump of Mr. Robertson's body hitting the floor. Unable to believe he'd survived, when he finally dared to open his eyes the fire had already begun to smolder.

Mr. and Mrs. Robertson were dead. Or if not dead, well done.

He was *saved*.

Saved by a nail.

And he had to wonder if it was a coincidence that nails had very near killed him, but a single nail had spared his life.

NOW YOU WON'T SEE Harry Maitland around the Ram's Head these days. Harry doesn't come in here anymore, not since he found God that night at the Robertsons's house.

The fire alarms were tied to the Robertsons's home monitoring system, you see. When the voice of the customer service agent called over the box Harry thought he was hearing the voice of God. It was not God, it was a man named Jim from AlarmSquad Home Security.

Now I have to ask you, do you think what happened to Harry Maitland on the night of December 28th 2015 was an accident of fate? Or was it "divine intervention"?

Would you call that a "Christmas miracle"?

Heck, don't ask me.

But you have to think, if God was there to save him, then didn't God also let the Robertsons kidnap him in the first place? And if a god would put someone through so much torture just to teach them a lesson, then what the hell kind of sick, depraved sadist have we been praying to all these years?

Not any kind of god I'd want to stand before awaiting judgment, that's for damn sure.

WHERE THE MONSTERS LIVE

I T WAS RAINING the day I brought my daughter's CD player back to the sex offenders under the bridge, and everyone was in a crummy mood.

Miami's weather is a blessing to those of us living on the street—at least until the rainy season, those summer months when you've got to get a roof over your head that isn't just a doorway alcove or the underside of a bridge, or you'll be soaked to the skin in seconds. The day I'd decided to go back home for the first time in months, it had already been raining three days, and most of us were sure the sun would never come out again.

By then I'd narrowed my search for the Rabbit Man down to three suspects: Tony Walker, Alejandro Gonzalez, and Orville "Popcorn" Perry, the convicted pedophiles I'd been living with for the last three months. Not everyone in Bookville had committed the sort of vile crimes these men had. Some were rapists, others were molesters, but most had been stuck there for petty sexual assaults, hadn't even spent a day in jail but had been forced to register anyhow. Forced out of their homes, into the shadows, and under the bridge.

Statutory cases, groping, sodomy. Some drunk guy caught pissing in public near a school yard. You could almost laugh at a creep who's exposed himself to old ladies, so long as one of them wasn't your grandmother or your great-aunt. It's sick, sure, but it doesn't physically *hurt* anyone.

Regardless of their crime's severity, lobbyist Ron Book's ordinance forced these men and women to live 2,500 feet from any school, park, or bus stop. Without violating parole or removing their ankle monitor and skipping town, the Tuttle Causeway and the Everglades were the only places left for a sex offender to live.

Ron Book's folly had pushed them underground and off the grid. Instead of making Miami safer, he'd made the city a thousand times more dangerous.

Walker, Gonzalez, and Popcorn Perry—these monsters had done hard time. Gonzalez liked little girls. Popcorn preferred boys, but he'd gotten arrested for trying to diddle one of the girls on his school bus route. He told us she had a short haircut and had yet to hit puberty, so it was easy enough to imagine her as a boy despite not having the parts. From my understanding, Walker was a pinch hitter.

None of these men had ever killed anyone as far as I knew, but together they'd strangled the souls of at least half a dozen children. What had sent me rushing home that morning was Gonzalez had told a story the night before about the rabbit he'd had as a boy, reminiscing about how soft its fur had been. I could easily imagine it reminding him of the silken hair of his victims.

To ingratiate myself to them early on, I'd told a lie about how I'd done two years in Alamosa County for assaulting my niece. Popcorn and Walker had wanted details, so I fed them details: said I'd been grooming her for years before I actually got up the courage to go through with it. That I'd babysat for my brother and his wife—in truth, I have no siblings, only in-laws—for months just working up the nerve to touch her.

With my theater background, I've played everything from Hamlet's oedipal interests to Titus's cannibalism, but the part of pedophile was by far the most loathsome—particularly in light of why I was there. Popcorn had wanted to know about her underwear, if it had "decals," which I took to mean prints. Walker hadn't even bothered to conceal the erection in his frayed jeans. But Gonzalez had just stared, open-mouthed.

Afterward, I'd excused myself for a piss and ended up being sick in the shadows behind one of the big pillars.

One of those men had raped my six-year-old baby girl.

One of them was going to pay.

I left camp early the day I returned home, walking a little over three hours to the house where I used to live. My feet hurt and my clothes ran with a hundred rivers of dirt, but I hoped it would be worth the trek. There was a method to the madness, as they say. Or so I'd thought then.

Marnie was just pulling out of the drive when I arrived, our little girl Nola in the backseat playing with a doll I didn't recognize, making it dance. Neither of my girls saw me hiding behind the sprawling gumbo limbo in the Garrisons' front yard as they drove past, the two of them smiling and singing. Tears clawed out from my eyes, seeing the both of them looking forward instead of back, the way I thought they ought to be looking, toward a life when all three of us were still together. Toward the past I'd left behind in pursuit of my singular goal, this burning obsession. I'd been gone a little over four months by then, and it wasn't as though I'd expected life to stay in a sort of freeze-frame with me out of the picture. Still, seeing them singing along to one of Nola's CDs, seemingly as happy as you please... it was a blow.

Once the car disappeared around the corner, I did what I could to smother the pain. I drew the hoodie up over my head and crossed to the house, looking both ways, skirting the garbage cans lined both sides of the street, glad the municipality hadn't changed trash pickup to another day while I was gone. If Marnie had re-keyed the locks, God forbid, I figured I could wait around and break a window when the truck came rumbling up the street. But I didn't need to wait. My key slid in effort-lessly. Twisting it in the lock, I let out a sigh of relief.

The house was just like I remembered it, if a little messier. It smelled nice, like the lilac shampoo both Marnie and Nola apparently still used. It smelled *clean*. Even the hints of last night's dinner in the garbage—a spaghetti sauce starting to turn—smelled terrific. Smelled like *home*. Stink permeates homelessness: the smell of trash, the smell of dirty streets, of fire bins and piss and other people's body odor, the wet dog smell that saturates your clothes and bedding, the smell of rust and dirt and decay.

It felt good being back here. Felt right. I wanted to strip off my clothes and climb into the shower, wash off the layers of grime the rain hadn't been able to make a dent on. Wash off all the hell and scum I'd had to wade through to get to where I was now, with the Rabbit Man almost within my reach, and stretch out on the fresh clean sheets. To wait for Marnie to come home and tell her I'd been stupid, that I'd give it all up if only she'd let me stay.

Our bedroom was exactly the way I'd left it. If she'd taken down the pictures of the two of us together, the trips we'd taken before we had Nola, our engagement and wedding and honeymoon photos, I might have paused to reflect on its meaning. That they were still right where they'd been when I left made me think I could still come back if I wanted, if I could just summon the courage to quit. To give up on death and allow life and love back into my heart.

Anger rushed into my veins, and I pushed these thoughts away. Useless speculation. The thoughts of a coward. I had to protect my family, and the only way I knew how to do it was by leaving them behind.

I headed for the closet.

The night before I left home, Marnie had been off at a parent-teacher conference, listening to "suggestions" from parents who seemed to believe their fourth-grade children weren't receiving an adequate learning experience. As part-time drama teacher at her school (and sometime screenwriter), I was exempt from such proceedings, and so Nola and I were home alone, which happened every so often. While Nola read her favorite book for the hundredth time, listening to her little CD player, I watched the Yankees get their asses fed to them with the sound turned off.

After a while I headed out to the garage, fed up with the lousy game and Nola's repetitive pop music. She'd always been curious about the music Marnie and I used to listen to when we were young, and so I hunted down a handful of mixed CDs I'd made in college, most of them for when we'd turned the overhead lights off and the Christmas lights strung up around her dorm room twinkled over the bed like stars.

I came back to the living room with the box and hunkered down in front of Nola. She scowled when I turned off her music, but when I showed her the words I'd written on that first CD, her eyes lit up and she tented her fingers in a devious manner reminiscent of her mother hamming it up over some cunning plan she'd devised to rope me into something I didn't want to do.

The first song was "Sweet Child O' Mine." Nola seemed to enjoy it, even though she said Axl Rose's voice was funny. After that were a couple of songs I don't recall—one-hit wonders, most likely. Then came "Sympathy for the Devil," and it wasn't long before Nola and I got to howling along with Mick Jagger—"Hoo hoooo! Hoo hoooo!" I skipped the Chili Peppers' "Under the Bridge" since it's about suicide or heroin —or both—and even though Nola had already been through more than most kids had by sixteen, she was still only six.

Near the end of the CD, Nola and I had nestled down on the rug with the ball game flickering unwatched on the TV. I'd been staring up at the ceiling with my arms behind my head while Nola talked about what she liked and disliked about each song, a running commentary that was amusing at first but then sort of droned on as I began to daydream about grabbing the Rabbit Man by the throat and feeling his trachea splinter between my fingers. The image made me smile.

The cops still hadn't caught him, the man who'd assaulted my child, my little Nola, and I'd been spending most of my waking hours daydreaming about choking a man in a bunny suit to death as if the whole thing was a joke when the truth was far more sinister. Even then, I'm sure some dark part of me knew I could never move beyond the blind hatred, beyond thoughts of bloody revenge. That the wound he'd opened in me would turn gangrenous. Deadly.

I'd found myself sympathizing with those hovering parents Marnie and I used to berate. I heard the truth in meaningless catchphrases like "stranger danger." Buffer zones like Ron Book's sex offender ordinances, barring perverts and pedophiles from living within a short distance of any place children gather, seemed to make some kind of logical sense to me. I was deluding myself, because I couldn't live with the truth: that I would never feel Nola was safe again without my constant supervision.

When I snapped out of it, a song I hadn't heard since Marnie and I were in grade school had come on, and I realized Nola had grown silent. I rolled over onto my stomach to see she sat frozen, her face, framed under the little brown bangs Marnie cut with scissors on a kitchen stool, twisted into a rictus of fear.

"Nola," I said. She didn't respond, didn't take her eyes off the CD player we'd gotten for her fourth birthday, the little pink one with *Dora the Explorer* stickers plastered all over it. I snapped my fingers in front of her face and she didn't flinch. A runner of drool spilled from her lip and pattered on the carpet.

Was she having a seizure?

The chorus kicked in then, the choir singing of tiny hands in larger ones, of a love that could be seen as a crime. The words struck me like a hammer in the chest. Wanting to be her daddy. Her preacher. Suddenly the love song seemed sinister. When I reached to turn it off, an odd creeping sensation like when you're about to crush a particularly large and wriggly insect crawled up my spine.

The song stopped. Nola snapped out of her trance.

"Nola," I said. "Sweetheart, have you heard that song before?"

Nola shook her head violently, wide blue eyes obscured by her bangs as she looked down in curiosity at the drool spots on the floor. Though she'd never spoken a word about the monster who'd assaulted her, the trauma still far too pervasive, I felt certain he would have told her never to tell, that if she told on him he'd come to her house and murder her family or something equally abhorrent. I understood that fear, but rage overcame me, and I grabbed her arm, much rougher than I'd meant. "Nola, don't lie to Daddy."

I didn't realize Marnie had come home until I looked up in that awful moment to find her standing in the doorway. My hand fell away from Nola's tiny arm, the skin red in the shape of my fingers. Tears stood in Nola's eyes, though the look on her face was not pain but surprise. I'd never laid a finger on her for discipline until just then. Quite frankly, the look on my face in that moment probably mirrored hers.

There was no argument that night or ever. Marnie simply looked at me, straight into my heart where the poison had been festering. She took Nola by the hand, who'd run to her crying as the shock of what had happened finally struck her, and the two of them went upstairs to bed. I spent a few sleepless hours twisting back and forth on the couch under a small throw blanket. Eventually, I crept upstairs to my office and picked up the journal the family therapist had suggested I use to jot down what she'd called "irrational thoughts and/or behavior." I'd had neither the time nor inclination to use it, just left it on my desk to gather dust. What good would writing about it do? I needed *action*, not *words*.

When I opened it that night, I realized I'd been wrong about that. Marnie had been filling in the journal for me, and her words were exactly what I needed in that moment. Reading it made me sick, looking at my transformation through Marnie's eyes. In her words, it was like I'd been holding the family underwater, drowning us in my grief, determined to make Nola relive what that monster did to her over and over so she'd remember something, *anything*, about him: a smell, his voice, something about the place he took her, something about the rabbits. Dr. Ambrose might have held similar suspicions, but Marnie had known it in her bones I would never get past it, that I'd never wanted to. She'd known before I fully understood myself just how badly I'd wanted to hurt him, even *kill* him—to make the Rabbit Man suffer for what he'd done to our little girl. Our sweet Nola.

The next day I told Marnie my plan. All she did was sigh. As if it had been inevitable, like she'd been waiting for me to admit it. Finally she'd asked me, "Do you really think it's going to help her? Nola needs a father, not a vigilante." She'd told me if I went through with it to never come back.

That was just about a third of a year ago. This rain-soaked morning was the first time I'd been home since.

I FOUND THE little pink CD player right where I'd hidden it that night, under the musty old sleeping bag we'd used at the Grand Canyon the summer before Nola was born. I took that, too, and returned to Bookville shortly after one, dog-tired but eager to share my "find" with the others. The battery had died in Walker's RV a few weeks back, and our little area of the camp hadn't had music since. I was sure they would be pleased.

As I trudged down the concrete shoulder toward camp, I was reminded of a phrase from one of Nola's favorite picture books: *Under the bridge, where the Monsters live...* A story about a family of nice, cuddly monsters. *Here is that fabled place*, I thought. Only the monsters down here were most definitely not nice, and trying to cuddle one would be dangerous, like kissing a piranha.

"Look what I found," I said, holding up Nola's CD player.

The three of them looked up from their game of Rummy on a table made of plywood and wooden cable spools. Gonzalez's eyes lit up like a kid who'd just found the bra of his best friend's mom on their shower rod (though I suppose that wouldn't have interested him much even as a child). I plastered on a smile to cover for the sneer I felt trying to creep its way onto my face, having placed all bets on him.

He was my Rabbit Man. I was sure of it.

"Got batteries?" Walker asked.

"These ones still work," I said, and put it on the table by the discards.

"What's all this pink shit?" Popcorn wondered, eyeing me with suspicion. "You break your parole, or what?"

I pretended to be shocked. "Nah," I answered Popcorn. "Just found it. It's amazing what people will throw out on the street these days."

I popped the top open, revealing the mixed CD. The words *FOR MARNIE* had long faded, printed in block letters eleven or twelve years ago, the same words that had made Nola's eyes light up the night before I left her and her mother to live under the bridge with these animals.

"Still got a disc," Walker said. "Wonder who the fuck Marnie is?"

Again, I held back an unconscious sneer.

"That's the kind of question could get your ass in a whole lot of trouble," Popcorn said, before turning to me. "A'ight. Play that fuckin' music, white boy."

I sat down beside Gonzalez, who continued to eyeball the CD player the way Nola had that night in the living room, albeit somehow managing not to drool. One of the benefits of camping out close to the Bay, we could rinse our clothes out regularly or use laundry soap when we could find some. Hell, we could even give ourselves a good wash once in a while. Gonzalez wasn't most of us. He reeked of cigarettes and an omnipresent aroma of unwashed asshole. He hadn't brushed his teeth in months, maybe years. Sitting next to him you could imagine stink lines rising from his body, like that kid from *Peanuts*. It was difficult to sit so close to him, but I wanted him close when it happened.

This mound of dirt and repurposed trash under the Julia Tuttle Causeway was our living room. Graffiti on the pillars was the art on our walls. I pushed PLAY.

"Sympathy for the Devil" came on, over the shouts and laughter and music from the other encampments. Popcorn bit his lower lip and began to bob his head to the music.

Walker—who fucked girls, boys, adult women and once, according to his own account, a sedated gator—grew a sick smile. "I used to fuck to this song," he said, and stood up from the broken sofa to demonstrate, gyrating his hips with one hand at his side and the other holding down his imagined victim, be it human or animal.

"Sit your ass down," Popcorn said.

"You want some of this?" Walker said, thrusting his crotch toward the larger man.

"You best be gettin' your skinny dick outta my face." Popcorn picked up the discard pile from their Rummy game and threw the cards at Walker, who giggled and flopped back down on the couch.

"Man, you're pickin' those up!"

"Bull*shit*."

Popcorn and Walker left the cards scattered on the ground and the ratty old sofa. I let the song play out, then skipped the next two. Still couldn't remember them, even if I tried.

"Hey, I like that song," Walker groaned about the second, but the next song had already started, the haunting chords on a keyboard, the *tss-tss-tss* of a hi-hat.

When George Michael began to sing in his raspy whisper, Gonzalez turned to me. He met my eyes for only a moment, but the shock was palpable, the guilt evident. He returned his gaze to the CD player, and as the song played out my eyes never left him. I felt them tearing up, thinking about what he must have done to my Nola, but I blinked it away. I couldn't let my grief, my anger, and a sudden disturbing rush of exhilaration from being so close after searching for so long come between me and my revenge. I studied Gonzalez with glistening eyes: this bland monster, this mild-mannered beast. I watched him and pictured my knife slipping into the hot meat between his ribs.

"The fuck is that shit?" someone called over, tearing me from my fantasy. I allowed my gaze to move beyond Gonzalez to the black '80s Chevy Impala resting beside a spray-painted entreaty that had once made the papers: *WE ARE NOT MONSTERS.* A guy I'd seen around a few times sat hanging out the driver door. He had a little mustache and silky blond hair like a man on a box of hair dye, except the circles under his eyes were so dark they could have been bruises.

"It's called music," Popcorn shouted back. "The fuck you think it is?"

The blond dude got out of his car and approached, snapping bubblegum. "Why you listenin' to that faggot, huh?"

"Actually, he's bisexual," Walker answered. "Not that it makes any goddamn difference."

"You listen to that shit, you're no better'n a faggot yourself." Blondie came right up to the table and reached for the CD player.

Popcorn swatted his hand away.

"Don't you fuckin touch me, nigger."

Popcorn's eyes narrowed. He grabbed the blond guy's arm and jerked it up behind his back, the kind of move a cop or someone who'd been trained in military might use, and I found myself suddenly glad to be up against Gonzalez instead of Popcorn.

"That's uncalled for," a woman I knew only as Pip shouted over to us.

Others crowded around. A man with a lisp and cargo shorts cinched high on his waist by a frayed piece of rope asked why we couldn't all just get along.

In the fracas, the blond dude stomped down on Popcorn's foot, chewing his gum with a gleeful. The heels of his cowboy boots sounded hard, and Popcorn's sneakers had seen better days. They were bound together by duct tape and falling apart at the seams, his tube socks so dirty they were black in places visible at the sides. Popcorn's howl of pain just about matched Mick Jagger's, and he let go of the blond dude's arm.

Blondie shook his hair as if Popcorn had just ruffled it instead of nearly breaking his arm, and then locked eyes with Gonzalez. The wretched little smelly man looked behind himself, shrinking from the cold gaze. Blondie had found his prey, a victim to reclaim his dominance. Before Gonzalez could scramble over the back of the couch, Blondie had yanked him back by his filthy jeans and began raining down on his back with balled-up fists, calling him *queer* and *runt* and *pussy*.

Whatever he was, Gonzalez was *mine*.

A surge of frenetic energy ran through me as I grabbed a fistful of Blondie's hair and yanked him away from Gonzalez, who used the distraction to squirm away. I threw a punch before Blondie could swing at me, clipping him in the jaw. Having never been in a fight before, only ever using my fists against inanimate objects, it stunned me how much of a rush I got from the feel of his jaw against my knuckles. The feeling was short-lived as Blondie slugged me hard in the gut. I staggered back, the breath knocked out of me, while Popcorn and Walker jumped in to pull Blondie back from doing me some real damage.

In all the commotion, Gonzalez had gotten up and was slinking off. I gathered up my strength and followed him. The ruckus of the other three men struggling and the crowd either egging them on or jeering them grew quieter the further Gonzalez and I ran.

This is it, I thought, feeling stronger and almost hyperaware the closer I got to my quarry. I didn't think about going back home. I didn't think about Nola. All I could think of was *blood* and *blood* and *blood*...

I SUPPOSE I should tell you about the rabbits.

The day Nola ran away, Marnie and I had been fighting. Silly argument. She'd caught me smoking, something I hadn't done since she was pregnant—as far as she knew—and we'd gotten into it. She accused me of not caring to live long enough to see Nola graduate from college, and I accused her of not letting me relieve my stress the way I wanted. Nola heard us. She'd packed up some things in her knapsack: her stuffed lion

Julio, which she spelled with a W-H-O, her favorite book about the elephant king, a bag of marshmallows (*mushmellows*, she called them), and a flashlight. I suspect she was going to camp out and roast her mushmellows over a fire, but how she'd planned to light one, I don't know. I suppose the thought might never have crossed a six-year-old's mind.

Whatever she'd gotten in her head, Nola sneaked out the back door while Marnie and I argued in raised whispers, knowing full well she could hear us despite the closed bedroom door. Somewhere after the corner of Day and Matilda, where a crossing guard told police she'd scolded Nola about crossing the street without looking both ways, our little girl disappeared.

Marnie noticed she'd slipped away just when we'd gotten to the root of the argument. At first, we thought she'd been playing. Nola had always loved hide and seek. So we looked in all the usual spots we might find her: behind the curtains, crouched behind the big ficus in my office, in the basement shower, or in her closet, under a pile of stuffed animals.

Nowhere. Anxiety grew to full-blown fear. She knew enough not to run away, but if she'd heard us arguing...

We searched outside, in the front and back yards, Marnie running out into the street and calling out her name. We phoned her friends, spoke to baffled, concerned parents. Finally, we called the police. Fifteen minutes later, officers showed up at our door. Marnie kept tugging at her shirt sleeves, pacing the room while the two officers took down what we had to tell them: what she was wearing, how old, hair color, about how tall, could she have gone to a relative's? I'd been watching Marnie unravel the whole time until she finally exploded, screaming at the officers, "Somebody's taken my baby and you're wasting our *fucking time!*" They'd looked at each other, offered their apologies, and then put out an AMBER alert.

While Marnie waited at the house for Nola to return, the both of us sick with the absolute certainty that at any moment they would call back to tell us they'd found her body in a ditch somewhere, I drove up and down the neighborhood. I scoured the grounds at Liz Virrick Park, where we often took her when neither of us were busy on the weekend. I even went to Nola's school, where Marnie taught the fourth grade, and

I taught drama part-time to finance a failing career in screenwriting. Being there filled me with the dreadful certainty Nola would never have her mother as a teacher because some monster had taken her life.

Lost. Gone. Dead. My little girl is dead. These thoughts circled my mind as I drove through the neighborhood, once, twice, three times, certain I'd missed somewhere, hoping to return home to find her eating peanut butter out of the jar with her fingers, laughing at cartoons with her mother. But each time I returned, Marnie had been pacing the porch, or sitting, tugging at her shirt sleeves, and the house had been empty. I feared—*we* feared—there would never be laughter in that house again. So, back into the car, driving down the same streets, shouting her name as the neighborhood darkened.

It was just after 8 p.m. when the police called. My sweaty hand shook so badly the phone slipped into my lap. I pulled the car over and listened to the officer speak, holding the cell in a trembling hand as my heart pounded in my throat.

Imagination can be a terrible curse. I never saw it with my own eyes, but the image still haunts every waking moment of my life. It drove me to live among the sex offenders. It compelled me to find the monster who did it, the Rabbit Man, and to put him six feet in the fucking ground.

The sick fuck had left Nola naked beside a trash bin on the bare asphalt in an alley in Little Haiti. Eventually a busboy from a nearby restaurant had come out to dump his mop bucket and saw her shivering there. He'd called the police without going to her—worried, perhaps, that even attempting to help a naked child might be misconstrued as sexual abuse.

When Officer Sam Higgins arrived, he found a feral child huddled with her arms around her bruised knees, matted hair tangled in her face. Bleeding not just from the places she'd been violated, but from dozens of raised marks forensics later determined to be tiny scratches. Higgins wrapped the emergency blanket from his trunk around Nola, told her everything was going to be okay, that he was going to bring her to her mom and dad. At these words she leapt into his arms, latching around his neck, smearing his uniform with her blood.

The police were taking photographs of her injuries when I burst through the door, demanding to see her. Officer Higgins got in the way. Three officers had to hold me back from punching him, and if not for Sam's interference, I might have been charged with assaulting an officer. Sam and I hashed it out later. With two daughters himself, he keenly understood my rage. The Special Victims Bureau had taken over the case, but he'd promised to update me personally.

Marnie, Nola, and I went to the family therapist together. Dr. Ambrose had us explore our emotions in excruciating detail. She wanted us to open up, to work through our feelings, but each Thursday at 2 p.m. I begrudgingly entered her office and sat on that plush sofa entirely numb while Marnie droned and Nola played with toys in the corner. I saw no point to those visits; we were picking at scabs. While their meaningless words filled the terrifying silence, I sat alongside my wife, brewing hatred. My most violent fantasies were born in that room: gruesome acts I suspected I'd never be able to stomach even if the opportunity arose—thoughts which belonged to the monster growing inside me.

Eventually Dr. Ambrose accused me of stalling progress. I questioned her methods, her motives, called her a sadist. She asked me to leave. I apologized and she'd allowed me to return to the room. I'd lose myself in fantasy again. Several sessions passed this way, until our time was up.

Detective Rosario called a few weeks into this routine to inform us the lab had analyzed the white hairs they'd found on Nola's skin. Turned out to be animal fur, not human hair. They suspected the rapist kept rabbits, which kicked off a wide search for rabbit hutches in backyards and on rooftops.

Rosario didn't seem hopeful. By then, most registered sex offenders were living under the Tuttle Causeway, many of them already wearing ankle monitors.

I found myself driving several miles out of my way after work, slowing down over the water, catching a look at their tents and vehicles before driving ponderously back home. I'd seen them gathered down there, huddled from the rain, sharing food they'd scrounged, arguing, laughing. It all seemed normal and yet so alien to me. I wondered how they lived.

I wondered how they'd *bleed*.

Since I couldn't deal with the injuries to Nola's privates, I'd saddled Marnie with the unenviable task of applying ointment for several weeks before they healed. We spoke to each other less and less. We ate in front of the TV. I spent hours each night in the garage, pretending to work on the car. Mostly I would read my dad's old hunting magazines, fantasizing.

Late one night, Marnie entered the garage where I'd been sitting on a stool reading an old magazine, not even bothering to cover for the work I wasn't doing, and handed me the portable phone with no discernable expression in her gaze. I took it, listened to Sam Higgins apologize while feeling the floor drop out from beneath me, and mechanically thanked him for his help. Special Victims had made no progress in their search, and Nola had been unable to remember any details despite my coaching and our increasingly acrimonious sessions with Dr. Ambrose. Barring anything new, the case had effectively fizzled out. Went cold, like the darkened corners of my heart. After that, we never heard from him again. The Rabbit Man had gotten away.

That night I aimed to make sure it never happened again.

BREATHING HEAVILY, I caught up to Gonzalez near the fence at the base of the bridge and jerked him around roughly to face me.

"Hey! What gives?"

My vision was on a dimmer, timed to the unsteady beat of my heart. After that sucker punch from the blond dude and chasing after Gonzalez, I was on the verge of blacking out. But I would make sure he looked me in the eyes as the life drained out of him. I would make sure he knew what he'd done.

"*Nola*," I said. I shook him by his lumberjack jacket, raising a cloud of dust. "Nola, Nola," I blubbered, "my fucking *daughter*, you sick *fuck*!"

Mortified, Gonzalez threw his filthy hands in the air, a gesture of innocence. "Hey, no wait, man, I haven't—*done that*—for ten years! I slipped up *once*. I would never—I've *never*—I..."

I saw it dawn on him: first disgust, then fear, shock... and then confusion, suspicion. He looked over my shoulder, where the altercation had died down and Blondie was walking backwards to his car, shouting curses and kicking the dirt. "You have a *daughter*?"

My grip on him lessened. I grabbed him harder, attempting to embolden myself. "Bullshit!"

"I swear, I haven't—" Gonzalez couldn't say the words, as if his own crime disgusted him. "Not since, you know, back then. I served my time. She's *forgiven* me. I swear to Jesus, man, I haven't done it again since!"

I felt the monster inside me step back from its cage. Gradually, I let Gonzalez go. He brushed his jacket off as if I was the one who'd made him dirty. "I'm sorry," I said as a cloud of dust rose around us.

"It's okay. I'm fine." With another look over my shoulder his eyes narrowed, and he returned his gaze to me. "You know, I knew there was something not right about you when you first came down here. Something about the way you moved. Not quite Walker's swagger, more like you were looking down your nose at us." He shook his head. "And that story about your niece? The things you said you did to her..." Gonzalez trailed off, swallowing hard, avoiding the unpleasant terminology.

I'd noticed him wincing as we listened to Walker describe his escapades in nasty detail. All this time I thought Gonzalez had just been putting on a show, the way some of the most vile politicians and religious figures act sanctimonious when inside they were repugnant.

"I didn't buy that for a second," he finished.

"You didn't?"

Gonzalez shook his head.

"Why not?"

"It's like there was nothing there," Gonzalez said, and gestured toward his own face. "In your eyes. No regret. No pride. No *lusting*, like the way how Walker talks about his..." Another hard swallow. "Just this blank look. A *dead* look."

I regarded him silently.

"So you think somebody here—what? They—*did something*—to your little girl?"

I nodded, feeling like a fool. All this time it had been so plain to Gonzalez I was a fraud, it must have been obvious to the others. Fear crept into my nerves, setting the monster back on edge. I would have to be more careful.

"Why did you think it was me?"

It took a moment for me to realize what he was asking. "The song," I told him. "The way you reacted to it, I just figured..." I didn't need to mention the rabbit. It didn't seem smart to reveal such evidence.

"Which song? That '80s one?"

I'd nearly blown it all because of that song. Again, I nodded.

"It wasn't the song," Gonzalez said. "It's the tape player. It's the exact same..." He shook his head, his eyes downcast, and with that look I understood. His own victim must have had the same CD player. He hadn't been reacting to the song at all. "Anyway," he said, "I wasn't the one acting strange. Popcorn and Telly, those guys started a fight over it."

"Telly? He the blond guy?"

Gonzalez was about to speak when the blip of a siren startled us both. We turned to look as a police cruiser crawled into the center of camp, parting the crowd. Miami P.D. swinging by for a routine check, although just as often they came through to harass the residents. Some of these men and women had parole terms stating no alcohol or illicit drugs. Others weren't allowed to be within a certain distance of other offenders, which didn't make much sense under the bridge, where everyone was here for the same basic reason. Most of the cops who came through here were just looking for a reason to use unacceptable force. For the most part, I wouldn't say I could blame them.

Gonzalez shifted nervously in the dirt. The cop got out of the car and headed over to a huddled group of sex offenders. As he turned in the direction of the scuffle, fear struck me and I hid my face, muttering, "Shit!"

Officer Sam Higgins' bald head gleamed as he patted a woman in boxer shorts and galoshes on the shoulder and passed a bottle of water to an elderly man I didn't recognize. New people wandered in here every day, as more and more were forced to sign the registry, many for petty offences. Higgins checked on a guy's ankle monitor. The guy—Dolph, I think—offered his hand, and Higgins shook it without hesitation.

It amazed me to see how humanely he treated these people, knowing some of them could easily have victimized his own children. It was clear he believed in basic human decency, though if he'd caught these same people in a crime I was certain he wouldn't hesitate to tackle the prick and put him in the back of his cruiser, maybe put a little more elbow into the bust than was necessary. He was a cop after all, not Gandhi. But the fact that a man who dealt with the absolute worst of humanity every single day could still find a moment to be charitable gave me a glimmer of hope.

As I watched him smile and shake hands, I felt like I could forget about the Rabbit Man. I could leave here and never come back. I could return to my long-suffering wife, to my courageous little girl who had somehow managed to put her assault in the past while her father continued to grieve.

Sam laughed at something one of the men said and got back in his cruiser. I watched him drive back to the topside of the Tuttle, watched everyone return to whatever they'd been doing. I felt myself relax.

"You know, if it's anyone here, I'd put money on Telly," Gonzalez said, dragging me right back down.

"Why him?" I snapped.

"I just overheard him bragging once, about all the stuff he'd gotten away with. He said he—"

It was clear he couldn't repeat the actual words Telly had used. "You don't have to say it."

Gonzalez gave a brief smile. "Thanks. He did it to a little girl, and all they got him on was grooming some cop on the 'net posing as an eight-year-old."

Down there among the others, the blond guy, Telly, chucked a stone in the direction the cop car had gone, having since recaptured his bravado. I watched him swagger back to his own car, chewing his gum with his mouth open. He climbed in and slammed the squeaky door behind himself.

"You're gonna kill him, aren't you?"

I thought about the scratches, the rabbits. My mind ran through all the gruesome scenarios I'd dreamed up during our sessions with Dr. Ambrose. "What if I said yes?"

Gonzalez followed my gaze. Telly had his dirty work boots rested on the driver's window. Behind the windshield, the orange ember of his cigarette burned.

"I won't tell," Gonzalez said. "He'll just do it again, the second he gets a chance. You can tell just by looking at him. Heck, I wouldn't be surprised if that's what he does at night, driving off all by himself."

I considered this in silence, knowing the decision had already been made for me.

EXCEPT FOR THOSE times he left camp well after sundown, I didn't let Telly leave my sight again for over a week. He'd recline the driver's seat and nod off as the sun began to sink beyond the skyline, well before anyone else had even considered sleep. Later, when most of us had been out for a few hours, I'd watch him light up a smoke in the dark behind the windshield. Then he'd creep out with the running lights off. A few hours later, he'd pull back into his spot. I'd watch him fire up a butt with his Zippo, lighting a dark smile on his face. The little orange ember of his cigarette would wax and wane. After a few minutes, he'd flick it out the window in a shower of sparks, put his booted feet out the window, and go back to sleep. Once, he'd gone directly to the water and washed his hands. To wash off what, I don't know.

But I can guess.

About a week into this routine, Telly left the car to go down to the water to fish. (We caught a fair few down in that part of Biscayne Bay. Going hungry was never a worry for us living under the bridge, though I lost the taste for fish quickly.) I wandered over to the car, curiosity getting the best of me, and peeked in the dusty window. The passenger seat was covered in cassette tapes, mostly metal and hard rock bands: AC/DC, Iron Maiden, Metallica, Slayer. With a collection like that, it wasn't likely he'd have ever listened to George Michael, but I considered it might be a part of his pathology, like maybe he'd been abused to it when he was younger. Or maybe it reminded him of a junior school crush. Parking tickets were scattered on the floor like the bottom of a birdcage.

I spotted what I'd been hoping to find hanging from the rearview mirror. Due to the fine layer of dust on the windshield, I hadn't been able to see it before. A little white rabbit's foot swayed gently on a bathtub chain, a few spots of something dark on its fur. I shaded my eyes against the glass for a closer look, thinking it might just be blood.

"Lookin' for somethin', asshole?"

I stepped away, caught. Telly sauntered back with the fishing pole over his shoulder and no fish. I stammered something about looking for cigarettes, and Telly narrowed his eyes.

"You want a smoke, you coulda just ast." Chewing absently on a wad of pink gum, he reached into the back pocket of his jeans and pulled out a pack of Camels, shifting the pole to his other shoulder. He shook one out and flicked it at me.

I caught it, fumbled it into the dirt. I picked it up and blew on it, then nestled it between my lips. The sweet smell of tobacco filled my nostrils. Marnie and I had quit when we found out she was pregnant. I'd sneaked a few puffs here and there after Nola was born, but after Marnie caught me lighting up the day of the argument, the day Nola ran away, I hadn't smoked since.

"Got a light?"

He threw a Zippo at me, and I caught it deftly. Lit the smoke. Inhaled. The first drag felt like pins jabbing my lungs. After that, the drags were smoother. "Thanks," I said, holding the cigarette between my teeth as I handed the Rabbit Man his lighter.

"No problem." A buzz had him reaching into the back pocket of his jeans. He opened the flip phone and studied the message. "Gotta split," he said. He opened the car door, then squinted at me. "Hey, no hard feelings about that love tap last week. I woulda hit me, too, if they'da been my buddies you was messin' with."

"They're not my buddies. Thanks again for the smoke," I added, walking away.

"Any time, amigo. Just stay the fuck away from my car next time."

I lied and said I would.

IT WAS TWO nights later when I dared approach his car again. He was asleep inside, his boots on the dash. I crept up to the driver door and listened to his slow, deep breathing for a while, maybe too long. I needed to be sure he was sleeping. I wanted to catch him off guard. He looked at peace. Like he'd slept well. It enraged me to see that, when my own sleep was so fitful because of him.

I wondered how many other children he might have abused since the police sent him down here, how many childhoods he'd taken away. How many families he'd destroyed. How many fathers he'd poisoned, the way he poisoned me. I still knew nothing about him, but none of that mattered. I could have called in with Officer Higgins' badge number, got them to run Telly's plates. I could have found a previous address. I could have rented a car—unless Marnie had cancelled my credit cards, which was possible—and followed him the next time he left camp. I didn't do any of these things. I didn't want to know about his life. All I wanted was for it to be him, and for it to end *tonight*.

I rounded the dirty front of the car to the passenger side. Ever so gently, I pulled up the handle. The door came open an inch with a click that seemed to rebound off the cement pillars and the underside of the bridge. Telly snored and shifted in his sleep. I froze, blood hammering. We were mere feet from each other, but his car was far enough away from the rest of Bookville, a pariah among pariahs, that I thought I'd be safe from potential witnesses. Despite the distance, if he woke up and saw me looming over him, no doubt he'd shout, and my whole stupid reckless plan, the months of research and preparation and time away from the girls, all of it would have been for nothing.

I held my breath.

He didn't wake.

Slowly, I pulled the door open. The amount of times I'd watched him open it to get one thing or another, I knew it wouldn't creak, not like the driver door. I knew the dome light wouldn't come on, either; it had burned out or didn't work. I slipped in cautiously beside him and pulled the door closed.

Telly slept with his seat reclined, his knees curled up to his chest. He breathed deeply, a sure sign he was either asleep or faking it, ready to gut me like he gutted fish with the jagged hunting knife attached to his belt.

His eyes suddenly snapped open and he scrambled up against the door, sucking in a breath with childlike terror before squinting at me coolly. His breath smelled like cinnamon when he said, "What the fuck do you want?"

"Roll up your window."

"Why the fuck should I?" He looked in the direction I indicated: the tip of my father's old buck knife aimed at the faded crotch of his tight jeans. "*Jesus*, man," he said on exhale and rolled up the window, not taking his eyes off me. "You mind tellin' me what the fuck you're doin' in my car? And don't say you're lookin' for a cigarette, amigo, 'cause I know you ain't a smoker."

For a long while, I said nothing. All the time I'd spent dreaming about this moment, it felt like he should know why I was here before I took his life away. It felt like I should make him aware, for Nola's sake if not mine. But everything I started to say seemed wrong. Like I'd be offering him an explanation he surely didn't deserve. Like I'd be allowing him the opportunity for forgiveness when forgiveness had never been an option.

"Take out the tape," I said finally.

"What?"

"*The tape. Take out the fucking tape.*"

"All right, man. *Shit.*" Eyeing me the whole time, Telly reached for the cassette player in the dash. His dirty fingers found the eject button and he pushed it. The tape popped out with a satisfying clunk. Telly fumbled it into his hand, then held it up for me to see. "All right?"

"All right," I said, and thrust the knife at his crotch.

Telly's eyes opened wider than I'd thought humanly possible, like something you'd see on a Saturday morning cartoon. He made to cry out, but I pressed a hand over his mouth, his mustache prickling against my palm, his tongue flicking out, probably involuntarily, as I mashed his head against the doorjamb.

Relishing the agonized terror in his eyes, I missed the sight of his hand scrabbling for the knife at his hip. He had it pulled out and pain tore up my chest before I could react. Smashing his head back against the door, I thrust my elbow against his wrist, pushing it back. I shoved my knee down hard against his legs, yanking on the knife in his groin. It came free with a jet of blood that splashed my wrist, his jeans already dark with it.

The wet blade gleamed in the arc lights as I pulled it back to strike again, and I shoved it straight into his throat, to the hilt. The monster's tongue flicked against my palm as his life spurted out from the hole in his neck, soaking my shirt. His legs kicked weakly, like a dying insect's. A gout of blood poured from the hole as he gagged. His fingers relaxed, dropping his knife. The life left his eyes.

I sat there a moment longer, watching his body leak blood, listening for his breath. I couldn't believe he was dead, that it was finally over and I could leave this godforsaken place and return to my family.

His cell phone buzzed.

I wondered who would be texting so late. I couldn't imagine it being a booty call, although I supposed like Walker he could have had a thing for women and men as well as children.

I told myself it was over. But the cell phone buzzed again, and I couldn't resist opening the glovebox, from which I'd located the sound on the second buzz.

Two items fell from the glovebox on a landslide of junk paper and Big Red chewing gum wrappers: Telly's crappy flip phone, and a heavy black revolver.

I picked up the phone, giving the gun a wary look, as if it was a dangerous animal.

Two new messages awaited, both from Unknown Number.

The second message was an address. I knew the area. Somewhere in Coconut Grove, where the rich folk live.

The first message said: ARE U IN?

Was I in? Hell, I didn't even know what I was in *for*—but I'd already come this far.

What if Telly had an accomplice? I thought. Someone with the resources to keep him from falling under the scrutiny of the Miami-Dade P.D. Someone rich enough to live in Coconut Grove.

I had to find out.

I scrolled through prior messages phone, looking at his responses. They were curt replies, mostly written in text-speak. No wonder, with the ancient buttons on the thing. Heart hammering, I thumbed the

buttons, clicking ponderously through numbers and letters to type out:
B THERE IN 1 HR

I wasn't sure how soon they'd be expecting him, but I wanted to give myself enough time to get cleaned up first.

The phone buzzed again in my hand.

MAKE IT TWO, BACK DOOR'S OPEN

Even better, I thought.

Telly's body slid another few inches toward the floor. In the dim light beyond the space he'd left, I spotted Gonzalez huddled against a pillar, watching us with wide eyes. I wondered how long he'd been standing there. Long enough, I guessed.

His eyes met mine, and he nodded. Somehow, I managed to nod back.

I dragged Telly's lifeless body out of the seat and climbed over him, then sat him up in the passenger seat. Reaching over him, I half-expected him to snap awake and grab me around the throat. Of course he didn't. And when I yanked on the seat adjuster, he dropped back along with the seat.

I flicked the dome light to its off position, and started the engine. The Impala purred like a panther. The running lights already off, I backed up, and drove out up the embankment, leaving behind Bookville for good.

As I drove west on I95, the rabbit's foot jingled on its chain from the mirror. In all the commotion, I'd forgotten about it. I tore it down to get a better look. The dark stains were no doubt blood. Whether it was old blood or new I couldn't tell, not when I'd just smeared Telly's blood onto its dirty off-white fur.

I tucked the totem into my pocket and looked at myself in the rearview. A few streaks of blood had spattered my face, and I wiped them off with the back of my hand. I didn't plan to go home looking like I did, anyway.

At my old 24-hour gym, I parked the car at the far corner of the lot, under a broken streetlamp. There was a blanket in the backseat, which I threw over Telly's body. When I got out, it felt like I'd given my whole body a workout, every muscle aching.

I staggered to the brightly lit gym. The doors slid open for me.

The attendant, a young kid with clear, tanned skin, gave me a funny look. When I got into the showers, I understood why. I hadn't been into the city for a week, hadn't shaved, hadn't slept. My shirt was gouged open at the chest, matted to my skin with blood. I looked like a man who'd gotten lost in the jungle, fought a wild animal, and narrowly escaped with his life. I left the showers clean and shaven, my wound— Telly's blade had cut my left nipple in half—washed and dressed with paper towels, surprised that the kid wiping down the equipment hadn't called the cops. Far enough away from the mess I'd left under the Tuttle, I had no worries they would finger me for the crime even if the kid called in my appearance and had them pull the security video. For all they knew, I'd taken time off work to deal with the aftermath of what had happened to Nola.

Back at the Impala, I rooted through a duffel bag of clean-smelling clothes in the trunk. Telly was about my size, and always seemed to be dressed in a t-shirt and a fresh pair of jeans. I assumed on some of his excursions he'd been to use a laundromat, but I suppose his friend in the Grove could have easily gotten them washed for him.

I found black jeans a t-shirt and as worn Miami Heat cap, and put them on in the dark below the burnt-out streetlamp. The jeans were snug and a little short, but the t-shirt fit well enough. Though they were clean, they felt slimy on my skin and scalp. To be wearing the clothes of the man who'd assaulted my little girl... but it was a necessary evil.

Walk a mile in a man's shoes, I thought. When I got back in the car, I gave Telly's pale, dead face a long hard look.

This was somebody's son. Someone had given birth to this monster. Had *raised* it.

Not wanting to give him another moment of my time, I started the car, and headed toward the Grove. He was fertilizer now. Worm food.

The streets out here were bright even in the dead of night. Palms in front of multimillion-dollar homes swayed in a breeze from the bay. I read house numbers on pillars and porticos and wrought iron arches until finally I found the house.

I parked the Impala on the next block, left it there, and headed back on foot.

The whole neighborhood felt eerily quiet, aside from the gentle swish of the tide, and the palm fronds above. I imagined the people who lived here, in their Xanax-induced slumbers, some maybe burning the midnight oil to keep the creditors at bay. Was it possible a predator lived among them? I was certain there were tax-evaders. Philanderers. Pill addicts. Spouse abusers. Investment swindlers. Perpetrators of criminal negligence—even potential vehicular homicides.

I wondered how many sex offenders had once lived on my own street.

The house stood silent before me, the moon casting a diamond glint trail on the bay beyond. A security camera watched over the gate, the stone wall around the perimeter lined with bushes. Spotlights lit the glass house's exterior, but inside the only room that appeared lit was the kitchen.

As I headed along a red clay path toward the beach in the darkness below the wall, the sound of the ocean grew louder. My feet more sore than they'd been the day I'd walked home, I longed to take off my shoes and walk in the sand. But more pressing business was at hand.

The gun felt heavy against my spine, tucked into the back of Telly's jeans.

On the beach, I crept close to the wall, looking for a point of egress, certain the owner had access to the docks dotting a strip of white sand. Finally, I reached a small gate where the wall dipped down on either side. No camera in sight. The gate locked, I climbed over the wall and jumped down on the other side, praying they didn't have dogs.

The water beat against the shore, almost as loud as my heart thrumming in my ears.

The house, a series of stacked white stucco-and-glass rectangles, stood quiet and stark against the moonlit sky. I could see a camera above the back door, and I slowed my approach, pulling the peak of the Heat cap down to hide my face. I rounded the pool, spotting children's pool toys floating in the blue-green water, lit from below. Stepped over a damp towel left bunched on the concrete, and a small pair of sopping wet board shorts with little flamingos printed on them left halfway to the door, as if they'd been cast off on the way to the house.

I stood under the camera, and jiggled the handle. No luck.

Out of options, short of smashing one of the window walls and announcing the presence of an intruder, I thumbed the doorbell.

As I waited for a response, I felt sick creeping into my throat, and swallowed it down, hard.

"That you, Tell?"

A male voice over the intercom. Deep. He sounded drunk.

I nodded, not wanting to show my face but desperate to make the man believe I was Telly. Inspiration struck, and I dug into the jeans, thankful I'd thought to transfer it from my pants when I'd changed out of them.

I held up the rabbit's foot. Jingled it on the chain.

The door buzzed.

"C'mon downstairs," the man said. "The party's started."

I stepped inside.

The darkened house smelled of burning incense. Beer. Lit dimly by the moon over the bay, the living room looked as though someone had been having a party. From deeper inside the house, music thumped. Just the bass, but I recognized the song. I'd heard it in nightmares so often the beat was seared into my brain. I swallowed bile, and continued toward a brightened doorway.

Stairs led down. Basements were rare in Miami—hell, in most of South Florida. Near the beach, you'd have to drill through several feet of coral rock before you hit water. It was difficult to dig, and even more to keep them dry.

I drew the revolver from the back of Telly's jeans. I'd already checked to see that it was loaded. I wasn't sure what I would find down there, but with the boy's swim trunks at the pool, and whoever lived in this house being a friend of Telly's, I felt it best to err on the side of caution.

Creeping down, I held the gun pointed at the doorway, expecting someone to step out at the foot of the stairs with every step down, the song so loud it felt like the music penetrated every pore in my body. I realized halfway down the stairs that I'd been crying.

As I descended further, a room came into view below, oddly incongruous to the modern style of the house above, as if someone had torn it straight from a magazine from the '80s. Faux wood paneling. A brown tartan sofa with colorful afghan throw pillows. An ancient game system resting on the floor, hooked up to a large tube television with knobs instead of buttons above the brown speaker panel. The smell of beer was even stronger. Several empty bottles stood on the coffee table, some with the labels peeled off.

I reached the clean concrete floor, and turned.

The boy was stretched out naked on the red fabric of a pool table, his frail limbs spread wide, hands and feet pointing toward the corner holes. He looked about nine or ten, the conspicuous lack of pubic hair at his groin and under his armpits evidence of his young age. He appeared asleep, but was more likely passed out or drugged. If so, he was lucky not to be subjected to the sight of the two men watching him.

On either side of the boy, two deeply tanned men stood stripped down to the waist. One wore boxer shorts, the other tight blue briefs, his erect penis sprung from the y-front. The man in boxers, his hair slicked back like Gordon Gecko, stroked himself with one hand while leering down at the boy, taking a swig of beer with the other.

"Father Figure," blasting from a large wood cabinet stereo, ended.

The man in the briefs kneaded the foreskin-hooded end of his penis as if he were chalking a pool cue. In the silence, he groaned. Neither man had seen me—yet.

I snapped back the hammer.

The man in boxers turned to me, the bottle dropping from his hand as he realized I wasn't Telly.

"What the—?"

The pistol silenced him before the bottle hit even the floor, the bullet tearing into his shoulder and spinning him around on his bare feet with a spray of blood, DayGlo under the fluorescent track lights. He fell back against the pool table, his arm squeaking as he slid down to the floor on his butt in a puddle of beer and broken glass.

The song started up again, on repeat: *Tss-tss-tss...*

Briefs had reached into one of the pockets and grabbed a pool ball while I'd watched the Boxer Shorts fall. As he threw it at me, his hard-on bounced in an almost comical way, making me think of those Follow the Bouncing Ball singalongs from old cartoons.

I ducked, but not before it struck me in the chest, just above the nipple Telly had slashed open. I fired again. The shot went wild, striking the wall a foot from his face, taking a chunk out of the wood wallpaper.

He tore a pool cue off the rack and gripped it in both hands, holding the felt-tipped end pointed at the boy's scrawny chest.

"Don't fucking shoot, man, I swear to God—"

This time, my aim was true.

I approached Boxer Shorts as he tried to pull himself to his feet, his blood-streaked hand constantly slipping on the wood of the pool table so he kept falling back on his ass in the spilled beer.

"Please, don't kill me, man," he wept. "I'm sick." He blubbered, lips quivering, tears streaming down his face. "I'm just sick!"

"I know," I said, and shot him in the head.

THE WALK BACK to Telly's Impala was excruciating. I kept thinking somebody must have heard the shots. Someone must have called the police. But the cops never showed. The streets remained empty and silent, just the sound of the breaks hitting the sand accompanying me to where Telly's body awaited disposal.

I filled the small gas can from the tank with a syphon I found in the trunk, and splashed the gas around the front and back seats, drenching Telly. I tossed the gun in through the passenger window, followed by the gas tank.

Telly's Zippo lit on the first strike. I stepped back, and threw it in.

The fire caught fast. I was already on my way back to the beach when the gas can exploded, and I turned back to see the Impala shoot into the air, flames spewing from shattered glass as it crashed back down on burst tires.

The boy was sitting where I'd left him. I'd carried him upstairs and dressed him in the living room, where they'd left his clothes. He didn't weigh much, maybe sixty pounds soaking wet. His eyes fluttered as I carried him down through the darkened residential streets. Police sirens blared by on the block opposite, heading toward the fire, but somehow we remained unseen.

I carried the boy as far as Mercy Hospital. With the cap peak still obscuring my face, I brought him into Emerg, which seemed eerily empty. As I laid him out on a gurney, a night nurse came down the hall with a clipboard. She called after me as I rushed off, ignoring her, glad the boy would be safe in her care.

As I walked home, I thought about what Marnie had said to me the day I left. Nola may not have needed a vigilante. She would certainly have preferred I'd never left, that I'd stayed home to be a father to her and watch over her. But I'm certain the boy, had he known how close he'd come to being violated and most likely murdered that night, might not feel the same.

It broke my heart to know things between Marnie and I would never be the same, no matter how hard I tried. Even if she'd have me back, our time apart would always be between us. The Rabbit Man's death, and those nameless men whose lives I'd taken in a basement in Coconut Grove, would seep into every seemingly pleasant conversation, every social engagement, every one of Nola's milestones. In the back of my mind and hers, the Rabbit Man would still be running.

Back at the house in Coral Gables, I used my key in the door, pleased for a second time to find it still worked. I crept up to our bedroom, saw Marnie sleeping with legs stretched over my side of the bed. It had been four months since we'd slept in that bed together, and she still slept mostly on her side.

I slipped by into Nola's room. The moon illuminated her head against the pillow. Nola had a thumb in her mouth, a habit she'd grown out of at age four but had taken up again in the wake of her experience with the Rabbit Man.

My sweet little girl's eyes opened wide as she drew the covers up to her chin, and for a terrible moment I flashed back to the eerily similar look Telly had given me when I woke him with the knife. Nola relaxed, seeing it was me.

"I thought you were a monster," she said.

I wondered, *Am I?*

Could I tell her there was nothing to be afraid of, that there were three less monsters in the world because of what I'd done that night? I flashed on the tape in Telly's hand, completely unreadable in the dark. It could have been a polka album for all I'd cared. That splotch on the rabbit's foot could have been dirt or paint or just about anything.

Could I tell her I'd taken pleasure in killing those two men?

There was no doubt in my mind what they'd intended to do with that boy. But what was Telly's role in it? Had he in fact been the Rabbit Man I'd so wanted him to be? I'd *needed* him to be, so I could come home to my wife? To our daughter?

Marnie had been right after all: Nola didn't need a vigilante. I'd needed to *be* one.

I'd fooled myself into believing that killing the Rabbit Man was about seeking justice for my little girl, but it had never been for her. I'd needed to take him out of the world to feel strong again. I needed to erase him from our family history to cover for my own shame, my own weakness. So I wouldn't feel like a coward anymore.

So *I* would feel safe.

It had never been about justice. And the fear, that *shame*—it would never end.

There were more of them, you see. I'd forgotten about Telly's cell phone tucked into the back pocket of his jeans. And as I crossed the South Dixie Highway on my way back home, it had buzzed against my pelvis.

TOMORROW NIGHT, the text said. U IN?

Was I in? No question.

But first I needed to buy a gun.

I smiled down at Nola, her face half in darkness, my shadow drawn long over her bed. "No, honey," I told her, faking a reassuring smile. "It's me. Daddy's home."

Skin Flicks

Published 2023

SKIN

1

The two-tone '78 Camaro sped down Mulholland, barely slowing to take the corners, the refurbished small block 350ci engine making more of a choked growl than a purr.

Larry Walker spun the wheel, leaning into another corner. The rocker panels rattled, flecks of rust speckling the road. The Camaro had seen better days. So had Larry. In the '70s and early '80s, it had been featured in gatefold magazine spreads and billboards on Sunset and Rodeo Drive, in Melrose and Fairfax, on freeways in and out of town. During that time, Larry Walker's presence—but above all his giant cock —had covered the pages of dozens of magazines and filled the screen in hundreds of films. He'd been one of the most sought-after stars during the Golden Age of Porn, from old stag film loops to the era of VHS home video and DVD. Now, he was lucky to land a paying commercial to pay his rent. If that hadn't been the case, he'd never have come out here tonight.

Larry glanced at the needle, hovering well over sixty, like himself. "C'mon, baby, c'monnnn," he cooed.

A bright, fat moon shone through the cracked glass T-top, the sycamore and oaks he passed as silent and still as the bones buried beneath Mount Sinai Memorial.

Twin headlights flashed over his grizzled features in the rearview. Stunters often cruised Mulholland at night on motorcycles, reaching dangerous speeds far higher than Larry's Camaro could handle. Two lights could possibly be competing bikes. Was it just another late-night cruiser? Or had that psycho in the mask caught up to him?

Distracted, he took the next corner too fast, bumping up over the curb and struggling to right himself. The redline tires peeled rubber on asphalt, squealing like one of his costars when he'd inched his tool in as deep as it would go. They'd called him the Sex Machine, back then. That or The Piston. It was a term of endearment and respect but often used as a sly insult. In those days he could fuck and fuck and fuck and only the sound of the director shouting *"Cut!"* would stop him. Like he wasn't a man at all, just a hard dick walking on two legs. Like he had nothing behind his eyes but a constantly looping stream of pornographic images, sucking, licking, rubbing, fucking.

The vehicle behind him took the same corner with ease.

"Fuck!" he shouted, slapping the steering wheel.

The bright pink face of his hunter was visible through the car's windshield, even in the dark, its mouth and eyes wide as if in perpetual shock. His years of taking 'ludes recreationally may have kept his mind sharp enough to temporarily escape, but he'd never be free, not driving this rust bucket.

Maybe twenty years ago she'd have had it in her. *He'd* have had it in *him*. Not now. They were too old. Too out to pasture. This creep had youth and wealth on his side. He had a hacienda in the Hollywood Hills set far enough away from its neighbors that no one would notice him coming and going with walls made of foot-thick concrete so no one would hear the screams.

With an enraged boost of adrenaline, Larry slammed his foot down on the accelerator.

The Camaro roared forward. He took the next two turns without risking a look behind him, and when he reached a third, the other car was right on his tail.

"Shit! Come *on*." He rubbed the dash in concentric circles with his long, thick fingers, the way he'd stroked hundreds, *thousands* of clits. The engine roared. "C'mon, girl. Just gimme this one last stretch."

The lights at Laurel Canyon were red.

"Shit!"

Larry had a split-second decision to make. The traffic looked sparse. He pressed his foot down on the pedal as hard as he could and blew past the lights at top speed, narrowly avoiding a motorcycle crossing the intersection.

"Yes!" He slapped the dash. "Fuck yeah!"

The car behind him hit the light on the green and didn't slow. It kept pressing forward, and Larry didn't notice the fresh-laid patch of asphalt in the road until he hit it. The Camaro bounded and swerved. He fought to maintain control but overcompensated—like critics accused him of later in his career, leaning too far into self-parody to survive the unforgiving film and TV industry—and the car spun out, tires screeching.

"NononoNO!"

SLAM!

The Camaro hit the ditch and struck a sycamore at high speed, the windshield shattering inward in a rain of glass. Larry's head struck the driver's window with blinding pain, cracking it. The front end was totaled, the mangled hood popped like a virgin's cherry. The back left wheel spun six inches above the asphalt. Oil leaked in a puddle in the dirt. The vanity plate had fallen off and lay against a nearby tree, SX MCHEN spelled out in blue letters beneath *California* written in red script.

Larry nearly lost consciousness as his forehead dropped against the wheel. The horn blared out into the night but he couldn't seem to lift his head. It felt too heavy for his shoulders, as if it belonged to someone else.

A black-gloved hand smashed through the remains of the driver door window, brushed aside broken glass to grab Larry by the hair—something Larry had done dozens of times to dozens of women—and pulled him back to the seat. He couldn't move. His breath came shallow. A crushing silence filled the space left by the horn.

The gloved hand reached past Larry. He watched through dazed, blood-tinted eyes as the hand turned the keys, shutting off the engine, retracting from the glassless window with the keys held between pinky and thumb. There was a jingle—barely heard over the ringing in Larry's ears—as the man threw them into the woods. The engine ticked rhythmically in the semi-dark.

"What are you—" Larry swallowed, the dry click of his Adam's apple audible. "What do you want with me?"

The man leaned in, turning slowly toward Larry until his dark blue eyes were visible within that ridiculous mask, the one made to look like one of those yellow-blonde inflatable sex dolls with the too-pink skin and red lips perpetually opened in an exaggerated O. The freak behind the mask blinked, as if the answer was obvious.

"We're going to make a film together, Larry," the man said, his voice muffled by polystyrene.

As Larry lost consciousness for the second time that night, the man in the mask unlocked the door and began wrenching it open.

2

Yesterday.

Larry got the call a little after noon. He was already two whiskies deep, having seen the news early and read the story several times. He cleared his throat, swallowed an acrid belch that tasted like orange juice and vodka filtered through an ashtray, and picked up the phone.

"Sorry to call so early, Lar," his manager, Thom Gorski, said.

"I was already up."

It was true he rarely woke before noon, but today he'd shot up around nine and hadn't been able to get back to sleep. Something had been nagging at him, the tail end of a nightmare or a vague intuition he couldn't put his finger on.

When he saw the story in the morning paper, he set down his espresso—which he always called *expresso*—and broke out the Absolut vodka from the freezer, poured it into a jug of orange juice, dumping in Galliano, and making himself a stiff Harvey Wallbanger.

"I guess you heard about Linda," Thom said.

Larry swallowed another mouthful of liquor. "I heard. You still haven't heard from her?"

The *Times* had reached out to Thom, her manager, for comment.

He'd told them they hadn't spoken in a week. Her distraught husband put in the call to the cops two days ago. When she didn't come home a second night, her husband—Chet Daniels, a low-budget shlock horror director who'd been casting Linda Flint in his films for over a decade—decided to contact the press. They were just finishing up pre-pro for his new flick, he'd said, and were supposed to begin shooting in a few days. He couldn't shoot anything without his star, or as he was quoted as having said in the article, his "muse."

The headline read *FORMER PORN STAR MISSING*. No mention of her charitable foundation or the years she'd spent in her husband's "legitimate" films. It was always the same. Larry had seen his friends and former colleagues reduced to the same three-word moniker over and over in the news. *FORMER PORN STAR FOUND DEAD. FORMER PORN STAR IN REHAB. FORMER PORN STAR ARRESTED. FORMER PORN STAR DEAD IN SUSPECTED SUICIDE.*

When Larry had first noticed this, he'd started thinking of his life told in third-person headlines. Former Porn Star Ruins Pot Roast. Former Porn Star Takes a One-Wipe Shit. Former Porn Star Rubs One Out in the Shower. Former Porn Star ODs on Cheetos Watching *Dancing with the Stars*.

"No," Thom said. "I haven't heard a peep. You haven't, have you...?"

Linda and Larry used to date off and on back in the day. They met on Linda's first picture, one of those fantasy ones where Larry was given three wishes and ended up fucking every woman in the film. He'd taken Linda's porn cherry and he couldn't even remember the name of the movie. But he remembered Linda. She'd been a sweet little piece of trim with a ginger-blonde bush and long shapely legs. She'd worn nothing but cowboy boots in the scene and the image of her standing in the pizza parlor set in her birthday suit, even after he'd slept with literally *thousands* of women, was indelibly imprinted on his mind.

Larry got up from the kitchen table and wandered into the sunken living room in his silk kimono. Just thinking about Linda back in the day got him at half mast, his tool slapping against either thigh like the pendulum in a grandfather clock. Given the circumstances it wasn't an entirely welcome hardon—she could be dead for all he knew—but at the ripe age of sixty-eight he took any chance he could get to rub one out.

"No, Thom, I haven't seen her," he said, scanning the shelves of videotapes embedded in the eggshell white wall.

His tapes weren't sorted alphabetically by title or chronologically but by the first name of his most prominent co-stars for easy masturbatory access. Annette Haven, Amber Lynn, Asia Carrera, Becky Savage, Bunny Bleu, Candy Samples, Constance Money, Desireé Cousteau, etcetera, etcetera, etcetera. He found the one he was looking for on the second shelf from the bottom, not their first scene together but the one where the two of them fucked in the middle of a raging orgy, a key party they'd been invited to, the nerdy accountant with a massive dong and his shy yet sexy wife coerced into half a dozen scenes of wanton debauchery throughout the film.

"Well, if you do see her, Lar, call me right away, you got it?"

"Will do, Thom," Larry said absently, the phone tucked between shoulder and ear so he could pop the cassette to the VCR while stroking himself through the silky kimono with his free hand.

"Speaking of calls," Thom said, "have I got a project for you."

"Oh yeah?" Larry stopped touching himself. His boner throbbed away pleasantly while he waited for Thom to reveal his secrets.

"Yeah. Guy called me this morning. Wants you to read for a part in a film."

Larry plopped down on the white leather sofa in front of the TV. "What kind of movie?"

"A lee-gitimate motion picture, Larry. Not a cameo, either. A *starring* role."

"A lead? No fucking way."

"Yes frigging way," Thom said, matching Larry's excitement, but omitting the curse as a self-professed Good Catholic Boy. "Some kind of serial killer thing. You'd be the grizzled detective on the case. I flipped through the script this morning. Sort of a '70s throwback, cat-and-mouse picture. Think Popeye Doyle, Jim Rockford—"

"Dirty Harry," Larry added. "I'm fuckin down, Thom. When and where?"

Thom rhymed off the details. The map showed it was in an office plaza in Beverly Hills, not too far from Larry's Hollywood apartment. He could walk the distance if he wanted to look like a chump.

He hung up with Thom, promising again to call him if he heard anything from Linda, and pressed Play on the remote.

On the big screen, baby oil-slickened bodies rolled and writhed over one another, genitals mashing, lips smearing, hands caressing. And at the center of all of this, a young and virile Larry Walker and a vibrant, toned and tanned Linda Flint laughed, shrugged up their shoulders, and began to undress each other. The theme of the film was "if you can't beat em join em," summed up by an early line in the film from Larry's neighbor, played with characteristic aplomb by the great Mike Horner: "If you can't beat em, beat off with em."

Larry squirted lube into his palm and took the advice in hand.

3

Tonight.

The scene was playing when Larry awoke. The orgy. Only it wasn't on his TV this time. It looked like it might be an actual 35mm print, screening from an old projector onto a big blank white wall. The room was otherwise dark. The projector rattled away pleasantly somewhere behind him, and if not for the pain in his head and the fact that he appeared to be strapped around the chest to a hard plastic chair set up to face the scene, his wrists and ankles zip-tied, he might have lost himself in the nostalgia it conjured up.

"Where..." His voice cracked. "Where am I?"

For a split second he'd forgotten about the psycho in that fucked-up blow-up doll mask, until the man stepped between him and the film. He was dressed neatly: black pleated pants and a black shirt. A strange counterpoint to the mask.

Back in the '70s, when the ads for them were in the backs of pretty much any publication, Larry remembered his friends calling them Suzie Q dolls or Blow-Up Betty. Neither name fit the freak in the mask, so he thought of him as The Doll.

"You're awake," the Doll said, his voice muffled, yet somehow familiar. "Good."

"Why are you doing this?"

"I told you, we're making a movie, you and I."

"That's what I *came* here for, man. Why did you have to *drug* me?" Raising his voice, the pain in his forehead came back with a vengeance. "You made me crash my car!"

"I didn't *make* you do anything. Not yet. You have free will, Larry." Larry sensed the man smiling behind the mask. "For the moment."

He remembered the horror he'd seen in the basement and tried to spring up from the chair, but all he did was hurt his wrists and legs, pulling against the tape. Peering down, he saw the chair was bolted to the floor.

"Relax, Larry," the Doll said, brushing Larry's sweat-and-blood dampened hair out of his eyes. Larry flinched and reared back as far as he was able. "Oh, don't be so uptight. This is your very own private screening room. I hoped you'd like it."

Larry said nothing. The man in the mask stepped aside, allowing him to see his performance. The quality of the projection was quite good, almost like the original 35mm they'd screened at the 57th Street Playhouse in 1979, with a gala opening for the press and cast at the Four Seasons. The picture—*The Awakening of Mr. and Mrs. S*—had done well at the box office, but had reviewed poorly, called a "lesser, cheaper *Misty Beethoven*" by bourgeois New York film critics. "Walker is certainly no Jamie Gillis," a writer for the *Village Voice* proclaimed. "His acting isn't even up to par with 'farcical' stars like Randy Rockhard and Harry Reems."

"I blame myself for your escape," The Doll said, drawing Larry from his reverie. "I should've known with your tolerance level I'd need to give you more drugs."

Curiosity finally got the better of Larry. He had to know. "Where did you get that?"

"The film? It's the last of its kind, a rare 35mm print. They don't make them like this anymore, do they, Larry? Not since videotape."

Larry didn't reply.

"What you saw in the basement. My *tableau vivant*," The Doll said, with an air of pretention. "Did that excite you?"

Larry remained quiet. On the screen a much younger version of himself ate twenty-one-year-old Linda's pussy from behind. He remembered the smell of it, like fresh sweat and baby powder, and the savory taste, unlike any he'd eaten before or after. Without warning, he felt his member start to throb beneath his jeans.

"It did excite you, didn't it?" the Doll said. "I'm glad. I made that tableau just for you. It's all for you, Larry."

"You're a sick fuck," Larry spat.

"You call me sick. I'm merely a seeker of pleasure, like yourself. If that's depraved, then I'll gladly join the club." The Doll turned and began to walk away. "Relax, Larry. Enjoy the film. I'll be back soon and we can discuss your triumphant return to the big screen."

The Doll crossed the room to a closed door, the clicks of his hard-soled shoes echoing in the large space. He unlocked it, unlatched it, and pulled it open with a squeak of metal hinges. It looked heavy. Impossible to kick down.

"What is this fucking place?"

"It's a shrine," the Doll said, stopping momentarily in the doorway.

"A shrine to what?" Larry called out.

"To you, Larry. It's a shrine to you. Honestly, I'm surprised you haven't grasped that by now."

4

Yesterday.

The office complex was easy enough to find, even with a few drinks in him. Several COMMERCIAL PROPERTY FOR LEASE signs plastered the glass front. Only one car was parked in the lot, close to the doors, but it was covered in a thick layer of dust and looked like someone might be sleeping in it at night. It wasn't an uncommon sight. So many people slept in their cars in L.A. it might as well have been considered its own community.

Larry hadn't driven this way in a while and couldn't remember if this complex was occupied the last time he had or if it had been abandoned for some time. A few broken windows, boarded up from the inside, made him think the latter. He supposed he could look it up but what did it matter? He'd been to worse places looking for work. Often they were in dubious, cramped office spaces above stores in Culver City or the Valley, with posters of films no one had ever heard of covering the walls and seemingly the same blonde women seated in every waiting room, like a glitch in the Matrix, subvocalizing their sides.

Larry shrugged and turned off the ignition.

He climbed out, pushed his longish hair out of his face, and swag-

724

gered to the front door. A part of him expected it to be locked when he tried the handle—it wouldn't have been the first time Thom had gotten the address wrong to an audition. But it pulled open with ease.

The foyer smelled like cleaning supplies. There was a security desk with no one stationed at it. Two elevators with chrome doors. One of those folding WET FLOOR signs. That was it.

On the wall beside the elevators was a directory, like in a medical office, with every space blank aside from one. The name of the plaza— JCL Properties Inc—etched at the top. The one filled slot was for AUTHORITY PICTURES - SUITE 201, the company Thom had mentioned.

Larry shrugged again and thumbed the up button. The elevator to the right chimed immediately, the doors sliding open on a mirrored interior. Larry stepped in, checked his hair, straightened his collar, and pressed 2.

The doors closed and the car lurched. He gripped the rail. Above the door, the digital floor indicator flickered between zero and eight like an alarm clock on the fritz. Larry caught a look at his fearful expression and tried to remain calm. He didn't like cramped spaces. The last thing he'd want was to get trapped in an elevator. Especially if it meant losing out on a starring role in a serious picture.

The floor shook, the structure groaning. Finally it settled, and Larry's heart rate slowed as the ding indicated he'd reached the second floor.

The doors slid open.

Larry stepped out into a small atrium with the glass doors to Suite 201 directly ahead of him. He stepped through to a small waiting room. A young blonde woman in a beige blazer with a low-cut cream top sat behind the desk. She looked up when he entered. The interior office was separated from the waiting room by a panel of frosted glass, with a wood door to the left of the desk.

"Hi, I'm—" Larry began.

"Have a seat, Mr. Walker. Jason will be right with you."

Larry sat in the single chair in the room, set up across from a small table with a few magazines on it. He waited, glancing up at the woman behind the desk every so often, not enough that she'd think he was a creep. Something about her looked familiar. Maybe it was just that she looked like every other attractive blonde woman he'd seen in every other audition all across town. Only instead of looking at her lines on a script, she was grinning at her phone. He supposed she could be reading sides on a phone, these days. Less and less he'd see actors holding physical pages at casting calls.

"Have you worked for Mister..." He realized he'd forgotten the director's name on the way here. "...for Jason long?"

She glanced up from her phone. "What's that?"

Larry cleared his throat. "Have you worked here long?"

"Oh." She shook her head, smiling slightly. "No, not long."

Larry nodded. He looked around the barren office. Drummed his fingers on his thigh. "You look familiar," he said. "Are you an act—"

A beep interrupted him. The assistant picked up the desk phone. She listened. "Yes, sir. Right away." She hung up and her blue eyes settled on him. "Jason is ready for you now."

He stood. "I'll just—"

She gestured toward the door. "Go right in."

Larry went to the door. He felt woefully unprepared, no idea what awaited him, no lines to read. Then again, he was the only one here. And the director—Jason Whatever His Name Is—had called for him by name. Maybe this wasn't an audition at all. Maybe this Jason guy just wanted to see him in person, shake his hand. Maybe he was a fan.

Larry gave the woman a smile. "Wish me luck?"

She looked up from her phone briefly enough to say, "Luck."

He opened the door.

The office was empty, just a long conference table with one chair at the far end, near a bay of windows overlooking the used car lot across the street.

Larry looked back at the assistant, then again into the room. There were no other doors. Feeling somewhat foolish, he ducked to be sure no one was hiding under the table.

"I'm sorry, *where* is Jason?"

The assistant sighed, fluttering her eyes dramatically. If she wasn't an actress, she should be. "Go right in, he'll be with you in a moment."

Larry entered the room and pulled the door shut behind him.

Standing there in the wide, empty room with nothing but the hum of air conditioning made him anxious. He wondered if he shouldn't have left the door open for Jason, whenever he arrived.

"Mr. Walker," a crisp male voice called from the middle of the room. Even before he noticed the conference call phone at the center of the long desk he could tell from the hollow tinniness that it came from a speaker. The assistant must have signaled his arrival in the room.

"Hi," he said, approaching the speaker. "Can you hear me?"

"I can hear you just fine, Larry. See you, as well."

Larry looked up and noticed the camera in the far, high corner of the room.

"Please, have a seat."

He crossed to the chair, spun it around, and sat facing the camera.

"That's a great shirt. Perfect for our lead detective."

"Thanks, Jason."

"Call me Jay."

"Will do."

"And relax," the man said. "This isn't a job interview. If anything, with your pedigree you should be interviewing me."

Larry chuckled amiably. He felt like he was being flirted with. It was a nice ego boost, no matter who it came from, even if the guy was just blowing smoke up his ass.

"You know what? Why don't you come out to my place tonight?"

"Tonight?"

"Sure. We'll have dinner. Discuss the film."

"So... does this mean I got the part?"

"Do you have the part? Larry, this role was written with you in mind. You *are* the part."

5

In retrospect, he should've known going to the house of someone he'd only ever met over the phone, in an office that could very well have been broken into just to set up the conference call, with an assistant that could've been hired for the day, was a bad idea.

Unfortunately, the ego boost and the thought of landing a lead role in a legitimate film made him careless, and when the gates rolled open at the estate in the Hollywood Hills seemingly of their own accord—though Larry could see the camera pointing down at him, perched on a high pole—he realized he still didn't know the director's last name.

He could very easily disappear in a place like this and no one would even know. People disappeared in this city all the time. He remembered reading a stat like twenty-five thousand adults and children went missing in L.A. County every year. Some people *came* here to disappear.

Larry glanced at his watch. Just after eight. This deep into October, the sun had already set hours ago. It wasn't quite dark—L.A. never got *full* dark, not without a major blackout—but it was dark enough to be sinister. He never drove out to the Hills at night. If he went anywhere after dark it was usually to some club in West Hollywood or the Fashion District.

Should probably put in a call to Thom. Let him know I got the part.

"Park in front of the house," came Jason's voice from the speaker beside the gate, making Larry fumble and drop his phone. It bounced off the passenger seat and landed in a heap of discarded fast-food bags, cups and crumpled receipts, along with dozens of flyers and business cards he'd found stuck in various places on his car a couple of times a week.

"You haven't changed your mind, have you?" the voice on the speaker said. It only now just occurred to him he still hadn't seen this guy's face.

"Nope, just..." Larry glanced down at the junk in the passenger footwell. He was about to add, *dropped my phone,* but said instead, "Be right up." He was already a few minutes late. Best not to keep the man waiting.

He touched the gas, and the Camaro lurched forward between the gates, gravel crunching. Driving slow down the long drive lined with tall trees, he watched in the rearview as they rolled shut behind him.

The house, when it emerged from behind the trees, looked like a jumble of light and dark children's blocks inlaid with horizontal rectangular slots of glass for windows, seemingly at random, from which a bright white light shone through. It looked like some kind of Brutalist alien spacecraft landed in the woods. Thinking about that reminded him of the *E.T.* porn parody he'd done in the '80s. He'd worn a store-bought E.T. mask and screwed Elliot's (adult) sister, his mother, and half of the scientists trying to study him. His catchphrase, uttered in the weird raspy goat-like voice he'd used for the character, was "E.T., bone ho." Amblin had sued and the film had been barred from release.

Larry pulled up behind a shiny black Audi parked in front of the odd-shaped structure and turned off the engine. He shoved the keys in the tight front pocket of his jeans and stepped out of the car.

The night was cool, the warmth and smog of the day cleared, the air perfumed with sage and jasmine. The Hills always smelled like a classy lady at night—except in the few weeks leading up to the winter rainy season, when gardeners sprinkled the lawns with manure. She didn't smell quite so classy then. She smelled like shit.

Larry checked himself out in the cracked side mirror, smoothed his bangs to the side and straightened his collar, then casually strode up the steps to the front door.

He thumbed the buzzer. A musical chime echoed through the house. Through the vertical slot of frosted glass in the door, he saw a dark shape moving toward it. A moment later, the door opened.

A man slightly taller than Larry's five-foot-ten stood in the door, gazing at him. He was dressed neatly in a black blazer and plain black shirt, with black pleated pants, his dark hair swept back from a receded hairline. His lower jaw was long, making the lower half of his face look somewhat gaunt, but his eyes were bright and inquisitive, his complexion shiny, healthy-looking.

"Come in, Mr. Walker." The voice didn't match what Larry had heard from either speaker today, again putting him off kilter. There was a slight Britishness to it. "Jason's expecting you."

Larry stepped across the threshold. "Thanks, uh..."

"Reed," the man said. "I'm Jason's... well, I suppose you'd call me his butler, though we never use the term."

"Right on," Larry said.

"Have a seat in the drawing room, please." Reed gestured toward the sofas and chairs set up in front of a roaring stone fireplace.

"Sure thing." Larry stopped a few steps into the foyer, glancing down at his vintage Tony Lama snakeskin boots. "Should I take off my shoes?"

"Don't worry about it," the butler said, the corners of his eyes wrinkling, though he wasn't smiling. "In fact, he'd prefer you leave your boots on."

"Great," Larry said, though it did seem like an odd thing to mention. Maybe it was part of the character.

"I was just leaving for the night," the butler said. "But please, make yourself at home. Pour yourself a drink. Harvey Wallbanger, that's your drink of choice, isn't it? I've added Galliano and Absolut to the bar."

"Rock on. Thanks, brother."

Reed smiled lightly. "Don't thank me, Mr. Walker. Good night," he said, and stepped out into the night, closing the door behind him.

Larry wandered into the drawing room—it made him feel silly and pretentious just thinking that word—his bootheels echoing in the large space. Rich people really liked to flash it in your face how much money they had. The ceilings were always high, the rooms large with very little furniture to take up space. The homes of the rich and famous were more like fashionable boutiques. You could throw a party in a single room, mingle the entire night, and still not meet everyone who'd attended.

Quit being jealous, he thought. *If you had this kinda money you'd be living like Rocky in* Rocky II. *Have your own robot butler.*

He chuckled and looked over the various animal heads on plaques and full sauntered over to check out the bar.

Outside the Audi's headlights came on. He couldn't hear the engine. Whether that was a testament to the car or the soundproofing of the house, he wasn't sure. Regardless, Larry figured the butler must be paid handsomely to afford a car like that. Larry's net worth was sometimes estimated at upwards of a million dollars on the internet, but even he couldn't afford to drive around a car like that. In truth, he had some money tucked away in stocks and bonds but he needed to keep working to pay the bills. The guy who owned this house probably had enough wealth to be passed down for *generations*.

The Audi's taillights cast their red glow over the trees as it ambled down the drive. Soon even they weren't visible, and Larry was left alone in a stranger's mansion—although he supposed he wasn't *entirely* alone. Jason was here somewhere. It was only a matter of *when* he'd make his appearance.

Larry fished out two ice cubes from a silver dish with a pair of small silver tongs, dropped them into a tall glass, poured from a crystal decanter what he assumed from the smell was vodka onto the ice, then the Galliano. He'd just reached for the jug of chilled orange juice, condensation dripping from the glass, when a sound caught his attention.

He paused with his fingers hovering near the handle, listening.

Larry just about gave up but the sound came again. This time he heard it more clearly. It sounded like a voice, from somewhere inside the house. A child, or a woman with a particularly high voice.

Maybe Jaybird's gettin laid, the old dog.

He grinned, dismissing the sound. He poured some juice into the glass, and shook it around as he returned to the sofas. They were hard and uncomfortable, nothing like what he was expecting a rich person's furniture to feel like. If he ever got rich—won the lottery, for instance—he'd make damn sure the seating *pampered* his guests asses. This was like sitting on slightly spongy boxes.

Where the hell is this guy? I mean, you tell me to be here at a certain time, and I'm here fuckin late, and you're still upstairs balling some bimbo with a voice like Minnie Mouse? Finish up already and—

"...*ah*..."

Larry stood up ramrod straight from the sofa, the contents of his glasses spilling over his hand. That one *definitely* sounded like a muted scream. And not a good scream. Not an *I'm-about-to-cum* scream.

It sounded like a scream of terror.

Okay, fuck this place.

Larry placed the Wallbanger on a coaster on the glass table and crossed the room to the door.

"I'm outta here. I don't need this shit that bad."

The scream came again as he passed an open doorway. It led into a room he hadn't noticed when he'd entered the foyer. He stepped through, marveling at a dozen animal heads mounted on the walls, from deer to a pair of lions to a white rhino. A gray wolf stalked a caribou, both animals mounted on pedestals. A cheetah bared its fangs at an owl. A black stallion stood frozen in mid-trot across the room, its mane cascading back over its withers as if caught in the wind. Every animal was perfectly preserved, such flawless representations of their live counterparts in the wild they could've belonged to a museum.

Larry reached out and stroked the horse's flank. It was equally smooth and bristly, like Dimples, the horse he'd ridden as a child. They weren't statues or replicas: they were taxidermied, all of these animals. Their hides and feathers and fur stuffed with sawdust or cotton and shaped with armatures.

When he was a little kid he'd loved animals. His uncles had been hunters, and he'd convinced one of them to save him a strip of deer fur, which he'd stroked lovingly every now and then for months, rubbing it against his cheeks and skin, until the strip of fur was as ragged as an animal with mange.

"...*ah*..."

The sound startled him. He'd been so absorbed in his memories and the sight before him he'd nearly forgotten what had drawn him in here in the first place. At the far end of the taxidermy room, a set of white stairs wound down into what he assumed was a basement or wine cellar. The voice appeared to be coming from there.

"Fuck," he muttered, already aware he was going down those stairs whether he wanted to or not. If someone was getting hurt down there, if some kind of casting couch bullshit was going on, he wasn't about to walk away and let it happen. "Fucking fuck."

He crept to the stairs, wary of every creak and groan his boots made on the wood floor. At the top of the stairs he peered down. He couldn't see around the column. The walls were painted a flat white, but unlike the pristineness of the other walls on the first floor, the flaws in the plaster became visible as it descended into the dark.

The scream came again. This time it was a word.

"*...help...*"

Larry suppressed the urge to run down the rest of the way and crept as slowly as possible to avoid being heard. His own heartbeat thudded in his ears.

Shit, this is just like outta one of Chet's movies. Oughta pitch it to him next time I see him and Linda.

He'd been thinking about Linda most of the day but her disappearance had slipped his mind after the thing at the office. He tried not to think it, but the thought came anyway: *If I ever see them again.*

Christ, she could be dead...

The stairwell ended at a short corridor. Opposite the stairs was a single heavy door, locked and bolted. To the left the hall opened on what appeared to be a vast, dark space. The urge to shout just to see if it would echo nearly overcame him.

"*...AH...*"

There it was again, much louder this time. His eyes had adjusted to the light and now what looked like two giant cubes were just barely visible to the right and left of him. The sound appeared to be coming from the one on the left.

What the fuck is this Joe Goldberg shit?

Larry crossed to it, reaching out ahead of him so he wouldn't walk into something he couldn't see. When his fingers touched a smooth, cool surface they made a hollow plunking sound, like tapping an empty fish tank.

Glass.

"...AH..."

It was so close to him now, maybe a foot away. It was odd how steady they came. The space between them almost seemed like the sound was on a loop.

His fingers danced across the glass until they reached a different surface. Cooler with striations. Plaster, maybe. Cement.

He slid the hand down the—column, pillar—until they found a switch.

"...AH..."

Do I really want to see what's in there?

He didn't, but he had to know what was making the sound. If someone was in there, if someone was *hurt*—he couldn't leave without doing something.

He flicked the switch.

The inside of the cube illuminated. The wall was indeed glass, the columns cement.

Larry took a step back in surprise.

Within was a set made to look like a doctor's office from the '70s or '80s, with all kinds of medical drawings and posters on the wood paneling. In the middle of this was a woman in a hospital gown seated in a gynecology chair, her legs spread with her feet in the stirrups. On the floor between her legs, some kind of robotic piston arm thrust a dildo in and out of the woman's vagina. Her eyes were wide and glassy, apparently staring at him as the dildo rammed in and out, her mouth open in an "O" of apparent pleasure.

It looked like some kind of pornographic art exhibit, reminding Larry of the Endangered Species section of the Natural History Museum he hadn't visited since the '90s. The colors seemed to pop, especially the rosiness of the woman's cheeks and pussy lips, the mint green hospital gown, and her bright blonde hair in a teased Farrah Fawcett look.

The sound of her moans assaulted him suddenly from a speaker below the switch: *"...AH... AH... AH..."*

Now the sound made sense, but it seemed off from what he was seeing, like an old porn reel with the sound out of synch. The O of her lips widened and reduced slightly out of time with the moans. An untrained eye might not have caught it. Having dubbed dozens of porn films before the industry switched to VHS, Larry noticed it right away. The effect was unsettling.

What's going on here? Some kind of kinky submissive shit?

The dildo pistoned. The woman in the chair moaned. Larry felt himself beginning to stretch out the right thigh of his jeans. Her glossy eyes looked dazed, either out of her head with ecstasy or drugs.

She can't see me. She's looking right at me... but she can't see me. Gotta be one-way glass.

Unaware he was doing so, Larry began stroking his cock through his jeans. Up and down the length of it, matching the rhythm of the dildo plunging in and out of her pussy. In and out, up and down.

"Larry, look out—!"

Larry turned toward the voice, somewhere in the dark beyond the cube.

Before he could investigate, he felt a sharp sting in his neck, and a gloved hand smelling of clean leather gripped him around the nose and mouth. He tried to fight but the effect of whatever he'd been stuck with was immediate. The light began to dwindle around scene in the cube, like an old vignette fade to black.

It only occurred to him as his lights went completely out that the scene in the cube was from one of his movies. And not just a random film, either: it was *The Awakening of Mr. and Mrs. S*, the one he'd been watching that very morning.

6

The memory of the drugged woman in the basement came back to Larry as The Doll closed and bolted the door behind himself. The drugs must have messed with his short-term memory, like a drunken blackout. He remembered the whole thing now, but just bits and pieces from when the needle pierced his neck to when he woke up here in the chair.

A highlight reel of the time in between played out in his mind now: waking briefly as the leather-gloved man—obviously The Doll— dragged him up the stairs, and again as he sat him in a chair—*this* chair —in the screening room. The sound of The Doll humming behind him as he set up the projector. Then leaping up from the chair with a sudden burst of fear-fueled adrenaline, flashes of running through a maze of endless white hallways, finding himself back in the drawing room some- how, then outside, then behind the wheel of the Camaro.

His mind had started to clear once he was driving. He remembered the gates coming open as he neared them, thinking they must be auto- mated but not caring to think too deeply about it, just blowing through them as fast as the Camaro would allow. Everything after that was fresh in his memory, despite the head injury, until he blacked out while The Doll tore the car door open.

From there, he'd woken up here, with the last reel of *Mr. and Mrs. S* playing on a loop.

The Doll wanted him to make a film. Judging by what the psycho had said before he left the room—claiming this place was some sort of *shrine* to him—and what he'd seen in the basement, the recreation of the expectant mother scene from *Mr. and Mrs. S*, with the pistoning dildo in the place of Larry's own member, he had a pretty good idea what kind of picture they'd be making.

Larry didn't suspect it was a detective movie, no matter what script he'd sent Thom.

Whatever the script had been, it was merely bait. The Doll—was his real name even Jason?—knew Larry was looking for work in legitimate films. It was common knowledge, particularly to someone who appeared to be a fan of his work. The office space was likely a front, either rented for the day or broken into. The assistant was likely an actor, as he'd suspected he remembered her face from some audition or another. It was even possible they'd worked together on some commercial or film background.

Lure him in with a promise of work. Switch the location to somewhere not communicated through the manager. Lull him into a false sense of security with the butler—likely another actor—and the Harvey Wallbanger.

Then what? Did he *want* Larry to find the woman in the basement? Was that bait, too? Did he want him to witness his devotion to Larry's career, or at least to that film? Did he *let* him escape?

Was all of this part of the performance?

Is he filming me right now?

Larry wrenched his head around as far as it would go in both directions. He didn't see any cameras, but the flickering light from the projector was too bright to see all the way back into the far corners. It was possible an entire crew was back there in the dark, filming him, though he had to admit even at his most paranoid as he was now, it wasn't very likely.

So, The Doll wanted him to make a skin flick, a porno. He'd quit the business a decade ago, when he'd started having to take boner pills just to keep from going soft mid-shot. Not much more embarrassing to a man who was once a legitimate "woodsman"—which in the business meant he could command an erection at will—than trying to cram his semihard dick into someone's asshole on camera while an entire crew watched and waited. After a while, the pills had started to give him concerning palpitations and vision loss, and sent him to the emergency room twice for priapism, so he'd quit taking them and left the industry.

But he *could* take the pill and fuck whoever he needed to fuck if it meant it would save his life.

The only real concern was just who—or *what*—The Doll wanted him to fuck.

He'd seen *A Serbian Film*, the brutal tale of a faded porn star like himself, although much younger, paid to star in an art house film which ends up being a snuff tape. The director drugs him and tricks him into having sex with his own young son. It was shocking and disturbing and Larry had walked out halfway through the screening—the baby rape scene had been the final straw—at a party with some of the more unsavory elements in the gonzo porn market, who'd been laughing and cheering during the worst parts. It seemed like some of them had seen it multiple times.

There was no way he'd fuck a kid. Bad enough that he'd worked with Traci Lords when she was underage, but at least she'd been in her late teens.

He wasn't fucking animals, either. No zoophilia or bestiality or whatever fancy name they wanted to give it. Not barnyard animals or domesticated. Judging by the taxidermy room he'd seen earlier, it was obvious The Doll had an obsession with them. Larry had experienced a close call in the '80s, when a director paid to fly him out to Spain, where it turned out he'd wanted him to star in a film where the actors were fucking sheep and pigs. Just the smell of these animals when he'd walked on set was atrocious, a musky odor he couldn't get out of his nostrils for days, no matter how much coke he'd snorted afterwards to obliterate the memory. He'd seen one of the farmers, he guessed, going around with a broom and a dustpan cleaning up their shit, while one of the background actors spit into his hand and slathered up his dick, gripping an animal's tail. Larry had found the director, told him to fuck them himself and stormed off set. He'd gotten on the next flight back to the States and never gone back to Europe, not even when he'd been nominated for a Ninfa award and the Hot d'Or for Best American Actor almost a decade later.

But... if the director had put a gun to his head back then... he supposed he would have had to grin and bear it. With a gun to his head, he'd probably fuck just about anything.

No gun had been produced here yet. It was possible there wouldn't ever *be* a gun. The Doll hadn't threatened him with violence. But he'd been drugged and kidnapped. He'd been strapped and zip-tied to a chair. The implication of violence bubbled under the surface of every detail, every word.

On the screen, his and Linda's younger selves shrugged up their shoulders and undressed each other, choosing to join the orgy their friends, colleagues and neighbors wouldn't let them ignore.

Wait a second, hang on a damn minute... a woman called out for me down there, right before he stuck me with the needle. Called me by name. Told me to look out. I knew I recognized the gynecology scene but that voice was familiar, too. Fuck me...

The revelation hit him like the strike of a match. Down in the basement, possibly in another of the glassed-in cement cubes he'd seen in the dark, Linda Flint was trapped just like he was.

7

L arry had to piss.

The Doll let the film run three more times before the latches unlocked and the door came swinging open once again. By then Larry had been calling out for at least half the film, on the verge of pissing his pants.

"Please. I gotta piss real bad, man."

The Doll cocked his head. "So piss."

"I'm not pissing my pants."

"Then you're going to have to learn self-control. It's been a long time since you were in the industry. When was the last time you exercised your pubococcygeus muscle?"

"My what? What the fuck are you talking about, man?"

"Your PC muscles, Larry. When was the last time you did Kegels?"

"Kegels? Isn't that for chicks?"

"Larry. A good manager would have informed you, if you'd done regular Kegels you never would have needed to take those awful pills to keep an erection. You'd still be at the top of the industry."

"Great! That's really helpful! Now can I please just use the bathroom?"

The Doll remained silent, then stepped around him, out of sight.

The sound of something hollow and metallic scraped on cement. He returned with a bedpan, which he placed on the floor between Larry's feet.

Larry jerked his arms and wriggled his fingers. The zip ties were tight enough to cut off much of his circulation, giving him pins and needles. "Cut my hands free, man."

"I'm afraid I can't do that."

"What? How am I supposed to piss?"

"You'll just have to trust me. Do you trust me, Larry?"

Fuck no, I don't trust you, his mind screamed. But he said, "Sure. Okay. I trust you."

The Doll reached for his zipper.

Larry pulled his hips back as far as they would go. He wasn't a homophobe. He'd done some gay-for-pay flicks in the '80s, and while it wasn't really his thing he'd had a bit of fun and made some cash. But the thought of this psycho getting anywhere near his dick inspired nothing but terror.

What do I do if he tries to jerk me off? What if he tries to crush my balls?

The Doll blinked behind the mask. "You said you trust me. Let me help you."

Larry relaxed his hips. The Doll grasped his zipper with a gloved hand and jerked it down. The anticipation of finally being allowed to empty his bladder made his back teeth hurt. The Doll reached into Larry's pants and grasped his cock around the root. He pulled it out and let it hang over the edge of the chair. Then he picked up the bedpan.

"Okay, Larry. You can urinate now."

Larry let loose. The urine splashed the pan with the sound of a power washer spraying empty paint cans. He sighed heavily, his whole body relaxing into the stream leaving his body.

"I'm going to take the pan away, Larry. If you piss on the floor, even one single drop, I will hurt you."

"What? Dude, you can't—"

"One... two..." On three, the Doll pulled the bedpan away. Larry tensed immediately, clenching as hard as he could to stem the flow. But he was in his sixties. He couldn't even use the toilet on a regular visit without two or three drops staining the inside of his undershorts. It was bound to drip at least once or twice.

He didn't want to find out what The Doll would do to him if that happened.

God, please, suck that piss right back up into my dick.

"Very good," The Doll said, returning the bedpan to its position below Larry's penis. "Okay, you can finish now."

Larry let the last of the urine out in a torrent, gasping audibly. When he was finished, The Doll placed it on the floor and tucked Larry's cock back into his jeans.

"You see? Self-control. I knew you had it in you."

"Yeah, great. Thanks."

The Doll stood with the bedpan, its dark yellow contents sloshing. "Looks like you'll need some hydration. I'll get you some water. Do you like LaCroix?"

Larry hated sparkling water and didn't understand the obsession with it, but he nodded, if only to get some moisture in his body.

"Very well. One LaCroix for my star coming right up."

The Doll turned with the bedpan and headed for the door.

"Jason?" Larry called out.

The man stopped in his tracks but didn't turn.

"Yes, Larry?"

"Who's the woman in the basement?"

"Which woman, Larry?"

"The one that called my name right before you stuck me with the needle. The one that said to watch out."

The Doll's shoulders sagged as he exhaled a sigh. "I suppose it wouldn't hurt to meet your costar before the big scene. Even though I'd wanted it to be a surprise."

"You'll take me to her?"

The Doll looked back over his shoulder. "I'll bring her to you. But you'll have to be ready for her, and in that regard, I have a surprise for you. But you'll need to be hydrated first. We need to make that money shot count."

"Money shot," Larry repeated.

"You know what I mean, Larry. Don't be coy. Oh!" he said brightly. "I nearly forgot. I brought someone to keep you company."

Larry felt his hope rise, though he knew it was foolish. The Doll stepped behind him again, out of sight. Larry turned as far back as he could but couldn't see the man in his peripherals. He turned back to face the screen, his neck strained. He'd learned sometime in his mid-forties than sudden movements were no longer advisable.

A furry, fanged snout entered his field of vision, and he reared back, straining his neck further. The Doll leaped into view, holding a fox mounted on a stand, uttering a high, creepy giggle.

"Oh, I'm sorry, Larry. I just couldn't resist." He turned a key on the fox's flank, gears inside the animal winding. When he set the fox down between Larry and the screen, facing him like a menacing guard dog, the animal's legs began to move on its stand with a sluggish gait while its head swung from side to side, the jaw opening wider and partly closing. "This is Reynard. Reynard is what they call an *automaton*. I know how much you love foxes, though I suppose this wasn't quite what you had in mind."

Again, that high giggle, muffled behind the mask.

"I leave you two to get acquainted," The Doll said, and left the room.

Larry watched the fox as it wound down to a crawl and finally stopped altogether, the light from the projector flickering over its fur and shining in its glassy eyes. Something about it made him think about the drugged woman in the basement. He supposed it was the movement, reminding him of the pistoning dildo, some kind of perpetual motion fucking machine. But that connection didn't feel exactly right, and once he'd noticed, it was impossible to push the thought out of his mind.

8

The Doll returned three sex scenes later with the can of LaCroix. Larry had watched himself cum so many times tonight, he felt like a boxer psyching himself up for a fight by watching his wins over and over again.

I haven't cum like that in a decade, at least. Usually one weak pop and a few dribbles. What's this guy expecting? A load like this? Will he hurt me if I don't cum buckets?

The door opened and The Doll popped the top on the can with a satisfying hiss. Despite his dislike of sparkling water, Larry salivated. The fox watched them as The Doll nursed Larry straight from the can.

"There you go."

The cold liquid bubbled all the way down, with a slight lime taste, moistening every inch of his mouth and tongue and throat. When The Doll removed the can, Larry let out a satisfied gasp.

"Goddamn, that's good. I never liked sparkling water before but I get it now."

"I'm very glad to hear that, Larry. And there's more where that came from. If you cooperate with me, if we trust each other, this doesn't have to end poorly."

"You mean if I play along, I won't get hurt."

The Doll's head tilted, regarding the stuffed animal on the floor. "If you'd prefer," he said.

"Well, I'm ready to play along," Larry told him, just hoping for the chance to get out of this chair. He didn't dare believe this man would let him and Linda go when they were finished the movie. That was giving in to a false sense of security. Best to think the end goal was to kill them both whether they played along or not, and to cooperate until the first opportunity to escape came up.

But he couldn't do that until they were together. Unless he was somehow able to kill The Doll, there was a distinct possibility he'd murder her if Larry escaped on his own, and by the time the cops showed up there would be no evidence left of any of it.

"That's wonderful to hear, Larry. Let's hope your costar feels the same."

9

Larry woke with a start when The Doll came back into the screening room. He hadn't been asleep long, judging by the scene in the film, unless it had already played through again. Maybe twenty minutes, tops. He'd had a nightmare about a menacing shape chasing him through twisting white corridors in the dark. When it finally caught up to him at a dead end, he'd turned to find the shape was a giant sentient version of his own penis, mole and all. The urethra had opened like a mouth and swallowed him whole.

The door opened then, waking him, and for a moment Larry thought his captor had walked away and left the door open, like some kind of test.

After a moment a squeak of metal came from behind the door, followed by another. The door came all the way open, pushed by something on wheels that Larry couldn't quite place at first.

As it neared, with The Doll pushing it, the same wheel squeaking, Larry realized he'd seen this thing before, down in the basement.

It was the gynecology chair. The same woman sat in it, her legs still in the stirrups, still naked beneath the gown. In the light from the projector he saw her cunt clearly. It appeared to be gaping, like her opened mouth, as if it had stuck that way or she was somehow holding it open by sheer force of will.

"Tada!" The Doll said, gesturing toward the chair he'd rolled to a stop directly in front of Larry. The projector image flashed over the woman's pale skin and glassy eyes. She didn't blink.

"What the fuck?" Larry gasped.

It was a doll. Some kind of doctor's manikin.

But what kind of manikin had such realistic features? Why did the skin appear slightly powdered, the lips and eyes glistening with moisture?

"Meet your costar, Mindy St. Pierre."

Larry remembered the name. She'd played the young expectant mother in the doctor scene. The manikin looked somewhat like her, but like a statue in a wax museum it wasn't *quite* the same. It could've passed for a stunt double or a sibling.

"What do you mean, costar?"

"I mean," The Doll said, picking up Reynard the Fox and moving it out of sight, "you're going to fuck her. We've got to get you back in fighting shape before we film the main event."

"I'm not fucking a doll."

"It's never stopped you before. What is it you call the Love Doll you've got tucked away in your closet? Jessica?"

Larry reeled. Nobody knew about Jessica. He hadn't told anyone, not even his closest friends in the business. He hadn't even taken her out of the closet in ages. So how could this freak know about her? Unless he'd been watching Larry long before they first met. Unless he'd been inside Larry's apartment.

"And anyway, Mindy *isn't* a doll. She's a woman."

"Look, I know the difference between a woman and a fucking doll—"

"What I'm telling you, Larry, what you're *failing to grasp* here, is that Mindy St. Pierre isn't a *doll*. She's a real woman. *Was* a real woman. Like Reynard and the animals in my menagerie."

"No," Larry said, the truth of it beginning to sink in.

"Yes." The Doll nodded slowly. "She came here just like you, Larry, looking for a part. She thought she could seduce me into some casting couch nonsense. But she was wrong. *Dead wrong*, you might say." He tittered, that high, creepy laugh Larry had heard when The Doll had shown him the fox. "I drugged her and skinned her alive. Yes, the structure beneath her skin is technically a manikin, and the eyes are glass, but the *rest* of her—the *essence*—is real."

"What the fuck...? What the fucking fuck!"

"Taxidermy is a very *Zen* activity," The Doll said, stroking the dead woman's cheek with the back of a gloved hand. "It's very meticulous. It takes a trained eye and a skilled hand." He returned to Larry, crouching at his knee. "There's something... *sacred*... in knowing you've preserved a thing forever."

The Doll laid a gentle hand on Larry's knee. Larry jerked it away. "You're a fucking psycho."

The Doll shrugged, standing. "Maybe. My point is, if you love something, *lean into it*. Like you did with fucking. You found your niche in a world where most people never discover their purpose, their *raison d'être*, and you *embraced* it, you *made it yours*. Some may have compared you unfavorably in your heyday to court jesters like Ron Jeremy and Harry Reems, but you were a *lion*. King of the Cock." He leaned down, his eyes flickering in the light from the projector. "*Nobody* could fuck like you, Larry. Not Peter North, not John Holmes, not Mandingo. *No one*." He laid both hands on either knee. This time, Larry let him. "You were a *legend*, Larry Walker. You *are* a legend."

The Doll reached behind himself, the hand returning with a pair of clippers. Larry cringed, slamming his knees together to protect his junk.

"Why would I do that?" the freak asked. "I'd no sooner cut off your prick than paint eyebrows on the *Mona Lisa*, or add arms to the *Venus de Milo*."

He opened the blades and slipped them under the zip tie on Larry's left wrist, glancing up to catch Larry's look of anticipation.

"Can I trust you, Larry?"

Larry nodded firmly.

The Doll snipped the zip tie free. Larry raised his hand and wriggled his fingers, loosening the muscles, shaking out the pins and needles.

The Doll scooched over and snipped the tie on his right hand. With two hands free he could choke the man if he wanted to. But what good would it do? His ankles were still tied, the leather strap was still tight around his chest. He could kill the man and still end up stuck here, starving to death while his most famous film played on an endless loop, driving him to insanity.

He massaged his wrists while The Doll snipped the ties on his ankles. Then Larry twisted and rolled his feet. With all the pain in his wrists he'd barely noticed how bad off his feet were.

"I'm going to let you out of the chair now. If you try anything..."

"I won't."

"Good. Because I won't harm your face, Larry. Or your genitals. But there are things I can do, *techniques* I've learned, that would make emasculation feel like a day at the spa. You do not want to test me."

Larry nodded.

The Doll nodded in response. "Good," he said, then moved behind Larry. The sound of chains rattling, and a padlock being opened. Then, suddenly, the pressure on Larry's chest loosened.

He grabbed the back of the chair and pushed himself to his feet. He staggered, walked a few steps. The Doll continued messing with the chains behind him, making a racket. How many hours had he been strapped to that chair? What day was it? He stretched his arms. The dead woman stared at him. He stayed as far away from her as he could.

"That's better, isn't it?"

The door was still open. He could run right now if he wanted to. But Linda was somewhere in the basement. If he ran, she would die.

What if it's not her? What if that was a trick? The whole thing felt like a setup, didn't it? Just go, *man. Make a fuckin run for it.*

He took two steps to the side, testing the limits of his freedom. With two further, more confident steps something yanked back jarringly, causing him to stagger backward and almost lose his balance.

He caught the back of the chair and peered behind it, not understanding what had happened. Now it made sense. He wasn't free. The strap around his chest was connected to a length of chain that ran through a hole in the back of the chair. The chain ended at a metal loop bolted to the cement floor.

The Doll watched him from behind the mask. "I hope you weren't planning to walk away."

Larry shook his head.

"That's good, Larry. I've given you enough chain to do what I've asked. Please don't use it to hang yourself."

Larry regarded the dead woman. Aside from having once been a live human being, how much different was she from Jessica the Love Doll?

"I can't."

"You *will*."

He shook his head, his body beginning to tremble uncontrollably. "Why? Just... just tell me why."

"Why is not your concern. You're an actor. *Act*."

He shook his head again. The woman stared at him, her glassy eyes judging him.

"Larry. *Larry*."

Larry looked up at The Doll.

"How many women have you treated like objects? How is this any different?"

"It *is* different!"

"*Why?*"

"Because I'm not a fucking necrophiliac, you psycho! She was a fucking living *human being*! All she wanted was a role in a goddamn movie, just like me, and for that you *skin her alive*? Make her into a fucking sex doll? What kind of sick-fuck logic is that, huh? Why do you wear that fucking mask? *What the fuck fucked you up in the head so bad?*"

The Doll stared at him for a long moment. The woman stared at him. Finally, the Doll blinked.

"This isn't going to be a confessional, Larry. Either you fuck Mindy, or the two of you switch places in the stirrups and I wheel in her robot friend. I could leave you to its mercy for days. How long do you think you'd last before you develop the first fissure? How long until you pass out from the pain, or internal bleeding?"

"*Fine.*"

The Doll cocked his head. "Beg pardon?"

"*I said I'll fucking do it.*"

"Well, that's very good to hear, Larry. I'm glad you've decided to come around." The Doll approached the woman in the chair, reached for something beside her and held it out to him.

Larry regarded the bottle of oil-based lube for a long moment. He still wasn't sure he could go through with this—the dead woman would be staring at him the entire time with her glassy eyes. But he snatched the bottle from The Doll's gloved hand and reached for his zipper.

This was a line he'd never even *considered* crossing, forced or otherwise. Of course there were half a dozen dark tales of snuff sex tapes passing around the industry, but no one he knew had ever seen a *real* one. They were rumors. Things to frighten the newbies.

Now here he was about to *star* in one.

If this ever got out... if this ever hit the public...

But it wouldn't. That wasn't what The Doll was about. This was meant to be private. He'd called it a "shrine." He'd never be able to show it to anyone because then his secret life would be revealed.

It was cold comfort. It still meant Larry had to fuck a corpse.

He pulled his cock out through the y-front of his underwear. He swallowed hard, closed his eyes, licked his dry lips, and began tugging on his foreskin.

I can do this.

"Open your eyes, Larry."

He did. The Doll held a high-end prosumer video camera to his left eye, pointed at Larry's face.

"Fuck her like you mean it. The camera wants to see that famous Walker passion in your eyes."

Larry gazed over the top of her head, unfocused on the film, not daring to meet those glassy eyes, and got himself hard.

"Touch her, Larry. She's ready for you."

It's skin. Real human skin.

He reached out and touched her stomach, surprisingly smooth and firm yet yielding, like touching a pillow made of lambskin.

I can do this.

He grasped her hip, smooth, firm, the feel bone under the skin. Or an armature, he supposed. His fingers pressed into it, making slight creaking sounds, like easing into a leather couch. The effect was nearly enough to make him lose his erection.

You've fucked in front of a thousand strangers. You've cum in high-heel shoes and peanut butter jars and potted plants. Pretend it's a doll and fuck it, you coward.

He tried pushing the head of his cock into her open hole, but it stuck against the sides.

The lube.

He reached behind himself, still jerking off, not wanting to lose this rod. His fingers touched the bottle and he grasped it, brought it over and drizzled some onto his prick. He worked it over the head and down the shaft, reaching back and placing the bottle back on the chair.

"Good," The Doll said.

Okay. Here goes...

He pushed into the leathery hole. This time, with his cock sufficiently lubed, it slid in not quite easily, due to the width of the hole, but with a grip that felt *almost* real. He supposed if he turned a lambskin glove inside out and filled it with lube, fucking it would feel something like this, which—if he pushed away the thought that it was human leather, that those glassy eyes weren't real but the teeth and hair and fingernails probably were—he had to admit felt almost... *good.*

Instinctually, his eyes fell over the dead woman's body, moving quickly past her perpetually staring eyes to her glossy, half-parted lips—the tongue inside, probably fake, moist and touching the backs of her upper teeth—her long, smooth neck, her perky tits which would never sag with small puffy nipples, her belly a smooth slight paunch, her cunt plucked hairless, the folds rosy pink as he plunged in and out. The Doll must have measured the length of it perfectly because when balls deep, the head of his prick hit its rounded end, like pounding against a cervix.

Larry thrust and thrust, getting into it, doing his job, playing the role, and The Doll shot the scene from various angles. He had to admit she had a passing resemblance to the woman on the screen. But she *wasn't* her. Larry had seen Mindy St. Pierre at the AVNs in the early 2000s. After a few DUIs and a brief stint in rehab she'd gained about a hundred pounds. She'd looked healthy but *nothing* like she did back then.

This dead woman was somebody's daughter, someone's sister. A Missing Person. Gone to an audition at some empty office park in

Encino or Culver City and never heard from again. Yet another wannabe starlet used and abused by this heartless city and left a literal empty shell, a shell stuffed with sawdust and doll armature and, currently, Larry's rock-hard, lubed-up eleven-inch cock.

Despite these thoughts and the uncanny valley quality to her face and skin and the inhuman texture of her vagina, Larry felt a tingle in his balls signifying his imminent climax. He reached out and grabbed the dead woman's hair. The soft, silky texture—far more human than the rest of her—pushed him over the edge and he came hard, filling her hole, shooting gouts onto her stomach, into her belly button. The force of his cum was so powerful his whole body seemed to deflate, and he fell over her chest, breathing heavily.

An incessant buzz filled the room, so loud Larry at first thought he'd been struck by lightning, some kind of moral punishment for ejaculating on a dead woman's corpse. Fistfuls of her hair came away from her head, twisted through his fingers. He shook them away in disgust and got to his feet, panting, his erection wilting.

The Doll lowered the camera from his eye and craned his neck toward the plain white ceiling.

"*Fuck*," he muttered. "Stay put. I've got to get the door."

With that, he crossed the room, leaving Larry alone with the lube and the cum-drenched dead woman and his film—currently the "Mrs. S. Fucks the Milkman" scene—playing on an endless loop. He waited to hear the sound of the latches and locks, but there was nothing beyond the click of the door as The Doll pulled it shut.

The door was unlocked.

Larry tucked his sticky, wilted cock back in his jeans and hurried back to where the chain met the link on the floor. He grabbed it close to the base and pulled as hard as he could, gaining nothing but a strained shoulder.

"Okay, *think*, Larry, fucking *think*."

The chain looped from the floor through a hole in the back of the chair. He'd never actually been strapped to the chair itself, only pulled so taut against it that it felt like he'd been strapped securely to the chair. There was a good... maybe five feet of slack sagging between the chair and the floor. He could reach the giant projector looping cabinet from here, if not for the chair. *Turn off that fucking film.*

But what if he did, and The Doll came back before he'd gotten free? What then? He'd already made him fuck a corpse, and even though he didn't technically *enjoy* it, he *did* ejaculate. What worse could he possibly do to him?

You want worse, he already promised it.

He'd strap Larry to the *other* chair, that was worse. He'd use her pistoning dildo friend Robocock on Larry's poor hemorrhoidic pucker until he passed out or died.

So... what then? Keep pulling on the chain? Pray to God he could break free?

Someone's at the door, right? Should I scream? Would they hear me?

He shook his head.

Nah. If nobody heard his other victims, they wouldn't hear me. The house is concrete. The basement's probably got better soundproofing than a Melrose recording studio.

"You gotta do *something*, man, don't just stand here like a prick."

He looked around the room. The dead woman. The chair, bolted to the floor. The projector cabinet. The lube.

"*The lube.*"

He hurried back to the chair and grabbed the bottle, turned it around and read the instructions. DO NOT INGEST. DO NOT USE NEAR EYES OR MOUTH.

Larry briefly wondered how many quarts of personal lubricant he'd swallowed in his lifetime. Then he gathered up the slack of the chain, making sure it was easily accessible on the far side of the chair, where he stood awaiting The Doll's return.

He stood poised with the lube in his right hand, only realizing he was gripping it too hard when he noticed his hand shaking. He steadied his hand, did a bit of meditative breathing. In through the nose, out through the mouth.

The door finally unlatched.

Could he do it? Would he chicken out?

What if nothing happened? What if he got the lube in The Doll's eyes and it didn't do anything? What if he squirted the entire bottle at the freak and it missed the eyeholes of that fucking mask?

The door swung open. The Doll stepped in.

"Fucking lawyers," he said with a dramatic sigh. "Am I right? Now, where were—"

The moment The Doll came within spitting distance, Larry snapped open the bottle with his thumb and squirted it squarely between the eyeholes on the mask.

The Doll cried out, grasping at his face.

Larry grabbed the length of chain and ran at him. He swung it over the freak's shoulders once, twice, and pulled.

The Doll grabbed at him, clawing and screeching, eyes red and raw through the eyeholes. Larry held fast, ignoring the freak's manicured nails digging into his throat, bringing blood. He'd kill the fucker even if it was the last thing he'd do. Just hope to God he had the keys on him somewhere.

The Doll grabbed him by the shoulders and launched the two of them into the gynecology chair. The dead woman toppled, sprawling on the floor in the same seated, spreadeagle position, like a statue made of human leather. Larry noticed neat lines of stitching up the backs of her arms and legs and along the spine as his jism oozed from her perpetually open hole onto the floor.

He slammed The Doll against the chair, pressing his face into the hard, mint-green Naugahyde, choking harder. The man gagged. The mask came off as they struggled and Larry startled at the face he'd revealed.

Though his hair was a sweaty mess and his eyes were raw, streaming tears, behind the mask was the same man who'd let Larry in the night of the audition, well dressed, with the slight British accent. It was Jason's "butler," Reed.

"What the fuck...?"

Reed or Jason or whoever the fuck he was reached down. At first, Larry thought he was reaching for his junk and he took a single step back. Then the hand shot up, and he felt a sting in his midsection. He looked down just as the freak depressed the plunger, filling him with whatever he'd shot him up with that first night, though likely at a higher dose this time.

Larry squeezed, pulling the chains as hard as he could. The Doll gasped and choked and his red-raw eyes were beginning to dilate, but his lips upturned in a smile, his teeth pink with blood. Larry was losing his fight against the drug coursing through his system. Either one of them would survive, or they would die together. The freak seemed to be betting on himself, or neither.

Larry's arms grew numb. He pulled with every last bit of strength. How long did it take to choke a man to death? How long until his arms became so numb he could no longer hold the chain?

His vision began to gray, slipping away at the sides. The last thing he saw before passing out was his captor's blood-pinked smile, and the flicker of the film in his insane eyes.

10

Awakened from another dreamless sleep, Larry found himself restrained and sitting again, only this time he appeared to be moving.

He heard the squeak and rumble of wheels beneath him. Smooth white walls stood on either side of the conveyance, whatever it was. For the moment, his head seemed to be as immobile as the rest of him. The occasional inset bulb illuminated the corridor from the equally white ceiling.

Were these the halls he'd run through the other night, trying to escape after The Doll had hit him with the drug the first time? No wonder he'd had difficulty. They took one corner after another, as if heading deeper and deeper into a labyrinth.

Finally, they entered a large, dark room with a very high ceiling.

"Oh, you're awake," The Doll said. The sound of a switch being thrown was followed by dozens of track lights coming to life twenty feet above Larry's head. He squinted against the brightness.

"Where are you taking me?"

"I'm afraid this is your final stop, Larry. The end of the line. You really shouldn't have tried to hurt me."

The freak leaned over him. Behind the mask, his eyes were clear and

757

no longer red. But the marks on his stubbled throat would be impossible to ignore. Someone would ask questions. Maybe someone who was already curious about Jason Reed's private life.

Larry giggled.

"What are you laughing at?" came The Doll's muffled response.

"You, you fucking psycho *freak*," Larry said, through his laughter. "Why the fuck are you still wearing that thing, huh? I've already seen your face."

"But your costar hasn't."

"Is she here? *Linda!*" he called out. "*LINDA!*"

"Linda is sleeping right now."

"I want to see her."

"You've got no right to make demands."

"I'm the *star*, goddammit! I fucked your Frankenstein, now fucking let me see *Linda*!"

The Doll stopped rolling him forward. After a moment, he said, "Very well." Then he rolled Larry forward again, stopped a moment later and turned him around. "Here she is. You see? She's sleeping."

Larry managed to lower his head, resting his chin in his jugular notch. The scene displayed before him, set inside another glassed-in cement box, looked exactly like Mr. and Mrs. S's bedroom from the film, down to the pea-yellow color of their sheets and the black and white photographs on the night stands. The amount of detail the freak had gone to, whether himself or some interior decorator, unaware of their intent, possibly believing them to be some sort of art installation, was incredible. Like the doctor's office, it looked like a scene pulled straight out of the 1970s, like a strange cubed time capsule.

Linda Flint lay on the bed, her curly blonde hair pulled up, dressed in a silky nightgown. Her chest, which she'd never gotten augmented, even when most women with small breasts in the industry were doing it, rose and fell beneath the retro flower-print duvet.

He called out her name again. Her eyelids didn't flutter. She didn't even stir under the covers.

"I told you, she's sleeping. She's been very busy."

"She's okay? You haven't hurt her?"

"Does it look like she's been hurt?"

She looked fine. She looked like an angel.

It hurt to see her trapped in a box, like The Doll's other women—at least he assumed there were others. There were five more cement cubes down here, each likely containing its own scene from the film. Each with its own manikin made from human skin.

The chair began rolling slowly down the corridor between the cubes. Larry examined the first as they passed, slow enough to see that while The Doll hadn't been in the screening room with him, he'd been busy down here filming Linda's "scenes." On TV screens set up on either side of this tableau the original scene played in-sync with a newly filmed version, in which Linda blew and rode the quarterback reverse cowgirl. Within the locker room set, a young man lay across the bench in football gear, his arms raised to remove his helmet from his shaggy hippy hair. His bare chest, lean arms and face had the same leathery, not-quite-human look as Mindy St. Pierre's, his glassy eyes looking down as the large erection protruding upward from his knickerbockers, where Linda would've been during the filming.

In the scene on the left screen, filmed during the '70s, Linda's enthusiasm was infectious. She'd been one of the best in the business. Colleagues called her "Eveready," after the battery, because she'd had the uncanny ability to get wet without any physical stimulation, like a dramatic actor able to cry on command. She'd been the female equivalent of a woodsman, a perfect pairing for Larry.

In the scene on the right, Linda was clearly disturbed. She gorged on the leathery member, cradling the dead man's hairless balls, as a single tear spilled from her one visible eye.

"Why are you doing this to us?"

The Doll slowly turned the chair, and began rolling him toward their destination. "I suppose I owe you *some* sort of explanation, don't I? After all, you are my muse, Larry. Do you know the story of Pygmalion?"

"Yeah, the uh... isn't that what they based *Opening of Misty Beethoven* on? 'The rain in Spain stays on the plain' and shit?"

"Not the play. The figure from Greek mythology."

Larry shook his head. "Never heard of him."

"Well, Larry, in Ovid's *Metamorphosis*, Pygmalion was a sculptor so disgusted by prostitution he became celibate, choosing instead to spend his time with a woman he'd carved from ivory. He named her Galetea. He became so enamored by Galatea he began kissing and fondling her, and eventually fell in love with his own creation.

"One day, the day of Venus's festival, Pygmalion made a wish that he would find a woman who was the living embodiment of Galatea. When he arrived home, he kissed his ivory lover and discovered her lips were warm. Her breast warms and softens to his touch 'as wax grows soft in sunshine.'"

"Then what happens?"

"Then she wakes and they have a daughter together. It's a very brief and unsatisfying conclusion."

"So, what? You get in the boxes and fuck these things?"

"Don't be distasteful."

"Then what? Give me *something*. You said this is a shrine to me, you said I'm your muse, don't you *want* to tell me?"

"That's not entirely true. It is a shrine to you, but not *just* to you. When I was a young boy, maybe eight or nine, I fell in love with a picture in a magazine. I found it in the woods, in what looked like a hobo's encampment.

"The story that went along with the pictures called her Denise. She had curly blonde hair in a high ponytail and wore workout clothes from the era, which was the 1980s: a red one-piece bikini with blue leggings and white sneakers and a yellow sweatband. When I got a little older some boys and I managed to sneak into the adult section of the video store. It wasn't too difficult. Someone distracts the clerks while another plays lookout, and the rest sneak through the curtain. I searched and searched for my Denise among all the videotapes, and when I finally came across one that looked something like her it turned out to be a different woman altogether. Her name was Amber Lynn. But I still couldn't find Denise. I later discovered her name wasn't Denise at all. It was Linda Flint."

As he said this, he rolled Larry to a stop in front of another diorama. This one contained the kitchen set for the Milkman scene. The milkman himself stood against the kitchen island. Bottles of milk lay spilled on the floor around his feet. On the screens, Linda took the Milkman's hot load on her tits, already glistening with the milk she'd poured down them. In the original, Linda laughed as the Milkman covers her face and tits, smearing it all over herself and rubbing the glistening head of his cock on her face. In The Doll's version, Linda startled as a geyser erupted from the dead man's prick. It looked as though she wasn't expecting the thing to actually ejaculate. The stream of pearlescent fluid struck her eyes, down her throat—she gagged—and basted her breasts, heavier than they'd been during her porn career, plumped from two pregnancies and the baby weight she'd never managed to fully lose.

Linda reacted to something off camera—verbal cues from The Doll, most likely—then forced a smile as another spurt of fake sperm splashed her forehead.

Larry felt himself stiffening again, despite whatever drugs The Doll had pumped into him, what he'd just been forced to do with the dead woman, and what Linda had been subjected to in the film. It was an animal reaction. He could no more prevent it than stop his heart from beating. The scene disgusted him, but disgust had rarely prevented him from getting hard in the past. Call it the Curse of the Woodsman.

"From then on," The Doll said while the scene looped back to the beginning, "I began ordering pornographic films through the mail, pretending to be the owner of a video rental house. The tapes always came in large boxes filled otherwise with mainstream theatrical releases. I told my parents I was studying them so I could be a director. They were likely just pleased I was no longer interested in creating automatons and *tableau vivant* from dead animals. I believe they found that hobby *strange.*"

As the Doll continued his story, he moved the chair onward, passing a bedroom set that Larry didn't recognize. Though it looked like the same era as the film, it was much more extravagant. The two screens in the high corners were turned off, their screens black.

"While I amassed my film library in an east-wing room my father soon designated my screening room, for which he bought a projector and screen and all sorts of state-of-the-art equipment to encourage what they saw as a 'safe' hobby, I kept my *secret* collection in a hole in the wall of my walk-in closet. When my parents left for whatever it was they did together on the weekends, play tennis or lunch at the club, I brought one or two tapes to the screening room, locked the door so Reed, our butler, wouldn't walk in on me, and watched the tapes with the sound turned off."

Larry absorbed the fact that The Doll's butler's name was Reed and clearly couldn't have been his own, but didn't acknowledge it. "Didn't he have a key?"

"My parents made sure the staff weren't to disturb me while I was 'studying.' And anyway, I was too young to masturbate. They would only have caught me watching the films with the rapturous attentiveness of a young acolyte hearing the Gospel. I *was* studying, you see, but not to be a director. I wanted to be a *star*."

"It's not all it's cracked up to be, believe me."

"But you got to fuck Linda Flint *in her prime*. Kay Parker, Jeanna Fine, Bambi Woods, on and on—"

"It's a job." Larry managed a shrug. "I also fucked a lot of ditch pigs."

"Larry, I'm aware the adult industry isn't everything a pubescent boy imagines it would be. I've also had my share of porn stars. Big names. Their tapes are in my library, if you don't believe me. But it's not about the *act*, Larry, it's about the *fantasy*."

He stopped the chair again just close enough for Larry to see the gynecologist's office set in one of the last two cubes. The cube to the left of it was dark. It was impossible to see through its glass, only the reflection of the other cubes and the two of them standing between them on its surface.

"When I discovered *The Awakening of Mr. and Mrs. S*, it was *my own* awakening. My parents were heading toward a divorce at the time. Even the staff were talking about it, in hushed tones, when they thought no one was listening. But I was listening, Larry. I loved my parents, as much as I was able, despite not having very much to do with them. I knew something had to be done.

"Do you remember the film *The Parent Trap*? Not the sequels or the subpar remake. I mean the original 1961 film with Haley Mills playing the twins."

Larry remembered it. The film had come out when he was eight or nine. He'd seen it with his mother and little brother in the theater. His mother, who'd recently gone through a very ugly divorce after catching his father "in the act" with another woman, had been very vocal about the film after they'd left the theater. If they hadn't lived on a fixed income she likely would've made them leave halfway through.

"It's important to bear in mind that I was quite young and naïve at the time I came up with my plan to prevent my parents from getting a divorce. I based it on Mr. S's scheme to trigger his wife's sexuality in *Awakening*. I paid to place an ad in the classifieds of a local newspaper known for its risqué back pages. In it, I asked for a man looking for a discreet encounter, no names and no strings attached. They were to call the number I provided, which was to the payphone across the street from where I grew up.

"I figured it would receive a handful of calls at most. You wouldn't believe how many men called that payphone, Larry. Day and night for days. Or perhaps you would. Suffice to say, I found who I imagined would be the right fit quickly, and canceled the ad the same day. I pitched my voice up high to sound like a woman, which wasn't too much higher than my voice at the time, since I was young enough that it hadn't changed yet."

"Wait a minute," Larry said, trying to look over his shoulder at the freak in the mask. "I remember reading about this in the late '80s. That kid was *you?*"

"It's rude to skip ahead, Larry. Fortunately, most people don't remember the story. It was a blip, coming as it did during the heat of the Menendez trial. But I'll never forget, Larry. As I'm sure you can imagine.

"I was home when it happened. I told the man—I never got his name but I discovered it later, after everything was said and done—I told him to enter through the back door. I said—using what I thought was a sultry female voice—that I'd leave it open. That I'd be horny and waiting for him. He was to go upstairs and ravage me, and not to take no for an answer: just like Mr. S told the Milkman. I knew my mother would be loaded up on so much Valium she'd have passed out in front of *All My Children*—"

"And you thought she'd be fine with some guy breaking into her house and *raping* her?"

The Doll stepped out in front of him, staring down through the eyeholes of the mask. "My only awareness of sex was from pornography,

Larry. How could I know what you did was wrong? It worked out well for Mr. and Mrs. S, didn't it?"

"You're blaming Linda and me for some movie we made for a few thousand bucks forty years ago! That's what this is all about? That's why you kidnapped us? Forced me to... to fuck that *thing*?"

The Doll didn't respond, merely continued with his tale. "The man entered our house through the back door at three-thirty-seven pm," he said. "Police found no sign of a break in, of course. From the back door, the man entered the kitchen. He opened the fridge, took one of my father's imported beers and drank it on the way upstairs. The police found the bottle cap discarded on the kitchen floor.

"As expected, the man found my mother passed out in bed. He entered the room and turned off the television. He took off his clothes while he approached her."

"Is this from the police report?" Larry asked. The level of detail had to either be from the report or imagined.

"I set up cameras, Larry. Remember? I was studying to be a director, or so my parents thought. I had cameras in the kitchen, the foyer, the master bedroom. He was fully undressed before reaching my mother in the bed. He was masturbating."

"*Jesus*, dude. It's your mother."

"The police never discovered my tapes. In fact, I still have them. I watched them, afterwards. I had to know what happened. I had to know *why* and *how*. My mother woke up with him on top of her. He'd already climbed under the duvet and was fondling one of her breasts, like Pygmalion and his Galatea. Only my mother didn't warm to his touch. What she did was *scream*. He forced his lips over hers and she continued screaming into his open mouth. I heard her from the screening room in the east wing. I was terrified. I'd never heard my mother scream like that before. Or after.

"Why didn't you help her?"

"I was twelve years old, Larry. Alone in a palatial estate filled with valuable items and a safe full of cash. I'd sent Reed out on an errand. It was just my mother and me in the house. And the man, of course. The man I'd told not to take no for an answer. The man who likely wondered how he'd gotten so lucky to stumble into some lonely house-wife's rape fantasy. No names. No strings.

"It was several minutes later according to the timecode on the tapes, when my father returned home early from a business meeting, though in my mind it felt like *hours*, sitting alone in my screening room, waiting for it all to be over, while my mother was being raped. I saw him arrive on the tape from the foyer camera after the police left. He heard noises from upstairs. The moans and grunts of a man and a woman. He retrieved his gun from the table in the foyer, a snubnosed .38-calibre Detective Special, and crept up the stairs.

"He found the man and my mother in bed together. I can only imagine what he must have thought, because he didn't hesitate. He shot the man in the head. His entire face exploded over my mother, showering her with blood and teeth and brains, and when she managed to push the dead man off of her, my father shot at her three times. The camera in the bedroom didn't catch his expression, only the back of his head as he determined what must have been happening there that afternoon. The first two shots missed. Feathers burst from the pillows. The camera did capture my mother's look of fear turning to hope as she reached out to her husband, my father, readying to plead for her life. Her mouth had barely opened before the third shot struck her in the chest, puncturing her heart. She died almost instantly.

"My father approached the bed. He stood over his dead wife and what he imagined must be her lover, the man who'd been slowly pushing her away from him for almost a year, edging them closer and closer toward divorce. With his face half turned toward the camera, it did capture his look of resolve as he put the pistol to his own forehead and pulled the trigger. The gun fell from his hand and his body collapsed over my mother and the man in the bed. The rest you already know, since you read about it in the paper."

"Jesus fuck, man," Larry said. "Look, I'm sorry that happened. But that's not our fault. It's *nobody's* fault. You didn't understand what you were doing and we just made a fun little skin flick. I mean, who the hell could imagine some kid would copy that scene? What are the odds?"

"I don't know the odds, Larry. What I do know is that my final tableau requires a happy couple."

"You're gonna kill us, aren't you? Skin us alive. Make us into one of them?"

The Doll tilted his head against his shoulder in what Larry thought looked like sympathy. "Oh, Larry, I would never hurt you. At least not like that. You were my TV father. Other boys had Steven Keaton or Danny Tanner or Uncle Phil. I had you. And Linda was my TV mother."

Larry considered mentioning how warped that was, that two actors who'd worked in a few skin flicks together would be surrogates for anyone's parents. But he was pretty sure The Doll already knew it.

"I just need the two of you to work together one last time. Let me preserve it with my cameras. And then I'll set you free, I promise you."

"Both of us?"

"Both of you. You'll be happy to know your costar has already consented."

Larry didn't believe him, but it wasn't as if he could do anything to prevent whatever came next. He'd already tried to escape and been caught, tried to kill his captor and failed. What else could he do but play along and hope the two of them together might be able to overpower the freak or convince him to let them go?

He looked at his reflection in the dark surface of the glass in the final cube. He looked for a long time. The years had taken their toll. The booze and drugs hadn't been kind. What if he could relive that Golden Age of youth, right here in The Doll's basement? Larry and Linda together again. Not on the screen, but in reality. Not exactly consensual, but on a level playing field of coercion.

How many times had he imagined being with her again, the way they were then, while he watched their scenes and jerked himself to climax? Her smell. Her taste. Her eyes and smile and every inch of her body.

"Okay," he said finally.

The Doll nodded. "I'm very glad to hear that, Larry. One last shot and you'll be free. After everything I've put the two of you through to prepare you for your Big Scene, isn't it wonderful to know you'll be freeing each other?"

11

The Doll wheeled Larry back to the screening room with no punishment for attempting to murder him, despite the prominent bruises from the chain visible on his stubbly neck. Larry supposed the freak was feeling generous, that the implication of violent penetration the gynecologist chair threatened had only been to facilitate his compliance in the "Big Scene," which he imagined would take place in the final cube.

Whatever the reason, The Doll whistled a cheery tune as he rolled Larry back to the white room. Larry didn't recognize the song until he was secured again to the chair bolted to the floor, and the freak was hefting the dead woman—Larry's sperm dripping from her hole—back onto the gynecologist chair.

It was the theme song from *The Parent Trap*.

He popped the top off another La Croix and offered it to Larry. Larry nodded, his thirst almost overpowering. The Doll nursed him. Larry guzzled the fizzy liquid, feeling it hydrating every crevasse of his body.

"I'll be back soon," The Doll said, a smile in his voice as he returned to the dead woman in the chair. "Take five, as they say. Do whatever you need to prepare. You'll be in front of the camera again very soon, Larry.

The climactic return of Larry Walker to the pornographic film industry!" He shook his head in awe. "You can't *begin* to imagine how excited I feel right now...."

Uttering his high-pitched giggle, he rolled the chair toward the door.

"'Prepare,'" Larry muttered to himself once the man had left. He raised his hands the half inch they would move from the armrests, held with zip ties. "Yeah, how the fuck am I supposed to do that?"

Even if his hands hadn't been zip-tied to the chair, the current scene playing on the wall, in which a young Linda Flint was ravaged by a man credited as The Milkman, no longer aroused him. It was doubly tainted, by the horrors Linda had been subjected to in the cube room, and the terrible secret The Doll had revealed about his shattered childhood.

If by some miracle he made it out of here alive, Larry doubted he'd ever be able to jerk off to this film ever again. A small price to pay, he supposed, for the trauma it had put the three of them through.

"Now what?" he said aloud.

He glanced to the left of him, startling at the sight of Reynard the automaton. He'd forgotten The Doll had moved it out of the way when he'd wheeled in the dead woman. It stared up at him with its mouth half open, baring teeth in a wolfish smile.

"Shut up," he told it.

The fox continued smiling.

Several minutes later, once the Milkman had emptied his balls on Linda's face and chest and the next dialogue scene began in Larry's office, The Doll returned. He carried with him a set of clothing draped over one forearm and a packet of boner pills.

"I wasn't sure if you'd need these but I brought them just in case," he said, approaching the chair. "I know in your interview with Luke Ford you said you quit acting in porn because of what the pills did to you, then I figured one last time couldn't hurt, right? I'm going to untie you so you can change into your costume. You'll be good, won't you?"

Larry nodded.

The Doll nodded back. He began by snipping the zip ties, like before, then undid the chained strap from around Larry's chest. Larry stood and took the neatly folded pile of clothes when The Doll offered them.

"I never wore these in the movie," he said, looking at the faded denim jeans, a pair of tighty-whities—a rare item in porn—white tube socks and a Def Leppard T-shirt with the sleeves cut off.

"No," The Doll said. "You didn't."

Larry frowned, not getting it. This was supposed to be the recreation of a scene from *The Awakening of Mr. and Mrs. S*, wasn't it? Why would he make him wear something that wasn't from the movie?

"Put them on, please."

Larry undressed, glad to be out of his soiled clothes and to put on something fresh, whether it was from the film or not. "I guess it's too much to ask for a shower?"

"No need." The freak produced a small, long-necked green bottle from the right front pocket of his slacks.

"Brut for Men," Larry said, reading the label. "There's a throwback."

"Yes," The Doll said. He spritzed some at Larry's armpits and groin as Larry pulled up the fresh underpants. It permeated Larry's nostrils, a spicy woodsy scent with an undercurrent of citrus. Better than his current musky funk, he supposed.

"Better spritz the b-hole to be safe," he said, turning and slipping the underwear partway down. A light hiss was followed by a cool misting on his ass cheeks and pucker. He tugged the underwear back up, then pulled on the socks one by one.

When he was fully dressed he felt ridiculous. He hadn't worn a muscle tee in decades, and the wrinkled skin hanging from his pallid biceps didn't quite fit the style. He shrugged. "How do I look?"

"Almost perfect," The Doll said. He stepped forward and pressed something over Larry's upper lip. It felt sticky and tickled his nose.

"Is that a fake mustache?"

"It is," The Doll said.

"I didn't have a mustache."

"No. You didn't. Are you ready for your Big Reunion?"

Larry was. Aside from just a little while ago in the cube, he hadn't seen Linda in a few years. She'd always been busy with one of her husband's films, and when they did get together Chet was always there, like a chaperone. Though he claimed to be "cool," Larry had always figured Chet Daniels was a little jealous of their friendship. The kid was in his thirties. He hadn't even been a gleam in his father's eye when Larry and Linda had acted in their first scene together.

"Let's go meet your Leading Lady," The Doll said, ushering him forward.

Larry had never left the room without being under the effects of the drugs. On the way back from the cube room he'd been lying down, strapped to the gynecologist chair. He hadn't seen that the winding stairs stood right across the corridor from the door to the screening room, but from what he remembered of his first time down here, it made sense. The cube room stood a short distance to their right, the room fully lit.

The Doll led him forward. He felt like a groom walking up the aisle with his father. But where was the bride?

The cube to their left, the doctor's scene, was set up as it had been when he'd first come down here, with the piston pumping the dildo in and out of Mindy St. Pierre's leathery vagina. The one to their right remained unlit. He paused a moment to look at himself in the dark glass. He looked strange. He hadn't worn a mustache or a cut-off tee since the late-'80s. The only thing missing was his sweet mullet.

"What's in that box?"

"Would you like to see the tableau, Larry?"

Larry looked at his reflection. The Doll standing next to him, his head tilted quizzically to the side. He nodded.

The Doll draped an arm over his shoulders. "Very well. But you know what they say, Larry: curiosity killed the cat. Are you sure you want to see?"

What could possibly be inside? From what he'd seen of the other cubes, the last scene of the movie was the only one missing: the orgy at the neighbor's house, played by Mike Horner and Annette Haven, set in a sunken living room like the one in Larry's apartment, with shag carpet, a disco ball and lava lamps, the stereotypical swingers' pad from the '70s.

Could it really be that bad?

Considering what the others had inside? Yeah, he thought. *Pretty sure it's gonna be bad. Are you sure you wanna see this?*

He nodded again.

"All right," The Doll said. He removed his arm from Larry's shoulders and approached the box. "Now, Larry, I want you to understand that what you'll see inside is my masterwork. Everything I've done in my entire life led to this creation."

"Just turn on the fucking light."

The Doll chuckled once, then pressed a button on the side of the cube and stepped aside.

Larry's anxious reflection vanished from the glass as the inside of the cube illuminated. If it hadn't he would've seen his expression shift from apprehension to realization to panicked terror in a single blink. He stepped back in horror, bile rising in his throat as the scene within the cube came to life.

As he'd expected the set was a prefect replica of Horner and Haven's living room, only what was on the set he could never have imagined. Mounted on the floor, on the sofa, on the La-Z-Boy recliner and propped up on throw pillows, six men and six women flayed alive by The Doll, their cured flesh stretched over animatronic armatures and pillow stuffing, writhed, grinded, humped and thrust their crotches into the dead-eyed faces of their partners. The eyes, susceptible to decay, replaced with prosthetics, glassy and unblinking. Their open mouths, tongues protruding in orgiastic ecstasy, made of plastic or plaster glued to the inside of the skulls. Their gears and pulleys whined and buzzed as their leathery bodies moved without rhythm, permanently erect members plunging into always wet, always open mouths and vaginas, fingers stroking back and forth like clockwork cuckoos, hands jerking up and down mechanically. From the speaker came the moans and grunts of the film's soundtrack, playing on the TV monitor at the far left of the cube. The monitor on the right remained blank.

Buzzzzz—click-click-click and a cock entered an open mouth to slurps and moans from the film.

Whirrrrr—chug-chug-chug and a dead woman's head descended jerkily between another dead woman's legs. The lips smacked on the soundtrack as the automaton simulated cunnilingus.

Despite the horribly unhuman quality to the movement, Larry found he couldn't pry his gaze away. It was repulsive yet fascinating. The more he looked the more details he noticed: the stitching under a breast, at the backs of the arms and along the spine like the dead woman he'd been forced to fuck in the white room. The fake facial hair and pubic wigs glued to their desiccated skin to recreate the era and actors whose roles they were playing. The cracks and aging in their skin like old leather, some much more noticeable than others. Early kills, Larry assumed, several of which were sewn up with thicker thread, leaking bits of stuffing. He was certain he recognized at least a few faces from auditions, though none of them were actors from the original scene. The blonde between another woman's legs looked almost exactly like the woman behind the desk at the empty office, and though the skin itself looked fresh enough, he couldn't get a good enough look to be sure with her head bobbing jerkily up and down.

"Fuck..." he croaked. "What the fucking fuck?"

"Does that mean you like it?"

"Turn it off. *Turn it the fuck off!*"

The Doll flicked off the switch. Immediately the cube darkened and the film's soundtrack stopped, but it took a few moments for the automatons to wind down. Their buzzes and clicks slowed and eventually ceased as Larry stared at his own mortified reflection.

"Come now, Larry. Let's not keep Linda waiting."

The Doll ushered him toward the cube containing the fancy bedroom. The camera he'd used earlier stood on a tripod in front of it. Within, Linda lay in in the large four-poster bed, her hair up in rollers, dressed in a baby blue nightgown with a ruffled collar that looked like it was made out of Larry's grandma's doilies. Neither the set nor either of their costumes were from any of the films they'd been in together, at least to Larry's recollection.

"She's still sleeping."

"Galatea awaits her Pygmalion," The Doll said.

Fucking creepy thing to say, Larry thought. *But what does he say that* isn't *creepy?*

The Doll approached the right side of the cube. He removed a key from the same pocket he'd kept the cologne and unlocked the inset glass door. He stepped back and gestured toward the doorway.

Larry approached the cube cautiously. Why didn't he recognize any of this? He'd been in several hundred films, he supposed whatever this scene was could've slipped his mind. But he remembered every film he and Linda had starred in together. He watched them regularly on his big-screen TV, reliving the moments like an erotic highlight reel. Pornography was his home movies. If Ralph Edwards said, "Larry Walker, *This Is Your Life*," the entire broadcast would have to have been censored. The audience would've required rain slickers.

"Action, Larry," The Doll said. He stood behind the camera now, his left eye on the viewfinder.

Larry stepped into the box.

On the bed, Linda's chest rose and fell. She was alive. That was something, at least. Maybe they could hatch a plan while they fucked. If they kept their voices low and their mouths close, The Doll might not even notice. How many conversations had they had while on set that hadn't been caught? Granted, The Doll's camera recorded sound, unlike the 35mm cameras back in the day. But he wasn't wearing headphones. He'd hear whatever was audible through the glass to the human ear.

The door shut behind him. He turned to see The Doll tuck the key back into his pocket.

"Hey!" Larry pounded on the glass. "You never said you'd be locking us in here!"

"I never said I wouldn't." The Doll returned to his place behind the camera. "Please remove your clothes while slowly approaching the bed. Shirt first, socks last."

"Unlock the door and I'll do whatever the fuck you want!"

"It doesn't work that way, Larry. If you don't do as I say you can watch as I remove your costar's skin while she's still alive to feel it. I'll start with her face, work my way down to her beautiful breasts—"

"All right, for fuck's sake!" Larry started lifting his shirt over his head.

"Act like you mean it, Larry." The Doll's voice came over a speaker above the bed. "You've just stumbled across Sleeping Beauty and now you're going to fuck her awake."

Larry tossed his shirt aside and unzipped his jeans, moving toward Linda on the bed. He kicked off the shoes—a pair of scuffed-up Adidas, white with blue stripes—and swaggered toward the bed while tugging down the jeans and undies together, the way he'd always done when the costume required something under the pants. If that wasn't how The Doll wanted it done, he didn't voice his concern.

The socks came off last, one at a time, at the side of the bed. He looked down at Linda. Her eyes were sunken, puffy and raw from tears. Her face was scrubbed shiny and clean, the rise and fall of the few visible inches of her lightly freckled breasts above the duvet mesmerized him for a moment. He'd been at half-mast as he crossed the room but now he was fully erect, his cock bobbing slightly up and down in time with the pulse of blood to its thick purple head.

He licked his lips. The fake mustache prickled his tongue.

"Get under the covers, Larry."

Larry lifted the blanket. Linda didn't stir. Her eyes didn't move from side to side behind their lids. She wasn't sleeping. Either she was unconscious or she was doing a great job faking it. She'd always been one of the better actors in the porn industry, and in her husband's films she was one hell of a scream queen. It was just as likely she was acting as unconscious.

You can't do this, Larry thought.

You have *to do this*, he told himself. *If you don't, he'll kill you both. But he'll make you watch him kill Linda first.*

Larry raised the covers and climbed over Linda. Again, he wasn't sure if that was The Doll's intent for him but he performed better when working from the left of his costar. A cloud of orange-and-floral scented perfume and light sweat rose as he let the duvet fall over them.

"Caress her breast," said The Doll over the speaker.

Larry watched Linda's eyes for movement. He was so close he could hear her breathing, slowly in and out through her nose. Her lips were thinner than they'd been when she was in her twenties but they were moist and glistening, half parted with the tops of her lower teeth exposed and just the tip of her tongue. His rock-hard rod throbbed against the underside of the blanket, imagining her hot tongue circling the head of his cock, licking the base of it, slurping up his balls.

Fuck, I might just cum right now if I touch her.

Larry reached out and gently cupped her right breast. Warm and yielding, he felt her heart beating beneath his palm. But her breathing didn't change at his touch. Her eyes didn't open. Either she was still out of it or she was doing a hell of a job pretending.

"Linda," he whispered, certain his face was turned far enough from the camera it wouldn't catch the movement of his lips. "Linda, if you're awake move your eyes."

Her eyes didn't stir beneath the lids. Unconscious, then.

"Now kiss her."

The mustache tickled as Larry licked his lips. He leaned over her, opening his mouth, moving closer to hers. He could smell her breath now, acrid and slightly sweet. He imagined his own was worse. When was the last time he'd brushed his teeth? He didn't even know what day it was.

"Squeeze her tit and kiss her."

Larry squeezed her breast and put his lips against hers, not kissing exactly, just sort of mushing them together. Back in their porn days many directors would require them to flick their tongues against each other's, like they were jousting. Larry kept his tongue in his mouth.

Linda's eyes sprang open. She reacted with shock to seeing him on top of her, his lips pressed against hers.

"Larry?"

"It's okay," he whispered into her open lips. "We can figure this out."

She pushed at his arms, trying to shove him off of her, shock turned to anger. Larry held her down, the struggle making him harder. A vague thought that he could reach down between the two of them and jerk up the nightgown and shove it in her before she could stop him arose, but he pushed it away as he held her down. He was no rapist, not even if The Doll forced him to be one.

"We have to get out of here," he said.

"Larry, look out—!"

"I have no guilt in my heart, Larry," The Doll said, not over the speaker this time. His voice came from directly behind him. "Do you?"

Larry's back screamed as he wrenched his head around to look over his shoulder. The Doll had entered the cube while he'd been struggling with Linda. The freak held a black, short-barreled revolver that looked like something out of an old cop movie.

Larry did the only thing he could think to do in that moment: he threw himself over Linda, hoping that if The Doll fired she'd survive the initial blast and have a shot at getting out of here.

He had less than an instant to prepare for the pain. The crack from the pistol and the explosion of fire in his ribcage were simultaneous. For some reason he'd expected one would precede the other, like lightning before the thunder. It was a strange thought to have in the moments before dying.

Linda screamed. She pushed Larry off of her, and he rolled onto his back on the bed, his head propped up by frilly pillows. Two more shots fired. In the glass he saw Linda's body jerk and she fell forward, two dark red holes marring the blue nightgown.

Larry gasped. The hole in his chest whistled, making a sucking sound as he breathed in, like someone giving head.

In the reflection on the glass, he saw images on the two screens above his head. He hadn't noticed anything playing on them before. He'd been too focused on the scene itself. Now he saw that both images were of the same bedroom. Only in one a man and woman he didn't recognize lay dead or dying on the bed. In the other, he and Linda were in a similar state, though in different positions.

On the first, a man in a suit stood with his back toward the camera. On the other, The Doll did the same.

As both the man—The Doll's father, from the video he'd shot when he was a child—and The Doll himself stepped over the beds.

"You're free now," The Doll said. "Both of you."

The Doll and his father raised their pistols to their heads the scene playing out before Larry's eyes faded to black.

"Cut," The Doll said finally. But neither Larry nor Linda was alive to hear it.

12

The Doll—who called himself Jason, though that wasn't his name —dragged a chair over to the Orgy tableau vivant, his "living photographs," though he preferred to think of them as living films. He sat and stared into the cube for a long time, sipping from a tall, cold Harvey Wallbanger, his erstwhile mentor's favorite drink. With the last two human automatons mounted and set in place, he could finally put the past behind him. The final pieces of the puzzle had fallen into place. There was no more work to be done.

Jason picked up the newspaper and reread the headline below the fold, alongside a not-so-recent photograph of Larry: *SECOND FORMER PORN STAR MISSING*. He found it so reductive. As if there was nothing more to a life than what they'd accomplished. The headline for his parents' deaths had read *SOCIALITES DEAD IN DOUBLE MURDER-SUICIDE*. A horrific family tragedy dismissed in a mere six words.

Whirrrr—chug-chug-chug and dead Larry fucked dead Linda doggystyle while the other automatons buzzed and clicked around them, a lifeless, mechanical orgy of cured flesh and oiled metal workings.

The theme of *The Awakening of Mr. and Mrs. S* was "if you can't beat em, join em." This scene was the culmination of that theme, at the climax, so to speak. Linda and Larry had joined the others. They were together again, forever, reenacting their final scene together endlessly.

A happy family. Reunited.

Jason smiled and raised his drink in a silent toast to the men and women who'd made him what he was today, whether they'd know it or not: to his mother and father, to Linda Flint and Larry Walker, to the thousands of actors in hundreds of pornographic films. He smiled, stroking his erection through his pants and sipping the drink, as the scene played again and again and again...

PEG

Peg wuddn't a real unicorn, that's the first thing I s'pose I ought to tell ya.

Jed Hapscomb's daughter Rowena May called 'er a "Pegasus" when she come out just a foal with a big ol bone stickin out the top of 'er head—Peg, I mean. After that, the name kinda stuck, even though Peg was actually more like a unicorn than a Pegasus. Hap hisself—that's what folks round here call him, Hap, not Jed—called the horse "Peg" on all the scrap wood signs he painted by hand and stuck out yonder on the county road, same as the ones pointin back five miles both ways from his farm. Come see the freak o' nature, get yerself some corn or taters on yer way out, maybe a slaba hog if you're feelin peckish.

Cost you five bucks just to see Peg and ten bucks to pet her. Twenty if you wanna give yer kid a ride and forty for a ride and for Happy to snap yer pitcher with his dead wife's Lucille's Polaroid. In the three years since Peggy was born to that old nag who passed giving birth to her—on account of the rupturing that foal's horn did to 'er lady parts—Happy made more whoring out that abomination of a horse than he did the past five years selling corn and taters and raising sows, now that's the truth.

Few months after she was born, when the weird protuberance on 'er forehead Hap figgered was some kind of abnormal skull growth actually *kept growin*, he called the vet to take a gander. They brought 'er into Doc Embry's office and got x-rays done of 'er head and ol' Doc Embry come to find it was cartilage stickin out, not bone. Same as like you got in yer nose or yer ears. Never seen nothin like it before, probably never would again, or so he said.

The second thing y'ought to know is, Peg didn't eat like no normal horse.

That expression bout not lookin a gift horse in the mouth? Doc Embry shoulda never looked inside Peg's. What he found there was damn near more peculiar a sight than that horn of hers.

Turned out them wolf teeth of hers—of which she had six, three on each side—were fully developed at three months old, and sharp as razors. If she'd been conscious at the time o' the examination, she coulda taken a good chomp out of the doc's hand and he mighta lost a finger or two.

But she hadn't been, and she didn't, or Embry woulda likely had to put ol Peg down and this story woulda turned out a whole lot different than it done.

See, Peg was a carnivore, which is odd for a horse but them wolf teeth made it easy for 'er to chew up meat. Ol' Happy fed 'er scraps, the stuff the butcher scraped off his pigs' bones after he broke 'em down for the shop. Hoof and cheek and innards. The gray, slimy meat on their curly little tails. Peg enjoyed meat so she ate up every bit of it Hap slopped in front of her.

Up til then, Hap's little girl Rowena rode all the horses on the farm, but he wouldn't let 'er anywhere near the stable or the pen when Peggy was out stretchin 'er legs. He was worried about that horn, first of all. As Peg got older the horn seemed to get sharper. But second of all it was Rowena who got Peg started on eatin meat, feeding 'er scraps she snuck out from the table. She only admitted to it after the horse got so skinny from not eatin nothin but table scraps Peg woulda died if she kept 'er mouth shut. Rowena, I mean, not the horse.

After that, Peg wouldn't eat a damn thing *other* than meat—no oats, no carrots, not even 'er salt lick. Them shits of hers stunk to high heaven. I could smell em from here, now that's the truth, and Hap's farm is a good half mile yonder as you prob'ly seen drivin out here.

Ol' Hap figgered Peg'd take a bite outta them pigs if she had half a chance, and outta his girl too, if he let 'er near. That's how come when you paid to see Peg she'd have on that grazin muzzle she always wore. Last thing Hap needed was some litigious out-a-towner slappin him with a lawsuit for bitin off one of their kidses fingers, only it turned out that's exactly what he got later on. A lawsuit I mean, not a bit off finger.

I s'pose all this is besides the point. You're here on accounta what happened to all them city fellas so I'll spare ya my meanderin. Sometimes I forget you big city folk like to cut the bullshit and get straight to the point, least when it suits ya.

Some local boys, according to the story, they come out drunk as skunks to Hap's farm late one night to do a little cow tippin. Story has it they was out earlier that day to ride Peg but Hap wouldn't let em on account of they was too big and already reekin of grain alcohol or shine. So they come out again in the dead a night to teach Hap a lesson, or so they thought.

Well, after a couple or three futile attempts to get Hap's bovines to roll on over, one of them boys got the brilliant idea to get Peg outta 'er stall an take that ride Hap wouldn't let em have earlier in the day.

They was tryna get the stall door opened, from what I understand, when one of them boys thought it'd be wise to take off Peg's blinders. That was their first mistake. Actually, climbin into that stall was the first mistake. Takin them blinders off was mistake número dos, as them migrant fellas Hap used to hire might say. Hell, let's be frank: that whole night was one big mistake, and them boys was about to find out just about how much.

See, Peg could *smell* them drunk sumbitches, but she couldn't *see* em. And she was an ornery horse, even when she was a filly. Hell, when she was just a foal she done bit the titty off one a Hap's other nags, the one that had a newborn 'round the same time as Peg's mother shat that horned abomination into the world.

They say don't blame the horse, blame the trainer. But in the case of Peg, Hap did just about all he could. Even had a Native American feller come out to try an' break her, but all he done was break his own tibula or fibia or whatever damn bone it was, maybe both.

What's that? Right, I was talkin about them boys started it all, wuddn't I? Ol' gray mare ain't what she used to be. My mind, that is, not Peg. We all know what happened to her. My mind is kinda soupy these days, or so the wife likes to tell me just about every chance she gets.

Well, okay. One a them boys was already in the stall with Peg, takin off 'er blinders. The other boys was fiddlin with the latch like a couple of virgins tryna unclasp a lady's delicates. That's when Peg starts chasin that first boy around the stall like a Benny Hill sketch. He's shriekin and hollerin and Peg's whinnyin and nayin and finally them other two boys get the latch open, and out he come with Peg hot on his tail.

Turns out one of them virgins musta fancied himself a rodeo clown instead of just a reg'lar ol' clown so he starts runnin distraction, and from what everyone saw in the news a week or so later, the same thing that brought all them city fellas out here in droves, you know what happened next.

Them boys said ol' Peg damn near tore that poor boy's soul right outta his body. Say he was ridin 'er like a buckin bronco that night, 'cept he wuddn't holdin on to nothin but the frayin shreds of his own dignity, and he weren't sittin on no saddle, he was horn-deep up the keister right on Peg's forehead with 'er eyes rollin around in 'er head like she needed an exorcist and his own just about poppin outta his skull.

Well, it was about that time Happy come out with a shotgun and a lantern, and suffice to say he was decidedly *un*happy 'bout what he saw. According to him, them two virgins was holdin hands with their recently deflowered partner while Peg bucked and brayed, reamin out his anal canal like a core drill, as the French say.

After a while, Hap managed to get the ornery ol' girl settled down enough so the three of them could pry the boy's tarhole off'n Peg's horn, which was slick with shit and blood and undigested bits of what the boy likely had for supper that night. Boy was bleedin pretty good too, like a stuck pig accordin to Hap, who ought to know considerin he slaughtered enough of em in his time.

Hap brought out some cotton balls and a rag and bucket and told them boys to warsh up Peg's horn and to pack their friend's ass crack so he didn't bleed to death, probably in that order. Said he'da done it hisself 'cept he wanted to teach em a lesson their daddies shoulda taught em a long time ago. That lesson bein, you don't mess with another man's livelihood, especially if that livelihood's a grumpy ol' nag with a horn on 'er head.

Well, them boys left the Hapscomb farm reekin o' shit with their tails tucked 'tween their legs—and a wad of blood-soaked cotton between one of em's. Hap promised he wouldn't say peep to their folks but lo and behold one of them boys had to run his big mouth, and it ended up the mother of the boy who lost his anal virginity to a horse with a horn on 'er head decided it'd be in 'er best interest to sue ol' Hap for every penny he had to his name.

Come to find out, Hap didn't have much money after all, which was a surprise to no one apparently except for the kid's mama. The farm'd barely broke even back then, what with the goddamn Democrats cuttin subsidies an' all. Still, what Hap made whorin out Peg kept em afloat, and that boy's folks knew that much, at least.

Somehow or another, the local rag got wind of all this and published the story—probably the same one that got you interested all them years ago. Letterman read about it on his show, made a worldwide laughin stock outta them boys, and got a lot of folk drivin all the way out from the city to see the horse that done it, to see Peg and get their pitcher took with a "genuine unicorn."

Business was booming after that. And Judge Crawford done threw the lawsuit outta court, said if them boys hadn't gone out to Hap's farm stinkin of shine an' provoking Peg, she'da never assaulted him in the anus.

Now I believe they call that "blaming the victim" these days, but back then it was just plain ol' common sense not to poke a bear. Course, nobody woulda expected a lady horse to penetrate the anal pucker of a teenage boy but there you have it. Stranger things, an' all that.

It was 'round this time the government come a-sniffin aroun, as they do. They smelled money, and untaxed money at that. Turns out, Hap hadn't been filin his taxes in years. Owed em more than he could pay with his earnins, and if he didn't make that money back quick the bank was fittin to foreclose on the farm, or as Hap put it, they was "fittin to bend him over an go in dry." Add to that a li'l girl smart enough to eventually go off to college someday, an Hap found hisself in quite the conundrum.

That's where you come in, I guess. This *documentary* you're makin bout them city fellas and what happened to em.

Now I ain't the judgin kind. Leave that happy horseshit to the Almighty, is my credo. But any o' them fellers come out here lookin to get cornholed by a filly with a horn, I figure they got what's comin to em. Poor Hap was in a tight spot, and I know he done what he had to do to get his ass unstuck, so to speak.

But Lord I cannot begin to fathom the horrors he musta seen when those city fellers come a-hollerin. I know they showed them tapes at his trial. Damn thing was a three-ring circus, includin the horse tricks. They never showed em on the news, mind. Always had em blurred out. But you could hear ol' Peg whinnyin like a horse in a burnin barn and all them fellers groanin and moanin while they used that damn demon horse's head to get their jollies.

Now Sheriff Deacon an me go way back. That poor sumbitch had to watch every one o' them tapes 'fore he turned em in for state's evidence, and his face was still green when he passed on what he saw to yers truly. Ghastly stuff, I can tell you that much. Stuff that'd make ya sick just to think about.

I tell ya, I seen my share of farm animals ruttin. Hell, back when I was a boy bout the same age as them kids from the beginning, I seen a feller stick his pecker in a cow's cooter. The stench that wafted over from that unholy congress nearly made me upchuck my lunch, but it's the God's honest truth. Now the Bible says thou shalt not layeth with a beast as thou layest with a woman, but it doesn't say nothin about doggystyle, and it sure as shit don't say nothin bout gettin it up the cornhole from a horse with a horn.

Ol' Hap, all he done, or so he says, was keep a hold on Peg's reins while them boys slipped off their kicks and took turns easin their hairy assholes onto that horn and some other feller, the guy who wore the hangman's mask in them videos, recorded it for posterity like it was Christmas mornin. Hap says he tried to think o' nothin but the money, which meant he'd be able to hang on to his livelihood and make a decent life for Rowena May. This business, though, was *anythin* but decent. Fella with the hangman mask was the one who paid him. Hap got to thinkin it was sumpthin like them big city fellers who pay a ridickless amount o' cash just to shoot wild animals in a pen. And this feller in the hangman mask, he was the ringleader, takin a hefty cut 'fore Hap saw any money at all.

That in mind, Hap got to wonderin, while he held Peg back from murderin those boys via the rectum—which reminds me of the punchline to that ol' joke: "Rectum? Dang near killed 'im!" But ol' Hap, holdin on to them reins and holdin back his gorge from the stink of human excrement—funny how you get used to all manner of animal shit but people shit don't ever seem to get any less foul. I s'pose there's a lesson in that. Anyways, ol' Hap starts a-wonderin just how big a cut the Hangman was takin, an' if'n he kept that cash on his person or elsewhere.

But Hap don't act on that thought this time. This time he just holds them reins tighter than his pecker when he's holdin in a piss with them kidney stones he had a while back, an he keeps his eyes shut to stop hisself from pukin while them city folk took turns ridin Peg's horn.

Now I should mention, Happy never had much love for that horse. Way he tells it, he done put a rifle to Peg's head more than once an willed hisself to pull the trigger. He knew she was an abomination just like the rest of us did. But he stopped short at the last minute on account of, a) despite bein a horse, Peg also happened to be a *cash cow*, and b) Rowena loved the thing, even though she weren't allowed to ride 'er.

Still, that night Hap found hisself sympathizin with that retched nag. Watchin all them city boys take off their weddin rings 'fore they pulled down their underpants made him realize this was more than just an unholy covenant between Man and Horse. This was *rape*, pure and simple, not unlike if them fellas was stickin their willies in Peg's holiest of holies. And it was clear, the way the ol' gal whinnied and neighed, them eyes rollin around in 'er head while them fellers eased their puckers down on that horn, deeper and deeper, that ol' Peg had no interest in bein part of this.

Up til then, Hap had made his peace with the fact he was pimpin out Peg's horn to them perverts. But Peg was a lot more than just 'er horn. Folks who been around 'er long enough for their kid to take a ride or have their pitcher took, they didn't see the same things Hap did. Peg was strong-willed, too.

And she was *teeth*.

That's when Hap come up with his plan.

Damn sure wuddn't the smartest of plans, as far as plans go. But Hap wuddn't exactly the smartest o' fellers. Come from a long line of pig farmers and not much in the way of schoolin. He aimed to change that for Rowena May. She was doin pretty well for herself at the public school despite the handicap of bein born to a mental midget like Hap. But she had 'er mother in 'er too, an 'er mother'd been one of the smartest gals in town, which was why it come as such a shock when Margaret Ellis became Margaret Hapscomb. Folks who knew 'er said it was to spite 'er daddy. But they're both gone now, so who can say for sure?

What's that? Well, that is odd, can't say I ever thoughta that. Always seemed peculiar Peggy bein short for Margaret, wuddn't ya say? Prob'ly don't mean nothin in this partic'lar situation but it sure is a odd coinkidink just the same.

Anyhoo, to make a long story a might bit shorter, Hap decided that very night if he was gonna take any more of the Hangman's money he'd let Peg have a go at em. Nip em in the butt, if you catch my meanin.

Next night come round, and out come the Hangman with a busload a horny idiots. All of em had on them li'l Zorro face masks to protect their identities if the tapes ever got leaked, just like th'other night. This was a while before the TicketyTok an all that, but shit like that seem to make its way to the public eye anyways, don't it? Like maybe it's too terrible to keep secret for long. Like the universe or Fate or some other hippy-dippy shit *wants* people to see em.

So just like the last time, Hap straps Peg down with her blinders an grazin muzzle on. An as them city slickers get their puckers nice and slick with the lube the Hangman passed around, little do they know that this time Hap lef one of them buckles on the muzzle loose.

The men all had their skivvies off by the time the Hangman brought Peg's head low enough for the first feller to climb atop. Hap watched this time, despite how disgusted he was by the whole ordeal he got hisself caught up in. He watched an he bided his time. He said those deviants were tuggin on their willies and squeezin their balls, just a-waitin on their turn. Meanwhile, the prevert on the horn was ten-inches deep, ridin up and down, his eyes rolled back in his head.

I don't wanna say what happened next, but I believe it was the proverbial straw that done broke the camel's back, the camel bein ol' Hap and the back bein the limit of his tolerance.

So what Hap done was simply flick the buckle. The muzzle come loose just as the first of them sickos shot his wad in the dirt, and ol' Peg turned her head and bit that Hangman feller's hand clean off.

Well the Hangman started screamin, naturally, holding on to his wrist, tryin to stem the geyser of blood, while Peg jerked her head up, lifting the feller on her horn, skewerin him up to his lungs. Meanwhile, at least accordin to the video they showed at the trial, and what Sheriff Deacon related to me prior to that three-ring circus, Hap stepped back and let go of the reigns and let nature take its course, as the French say.

Well, Peg took the opportunity to leap forward, the feller on her horn floppin around on the top o' her head like a puppet. Coroner said he was dead prob'ly the second he took that horn all the way to the hilt. That didn't stop him from havin a hardon that'd shame a porn star. The other fellers knew their time was up and got to runnin, only half of em had their pants around their ankles, and tripped the second they started, fallin face-first in the hay n dirt. One feller did a faceplant in a heap o' Peg's shit, an he was one of the lucky ones.

Peg went right for the closest feller's pecker, chomped the sumbitch right off. But she didn't eat it. Figure she was too riled up to eat. The guy dropped like a gunny sack full o' corn and Peg kept on chargin ahead. One feller thought he was clever. Took off his red T-shirt and started flappin it like a matador. I s'pose he was tryin to distract 'er, but she ran right at the dumb sumbitch and took a good chunk out of his ass 'fore he managed to climb over into one of the sow's pens.

Peg got one of the fellers on the ground before he could stand back up. Bit off half the poor sumbitch's face. I can scarcely imagine the last thing that feller musta seen, Peg's jaws closin in on him with all them sharp teeth while the dead man with the hardon hung over him, arms and legs akimbo.

Them other fellers went runnin from the barn hither and thither. The smart ones ran for the bus, 'cept the Hangman held the keys, and he was passed out from blood loss. Hap claimed at the trial he didn't want no one to get hurt. Now I can't speak on whether or not that's the God's honest truth but I do know while Peg was distracted he climbed out a winduh and went to get his rifle.

He said it was time to put the ol' nag out o' her misery.

Peg, in the meantime, went after them fellers runnin out the barn with their pants still unzipped. She was voracious, galloping back and forth, hungry for blood, the dead man with a hardon still bouncing around on her head like a kid on a carousel.

"Stay in the house, Rowena May!" you could hear Hap shout on the tape, over the screams and whinnies and cries for help. "*PEG!*" he shouts.

On the tape you can hear the horse neigh, almost like she's replyin.

"This is for your own good!" Hap shouts then.

That gunshot cut through all the screams. *PA-POW!*

You could hear Peg whinny then, but accordin to Hap he just winged 'er. She went off runnin, gallopin down the drive to the road.

Hap got in his truck and drove off after 'er. She made it all the way to town by the time he caught up. Peg was gallopin down Main Street. Some folks who saw 'er later said they thought she was a blood-streaked Sagittarius at first. You know, the Zodiac sign.

What's that? A center? Oh, a cen*taur*? Well, okayden. Whatever them thing's are called, that's what they said. Folks didn't see Peg's head at first, ya seen, her runnin at a gallop. Just Peg's body with a man perched on top, his free willy flopping back and forth like a conductor's wand at Carnegie Hall. The same damn fools kids who'd set this whole ordeal into motion was smokin reefer outside the pool hall and likely thought "there but for the grace o' God," or whatever the modern yo-yo equivalent is.

Hap chased Peg all the way to town hall, and while she trotted right up the town hall steps an swung her head round and flung that dead naked feller right through the front winduh, almost like she was makin some kind of formal protest, Hap jumped out the truck and lined up his shot.

Ol' Mayor Burton come to the winduh just about then and seen that blood-drenched nag snortin and sneerin out on the steps. Likely figgered Peg was a Horse of the goddang Apocalypse come to tell him his time was up, 'til he seen the naked feller sprawled out at the foot of the front desk like he done dropped dead from priapism on his way to payin his property tax. An he mighta seen Hap standin out front of his truck, if Peg herself hadn't been in the way.

But she was, an it was the crack of the rifle that signaled Hap's presence. Then her head burst open like one o' them Mexican peenatas, only instead o' raining candy on Burton, the litigious sumbitch got painted with blood and brains and pelted by the sharpest damn horse teeth anyone ever saw. Out on the campaign trail, Mayor Burton liked to make a point 'bout how he wuddn't afraid to get his hands dirty, but I can't he'p but wonder how he felt bout gettin the rest of him covered in the stinkin insides of a dead nag. Not too favorably, is my guess.

Well, Hap got the job done finally but his part in this song and dance was far from over. They say a feller who represents hisself in court's got a fool for a client, and never has that been more accurate than at Jed Hapscomb's trial. I s'pose y'all know he's servin five to ten at Nebraska State Penitentiary for animal cruelty and criminal negligée causin death, o' that Hangman feller an the human half of your centaur, them an a couple others. Feller without a face survived, by some miracle or trick o' the Devil. But who would want to, seein what he seen?

Bank took the farm a short while later, and Rowena May got took in by her grandma. Better off than with her halfwit father, most folks agree, 'specially after the trial. Folks round here, when someone fucks up, they call it a "Peggin." Feller blows up his trailer cookin meth, he got Pegged. Mayor's wife caught cheatin with their undocumented gardener, all three of em got a Peggin.

Now I wish I was the type of feller who could sum all this up for you folks like some shaggy dog story with a pithy comment or a clever one-liner, but truth is that just ain't me. Save it for the barstool philosophers down at the Tartan Tap, is my credo. Heck, maybe y'all can give the story a spit shine in that documentary o' yers. That'd be real nice.

What you said 'bout Peg bein short for Margaret got me thinkin, though. There was a time when Mags was alive an Hap used to come to me to gripe 'bout how she was gon' "nag him to an early grave." Turned out a nag horse just 'bout put him there instead.

And I can't he'p but wonder if Mags hadn't gone early to the grave herself if'n all that Peg stuff never woulda happened. She prob'ly woulda put the horse down when Peg was born, I figger. Better to put it out of its misery quick than let the poor beast suffer as a carnival freak. Mags was sensitive that way. Even if she hadn't, she likely never woulda let those city fellers take turns ridin on that horn. Or if she had, she woulda had the brains to get the Hangman's money up front an take a steeper cut.

Makes ya think though, don't it? 'Bout how close any of us might be to a Pegging of our own? Metaphorically speakin, of course.

Really makes you think.

Bait

When Alexa and I were little and we used fish in the Paintbrush sometimes after school, she'd never had trouble baiting a hook.

Most childhood skills disappear over time if they're not kept up. That particular skill—baiting a hook—it never left Alexa. Maybe if I'd known what she had in mind, I might not have gone to see her the night she texted me. I might have had better things to do with my time. But she'd had that effect on people. A part of me had always wanted to be her, wanted to be *with* her. If I'd been conscious of it, I might have spared myself a lot of pain. Then again, I might have gone to see her anyway.

Once she'd blossomed, men began to gravitate toward her wherever she went. Women, too, though she'd never been with a girl as far as I knew then, which was one of the reasons I never imagined she'd have any interest in me. She didn't need to put on makeup or doll herself up at all. Jogging pants and her hair in curlers, on a brief trip to pick up something from the corner store, some eggs or a chocolate milk, she'd get wolf whistles. She'd get strange men in white vans slamming on their breaks to try and give her a ride. Or to try and get her to give *them* one.

When she did doll herself up—*watch out, sister*. It was like a nature video the way guys would vie for her attention. Trying to be the first to buy her a drink. To chat her up. To take her home.

Alexa and I grew up on opposite sides of the same city, in the same school only because I bussed in. Where I lived, carrying around books like I did got you marked as prey. So, I traveled halfway across the city to her school, where I could pursue academic endeavors without the threat of my five-foot-fuck-all frame getting a beatdown—verbal and physical —from every girl who wanted to prove *they* were the alpha.

After high school, Alexa and I went our separate ways. I stayed to take journalism at a community college. Alexa left town, getting her Masters in Psych at NYU. Nobody had ever expected any less from her. I could have ended up on the street and the kids we went to high school with wouldn't have batted an eye. They all saw me as gutter trash despite my GPO, simply because of where I'd grown up.

I hadn't seen Alexa for a few years since we both went our opposite ways, but we'd emailed each other every so often just to keep up. When I moved to the city for a full-time writing gig that had since fallen through, we tried to get together on a handful of occasions, but circumstance always got in the way, raincheck after raincheck. It got so we were apologizing to each other in those emails more than we were catching up, and it'd begun to feel like a chore—if not for me, certainly for her. Months went by like this. I'd considered just not responding to her last email but of course, sappy me, I did, and Alexa left me hanging, waiting on her reply for *weeks*.

Until one night a few weeks back, she texted me out of the blue: *I NEED YOU ASAP!!*

My blood pressure spiked when I saw those two words in all-caps: *NEED YOU.* I'd seen her brush off so many ostensibly hot guys over the years, from the high school parties to the club scene, the idea of being with her had never even crossed my mind. Okay, not *never*. There was a lonely night or two when my thoughts went back to the two of us skinny dipping at that lake up north and I'd caught a glimpse of her pale slim body in the moonlight. But the thought that she would ever take *me* home—you can imagine how crazy that must have seemed to a Plain Jane like me.

Somehow, I managed to play it cool, even though my heart was drumming in my ears. We were *friends*, after all. Or *had* been. No reason I shouldn't assume she just wanted me to help her move some furniture.

I chose my words carefully. Deleted the text and tried again. I asked her where she was, trying not to seem too eager, trying to play aloof. She had, after all, stood me up the last time we were supposed to meet.

This time she replied back instantly: *my apt pls hurry!!*

I saved the article I'd been working on, a freelance job, and tossed on my jean jacket. The streets were slushy. Some snow remained on garbage bins and trash bags. I'd already walked several blocks in the cold when I realized I'd forgotten my phone—the very thing that had gotten me into this mess—but by then I'd just flagged down a cab and I'd gone too far to turn back. I didn't know at the time how true those words would become.

I wouldn't need the phone, anyhow. I knew where she lived, or at least where she'd lived the last time I'd seen her. If she'd changed her address, well... I'd lived through a lot more embarrassing moments than knocking on the wrong door.

Alexa lived in a townhouse off Amsterdam in Hell's Kitchen. I'd dropped her off there in a yellow cab one night after she'd had a few too many drinks, and the cabbie had continued to my damp, cramped basement apartment in Greenwich, a not entirely unpleasant biographical note I share with the late-great Hunter S. Thompson.

I got out at what I hoped was still Alexa's townhouse, paid the driver, and looked up at the darkened windows as he drove off, the sound of rain slashing under his tires. If she was home, she must have been in one of the back rooms. Otherwise she was sitting in the dark, and I should probably confess, the image of her creamy skin gleaming under the streetlights gave me a thrill.

The second-floor buzzer said KEACH: Alexa's last name. I pushed it and waited to hear her voice. Instead, the door buzzed like an angry insect. I tore it open before the maglock could decide I wasn't worthy of entry—I certainly didn't *feel* worthy right then, especially when I caught site of my reflection in the door glass. I quickly smoothed my hair—a sharp bob in need of a trim—wiped a smear of ink from my cheek and stepped into the small (yet loads bigger than mine!) foyer. From one of the two doors on either side of me, the smell of jerk lamb or goat filled the enclosed space. Even if I hadn't forgotten to eat dinner in my rush to finish the article, I would have been salivating.

Like I said, she knew how to bait a hook.

The stairs creaked all the way up. From the outside, the brownstone gave the appearance of affluence but little of that remained indoors. The wallpaper had peeled, the paint cracked and flecked. Cobwebs covered the wall sconces like handcrafted lampshades, the floors stained and layered with dirt and crumbs as if no one had cleaned in months. At the top of the stairs, Alexa's mailbox was crammed full of envelopes and junk mail. The door number—3—hung upside-down from a single screw. Up here the spicy food smell had given way to the dank stench of someone's clogged sink and/or toilet.

I knocked.

From inside I heard heels cross a wooden floor toward the door, followed by the slight squeak of a rusted hinge I assumed to be the peep-hole guard. Then the rattle of a door chain, the clack of two bolts unlocking. Finally the door swung open six inches or so while the over-head light in the hall, its dome filled with dead flies, crackled like a bug zapper.

Alexa peered out at me from the darkened apartment. She looked past me, blinking at the cracked stairwell ceiling. "Are you alone?"

"Of course, I'm alone. Alexa, who the hell would I bring?"

She looked over my shoulder again, then nodded and dragged the creaking door halfway open, just enough for me to step inside. I stayed in the hall, suddenly unsure I wanted to be here at all. It seemed like the pungent smell was coming from *inside*.

"Are you gonna come in, or not?"

I thought, *What's the worst that could happen?*

In nights since, I wish to hell I'd taken a moment longer to ponder that.

Because the worst thing that could happen is often far worse than you could ever begin to imagine.

<hr>

Alexa closed the door behind me and began pacing the room while I tried to acclimate myself to the darkness, everything in silhouette from a streetlamp shining dull yellow through the curtains.

"Alexa," I said, crossing toward her dim, moving shape. Her dark hair had fallen over her shoulders like a hood, much longer than the last time I'd seen her. Back then she'd been trying anything to keep men's attention away from her. One summer, she'd returned to high school with a shaved head. We'd called it her "Sinead" phase. The boys had called her "dyke," which had gotten more under my skin than it had Alexa's for obvious reasons. It was easy for her not to care about labels like that.

"What's going on?" I asked her. "Are you okay?"

The dank smell was stronger in here, though I could also smell a men's cologne, sweat, and the faint flowery talcum scent I'd long ago come to associate with Alexa. As I reached out for her, my shoe struck something soft and solid and I barely managed to catch myself before tripping.

If Alexa hadn't been making me edgy the way she'd kept pacing, muttering to herself the way she was, I might have wondered what I'd hit. My shoe came away tacky from the flooring. With the smell in here, it wouldn't have surprised me to discover I'd stepped in shit.

"I'm turning on the lights," I said.

"*Don't!*" she cried out. She'd stopped moving just long enough for me to make out the fear contorting her features, amplifying my own nervousness. Then right back to pacing, as if the constant movement was the only thing keeping her from jumping out the window.

"Alexa, would you stop clomping around and tell me what the hell's going on?"

"I can't do it anymore," she said. "I *can't.*"

"Can't do what, Alexa?" Anger got the better of me. "Would you fucking *talk* to me, already? I came all this way—"

"Okay," she said, seemingly resigned. Her pale silhouette sank with a springy sound into what I assumed must be a chair. "Okay. You can turn on the light."

"Good." I moved back the way I'd come and ran my fingers along the wall. When I found the switch, Alexa said, "Don't scream."

It was a strange thing to say, I mused, as I flicked on the lights. But turning back to her with the light on, I almost did exactly what she'd told me not to.

A man lay on his back on the carpet. Pale-skinned and hairy, his fat, uncircumcised cock stood erect against the mound of his stomach and yellowish pubic hair. His blank eyes stared up at the ceiling. Not blinking. Not breathing. In my shock, I staggered back against the door. The pool of congealing blood surrounding him, spreading out from between his legs, was marred by a single footprint—*my* footprint. My thoughts buzzed with legal terms: *Forensic evidence. Accomplice.* This guy was young, barely older than me. But there was no doubt in my mind he was dead and the stench filling the room had come from him.

Retching, I staggered back, making a home for myself against the door like a frightened spider. I looked up at Alexa. She was watching me closely, gauging my reaction.

"Alexa," I said. I was barely able to look at her with the dead man's prick within my field of vision. It was hard enough to maintain eye contact with Alexa in her lingerie and high heels, like a pinup in some men's magazine—and what the hell had they been doing here, exactly?

"Alexa, were you...? Did you *fuck* this guy?"

She looked at me as if I'd slapped her. I'd struck a nerve, despite my misplaced revulsion. I couldn't explain why my mind had gone there, why the idea of her having slummed it with a man so clearly beneath her seemed more shocking in that moment than the fact that the man was dead. Was it jealousy? Was it insane to feel jealous when the man she'd been screwing lay dead on the floor between us?

I reached behind me, fingers scrabbling for the door handle, eager to leave before Alexa could reel me further in.

"Brook..." she said, the plea in her tone fixing me in place. "*Please.* I need your help."

"What did he do to you? Did he try to... to *rape* you?"

Shame in her red-raw eyes, Alexa tugged at the hem of her high-waisted black panties, as if it had only just occurred to her she was practically naked. She shook her head no.

"What then?" I demanded, struggling to understand, to comprehend the incomprehensible. *She murdered this man.* The notion had finally sunken in.

"It's more complicated than that."

Whatever "it" was, her shock seemed to have subsided. Seeing this made me even angrier. "So, what? You called me here to help *clean this up*, is that it? Haven't had time for me in nearly a year, now you need an errand girl?"

"It's not like you were any more communicative," she snapped.

I needed something to drink. Fear and anger had dried out my mouth, making it difficult to talk—and the *need* to talk, to ask questions, felt compulsive. I moved laterally to the kitchenette, giving the man on the floor a wide berth. Running the cold water, I splashed some on my face, not daring to turn my back on the dead man in the living room.

I caught movement from the corner of my eye but it was only Alexa, standing briefly to snag a glass of red from the coffee table. The glimpse of her bare ass, barely concealed by flimsy, lace-bordered panties, managed to stir feelings in me despite the clear mental image of what must have happened to the dead man. *She killed him,* I thought again. Alexa sat back down, crossed her legs, and downed the glass in one gulp.

I drank greedily from the faucet, then returned to the living room. I sank into her leather sofa, the dead body between us. "Alexa... what the fuck happened? Why did you...?"

The man's penis began to flop.

Not just flop—it was doing a goddamn *jig*.

As we watched, me horrified, Alexa strangely calm, the skin of his penis stretched out, like someone trying to shove their head through a tight turtleneck. I looked up at Alexa. She was eyeing me with a strange look. Curious, as though she was gauging my reaction again rather than reacting to the horror herself. The shock of it was doubled for me. I'd seen two, maybe three penises in my entire life—and certainly none as big or as *excited* as this one.

Suddenly the flesh burst open. Chunks of yellow fatty tissue splattered against the coffee table and the man's testicles oozed out over his freckled leg. I flinched at the sight and managed to hold back a wretch, just glad none of the spatter had landed on Alexa or myself.

Again, movement caught my eye: the black, scabrous legs of an insect. A *large* insect. My reaction to this was more primitive than to the sight that preceded it. I crabwalked over the back of the sofa in horror as the chitinous creature clambered over its host's viscera-splattered thigh and plonked down on the carpet.

I couldn't help myself. I screamed.

Black compound eyes stared into mine as it scuttled toward me on what looked like a dozen legs, tentacles thrashing, its blood-slicked carapace glistening under the lamplight.

Alexa moved quickly, leaping up from the sofa, and stomped down hard on the thing as it reached my feet, where it had been heading straight for what I assumed must have been its destination—my pantleg. Its mucus-like insides squirted out and it squealed like a boiled lobster, writhing under her stiletto heel, its horrible limbs flailing.

She offered me a sympathetic look while she slipped off her shoe, but no explanation. She brought the heel to the kitchen sink, walking awkwardly—one heel, one bare foot—and rinsed the shoe under the tap. I remained where I was, crouched by the door, staring open-mouthed at the mess between my feet. Finally, I managed to put my thoughts into words.

"*What the fuck was that thing?*"

"The males never mature properly," Alexa said over her shoulder, and I wasn't sure I'd heard her correctly at first. "It's best to just put them out of their misery."

"Alexa... what's *happening*?"

"They need hosts," she said, not answering my question. "If they inhabit a suitable host, the relationship is symbiotic. With a non-suitable one... well, you just saw what happens. Paratenic hosts—they don't live long."

I looked at the man on the floor between us, his genitals like a burst piñata of blood.

"Where did it *come* from, Alexa?"

"From me," she said, as if it were obvious.

"You..." I swallowed hard, inadvertently glancing at the lacy material between her legs, pubic hair visible through the fabric. "...that thing was *inside* you?"

She shook her head patiently. "I was born with another living being inside me. A symbiont. *That—*" She pointed to the mess on the floor. "—was one of her brood. Her offspring."

"Why *me*, Alexa? Why did you call me here tonight?"

"I need to confess what I've done. You're the only writer I know."

"How lucky for me," I scoffed.

"And because you're my friend," she added. I saw a deep sadness in her eyes. I tried mightily not to feel sorry for her in that moment, but it was difficult. We'd grown up together. But I wanted more than anything to hate her right now. For what I saw as a betrayal. Not just roping me into a murder, intentional or not, but for making me a witness to this atrocity.

"I wanted you to know about me. Why I've seemed... distant. Why I've held you at arm's length."

"I'm not one of those 'friend zone' assholes, Alexa."

"Of course, you aren't. But you have feelings for me. I've seen it."

I shook my head.

"I have feelings for you, too, Brook. This is what happens to the men in my life. Women, too, if they're incompatible." She jutted her angular chin toward the man on the floor. "*That's* what happens."

"If you knew that, why did you sleep with this bozo?"

"He's not a bozo," she said with a scowl. "He was kind. Besides, it's not like I have the luxury of choice. You've heard of zombie ants?"

I told her I hadn't.

"There's a fungus," she explained. "*O. unilateralis* it's called. It infects the ant's brain, makes it crawl to the top of a leaf blade to spread its spores and infect other ants."

"Okay," I said, not quite getting it. I looked it up later. It's a strange and complicated process, essentially how Alexa described it except that she'd left out the fact that it kills the zombified ant after the insect reaches the leaf and grows a stalk out of its skull to infect other ants. This is the fungi's *raison d'etre*, a perpetual cycle of mitosis to create endless versions of itself.

"You're saying this... *thing*—this symbiont—that it *controls* you?"

"During its breeding cycle... to a point..." She made a gesture between a nod and a head shake. "...yes."

"It—*she*—made you fu—" I changed tact. "—*have sex* with this—" I almost said *bozo* again. "—with him."

Alexa nodded with a downcast look. "I don't want anyone to die. If I could stop myself—"

"Have you tried to remove it?" I still couldn't think of this thing, this parasite, as anything but an 'it.' My disdain for this 'living being' must have showed because Alexa sneered.

"*She's a part of me*, Brook. Our nervous systems are connected. I can't live without her."

"But it's *killed people*, Alexa. How many?"

She wouldn't look at me. Her gaze was held by the man on the floor.

"*How many*, Alexa?"

"Six," she said, then shook her head. "Ten."

"Ten people."

She was a serial killer. A *multiple murderer*. And here, now, I was her accomplice. It was already far too late to turn back. I considered asking her to turn herself in—but the thought of her in prison broke my heart. That left us with only one choice.

"What did you do with the rest of them? The other..." I didn't want to say it. "...the others like him?"

She told me.

Deep in the woods on the outskirts of Twin Lakes, where Alexa and I grew up, Paintbrush Creek widens to a river. And soon we were on our way in Alexa's Volvo, to the clearing in the woods where we'd baited our hooks as kids. We'd caught plenty of brook trout there, over the years. Late one night, when we were sixteen or seventeen, we'd had a little too much to drink at a bush party and shared our first and only kiss on a park bench carved out of a felled sequoia.

Oh, I'd been hooked all right. From the very first day we met.

All she had to do was reel me in.

During the drive, I'd asked Alexa to tell me everything she knew about her parasite. She hadn't wanted to talk, saying she needed to concentrate on the drive. She said she would tell me afterwards, and I believed her. So we'd listened to the radio while she drove, and every time a set of headlights flashed in the side mirror I worried a cop would pull us over and we'd have to explain why there was a dead man wrapped in a white linen tablecloth in the trunk with his genitals torn to shreds as if he'd slathered them with peanut butter and let a Rottweiler go at him.

At three A.M. we pulled into the gravel lot at the southern entrance to the park. It was over a hundred acres of land, some of it trailed, much of it untouched. The clearing was a bit of a hike. We had a single flashlight and our phones to get there in the dark but it was carrying the body that troubled me. We couldn't exactly drag him without leaving forensic evidence.

Turned out we didn't need to. There was a park maintenance shed that was new since the last time I'd been here. Alexa surprised me by using a couple of bent hairpins to jimmy the padlock.

"Where the hell did you learn that?"

"Remember my parents' liquor cabinet?"

I'd always wondered how she'd gotten into it. Now I knew. She'd been practicing.

Inside the shed were all the tools we'd need. A shovel, a pick, a wheelbarrow, even a bag of lime. It was almost too perfect.

We lifted the dead man out of the trunk and placed him on trash bags we'd laid out in the wheelbarrow. Then we got moving, rolling him into the woods.

This might surprise you, but I've never buried a human being before. When Alexa and I were kids—I think I was about twelve or thirteen—my cat Meowzers died. I cried so much I thought my little heart would burst but when my dad told me I could take her into the backyard and bury her there, I remember I got really quiet. I didn't stop being sad immediately, but just knowing that Meowzers would be there in the backyard, a few feet under the ground, where I could talk to her if I wanted to, it *calmed* me.

We took her to the backyard in a tin box lined with the case for the old pillow she used to sleep on and I helped my father dig the hole. I said something silly as a eulogy I'd probably seen on TV, and together we buried her, under the apple tree. The cement marker my father made is still there in the backyard, only visible when the kid from down the street comes by to mow the lawn.

This was not like that.

For one thing, this guy *smelled*. He stank like rotting vegetation clogging a sewer pipe. The sheet we'd rolled him up in was soaked through with gore and when we finally managed to heave him into the hole, it unraveled, exposing himself to us. Whatever had happened to his body in the time since we'd left Alexa's apartment, under the light of the moon all the veins leading toward his crotch had turned black, the flesh around the wound itself a sort of yellow-green slop.

Alexa climbed down into the hole—she'd put on proper footwear and a tracksuit—and tucked the body back into the sheet.

The body. Just thinking of him like that, like this man was no longer a person, made me sick to my stomach. This was a *human being* in that hole. I didn't know the circumstances leading up to him being in Alexa's apartment and I didn't *want* to know, but even if he was cheating on his wife with a newborn baby at home, this end—a mangled body discarded in an anonymous hole in the woods—it wasn't deserved. And there were ten other people out here, rotting in the earth.

The soil eroded and Alexa slipped climbing out of the hole. She fell face down in the dirt and when she raised her head, she was covered in it: smeared makeup, dirt, blood under her fingernails. That was when Alexa finally broke down crying. When I knelt to console her, she brought her hand to her throat.

When did she get the knife?

"I can't do this anymore!" she said, her voice high and tight, her larynx straining against the edge of the blade.

She was going to kill herself, right in the fresh grave. And there was nothing I could do to stop her. I'd forgotten my phone at home. I'd be burying two bodies instead of one.

I said her name. Sharp as the knife to her throat.

She looked up at me, tears streaking the dirt on her face.

"You don't need to do this," I said.

She sniffled. A runner of snot ran from her right nostril to her lip. It brought me right back to when we were kids. The time she skinned her knee on our skateboards. The time she'd gotten trashed and picked a fight with a school bully at a party in these very woods, got her ass kicked and came running to me, who hadn't even been invited.

"We can..." I started to say, but I didn't know how to finish. What could we do? "We can figure this out. You don't need to *kill yourself*, Alexa."

"I *do*," she moaned, shaking her head at the dirt. "It won't stop, never, not until I'm dead."

"Or until you give it what it wants."

She looked up, curiosity in her eyes. Still, the knife never left her throat.

"You said the thing inside you, this... symbiont, that it needs a suitable host. *Compatible*."

She nodded, sniffling.

"You're a compatible host. That's why it lives inside you. But what would happen if it found another compatible host?"

She looked at me. Curiosity became realization. "It would breed."

"That's all it wants, isn't it? To breed? To make a perfect copy of itself in some other body. Some other *host*. Has this ever worked for you?"

She shook her head.

"And did the people you... slept with... did any of them know what they were in for? Were any of them *prepared*?" I meant to ask *Did they consent to being violated by a parasite?* but I didn't want to imply she was some kind of rapist. Which was odd, considering she'd been party to multiple murders, involuntary or not.

Again, another head shake, this one almost imperceptible. Ashamed.

"What if..." I didn't know how to say it. How to boil down everything I've wanted for decades into a single question. "What if we tried it? Together?"

She blinked up at me. "You... I could never do that to you, Brook."

"I can't just let you kill yourself. I've... *wanted you*... for as long as I can remember." The shame of never having come out and said it before burned in my cheeks and neck. "You called me, I came. Let me try to help you."

After what seemed like an eternity, she lowered the knife from her throat and started to climb up from the grave. I took her hand and helped her out.

"You understand what that means. If you're incompatible."

I nodded toward the hole in the earth. "I end up in a plot next to—" Here I was about to lay dirt on the man's grave and I didn't even know his name.

"Derrick," she said.

"Next to Derrick," I agreed.

Alexa shook her head. "I would bury you in a special place. *Our* place. Under the old sequoia bench."

Somehow, that was just about the kindest thing anyone had ever said to me.

We went there shortly after we covered over Derrick, Alexa guiding me by the hand through the dark woods, sitting me down on the bench carved into the massive, ancient log. Once, we'd tried counting its rings. We'd lost count but had it figured for at least a century old, likely more.

She sat down beside me. I could barely hold her gaze. This was awkward. We'd been friends forever. Kids together. She slipped her right leg behind me and held me around the waist. I felt her breath hot on my neck, prickling my spine.

From behind, she unsnapped the top button of my jeans. I jerked away nervously. "What are you doing?"

"You'll need to be aroused for this part," she said.

That shouldn't be a problem, I thought. Despite the circumstances and the very real possibility this might be the last sexual encounter I'd ever have—the last *anything*, really—every part of me felt electric. I'd waited for this moment most of my life. I nodded, as imperceptibly as she had earlier. "Okay."

I helped her unbutton me. Helped her slip the jeans off my legs and lay them beside us on the bench. The old wood was cold and slightly damp under my ass but I didn't care. The tips of her index and middle fingers found my clit and began to stroke rhythmically. The electricity streamed down from every part of my body and focused itself on the motion of her fingers. My toes curled. In moments, I was crying out in ecstasy.

In the distance, a wolf matched my cry.

Alexa leaned around and kissed me then, slipping her tongue between my lips. I kissed right back, already exhausted, panting and wet, hungry to taste her but knowing her arousing me was mostly utilitarian, a means to an end.

She stood and pulled down her track pants. Laid them out on the bench, slipped off her underwear and set them beside her pants. She sat on them, beckoned for me to come to her.

I slid over. Alexa put her left leg over my right and pulled me closer, so our bodies were almost touching, and lifted my left leg over her right. I knew the position she was trying to get me into and almost giggled—actually *giggled*—but thankfully managed to hold it in.

"What's wrong?" she asked.

"Nothing," I said. "It's just... lesbians don't actually scissor."

She gave me a calculating look. "Have you ever tried it?"

I'd tried. *Of course,* I tried. I'd gotten myself off using just about every part of my partners' bodies, among other things. But had I ever really given scissoring a fair chance? I shook my head, embarrassed by the admission.

"Then how would you know?"

She had me there.

Alexa took my hands. Drew me in until we were pressed together, her razor stubble grazing my labia. With our lips pressed together—both pairs—Alexa began grinding me. I had to admit it felt quite good, especially with her, though nothing like the stimulation of a hand or tongue. Still, my long-withheld desire for her overwhelmed me and I gripped her ass, her smooth flesh cold as the wood beneath us, pumping my hips, pumping against her ripe mound. I felt her clit hardening against mine, and then...

And then.

I'd only ever been penetrated once by a man. I'd had a boyfriend for a brief period in college, an experiment, so to speak. We'd fucked once, and it had ended almost before it began, with a gooey mess on my belly and an allergic reaction to latex. Of course, I'd used toys of all kinds. Dildoes, vibes, G-spot stimulators. I was inexperienced but I wasn't a *prude.*

This felt nothing like any of those.

Something slick and spongy parted my labia and entered me. At first it felt like a tongue, flicking up and down inside of me, only ribbed and much longer. I freaked out, and nearly pulled away. But Alexa's gaze held me. I stayed fixed to her, and the *thing* inside of her, the *symbiont*, began probing the walls of my vagina, hitting my G-spot like nothing and no one had ever done before.

In moments I came harder than I ever had in my life, this alien creature tongue-fucking me as Alexa's clit rubbed against mine, our thighs intertwined, our bodies so close it was like she was penetrating me herself, and fireworks exploded in my brain as I howled into Alexa's wet, open mouth.

The moment I did, the symbiont must have sensed my full arousal. The tongue-thing was just the tip of it, and with my pussy all but gushing it squeezed itself all the way into me. I felt the *fullness* of it widening me, so large it actually pushed my legs even further apart. I gasped, feeling the flesh split, a wound I'd experience over the next two weeks while sitting, using the bathroom, even walking from my desk to the kitchen and back. I felt the alien *thing* inside me, *filling* me, pressing against my bladder, widening the narrow opening of my cervix and nestling into my uterus. I felt it settling there, making itself cozy, making a home in me.

I expelled the breath I'd been holding in a single burst, my whole body shuddering as I fell into Alexa's embrace.

"She's gone," she said after a moment. There was relief in her voice, but also sadness. Like the miscarriage of a child she'd never wanted.

"What do you mean, *gone?*"

"She's not in me anymore. I can't *feel* her."

She couldn't feel it, because it was in me. *She* was in me. Not just an egg or a copy of itself. The whole symbiont.

And I'd *survived*.

We put our clothes back on in silence. The symbiont felt heavy between my hips but by the time we reached the car, with the wheelbarrow and tools back in the shed, safely locked up, it was like there was nothing there at all. I put in a pad from Alexa's glovebox, the blood from the fissure soaking into it. When she dropped me off at my apartment a few hours later—thanking me, promising to call *soon*, but not kissing me again, leaving me hanging—the wound had stopped bleeding altogether, even though, as Alexa drove off, my heart still was.

ALEXA CALLED me several times a week that first month. Wondering how I was doing. How I was handling it. If I thought I'd be okay with the "responsibility." Thanking me over and over for changing her life. After that, the calls grew infrequent. I didn't mind. We'd grown apart, and that was fine. What we'd shared was more important than any short-lived fling might be. Even more than if we'd somehow managed to make the two of us work. We'd been friends for as long as I could remember, but friends often drifted apart, especially if the elephant in the room was far too big to ignore.

I never wrote her story, not as anything I'd ever try to publish. I *couldn't*, even if she'd still wanted me to. The last thing the world needed was another barely disguised parable about the dangers of female sexuality, more sex-negative antifeminist bullshit to pick away at all the progress we'd made over the past century. Even if that story was one-hundred percent fact.

Instead, I did what she could no longer do herself.

When Alexa and I were kids, fishing in the Paintbrush, it took a lot of patience and practice to learn how to bait a hook myself. I pricked my finger countless times, grieved for every lost leech and worm, but eventually I managed to make it work. I remember how proud she'd been of me, that first fish I'd caught—barely bigger than a minnow—once I'd baited the hook on my own.

I had no idea how to pick up a man, or a woman for that matter. But soon it became second nature. I don't know if the symbiont changed me, if it exuded some kind of attracting pheromones while it was in heat or if all I'd ever needed was the confidence boost from finally being with Alexa, finally *getting over her*... Whatever the cause, once those scars healed I felt more sexual, more *in charge*, than I ever had in my life.

Eventually, they were vying for *my* attention.

All I had to do was cast out the line, and wait for someone to take the bait.

THE MOVING HOUSE

A PREQUEL TO THE GHOSTLAND Trilogy

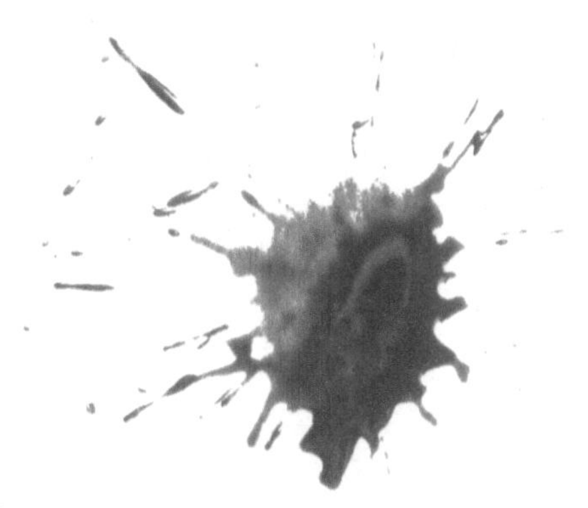

THE MOVING HOUSE

Winter, 2014

Long before it was called "Garrote House," superstitious neighbors had called it "the Moving House," though the house at 1 Hedgewood Crescent had stood unmoved at the end of the cul-de-sac, crooked and silent, for over a hundred and seventy years. From the outside it had a certain charm—it was the sort of house realtors might say had "good bones," but only if they were unfamiliar with its history.

Because The Moving House had seen its share of bones... and flesh... and blood.

Christopher Hedgewood pulled the rented van up to the curb out front and peered through the cracked passenger window at the darkened house. It had been passed down to him through the generations—though it had seen its share of interlopers, each of whom had met an untimely and violent demise. His own ancestors hadn't been immune. The house knew only violence. It bred it.

Garrote House was his birth right. The Hedgewood family legacy and its curse.

"I've gotta be nuts," he told himself. Through a long sigh, he said it twice more. The seatbelt alarm dinged as he climbed out. The biting night air chilled his breath.

"You made it."

Christopher wheeled at the voice. Sara Jane Amblin stepped out of yet another new car. The streetlights at this end of the cul-de-sac had burned out. Backlit by the moon, his business partner had a sort of hazy glow like the female lead in an old black-and-white movie, her dark, high cheekbones shimmering. Christopher didn't much fancy women, but he knew a work of art when he saw one.

"I wouldn't dream of missing out," he said, hugging her briefly. Though the truth was he nearly hadn't come at all.

Sara Jane looked up at the house, its gables like teeth gnawing at the black edge of midnight. "Shall we?" she said, holding out an arm for him to take.

He slipped his through hers, and felt her shiver through her puffy down-filled coat—more out of fright than the cold, he suspected. They gave each other challenging looks before starting toward the gate.

Stopping there, Christopher brought out his flashlight and shined it over the wrought-iron arch. Rusted paint-flecked letters spelled out GARROTE HOUSE, entwined with the same sturdy Boston ivy— which grew as eagerly in Seattle, despite the name—that smothered the low brick walls on either side of the walkway, and clawed its way up the front of the house to the windows on the second floor. Its dead leaves skittered along the cobblestones in the cold night air.

"This gate will have to come," Sara Jane said.

"I was just thinking that."

Relying on each other's courage, they passed under it arm-in-arm.

The Moving House didn't so much move as *shift*, and then only in subtle variations. Sara Jane's people had taken measurements in fifteen-minute intervals throughout the day, confirming that the interior walls would widen and narrow, widen and narrow again—almost as if the house itself were breathing. The movement was undetectable by the naked eye, but through the course of a day, the sofa, for instance, could be several inches from the window, and hours later flat against it. The effect on the occupant was a general uneasiness, a sense that something was *not quite right*, and whether it was this effect that had driven the house's occupants to madness was anyone's guess.

1 Hedgewood—the street named after the man who'd built the house, Christopher's great-great-grandfather Oliver Hedgewood, when it was the only house for miles—was what realtors would call a "stigmatized property." Over the years it had seen its share of tragedies: the usual deaths and injuries during construction, when such things happened regularly, the tuberculosis outbreak of the early 1900s, several suicides, homicides, and very few deaths stemming from old age. It was suggested by some to be a "sick building," a structure itself which caused illness as if by accident of shape and fate. But the final blow to its reputation was when it entered the public's consciousness as a "murder house."

Clayton Odell had been a sculptor with a reputation for challenging established conventions. Considered by some to be "a modern Picasso," his art, particularly his sculptures, had sold well enough for him to purchase the house at 1 Hedgewood in the late-'70s at a then-whopping $1.8-million. Odell's ironworks were monstrous caricatures of human invention throughout the ages. Odell's *Man and Machine*, merging da Vinci's *Vitruvian Man* and his invention, the "Aerial Screw," had stood in the lobby of the Metropolitan Museum of Modern Art for several years. It might have stood there today had the artist not made his final project the murder-suicide of his entire family in the summer of 1984.

Odell's estate sold off his entire body of work and belongings. Sitting on prime Seattle land, the writer Rex Garrote—now also deceased—had snatched 1 Hedgewood up after a string of successful horror novels. Christopher had never had much interest in Garrote's books. The covers made them seem lurid, and even though his ancestors' house had seemingly been the inspiration behind a trilogy of novels, Christopher still couldn't bring himself to read them.

He felt it would be like reading his family's history through the lens of a man obsessed with serial killers and monsters.

Garrote himself suffered a particularly gruesome death. The police believed it was self-immolation, though Christopher—who'd been a child at the time it happened—seemed to recall a detective suggesting the author wasn't dead at all, that he was merely in hiding. It would explain why no one who'd been in the house in the intervening years had seen his ghost, many despite claims of seeing the others: the Odells, several builders, the house staff, and much of the long line of Hedgewoods leading all the way back to Ollie in the 1800s.

Christopher didn't think it was likely, anyhow. How could a man with his level of fame—he'd had a TV show, after all, though it had only run for a single season—have kept himself hidden for nearly a decade and a half? It was far more likely that the house had claimed another victim. That she'd fed upon him psychically until she could finally feast on his physical remains, as she had the rest.

After the horror writer's death, Christopher's father, Fox Hedgewood, snapped up his family's former estate for a song and seemingly on a whim, with no real plans for the property. In the following years the house remained empty, slowly falling into disrepair.

Christopher Hedgewood had been fascinated with houses since a very young age. His father—whom he loved but could not abide—had no appreciation for architecture, only money. It wasn't until his early twenties that Christopher discovered the old Garrote house was a part of his father's estate.

Like his father, he'd had no idea what to do with it, only that he wanted it to be *his*.

In the years since the horror author burned himself to ash, neighbors reported hearing noises from inside, seeing strange lights. Ghouls obsessed with murder and a quick shot to fame broke in from time to time and came out terrified, banging on doors down the block, raving about becoming lost in a maze, asking startled occupants if they could *see* them. If they weren't, in fact, dead.

Just last year, a group of teenagers were interviewed on the local news after the disappearance of their friend, claiming the young girl hadn't been kidnapped, as was believed by police, but had ventured into the Moving House alone and never come out.

Christopher had put a guard on the premises, worried there might be another incident. While genuinely concerned for safety, the same ambition that flowed through the blood of his ancestors burned in his, and he felt secretly delighted by the unpaid publicity. By the time Jennifer Lynn Daniels went missing in 2009, Christopher had already begun toying with the kernel of an idea.

If so many people wanted to enter the Moving House despite the reported dangers, why not give them what they wanted? An authentic, yet safe, haunting experience.

It wasn't until he met inventor and parapsychologist Sara Jane Amblin that Christopher decided it was possible. With all the strides she'd made in paranormal science during her work with the Hedgewood Foundation, Ms. Amblin was certain that with proper funding, she could provide him exactly the sort of experience he desired.

As it turned out, they'd already been working on that very thing—with Garrote's estate as a silent partner. It had been Garrote's idea to construct a haunting-themed amusement park, one filled with haunted buildings and objects he'd apparently been collecting throughout his life. It was Christopher's idea to thrust Garrote's posthumous involvement to the forefront. To use the writer's infamy among horror fanatics as a selling feature.

He was sure the maniac himself would have approved.

"What the general population thinks of as 'ghosts' are essentially energy imprints," Sara Jane had told him during their initial meeting. "They're echoes. The detection equipment I've designed works the same way as a crime scene lamp illuminates trace evidence, after a fashion. What you see is the *imprint* of past life, like footprints left in the sand. When combined with my Recurrence Field, those echoes, those *imprints*, could theoretically last forever." Her dark eyes had lighted. "Like photographs. Like moving photographs."

"This Recurrence Field," Christopher had asked, "you've seen it work?"

Back then the answer had disappointed him. In 2011, the Recurrence Field had been still a theory, though the Hedgewood Facility's newfound understanding of what Sara Jane often referred to as "spiritual imprints" would bring it that much closer to reality.

"When you're dead you're dead," she'd explained. "That's the end of it. What I'm giving you is not life after death, but energy *beyond* death."

Naturally, Christopher had been skeptical. Encoded in his DNA was the legacy of his third great-grandfather, legendary American showman John Purdy Hedgewood, proprietor of Hedgewood & Son Circus. The man had known how to spot a sucker, and how to prevent oneself from becoming one. Sara Jane had assuaged Christopher's doubts with a demonstration.

"Was that window there before?"

Her voice startled him from his thoughts. Still approaching the house, she was looking up at a second-floor window, fear in her eyes, her breath hurried. He followed her gaze. In the years since he'd discovered his father owned the Moving House he'd come here dozens of times: watching her, studying her. He knew every inch of her brick-and-mortar surface, of her wraparound porch, her gables, her hedges. He knew immediately Sara Jane was right. The octagonal window, each pane a stained-glass pastoral scene, had shifted a good three feet to the right, so it no longer rested below the middlemost gable. This phenomenon had never been recorded, only reported. The interior walls were constantly moving, but the exterior had always remained fixed to the same dimensions.

Impossible... but the proof was there, right before his eyes.

Her claws were already outstretched, burrowing into their minds like the twists of ivy clinging to her façade.

"It's a trick," he said. "She wants us to stay out."

"She?"

"All houses are female," he said. "Especially the crazy ones," he added with a wink.

Sara Jane narrowed her eyes. "You've never gone inside at night, have you?"

Christopher shook his head.

"Are you sure you're ready?"

I've gotta be nuts, he thought again. He remembered the sweet elderly lady ironing her husband's shirts in the moment before the man stepped in with a shotgun and splattered her brains across the spotless kitchen. He'd watched her eyes widen in horror again and again in the little post-war bungalow in Detroit, courtesy of Sara Jane's Recurrence Field. He saw the back of her head splinter, her blood and gray matter soil the fresh laundry—then a stutter as the scene "reset"—her shock again, her fragmented skull, her blood—*stutter*—shock, skull, blood. On the fourth repetition his guts had twisted in knots, and he'd run to the cramped bathroom to vomit. When he returned to the kitchen, the woman and her visible insides were gone. Sara Jane had turned off the Recurrence Field, apologizing.

"It never gets easier," she'd told him, though the emotion connected to the words had not been evident in her face or tone. Her expression had remained guarded as she packed away the heavy equipment. He'd helped her, eyeing her with suspicion.

"I'm ready," he said now. A sigh plumed from his lips as they stood on the creaking porch of the Moving House, where many a Hedgewood before him had lost their life.

He put the key in the lock and twisted it. The double doors swung inward with a gasp of musty air. He and Sara Jane shared a fearful look, then stepped across the threshold together.

Inside, blackout curtains covered the windows. Even the octagonal skylight in the rotunda's ceiling—the one that had appeared to have shifted outside, now back in its proper place—was covered. A double staircase wound its way up to the second floor on either side of an antique verde marble floor. Their flashlights skittered over disorienting patterns of white veins in the serpentine green stone. Having stood here hundreds of times in the dazzling light of day, neither Sara Jane nor Christopher marveled at its moldering beauty.

"Where should we start?" he wondered aloud.

"In the master bedroom. Where *he* started."

Sara Jane and her crew had thoroughly researched the Moving House Murders from virtually every angle. Odell had begun in the workshop, grabbing up his tools in the middle of the night, while his wife Laura and their two children slept. Placing a hand over Laura's nose and mouth—blood-spatter evidence confirmed this long before the Recurrence Field would prove it—Odell stabbed his wife sixteen times in the heart, leaving nothing but bloody pulp.

Cries arose from the nursery next door. The boy had woken to his mother's muffled screams. Odell's bare feet left sticky red prints on the shiny hardwood on his way to the nursery.

He entered the children's room, moving like a sleepwalker, arms hung loose at his sides, the chisel dripping blood on a shaggy, cow-shaped rug. He plodded over to his son's crib. Without a moment's hesitation, his arm rose and fell three times. The cries stopped abruptly. He did the same to his daughter, the boy's twin. He left the chisel in her tiny chest, carried her lifeless body like a skewered roast to the octagonal library at the epicenter of the house, laid it down then went back for the others. Once the entire family was reunited, Sam Odell set about taking them apart piece by piece with his sculpting tools: a hacksaw, an acetylene torch, a chisel.

Once he had finished, he sat surrounded by the hacked and bloody pieces of his wife and children. His eyes and teeth gleamed white amid the glistening red of their blood drenching him from head to toe as he laughed.

And then he began to sew.

Christopher and Sara Jane rose the stairs, fully aware of what awaited them on the floor above. She'd played back the scene a dozen times or more, following Odell from room to room on his brutal rampage... and not once did it ever get easier. He'd never desensitized to it, as he assumed he would. The sorrow was always as deep as the first time, and he wondered now if he'd made the right decision, if he should have used his influence on the chairs and shareholders to stop this thing before it went too far.

This was their gift to the world: proof of life after death. Life *beyond* death. But he worried he might be following in the ill-fated footsteps of his late ancestor, John Purdy, the circus showman. He worried it was too late to turn back.

I've gotta be crazy, he thought, rising the stairs. *Go back, Christopher. Go home. Gregory's waiting. Our bed is warm. There's love there—not death. This is madness.*

Sara Jane's words on the phone tonight echoed in his mind, reassuring him after he'd expressed his concerns: *They aren't alive. They feel nothing.*

He sometimes wondered if Sara Jane herself felt anything, if her dedication to scientific discovery hadn't suffocated some of her humanity. She was a good woman: intelligent, a caring friend, responsible. But empathy seemed difficult for her.

The equipment was already set up on the second-floor landing: a series of large, smooth plastic machines with rounded edges, heavy and sanitary looking, like MRIs or CAT scanners. Christopher started the generator. Within seconds its thunderous sputtering began to echo throughout the house.

Sara Jane flicked a switch on the larger machine. It powered on with a high-pitched whine, flooding the hall with unnatural white light.

Once again, they put on their clunky, heavy helmets, prototypes for the AR glasses which were in the development stage now at the Hedgewood Facility laboratories.

Footprints illuminated before them, the dull pink of echoed blood, bare feet padding down the hardwood hall from the master bedroom toward the twins' room as Sam Odell—still obscured by the veil of death—staggered from the first murder to the second.

When the footprints reached the doorway, the man himself shimmered into existence: wispy at first, like a hologram, but as his semitransparent, blue-hued hand grasped the door handle it appeared to solidify. It was not solid. Christopher had made certain of this during his initial experience with Odell, by stepping into the scene to grab the killer's arm, attempting to stop him from obliterating Laura Odell's heart. His hand had slipped right through Odell as though passing through a fog.

Odell's sleepwalker eyes stared into the middle distance as he opened the door. Sara Jane followed, skirting around the footprints. Christopher stayed with the machine. Its protected cables ran along the wainscoting into the master bedroom, continuing into the nursery, and down the stairs to the heart of the house, where Odell would soon spray his blood over the books lining the library walls.

"Where did he go?" Sara Jane said from behind the door.

"What?"

"Odell," she said, stepping out of the room. Her expression betrayed none of the confusion or fear present in her voice. "He just disappeared."

"That's impossible," Christopher said. "Isn't it?"

"Impossible or not, he's gone."

Christopher met her at the doorway. Sure enough, the echo of Sam Odell was nowhere in sight. Sara Jane pushed past him, hurrying toward the hall. He hung back in the doorway, watching young Jenny Odell and her brother Jack sleep peacefully—had the loop already reset itself? He didn't know. He followed Sara Jane back into the hall.

She kept walking faster, faster, peering into open doors as she passed, following the cables down the hall, muttering "Fuck, fuck, fuck," as she went. Christopher kept pace behind her, looking through the same open doorways she had. They rounded a corner. A single lamp illuminated the hall, throwing their long shadows ahead of them.

"We should have turned on the overheads," Christopher said.

Sara Jane ignored him, but he knew how she would have answered: supplementary light rendered the detection lamps useless. Without them, the helmets they wore could not pick up the dead energy left behind. It was the same reason they'd covered the windows. All of these kinks would be worked out before the technology was made public, of course. For now, they were stuck with its limitations.

Out in the rotunda, the generator sputtered and the light behind them began flickering. Suddenly the house became silent. One by one, the large lamps extinguished, plunging them into a darkness so complete it was as if they had stepped off the edge of the universe.

"Christopher...?"

"I'm here."

"Don't move. I'm coming back."

Christopher remember his flashlight. He flicked the switch. It came on weakly before winking out. "My flashlight won't work!"

"The Recurrence Field saps electricity from batteries within its range, remember? It works with energy."

He remembered—not that it had ever been a concern during their daylight visits. He tucked the useless thing back into his coat pocket. Blood thundered in his eardrums as he waited for her hands to reach him. As the seconds stretched out, he began to worry the hands that would eventually grab him would not be hers. His muscles tensed. The hair on his neck stood up.

"*Sara...?*"

Not even the gentle swish of a hand brushing the wall met his ears.

"Sara! Where are you?"

Her voice called back from a distance, "I'm almost there!" A brief pause. "Did you move?"

"I've been standing right here! Where are you?"

"I guess I must have got turned around. I'll come back. Keep talking, okay?"

He couldn't think. His breathing grew panicked. "I don't know what to say!" he shouted back.

"Then sing!"

Christopher racked his brain. Strangely, what came to mind was a song his mother had often sung as a lullaby, as it was one of few she knew by heart. He thought of her clear voice singing to him and his older brother when they were both young, a hand on her heart, and he called out, "'O beautiful for spacious skies—'"

"Really?"

"Do you want me to sing or not?"

"Keep going then." She sounded closer now.

"'For amber waves of grain, for purple mountain majesties, above the fruited plain!'"

His voice came less tuneful than frantic. The windows rattled. He reached out to the wall for grounding, tethering himself to his rapidly diminishing grasp on reality. He thought of Odell, sitting cross-legged amid a spiraling tower of dusty old tomes, dragging the hacksaw teeth across his throat. "I don't want to sing this anymore."

"I'm almost there, keep going!" But her voice sounded even further away.

Christopher sang faster, blood racing: "'America! America! God shed His grace on thee! And crown thy good with brotherhood, from sea to shining...!'"

The silence drew out. He felt suddenly, inescapably alone.

"*...Sara?*"

A sconce flickered on near his head. The leap from pitch dark to sudden brightness startled him, though not so much as the hulking presence before him. The nude creature stood eight feet tall, a totem pole of warped human anatomy, a smooth-skinned man wearing the upper half of a woman on his shoulders, her raven-haired head lolling left and right, with something like a medieval torture device covering her nose and mouth. The two infants had been raggedly sewn in place of her breasts. Between them, Odell's piercing dark eyes stared out from the wet, crimson hole in her ribcage.

Christopher had a single moment to wonder how he'd ended up in the library downstairs when he hadn't moved a muscle since the lights went out. Then the monster snatched out with its many arms, grabbing him by the throat, the shirt, his abdomen. As the air escaped him, he heard Sara Jane call out his name from an impossible distance away.

He wanted to shout to her *Stay away*. He wanted to tell her, *Turn back*, to say they'd made a mistake—all of this was a mistake from the very beginning. But the hands at his throat choked his words, and the world itself grew dim, until all he could see were the vacant eyes of a dead man, a sleepwalking spirit staring out from a jagged hole between two shrieking, murdered infants.

WHEN THE LIGHTS flickered on Sara Jane found herself standing above the stairs, barely an inch from what would have been a very bad fall. She stepped back hastily with a sharp inhale, marveling at how close to death she'd come. It would have been bitter irony to die here after all her work, in the house that had inspired it.

It took her several frantic minutes to find Christopher. By then rigor mortis had already begun to set in. She closed his eyes gently, and his mouth. His mask of terror was too much for her to bear. Though he had come here many times of his own volition, she felt some amount of personal responsibility for his death. It was her work that led to it, after all. But whatever had happened to him, she was certain Christopher would want that work to continue.

It was their legacy, both his and hers.

The author Rex Garrote's too, she supposed.

With her cell battery close to drained, she placed a call to Christopher's brother at the Hedgewood Facility. Someone would have his body moved off the premises. They would make it look like he died of natural causes, or suicide, or asphyxiation. No one would tie his death to this house, just one more in a long line of them, many from Christopher's own lineage.

The house had fed. Hopefully, it would not need to feed again for some time.

Very soon now, the Moving House would literally be moving to a new location. Plans were already underway to uproot the whole terrible structure from its poisoned foundation and transport it all the way across the country to a plot of farmland in Maryland.

Garrote's dream of a theme park showcasing the most-haunted places and objects in America had begun with this house, its star attraction.

Sara Jane and the Hedgewood Foundation would soon make that dream a reality.

They would call it Ghostland.

Like what you've read?
Continue reading with *Ghostland*.

Afterword

Horror Made Me Do It

When someone asks "What's your favorite (book, movie, TV series, song)?" I find the answer about as difficult as choosing what to order when everything on the menu looks good and I haven't eaten since breakfast. For the sake of this afterword, I've narrowed it down to the two books that influenced me to start writing, both of which happen to be short story collections. Stephen King's *Night Shift*, and Clive Barker's *Books of Blood* were my first journeys into their terrifying minds, and still resonate with me long after reading. They aren't necessarily my all-time "favorites," but they've inspired me to achieve similar heights in my own writing.

Night Shift was on the shelf at the old cottage, and its creepy cover called to me... You may know the one: the hand covered in eyeballs and wrapped in gauze (this was the double cover, with the eyes peeking out from holes in the flap). It refers to the story "I Am the Doorway," where an astronaut brings home an alien stowaway that uses him to peek into our world. *Night Shift* effectively blends science fiction, horror, terror (if you don't know the difference, pick up his seminal non-fiction book, *Danse Macabre*), and gross-outs. Most may not be the best King shorts, nor the most chilling, but they are memorable for the far-outness of their concepts, and the sheer amount of adaptations they've produced.

"Jerusalem's Lot" and "One for the Road" serve as a sort of prologue and epilogue to the novel, *'Salem's Lot*. "Children of the Corn," about a couple who stumble into a creepy religious town where there are no adults, was made into more sequels than it deserved. "Trucks" became King's directorial debut, *Maximum Overdrive*, with Emilio Estevez and an AC/DC soundtrack King probably listened to while he wrote the script.

My favorite of the bunch when I was a kid, "Battleground" (which I copied from memory for a school assignment on my dad's Tandy laptop), was adapted well in the *Nightmares & Dreamscapes* miniseries, with John Hurt as the hitman besieged by the toymaker's box of animated soldiers.

In a recent reread, I found two decidedly non-horror stories work very well for their surprising level of emotion and honesty. "The Last Rung on the Ladder" is a haunting story about siblings, trust, and suicide. "The Woman in the Room," adapted into the first short film by Frank Darabont (*The Shawshank Redemption, The Walking Dead*), is a sad tale of a man's inner demons and remorse as he prepares to pull the plug on his dying mother. I have a feeling King, whose mother had recently passed, wrote the story to purge his own demons, and those feelings shine through (darkly) on the page.

The book also stands out in my mind for two quotes about writing that have stuck with me, one from John D. MacDonald, and the other from King himself. In the Introduction, MacDonald wrote that when he met people at parties, someone would always said, "You know, I've always wanted to write," to which he began gleefully replying, "You know, I've always wanted to be a brain surgeon." I don't believe the two are comparable, but the path to each begins with plenty of study and practice.

In the Foreword, Stephen King answers a question in a similar fashion: when asked "Why do you choose to write about such gruesome subjects?" King responds, "Why do you think I have a choice?" I think he was on to something.

"I HAVE SEEN the future of horror... and his name is Clive Barker." This quote by Stephen King was splashed across the covers of Clive Barker's *Books of Blood* omnibuses I happened across at my local library. (For a small town, the Millbrook Public Library seemed to have just about everything a young horror fan required to keep himself sane.) Barker's short stories are still some of the most visceral and imaginative I've ever read. His prose is often spare, but always vivid.

I was 15 when I first read Clive Barker's *Books of Blood*, and I loved it so much I thought I'd try writing my own monster story. The first wholly "original" story I wrote that wasn't a school assignment was about a psychic forced to open a doorway into another "realm," who begins to bond with the demon there and uses it to take revenge on the man manipulating him. The second was about a hired killer who falls in love with his victim. It was a weird little S&M story with some cool twists and turns, the title story for collection I never finished called *The Blood Letters*. Aside from one or two more, I never finished any of the other stories. I really wish I'd pushed myself to finish them, but instead I kept starting new novels and never finishing them for years. I had no idea how to go about publishing something back then, aside from vanity press, and I never really thought of it as something I could do as a "job," so I got into the television business instead.

The *Books of Blood* omnibuses open with the eponymous frame story, in which we learn the Books have been carved into the flesh of a phony psychic by the ghosts of a haunted house. From there we take a ride on "The Midnight Meat Train," following serial killer Mahogany into the depths of depravity. "In the Hills, the Cities" contains some incredible imagery heavy with metaphor.

There are other stories that return to my imagination like the animated dead from time to time: "The Body Politic," in which our hands revolt, lopping each other from the oppressive shackles of our bodies and skittering off to conquer the world. In "Down, Satan!" a man seeks the attention of God by building a Hell on Earth. "The Age of Desire" is a chemical aphrodisiac experiment gone wrong. "The Forbidden," a story about the power of legends, became the basis for one of my favorite horror movies, *Candyman*. It was Barker's debut collection, filled with gruesome imagery, insane twists, poetic style, and in-your-face sex and violence, that made me decide to publish a short story collection of my own as my debut, *Gristle & Bone*.

Stephen King once wrote that short stories are becoming a dying art. Everybody wants longer novels, series, sequels. I believe there will always be a place for them.

Anthologies are becoming increasingly popular again, particularly in the horror genre. As are novellas, especially in the extreme horror subgenre. Short stories have the benefit of being read in one sitting. For a writer, there is no better spark for the imagination. Both Barker's and King's short stories have been and continue to be a huge inspiration for me and my writing.

Thank you for reading the 33 short stories and novellas within these pages. There's so much content out there right now, and the fact that you took the time to read most or all of these stories means a great deal to me.

While I've got your attention, may I ask a small favor? Reviews help other readers discover my books, and give me the motivation to keep me writing! So if you have some free time, please consider leaving an honest review on Amazon, Goodreads or your favorite review site. It's the cheapest and easiest way to support my writing, and I would be forever grateful.

DR, 2024

About the Author

Author of the cult smash-hit *Woom* and *Ghostland* and more than 15 other books that aren't the cult smash-hit *Woom* or *Ghostland*. His debut collection was blurbed positively by the legendary Jack Ketchum. His novel, *Pedo Island Bloodbath*, was nominated for a 2024 Splatterpunk Award for Best Novel.

For 7 FREE dark fiction short stories/novellas including the prequel to GHOSTLAND, "The Moving House," signed copies of Woom, bookplates and merch, please visit www.duncanralston.com.

For more delicious dark fiction, please visit
www.duncanralston.com and
www.shadowworkpublishing.com.

www.ingramcontent.com/pod-product-compliance
Lightning Source LLC
Chambersburg PA
CBHW030323010826
48973CB00004B/844